D0610215

A Londoner, Tom Barling has worked for the national press, in advertising, as an art director and a TV producer. For many years he ran his own production company producing commercials and animated films, mostly for the American market. His previous novels include *The Olympic Sleeper*, *Goodbye Piccadilly*, *Bikini Red North* and *Terminate With Prejudice*.

Also by Tom Barling

GOD IS AN EXECUTIONER

and published by Corgi Books

The Smoke

Tom Barling

CORGI BOOKS

For Smudge and Marion

THE SMOKE
A CORGI BOOK 0 552 12504 0

First publication in Great Britain

PRINTING HISTORY
Corgi edition published 1986
Corgi edition reprinted 1987

Copyright © Tom Barling 1986

This book is set in 10/11pt Paladium.

Corgi Books are published by Transworld Publishers Ltd., 61–63 Uxbridge Road, Ealing, London W5 5SA, in Australia by Transworld Publishers (Aust.) Pty. Ltd., 15–23 Helles Avenue, Moorebank, NSW 2170, and in New Zealand by Transworld Publishers (N.Z.) Ltd., Cnr. Moselle and Waipareira Avenues, Henderson, Auckland.

Printed and bound in Great Britain by Cox & Wyman Ltd., Reading, Berks.

For Smudge and Marion

PROLOGUE

AT THE DARK of the moon Micky Dogge took the money out of the deserted warehouse by an upper window. He went down a rope and dropped to the cobbles without a sound. There was just his breathing and the lazy slap of Thames water against the piles of Wapping Reach when he went to a waste lot behind stables where he had left his stolen car under a tarpaulin.

A gyppo's cob whinnied when he started the engine, and he caught a fox in his headlights when he turned east towards Canvey Island and the boat on his brother's mooring.

On the drive there were fog patches and patchier traffic.

Micky began to think like a millionaire.

He would be long gone before they opened the safe in Windmill Street and wondered where the money and their bookkeeper had gone. Monday morning at the earliest, and then they'd send somebody around to Micky's house to see if it was the old bronchitis again. Micky figured he had the whole weekend to lose himself on the Continent before slipping across the border into Spain. They didn't even know he had a passport.

Micky timed his arrival at the mooring as the tide turned and the river ran out to sea under a greying sky. He opened the cockpit slide with his spare key and lit the navigation lights before throwing the pigskin case of used notes into the small saloon. An early heron came off the salt flats and took silent wing as the first glow of Saturday came off the calm of Foulness and Micky primed the engine. He knew enough to set a course for Calais and to follow a car-ferry into the inner harbour. By Sunday morning Micky would be in the back of a coach knocking back the duty-free Scotch as it bombed him all the way to Rosas in Catalonia. Then he'd be sitting pretty, Jack the Lad with 20 million pesetas to see him through his old age. All those years under Archie Ogle's thumb paid off in golden spades, and it would be easier for the firm to swallow the loss than admit they'd been taken by a mouse who'd turned them over for a real bundle of money.

Micky loosened the stern-lines and thought he would whistle something fitting as he went out with the tide. Something appropriate. He had decided on 'Colonel Bogey' when he remembered he ought to let the bow-line go first and went along the waist to see to it. The cruiser's stern was beginning to yaw, and he had to move fast before he found himself reversing away like some beginner yachtie.

He was fumbling with the knots when he found himself head deep in water, diesel and rotten shellfish. Micky floundered, his feet hooked over the gunwale to keep the cruiser alongside the pontoon as he tried not to breathe and decide which line had fouled him. Then thumbs in his neck filled him with panic, and he knew he would drown poor if he didn't think very quickly. He kicked out and felt the cruiser swing away from him. Saw the sky through popping lights of pressure as his head broke surface. Saw slate eyes in a shadowed face as forearms lifted him from the sluggish race. Knew Charlie Dance when he saw him and felt fear cramp his torso and toes. By then he was plunged back into the tide and yelled the last of his air out in a plea for mercy.

He was trying to tell Charlie about the fat man who'd given him the idea in the first place, the man who'd told him how to launder the money for a small percentage. Micky felt the pontoon mash his face before he was flipped on to his back and a heel crushed his oesophagus. Micky tried to say Vic Dakin's name with a mouth that flooded with blood as Charlie tied Micky's ankles to the bow-line and pushed the cruiser out into the river. He lifted the pigskin case from the cockpit and stood away as Micky was slowly dragged from the pontoon, his hands scrabbling at the wet concrete. Micky thought 'Bastard' at Charlie's cold smile a moment before he flopped into the surf and was something of no importance being towed out into the North Sea.

Charlie watched a last kick roll Micky into the undertow and felt for cigarettes that weren't there; then he drove back to London, looking for vending machines on the way.

Wanting sleep more.

CHAPTER ONE

SUNDAY had dawned like a grey afterthought.

Charlie Dance lost Sergeant Quill in the backstreets below Shooters Hill and delivered Archie Ogle to what was left of Mafeking Street. He parked on rubble and let Archie out to shake hands with two tame councillors and the retired DS who minded them. The one with acne said he hadn't minded the wait and the one with moist eyes said rain was good for the complexion as Archie marched them off through scaffolding to a site-hut the demolition men used as an office.

Charlie ate a yawn and watched for Quill's car, wondering why he stood in drizzle instead of being tucked up with Ingrid and the quality Sundays. Thought: *So what if Archie was born here? The bulldozers would soon turn Mafeking Street into an unmourned memory. The sooner the better. Archie's wearing too many yesterdays to be wandering about in this weather.*

Charlie looked for cigarettes and didn't have any.

An hour dawdled past before Archie came back to make a marmalade stray run with a well-aimed brick.

'That's them finger-tamed. The sooner I get an office block up on this site, the better,' he said.

Dance hid his surprise.

'Didn't think this was a sentimental journey.'

'I didn't buy up half the mother's sons down the Town Hall for the memory of ten kids in one room and a bucket under the bed, the old mother scrubbing to put a cob of bread on the table with the old man all bones and eyeballs from galloping consumption — him too proud to steal a crust and free with his hands if he caught us kids at it. Morals ain't for the hungry, Charlie. This is 1963, not 1923, and in six months this heap of slag will be the Archibald Ogle Complex. And that makes the past well dead and buried.'

Archie chewed on an unlit cigar, and Charlie could see pink scalp through his thinning hair.

'Always ahead of the game, eh, Arch?'

'Don't butter my bread.'

Ogle punched Dance's shoulder.

'I can still box you three rounds, seventy-two or not.'

They traded friendly blows until Ogle's wind failed.

'Too many Havanas, Arch. Rest on this wall.'

Archie leaned against broken brickwork, his jowls mottled. 'Mind – don't nursemaid.'

'And who gets the edge of Queenie's tongue if you end up back in the heart ward? Me.'

Ogle sneered, breathless. 'My Queenie'd no more give you the hard verbals than pull our black cat's tail. You could be our own kid the way she bubbles on about "her Charlie".' He lit the cigar with a gold Dunhill. 'We're all going soft.'

'Sensible ain't soft, Arch.'

A bulldozer growled awake down the street and blue smoke drifted. Archie huffed bluer smoke and tapped his lined forehead.

'There's more to life than bashing pimps and publicans for a handful of sovs.'

Charlie thumbed an eyelid. Wanted his breakfast.

'Maybe. But a fancy office with your name up in lights won't hold the cobbles for us.'

'Who said it would?'

'And standing about in the rain makes no sense, neither.'

'Only if you make sense of it, Charlie son.'

'It's your twopence, Archie. You make sense of it.'

'Then, listen up hard. Look how things are changing. Porn's right out in the open since *Lady Chatterley* beat that obscenity charge at the Old Bailey; and little girls in gymslips give their cherries away in the playground without so much as a shrug; and so many housewives work the raincoat trade for pin-money the regular toms might just as well work a till at Tesco's; and the big money's gone out of off-course bookmaking now you can write a bet in any high street. I mean, when was the last time you saw a bookie's runner eat his betting-slips with Tall John trying to make him cough up the evidence? Even the government's into gambling with their bloody premium bonds. There's only so much dough in a punter's pocket, Chas, and everybody's reaching for it with both hands. And if a thing's legal it can be taxed rotten by them faces in Whitehall. It's a wonder to me Downing Street ain't running state-controlled brothels like the Eyeties do in pastaland. How's your average villain to make a dishonest crust if immoral gets to be legal?'

Dance bit on an unwanted grin.

'You'll think of something.'

Ogle pointed a finger along his cigar.

'When there's a war there's a black market. You sell at your price.'

'The war was eighteen years ago. Gone are the days when a smart face could buy up half a million left-footed army boots, reverse the soles on half of them and end up with 250,000 saleable *pairs* of boots. Rationing went out with the Coronation. And that's ten years back.'

Archie grinned at the memory and the pain in his chest.

'Same principle applies, Chas. We have to control what controls everything else. The top commodity.'

'And what's that when it's at home?'

'Drugs, Charlie. Hard drugs.'

The ground shook as a wall toppled.

'Funny pharmaceuticals? Leave it out, Arch.'

'They're the route to the big money, Charlie. I didn't make the times, but I take my profits from them. Ten years gone you never saw a muggle outside a Chinese mah-jong parlour, never heard of faces shooting up on horse or coke, unless it was some black trombonist or a tosspot Lascar off some Panamanian rustbucket. The dockside brothel where you could get a pipe of opium was the exception, Charlie. The real exception.'

'So let it stay that way, Archie.'

'But it ain't that way no more. That's what I'm saying.'

'Still your twopence.'

'But you ain't listening.' Archie blew smoke near Charlie's face.

'I thought you'd just got through telling Toronto we weren't interested in supplying them from Europe?'

'That was before I went to Pakistan to see for myself. And I never say "Yes" when the Tonna brothers first bring anything to me. Not straight off. Never be predictable, Charlie. Keep them off balance.'

'Meaning you'll say "Yes" when you're good and ready, right? And before somebody else gets in ahead of you.'

Archie shrugged. 'You want the Harolds or the Troys sitting in my chair?'

Charlie watched Archie's faded green eyes chill beyond cigar smoke, saw deep squirms of anger writhe below the surface, and answered 'No' with a forced smile.

'Then, be a realist, son. It's that road or none. If we don't control it, some other set of heavy faces will.'

'Maybe.' Charlie shrugged his arguments away, seeing no profit in them.

'Definitely,' said Archie.

'That don't mean it sits right, Arch. We've already got the heavy filth up our bumper for breakfast, dinner and tea. And wouldn't they just love to nail us to the wall for any-sodding-thing!'

'That's as bloody maybe . . . .'

Archie broke off to bow over the pain in his heart.

'Your pills, Arch . . . .'

'Brandy . . . from the . . . Rolls . . . .'

'Queenie won't stand for—'

'Queenie won't know!'

The hollows in Archie's face burned dull crimson. He listened to Charlie race away and fumbled a wolferin tablet on to his tongue. Waited for his world to right itself after familiar waves of nausea and the swirl of coloured light behind his eyelids. The vague heart fibrillations eased and he thought about Charlie walking the cobbles in his shoes.

When the time was right. And well after Queenie had made Archie retire to the villa in Malta she had spent an arm and a leg of his money on. A long time from now. When Archie was old enough to sit in the sun without suffering from the terminal fidgets. In a thousand years when he had outlived his enemies and being retired didn't mean lying in state with cosmetic surgery disguising the wounds that had killed him.

Archie picked up a clod of hardened clay and crushed it to powder as he laid his monument of glass and steel over the existing street. There was too much to do to let up now.

Hadn't he made the peace when he retired Kosher Kramer to Brighton and allowed Eyetie Antoni his small patch in Old Compton Street? Wasn't the East End peaceful with the Troys bottled up in Bethnal Green and the Harolds across the Thames in Camberwell? The Bellavers had Catford, Micky Raven held Fulham, the blacks were turning Brixton into a ghetto, and who cared if the Irish laid pennies on each other's eyes in Kilburn? Not the Chinese in Gerrard Street or Alfie Horrabin north of King's Cross, and certainly not Archie Ogle with Soho, the West End and Knightsbridge.

How bad is that?

Archie smiled and blew smoke into the drizzle.

All I need is time, and it's all Charlie's. Just as if he was the son me and Queenie never had.

Charlie was seventeen when Archie found him dealing poker at an illegal Harringay spieler near the greyhound stadium. One of Archie's off-course tic-tac men had squawked about losing a monkey to some flash kid, and would Archie take a team over to suss out how much sharping was going on? And there was Charlie, skinny as a scaffold and flicking pasteboard about as if he had been born in a blackjack shoe on green baize with an eyeshade nailed to his forehead. The cards shuffled and dealt themselves as if his long hands had nothing to do with them when Archie claimed himself an ante, and only after being low-flushed out of a ten-quid pot, beat out of a full house by four fat ladies did Archie make noises about a skimmed deck. That was when Charlie broke the seal on a fresh deck and predicted the next five hands without laying a glove on the cards; said Micky Raven would draw low as he always did, and that Manchester Freddy didn't ought to have had four spare bullets in his cuff since there was already four straight aces in the deck, and didn't a top face like Mr Ogle know that? The first kid to call Archie face to face over one of his strength pulling a stroke at a straight table, all politeness and no old buck.

Archie had pushed over all the money, and young Charlie just hadn't been there when Manchester Freddy tried to lace him across the table. Charlie armlocked Freddy and turned his own cut-throat across his windpipe, hooking out the holdout aces on to the baize as sweet as you please with Freddy turning all colours with no wind left to bluff as Archie dealt out the hands to prove Charlie right.

'So you've got card sense,' Archie had told him, 'but that still don't make this a smart move.'

Charlie had listened as Armchair Doris told him he could end up buried without a tanner's worth of violets on his grave, then had looked at Archie as if he was a two-high instead of the ace of trumps he'd expected and said, 'I play the man, not his cards, Mr Ogle,' tacking on a sigh like he hated wasting grammar-school ideas on somebody who ought to know better. As if Archie hadn't been backed by Nasty Nostrils, Sodbonce and Raven's faces from Fulham; six to one against him, not counting Bad Alice, who was laughing like a storm-drain.

'Come and see me,' Archie had told Charlie when he got Manchester Freddy back, but it had taken three years and a bad whacking before he had fallen into Archie's Denmark Street spieler. By then he had a modest rep at the tables and outpunched his weight in the ring. But that was about the time Kosher and Eyetie had their straightener and had kept Archie well busy ducking and diving and sorting . . . .

Lost in thought, Archie made cigar smoke and stared through it at nothing but old memories.

Dance sprayed soda into Courvoisier and took his time locking the Silver Wraith. Archie could wait for his brandy. He carried too much lard and too many years to spar up to a man forty years his junior. Angina pectoris didn't just go away but, even so, Charlie's deltoid still glowed from his first whack and reminded him that Archie must have been a real handful in his prime.

Charlie walked slowly as the rain petered out.

Back in the twenties, when Archie had been just another tea-leaf Jack the Lad, he had managed to make himself useful around the Elephant and Castle bookies who were well upset about an Italian firm who were making themselves busy around the big racecourses. Bit by bit the Mancini brothers had tied themselves up with the Romany families who thought they owned the public turf by right of tradition, and were ringing the casual bookies who went down there to earn a few shillings from the off-course punters who couldn't afford the silver ring. Squeezed out, the bookies could only grumble and bear it, until Archie got himself a small firm together and went down to Epsom on Derby Day in a 'borrowed' charabanc.

Archie took a pick-handle to the cordon of men around Antonio Mancini and wouldn't back away, even when a cut-throat opened him up from eyebrow to Adam's apple. After a fight that raged over a quarter of a mile, Mancini's faces did a runner and Archie's firm owned the gory heath. Antonio took an early retirement in Sicily, and his brother Placidio joined him there after a stretch in Maidstone for tax-evasion. They died together when their black saloon blew itself to smithereens on the road to Salerno after hitting a goat stuffed with explosives. Somehow the story got about that Archie had something to do with it, and he never tired of not denying the fact. A reputation was welcome wherever it came from, and Archie never minded publicity in the early days.

After Doc Rudge sewed Archie back together in Spitalfields, Archie collected dues from every racecourse south of The Wash, and wouldn't let the big syndicates squeeze out the small books by buying an 'exclusive' on his 'protection'. Archie figured that small bookies could only become bigger bookies in an open market, and that his share of their take would rise proportionately. A shrewd decision that made him popular. And wealthy.

When Mussolini made his alliance with Germany, all the Italians in London were interned, and Archie kept their places warm for a 'consideration' they had no choice but to pay, and their businesses were a natural outlet for his black-market fiddles. Rustled sheep were butchered on the road and served that same evening in many a legitimate restaurant, and how some of Archie's faces could tenderise the toughest piece of meat with a ping-pong bat studded with gramophone needles was one of the seven wonders of wartime cuisine. And, as 'banker' to the many faces reluctantly called to the colours for the duration, Archie was the face they naturally turned to when they came home to post-war austerity. But not all of them took their 'starter' with a smile. The chaps had learned more than drill and bull on foreign service, and taking orders in civvy street was something a few hard-heads couldn't swallow.

The Elephant and Castle mob gave Archie a legful of buckshot when they shot up the Back Hill café where he collected dues from the Smithfield bookies. Two days later, four faces nosed a Daimler into the tide from Beachy Head, and Danny Rosen went to Palestine for his health — only to drown in the Dead Sea, an accident nobody was able to explain.

Except in metaphysical terms, thought Charlie.
I shouldn't even know a word like that.

He topped the broken ground east of the way he had come. The shifting puddles on the rippled tarmac shone like wet seals, and dockland cranes were rusty frets above the riverside warehouses. The grey sky rolled in Sunday silence, and Archie leaned against a boarded café window making smoke-rings. He broke them into meaningless scribbles when he waved and yelled something over engine noise.

Charlie raised the brandy in salute.

Archie looked like a tough old uncle with nothing better to do with his time than dangle children on his knee.

Some uncle, thought Charlie.

His stomach rolled as Archie turned to look up and back.

A crane swung above the café roof, and the entire building shuddered. Roof slates scaled into the street, smashed to shrapnel on the cobbles. Upper brickwork bellied out, breaking into slides of brick and mortar as it toppled. An iron ball swung through the exploding hole and a stone lintel fell to break where Archie was coming to his feet, losing him in a stew of dust and bouncing stone.

Charlie lost the brandy-balloon and ran, his eyes fixed on the spot where Archie disappeared.

Then he was inside the rising dustball, and stuff struck down at him in vicious disarray. His right arm went numb as he hurled masonry aside. He choked on the filth of a century, tasted wet soot and the cat-stench of ruptured sewage-pipes.

He hauled at what could have been an arm and found a lolling head. Cradling it against his chest with fierce care he took the falls of debris on his own back. A black rush of fire filled his head with confused notions of up and down and around.

'But it's Sunday.' Charlie wondered why that was significant.

He heard his forearm break as a second fall of debris stole all the breatheable air.

He fell over what could have been Archie and did not see Quill's unmarked Q-car roll up beside the Rolls, or the man in a boiler suit drop from the crane. Agony opened ebony petals and drew Charlie into a limbo stink of brickdust and burned wood.

The anteroom of the intensive care unit was almost quiet.

Archie was just about holding his own, and Queenie pretended to knit at his bedside. Charlie smoked on a hard chair and dribbled smoke at the floor. He had already been interviewed by two CID busies from West End Central.

'Purple's your colour, Charlie.' Detective Inspector Lemmon had turned his hat and slouched to conceal his height. 'Have you thanked Sergeant Quill for finding you?'

'Oh blimey yeah.'

Charlie held his plastered forearm and died for a swallow of Jamieson's. His mouth was stagnant, and a toy tram yammered near his mastoid bone. He watched Quill grin at his swollen profile. Short dark Quill was known as 'The Prophet of Doom' both sides of the fence and was universally disliked – unlike Lemmon, who was too straight to be on the take.

'Accident, Charlie?' Lemmon's West Country burr had survived fifteen years in London.

'No other way to tell it.'

Charlie waggled electrified fingers, preferring pain to conversation with the filth.

Quill sniggered and looked wise. 'Archie's enemies fill a telephone directory. Am I witnessing the start of a lot of jockeying for the top spot, Charlie?'

Lemmon smiled his avuncular smile.

'You'd earn your pension then. Nothing special about thick navvies knocking down the wrong wall. Happens every day.' Charlie blew on swollen knuckles.

'An accident, then?' said Lemmon.

'And not you getting ambitious?' asked Quill.

'Now, ain't you the sly one?' Charlie squinted up at the

light-globe. 'You can judge a man by the company he keeps, Mr Lemmon.' He turned to glare at Quill. ' "And the pig got up and slowly walked away." '

Quill said something foul.

'You got to the DS there.' Lemmon sounded neutral.

'First in draws first blood.'

'Why were you in Mafeking Street, Charlie?'

'Walking down Memory Lane.'

'Looking for a dirty dark doorway to cuddle in, more like.' Quill bared irregular teeth.

Charlie smiled. Said nothing.

'He doesn't like you, Charlie,' said Lemmon.

'You don't drop buildings on yourself, Mr Lemmon. Tell Armpit that, will you?'

'Suicide pact? Lovers' quarrel?' said Quill.

Charlie's laugh hurt his taped ribs. He took one of Lemmon's untipped Player's and drew flame from a lighter.

'If you and Archie reformed, we could close a lot of fat files, Charlie,' said Lemmon.

'Save you dusting them off all the time.'

Charlie's head pounded. Lemmon's big face drifted in the tungsten light like a bland pink moon, and liver spots danced in the shadows behind Quill. Hospital astringents dried Charlie's mouth and furred his teeth. He hawked moisture from his throat and swallowed. The booth shimmered and darkened and lightened again. He must have slept because the policemen had gone and Lemmon's Player had burned itself out on the floor. Charlie shredded it under his heel and wondered if he had really heard Lemmon say: 'The funny thing is, Charlie, there was no navvy on that crane. The demolition contractor wasn't working a Sunday shift. You'd best think on that, old son. We'll be back.'

'And they will,' Charlie told the empty anteroom.

'Talking to yourself? First signs, Charlie.'

Queenie Ogle was there. Her eyes were bright from weeping and her brilliant white hair had strayed. She wore her best black and sharp patent alligator shoes. For

Queenie, the world of fashion had frozen in 1948. Her umbrella was with her knitting beside Archie's bed.

'Thank providence you were there, Charlie.'

'I'm always there.'

'And look at the state of you.'

'I'm better than I look.'

'Be a while before the dollies fancy your smiling ways. That eye's more rainbow than Selfridge's Christmas display – worse than when Troy's freelancers gave you that kicking three years gone.'

'I never told you . . . .'

'Archie whispered. What I don't know ain't worth spitting out with your gum.'

'This is nothing. Nor was that.'

'Don't tell Queenie porkies – and don't let the filth get to you. They made their usual noises at me. Like talking to a couple of blocked sinks. I want you out of the East End. Now. Matt and Sodbonce will mind me and Archie.'

'I should be here.'

Queenie knuckled Charlie's chin.

'I've seen more spark from a dead battery. Go and get cuddled up to your latest drop of ice-cream.'

'Ingrid?'

'Ingrid. Get down West and wait for my call.' Queenie's kiss was firm and fierce. 'And shave, or she'll think she's pulled a big yellow monkey.'

Charlie climbed the ten miles to his feet.

'I'm gone.'

When Charlie had swished through the rubber doors Queenie shook her head and went back into the empty private room. Archie was in another hospital five miles away undergoing surgery. His chances of survival were better than sixty–forty.

Queenie would have taken the bet in hundreds.

She sat on the stripped bed to wait for Matt and Sodbonce.

Ingrid Dakin reached the Savoy at dusk and was shown up

to a fourth-floor suite where Charlie showered. She checked the interconnecting rooms and settled herself on a lounger in a tan and chocolate sitting-room. Her oval face was drawn, and there were pearls of rain in her thick black hair. She worried her lower lip with small sharp teeth and crossed a long leg to watch Charlie towel off.

Her polished accent had got her out of Pimlico and into a few commercials, and the gold flecks in her grey eyes gave her a knowing look. Now she dealt blackjack and poker at the Philadelphia House in Mayfair.

She bit on an unlit More and flicked her quick eyes round the expensive room.

'All a bit high-flown for you, Charlie.'

Charlie skimmed a lighter at her cigarette and didn't explain that Archie kept the suite for foreign contacts like the Tonna brothers, who were due in from Toronto at the end of the week.

'Did you bring me some clothes?'

'You left some things at my place. I didn't go near yours. Am I to know what's going on?'

'No.'

Ingrid frowned at Charlie's denial and tried not to look at his bruised torso.

'So you tripped over your shadow and Archie fell over you.'

'I'm better than I look.'

'A face as colourful as a baboon's bum, and more winding-sheets than a mummy at the British Museum? You're a winner all right. What does a working girl have to do to get a drink around here — take in washing?'

'You could rub my back.'

'Which only leads to rubbing your front.'

'Gin?'

'Drowned in tonic. There's a no-limit game in the private suite tonight that could go on until dawn. Some high-roller from South Africa.'

'Good. You can come back with the early editions for scrambled eggs, smoked salmon and a cuddle.'

Ingrid's snort had humour.
'Don't make promises you can't keep. Get tucked up with a cup of cocoa and bread-and-butter soldiers for your three-minute egg.'
'I won't fall apart.'
Charlie iced a tall Beefeater and the cubes cracked when he added tonic. He built himself an Irish on the rocks as the toy tram rattled through the labyrinth on his inner ear and went away.
Ingrid sipped her drink and pulled his bath towel aside.
'Your friend seems glad to see me.'
'We both are.'
'Tell him to take a nap.'
Charlie killed a yawn. 'You ring his bells.'
'So that's what they are. I thought you were smuggling baby hamsters.'
Ingrid lost her drink and cigarette on a side-table.
'There's a trick to taming hamsters,' said Charlie.
'Like this?'
'Don't talk with your mouth full.'
Ingrid pushed her face into Charlie's thighs, glad she had masked her fear with a show of levity. The tape round Charlie's ribs was very white against the bruised and faded tan. Ingrid made Charlie shudder with slow passes of her tongue.
During the four months Ingrid and Charlie had come together with casual regularity for what he variously described as 'nosh and ice-cream' or 'nookie and nibbles', Ingrid had never known him to raise his voice or to ante-up at the gaming-tables; and when Charlie collected on an overdue marker for the club his 'finder's fee' never recrossed the baize on the turn of a card. Charlie made cards stand on their heads and could spot a ringer three tables away.
Ingrid had learned not to ask about Charlie when her curiosity nagged her. The idle talk about him was as persistent as the hum of cicadas in a distant summer field, and just as ephemeral.

Ingrid opened her mouth and drew herself up on to his swollen member. Panting into his strong brown neck she kneaded his hard shoulders and said meaningless things into his ear. His plastered forearm supported the small of her back and his good hand cupped a buttock, finding the dimpled trigger-spot with a gentle thumb.

Ingrid brought her legs off the floor and crossed her ankles behind his back. Drew him deeper and leaned out and away to see into his face. The mashed eye was in shadow and the clear one stared at something through the wall and beyond the sky, lost in private thought.

'Come back to me, Charlie . . . .'

'I'm here, love . . . .'

Charlie roamed mentally, conjured faces caught in the complex web of London's heartland, sought out those who did not fit – those who might just have become ambitious enough to oust Archie Ogle. He drifted through the confines of Soho, from the prestige offices of Warner and Fox to the glaring huddle of porno cinemas which ran explicit movies for the international raincoat set and employed tired toms to twirl their tassels for sweaty loners in faded cellar clubs. Each alley, every back turning, mews and cul-de-sac. Each arcade, bar and spieler. Up narrow flights of stairs where the Maltese pimped, laundered hot money or sold heroin cut with baking soda to zonked-out kids who would die old without gathering years.

Into Old Compton Street where skiffle had given way to rock, where Eyetie Antoni held on to his dwindling patch and dreamed of earning the kind of respect his father Alfredo had enjoyed, and still lived with the hope that Special Branch would not stop him attracting his New York Sicilian contacts into London.

Up along Dean Street, where jazz and seared kebabs flavoured the neon air. Where Cypriots, divided by their Greek or Turkish origins, ran their ethnic kitchens, toms and bars in uneasy tandem. Where small film companies flew by night and amateur toms of every hue gave their punters stand-up quickies in the nearest unlit alley.

Then Frith Street, where sleek Bentleys delivered diners from the City of London to Wheeler's Braganza for expense-account seafood. Where winos lounged beside saunas with topless masseurs for either gender or sexual persuasion. Beak Street, Windmill Street and Archer Street; the rats' maze of streets bounded by Shaftesbury Avenue, Piccadilly Circus and Regent Street. Where street-markets, kosher cafés and Stripperamas stood cheek by jowl with dodgy hostess clubs; where carbonated perry passed for champagne, the girls smiled their shilling smiles as their pimps talked in thousands, thought in hundreds and paid out in tens.

And the Chinese getting organised in Gerrard Street. Gradually ousting the few scruffy Indian restaurants and ticket agencies, airline bucket shops and jobbing printers. Building a ghetto where the Triads could trade impassively in angel dust and horse, in opiates and cocaine. Always suspicious of round-eyed whitey and the few blacks with standing amongst the West End brotherhood. Dismissing the Kilburn Micks, despising the shopkeeping Asians, on nodding acquaintance with the stallies and market moguls of Berwick Street, and flat-faced with officials of any kind.

Charlie moved east.

Past the City of London to Bethnal Green where the Troy brothers waited impatiently, ever jealous of Archie's holdings, building their reputation with a campaign of violence Charlie had dubbed 'Duff of the Month Club'.

The Troys had a money-man behind them now, if persistent rumour was to be believed, and they wanted a slice of the West End pie, whatever it might take. They used the Bellavers from Catford for team-handed whacks, paid off the local law in grands, and still kept in touch with the old faces Archie had banished to Brighton — men like Kosher Kramer, who had fought Eyetie Antoni for supremacy in Soho before Archie had marked both their cards.

Charlie crossed the Thames to Camberwell where

Connie and Wally Harold were the kings of scrap metal and the used-car trade; experts in long-firm frauds and convenient warehouse fires when Board of Trade officials took too close an interest in their 'stock'. The brothers who thought Sir Oswald Mosley's fascists had got it about right except for the phoney politics and the uniforms; who reckoned that Coons, Yids, Pakis and Chinks were fair game for shake-downs, and a floor brad through the genitals when the sovs weren't coughed was standard practice with their collectors of the long green.

The Harolds were given the pavement when they passed, but nobody ever crossed the road to shake their hands like Archie's punters did. As Archie always said: 'You can't punch respect out of people. You have to earn that privilege.'

Troys, Harolds, Bellavers, Brighton, Triads, Malts .... Names and faces pumped through Charlie's mind in time to Ingrid's urgent jogging.

'Come with me, Charlie ....'

'I'm here, love ....'

'Yessss ....'

Ingrid's back arched before she went limp and Charlie eased her down on to the bed to share one of her Mores as they sprawled on the cool counterpane, his thoughts as ephemeral as the mentholated fumes. There were no answers, only questions.

'What happens if Archie doesn't make it, Charlie?' Ingrid voiced the fear in both of them.

Charlie thought: *I know too much for what I do.*

In Canterbury in 1165 a group of monks witnessed an explosion on the moon one June evening just before vespers. Then it was believed that the universe was constant, incapable of change, and before their eyes, whack, Lucifer's bolt spread burning plasma into the infinite vault, blacking out the white crescent of reflected light. The Blessed Gervaise recorded the event from eyewitness accounts, despite the fact that his log may have gone against all previous precepts of the known immutable universe created by the Almighty.

Is Archie that to me?

An immutable universe?

'Archie will make it.'

Charlie breathed Ingrid's musk as she snuggled closer, not realising he had spoken aloud.

Ingrid was long gone.

Unable to sleep, Charlie took his arm out for a drink in company. Solitary supping was for alcoholics.

At five in the morning Covent Garden already throbbed with vitality. Handcarts ground on the cobbles, and sweating costers exchanged cheerful profanity as they offloaded lorries to build fanciful displays of wholesale fruit and vegetables in persistent drizzle, turning night into day with hard bargaining over prime, second- and third-class pippins, hothouse lettuce, Guernsey tomatoes, Egyptian potatoes and cantaloup melons, shaving farthings on their 'morning-fresh' for hoteliers and restaurateurs, wholesalers and shipping lines, swearing on their relatives' lives there wasn't a cheaper bargain in the western hemisphere.

All costers are born with a thirst, and the nine market pubs did Cup Final business every night of the week. Committed drinkers from all over London found their way into Covent Garden, hoping to convince the licensees they were bona-fide traders who could be served without penalty.

Charlie lined his stomach with tea and saveloys at the coffee-stall under the portico of St Paul's Church and sank a large Irish in the Nag's Head and the Enterprise before going on to the Kemble's Head opposite Bow Street magistrate's court.

A crowd of mourners with a coffin filled the saloon bar. Charlie pushed into the public where Stripes Flynn banged for service over the noise. An overweight man with fists like capons, Stripes wore a straw hat, a soiled apron, and boots caked with bloody sawdust. He had started as an 'empties boy' at the turn of the century, remembered the brothels in Drury Lane, the carriage-makers of Long Acre, when only Irish women were allowed to porter, and the last bare-fist prize-fight in the piazza. He and Archie had become partners in the black market in 1940, and he was fond of telling how he ran a Bentley, a house in Harrow and his butcher's and fruiterer's in Covent Garden and Smithfield meat-market — and still couldn't sign his own name.

'Glass of Bass and a ham on white. And Gawd have mercy on us sinners if it ain't Charlie Dance. Thought you was too high on the firm to trudge the cobbles to cop the subs.'

Charlie added whiskies to Flynn's pint and sandwich and paid with small change.

'What's the crack with the coffin?'

'Old Custard Sammy's boys giving their dad a proper send-off. Taking his mortals around every pub he ever drank in before they drop him at Kensal Green cemetery. There was a man who knew apples, Chas. Custards, biffins, codlins, cat's heads and leathercoats, pearmains and redstreaks. Knew 'em all. He was still humping a barrow when he was eighty-four, and was ninety-two when he dropped off last Friday. Five foot of iron he was, and never went a day without his fifteen pints of Burton. Reckoned he sweat sixteen pints, so he could never get pissed. Never did, neither.'

Charlie reached for a fiver. 'I'll send a drink over.'

'Not wise, Chas. They're market, you ain't. And seeing you with your face all chopped up might remind them you and Archie had a bit of a mishap. Give them ideas.'

'Accidents happen.'

'To the likes of you and Archie? They've heard different.'

'How different?'

Flynn drank Bass and chased it with Irish.

'Just what's being bubbled around the barrows. For what that's worth.'

'How about not a lot? Nothing.'

Flynn laid a stub of a thumb against Charlie's chest.

'I'll write that out and hang it in the shop with my old dad's Victoria Cross, shall I? Old jessie's gossip from round the parish pump, right?'

'You're the only jessie bubbling, Stripes.'

'Hardnose the slags, Charlie. Accident? My grannie's armpit.'

A slow fire built in Charlie's head.

'You're wearing a lot of mouth, Stripes.'

Flynn wolfed half his sandwich and wiped a shred of ham from his chin.

'Nobody reckons Arch more than me, Charlie, but business is business, right? Changes come, us traders will grin and bear it.'

Charlie's good hand found Flynn's shoulder.

'You mouthing for you or the whole market?'

'I'm *saying* it, Charlie, but it's being *thought* all over. Walk through the barrows for the crack. See who looks at you direct like old Stripes does. And then count them whose eyes scuttle in the gutter with the orange peel.'

'Goodbye, Sammy,' chorused the saloon bar.

Charlie heard the tram in his ear. Nerves in his plastered arm jumped like fledglings on a log. The mourners were beyond an opaque glass screen rich with etched herons and bulrushes.

Flynn sighed and pulled his nose.

'That's how it is, Chas. Any pissed-up barrow-boy with a bellyful of beer thinks he can take a poke at your firm. You just show us some hard. And don't just half-mind Archie when he comes back to the cobbles. Get tooled-up and mind him proper.'

'Shooters, Stripes?'

'Can't make mutton without topping sheep.'

'A flashed shooter has to be used, Stripes.'

'Ain't stopping the Troys. They hit a face that way last Tuesday week in Hoxton. Shoved a twelve-bore down his Y-fronts and blew his calves off. And for what? A ten-car forecourt not worth a tenner a month. Mindless that — maiming a punter when a couple of moody digs would have brought him round to coughing subs.'

Charlie let Stripes talk.

'Before the war it was different. Then your local manor was six streets square and you knew everybody. We all lived in the street with our chairs on the pavement and the front doors wide open. Sorted aggro with the rival manors on a bit of neutral ground. The hard lads never caused bother in the pubs they drank in, and protection was a few half-crowns and some giblets for the cat.'

Stripes stopped to kill his pint.

'Now the heavy mobs duck about in motors and talk in grands. They don't care who they hurt so long as there's profit in it. Don't even take care of their own punters. The good-bad old days are dead and gone like old Custard there. And more's the pity. I don't want to see old ladies starving and kids with the arse out of their trousers queuing for Sally Ann soup and dying for a florin's worth of medicine, but all this hard-bad-and-nasty ain't no change for the better.'

'No shooter cured a kid's whooping cough.'

'Happen you ain't wrong, Charlie. But fire with fire, son. I've seen you bare-fist on the cobbles. You're tasty. But fists against shooters ain't no contest, right?'

Flynn laid a hard paw over Charlie's hand.

'Can I have my shoulder back now?'

'Why not?'

Charlie drank his Irish down. It tasted of nothing. His anger passed as quickly as it had come. Smoke in the wind.

'See you, Stripes.'

'My best to Arch . . . .'

'Oh blimey yeah.'

It was 5 a.m. at the Philadelphia House in Mayfair.

Ingrid relined her lips in the staff powder-room. Jaded by six hours of dealing five-card stud, she lit a More and let it burn in the ashtray, wishing she was back at the Savoy with Charlie. Jorgesson the South African had killed a bottle of hollands gin whilst he lost £20,000 in cash and markers. He'd called Ingrid a 'rooinek dassie' when she left the table. Made it sound foul.

'So I'm a rednecked rabbit.'

Ingrid poked her tongue at the bronzed mirror and retouched her lashes.

The door banged inwards and Dotty Machin flopped into a chair, blonde hair tousled, face glowing.

'I'm finished, but you're wanted. Your high-roller is ready to start losing again.'

Dotty took Ingrid's lit More and ate smoke. She served cocktails in the private suite and charged a hundred a night to rumple her bedsheets. Her black pimp Jonas was serving a five stretch in Durham for demanding money with menaces and aggravated assault, but she salted his percentage away and visited him every second month.

Ingrid lit a second More. 'Let them get somebody else.'

'Won't wash, Ing. Jorgesson wants you and only you to empty his pockets. He couldn't keep his minces off your muffins. I reckon he'd pay a year's rent for a bit of rumpo with you.'

'Nonsense.' Ingrid swept make-up into her dress bag as Dotty giggled.

'If I had your legs and looks, I'd earn real poppy. You're the only model I know who's really modelled. You know, with your clothes on? Tommy Troy offered me some of that lewdie-nudie stuff, but I turned it down. That faggoty brother of his wanted it up the back the wrong way. Know what I mean?'

'Only too well.'

'My Jonas said to stay away from the Troys. "Them slags ain't healthy," he said.'

Ingrid patted Dotty's hand.

'For once, Jonas was right.'

'The money was good, though.'

'Machin, you're an idiot.'

Dotty pouted at Ingrid's expression. 'I only said it to see your face go funny.'

The table captain's face came round the door, said, 'Five

minutes, Ing. No lady's excuses or female toffee. Clean this tosser and you'll be home within an hour, right?' – and the door sighed closed.

'Smooth,' Ingrid sneered.

'Maybe there'll be a choice if Archie don't make—'

Dotty spilled ash down herself as Ingrid's fury reared her back.

'Don't even *think* that. If the Troys got hold of you, you'd look fifty, act ninety, and be finished as a human being before next Christmas. You think my Charlie would let—?'

Dotty's grin almost touched her eyes.

'*My* Charlie, Miss Dakin? Get out the orange blossom and book a bloody church.'

'You know what I mean.'

'Look, Ing, I only meant—'

'Save it.'

Ingrid stubbed her cigarette. Charlie hated tobacco on her breath and ashtrays in the bedroom. His flat in Pimlico gleamed without a thing out of place, and she knew he would have hated her mother's house: the stale air and staler bedlinen, the men who came and went after her father deserted them.

'Go home, Dotty. There must be *someone* waiting.'

'Only the canary. All right, so I'm just a cheerful daft whore . . . .'

Dotty's eyes had misted, and Ingrid kissed her. Pink with contrition.

'No, you're not. You're a friend and I'm sorry. Truly really.'

'And I'm too ignorant to be insulted, right?'

'That makes two of us.'

Ingrid followed Nasty Nostrils into the private suite where the big South African called for new cards and snapped his fingers at a small bald man who brought him drinks. Ingrid broke the seals on three new casino packs, spread them for Jorgesson's inspection, idly taking in the bald fatty at his side. He built Jorgesson a tall iced gin as if he'd done it many times before and sat with his hands washing themselves in his lap. Ingrid knew him from somewhere, and dealt the first hand, knowing she would remember. He might have been a shill from one of the suburban clubs, scouting for a floating gang who planned to ring the tables.

Jorgesson drew three cards and bet with £50 chips to win the first hand. He won twice more and had the fat man trim him a cigar. He drew two cards to his fourth hand, watched Ingrid draw one, leaned sideways and said: 'Light me, Vic.'

The fat man snapped a cheap Colibri at Jorgesson's Havana.

'Instant death, eh, Dirk? The little lady brings you luck.'

His voice rolled Ingrid back fifteen years, and she saw him with more hair and less belly. The toothy smiles when he took her on his knee to tell her fanciful stories of his own childhood in his lilting foreign accent. Sometimes he had been Armenian or Georgian, other times Dutch or Belgian. He had even shown her his many different passports. But that was before his factory failed and Mother entertained at home to make ends meet. By then Ingrid was twelve and Vic Dakin was just another sometime man who left money on Mother's pillow.

Nausea rolled with Jorgesson's Cuban smoke.

Fifteen years, you running bastard.

Ingrid heard the bet, matched it and raised a further thousand.

Jorgesson's smile hung in a pale octopus of smoke, and Vic saw himself through his daughter's eyes. Wiped his moist lips with a manicured hand, his own eyes shadowed and unreadable.

'She's showing three hearts, Dirk. Possible straight?' he said.

Jorgesson pushed more chips into the pot.

'Just me and the little lady and her three lonely hearts. Bluffing for her straight.'

Her heart inside a blazing fist, Ingrid raised two

thousand more. Blind to Jorgesson's stare of disbelief.

Fifteen years ago, Vic Dakin's heavies had pushed Ingrid aside to take flash photographs of Mother and two black American airmen for his divorce evidence. Caught her *in flagrante delicto* in a black and white sexual sandwich, her eyes bleached by flash and fear and hopelessness. Ingrid had been twelve years old and still had nightmares about it.

Ingrid turned her cards in a dream. The royal flush snapped over, slackened Jorgesson's jowls, cleaning him out.

'The House wins.'

The table captain raked the chips aside, and Vic led Jorgesson away through the gold chairs like a huge pink baby.

'Told you,' Nasty Nostrils said comfortably.

Wind tugged Ingrid's coat as she walked to the taxi rank. The pavements dried and cumulus clouds rolled east without shedding rain. The moon was a scudding orange ghost lost in sodium glare. A tabby with mad eyes stared through basement railings before flicking away to rattle milk-bottles.

Rapid footsteps came from behind.

Ingrid swung her torch as Charlie had taught her. The beam blinded Jorgesson's plump shill just as Ingrid's bag slammed into his face.

'Killing me is patricide, girl.' Vic Dakin pinched bloody nostrils. His Continental accent and cockney phrasing were an odd mix muffled by his hand.

Ingrid was scalded by adrenalin and fright.

'What d'you want?'

'Nothing that'll cost you.'

Dakin sidled into the kerb.

'You're balling Charlie Dance, right? Just get me a meet with him. For old time's sake.'

'Old times nothing. You talked Mother on to her back for the milkman to get your yoghurt for free.'

'Mother Hubbard, girl. Your old man's got a tickle that

needs backing by a big firm. You seen Jorgesson; he's worth fortunes to me, you *and* Charlie.'

Dakin's pupils were blobs of slick mud.

'Go to the Harolds.'

Ingrid knew Vic had bankrupted a Milanese nylon factory in an involved export fraud, and that the Harolds had long-firmed the stock and squeezed Vic out of the huge profits. But that was just street talk, and the Fraud Squad had proved nothing.

'And earn three nails and a hammer? Vic's begging, Ing. My number's on this card. Get it to Chas and tell him I'll make the meet any where or when. Kosher.'

Ingrid quelled compassion. Dakin's fear was rank on the wind, the smell of her darkest dreams. She took the card and said: 'If you hear nothing, it's "No", right? No pestering.'

'On your mother's . . . . Perhaps not, eh?'

Dakin wiped his slack mouth.

Ingrid just switched off her torch.

Dakin went away, hurrying towards a parked Mercedes with foreign plates. Jorgesson was behind the wheel and he burned rubber pulling away.

Ingrid took a cab to Charing Cross and walked through to the embankment to make sure she wasn't followed, took a second cab round Parliament Square and on to the Savoy.

Charlie dozed over a copy of the *Daily Express*. Archie Ogle's picture had made the front page.

Ingrid showered, then kissed Charlie awake. He liked her damp, and Vic's problems could wait.

Charlie flicked a crumb of sleep from his good eye and reached the telephone across Ingrid's naked back.

'Yeah?'

'Cosied up in Archie's ice-cream parlour, are you?'

Queenie sounded tired.

'Ain't why Arch keeps this suite on.'

'Don't kid Queenie. Archie wouldn't be Archie without his quota of crumpet. Marriage is knowing and caring — not making bones for soup.'

Ingrid rolled and exposed a full round breast. Charlie kissed it, and she frowned without coming to the surface.

'Makes you a bit special, Queenie.'

'Soft soap don't roll me on my back. Bad news travels fast. The Tonnas are staying home in Toronto.'

Charlie itched under the plaster.

'Ain't Roger and Jesus the loyal ones? What's the SP on Archie?'

'Doctors tell you nothing but nothing.'

'Want I should mark their cards?'

'They'd need permanent bedspace. There's others need sorting your way, Charlie.'

Charlie's torso ridged with hard muscle.

'Just name faces.'

'Two wreaths came to the house. One from Bethnal Green. One from Camberwell. Subtle they ain't.'

'I'm on my way.'

'The bandstand. One hour.'

Queenie rang off. Charlie dropped the phone in its cradle, and the cord climbed itself like a contracting snake.

'Breakfast?' Ingrid yawned.

'Later.'

Charlie padded into the bathroom and turned the shower to full, his sweat colder than the spray.

Lucifer's bolt had hit him in the stomach.

The great horse-chestnut was already ancient when the small parish park of Westcheap Within was created about it. Now it bowered over neat lawns and symmetrical gravel paths and threw cool dappled shade on the hottest summer days. Taller than the modest Inigo Jones church sited at the eastern corner of the park, the tree dominated a contemporary engraving of the church's sanctification which hung on the building's south transept wall; had silently witnessed the interment of hundreds of contagious corpses during the Great Plague; had survived the Great Fire of London the following year; and now heralded spring with budding spears in the grey overcast above the

Edwardian bandstand on the central lawn.

The slatted wooden benches bore dedication plaques and had been donated by people who had found tranquillity in this small green oasis in the industrial heart of East London. The lower foundations of the Georgian boundary walls were faced with old headstones, their carved commemorations mostly weathered away. Only in the lee of the covered entry-gate were the names and dates visible, and Charlie, who would have liked a sovereign for each time he had met Archie there, knew them all by heart.

Queenie kissed Charlie hello and sat on a bench to feed the pigeons.

'Archie proposed to me here.'

'He said.'

Charlie stood, favouring his ribs, unwilling to put up with another walk down another memory lane.

'Old means you repeat yourself.'

Queenie broke bread into squares.

'Not many,' Charlie said for something to say.

'What's it like to have men's fists, Charlie – to hit and hit hard?'

'You can't hit what hurts inside. That kind of pain you swallow.'

Queenie hit a hen on the head with a crust.

'They won't let Archie up now they've sent the wreaths.'

'Who's down? Him or you?'

'You ain't grinning like nothing's happened.'

'Nothing has I can't handle.'

'You'd have to cheer up to look miserable.'

'Says who, Queenie?'

'Archie wants you to play the waiting game.'

'Oh yeah? Like he wouldn't be out there with a sockful of pennies if he wasn't so banged up?'

Charlie snorted, and Queenie licked her lips.

'Twenty years ago maybe.'

'That's you talking, not the governor.'

'Maybe.'

'No "maybe" about it, Lady.'

An old woman led her mongrel round the park and went away. Young sparrows squabbled in the eaves and a bell marked the hour from the nearby Salvation Army Hostel. A watery sun cast soft shadows through the chestnut and traffic purled from the confines of Smithfield market.

The real world seemed a long way away.

Charlie made fists in his pocket and said: 'This never was a nice business, Queenie. Hail Marys don't make the sovs tinkle. Our firm stays top or we lose the street talk. The Troys can't buy what we get for nothing, and Connie Harold can't tickle the West End for the same reasons. By the time we've been to a première they're busking to an empty street. We can lose Archie's fifty years in as many minutes if we don't hold the cobbles.'

'Shooters, Charlie?'

'Shooters nothing. I've shot golds at Bisley and can knock the pips from all the playing-cards you pin to a fence. That's cards not men. Shooters make noise and wake up the Heavy Filth, and there's hundreds who'll pull a trigger for the right poppy. And their loyalty lasts as long as the money.'

'Who's to trust, then, Charlie?'

'There's me. And maybe me.'

Queenie pulled Charlie's face down and pecked his nose. 'Hold the cobbles, Charlie.'

'Oh blimey yeah,' Charlie told the pigeons.

CHAPTER TWO

THE FASCIA BOARDS of the Martyred Thomas were freshly glossed and lettered in gilt, and the marbled Corinthian columns between the Edwardian windows were scoured of grime. The bar doors had been marine-varnished and fitted with new brass furniture. The interior had been refurbished in mahogany and brass and acid-etched glass, and carpeted throughout in maroon Axminster.

Although their names did not appear on the magistrate's licence or the brewer's manifest, the Troys had spent big money on the Mile End Road pub.

The famous first-floor gymnasium was altogether different. Approached through a side-door and a steep flight of stairs, it smelled of resin, old leather, hot unwashed manhood and disinfectant. Period boxing posters yellowed by nicotine and sepia'd by flies had been greased by a million curious fingers. Tommy Farr and 'Bombardier' Billy Wells, Joe Louis and Bruce Woodcock, Freddy Mills and Randolph Turpin, Georges Carpentier and Rocky Marciano hung beside many dozens of forgotten featherweights, lightweights and heavyweights lost in obscurity and untouched by fame. Very few had fought for West End money, most had grunted through midweek three-rounders, their modest achievements as faded as the discoloured oblongs of cheap print.

Dusty light seeped through unwashed windows on to the full-sized ring, the rows of rusted and defaced lockers, canvas punchbags and weights, the shower room with its cracked tiles and lukewarm water; the hungry hopefuls and their hopeless trainers, who fouled the laden air with empty bragging and pungent expletives.

Has-beens, never-weres and no-chancers gathered there to watch for the shadowy big-time break that would never come their way.

Above the gymnasium were the Troys' offices. Unlike the bars of the Martyred Thomas they were decorated to their own personal taste, and violent primaries overpowered pastels, flock Regency stripes clashed with wildly patterned carpets, and lumpy furniture imitated leather under lights Ida Troy bought from fast-talking street traders. Plaster ducks flew, and a cocktail cabinet played tinkly tunes when it was opened.

Tommy Troy showed Vic Dakin his capped teeth and said: 'You give me a thirst, Vic.'

Dakin sat on a hard chair licking his mouth. Limehouse Lou and Gay Gordon had hauled him out of bed just before seven and hadn't allowed him his shoes. He wore trousers over his pyjamas, and his bare feet ached with cold.

Tommy ordered drinks all round, and Limehouse Lou mixed vodka martinis to 'Tulips from Amsterdam.'

'Except Vic here. He needs a clear head.'

'And he didn't get breakfast, neither,' added Jesse.

He took his drink and winked at his brother Tommy.

'Two years you've owed us, Vic,' said Tommy. 'Where you been hiding?'

'Only been back a couple or three days, Tom. Honest.'

'Three weeks, ain't it, Jesse?'

'Right, Tommy.'

Jesse watched Gay Gordon strop a naked razor against his palm, and Tommy scratched a sideburn with a letter-opener.

'Two years ago me and brother Jesse came all the way out to Milan on your say-so, Vic. To look at some genuine bent Old Masters. Florentine, wasn't they, Jesse?'

'More like Andy Capps with a few candles thrown in.'

'Twenty-four months ago, Vic. But we remember all them paintings in that garage in Milan, don't we, Jesse? You must have spent weeks getting them cobwebs to hang right.'

'Work of art,' said Jesse.

'More than we can say for the pictures themselves.'

Tommy leaned on the *Daily Express*, his elbow on Archie Ogle's forehead. Dakin squirmed in his chair, looking for the right words, knowing there weren't any.

'Tell him your favourite,' said Jesse.

'Belshazzar's Feast?' said Tommy. 'All of ten feet long. In that garage in Milan where Vic said it'd be? Big picture. All them biblical geezers swilling down the old holy vino with all them topless birds. And there's this hand – no arm, just a hand – and it's writing on the wall. You know, like God telling them it's drinking-up time. Anyway, there it was. All painted on canvas. In a big gold frame with curly bits all round it. Very old. Very impressive-looking.'

Dakin watched the letter-opener tease Tommy's hair.

'Good, weren't it, Jesse?'

'Handsome,' Jesse agreed.

Tommy pointed the letter-opener into Dakin's face.

'Only there was hardboard under the canvas and the gold frame was painted plaster. Well, Vic, me and brother Jesse just had to laugh. Didn't we, Jesse?'

'All the way to Vic's hotel.'

'Only he'd booked out and gone missing.'

'Leaving the brothers Troy with the paper hat.'

'And out a good few sovs in expenses.' Tommy rounded his desk to lean over Dakin. 'And still wearing the paper hat two years later.'

Dakin took a kick to the chest and dropped to drool on the carpet.

'Lucky he came back for a last laugh, eh, Jessie?'

'Lucky ain't in it. Give him to Gordy.'

Gay Gordon inspected an immaculate nail. 'I'll make him laugh.' His Gorbals accent had an effeminate lilt.

Tommy flicked Dakin behind the ear and drew blood.

'Gordon came on the firm after you done your runner, Vic. He dishes out more than paper hats.'

Tommy went back behind his desk, and Dakin was lifted

back on to the hard chair. He tried not to cuddle himself or gabble as he said: 'Those Milanese art dealers were Cosa Nostra, Tommy. They wanted me for that nylon export deal Connie Harold stitched me up over. He never paid them out and left me with my thumb up where the sun don't shine. I left a message at your hotel, didn't I? If I'd made the meet with you at that garage, we'd all have ended up with the paper hat.'

Tommy patted pomaded hair. 'It was you done the runner on Connie Harold, not the other way about. You ran out owing us. You run out owing everyone. And that makes you a slag who's run out of time.'

Dakin tried not to squirm away from Gordon's blade. 'You don't mean that, Tommy.'

Tommy said nothing with a show of upper teeth and a lot of gum. Dakin's scrotum tightened, and Jesse cracked knuckles.

'Look at us long and hard, Vicky boy, and see if we ain't serious.'

Dakin found Limehouse Lou by the tinkling cocktail cabinet, red hair over a pale freckled face, eyes that could have been holes in putty, paring his thumb with a razor as though it belonged to somebody else.

Gordon smelled of expensive Harrods Cologne, and white-blonde hair cropped close to his skull formed a hard V over his forehead. His no-colour eyes read Dakin's face like a dull book with no pictures, and the razor stropping his palm seemed to steal all the light in the room.

Jesse had put on weight since Milan. His features had coarsened and his eyes had a dead look. Only his plump mouth seemed alive and reminded Dakin of a red anemone ready for another small silver fish.

Tommy was unchanged when Dakin faced him to plead.

'We'll work something out, eh, Tommy?'

'How? When you've earned the paper hat and a wreath?'

Dakin wept when his pyjamas were ripped away. His shrunken penis was pinched between thumb and forefinger and Jesse's breath was warm on his belly as the ceiling lights flared like mad suns.

'Please . . . Tommy . . . .'

Jesse stroked Vic's member with Gordon's cut-throat.

'A nice little kosher trim. An inch out of the middle to feed to the goldfish. How'd that be, Vic?'

'I'll trade, for Chrissakes . . . .'

'Like what? There's nothing left.'

'I've got . . . Jorgesson.'

'Sounds like the foreign clap.'

A kick to the groin doubled Dakin up. He smelled his body hair singe as a candle played along a calf. Tommy leaked smoke and said: 'Give him some around the jewels.'

Dakin burrowed into carpet to get away from screams that came from somewhere deep inside him. The slap and thump of skipping came from the gym below. To stop the pain he talked of mineral rights in Namaqualand. Of Dirk Jorgesson and diamonds. Rare earths and bauxite and perlite. Clays rich in aluminium. And more about diamonds . . . .

Tommy half-listened as he wondered if Jesse and his young boys didn't have the best of it. He got his oats his way and Tommy's wife Helen laid there like a dead cod when his leg went over, even though he let her moon about down the local RC church and hang crosses all over the house. Grudging conjugals and all that religious palaver were enough to send a saint off to the local tomshop, and listening to Dakin sprinkle a primrose path with precious stones was pathetic if it hadn't the ring of truth.

'Let him up.'

Slammed upright, Dakin stared into his naked lap. Blood welled from a cut he had not felt and turned pink when he was doused in water.

'Is this straight?'

'On my baby's life, Tommy.'

Dakin pictured Ingrid in pigtails and hated the graceless cow of a woman she had become. Tomming around with Archie Ogle's top monkey and looked at her father like he was something she'd wiped off her shoe.

Blood dripped on to the *Daily Express* Lou had put under the chair to save the carpet, and Tommy winked as the red stain obliterated Archie's image.

'I take that as an omen. Clean lard-arse up and take him back where you found him, Lou. You're his minder. Our new partner needs protection, don't he?'

From you more than anybody, Dakin thought drearily.

Charlie took a cab to Frith Street and gave his name into a doorphone. Kensington Kate's Mother's Club was in a double basement below a cinema cutting-room Archie used as a front for his local collection agency. Kate's members worked the amusement arcades and pubs after dark, and came to Mother's to sway to Johnny Mathis records on a postage stamp of a dance-floor.

Kate had served a ten stretch in Pentonville before the war and wore a leotard top to show off his severely scarred back. He had been one of the last prisoners birched in a mainland prison and was proud of it. There wasn't a regular West End face with half a brain who did not respect him and, as one of the few 'straights' welcome in Mother's, Charlie reckoned Kensington Kate could give hard lessons to a flint quarry.

Kate and Electric Raymond watered the optics, joss-sticks burned on the backbar and a muted Mario Lanza came from the jukebox. Pink cherubs frolicked on the stucco walls and a life-sized naked man stretched his naked limbs on a couch inside a gilded frame, an excellent parody of Goya's *Maja Nude*. The silk pillows under the reclining buttocks were real enough to stroke.

Kate raised his watered Pernod.

'My favourite butch villain. Give us your face.' He kissed the air near Charlie's swollen eye. 'Well, somebody did your profile no good when they turned you and Archie over.'

Charlie shrugged on to a stool. 'That's what the papers say.'

'Drink?'

Electric Raymond's face was without make-up and shadowed by beard stubble.

'Too early. A word, Kate.'

'Flounce off and get Charlie some coffee, Electric. And take your time coming back. This is serious girls' talk.'

Raymond grinned and went.

'He's a sweet old thing, Chas, but I do miss my lovely drink of chocolate. Fancy going back to Nigeria without a word, the bitch,' Kate still missed the willowy black he called 'The African Queen'. 'Whatever goes down, we're solid with you and the firm, Chas.'

'I need a favour, Kate.'

'Pink Parisian underwear?'

'The stuff you knock out to the transvestites? The closest that stuff got to Paris was the French pub in Dean Street. Manny Manson knocks it out in his shmutter shop in Marlborough Street.'

'You would know. Eyes everywhere.'

'Not everywhere. That's the favour.'

'Sounds expensive.'

'A thousand sovs for openers.'

'I'd drink petrol for that.'

'Too easy.'

'And light the blue touchpaper myself?'

'Child's play.'

Kate arched a pencilled eyebrow, and Electric Raymond clattered cups as Fred Astaire crooned 'Funny Face'.

'Ante up, then, Charlie.'

'I want one of your finger-tame fairies to get kissing-cousin-close to a certain face. Close enough to count his snore rate and how many man-sized tissues he uses for the serious sniffles.'

'That close.'

'Just that close.'

'Does this certain face have a name?'

'Only if you get me the right fairy.'

'Describe this doyen of the dildo.'

'Seventeen — eighteen years old. Good teeth, good skin.

Well endowed in the jewel department and no temperament that can't be controlled. None of your theatrical vapours, no snorting or shooting up. No pill-popping or funny cigarettes. He'll have to take physical abuse without needing it, and his lips stay closed unless he's bubbling up to me. Even if he does end up in hospital without his thumbnails, right?'

Kate looked thoughtful. His hazel eyes gleamed like fake seed pearls.

'You're talking about a slice of West End prime rib.'

'Someone you just might be saving for yourself.'

'Listen, you heterosexual waste of a pair of legs, I'd give my eye-teeth for a little darling like that.'

Electric Raymond served coffee in good china and minced away.

Charlie added milk to Java blend and stirred.

'I'll up it a monkey.'

'A grand plus five is dough. Got to be double dodgy. Who's the special face?'

'Jesse Troy.'

'Jesse-fucking-Troy? You know what that arse of a face is capable of?'

Charlie swallowed coffee and rubbed his bruised eye.

'Never known you to verbal up on the swearing stakes.'

'Then, have it double.' Kate repeated the expletive.

'And another monkey.'

'Two grand? Not for three.'

'Three it is.'

'You mean it, you soft sorry sod.'

'Not many,' said Charlie.

Kate laid his lean hand over Charlie's fist.

'Listen — and this ain't fairy tales — last Christmas, Jesse Troy got his hands on a new stray in a Gerrard Street club. You know, jazz and muggles. Kissy-mouth, touchy-thigh, see what I'm carrying on my hip for a little virgin like you? The stray was only sixteen. Just another almost-fairy down from the provinces where the butch locals threw coal at him because he had a lisp and a bit of a walk on him, right?'

'I'm listening.'

'Jesse took him back to the Troy Fortress and gave him a seeing-to in every orifice until the kid's seeing and thinking double. Jesse even covered him in Golliberry jam and licked him clean.'

'So Jesse's got a sweet tooth. I thought he was into Marmite.'

'Gag away, Charlie. That was only for openers. Jesse passed out from the booze and smack — came to with the horrors. The stray's face down in the bath with claret up the walls and a loo-brush up where the sun don't shine. The kid's well dead with a ruptured spleen and other forensic delights. Jesse has the screaming abdabs and Gay Gordon finds him well ready to eat buttons off the furniture. Gordy gives Jesse a coke straightener and the good news that the stray's brown bread, dead. They have a snivel together, pack the stray into a trunk and drive him off to the seaside — lose his mortals on an outgoing tide from Foulness and go home for a quiet cuddle and some trouble-free sleep. That's three grand's worth right there.'

Charlie's ribs ached, and he saw Micky Dogge wave before he went under for ever.

'Where'd you get that sweet little bubble, Kate?'

'Gay Gordon himself. He got pissed up and bragged it all to one of my fairies. And made it sound like he'd set Jesse up. Hell hath no fury like a scorned iron, and you know how Gordy and Jessie was cosied up. Thank whatever that pricks like Gordon don't come in packets of three like condoms.'

'And they sent Archie a wreath.'

'Did they just?'

'Not many. Where does that leave our deal?'

'Well on.'

'Good.'

'And not just for the dough. Gordon went potty when he he remembered he'd talked out of turn and looked for the ear he'd whispered in. We got the fairy away to Amsterdam just in time, and the last I heard he was swanning about the Med on a yacht with some Lawrence of Arabia from Cairo.'

Charlie nodded with lidded eyes.

'Were the Troys in on that iron-ball trick with you and Archie?'

Charlie turned his cup on its saucer.

Kate bit his drink and scratched a delicate nostril.

'OK, Charlie. If you weren't carved from stone, you wouldn't be Archie's top bastard. I'm an old queen who wants to see Jesse and Gordon under six feet of sod. Or in Broadmoor mental hospital where they belong. And either suits this kiddy. You want that drink now?'

'When you've squared a special fairy.'

'Hold anything but your breath.'

Charlie took the stairs two at a time, suffocated by incense.

Archie Ogle relived a long-gone Sunday in a medicated fog.

Nurses fussed professionally outside his oxygen tent and Queenie's needles clacked with Archie's heels as he scattered Soho Square pigeons in the long-gone Coronation year of ten years before.

'He's mumbling. Trying to speak,' Queenie told a nurse.

'Some sing or think they're swimming the Channel.'

The nurse adjusted a saline drip.

Archie walked away from the present as a younger, stronger man. Four old men and a big woman waited in November mist by Cibber's statue of Charles II. Old Alfredo and Tessio for the Italians, Jewish Bob for the Hatton Garden diamond merchants, Cubby Colleano for the Maltese, and Bad Alice for the local clubs and spielers.

They were all dead, but Archie could see them as plain as day.

Archie sweated into his pillow as Cubby hurried forward to slow his pace. Archie was impatient, still jaded by the long flight from North America.

'Trouble,' said Cubby. 'Alfredo's son Antoni is facing off Kosher Kramer for who runs Soho.'

Archie knelt to retie nonexistent laces on his casuals.

'Eyetie Tony and Kosher? From soldiers to generals inside a month? I've been gone thirty days, not thirty years. Hitler didn't declare war so fucking fast.'

Cubby waved his arms and looked sad.

'Talk slow and think fast, Arch. It's taken ten years to get the firms talking, and them two nebishes have spread enough acid to erode all you've built. If their mouths cast shadows, the sun wouldn't rise for three generations. There isn't a twopenny tom or a ratbag wino who hasn't taken sides.'

Archie glared at the group by the statue.

'That lot look like they want answers. Say something I can bite on.'

Cubby put a Remembrance poppy in Archie's buttonhole.

'Alberto's folding with the big C. His son Antoni can't wait to play the Don like he's in some chicken-shit village in Sicily. Uncle Tessio's playing the first brass monkey as usual. He's tried talking to Antoni, but the shmuck won't listen.'

'And Jewish Bob?'

'Bob's well displeased with Kosher Kramer. Any more of Kosher's antics and we'll lose our money laundry through Amsterdam. Kosher's muscled some of the smaller Hatton Garden merchants for subs and figures the bigger ones will play along. He's got himself a small army of arm-breakers lined up east of Smithfield, and figures to turn over all the Eyeties in one go; figures that'll give him Soho on a plate and you'll swallow it.'

Archie punched a thigh.

'He never was the cleverest yiddle on the fiddle. What do Antoni and Kosher think they're playing? Ethnic Monopoly? "You give me Greek Street and I'll swap you Leicester Square and two dozen used toms"?'

'Ain't no laughing matter, Arch.'

'Ain't "Spot the Virgin", neither. I take it you've smiled at both sides and kept your khyber to the alley wall?'

'Does it rain downwards? Smooth Bad Alice first.'

'Her? Pound to a magpie she'll take care of herself. Come on.'

Old Alfredo turned a fedora and Tessio leaned on a walking-stick. Alice wore her best black and Jewish Bob had his thumbs in a yellow waistcoat. There were nods without handshakes. They might come later with agreement.

Bad Alice stripped a glove from a bandaged hand.

'That was my earner last night. Ten stitches and a club that won't open for a month. Plus squaring the law for *not* investigating what didn't ought to have happened. And this is Remembrance Sunday, Arch. I should be at the Cenotaph. Her up the palace is there for the first time as queen. And you know what that means to me.'

Archie made fists, and his leather gloves squeaked at the seams.

'I know, Alice girl. The damages are my shout. Just name me the guilty toerags.'

Alice jerked comfortable chins at old Alfredo.

'His idiot son's oppos took the needle to Kosher's tearaways from Bethnal Green. Wouldn't drink side by side. Wouldn't leave peaceful. Next thing it was bottles, fists and hot verbals over who runs Soho. You and yours should have been there to crack down, Archie.'

Tessio leaned on his stick and looked pained. 'There's a new breed of mongrel pissing up lamp-posts to claim territory. Antoni was born in Old Compton Street; he was defending his turf for all of us.'

'Who asked him?' snapped Bad Alice. 'Soho ain't private turf. Never was.'

Old Alfredo turned his hat in silence, and Jewish Bob said: 'With respect, talking business on somebody else's Sabbath is no skin off my proboscis, but all this talk of turf and manors gives me hives. This is Soho, not Hackney or Crisp Street Market in the Dark Ages. Can't go back to the days of Jack the Lad leaning on a widowed tobacconist for his beer money. Leave "Ten bob — seven-and-six or under the chin it goes" to the Petticoat Lane tossers. This is the Square Mile and there's no profit in broken bones.'

'Jewish Bob's got that right,' said Cubby. 'This is racial as much as it's territorial. The Eyeties against some East End yids. Let them have their straightener in the traditional way: pick their champions, choose barefist or tools, and go to it on neutral turf. I vote Hackney Marshes as the venue, and vote that Archie's firm chides them as thinks different.'

'No arguments from me,' said Jewish Bob.

Bad Alice looked at her watch.

'The spielers buy that. Half-hour to the gun and two minutes' silence.'

Tessio nodded agreement.

'Alfredo?' Archie prompted.

The old man dug at a wormcast with a heel.

'I apologise. My family apologises. But there is the matter of pride to be considered. The pride of my son. Am I to disown a son who never saw the old country except on postcards — a son who *thinks* in English? To him I am an old dinosaur from another time, another country. He's egg and chips, and I'm pasta and olive-oil. And you people want to push him further away from his father. For acting the man in his own right. If Archie Ogle had a son, he would know better how it is for me.'

Archie thought of Queenie's miscarriages and anger chilled his voice.

'Look at me like a man, Alfredo. You think an erection and a pregnancy in your dotage makes you a father? Passing cigars and getting legless on vino at the Christening? Boasting when he grows hair one between his legs and gets tall enough to see over a saloon-bar counter? To take pride in his banging up some nippy from Lyon's Corner House? In paying off her parents for an abortion, and laughing when he bends the family saloon on a Southend piss-up with his tosspot mates? Celebrating because his old man's got him off the hook again?'

Archie's pointed finger trembled.

'You *should* apologise, Alfredo Dimento. Apologise to yourself for being an apology for a father. Apologise to Cubby Colleano, who keeps his sons off the street and beats them crooked if they answer their mother back. Apologise to me for the son I never had. And apologise to Alice for the son she lost over Dresden on a bombing mission so your precious son could play with his toy soldiers. Sons and respect are the same. You have to earn them. You have a son, Alfredo. Now make him the man you once were. Or was that too long ago for you to remember?'

Alfredo had stiffened inside his coat, and his face was a bleached mask. Knuckles of hard muscle pulled his mouth down at the corners.

Tessio said, 'You shame my cousin.'

'He shames himself.'

Cubby looked to Archie to sum up for the entire council.

'Mark your son's card, Alfredo. There is more here to consider than your family, old friend.'

Archie's hand was ignored, and Alfredo walked away on Tessio's arm as though he had heard nothing. Cubby shook his head sucking his teeth.

'Eyetie Antoni won't listen to that poor old carcass. Cancer and a fiver says he won't see Christmas.'

Alice nodded and went through the gate to lose herself in the mists of Greek Street.

Jewish Bob said, 'Kosher cowboys against the Cosa Nostra is badder than bad, Arch. Better get it sorted.'

'It stops here, Bob.'

Archie and Cubby watched him stroll into Sutton Place.

'What else don't I know, Cubby?' Archie looked and sounded bitter.

'Kosher's come a long way since the boxing-booths and half-minding a few bookies. He knows enough to be dangerous, and he's backed by more than a couple of tasty lads.'

'They have names?'

'There's three outstanding: Johnny Parsons from Pimlico, and Tommy and Jessie Troy. Fair amateur boxers, the Troys.'

'Never heard of them,' said Archie, 'but they'll soon have heard of me.'

'We'll sort it over a good drink,' Cubby said with relief.

They were chinking Scotches in the Nell Gwynn when they heard police Citroëns bell past at speed, and by that time it was all over. Eyetie and Kosher had fought the length of Wardour Street and ended up carving each other stupid on the waste ground at the back of St Anne's Church. A tame DS from Bow Street brought Archie the news along with complimentary tickets for a formal dinner and dance.

'Baby-brained bandits,' Archie had snorted. 'I'll castrate them and play marbles with their orchestras.'

After he'd made some heavy calls he went off to dine at the top table with a chief constable, donated generously to a police charity to applause, knowing his faces were delivering naked men to Smithfield market to await his pleasure standing on cold marble.

Archie drifted back to his hospital bed and, lulled by Queenie's needles, slept the clock round.

An unmarked Q-car cruised Frith Street and two plain-clothes busies were busy being casual outside Mother's when Charlie hit the street. He asked them the way to Shaftesbury Avenue for the crack and reddened their necks by walking in the opposite direction.

An Asian tom from Meard Street catcalled from a door-way and a Greek waiter hosing the pavement sprayed their shoes accidentally on purpose to see them jump.

The Dog and Duck was empty when Charlie climbed to the public phone on the first floor. He made two short local calls to check the line for bugs, then reversed the charges to Dublin Gerry in the Irish Republic for want of small change.

Vinnie Castle and Fast Frankie Frewin cuddled stouts in the bar when Charlie went down, two bantams under a framed photograph of Henry Cooper banging Joe Erskine out of the ring. Big Peter pulled Charlie a small bitter and went back to polishing glasses, his expression as neutral as his pub.

Ten years before it had been different. Then the Raphael brothers had the tenancy and had backed Eyetie Antoni against Kosher Kramer, had watched Eyetie's back whilst he worked on Kosher's body with the blade they'd stashed for him. They even held Kosher's throat together long enough for the ambulance to get to him, and after the Old Bailey trial where perjured evidence flew like dirty flags and a local vicar told naughty porkies in the witness-box they faded away to Fulham and got cosied up with Micky Raven's firm. Eyetie stood on cold marble in Smithfield for Archie to keep his patch on Old Compton Street, and Kosher Kramer retired himself to Brighton when the surgeons had put his face back together again. The Troys crept home with chilblains, and Johnny Parsons was laid up in Pimlico for weeks with double pneumonia.

Charlie warmed himself at the fire across from Vinnie and Frankie. Vinnie minded Frankie's chain of betting shops for the Ogle firm and traded hot bubbles with Archie's finger-tame busies. Now and then he dealt with the straight filth if there was a need.

Frankie tapped his *Greyhound Express.*

'The Russians shoot their dogs into space. Mine can't make it round the first bend at White City. Science ain't what it's cracked up to be.'

Charlie nailed him with a look.

'Nor's your promise to stay off the bevy.'

'Stout ain't *drinking,* Chas.'

On paper Frankie was wealthy, but he wasn't allowed money or credit on Archie's orders. He was the only bookmaker in London who was barred from his own premises because he hated brewers' output gaining on his consumption. Frankie drained his glass and looked hopefully at Charlie, who said: 'What have you got for me, Frankie?'

'A headache. Somebody's muscling in on my chain

through straight brokers. Villains don't come through the front door with pick-handles no more. In the old days you could see who was trying to give you a good hiding.'

Charlie tapped his wristwatch.

'Cut the toffee.'

'I'm getting there. The brokers are Goldman's, but that's just the trading name. I fiddled around down at Companies House and came up with two names: a Malcolm Sadler and a Dirk Jorgesson. I dunno this Jorgesson from a bar of coal tar; but Sadler's one of your lahdies from the City, and he's playing both sides of the Thames. With the Troys *and* the Harolds. He's gotta be fronting for some naughty finance fraud, right? Or why else would he want my betting shops? Unless it's to launder funny money.'

'Has he got this straight, Vinnie?'

Vinnie smiled his whitest smile.

'That's his first bevy in three days.'

'And talking's thirsty-making, Chas.'

Charlie pushed his bitter across.

'Sup on that and keep talking.'

'Sounds double Dutch, Chas, but this Sadler's on the board of a whole raft of holding companies. All financial. All international. And Sadler's got a name for asset-stripping, gutting sick companies for quick profits. It's been whispered Tommy Troy's pulled himself a funny-money man. This just has to be the face.'

'I'll get J. C. Hatton on to it.'

Frankie swallowed bitter.

'Rather him than me. I ain't looking down Tommy's throat with Archie out of things.'

Charlie's eyes were grey stones.

'Without Archie you'd be a broken-down ex-jock dossing in a stable. Or have you forgotten what the Troys did to your brother Bobby? You want to digest your food through a plastic bag like him? Be a talking mattress too paralysed to hold a cup or go to the pisser on your own? And who picks up the nursing tab for him, Frankie?'

'Archie does . . . .'

'Right. And I'll tell him how grateful you are when I go back to see him.'

Frankie grew watchful. 'You seen Archie?'

'Had breakfast with him. He asked where your get-well card was.'

'That's handsome. The old tosser's made of concrete. Tell him I'll get the full SP on this Sadler.'

'You bet you will. Won't he, Vinnie?'

'You got it, Chas,' said Frankie.

Vinnie ran a nail across his frown.

'This Jorgesson. Ain't he the one Vic Dakin's been swanning around the casinos? You knew Vic was back amongst us, didn't you, Chas?'

'I knew,' Charlie lied. He slipped a ten-shilling note under a beermat. 'Have a drink on Archie.'

Frankie itched to hold the note up to the light as Charlie pushed into the street and smiled at nothing.

Sergeant Quill ducked below the dash of his Q-car when Charlie crossed to the Carlysle Arms for an Irish on the rocks. To his mind, Charlie Dance looked too happy by half for an overcoat whose governor was on the critical list.

'One day I'll feel your collar, sunshine,' he said aloud.

The dark waters parted and Ingrid drowned in twilight on a hotel bed. A shimmering sword of light became a chink in drawn curtains and Charlie's weight depressed the springs beside her. Ingrid shuddered as the nightmare brushed her with a dying wing.

The thing in the labyrinth had gained when she looked back, raked her heels with unseen claws. It had already smothered Vic and Mother in decayed filth that had once paraded as bright hope and ambition. She smelled coffee, fluffed eggs, hot buttered toast and the Irish on Charlie's breath.

Charlie poured coffee and Ingrid blurred his outline with lowered lashes, explored her ambivalent feelings for him and wondered if she felt anything more than an abiding lust. He was a pretty shape undressed, and she missed him when he wasn't around. When he read aloud from Pablo Neruda or Andrew Marvell his voice resonated through her like supercharged static, made her want to bite and scratch and own him completely.

'Same old dream, Ing?'

'You'd think I'd have grown out of all that fear of failure by now.'

'Who said nice earns nice? You could be worse off, dropping your third unwanted kid in some hole of a council flat, whining down the Welfare for milk and shoes for the brats because your hubby's done a runner with a younger bird.'

'Nice talk this time of the morning.'

'It's afternoon and your dream, right?'

'Feed me, you bastard.'

Ingrid snuggled and watched Charlie cut her toast into buttered squares. He was an untutored sponge who had good taste without caring, and rejected the bland and esoteric with the same shrug. Ingrid often found matinée tickets in his pockets, and when questioned about the plays he said: 'Killed a slow afternoon.'

Charlie tapped his teeth with a spoon.

'Eat your eggs. They're good for the bust.'

'And you've never seen a flat-chested chicken. That isn't one of my problems.'

'That goes double from here. What's this?'

Charlie turned the pasteboard Ingrid flipped at him. On the back was a scribbled telephone number and the front read:

GOLDMAN ASSOCIATES
Management Consultants to Turf Accountants

Ingrid described her meeting with Vic Dakin, leaving nothing out.

Charlie looked at her with dead eyes.

'Get dressed. We're going calling.'

It was an order.

Connie Harold swerved past an articulated lorry with his horn blaring and forced his Vanden Plas into a power-wobble to get his own back on his wife. Pauline's stupidity and lack of social grace had spoiled their weekend at Sadler's manor-house in West Sussex, and Connie lost his temper on the outskirts of South London when Pauline whined: 'And who does that Margot Sadler think she is? Looking down her long nose at me as if she was God's bloody gift.'

'Compared to you, she is.'

'Money don't give her the right to come the acid.'

Connie dropped the cigar-lighter and told Pauline to scrabble for it as he powered into the fast lane.

'Listen to Brainy Bum. All you had to do was wear your hundred-sov frock and keep your fat moo shut. Margot Sadler's got class and old money. So she don't need your flaming recipe for bread pudding, right?'

'I was making polite conversation.'

'You wouldn't know polite if it bit your bum. Your daft verbals made last night a fortnight long. One sherry and your mouth was off and flapping like the lead dog out of trap one.'

'Hark at Brewery Balls. When did you last come to bed sober and give me a bit of comfort? How we made three kids is a mystery.'

'Three kids ago you was worth comforting. If you wasn't all flab and headaches, I might act different. You've let yourself go, Pauline Harold. With your knickers off you look like a bloody blancmange left out in the weather.'

Pauline wept and beat at the dash with a plump fist.

'It's my glands. The doctor said.'

'Glands my elbow. It's eating ten square meals a day and watching the dust turn fluffy on the furniture. Christ, from the back you look like you're smuggling elephant bums for Chipperfield's Circus.'

'Take that *back*!'

'Why? If you could eat it, you'd swallow it.'

Connie slewed the Vanden Plas into Torrington Avenue and scraped to a halt at the kerb.

'Out. I got business.'

Pauline fell out on to the pavement and holed her tights.

'And I know what business. All you've got in your trousers for me is a cheap label. But for that secretary of yours . . . .'

Pauline ran up the front path, her calves and thighs in frantic motion.

Connie stayed at the wheel for a long count of twenty, rolled his heavy shoulders to feel his muscles harden and slacken, needing to use his fists on someone. Any-sodding-one. To burn up anger and adrenalin he took the suitcases up to the bedroom and emptied them out on to the unmade bed. The hundred-guinea dress tumbled out like an expensive rag.

Connie saw a harpoon-grenade hit Pauline in the belly as she floundered in an Arctic sea. Blood exploded into the icy waters as air escaped from her ruptured body, and hissing waves of crimson rolled outwards as she sank, staining the towering cliffs of impacted snow the red of a million sunsets.

He went down to the kitchen with the dress balled in his fist. Shook it out to show the food stains.

'You've turned tinsel to totters' tat, you gross cow. You're all meat and no gravy.'

Pauline crammed her mouth with iced cake, and flecks spattered the table as she screamed: 'Give it to her, then. Give it all to her.'

'Lower your clack. You want the whole street knowing our business?'

Pauline swivelled to open the window.

'I'll tell the whole sodding world what a bastard—'

Connie's fist arced upwards as he pulled her face into it. There was no sound for the interminable moment she hung suspended. Her hair spread out from the shock of the blow, and she fell away to slam into the new Moffat cooker.

Plates jumped from the warming-rack to chime apart on the composition floor, and Pauline's squall of pain was loud enough to end the day shift at the local soap factory. Bloody clots of cake flew from her ruined mouth, plopping into a pan of boiling eggs she had knocked to the floor, turning the water the dull red of an unlit stop-sign.

'I'll cost you . . . you bastarrr . . . .'

Pauline drooled, and a ham of a knee showed through her ripped dress.

'Go to your fancy woman . . . . Dirty whorrrrr . . . .'

Her wails followed Connie as he repacked a case with anything handy, her inarticulate tirade too close to the truth for denial. Stung, Connie went back downstairs to yell: 'Get her name right. It's Kelly, right? Kelly. And she's smart where it counts. In the office *and* in bed. That girl can figure the price per tonne of crude copper without losing her stroke when she's pulling my chain. And *she* don't have your answer to conjugal rights: the twenty-eight-day period and the five-day headache. She comes across when I want it. And now she's got the other thing you never had. Me!'

'Bastardinggg bastarrrrr . . . .'

Connie had no memory of driving into the scrapyard beside brother Wally's Bentley. He was just there staring at it. Mud had dried in fanciful ochre sprays on the black and green enamel, and Kelly's Mini was the red of blooded cake, forcing Connie back into the disordered kitchen.

'You'll never see me or the kids again . . . .'

Connie squeezed the wheel and watched the wipers saw through spotting rain.

The scrapyard was fenced by railway sleepers topped out with barbed wire. Two Alsatians in a wired run guarded the main gates and an old Pullman coach served as an office. Canadian willow-weed bobbed between the aisles of rusted cars, and a chalked sign near an old tractor read:

DRIVERS WANTED

APPLY WITHIN

It was one of Connie's running gags, and unemployed blacks did come into the yard from time to time.

Connie skipped through puddles, and shed rain from his hat when he banged into the office. Wally looked over a morning paper, and Kelly barely nodded from the kitchenette where she brewed tea.

Wally leaned back in his swivel.

'Don't tell me. Your Pauline won the paper hat at Sadler's castle, right?'

'Surprise, surprise,' Kelly hissed, stirring the pot.

Wally mouthed 'Jealous' at his brother's look of enquiry.

Connie sat at his desk to shuffle invoices.

'Looks like you been here all weekend, Kelly love.'

'Nothing else to do, was there? Not with a certain trader away playing happy families in the country.'

Kelly speared a teabag and flicked it into the wastebin, her thin face frigid with disapproval.

'It was business.'

Connie stopped himself ripping the neat invoices into confetti and snapped fingers at Wally.

'What's the SP on Ogle and Dance?'

'Archie was never at the City Hospital. Queenie pulled a switch with two ambulances. Archie had a police escort into Essex someplace and went missing. Charlie Dance is hobbling around like nothing happened, and when I went to your favourite bent busy at West End Central he was off drowning worms in Ireland.'

'Never a copper around when you need one.'

Kelly slammed a mug of tea on to Connie's blotter and let it spill deliberately. Connie dabbed at the spreading stain.

'Who poisoned your breakfast?'

'Your *business*, what else?'

'I can't scratch your back when I'm scratching Sadler's. Dakin's nylon deal went sour for want of laundering dough abroad sensible. Profit I can't keep ain't worth a box of monkeys. And you screaming like a bird up the dove don't help none, neither. With a shooting-war up our jaxies I need a lot more than your belly growling at me, Miss. Right?'

Kelly sniffed into a filing cabinet.

Wally sipped scalding tea and said: 'Not only did Ogle and Dance fall under a building, but their bookkeeper Micky Dogge went missing about the same time and ain't surfaced yet. Not only that, but there was two wreaths left on Archie's doorstep. One from us, and one from the Troys.'

'Who's the bloody joker?' Connie wondered.

'Tommy's the one for floral offerings. Maybe the wreaths is his way of making the Ogle firm think we're coming at them side by side.'

Connie made fists and looked at them. 'Us and Bethnal Green on the same bike? That's about as sensible as a chocolate fire-guard.'

'Or you taking Pauline to Sussex,' said Kelly.

Connie ignored her. 'Sadler said Vic Dakin's slid back into the Smoke, and he's working on Jorgesson behind Sadler's back. I want that monkey under my thumb as soon as you like, Wal.'

'Vicky Dakin? Why don't I just have Harry the Crack and Sailor give him a basket of lumps and lose him permanent?'

'Because I want *my* thumbs in his neck.' Connie turned to watch the dogs fight over a bicycle tyre. 'With Sadler behind our firm and Ogle down the Swanee there's only the Troys to spank before we have the Smoke to ourselves. I can see that clearer than that black bastard standing out there.'

Wally peered over his brother's shoulder. 'Well, look at him and his dreadlocks.'

'Don't like the dogs snapping, does he? If he's got the bottle to come inside, he'll be worth a laugh or three.'

The Negro sidled past the dog-run, and rain made his

coffee skin shine.

Connie pulled on rubber gloves.

'Run out the power cable, Wal.'

He stood on the step to watch the Negro approach the office with Kelly peeping from behind the curtain.

'The sign says you want a driver.' The Negro's smile was wide and white.

'Clean licence?'

'Yeah.'

'Heavy goods?'

'Still waiting for the Ministry test.'

Connie pointed at the tractor, and anticipation hardened his stomach muscles.

'Think you can drive that thing?'

'Give it a go, man.'

'Climb into the saddle while I get the jump leads. Battery's a bit flat from standing. Accelerate hard when you work first gear. She likes a bit of a help to start.'

'You got it, Mister.'

Connie hauled the cable out to the tractor and connected terminals to the bucket seat.

'Pump away, then.'

Connie raised his hand and stood back.

The Negro hit the pedal twice before Wally sent power down the cable. There was a crackling violet flash and the black man was hurled upwards and sideways in a loose flail. He skidded in mud and gravel and lay still for a long moment before raising his head.

Connie toed him in the side. 'That's what you get for climbing after British coconuts, Sambo my son.'

'I done busted somethin' . . . .'

'Only my heart.' Connie's smile was as phoney as a Christian mosque. 'And my dogs love a bit of dark meat. Won't eat any other part of the turkey.'

Wally rattled the wire to make the Alsatians bay as the Negro kneeled up holding his torn shoulder.

'You white shits. Doing dirt to a man trying to put a bit of meat on the table.'

He got a foot under him and swayed upright, his face twisted in pain.

'Go back to bananaland, Sooty. Play cannibals there if you want meat.'

'Honky Charlie-horse bastards . . . .'

Connie saw Pauline as he kicked the Negro in the stomach. Brought a knee up into the gaping mouth. The dogs went berserk when the Negro flopped against the gate and Wally threw him out on to the broken paving.

'Tell your tribe to come round. Ask for the Harolds.'

Connie was almost at peace with the world when he shucked the rubber gloves.

'See him on his way, Wally. Then keep going. I want that slag Dakin here fast. Try his sister's in Camden Town.'

'I've gone, Bruv.'

Wally drove his Bentley through the gate, his bonnet inches from the stumbling Negro's spine.

Pauline's manic gobble faded as Connie pulled his suitcase from the Vanden Plas. A stray pyjama leg dangled in the mud and a fishing sock slapped his wrist. He reminded himself of the old derelict he and Wally had taken to Savile Row for a new suit and then on to a champagne supper at the Astor Club. Had all the waiters bowing and scraping to the old tosser before the hired Rolls dropped him back at the Seamen's Mission in Rotherhithe. The old clown had come back the following day when there were hangovers all round and nobody had a sense of humour. They had dragged him out to Clapham Common and doused him in paraffin. The old tosser had tried to run with his coat and hair alight. Rolling in the grass, running on, patting at himself, rolling some more . . . .

Kelly laughed from the office doorway. Connie could have been seeing her for the first time, both familiar and strange.

Kelly's chin was too pointed for her narrow jaw and high cheekbones, and her enlarged Latin eyes were set too wide for her short snub of a nose and pinhole nostrils.

Her full red mouth needed no lipstick, and there were two moles on her long neck. Her high bust was too generous for her thin torso, and her ample hips curved into slender legs with small square feet. She had scraped her black hair back from her face with an elastic band, and Gestetner ink blacked the tip of her nose. Her laugh wound down when she took in the suitcase.

'You finally went and left the cow?' Kelly's cockney accent was as blunt as her manner.

'And who asked you to work through Sunday?' An excess of adrenalin swung Connie from violence to desire.

'That ain't jam on your tie. Her blood or Sambo's?'

Suddenly drained, Connie just shook his head.

'Get inside. You look done in.'

Connie lost his suitcase in a corner and sat. Sweat soaked his shirt.

'Shouldn't have worked Sunday.'

'Had to get that quote out for the Ministry of Defence. You done good buying yourself an under-secretary, and Wally's a grafter on the lorries, but you're both up the pictures over paperwork. And that's where money's made and lost. I know, I've saved you bundles.'

Connie let Kelly strip his shirt and tie. Her cool hands on his chest roused him and he cupped a breast.

'You looking for a bonus?'

'Not if you're walking me down the Road of Life.'

'You never talked like this before.'

'You never left home before.'

'Don't push me away, Kel.'

'First things first, Harold.'

Kelly slapped Connie's hand away and settled on her haunches to hold his marbled stare.

'You're cracked bringing Vic Dakin back with all these tickly long-firm deals going through, even if you do owe him some tasty whacks. And with Sadler playing you against Bethnal Green there's no profit in a baby straightener. Just ask yourself how Vic got to Sadler without your knowing it. And, if Sadler was straight, how come he's shopping about amongst the heavy firms?'

'Everybody's bent. Business is getting three-guinea names on your board and making your killing before the Board of Trade gets a smell of what's up.'

'You can do that without Sadler. Or bloody Dakin.'

'This is the second time today I've seen you for the first time.'

'Time you looked proper, then.'

'Lose that frock and I'll look all you want.'

'Forget Dakin and I will.'

'I need him until I square things with Sadler. This South African deal is too big to let Tommy Troy haul it into his corner.'

'You want it that bad?'

'I can taste it in my toothpaste.'

Kelly opened Connie's fly and rested her palm on his jockey shorts.

'Together we can do it.'

'Big jump for a Camberwell boy.'

'And an Islington girl from Woolworth's threepenny counter.'

Kelly felt Connie rise through the thin cotton.

'Lock the door and give us your mouth, girl.'

Fresh rain smashed against the windows as they found each other.

The Camden Road tower block had been built to mark the Festival of Britain and the start of the brave new post-war boom of urban renewal. The balconies were panelled in dull blue, and the Crittal windows stared from walls of soiled yellow brick. The trees planted with a silver shovel in 1951 had long ago been vandalised to death, and the railed lawns were mostly mud and neglect.

Charlie had traced the address from an unlisted number through a bent contact at Directory Enquiries. As he paid off the taxi Ingrid said: 'Aunt Rosie's place. Vic's half-sister. Or my mother's. I was never sure. Everybody was ashamed of everyone else.'

'Vic ain't backward in using the family, is he? Come and find me when you're ready.'

Charlie watched Ingrid up a cement path between hedges before going into the Eagle where muddy Paddies watched television racing over slow Guinnesses. Charlie was served an Irish in a glass small enough for optician's eyewash, and the wall-eyed barman said there was no call for ice at lunchtime.

'And I'm the tenth person you've told that today.'

'How'd you know that?'

'I'm psychic, Pat.'

'Name's Brendan.'

'Never, that's my mother's name.'

Charlie smiled the sting away and bought Brendan a half.

Time sauntered by as the television flickered in Edwardian mirrors. A long-odds horse won the next race, and the Paddies bought hot pies from the cabinet.

Charlie went into a brown study over his Irish. Went back to Bad Alice's Club in Poland Street just days before Eyetie Antoni and Kosher Kramer's knife-fight made column-inches around the world. To the poker game that had started on a Tuesday and continued until the following Saturday. When Johnny the Builder had asked Charlie to sit in as second dealer when he wandered in off the street. Johnny had been rehanging the lavatory door when the mob from Old Compton Street came in wanting a game. Then the Troys and Pimlico Johnny rolled in loaded with dough from a heavy tickle at Doncaster Races, left their tarts at the downstairs bar and sat in. Since Johnny knew them all from his racing-gang days and their dough was as good as anybody's he nailed a blanket over the doorway and dealt fresh cards.

Wednesday went into Thursday, and by Friday morning everyone but Charlie and Johnny was down to trouser buttons and flash talk.

To stop the moody looks and hot mumbles Johnny gave both firms an hour to raise fresh rolls and get back before the seats went cold. Everybody made the deadline, and by Saturday morning there was just the one big pot Johnny won with four fat ladies. That cleaned everybody out, and somebody wanted all the money back in the middle of the table because nothing had been decided. That's when Johnny realised the firms had been playing for who owned Soho. The Compton Street mob called Eyetie and the Troys got a message to Kosher and the table went over as fists and boots lashed out.

Johnny got most of the money out through a back window, and Charlie made it down to the first-floor landing before a chair parted his hair and a face coming up from the street put a lacer into his thigh. The razor hit bone and snapped off when Charlie fell. He went all the way down to the street on his face, and Tommy Troy gave him a kicking for skimming the deck for the Ogle firm. Charlie was too busy bleeding to argue and stayed down when Tommy went off to mix with the fifty faces whacking at each other with pick-handles in the street.

Charlie came round in the lower bar with Doc Rudge sewing him up without an anaesthetic, went under again and woke up in Spitalfields to learn that Eyetie had carved Kosher into hospital before Archie had him and his faces turning blue on cold marble in Smithfield. From then on Archie had Charlie on wages and put the word around he wasn't to be touched by anybody.

Ingrid came out of the rain as Brendan called last orders, and Charlie sat her down at a corner table with a gin and tonic. She inhaled half of it and said: 'Vic is up there. And somebody's worked him over.'

'What did he say about Jorgesson and Sadler?'

'Nothing. I couldn't ask.'

Charlie waited without expression.

'There's a red-headed face minding him. Vic called him Limehouse between groans.'

'One of Troy's overcoats.'

'He wouldn't let me in until Vic said I was the croupier who helped him out over the Jorgesson con. Limehouse laughed and said, "Playing away games with your old daddy Vic without Archie's top monkey knowing? You toms are all the same." I swallowed that to get a private word with Vic, but Limehouse wouldn't have it. So Auntie Rosie made me a cup of instant something in a dirty cup and I came away. That place is a tip.'

'Who else is up there?'

'My cousin Sharon. Fat, pregnant, and a bit mental. Sucked her thumb over the pictures in a mail-order catalogue. Her idea of motherhood is to buy cuddly toys to play with.'

'What about Lou?'

'He's edgy. Vic's scared stoolless of him. Lou lit a Player and Vic jumped a mile. I think they burned him where the sun don't shine.'

'Figures.'

Brendan covered the pumps and called time.

'Don't think you're going up there without me, Charlie. Aunt Rose is a slag, Sharon's dim and Vic's Vic, but they're still family and I don't want them hurt.'

'Who does?'

They walked to the tower block under Ingrid's umbrella.

Charlie spotted a green and black Bentley parked at the gate. He pushed Ingrid against the hedge and kissed her as if they were courting.

Their breath mingled as they waited.

Glass smashed from four floors up and raised voices came and went as passing traffic threw up spray. A door slammed open and closed, and stumbling heels clattered down the stairwell. A woman in a facepack came out on to the first-floor balcony to stare at the glass on the muddy lawn.

'It's them upstairs again, Fred,' she called into a room darkened for afternoon television.

Charlie saw a bloated face at an upper window, eyes wide with shock.

'Sharon,' said Ingrid.

A woman swearing in fierce monotone must have been Aunt Rose. Sharon's face went behind a billow of curtain, and the woman in a facepack pointed down at two men coming out of the entrance.

'I'll know you two sods in court. See if I don't.'

Vic Dakin moved on rubber legs, pushed forward by Wally Harold. Vic's face was uncooked dough and he held his trousers away from his crotch.

'Mongrels,' yelled the woman.

Vic mumbled as he was shoved on to the pavement.

Charlie elbowed him towards Ingrid and drove his forearm into Wally's face. The crack of surgical plaster against Wally's skull was a cleaver chopping cabbage. Blood spurted from Wally's hairline as he was driven back through the hedge. He flipped on to the lawn in a thrash of legs. His feet drooped and his toecaps slowly pointed inwards.

'There's only more of them, Fred,' yelled the woman on the balcony.

'CID. Get back inside,' Charlie ordered.

'Fred?' The woman went into the darkened room.

'I've seen fast,' Dakin panted, 'but that was Millhouse in the Thousand Guineas.'

'Walk. Walk casual.'

A bus ground to a halt at the lights, and Charlie bundled Vic and Ingrid aboard as Limehouse Lou staggered from the entrance to stare at the legs growing from the hedge. He lit a cigarette and let it smoulder in his swollen mouth. A gaunt figure in the rain without an idea in the world.

You and me both.

Charlie fumbled for small change as he climbed to the upper deck.

CHAPTER THREE

DIRK JORGESSON focused the strobelight on the oversized golden bed, and the two girls flickered erotically as they waited for him. In the erratic dancing light the girls were inviting, perfect. Close up they would just be paid whores, and just as disappointing as the first Bantu girl he had taken into the starlit bush. She had coupled with the enthusiasm of a she-goat and had called him 'thorn penis' when she wiped herself off with a handful of straw.

Jorgesson's enlarged genitals throbbed as he moved towards the bed. The brown girl was heavy-breasted and had high dimpled buttocks. Tribal scars lined her high cheekbones, and her slanted eyes were the yellow of winter grass. Silver beads hung from her plaited hair, and her long shapely legs were as black as sin against the metallic counterpane.

She opened Jorgesson's robe and supported his gorged manhood as the blonde girl dribbled warmed baby oil on to his penis. The blonde was as slender as a boy beside the Bantu with Eurasian eyes. Her breasts were small and round, and her pink nipples stood out like diminutive fingers. Her eyes were blank and blue under lowered lids, and she pouted as she worked the oil into Jorgesson's member. Her mind flew with the cocaine she'd snorted in the bathroom, whirling her back to the summer days of convent school. Before coming south with a rock band and before her habit turned her into one of Maltese Maurice's girls.

Dirk sank on to the bed and stretched out to watch himself in the overhead mirror, almost jealous of the stranger reflected there. The yellow eyes hovered over him like flickering moons as deft hands introduced joy beads into his anus. The small blonde lapped his thighs, making him wait just a trifle longer.

Jorgesson began to shake.

The telephone rang as the brown girl rolled her big breasts against his open mouth. Jorgesson eased her on to her side with a muted curse. Laid his head in the small blonde's lap, her subtle musk reminding him of rain-washed earth. Of the Transvaal. Of his wife Alicia and her lover. Of the fortune he had lost at the tables.

The brown girl gnawed at his stomach, and the blonde put the receiver to his ear.

'It's important,' Dakin said. Jorgesson could almost smell his panic.

'You pick your moments.'

'Like I said . . . .'

'Where are you?'

'In the lobby. Downstairs . . . .'

Dakin covered the mouthpiece to speak to someone beside him.

Jorgesson squirmed. The brown girl's tongue probed his navel.

'Won't take but a moment, Mr Jorgesson.'

'You're alone?'

'Somebody asked the time.'

Jorgesson's desire became disbelief.

'Dirk?'

'Come up in fifteen minutes.'

Jorgesson dropped a leg to the floor, nodded to himself in the mirrored ceiling. The fat man's strain had fuzzed in the mouthpiece.

The brown girl clamped a leg around Jorgesson's waist and edged down on to his erection. Her nipples were as dark as walnuts.

'Another time. Now we shower.'

The girls knew how Jorgesson liked to be soaped and massaged. He carried them into the bathroom as if they weighed nothing.

When they had gone with their money Jorgesson dropped a ·32 Airweight into the pocket of his towelling robe and was sipping chilled Krug when Dakin came into the suite. The man with him was tall and wide-shouldered and handsome in a cold way. Had good teeth and eyes like wet slate.

Dakin introduced Charlie Dance and sat gingerly.

'He didn't give me no choice, Mr Jorgesson.'

'Clearly. Mr Dance has a wristwatch and there's a clock in the lobby.'

Charlie made a fan of markers.

'Pretty observant for somebody who let Vic help him lose all this money. You've dropped paper all over the Smoke, and all because Vic sees you as a nice little earner. Vic's into debt with some very heavy faces who owe him lumps for past naughties. He's sewn you up so he can deliver you as a down payment. You've got something they want, and Vic's made dead certain you'll deliver. Trouble is he owes you to one firm and has promised you to another, and because he couldn't wait for you to lose straight he helped the cards along.'

'Then, I simply renege on my markers.'

'Not sensible.'

Charlie poured champagne and slapped Dakin when he reached for a glass.

'The House played straight; it's Vic who didn't. We don't have to rig the shoes to skin high-rollers like you. I could take all the court cards out of a deck and beat you with a two high.'

'I'll take that bet.'

'What with? You're broke.'

'I've got a no-limit credit anywhere.'

'Mister, there's always a house limit. And as of right now you couldn't get a cup of coffee on credit. So you stay and you pay.'

Jorgesson told Charlie to do something physically impossible to himself.

Dakin shifted in the ornate chair, and Charlie looked sleepy.

'Now, what did that buy you?'

'Satisfaction.'

'Short-lived stuff that.'

'This says otherwise, Mr Dance.'

Jorgesson sighted the Airweight at Charlie's necktie.

Dakin went the colour of faded daffodils.

Charlie could have been looking at anything but a loaded revolver.

'I don't think I'm getting through to him, Vic.'

Jorgesson bared teeth and gold inlays.

'Now burn the markers, Mr Dance. Don't reach into your pocket. Use the table lighter.'

Dakin gaped as the markers caught and crisped black. Literally seeing money go up in smoke.

Jorgesson crossed a pyjama leg.

'Now go into the bathroom, lock the door and lie in the bath. I might put a round through the door just for the fun of it.'

'Funny old fun.'

Charlie sauntered into the bathroom and turned the key with a rattle; then sat on the toilet twining his fingers into a cat's-cradle. Drawers opened and closed. Dakin whined as he was ordered about, and a suitcase scraped a door-jamb. A door slammed and there was silence.

Charlie let himself out into the living-room and took Jorgesson's discarded robe into the bedroom. When he had played with the strobelight he poured champagne and toasted himself in the overhead mirror, too amused to smile.

A coarse voice yelled: 'You there, Chas?'

'In here, Soddy.'

Nasty Nostrils and Sodbonce dragged Jorgesson into the bedroom and dumped him on the shag-pile carpet. The blonde head smacked against the dressing-table without disturbing Jorgesson's peaceful expression. Sodbonce brought Dakin in by the ear.

'A regular scurrier is our Vic.'

'Any problems?'

'No. They made for the underground carpark like you said, Chas. Didn't see us in the back seat until I whacked Jorgesson a moody in the back of the head. Had to clock him twice before he behaved. Whacked a bullet through the windscreen and it whined off every wall before it got tired.'

Sodbonce cocked scarred eyebrows and rubbed his long chin.

'Witnesses?'

Nasty Nostrils grinned with crooked teeth.

'Not even the deaf, dumb and blind.'

He threw Jorgesson on to the bed and dumped flower-water into his face.

'Shower job, I reckon,' said Sodbonce.

'Do it.'

Charlie took Dakin into the living-room and sat him beside the telephone. Dakin fingered the burned markers.

'All that money.'

'Copies.'

Charlie heard Jorgesson choke as water streamed into his nose and mouth. He dialled Connie Harold's office and handed Dakin the receiver. Listened to him go through his rehearsed speech. Connie's voice was distorted electronic thunder as he bawled: 'Since when can Charlie Dance haggle? You're mine, Vic. And for free. And Jorgesson ain't worth no fifty thou, neither.'

There was a lot more of the same, and Charlie heard Kelly ask sharp pertinent questions. He lit one of Jorgesson's Dunhills and blew a smoke-ring when he took the telephone.

'You'll trade, Connie.'

'It was you put our Wally in hospital.'

'Shouldn't send wreaths, then, should you?'

'That's Bethnal Green's kind of a stroke.'

'Makes us both innocent, then.'

'Like you was in the bulrushes with Moses, you cowson. And fifty thou makes you something I scrape off my shoe.'

'That's the price.'

Charlie rang off and smiled at white knuckles.

'Jorgesson's awake. You ready, Chas?' said Sodbonce.

'Oh blimey yeah,' said Charlie.

Dusk overtook Limehouse Lou in the Mile End Road.

He sat in the Ship with a light and bitter and relived the last few minutes he'd spent in Camden Town. He had thought Ingrid had left something behind when the door-bell went. The next thing he knew he was backing down the hall with Wally Harold all over him. Lou put a good one into Wally's gut and felt it all the way up into his sinuses. But Wally came back with a bullroarer of a body-slam and Lou, Aunt Rose and the well-pregnant Sharon went down in a heap with what was left of the coffee-table and a couple of dozen yards of rucked carpet. Vic Dakin had tried to climb the rose-trellis on the wallpaper when Lou smacked Wally with a tea-tray and Wally ruined the living-room window with the chair he missed Lou's head with. Then Sharon hit Lou with a stuffed giraffe and bit half his ear off, and Wally finished Lou with a size-nine boot to the mouth.

Lou sipped a second pint through mashed lips.

Tommy Troy had hissed through two sets of pips when Lou had tried to explain, and cut him off with: 'You didn't lose Dakin. You gave him away. You're dead and buried, Limehouse. I've ordered your wreath.'

Lou couldn't believe he'd been kicked off the firm after four years of heavy overcoating without so much as a florin for busfare. He'd never stuck to so much as an Irish penny when he collected dues from market traders or stallholders, and he'd whacked his full share of Pakis who'd moved into the shmutter trade after the Jewboys moved up west. There wasn't an Abdul or a Probaka who didn't cough the sovs after a couple of sewing-room fires or a blade against the old epiglottis. Lou wondered if he hadn't really been rated on the Troy firm because he was a straight hetero who wouldn't give Jessie or Gordon a tumble and had looked hot for Tommy's wife.

When there were five wet rings on the counter, Lou changed to large malts and a jazz trio played 'Rocking Chair' on the stage. Lou's elbows spread wider and the optics grew fuzzy. He mixed brandy with his whisky and didn't notice. His thoughts were minor keys lost in jazz rhythms, spun into mad loops by stylised progressions of melody. He sang but his mouth huffed ugly monotones.

Lou's melancholy became outrage.

He'd been told to pick up his marbles and walk, and there was no future in his mooning after Tommy's Helen with her locked up in the Vallance Road fortress and him well out in the cold. He must forget those eyes filled with God and promise. Her hair rolled around her face like gold rope, and washing dishes like she was making paper flowers.

Lou decided nobody elbowed him that easily.

He lost the last of his drink near his mouth and wove across a bar that tilted and yawed like a raft in a Solent squall. Evening chill burned his punished face and the street-lights jiggled into blinding serpents.

The Martyred Thomas was a canopy of brilliance. A great shout of light hovering above rubbery ground. Lou skidded into a shopfront and mashed three cigarettes getting one into his mouth.

'No one elbows me,' he told the uncertain night.

An unmarked van came out of a side-street, mounted the pavement and ground to a halt. The rear shutter went up and men dropped out on rubber soles, running past Lou to the intersection.

Lou coughed up a bubble of whisky and tobacco.

A lorry blocked his view and he snarled at it.

Men jumped from that. Faces flattened by stocking masks, staves and pick-handles in their fists. Jostled aside, Lou slid to the ground to swear incoherent nonsense.

Glass boomed into flying shards and wood splintered inside the Martyred Thomas. Some of the canopy lights died and smoke boiled across the street. Somebody bawled in pain as a bottle banged out of a window and flame spattered the pavement. Burning petrol made violent holes in the night. Ragged favours of high-octane spread across the cobbles, bursting upwards as fiery scimitars of heat.

Lou half-stood, leaning into a nonexistent gale, fighting gravity and alcohol. The men without faces threw bodies into the street, lay about them with boot and stave; yelled through stocking mesh, the saloon bar a muddy brown glow at their backs.

Lou staggered into their path without understanding.

A man fell beside him, his jacket smouldering. His face was a bloody mask and an eye hung on his cheek like a cheap bauble.

'Put the lights on, son.'

The man flopped and his sighted eye rolled up under the lid.

A woman with torn stockings ran past, her mouth a black zero full of screams. She bounced off the side of a halted bus and lost herself in shadows.

Lou raised an arm against the heat. Fire rose as a crackling wall, and pearl smoke turned him into just another ghost in the burning fog.

An Irish voice said, 'Another Troy bastard,' and Lou's ribs caved in when a pick-handle smashed across his chest. He had no memory of falling and vomited where he lay, no breatheable air for his impacted lungs. The lorry ran over his hand when it sped off after the van.

Lou didn't know if bottles exploded inside the pub or inside his head. He felt nothing. There was a crystal wall between him and the fog and the pain. Hoses played on steaming brickwork, brass helmets bobbed and canvas snakes unrolled, snapping rigid with sudden water pressure.

Lou wondered who was elbowing whom. Somebody was hitting the Troys the way he wished he could, and on the night the brothers celebrated their mother's birthday.

Lou was stretchered to an ambulance and laid beside the man with an eye on his cheek. There were red blankets and whirling blue lights. A cool hand peeled a lid and found his pulse, reminding him of paper flowers. And somewhere within him Lou found absolution for a great and vague sin of omission.

He conjured Tommy Troy and leered at him before losing consciousness.

Rain blurred the lights of Cromwell Road and chuckled in the hotel eaves as Charlie watched Jorgesson sign papers for J. C. Hatton.

A small, fussy man with soiled snow for hair, tinted horn-rims and crumpled ears, Hatton knew corporate law and liked money the way a gourmand adores gourmet cooking; in quantity with second helpings. He'd given up a lucrative law practice to front for Archie's legitimate deals, and ran racehorses and an Ascot box on the proceeds.

Beside him, Dirk Jorgesson was a flaccid shell with an undershot jaw. The hole gouged in his cheek by a ring was a livid dimple in his tired face.

'Pleasure doing business with you, Mr Jorgesson.' Hatton locked his olive files in his briefcase. 'Congrats, Charles. We now own title to sixty per cent of a potentially lucrative mining operation in the Transvaal. The mineral rights sold without incurring development costs could be worth one million sterling to a big corporation in that field. I thought it was only White Russians of Imperial stock who gambled to lose.'

'How long's this gonna take to finalise?'

'I'll have all the bows tied in heavy Latin by the end of the week. There might be some flak from the South African government over a deal like this. Jorgesson must have sweetened a minister of the Department of the Interior to mine in what are legally tribal lands.'

Hatton mimed a bribe with thumb and forefinger.

Charlie sipped laced coffee.

'Just keep the firm's name out of it. This is just a trading deal for us.'

'But will Archie see things that way?'

'He can't fret about what he don't know. Archie should just worry about Archie.'

'But should he ask – what then, Charles?'

'You tell him, don't you?'

'You were always reasonable, Charles.'

'Whatever's good for the firm, J.C.'

Hatton peered at his Omega oyster.

'Time I was tucked up with warm milk and a soporific novel. The memsahib frets if I'm too late.'

Hatton drove his Jaguar back to his mock-Tudor villa in Esher, trailed by two DCs in a Q-car.

Charlie answered the telephone first ring.

'Vinnie Castle, Chas. I've been clocking the Troys' boozer like you said.'

'And?' Charlie scratched an earlobe.

'There's claret on the cobbles. The Martyred Thomas is a write-off.'

'I can hear the fire-engines from here. What about faces?'

'Under stocking masks? No chance. Smells like Camberwell, though.'

Charlie grunted, and Vinnie sucked a tooth in his ear.

'Want me to hang around?'

'Only if the brothers are about.'

'They went home a good hour before this lot went nasty. Ida's birthday, ain't it?'

'Swing round the clubs for loose bubbles, then, Vin. Could be someone'll let something slip.'

'Right.'

Vinnie rang off, and Charlie fanned banknotes between Dakin and Jorgesson.

'A last fling before mattress time.'

Jorgesson did not understand and said so.

Charlie winked, his face remote.

'Just another night for the Ogle firm. Just keep Vic away from your cards.'

CHAPTER FOUR

THE HOUSE SHOOK as a train crossed the viaduct, and Helen waited for it to pass before putting the sixtieth candle on Ida's cake. Tommy watched her put finishing touches to the lavish confection, his back to the kitchen door. A silver *60* stood out from a big crimson heart surrounded by iced forget-me-nots, and *Ida* was spelled out in yellow marzipan roses.

Helen wasn't half the woman Ida was, and Tommy wished she ran to him as readily as she ran off to the local Catholic church when her tight little world was upset. Why she wasted that nice little body on all that religion was beyond him, and he would have loved to know what she whispered in that priest's ear. The old tosser probably had more form on the Troy firm than the whole Metropolitan Police Force, Tommy thought, trying to feel the party mood. But Limehouse losing Dakin like he was a small boy who couldn't be trusted with a sixpenny errand was too big a shaker to be taken with a shrug and a grin. Even sending Lou's mother a wreath and a raft of bereavement cards wasn't enough of a punishment. Lou would have to open the door to real undertakers willing to discuss his own funeral arrangements. Then Tommy could have Lou worked over by faces he didn't know. Making sure he and Jessie could watch from not too far away.

Tommy's cigar crackled in his fist.

After running Bethnal Green, Soho and Mayfair had to be a real doddle for a man like himself. With Sadler behind him to buy what he couldn't readily take, Tommy was ready to give the heavy finger back to Archie Ogle, have *him* standing in refrigeration with frost around his balls like a deposed headmaster. Tommy had not forgotten how he'd had to grovel for Archie all those years before, and humiliating the hard old man was a pleasure to come. If the old tosser survived falling under that café.

Tommy had needed to be hard right from his schooldays when he and Jessie had been called 'resurrection men' by older youths. The old grandmother told Tommy his great-grandfather had come to England aboard a Dublin packet and lived on his wits in the Pool of London, and that 'resurrection men' was the old term for grave-robbers. Tommy and Jessie had taken tyre-irons to their tormentors, and their reputation for being hard men was established early.

When they weren't disrupting classes, taking public canings and avoiding the Schoolboard Man, they ran from the police and hid what they stole in a breached tomb in the old Brady Street burial-ground. Their first juvenile conviction came when a railway worker saw them lever the capping stone from their favourite monument. Ida had taken her copper-stick to them for getting caught – not for stealing the rings and gold sleepers from a jeweller's in Roman Road.

The brothers boxed ten-bob three-rounders and worked the travelling fairs in the summer months, and found a way of stealing pennies from the pitch-owners, who turned out their pockets at the end of the night. They kept their bicycle clips on and dropped coins into their trousers, trying not to clank when they biked off home.

Jesse barged in to break Tommy's train of thought.

'You should see the tributes to Ida on the sideboard. The whole manor's chipped in.'

'Who'd risk a broken leg for want of a card from Woolworth's?' Helen spoke without looking up as she set a last rose on the cake. A small ebony crucifix cast a shadow into her cleavage.

'Mouth,' said Jesse, trying to scoop marzipan from a bowl. 'Three generations of Troys were dragged up in this house. I'd like a pound for all the whacks Ida's handed out, eh, Tom?'

'She could hit, and she ain't dead yet.'

'Talk like that tempts fate, Tom. Spit and throw salt over your shoulder.'

'Not on my floor you don't,' Helen said.

'It's Ida's sodding floor.'

'So let her wash it.'

'And you're the Christian, Helen?' Jesse sneered.

'Just like you,' Helen sneered back.

Tommy was mesmerised by the black cross between Helen's breasts.

'None of us ain't. We used to nick the candles when the old grannie dragged us to Mass. Knock them out to the stallies in Middlesex Street. And the sacramental wine.'

'Didn't know no different, did we?' said Jesse.

'And we do now?'

Helen shook hair from her face. 'Then, it's a good thing they lock the church these days.'

Tommy's eyes narrowed against cigar smoke.

'Be glad it's Ida's birthday, Helen. Right?'

Helen suppressed a shudder. Tommy would be brutal in bed if she antagonised the brothers further. Sour breath in her face as he used her like some unfeeling thing. All the soaps and lotions couldn't wash his attentions away when the mood was on him, and with Limehouse gone none of the others would walk her to church or ramble across the marshes. She would miss his freckles and solemn silences.

'The cake's finished,' she said quietly.

Tommy lit the candles and led the way out of the kitchen. In the hall Gay Gordon listened to the telephone with a rigid expression and waved to attract Tommy's attention. But Jessie opened the living-room door and the party rolled out on a wave of overheated air.

Ida's bawling laugh came from a mouth as red as a fire-bucket. She wore a loose purple dress with a double train, and her arms were as muscled as someone who beat hot metal for a living. Her thick grey hair was stiff with lacquer and her drop earrings were as big as arrowheads. Heat and excitement had crackle-finished her make-up.

'My lovely boys. None finer in the manor. And our Helen, the jewel in Tommy's crown. If only your sainted daddy was here to see us together. A family.'

She pinched tears from her eyes and missed Helen's look of disgust.

'Save your breath for blowing, Ma,' Jesse said.

Gay Gordon pushed in to tug Tommy's sleeve.

'All out in one go.' Ida puffed her cheeks at the massed candles, drawing laughs.

'The phone, Mr Troy.'

'Not now, Gordy.'

Tommy told his mother to make a wish and handed her a knife.

'My wishes'd make you blush. I don't smoke or swear, but I'm a bugger for Woodbines. Plates and forks, Helen.'

Ida stabbed the crimson heart dead centre and opened the gift Jesse thrust at her, a heavy gold charm bracelet. Tommy pushed Gordon aside, gathered his mother under his arm and told somebody to open the curtains. Ida stared out at the pink Cadillac with her mouth full of cake.

'But I don't drive, Tommy son.'

'Him in the uniform does that, Ma. Anywhere you wanna go.'

'The phone, Tommy.'

Gordon's no-colour eyes held Tommy's.

'It can wait.'

'Not when they've turned over the Martyred Thomas.'

'*What*?'

Gordon almost smiled. 'Don't need repeating.'

Ida pulled Tommy to her, her kisses and tears as warm as spittle on his face.

'Nothing, Ma . . . .'

Tommy saw Jesse's naked jealousy. Saw Helen's nausea as she ran from the hot press of bodies. Saw rage as a red swirl of mist. His tongue and teeth tasted foul.

The party was nothing more than a bunch of nonentities sucking up to power.

'How bad?' he asked Gordon.

'They done a lot of our faces over serious.'

'And the pub?'

'Insurance job, Tom.'

Tommy let his mother kiss him until she was finished.

Archie Ogle had been hit on Sunday. The Troys' turn had come today. Tommy wiped a sweating mouth.

'Get the cars out front,' he said, wondering: *Who*?

Charlie watched the main salon with his table captains.

Watched the usual Tuesday-night drifters move through the tables in search of maximum action and minimum risk. The hard core of matrons and widows squandering their late husbands' estates, and the smart geriatric set with nothing to kill but time. Gents from Dagenham or Nottingham who sold cars, shoes or peanut-concessions shot their cuffs over the tables without knowing that brown shoes did not go with blue suits or that loudness didn't equate to wit. Dress-salesmen with bow-ties as big as black butterflies who ironed their banknotes to make them snap when they played 'Neighbours' at a thousand a throw. Self-made men ousted from their boardrooms by anonymous accountants who preferred discreet corporate images to the egocentricity of the singular entrepreneur; dull old men with the specious privileges money bought them, and the leggy girls who decorated their chairbacks for money and kudos. Mathematicians who thought in orderly progressions like binary calculators, quiet men who marked their plays in ciphers and codes; all calculation and no outward show of pleasure. Tourists who fumbled and blushed and needed to be told what they held, who squealed when they won and pretended they could afford their losses. Charlie knew all the types and understood them without like or dislike. They were bread-and-butter punters who meant either profit or loss on an evening.

Jorgesson and Dakin played table five with a commercials director and three lady publishers from New York. Jorgesson's gin was watered, and Dakin toyed with a beer between visits to the gents'.

An hour into Wednesday morning a red light in the lobby signalled strangers in the reception hall, and Charlie had Ingrid relieved at table five before he wandered through the tables with nods and words here and there.

The reception area had peach mirrors to reflect crystal, plastic blooms to spray up Corinthian columns, and thick carpet to muffle untoward noise. The receptionist had a Grecian profile and a degree in advanced business studies, and her composure had turned the Troy firm into sullen schoolboys without help from Nasty Nostrils or Two-tone Ted.

'Will you vouch for these non-members, Mr Dance?'

Charlie sent the cool Miss Newton away, dangled a leg over the Empire desk and offered the register to Tommy Troy with: 'You're welcome as my personal guests.'

Jesse's face was oily in the peach light when he said: 'Ain't you the formal one?'

'Been feeding him raw meat, Tommy?'

'Jesse's calm enough.'

'But is he tooled up?'

Charlie swung a gleaming patent shoe, and Jesse rolled his shoulders at Charlie's overcoats.

'They ain't patting my threads.'

'Then, you walk. Having a blade or a shooter stashed ahead of you won't work here, chaps.'

Charlie traded looks with Gay Gordon, and Tommy toed ash into the carpet without looking down.

'Don't hardnose us, Charlie. You're carrying too much canvas for a sick firm.'

'Not me who had the fire.'

Tommy's face lost resolution as it hardened.

'You've got good grasses or a lot of matches, Chas.'

'Bangs and sparks frighten my budgie, and I climb into his cage when Camberwell starts bonfires.'

'Don't lahdie us, Chas. I can still smell the cobbles through that starched shirt.'

Charlie found a smile and kept it.

'So who's tooled up? Jesse or Gordy?'

Gay Gordon bared teeth, and Jesse paled when Tommy held them back. Nasty Nostrils had found a sawn-off under his jacket.

'Nobody as it happens. We've gotta talk, Charlie.'

'I'll rabbit over a bevy if the Happiness Twins take a walk.'

'Don't go for chat without back-up, Tommy,' Jesse warned.

Tommy shunted Jesse into Gay Gordon with a forearm.

'Go play "I-Spy" in Bond Street. First one to spot a straight busy gets ten points. Pat me down, Chas, but don't get hysterical about my inside-leg measurement.'

'Ain't the tool I'm worried about.'

Charlie held a curtain aside and Tommy sauntered into a concealed passage with his hands in his pockets.

The manager's office was a warm womb of oiled teak with a splash of light over the partners desk. Tommy lounged in the manager's chair to be close to the Armagnac and ice. His cigar hadn't the class to travel the six miles from Bethnal Green, and his pomaded hair gleamed like a swash of petrified tarmacadam. Charlie leaned by the aquarium with a small Irish.

'Maybe I should be hunting the other side of the Thames, Charlie. But we'll drink Ida's health, eh?'

'To the old mum.' Charlie skimmed cigars across the desk. 'And, Tommy, smoke something that don't kill mosquitoes for UNICEF.'

'If that's a charity, put me down for twenty sovs.'

Tommy dropped his cigar-butt into sand and bobbed a Havana on a moist lower lip until he drew flame through it, watched Charlie toy with an unlit Senior Service and added: 'An up-market alky once told me handsome cigars smoke better if you know how to light them. But this alky draws wages from me, so who's got the class? He don't have the nous to come in out of the rain, neither – a bit like you.'

'What would I do without your umbrella, Tommy?'

'Get well rained on, that's what.'

'By you? Archie'd get the dead needle.'

Tommy pretended surprise.

'Gloves off already, Chas?'

'I never did time, so I don't know how to waste it.'

'With the organ-grinder finished his top monkey should know enough to join a firm that knows how to hold the cobbles.'

'Like you'd drop Jesse to handshake with me.'

'He's family.'

'So's Archie.'

'Same meat, different gravy. The Harolds ain't reasonable over four-star brandy, so cop my coat-tails before I grab off the Smoke without you.'

Charlie watched a swordtail take a thread of Tubifex.

'You slipped on that greasy pole before.'

'Backed the wrong horse, didn't I? This time I'm spurring the favourite, me.'

'I play the man, not his cards, Tommy. The last time I gutted you with a pair of jolly jakes I woke up with stitches from crotch to breakfast-time. Just before you ended up with frozen jewels and a heavy finger up your nose.'

Tommy smiled through fragrant smoke.

'Then ain't now, but if you want a baby straightener to clear the air you're on. Here's four and a thumb.'

Charlie did not shake hands.

'And avoid a three-way straightener, right? You can't handle us and Camberwell together, and you know it. You and Connie Harold can kill each other all day, every day, and twice on Sundays as far me and Archie are concerned. All we want is the face who does a ball-and-chain job on cafés, right?'

'My tar ain't on that brush, Charlie, and well you know it. I'd have dropped the last hod of bricks on you personal, and no mother's son comes back from the dead. Not even with a Ouija board and a gross of mediums.'

Charlie made a smile he could live with.

'And I wouldn't have made certain-sure you and Jessie were banged up inside the Martyred Thomas if I'd lit the fuse?'

Tommy nodded at that.

'So Connie Harold earns the paper hat. So why not flatten him between us?'

'Losing Connie permanent won't earn you the Smoke. That'd take big dough.'

Tommy shed careless ash.

'Dough I got.'

'Malcolm Sadler's dough.'

Tommy leaked smoke into his drink, unable to swallow.

'Who?'

'A clever stockbroker face who's playing you and Connie on the same rod and line. Trouble is you and Connie haven't got what he wants; I have.'

Tommy's crossed knee danced on a nerve.

'More front than the Bluebell Girls. I've got to hand it to you, Charlie, pulling my pud when you're potless.'

Charlie killed the office light and parted curtains from a two-way mirror. Table five sprang at them as Jorgesson folded a hand and Dakin scratched a wrist.

'A million in mineral rights ain't bluff.'

Tommy's eyes flared as he stood. Something vile flickered in their depths before he willed them to glaze. He nodded and freshened his drink as clumps of hard muscle knotted his jaw.

'So that's why Lou and Wally ended up in Camden Town without change of a pound. What do those two buy you apart from lumps on your lumps?'

'The quiet life. Nobody cosies up to Sadler without them. Not you, not Connie. So have your straightener. I'll talk to who's left standing.'

'No room for neutrals, Charlie.'

'Independent, not neutral. And ask yourself why

Sadler's waltzing with second-stringers instead of talking to Archie?'

'Stop talking and say something.'

'Sadler's the big runaround, Tommy. A café for us, a gutted pub for you. Us screwing around like rabbits on piece rates and Sadler in the wings with faces we don't know? Think on, Tommy.'

Charlie closed the curtains and the aquarium lit the gloom.

'Choose sides, Charlie.'

'I did that ten years ago. You want friends? Go to Brighton and shake hands with what's left of Kosher's firm.'

'That museum piece couldn't hit a fairground duck in the beak with a cavalry charge.'

'Then, stay in Bethnal Green.'

Tommy swallowed angry phlegm.

'Enjoy Archie's sunset, Charlie. That last dark alley is where me and Jessie'll be waiting.'

Charlie's shrug was a punch to Tommy's churning stomach. He dashed brandy to the carpet where it glistened until the fibres absorbed it.

'That's you, Dance. A damp spot on the cobbles.'

'That gets it said.'

Charlie watched the door sigh closed against Tommy's rigid back. The filtration unit bubbled and the fish darted in shoals. Neon fireflies in the dark as Charlie smoked the Senior and thought things through.

Tommy hadn't bitten on Kosher's name at all, so the answer to what was happening might not be buried in the past after all. Unless Charlie was dealing with the enemy within like a husband who finds his best friend in bed with the wife. Mafeking Street rubble bounced in Charlie's mind and his forearm ached under the plaster.

The PBX flashed red and Charlie heard Kensington Kate's baritone mellowed by Pernod.

'Burning boozers put prices up.'

'You've got me a fairy, then.'

'Casting call's tomorrow morning. Don't be late.'

Kate laughed and rang off, and Charlie sprinkled daphnia into the aquarium.

'I'm in a swimming-pool with two deep ends,' he told the fish.

CHAPTER FIVE

QUEENIE fed Westcheap Within pigeons, and the hard morning light was too honest for her larded make-up. She gave Charlie an empty look when he asked if she was tired.

'Only of you, you toerag.'

'There's no choice in the matter.'

'Says you.'

Queenie's closed face killed conversation. She threw Charlie the keys to her E-type and told him to take the Southend Road. He spun them out of Roman Road through back doubles and crossed the Essex border north of Woodford. Beyond Battlebridge, Queenie directed him down an avenue of elms to a grey Victorian building with enough chimneys to start a second Industrial Revolution. Lawns swept down to a lake where a false bridge crossed duckweed and wind-flurries to a small decorative island. Virginia creeper climbed a Georgian folly and waterfowl cruised the shallows under banks of weeping willow. Nurses walked wheelchair patients on the lawns and white breath ran on the wind.

A gilded and shadowed sign read: *Oldfield Sanatorium for Gentlefolk of the Masonic Order*.

Charlie checked his temper and parked on marble chippings beside limousines, a private ambulance, and a dog-cart with a roan mare between the shafts. Queenie stalked into the hospital and left Charlie to lock the car. The roan whickered and shared her sorrowing gaze with Charlie, the misery of the world in her brown eyes.

Charlie worried the cropped mane between her ears.

'That's life, horse. And being nice buys you less than

not a lot.'

He joined Queenie in the lobby and followed her into a secure area of locked doors and muscular orderlies.

Archie's sunlit room was decked out like the Chelsea Flower Show and greetings cards hung in gay lines above his bed. The picture-window overlooked the island and the russet folds of land beyond. The River Crouch shone through trees, and seagulls skimmed the mudflats.

Propped up on pillows, Archie lay with his blackened hands above the sheets, and his head-bandage gave him the look of a bleached Hindu. Face stubble was becoming a grey beard and his eyes were the green of old bank-notes. He let Queenie kiss him and waved Charlie into a pneumatic chair.

'No fruit?'

'When were you sick enough for grapes?'

Charlie caught the faint aroma of cigars and the ring of ash where an ashtray had nestled beside the squashes and medication. He smiled his polite visitor's smile.

'How's the food?'

'Comes on silver and tastes of greyhound straw. For the dough I'm paying they should leave me my tastebuds. And it don't stick to your ribs, neither. Like having a Chinese woman — an hour later you're randy again.'

Queenie plumped pillows, and Archie moved his head as if a barber trimmed his hair. Charlie's chair sighed when he crossed a knee.

'You're well enough to grumble.'

'Thanks to you, son.'

'And Sergeant Quill.'

'I don't like owing anything there, Chas. Pay it off fast.'

'How? By turning myself in?'

'Work on it. The punters have gotta look up to you.'

Archie's voice crumbled like stale breadsticks.

'I ain't the Man. The sooner you stride the cobbles the better.'

'With mashed ankles and busted kneecaps? No mother's son sees Archie Ogle hobble on sticks.'

'You can wave from the Rolls.'

'I'm a walker, Chas. The punters wouldn't swallow me waving at them from the back seat of a set of class wheels like they was yokels. They like me on the cobbles aside of them.'

'It's your face they want to see, Arch. Not mine.'

'Am I a nappy service for tired overcoats or what? Is he crying for me or for himself, Queenie?'

Queenie helped Archie sip from a beaker.

'I told him I didn't want you fretted. Now I'm telling him double.'

Charlie swallowed air.

'I can hold the local cobbles, but it's Arch who has to sort out Toronto and New York. And I don't like the Tonnas crying off their visit the exact moment we got hit with a café. You told them "No" on their drugs deal, and somebody close hit us, Archie.'

'Toronto ain't close.'

'Freelance faces are a phone call away, Arch.'

'That ain't your worry, right? You stay in the shadows and let the other firms sweat in the sun. You can do that, can't you?'

'Maybe.'

'That better be a definite maybe, son.'

'OK, Archie.'

'Well, then . . . .' Archie flopped back.

His eyes dropped and his mouth yawned open. Then he snored, asleep like an old rumpled baby. If it was an act, it was a good one.

Queenie tucked bedclothes.

'He overdid it.'

Charlie sipped from Archie's beaker behind her back, and vodka cut through the orange squash.

Finishing up, Queenie said: 'Let's go.'

After the heat of the hospital the parking-lot was as cold as nightclub ice. The roan nuzzled Charlie's hand and stamped a forehoof on marble chippings. Queenie skirted the horse with: 'I just hope you're satisfied.'

'Maybe.'

'That's your word for the day, is it? *Maybe*?'

'Could be.'

Charlie found a flattened Dunhill in his pocket and lit it with a Zippo. The roan wrinkled delicate nostrils.

'My old man had a dray like this. Used to keep it like new until he got too dozy on the booze and his lungs collapsed. I always wanted one as a kid, but I wouldn't kill for it.'

'That meant to mean something?'

Queenie had lost a thumb in her glove.

'Only to me.'

Charlie tossed the long cigarette-butt into the rhododendrons. The tobacco was as stale as an alderman's sock.

Queenie pulled at the car door with her tangled glove.

'You came out here to see if Archie had lost his bottle, you toerag. Maybe because you've lost yours.'

'And maybe because I wanted some answers. The truth. You remember that good old-fashioned stuff, don't you, Queenie? You and Arch used to set great store by it. Archie ain't overmedicated. Just dead drunk.'

Queenie rocked the car.

'It won't open until I use this. It's called a key.'

'Then, use it.'

Charlie's grin was as honest as an Oxford Street auction.

'Horses don't nag if you keep them in bran and carrots.'

'Open this door!'

The mare butted Charlie in sudden panic, and the air between then handclapped. An echo clattered out over the lake.

Charlie ducked in against the car. Reached for Queenie.

His knee-joint cracked with the cold as he threw himself across the bonnet. Half-rolling on his shoulders he brought his legs down on Queenie's side of the Jaguar. He skidded on chippings. Elbowed the hard metal to keep balance. Pulled Queenie in and down. She kneeled and tore a stocking as he shielded her.

The mare had stiffened all four legs. Her head extended

as she rolled bloody eyes. Red bubbles frothed in her nostrils and her teeth bared and clamped. With a monumental shudder she sank on her haunches with blood jetting from a massive exit wound in her withers. Hit again she reared. Then, with a long last look at Charlie, she rolled on her side and quivered until she died.

More shots gouged the chippings. Concussions fled with the startled mallards and racketed to silence. Mundane sounds came back. The squeak of an unoiled wheelchair. Wind in the elms. Dishes in the kitchens, and a porter hurrying to a telephone.

Charlie's finger curled around an invisible gun.

Queenie called Archie and fought Charlie's hold.

'Be still, woman.'

Charlie bundled Queenie into the car. Her handbag spilled in her lap. Things rolled into the well under the driving-seat, and she banged her head trying to retrieve them.

Charlie powered into a U-turn and drove west with wind mourning in the quarter-lights. Hedges danced in the backwash.

'You led them to Archie, You . . . .'

'Without knowing where I was going?'

'You had us followed.'

'Is that why they were shooting at us and not him?'

Queenie wept openly.

'Why, Chas? Why us?'

Charlie saw nothing but the roan dying and the road ahead.

'If I knew that, I'd be smart enough to be somebody else.'

A hand-lettered poster on the outer door of Mother's read:

CASTING TODAY
POOF IN BOOTS
OR
Homo is Where the Heart Is
A CHRISTMAS PANTOMIME

Charlie stopped dead in the lobby.

Halted by noise and too much perfume.

Ageing queens in suits watched young ones trade bitchiness at full volume. A group listened to a henna-rinse read poems and a beard in a caftan fed peanuts to a tame capuchin on a lead. A boy in green made dancer's spreads up a wall, and an effeminate in jeans and a boa talked into the public phone. Their musk washed around Charlie like decadent laughter.

Then the chattering and giggling stopped like a wave against rock as Charlie was looked over with feral antipathy.

'All right, troupe.'

Electric Raymond bustled from the stairwell, his jacket a shout of nubbed silk. His black trousers could have been sprayed on and his belt buckle was as big as the boss on a crusader's shield. He took Charlie down into the club like a guilty secret.

'We told you early, Charlie. *Early*.'

'This is bloody early.'

'This lot was here before nine. Bedlam.'

Kate sat at the bar. The cerise and veridian jacket made his blouse and trousers seem very white. He made room for Charlie and they watched a lean transvestite murder a Noël Coward number. An overweight Shirley Temple sang 'The Good Ship "Lollipop" ' and Charlie drank coffee laced with Irish.

'Bit of a circus, Kensington.'

'My dear Charlie, where does one hide an offertory candle but in a church? How else am I to show you talent of a special nature without drawing attention to the fact?'

'It's your twopence.'

'Just clock the little number to the right of the stage. Pink shirt and pants. Red leather wristbands. Next to the blonde gorilla with the swallow tattooed on his cheek.'

Charlie peered and said: 'Got him.'

Groomed white hair framed a cherubic face. The brilliant eyes could have been any colour.

'The little bitch is stagestruck. Shane the gorilla paupers himself to keep Lady Penelope in theatre seats.'

'Lady Penelope?'

Charlie scalded his mouth with laced coffee, still haunted by the roan's eyes. Shane was the kind of weight-lifter that wears short sleeves at thirty below and glories in wheatgerm. He hovered over the white-haired boy like a jealous cloak.

Charlie crooked a finger for a real drink.

'And this Shane won't roll over, that it?'

'Right in one.'

Kate's wink was fleeting.

'And I thought the shortest distance between two points was a straight line.'

'Not in my club, old dear.'

A skinny queen replaced Shirley Temple and sang well enough to amuse a cinema queue. A boy in black juggled and a nondescript tapdanced before Raymond called a break for lunch. Kate swept off to kiss the air beside special faces and came back with Shane and Penelope. Shane ordered fruit juice and Penelope wanted champagne cocktails. Shane's hand was a proprietary crab on Penelope's shoulder as the boy laughed at Kate's theatrical banter and oozed sexuality at Charlie as if Shane was just another shadow in the room.

Kate brought the conversation around to the theatre and how Charlie had a permanent box at Covent Garden. Shane's jealousy festered into blind rage under Kate's expert prodding.

'The Royal Court would go broke without Charles's patronage,' said Kate.

'I get a few tickets.'

'Such modesty for a financial angel.'

'I'd love to see *Canterbury Tales*. Chaucer is wondrous,' said Penny, needling Shane.

'He speaks highly of you, too,' said Charlie.

'B-movie dialogue,' sneered Shane.

'Manners,' said Kate. 'Charles is a friend.'

'If he has a box, he stole it. Or was it just another perk of the protection business?'

Charlie folded his arms and looked sleepy.

'Shane,' Kate warned.

'Leave it, Kate. I gotta go. Haven't sandbagged a granny all morning.'

'Make sure she's got her back turned,' said Shane. He drilled Charlie's chest with a finger and the roan rolled her eyes under Charlie's lids.

'I think you just went too far,' Kate told Shane.

Charlie stood and showed nothing.

'You can't insult me, sonny. I'm too ignorant.'

He laid a fiver on the bar.

'Here, buy yourself a new hair-ribbon and cheer yourself up.'

When he reached the foot of the stairs a bar stool glanced off the wall and took the drink from Shirley Temple's hand.

'My Bloody Mary.'

Charlie looked at Kate as if they were alone.

'You call it.'

Kate didn't move from the bar. 'Cabaret time, dears,' he said.

'It's your furniture.'

Charlie's hands hung at his sides.

Shane lumbered forward. A high loping right to Charlie's head was meant to duck him into an upswinging left. Both shots hit air. A palm slammed Shane's cheek and Charlie was gone.

Shane threw a fist at Charlie's forehead and burst his knuckles against the stucco wall.

Fingers flicked at his eyes and Shane was blinded by his own tears. His savage kick was blocked by a turning thigh, and a firestorm of pins and needles flared in his buttocks, numbed his lower back. A second toepunt turned a knee to water.

Charlie was behind him again.

Shane turned to smother Charlie with his bulk.

A blurring forearm snapped his head aside. Something

vital tore inside his throat and Shane tasted his own blood. When he blinked, overlapping images made no sense. He rolled a shoulder into a blind punch and steel fingers bit into his neck, lifted him on to tiptoe.

Roaring pain took the club away in a kaleidoscope of spangled nothing. He didn't feel two short punches break his thighs. He was a huge broken doll draped over a chair by somebody made of quicksilver.

Charlie could have been invisible for all the attention anybody paid him, so he went up to the street straightening his tie.

The boy with white hair was on the firm.

Charlie found Vinnie Castle and Fast Frankie Frewin in the long bar in Shaftesbury Avenue. Theatricals around the fire talked about the 'New Liverpool Sound' in carrying voices, and a dip sold a handbag he had just lifted from Selfridges. Fast Frankie asked for Scotch and got a small beer.

'All that ducking and diving to shake three mobiles and Inspector Lemmon's whole squad of busies for a lousy half-pint?'

'You shake them?'

'Does it snow in August? We ducked through Manchester Freddy's joint in Berwick Street – out into Duck Lane and done a hotsman down Wardour Street. Got as much chance of tailing us as Sally the donkey has of winning the Oaks.' Frankie buried his drink behind his bow-tie. 'They're paying us a lot of attention since Mafeking Street. Any news on where Micky Dogge disappeared to, Chas?'

'Gone on his holidays. How do I know?'

Frankie couldn't hold the narrowed slate eyes.

'He's Archie's bookkeeper, that's all. The wrong people tweaking his toes could get a lot of info out of Micky.'

'Don't worry about it. He'll turn up.'

Charlie bought more beer and felt for cigarettes he didn't have. Took and lit one of Vinnie's and blew smoke into Fast Frankie's face.

'Bottle tweaking, Frankie?'

Frankie's stomach churned, and fear took him back to rolling the second favourite at Newmarket eleven years before. He could still see Gallant Goose jerk when they finished him with a humane killer. Even if the Jockey Club had cleared Frankie, all the Scotch in the Highlands wouldn't get him back in the saddle. Brother Bobby had guaranteed the smart money from Brighton that the favourite would waltz home and hadn't laid off their bets to cover himself. But Gallant Goose had brought the favourite down with him, and a 16–1 outsider had romped home. Frankie was barred from racing for life, and Brother Bobby went on the trot with a topping contract on his head. The Troys took him off the Harwich ferry, took the £100,000 he'd run with, and dumped what was left of him on the estuary with his tongue in his top pocket. Archie Ogle was all there was between Frankie and those faces with long arms and longer memories, and if Archie went down . . . .

Frankie coughed on smoke and nodded.

'Scared ain't the word. But I ain't yellow or daft. You ain't one of them manic bastards who likes to draw on faces with a soldering-iron, but there's enough who do. And they'll come at you team-handed. Ten to hold you down and ten more to pull your teeth out through your socks. You and Archie go down, we all go down and dirty.'

Charlie leaned his broken forearm on the bar.

'That gets it said, Frankie.'

'And I talk too much, right?'

'Only all the time.'

Frankie jangled coins in a pocket.

'There's hundreds of little people tied up with the firm, Chas. From meat porters to market stallies, cabbies to publicans, they all bet with our firm, punt our gear or earwig the cobbles for hot bubbles. The toms keep their eyes open for us, and there ain't a first-storey man worth his corn who'd crack a crib in our manor without Archie says yes. Let the wrong faces get hold of that organisation and you've got Big Brother in spades.'

Charlie patted himself down, and Vinnie offered his cigarettes.

'If we're so bloody well informed, how come the iron-ball trick at the café came as such a big surprise?' asked Charlie.

'Freelancers,' said Frankie.

'But whose?'

'One of the seven things in the world I don't know.'

'So find out.' Charlie blew smoke into Vinnie's clouded eyes.

'You've had me out on the cobbles half the night, Chas,' said Vinnie. 'I've got us a contact inside Lemmon's squad. Trouble is he's straight.'

'Has he got a name?'

'Want me to write it in dayglo on the wall?'

'No, nor fly kites or send smoke signals. I haven't had a hot bubble out of you since the midwife decided I was a boy.'

Vinnie looked pained. 'There's a big tickle going the rounds I can't pin to the big firms as it happens.'

Charlie breathed more smoke.

'And? Or is that it?'

'It's what's *not* being said that's important. Faces who owe us won't hand out a weather forecast standing by an opened window. Bonar Tree's name got shuffled out alongside Ollie Oliphant's, so it has to be a train. They're the only decent rattler bandits in the Home Counties. And Ollie asked when Pimlico Johnny Parsons was due out of Durham, so they've got him marked down as second coachman, right? And the dough sounds big enough to buy us and sell us and give us back to ourselves.'

'Oh,' mused Charlie. '*That* big.'

'I get the bubbles, Chas. You have to make sense of them.'

Charlie ticked off points on his fingers: 'A rattler bandit who works the Brighton line. A top driver without form. A GBH merchant who was once cosied up with

Kosher Kramer and the Troys. About as useful as an unravelled string vest. Give me a knitting pattern that ties all this to Sadler and I'll be a happy overcoat.'

Vinnie dogged his smoke. 'If they need a laundry job, why haven't they come to us? Push the money out through Frankie's betting shops?'

'Sadler could be the answer to that,' said Frankie.

Charlie shrugged that away, needing time to think.

'And if they did have Micky Dogge they'd know how we launder through my shops,' Frankie added.

Charlie let that thought go without comment.

'Back on the streets. And be lucky,' he said.

Frankie turned at the door.

'And you, Chas. For all of us.'

'Oh blimey yeah.'

Charlie watched Vinnie and Frankie walk out into cool sunshine and pointed two fingers at the Irish optic. The barman short-changed the till in Charlie's favour and laid notes and silver on the bar.

'What d'you say, Charlie?'

'You know why it's easy to act the bastard, Dave?'

Dave shook his head.

'Because you use four hundred muscles to smile. And you only need one to fuck somebody. Cheers, son.'

CHAPTER SIX

TRAFALGAR SQUARE was alive with pigeons and the first flurry of spring tourists. Charing Cross Station was a hothouse of bustle, and the permanent shadows in Villiers Street turned Charlie's breath to vapour. He crossed to the basement coffee-bar in John Adam Street, ignoring the *Closed* sign.

The Gaggia was silent and the old Armenian washed last night's cups in a sinkful of steam. His uncombed hair was an untidy halo of floss around his bald scalp. Deaf and half-blind, he was grateful for the coolie wages Stavros sometimes remembered to pay.

Stavros and Sodbonce pawed the latest sex magazines in the scruffy back office, and the one opened on the desk featured adults and minors in grainy black and white.

'You'll go blind pawing that stuff.'

Charlie lit one of Stavros' Pall Malls and blew smoke across a woman accommodating three men, her eyes as dead as yesterday's oysters.

'This stuff is nothing in Istanbul.' Stavros scratched his unshaven chin, his pudding of a face as greasy as a marinated olive.

'So sell it there. Try punting that in the Square Mile and all you'll earn is a government-sponsored holiday at Her Majesty's expense. Then they'll deport you.'

Stavros said he'd mail-order the consignment.

He smelled as stale as a widow's bed.

'Listen up, you undesirable alien. Obscene literature through the Royal Mail will earn you a five stretch in Parkhurst. The firm would lose your earnings and we won't spring for a brief, neither. We've got enough claret on the cobbles without you slapping muck about, right?'

'I hear you, Mr Charlie.'

'You've had one stretch in a Turkish prison, and I know they'd love you back. Made yourself well unpopular over some young trusty with that shiv of yours. I don't have to go on, do I?'

'No, Mr Charlie. That Sergeant Mimi would cut off my buttocks 'cause I took a blade to his big nose . . . .'

'Yeah, yeah. How're Jorgesson and Dakin, Soddy?'

Sodbonce flicked ash from a stub.

'Sulking. I got Doc Rudge in to Vic. His leg was going a bit septic.'

'Like the rest of him. Did he call Connie like I said?'

'He did.'

The telephone jangled, and Stavros took a laid-off bet at 5—1 in hundreds without writing it down. He ran an idle nail across a close-up of siliconed breasts and irritated Charlie for no reason he could fathom. Stavros was as pathetic as the legions of dirty raincoats he catered for, and was probably his own best customer.

Sodbonce fired a fresh Player from his stub.

'There's a face waiting for you out back, Chas. I patted his threads and he's clean.'

Charlie clattered down into Stavros' bookstore and shook hands with Dublin Gerry. Gerry was in his middle forties and specialised in freelance arm-breaking. Two months had passed since his release from Durham's high-security wing and he flew over from Eire when his special talents were needed. His thick hair was the same dusty amber as the down on his forearms, and his eyes were the same green as the shamrocks tattooed on his wrists. He had served with the Irish Guards in Egypt during the Suez crisis where he had learned to kill in silence with or without a weapon.

Charlie winked and handed him an envelope.

'You did it up brown last night, Dublin. Earned every penny.'

'Wouldn't I have done it for nothing? I won't forget how you looked after Molly and the kids when I was inside.'

'A man's got to earn a crust, Gerry. See if you can't save some of that for a rainy day. You have enough of them in the old Emerald Isle. Your team have it away all right?'

'Sure and fine. Brother Dominic drove them down to Holyhead right after we turned the Martyred Thomas into Daniel's fiery furnace. They'll be supping good Guinness on the Irish Sea right now.'

'Any hurt?'

'One daft besom has an interesting limp from dropping a Molotov cocktail on to his foot. But, then, putting the boot into them Troys was worth it. And don't I owe them for how they squeezed me cousin out of the building game in Bethnal Green? Dropped him off his own scaffold into pre-mixed cement and left it to set around his broken legs? The Thomas was a fair deposit on what's owed me family.'

'Just forget you was there, right?' Charlie dropped his stub for Dublin Gerry to step on.

'I've no memory of nothing, me old Chas.'

'Uhuh. And what's this about Pimlico Johnny Parsons earning early remission and parole? You two shared a cell.'

'We shared the corridor, that's all. Johnny and me never got along, Charlie. Sure and wasn't he always cosied up with Kramer and the Troy bastards? A prideful man and difficult to know. He was forever at the screws over the slightest thing — talking prisoners' rights and all that old malarky. Until his wife left him, that is. Then he just closed in on himself. Prison takes people different ways. For me it was just a civilian glasshouse and nothing to get ragged about. But Pim was his own man and had nothing good to say about any man. Forget the man, he's a fuck-up looking for a place to really fuck up.'

'I heard Ollie Oliphant had something for him.'

Gerry grinned and winked.

'You heard about the mail train, then? I thought it was a Camberwell tickle, but with all those hungry mouths boasting about how big the money involved is I'd stay well out of it.'

'Could be you're right. Watch your back when you leave, Gerry. The law's all over me and mine like a blanket.'

Gerry's grin widened.

'Just think of all that law as minders acting unpaid. And who's gonna take a second crack at you with all that official interest you're attracting?'

Charlie smiled and nodded.

'One way of looking at it.'

When Gerry had gone, Charlie sat on Jorgesson's folding bed and quizzed him about his mining concessions in South Africa.

Connie Harold crossed a junction on red and amber and barrelled towards Smithfield. The May sun died in the upper windows of the new tower blocks, and a chill wind from the Essex marshes bobbed the street-lights on their wires. Wally snuffed through his bruised nose as Connie beat a double-decker into a roundabout. Harry the Crack and Sailor Mailer rolled with the car's motion, fists in the straps and faces carefully blank as Connie shaved a newsvan and powered the Vanden Plas into the fast east-bound lane. The governor was in a towering fury, and it was best to roll with the punches.

Wally's head was as fluffy as the hospital bed he had been dragged from. One moment he rested 'under observation' trying to work out how he ended up in the casualty ward – the next Connie was stuffing Wally into his clothes and ranting on about Vic Dakin ordering him to a meet.

Wally remembered giving Limehouse Lou a good hiding and hauling Vic Dakin out into the street. Then his head had exploded all over a damp lawn and rain had washed him into slamming darkness. Bed and rest called him, and Connie's monotonous swearing made his skull ache. Wally closed his eyes against the whip and glare of sodium lights and let the car carry him along.

He understood long-firm tickles with Sellotape and bleach and washing machines – even tractors – but

Connie's new schemes were over the moon and halfway to Mars. All the talk about owning a merchant bank in Malta and issuing their own banker's drafts to bribe government officials over some diamond mine was enough to do his brain in. All Wally wanted was a few dozen one-armed bandits up west, hand out a bit of protection on the side, and jolly along with a ready bird to help him brass away a few sovereigns on a Saturday night.

Wally held a pounding temple and refused a smoke.

If Connie wanted to get flash he could have financed the train tickle Bonar Tree and Ollie Oliphant were putting together. There was enough ready poppy in the Smoke without listening to Vic Dakin's old bunny about foreign investments. Wally was lost north of Tottenham Court Road, so playing banker in Malta and Johannesburg made as much sense as blowing up balloons under water.

Connie had braked and ripped his door open.

'Quit mooning, Wally. Out. Sailor's with me, so you and Harry cover the other side of the graveyard.'

Graveyard? Wally raised his collar against the chill.

The outer walls of Westcheap Within were slick with moisture, and a gas-lamp flickered on its standard. Wally followed Connie through a door in the east wall as Harry and Sailor went in under an arch. They crunched over gravel and crossed grass to a shadowed bandstand.

And waited.

Sailor's overcoat opened, and light slicked a shotgun barrel.

Wally leaned against the bandstand railing.

'Why're they tooled up when you can take Vic Dakin with a bloody winkle-pin?'

Connie's face flared in matchlight, and he bloomed smoke.

'Shut it and have another scout-around.'

Wally held his swimming head.

'Tasty talk, Con. You out here with shooters and temper all over your face is as sensible as banks and diamond mines. You can own all the best clubs and all the scrap from here to Aberdeen, have all the muscle and Rollers you can afford so long as you have them here, Con. Not in sodding Africa with a bunch of Dutch niggers.'

'Grow up, Wally. You can't afford to stagnate in business.'

Wally rolled his eyes at the lowering sky.

'Listen to Connie use three-guinea words like *stagnate*. Who cast you as a Technicolor millionaire? I've had your lahdie ideas up to my collar-stud.'

Wally held Connie's marbled gaze when his brother's hand clamped his wrist.

'Cain and Abel violence, Bruv? Raise a finger and I'll deck you so hard you'll clean your teeth through the top of your head.'

'It was you who lost Dakin to Dance.'

'That what I did?'

'And I've wiped your arse and tied your shoelaces all our lives. It's time you started paying back.'

Wally wrenched his hand back and flexed the fingers.

'You've had it all back in spades.'

'Now, listen, you . . . .'

'Forget it, Con.'

Wally stepped away and straight-armed a finger into his brother's face.

'Forget it all, Bruv. I'm through. Out. Done. Finished. You want to come down to earth again, I'll be here. But till then leave me out of it. Maybe I ain't got the class you want, but I'll be in the West End before you.'

Wally sidestepped and shouldered between Harry and Sailor. His footsteps died away, and it became quiet enough to hear river traffic from the Thames.

Charlie's quiet 'Good evening' was as loud as a shout of pain.

Limehouse Lou responded to Detective Inspector Lemmon's questions by whistling 'All coppers are bastards' through gritted teeth. There was no point in bubbling to the law to get the Troys tens and twenties at the Bailey. Lou knew they'd have him shivved before he opened his clack in the witness-box, and a dead grass is nobody's hero; even his old dad would buy Tom and Jessie the best drink in the house and boycott the funeral.

After an interminable half-hour the matron chased Lemmon away and left Lou with his morbid thoughts and a monumental hangover. The fire at the Martyred Thomas came back with every stab of pectoral pain. Lou shivered and took the names of three saints in vain.

'Lou?'

Lou squeezed his eyes closed. The voice did not belong. It belonged in church talking through the beads of a rosary. Or walking the marshes with wind streaming in yellow hair . . . .

Lou opened his eyes ready for a mirage.

And there were cornflower eyes and ropes of golden hemp. The oval face with its generous pout of a mouth. A glow of sundown set the hair alight, and the melancholy eyes burned with concern.

Lou's chest filled with secondary pain.

'Mrs Troy? How'd you know where . . .?'

'Police came to the house.'

Lou bet himself they were finger-tamed — Arthur Ax's boys in blue who danced to Tommy's tune — and he wondered how Helen had escaped from the Fortress.

'The chauffeur brought me in Ida's new car. He takes me most anywhere I want now you're not there to mind me. Ida's not allowed out until Tommy finds out who torched the Thomas.'

'Tommy should worry as much about you.'

'I'm not important.'

Lou wanted to tell her she was wrong. As far as he was concerned Helen was the entire universe. He wanted her hands under the bedclothes. Touching him where he hurt. Touching him where he lived . . . .

Desire flushed Lou's face and ears.

'Did anybody see you come in here? Tommy'd hurt you if he knew you'd wasted your time coming to see me.' Lou was breathless with fear for her.

'Save your breath for getting well.'

'Just promise you'll take care. Real care.'

'Don't fret yourself.'

'Promise, you daft bitch.'

Lou knew he had given himself away. Knew it was too late to pretend indifference. Saw mild shock in Helen's eyes. Saw it melt with compassion.

'You shouldn't talk . . . that way . . . to me.'

'It's done – ain't it? Ain't gonna see you carved by him over . . . me.'

'I'll be fine. Think of your own hurt.'

'You hurt – I hurt. That's bloody . . . it.'

Lou wished he could get up, shield her with his own body. Pain spun the room, and his chest was a smashed barrel without air.

'You even got to . . . *think* careful . . . .'

Helen said, 'Please get better.'

'What for?'

'For me.'

'Don't you kid me with words, Lady.'

'They aren't *just* words.'

Lou was confounded by dizzy nausea. Helen blurred, and her face was too close to focus on. Cool lips brushed Lou's mouth, and the pressure became a kiss.

'I'll be careful, dear Lou.'

And Helen was gone with the last of the sun.

Lou just lay there. Too frightened to hope. Too frightened not to.

'Good evening.'

Charlie aimed his voice at the glow of Connie's cigarette.

'Hold it!'

Connie threw his arms wide as the shotguns swung.

Directly in the line of fire, Connie became motionless. Choreographed drops, feints, rolls and falls. Rejected them with regret. Charlie Dance was close enough to touch.

'Where's Dakin?'

Charlie leaned where Wally had leaned.

'Three tooled up ain't you coming alone, Connie.'

'Like you have, Chas?' Connie wondered where Dance's back-up was.

Charlie shrugged with folded arms. 'Like I have.'

'When have *you* got that kind of bottle?'

Charlie's sigh was huge.

'I've just been down the road of threats with Tommy and his poofs. Leave it out, Con. Let's get straight to this face Sadler.'

'Who?'

'Tommy said *that*, too. Drop the toffee or I walk.'

'With shooters on you?' Connie wondered why he was wrongfooted and Dance could afford to show contempt. Something wasn't adding up.

'Trigger me — you've got nothing. When were you happy living off lesser villains' tickles like Troy and his slags, Connie? When you jumped bail on the purchase-tax fiddle and had it away to Canada? You didn't sit in the sun drinking yourself stupid. You built a new scrap business out of nothing. Sold it for a good profit when you crept back home.'

'The Tonnas must have given you that bubble.'

'Elbow the artillery and talk business, Con.'

'You talk a good fight.'

'I've got the hole cards. Dirk and Vic. Two fat aces like them got to be worth a hundred grand.'

'Suddenly it's double poppy? Fifty extra long ones? What for?'

'Hospitals cost, and Archie gets the best.' Charlie lifted an abrupt palm. 'And slagging me ups the price.'

'Shoot him, somebody.' Connie sounded strangled. 'Where do I get that kind of dough wholesale?'

Charlie chuckled. 'The Bank of Valletta? Or hasn't Vic sold you that phoney Maltese bank of his?'

'You're brassing me off with all these *maybes* and *alsos*.'

Charlie took a flyer. 'Or have you laid out too much dough on this train tickle?'

Connie looked blank. 'That's your firm.'
'And the Martyred Thomas is down to you.'
'Who's laying that at my door?'
'Same fella who laid it at mine.'
Connie's laugh was edged with derision. 'With Archie hiding under the bed your firm couldn't take a trolleybus at knifepoint.'
'Tommy didn't turn himself over.'
'We live in strange old times, Charlie.'
Connie drew smoke and made sparks with the discarded stub. He fumbled for Gold Flake and offered them. Charlie leaned in, and Connie lit cigarettes for them both with a Swan Vesta.
'And getting stranger.'
'Fifty grand for Dirk, Vic and the markers. Take it and run, Chas. The Smoke's getting too busy for your firm.'
'A three-way straightener and South Africa makes you a busy boy, Connie. Can you handle it?'
'Could you stop me?' Connie's question was harsher than his breath.
'I'll take the fifty thou.'
'*And* stand aside.'
Charlie could have been turned to wax.
'Archie and me under a café started the week badly. This morning I watched a horse die instead of me and Queenie. For lunch I crippled a butch poof, and had afternoon tea with faces I'd rather flush down the nearest po. And now it's you and the Happiness Twins shoving shooters up my hooter. Standing aside would be a pleasure.'
Connie Harold pulled an earlobe.
Wind sighed in the chestnut, stirred the outer branches with gentle clatters. Wooden sabres hacking at the night. Breeze skimmed the silent turf, and a clock chimed the quarter-hour.
Connie's marbled eyes were blank glass beads.
'We never turned you over, Chas. Not that I won't, rubbed-up the wrong way.'
'You ain't gonna offer me a change of firms, then?'

'A devious toerag like you on my strength? Leave it out.'
'Watch your back with Wally off on his toes.'
'He'll be back when the weather changes.'
'Vic Dakin's a greasy pole, Connie. He turned TWA and BOAC over for three hundred grand with his airline-ticket frauds, and bankrupted half of Milan over that micromesh-stocking swindle. I know you had some of the action, Con, but Vic was smooth enough to weasel a Mafia firm in its own backyard. They had a cannon up his nose and he talked his way out of it. Even left Tommy and Jessie in a garage with a heap of funny and phoney Old Masters before having it away on his toes with their poppy. You and Tommy think you're hard, but those Sicilians have memories longer than Grable's legs.'
Connie said nothing.
'The Fraud Squad are on to Vic's car-finance firm and that dodgy club of his in Marlborough Street. If they knew he was back in this country, they'd tear us all down to get to him. You could have Vic running scared since you shoved gelignite up his exhaust and left a stick tied to the letter-box of his Dolphin Square flat, but he'll run with your poppy if he can.'
Connie just listened.
'And don't fool yourself about his private banks, neither. The Bank of Valletta's as buoyant as a lead balloon. And watch the Sunday papers about his Merchant Guaranty Bank. Two straight faces are up for long stretches because they fronted for Vic. You ask yourself if Vic'd come back here if there was anywhere else to run? Just don't let him happen all over your shoes.'
'Why mark my card, Charlie?'
'Because dog-doody sticks to the most expensive shoes. And if your dominoes tumble they'll sure-as-eggs nudge a few of ours over. Just make money, not waves.'
Connie tugged his ear pink.
'Listening to you learns me one thing, Chas.'
'Oh?'
'Like I've bought the wrong coppers. You get lovely

straight bubbles, Chas.'

'Just have your dough at Windmill Street by noon. Hatton will sign the papers when I've counted the bundles.'

'No cheques, Charlie?'

'Signed by Vic Dakin, I suppose?'

'OK, so it's cash at noon.'

'Not many.'

Charlie backed away and turned from sight.

Connie picked a shred of tobacco from his lip, deep in thought.

In the car his sudden laughter made Harry and Sailor uneasy.

'What gives, Con?'

'Fight fire with fire. If the Troys can have a bonfire, why can't we? Where's Sad Sidney these days?'

'About the manor. Why?'

'Get him. And I do mean *now*.'

Connie drove towards Camberwell, stunned by his own brilliance.

Wally Harold passed three dress-vans parked in Archer Street without a second glance. All set for a three-day drunk he went down into the basement bar of the Troubadour Club and found himself a corner table, his mind filled with dark thoughts of filial betrayal. He was on his fifth large gin when somebody hovered to say: 'Wally son, it's Pim.'

'On your bike. Pim's doing five in Durham.'

'First day on the cobbles rates a hello drink, don't it?'

Wally squinted into eyes like frosted shellac.

Pimlico Johnny Parsons's long legs and squat torso gave him the illusion of height. A birthmark formed a small brown mouse above his right eyebrow, and his large head sat on a strong brown neck. He had heavy shoulders, and his knuckles were as white and hard as piano keys.

'You ain't done a runner, Pim?'

'Ate my last slop of porridge this morning.'

'Has to be. You was wearing that sod of an eyetalian jacket when you went down for five at Kingston crown court. So how come you didn't give me the chance of being at the gate with a bottle of bubbly?'

Pimlico turned his light ale and looked cautious.

'Things change in three years.'

'Between us, you tosspot? So I didn't visit you in the slammer, but when was known faces allowed in for reunions? We was Teds together when it meant something, jack-the-ladded the cobbles for the crack, not the sovereigns. Great old days, and they don't change for the likes of us, Mister. Large ones here, Barman.'

'Great old days ain't today,' Pimlico said without warmth.

Wally pinched the pain in his eyes. This wasn't the Pimlico he knew; this was shell with nobody home when Wally looked into his eyes. They were just bits of blue glass over nailheads. Forty-two months in the slammer after the Troys let him down couldn't surely have turned Pim into a zombie? Wally never did get the full SP on that roundabout, or how Pim's wife had done a runner whilst he was banged up.

Wally offered his cigars.

'Bad for the wind. Lost the habit when Miriam dear-johnned me in prison and done a runner with some tosser from Cyprus. Divorced me out there, and that gutted me, Wal. I took to weight-training to keep my brain straight.'

'You look tasty.'

Wally remembered Miriam as any milkman's friend. 'I thought Tommy was putting money indoors to keep her sweet?'

'Did for a while. Before Miriam upped and went and I figured the Troys had stitched me up over that GBH charge. How do a few moody digs suddenly get to be an empty safe and a half-murdered punter? And me inside on dodgy evidence and no appeal? I've had nothing but time to think, Wal. And they definitely stitched me. Maybe Tommy was having my Miriam and thought I was too much fella to turn over on the cobbles. I dunno the "why" of it. I only know I was stitched, and that gets paid for.'

'You got anything lined up?'

'Archie had Charlie Dance get me word I was welcome on their strength when I got my walking-papers.' A bitter smile cut Pimlico's cheeks. 'But I'm walking soft until I know how deep their cuts and bruises are.'

'I can slip you some tenners.'

'I'll earn. Not borrow.'

'Who mentioned lending, you tosser? This is me, right?'

Wally bought another round of doubles, his head slowly clearing.

'It still comes back when I'm earning, right?'

'Do it any way you want. All that pride and no gumption.'

'Nobody else gets to talk to me that way, Wally.'

'Who'd bother, you tosser?'

Pimlico's grin was a bright shaft of light.

'Nobody but a tosser like you.'

Wally watched the grin melt into a genuine smile. Pimlico's sudden laugh seemed to flush something inedible from his system.

'Know what's funny, Wal? Tommy had Miriam chauffeured up to see me religiously every month for the first half-year. Sent little messages. Saw I was all right with the snout-barons. All that old tonk.'

Wally was puzzled.

'Where's the cackle in that?'

'It was the chauffeur Miriam went off with. Shafted me and Tommy both, right? Time I laughed about it. Hurts your throat if you ain't used to it.'

Wally chinked glasses.

'Here's to you copping laryngitis, then. And thinking about Number One. You. That's what I'm doing from here on in. Wally for Wally. Cheers.'

'Meaning you and Connie had sudden words? Or does that head-bandage mean it went to an up-and-downer?'

'Just overdue verbals. I'm through being treated like a little boy. Now Con's got this uppity tart in the office I'm back working the carts like some totter's brat. You wouldn't think I had me own long firms the way I get the old toffee. Connie can have his lahdie-dah deals, I'll take a few machines in Soho.'

Pimlico laughed again. 'Ain't that just exactly what Chas Dance offered me? With a bit of crowd-control thrown in? You and me could carve that down the middle.'

'With Chas and Con locking horns in overdrive?'

Pimlico cracked bony knuckles. 'Charlie won't break his given word. And maybe he's shrewd enough to like the idea of you being off Connie's strength.'

'And the cow jumped over the moon.'

'Beats taking orders from an uppity bird.' Pimlico tossed off his drink and eyed the bar. 'Time for a casual retreat to the gents', Wal.'

'Don't feel the need.'

'You will. Don't crack wise, but there's something dodgy going down. A lot of faces are walking out too casual. Somebody's definitely marked down for a heavy pasting.'

Wally slow-eyed the bar without seeming to.

'Me being a Harold up west rates that. Spanish Joe still earwigs for Tom and Jessie, and he's off and running. And Silversleeves Sutton was supping with Barry the Blag. Them two have to be prised off the bar usually, and leaving bevy on the bar means they had their cards marked. That makes Silversleeves a Troy snout and us up the pictures.'

'A hotsman through the gents', then.'

'Dead end, Pim.'

Wally's eyes quickened in his bruised face as he mentally kicked himself. 'Those bloody dress-vans . . . .'

Boots pounded on the stairs. Double doors banged open in a bloom of shot and smoke. Drinkers scattered as exploding glasses showered the red carpet. Pimlico rolled the table on its side and crouched with Wally beside him.

The optics and backbar disintegrated above the Maltese barmen's heads. A second broadside skittered bar stools. A Greek pimp was bowled away with a peppered thigh, his trouser leg in tatters. Men in dark sweaters and ski-masks began breaking heads with staves, adding shrill screams and the thud of ash on flesh to the bellow of gunfire.

A booth erupted into shreds of bri-nylon and upholstery foam as a double cluster of shot turned the wooden uprights into kindling. The pearl ceiling-globes blew out in concert, and men and women milled in the narrow entry to the restrooms, shielding themselves from indiscriminate blows in the semi-darkness.

A tom with a badly lacerated face wailed, and the Greek called upon God in his own language.

Pimlico stiffened and swore. A masked man reloaded as he kicked his way through debris to their corner, snapped the breech closed and brought the shotgun to bear. Pimlico kicked Wally aside. Hurled the table. A double charge took the table dead centre and slammed it and Pimlico away.

Wally threw himself headlong with a long punch. Felt the shock of contact deep in his shoulder. The gunman's head snapped aside and he fell in a heap. Wally booted him for good measure, blocked a stave and headbutted another face. Hit across the shoulders, Wally made a painful kneedrop into broken glass. Called Pim's name and sneezed violently, his throat clawed by fumes. Stinking brown smoke rolled, covering the attackers' hurried withdrawal and blinding Wally with his own tears.

'Pim!'

'Here!'

Pimlico's Italian jacket was holed and bloody.

'Time-to-go time.'

Wally pulled a crescent of glass from a kneecap and helped Pimlico towards the stairs. They hit the double doors, and a last tongue of glass knifed into the floor. Wally's mashed cigar jiggled on his lower lip with a life of its own.

'Move, Pim. Before the law nosies in.'

They crunched up stairs frosted with broken glass.

'Could have blinded you, matey.'
'Couldn't blind a baby . . . .'
They stumbled into Beak Street. A Flying Squad saloon belled across a far intersection, and they leaned in a doorway until it faded into the traffic.
'Some tasty welcome home.'
Pimlico sagged heavily, and Wally's left shoe was spongy with blood.
Wally flagged a black cab and hauled Pimlico into the back.
'Spitalfields, Driver. Ten sovs if you make it fast.'
Pimlico pawed Wally's lapels.
'Did you see those slags whack that tom for no good reason? How can she earn with a busted boat? That bastard Jesse Troy and his favourite fucking fairy . . . .'
'You seen the tossers' faces?'
'Plain as the whack I gave Jesse. Least he'll whistle through a couple of breakfasts.'
Pimlico shuddered and drew blood as he bit his lip.
Wally threw his cigar into the whipping night.
'Must be they thought hitting the Troubadour was easier than going after one of Connie's spielers, even if it is neutral.'
'Christ, Wally . . . .'
'Soon have you tucked up at Doc Rudge's, matey. Make that twenty sovs, Driver.'
'And get run in for low flying?'
The cabbie saw Wally's face for the first time.
'You got it, squire . . . .'

Stabbed by fragments of his childhood, Charlie dozed in the Savoy suite. In his memory he lay in the Morrison shelter with his comic and shrapnel collection and listened to the buzzbombs from Peenemunde make their morning run over Aunt Maud's house in Whitechapel where his mother abandoned him when she ran away to Chislehurst Caves with daft Jimmy Irons, her 'nerves', and a blind linnet to warn of gas attacks from the air. She and daft Jimmy had been smeared dead by a lorry in the blackout after a pub crawl, but Aunt Maud hadn't told Charlie until they had been bombed out for the second time, and only because Charlie had tried to run away to find his mother. Then Aunt Maud had hugged him when he refused to cry and said nothing when he drank her Christmas port to find oblivion.

Charlie rolled on his side to cool his sweating spine.

Opened the door in his dream to a gaunt man in khaki who said he was Charlie's father and was nothing like the scuffed Kodak print Charlie kept in his biscuit-tin with his cigarette-cards of famous pre-war footballers. Charlie had turned gawky when Aunt Maud and the soldier hugged and laughed with brimming eyes and the soldier said: 'You're the sister I should have wed, Maudie.'

And left grey Bakelite German soldiers he'd liberated in Berlin on the kitchen table for Charlie to busy himself with when he took Aunt Maud into her bedroom and locked the door. Cold resentment sent Charlie into the backyard where he used a housebrick to smash the soldiers amongst the lupins on top of the flooded Anderson shelter.

Then listening at the kitchen window when the gaunt soldier drank tea from Charlie's Bonzo mug and told Aunt Maud he'd expected Charlie to be a small boy, 'Not a lad topping fourteen and six feet, all legs and eyes and scaffolding like somebody forgot the bricks', and laughing a bubbly laugh because of the tuberculosis in his lungs.

Then saying his bit of a pension wouldn't buy much of a business, but that he wasn't so much of an invalid he couldn't stand out in the fresh air and sell whatever to anybody who passed the half-crowns. Or make a small book if there was no real objection from the other bookies in the manor.

Charlie stirred in shallow sleep.

Walked the bombed sites thick with purple weed to stay out of the house when the stranger-father installed a telephone and took bets in Aunt Maud's front room with another man who made sums on a blackboard with his thumb in a ready reckoner. And later Aunt Maud got plump and serene after a mysterious trip to a registry office which Charlie avoided by bunking off to a Hoot Gibson matinée at the local fleapit, preferring cowboys to matrimony. Then the whispery little talks about a little brother for Charlie, and a party with a piano and crates of beer, and the confusion because Aunt Maud was Charlie's stepmother and looked nothing like the wicked ladies he saw on the silver screen.

Charlie stirred in sleep and remembered the dark day the telephone went away because a big bet hadn't been laid off and father and the man with a chalky thumb in his ready reckoner had been ringed by a snide bookie with the dead needle over their modest success. And Aunt Maud locked away in the bedroom with her swelling belly and a midwife, and the doctor popping in and out with worried expressions until a black limousine came with a coffin and a small white coffin, and Charlie's father cried over bottles of rum before he took Charlie to throw dirt over the black and white boxes in the cemetery. Which meant the little brother had taken Aunt Maud away and left young Charlie with 'Big Charlie', who coughed and shook the house when he tried to breathe in sleep and forgot to shave when he left the house to drink himself stupid.

Then the bad days got better when Blackie Bustin came to the house to get Big Charlie to sell Gestetnered racing-sheets outside Harringay greyhound track when there was still a paper shortage and newspapers were hard to come by. Big Charlie and young Charlie stood there in all weathers for threepenny joeys and held betting-slips for off-course bookies banned from the stadium. And, more often than not, Big Charlie stayed in the boozer with his bad chest and all the rum he could mump whilst young Charlie ran the pitch and learned how to turn a penny without punching a clock for a governor. He came to know the faces who earned around the tracks and travelled free on the rattlers by dodging the ticket inspectors, touted tips, tic-tacked or ran three card tricks, Spot the Lady or Crown and Anchor to part punters from the half-crowns. He learned to spot a shaved duck, turn aces at will, spot a shill in a crowd or cold-deck drunks for a penny a point.

Charlie turned streetwise as Big Charlie drowned himself in rum and small beer — learned every cobbles trick from a thousand bent uncles and, most important, how to hear the verbals without parroting anything back. Charlie might have grown into an adult unofficial runner selling papers on the side if Blackie Bustin hadn't got the dead needle because Big Charlie drank three weeks' paper subs and gave Blackie the drunk verbals in public when he was told to cough. Blackie brought his nephew down and told young Charlie there was a change of management. Blackie's fifteen stone and the nephew's razor left Charlie pitchless with no room for argument.

But Blackie had created a problem he knew nothing about and didn't let young Charlie explain. Charlie held a fat envelope of smart money to be laid off inside the stadium for the off-course heavies. Known as 'a scalp', the dog out of trap six was a ringer, and a lot of money rode on his back. To Charlie it was just another holding job, and he hung around for the Peckham bookie and his minder to collect. But Blackie's nephew hauled him into the shadows and kneed him senseless. Charlie came round in the groundsman's hut where a couple of punters had dragged him, and he got word inside the stadium a race too late.

The Peckham bookie took one look at Charlie and the unopened envelope, snapped fingers at his minder and went away looking like he breathed fire and brimstone. Two minutes later Blackie and his nephew tried clawing their way into a taxi with the minder bouncing them off half the walls in Christendom. A razor flashed and Blackie rolled on cinders with striped thighs and his face open to the bone. The nephew lost an ear and the tip of his nose, and fell down holding his thighs together.

The Peckham bookie came back to pat Charlie's head, and his minder looked on with scars forming a V from his cheeks to his chin. Charlie was asked if he knew Kosher Kramer, and he told the bookie he didn't.

'Or me?'

Charlie said 'No' again.

'Smart boy. Keep it that way.' The bookie nodded to himself. 'This ain't an earner, so you can't earn out of it.'

Charlie said he'd figured that.

'Smart again. You need to hang around that pitch?'

'Not so long as Big Charlie can, Mister.'

'It's his, right? I figure you for a lad with an itch to travel. Get on all them trains going places. Watch your gee-gees run for real.'

'Been on my mind, Mister.'

The bookie turned to Kramer.

'Smartness, see that? See young Charlie gets train money and cops the Newbury train with Barry the Blag and his team. And, Kosher, get the boy has some new clobber with creases and lapels, right?'

'I've got clobber.'

The bookie frowned at Charlie. 'Smart stays dumb, right? You ain't going back to your drum. You ain't going nowhere I don't say. And one day down the road you'll get asked about tonight. See you answer up prompt to the right face.'

Charlie tried not to look stupid. 'How'll I know it's the right face?'

'He'll be your uncle from Peckham. Got that?'

'Got it.'

'Smartness. See that, Kosher?'

'I seen it,' said the scarred minder, and put Charlie on the next train with a suitcase of new gear and a fat wad of folding money. It was six months before Charlie came back to the Smoke for Big Charlie's funeral. He heard the train whistle again and woke up reaching for the telephone in the Savoy suite.

Vinnie Castle said: 'They hit the Troubadour, Chas.

Done it up brown. Barry the Blag tipped me the nod when Silversleeves pulled him out of there. That puts Silversleeves firmly on the Troy firm. Barry ducked out on Silver and clocked Wally Harold and Pimlico Johnny staggering away all marked up. Means it weren't Camberwell, right?'

'Means just that, Vin. Call Doc Rudge and see if he's had some casualties in. Then creep round.'

'You got it, but why?'

Charlie chuckled and said: 'I'm popping a bottle of bubbly.'

Vinnie sighed. 'The day I understand you is the day I get hit with a smart stick, Chas.'

'Meaning you ain't thirsty?'

'Meaning that's me scratching at the door.'

Charlie grinned at the ceiling and shed exhaustion.

'The Troys have made their move,' he said, 'and that puts us on the side of the angels.'

CHAPTER SEVEN

DETECTIVE SERGEANT QUILL and his squad drank cocoa in a Post Office van on the corner of Windmill Street and Brewer Street. Wind flustered the litter and dry whirlpools of dust cartwheeled along the narrow pavements. Restaurants began to show light as they readied themselves for the luncheon trade, and for a while the vagrants and addicts had the streets to themselves.

Two winos walked a bottle towards Soho Square and an old woman with her belongings in plastic carriers came up from Piccadilly, shouting and mad and alone. A young heroin addict floated past the Windmill Theatre, blind to everything but his own drugged inner calm.

Quill drummed on the dash and said: 'The sights you see when you haven't got a gun. I hope your snout's right about this meet, Bulstrode. I haven't had a day off since Adam invented ale.'

Bulstrode mimed masturbation behind Quill's back. 'Who has? A CID officer without reliable information is about as useful as a three-legged greyhound,' he said, watching the barb redden Quill's neck. 'And Mr Lemmon passed it.'

'Like a dose of Epsom salts.'

Quill envied Bulstrode's underworld contacts and had no idea that Vinnie Castle's midnight call had come out of the blue. Unlike Bulstrode, Quill was a 'leaner' who gained information by duress, and villains literally spat at the mention of his name. He would do almost anything to see Charlie Dance banged up on a provable charge, and had cheerfully rousted the judge out of bed at six that morning to authorise surveillance taps and search warrants. Wishing the squad acted on his 'information received', Quill settled back behind the wheel, knowing that any success would be scooped by Lemmon anyway, and he transferred his dark hatred from Bulstrode to his DI. Behind him, Bulstrode traded glances with Payne and Dillman. To them, Quill was as transparent as twopenny villain's alibi.

'Off and running.'

Dillman adjusted his earphone tap.

J. C. Hatton came out of the National Car Park and crossed Brewer Street against the traffic. He let himself into Archie Ogle's office, and Payne's Pentax snarled through four exposures before the door closed. Charlie Dance was already inside.

Connie Harold left Sailor Mailer in the Vanden Plas and took Harry the Crack up to Archie's office where Charlie finished a long paragraph into a dictaphone and waved Connie into a chair.

Connie refused coffee and opened an attaché case on the desk.

'Used tens and twenties. No consecutives.'

Hatton pinched moisture from his mouth.

'Have you brought no legal counsel, Mr Harold?'

'And watch you and a brief screw me with legal chat? Forget it.'

Hatton disapproved and said so.

'Just sign the papers and give me the bodies. Save your flowery chat for the dowagers.'

Charlie pressed an electric door-release, and Dakin followed Jorgesson from the inner office.

'Satisfied, Connie?'

'Just count the dough.'

Charlie riffled the packs of notes, banged the blocks square and rebanded them into piles of a thousand. When he'd made fifty bundles Hatton gave Connie an olive folder. Connie put it inside his coat and watched Dakin shed sweat on to his shirtfront.

'Uncle Con ain't pleased with you, Victor.'

'Who is this man?'

Jorgesson eyed Connie with loathing and earned a bleak smile.

'Your own personal Father Christmas, Dirky boy.' Connie winked and held a nickel-plated ·22 Beretta in line with Charlie's blackened eye. Hatton's throat bobbed, and Charlie stayed where he was.

'The dough comes back, Chas.'

The Beretta stabbed forward.

Charlie heard men on the stairs and wondered if he'd hear the concussion that killed him. Connie jerked his head at Harry the Crack.

'See who that is.'

Harry swore when he had looked over the banisters.

'It's Quill and his merry men.'

'You sure?'

'Not fucking many.'

Connie eyed his gun. Almost threw it from him in rare panic.

'You're *dead* sure?'

Harry made fists.

'Is there up and fucking down?'

'Nice one, Chas,' Connie said.

Charlie just raised his hands above his head.

'And how's this gonna look when they come steaming in?'

Jorgesson brightened, anxious to see the *rooineks* lose face. Dakin tried the locked door to the inner office, and Harry waited for one of Connie's miracles as they all looked at Charlie.

'Stop reaching for the ceiling and lose that.'

Connie slid the Beretta across the desk. Charlie dropped it into the case with the money and handed the case to Hatton with: 'Out across the flat roof, J.C.'

Harry stopped Dakin following Hatton into the inner office. A fire-escape went down into a theatre backcourt, and the open street was only six paces beyond. Charlie poured twelve-year-old whisky into plastic cups, and Connie sipped Glenlivet when Quill, Dillman, Bulstrode and Payne elbowed in.

Quill's face shone as he said: 'We have reason to believe that there are certain substances secreted upon your persons or within these premises . . . .'

Connie raised an eyebrow.

'What's this, Chas? The law coming for their bunce in broad daylight? Must be well different up west.'

Charlie laid his wallet on his blotter.

'Take it out of there, Prophet. I'm a bit short this week.'

Quill continued his set speech, Dillman unscrewed light-switches and Bulstrode bruised his shoulder on the inner office door.

'Steel, ain't it?' Charlie said comfortably.

'What's "certain substances" when they're home?' Harry asked as Payne patted him down.

'Drugs,' said Connie. 'You dealing in heavy shit, Charlie? Well, well, well . . . .'

Bulstrode snapped fingers and held his shoulder.

'The keys, Mr Dance. We're on a kosher warrant, so save the old acid.'

'My secretary has it. And she's out to coffee,' Charlie said as Payne took wide-angle shots and Dakin hid his face. 'She likes the fresh-ground stuff, won't look at the stuff out of the machine. And with all the burglaries around here we keep everything locked up tight. You remember old Bertie Lodge, Con. Him who does all the auctions in Greek Street? They turned his place over rotten only last—'

Charlie was heaved from his chair and faced against the wall with Quill's hot breath in the back of his neck.

'Can the old bunny. Turn his pockets out, Bulstrode. And you, Harold.'

'You want *me* to go through Charlie's pockets?' Connie smoothed a camel-hair lapel.

Charlie laid his palms against the wall. 'Could be there's a spare Yale in the desk. I want a receipt for anything you take away.' He winked over his shoulder at Bulstrode. 'Do it by the book, son.'

Bulstrode finished searching Charlie and went through the desk drawers. They were empty.

Dillman took the lid from the toilet cistern and flushed it dry.

'Nothing, Sarge . . . .'

'Don't want the photos of the wife and kids bent,' Connie said when his wallet was taken.

Quill's sneer was savage.

'None of your fancy piece? Or don't she pose with her clothes on?'

Connie lost colour and his eyes marbled.

'Careful, Prophet. My brief loves harassment charges.'

Quill butted Charlie's head into the wall.

'I've got you both cold, so shut it.'

'Nothing, Sarge.' Dillman closed a filing cabinet.

'You've got nothing on anyone, Quill,' said Charlie.

'You're asking for a nice fall down the stairs, Dance.'

Charlie tasted blood. 'Not today, thank you.'

Dillman rummaged through the broom-cupboard and shone a torch into the fusebox.

'Nothing here, Sarge . . . .'

Quill tumbled plastic cups from the coffee machine and trampled them in temper. 'It's here. I know it's here . . . .'

Bulstrode faced Charlie into the office and their faces were close enough to whisper without being overheard.

'Somebody grassed you up, Charlie. The stuff's here and we'll find it.'

'What stuff's that, then?'

'Five kilos of heroin.'

'When have I ever touched that garbage?'

'How about now?'

'Tell Vinnie to get his facts straight next time, Buller.'

Bulstrode swallowed around a hot rock. 'You had Vinnie pull my pudden.'

'Not many, and only this once. Had to get Quill off my tail.'

Bulstrode's laugh was low and bitter. 'And have us get Harold off your back at the same time, right? You devious monkey.'
Charlie's shrug was eloquent. 'One way of not spilling claret. There'll be other straight bubbles, bank on it.'
'What's that, what's that?' said Quill.
Bulstrode turned away to light a Capstan. 'He's clean, Sarge. They all are.'
'Can't be. Keep clocking.'
Connie counted the money in his wallet with theatrical care.
'Down the station, is it? Nice cup of tea, suggestive biscuits and an official apology? Have you seen my new business cards, Prophet? By Appointment to the Ministry of Defence and the Ministry of the Environment. A man don't come more legit than that.'
Quill was pale with fury. 'You ripped out an old boiler and some wiring. A bloody demolition contract don't make you the blue-eyed boy of Whitehall.'
Dillman brushed cobwebs from his sleeve.
'Nothing, Sarge . . . .'
'You say that again . . . .'
J. C. Hatton chose that moment to emerge from the inner office.
'I'm sorry, Charles. I had no idea you were engaged.'
Quill and Dillman barged the old man aside and halted in the empty office. The single swivel chair looked very lonely on the bare boards.
'What utterly extraordinary manners,' Hatton said as Bulstrode patted him down. 'These *can't* be the people interested in the sub-lease, surely?'
Bulstrode shook his head and shot his cuffs.
'An official apology, Charlie?'
'Over a simple mistake, Buller? Never.'
'What mistake?'
Payne wondered if he had wasted a roll of official-issue Triple-X film as Quill swore and kicked paint from the skirting.

Charlie lifted the Glenlivet bottle.

'Another drop of Scotch, Mr Harold?'

Connie held out his plastic cup.

'One to you, Charlie,' he toasted. 'One to you . . . .'

'Shit and derision,' said Quill.

'Oh blimey yeah,' said Charlie.

The afternoon browned into premature twilight as the Vanden Plas crossed Waterloo Bridge. Ponderous black cumulus rolled east and thunder murmured distant threats. Sudden rain sluiced in and the gutters chuckled. The Elephant and Castle was a haze of oily spray and rain-dollies. The must of wet topcoats filled the car.

'No wonder the British Empire circled the globe. You people will go anywhere to escape this filthy climate,' Jorgesson said.

Connie exuded false good humour.

'Cold hands, warm hearts, that's us Brits. And I've got fifty thousand good reasons for going abroad, haven't I, Victor?'

Dakin shrank inside his coat, and Connie talked about the weather until they all sprinted through rain into the office where Kelly machine-gunned her portable.

Connie kissed the top of her head.

'Leave that, Kel. I want you to take our Dirk out to dinner. Sailor'll drive and hold Mr Jorgesson's coat.'

Kelly caught Jorgesson's eyes on her legs when she stood to smooth her skirt.

'Meaning you've got business I shouldn't see, that it?'

'Meaning I want you to make nice with Dirk, right? And you like the Astor, right? And I'm gonna be busy. Right?'

Kelly eyed Dakin up and down.

'Well, *hello*, Vic.'

'Hello, Kel. I could murder a steak diane myself.'

Dakin mopped his face with his scarf until Connie's fist took him full in the mouth. He went down covering his head and genitals.

'You're going nowhere, you bastard.'

'My God.'

Jorgesson sat without taking care of his creases and watched Dakin drool bile into the dust.

'Why, Connie? Why?' Dakin whined.

'Because we're partners. And *that's* your share of the profits.'

Dakin grovelled as Jorgesson stared and Connie sat at his desk.

'Off you go, Sailor and Kel. Take care of our Dirk. He's the diamond — not cut glass like tricky Vicky here.'

When they had gone, Connie told Harry to get some take-away Indian and to come back with his shock-box and a bottle of lemonade.

Dakin held himself and waited as the wallclock ticked and Connie played tunes on an elastic band.

'Gonna be a wet old afternoon,' Connie said placidly.

Thunder brawled over Spitalfields as Charlie watched Doc Rudge re-dress Pimlico's chest. The old man's yellow hands moved with professional economy as he used tape and dropped scissors into a kidney dish.

'You were lucky, young Pim. An inch closer to your pulmonary artery, and *pish* — dead in forty-five seconds.'

'What's owed, Doc?'

Pimlico sat up with a wince, and Charlie helped him into a new Simpson's shirt.

'Taken care of. How long does he have to rest up, Doc?'

Rudge inhaled snuff and scratched a discoloured nostril.

'With that physique, never. What can I tell you?'

'When your hundredth birthday was.'

Rudge suppressed a sneeze.

'Go, you toerags. Leave an old man in peace.'

In the white Rolls, Charlie said: 'Even Archie don't remember Doc as anything but older than God's Uncle Jack. And the old tosser still sounds like he just got off the cattle-boat from Europe.'

Pimlico said nothing, and Charlie laced hands around a knee.

'I hear Wally Harold brought you in.'

'He did. You making bones out of it?'

'Is there a need to?'

'Wally without his brother is ace-OK. Him and me was thrown out of everything together — school, Scouts, Boy's Brigade, the Church Army. Even the Sally Ann wouldn't spring us a bowl of soup we was so tasty. Him and me go way back, Chas.'

'Just wanted to hear you say it, Pim.'

'Then, you'll know why I want Wally with me on the bandits.'

Sodbonce took the Rolls away, and Pimlico trailed Charlie into Peter's Pelican Club in St Anne's Court.

'Wally's done a runner from Connie's firm. They're well divorced.'

Charlie ordered drinks and thought about blood and water without comment. Two butch lesbians in black leather played the machines and watched their brides strip on stage for the raincoats in the pews, and the barman went out of earshot to let Charlie and Pimlico talk in private.

'That Kelly has a lot to do with Wally elbowing the family firm, Chas. And I ought to know about dodgy birds after my Miriam done a runner with that bubble chauffeur. Could be she would have talked me into Tommy Troy's corner despite the stitch-up they worked on me over that dodgy GBH I went down for. I ain't the dumb hard-arse who went in for porridge three years back; prison changed all that, and what they done in the Troubadour last night don't make them my favourite faces.'

Pimlico broke off to watch the girls on the stage bump and grind through a scratched recording of '*High Noon*', hunger plain on his face. A fat girl in tights and a pink stetson did something suggestive with a Remington rifle and two skinny blondes did something similar with replica Colts.

'I could use some of that, Chas. My old man's nudging my collar-stud.' Pimlico's laugh was strained.

'Forget those slags. Look but don't touch.'

'Good advice, but I won't forget I owe you, Chas. You'll get every farthing back when I've worked on a little earner with Ollie Oliphant. Seems he's got some country-house caper sorted and needs a second coachman.' Scotch on an empty stomach had glazed Pimlico's eyes.

Charlie left him to make two calls and told Ingrid to bring Dotty Machin to Gennaro's Restaurant at 7·30.

'Wash your mouth out with whisky; I got you a girl,' he told Pim.

'I'm trusting you, Chas. Just hope I haven't talked out of turn.'

'Leave it out.'

'She's a natural blonde? Not out of a bottle?'

Charlie just winked.

'Hope I don't get the shrinks. A long stretch can do that to a man.'

'With Dotty Machin dancing on your eyelids with four-inch French heels? You may have to call the fire brigade, though. She's got a Phd in spontaneous combustion.'

Vic Dakin lay back in the marbled bathroom of his exclusive hotel suite in Milan. Up to his armpits in fragrant green suds, he drank fine champagne from an antique Venetian glass as three Italian industrialists hung on his every word. The dream was brighter than reality, and Dakin knew the more he owed these men the more they respected him and envied his panache and style. They had arrived demanding cash on the barrelhead for the previous consignments of micromesh stockings, and now they begged him to take a further million pairs on a ninety-day note unsecured by the usual banker's drafts. They ate the smoked salmon he'd flown in from Scotland and swilled the champagne as though Dakin had trampled the grapes himself. Not bad for a Hungarian Jew who had escaped from Odessa in broken shoes and without a wooden kopek to his name.

Dakin thought he would let more hot water into his

chilled bath before he got their signatures on the new agreements. He reached for a gilded tap and grasped agony as his high ululating screams shredded the dreams.

Dakin reared against his bonds. Stripped skin from his wrists and ankles as the portable generator fed voltage into his anus and testicles. There was vanilla essence on his gagging tongue and a lemonade bottle gurgled empty over his head. This time Connie's office did not go away. This time he could not plunge into the receiving past to relive old glories of great deception.

'See that, Harry? Lemonade damps him down and gives the electricity a chance. Give him a few more volts.'

Dakin bucked in the metal chair. Climbed away from exquisite pain.

Connie ate spiced food with his fingers and enjoyed the fat body flop and leap against the leather straps as if his penis was being stroked by erotic butterflies. His eyes were as green as phlegm on a pavement and he had ground chili peppers into Dakin's eyes with his thumbs. Dakin had stood on the slopes of Vesuvius and smelled the hot crater. Knew he stank as much as the sulphurous magma because he had fouled himself and begged God to give him back his Milanese bathroom.

Harry ground the generator handle in steady circles to make Dakin's muscles knot under shuddering fat, and stopped when Connie spooned dhal on to nan bread and told Harry to have some Tandoori chicken.

Dakin sagged to pant and wonder if his parents had suffered the same way during their last hours in the death camp when they walked naked on frozen ground and were forbidden to touch or make their last goodbyes. Whether they had tried to hold their breath in the concrete shower-rooms as the crystals rattled in the ducts to form the gas that killed them. He hung in the straps as if all his sand had run to the bottom and his swimming gaze was drawn to the glazed drumstick Connie pointed at him.

'You should see yourself, Victor my son. Dis-bloody-gusting. And your Uncle Con's gonna chastise you until you learn you can't sell him down the Swanee and come up smelling sweet. My meaning clear, is it?'

Dakin's distended belly shook as he nodded drearily. The smell of overspiced food sickened him.

Headlights swept into the yard, and Harry said: 'It's Sidney Salt, Con. You'd think he could afford something tastier than them old bangers he coaches about in.'

Connie licked a thumb. 'In the fire-insurance business you don't sport class motors people might remember. Sidney's a shrewdie, he's never even done juvenile bird. That makes him the best torch in the biz.'

Harry spat rice into Dakin's lap. 'You want Sidney in here with *that* on display?'

Connie bared teeth. His marbled eyes were hot fat spilled on cold stones.

'Sidney knows the score, don't you, Sid?'

Sidney Salt stopped shaking rain from his hat to stare across at Dakin's naked sprawl. His thin face grew hollows and he bit through the antacid tablets he habitually chewed.

'What's all that, Connie?'

'That?' Connie flicked curry sauce across Dakin's abdomen, chewed on chicken and a laugh that bared all his teeth. 'That, my old Sidney, is a nobody who thought he was somebody. And you're wrong, ain't you, Nobody?'

'Yessss . . . Connnn . . . .'

'See? He admits it. Get comfortable, Sid, I've got a double tickle for you.'

Rain lashed the windows to counterpoint Connie's casual air, and Dakin yearned for oblivion.

Dotty Machin rolled a joint as she straddled Pimlico on the water-bed Jonas had imported from America. Most of her tricks were rabbits in need of reassurance, and she had thought her black pimp the ultimate bull-stud. But Pimlico had brought her to a climax despite her professional reserve, and Dotty had decided she liked Pimlico almost as much as his insatiability.

'There you go, Pim. Best Paki black.'
'You shouldn't smoke that shit.'
Dotty was irritated.
'My drum. My house rules.'
'But it's my party, and I wanna go for another big one.'
'That's four. You been in a monastery or what?'
'Yeah, but I failed the physical.'
Pimlico waved drugged smoke from his face.
The girl's body gleamed like phosphorus in the subdued light, and his groin surged with need. Most long-term prisoners succumbed to self-abuse or consorted with queers, but Pimlico had not been tempted.
There was a saying in prison: Better a clean old man than a dirty whore. There were a thousand ways of deluding oneself in the chokey, and that was the least of them in Pimlico's opinion. The padre at Durham had got it right when he'd said: 'The only thing incarceration cures is heterosexuality.'
'And I ain't going back,' Pim said aloud.
'To the monastery, pet?'
'To prison.'
Dotty smiled with pinpoint irises.
'That's why you're taller lying down.'
She pinched out the joint and hoped Jonas would be as rampant when he was released.
'Let's make this a real coming-out party.'
Dotty trailed blonde hair across Pimlico's supine face and chest and gathered his quickening erection between her breasts, bored his navel with her tongue; gratified to hear his explosive intakes of breath, sure she was in charge again.
But when Pimlico lifted her bodily by the hips to introduce himself for the fourth time she knew she was wrong. She went with his surges of masculine need with a confused sense of wonder, and the moment she was exploded to the far corners of her bedroom she knew she'd make Pimlico the best breakfast he'd ever tasted.

Quill and Bulstrode swallowed yawns when Lemmon told

them that Micky Dogge had been caught in a trawl off the Southend coast, and then wanted to know where their brains had been that morning in Archie Ogle's office. It was close to midnight, and Lemmon had paused by Payne's desk on his way home to a late supper with his long-suffering wife. He pressed a heavy thumb to the damp photograph of Dakin in the Windmill Street office and asked: 'Where's this particular chummy at?'

'With Dance?' said Quill.

'Or Connie Harold,' said Bulstrode.

'Or in the shoe with Old Mother Hubbard?' said Lemmon.

'We can check, Guv. We still got wires into Ogle's . . . .'

'And Charlie Dance won't know that, eh?'

'Still . . .,' Quill started.

Lemmon rolled an unlit Player in his fingers.

'Micky Dogge's mortals coming out of the briny without you lot noticing is one thing, but not checking Interpol files is bloody criminal.'

His thumbnail scored the damp photoprint.

'This smiling individual is Victor Gideon Dakin. He's got more names than a war memorial, and he's not only wanted in Italy and France, but here in this sceptic isle. Now, does anybody want to do themselves and the Fraud Squad a favour by waking up, or is my supper going to wait yet again?'

Bulstrode picked up an internal and started to dial CRO.

Quill leaped to his desk and punished a knee against an open drawer.

'My shitty stick, Guv,' he said, only to find himself talking to a slammed door. 'I'm gone, too,' he added and made for the back stairs.

Alone in his radio car he pummelled the steering-wheel.

Now he had Dakin to add to his hate list his expletives were a mad litany of frustration that made no sense. But his course of action was as clear as the ebony patches of night above the thin rainclouds.

Charlie lowered the living-room blinds. His daily had

dusted through and fed his marine tropicals. The muted sound of a Telemann concerto was the perfect accompaniment to his very dry martini, and he lounged in a Conran chair, relaxed for the first time in an interminable week. It was good to be home, and he didn't need Ingrid wittering on about Vic Dakin.

'Now ain't the time, Ingrid.'

Ingrid worried the hem of her oyster satin nightdress.

'When, then? Tomorrow? Next week? Never? I need to know about . . . Vic.'

'If you mean your father, say your father.'

Charlie thought the pom-poms on her slippers looked like edible snowballs.

'I can't use that word. I just need to know he's all right.'

'OK. He's all right.'

'Liar.'

'So I'm a liar. I can't adopt the slag. He called it, and now he has to pay his dues. To quote Connie: "He took a liberty, we got the hump, he gets some tasty whacks." '

'Vic being a dreamer in Cloud-cuckoo-land doesn't make him . . . evil.'

'Like me you mean.'

'Your words, sport.'

'You want to yell at somebody? Call the talking clock.'

'Damn your glib humour and double damn you, Charlie Dance. Vic's not some *thing* to be bartered.'

Charlie lost his drink to crush Ingrid's wrists.

'That's *exactly* what he is. And he did it himself. Not me. Him. Your precious daddy is as nasty as they come. Two men are banged up on embezzlement and criminal conspiracy charges because they trusted him. Honest men. An entire Milanese factory is slammed closed because of him. And you don't get welfare in Italy. Out there you go hungry. And you can bet your safe little arse that nice Catholic girls are selling their cherries on the street because of dear old smiling Vic Dakin.'

'That's nothing to do—'

'That's *everything* to do with it. Grow up, Ing.'

Charlie threw Ingrid's wrists from him. When he spoke again his tone was icy.

'Live with it or don't. Your choice, Lady.'

Ingrid shook, and the poms-poms danced on her jerking feet. Words crowded her throat, jammed there by towering passion. Her neck convulsed and her eyes shone with unshed tears. Her long nails raked the air near Charlie's impassive face. She lifted the martini-jigger and emptied it over him. Ice-cubes skittered on the polished floor.

Charlie sighed. Expressionless.

'I know, I'm a bastard.'

'Don't rate yourself so . . . highly.'

Ingrid swept away for her coat and slammed from the flat.

The lift hummed in the shaft, and the automatic doors sighed open and closed far below.

Then there was silence.

'Well, goodnight, Vienna.'

Charlie put the trimphone to his ear when it warbled.

'Eddystone Lighthouse. Hang on, I'll turn up the wick.'

'Queenie,' said Queenie. 'Archie wants words. And, Charlie, he ain't exactly pleased.'

'Who is?'

'This is one even I can't straighten, Charlie.'

'Then, don't. Put the old tosser on. I may as well get it from everybody.'

'You been drinking?'

Charlie's snort of laughter was as sour as an old pot.

'Not nearly enough, Queenie love.'

'Well, watch your Ps and Qs; he's boiling.'

Archie snatched the phone and said: 'Have you tried explaining a dead horse to local wallies whose big night out is patrolling candy-floss stalls on Southend front? And looking like butter wouldn't melt when they told me Micky Dogge's carcass was swanning off to France behind a boat? I almost had a bloody relapse from baby-talking the tossers.'

'So endow an amusement arcade for delinquents. Micky

Dogge got unlucky and drowned, and it was me and Queenie who was being shot at, not you, Archie. You were safely tucked up with your Stolichnaya and orange juice. Just thank Christ that's the only bottle that's gone well missing. Yours sounds in good order.'

'I didn't lead that shooter here, did I?'

'They must have had you staked out. Any forensic?'

'Nothing. No shell-cases or footprints. I've got the local filth thinking it was some local ninepence-to-the-shilling who likes hurting animals. But that ain't the main event.'

'Just a couple of warmers, eh?'

'Cut the flip, Sherlock. I just had a long earful from Hatton. What possessed you to sell our markers to the opposition on a deal that's worth your legs cut off at the wrist? Favouring a slag like Connie Harold? Have you gone bent on me, or what?'

There was a good deal more of the same before Charlie cut in with: 'We got our dough. Be satisfied.'

'Don't get short with me.'

'Then, listen up with both ears. Not the daft deaf one. Even you couldn't work that deal. Especially you. Jorgesson's nothing but trouble on a stick. Another Vic Dakin. And this mining deal's more of the same in spades. It's a government fiddle, Archie. The South African government. And that means getting involved with their élite. Their equivalent of what went down in Nazi Germany.'

'What in hell are you wittering on about?'

'The Broederbond, Archie. Translates as "Band of Brothers". It's a secret society, and those faceless hardnoses run the country — the government, the civil service, the army, the secret service and right down to who gets to be the local schoolteacher.'

'So flaming what?'

'To get in with them you've gotta be a white Afrikaaner who can trace his bloodline back to the first trekkers to make it across the Drakensbergs, and be a devout Calvinist. That makes you a nebish kosher mouse in their eyes. What Jorgesson called an *uitlander*. They're more clannish than the bloody Sicilians and they've been in power out there since the end of the First World War. You know why?'

'You're gonna tell me, right?'

'They're tribal. And there are two forms of life they hate worse than the Blacks. The Brits and the Jews, Archie. And that's you on both counts.'

There was a kind of silence.

The line buzzed and Archie breathed heavily.

Charlie waited, and his ear sang from the pressure of the phone against his face.

'Well, Arch?' he finally asked.

'That's toffee.'

'Do I go through it again?'

Archie said nothing.

'Put Queenie on. I'll tell her.'

Archie cleared phlegm with an angry bark.

'You'll tell her nothing.'

'Then, you call it, Arch.'

'Maybe you did good. Maybe you didn't.'

'Say the word, Archie. One word and I'm gone.'

'Ultimatums yet?'

This time Charlie said nothing and let Archie breathe hard in his ear.

'Maybe we're all tired. Maybe I'll get back to you.'

Charlie crossed fingers round the receiver.

'Won't wash, Arch. You can't roll in on a tide of vodka and give me the heavy finger because I'm trying to think like you. Take the wheel or leave it to me. Can't have two bus-drivers in the same cab.'

Surprisingly, Archie laughed.

'Don't hand me all that snot-nosed stuff, you tosser. Like you was anxious to run round the racecourses again like you had to when that Harringay scalp went wrong in '47. There's no going back to the good-bad old days for any of us. You take your gall to bed and get eight straight hours.'

'And you, Archie.'

The line went dead and the tone burred in Charlie's ear.

He laid the phone in its cradle and stared at the ice-cubes on the floor. Then he stared at his steady hands. Turned them over and back, over and back. The recorded violins reverberated into silence after a contrapuntal finale and the machine turned itself off.

Charlie sat still for something to do. Then occupied his mind by going back to card schools on the trains with Johnny the Builder and Barry the Blag when they first taught him how to earn stake money for the races. And Barry the Blag with wild ginger hair and his face as pink as party blancmange shooting questions between stations to hone Charlie's betting sense.

'What's a Liverpool?'

'Three doubles, a treble, three double stakes about. Thirteen wagers.'

'Good. A Heinz?'

'Fifteen doubles, twenty trebles, fifteen four-horse accumulators, six five-horse accumulators and a six-horse accumulator. Fifty-seven wagers.'

Charlie learned the Poly, Roundabouts, Round Robins, Union Jacks and triple Yankees, betting with the field, Yaps, Trixies, and the incredible intricacies of the Goliath, a combination wager of 247 bets, and all of them off by heart.

He travelled from Perth to Newton Abbot, from Folkestone to Ayr, never once bought anything more than a platform ticket; slept rough and in luxury, took the boat-train to the Irish courses and met every dip, tout, tipster, mumper, off-course bookie, gambler and rattler-sharp in the business. All through a cold spring and a golden summer that came to an end at Ascot in September when the 'Uncle' from Peckham told Charlie he could return to the Smoke because the 'bad Harringay earner had been ironed', the smart money had been squared and the law had gone back to sleep. Also that Big Charlie had dropped dead over a double rum and his mortals waited to be interred.

Charlie and a bored vicar interred Big Charlie, and

Charlie dealt small midweek games in a Manor House spieler until Johnny the Builder got him working the Soho clubs for a cut of the take.

An old tom called Armchair Doris did Charlie's laundry, and Bad Alice gave him a room over her club whilst a couple of the younger toms squabbled over who served his Sunday lunch. An old queen known as Funnyface Phyllis had Charlie bounce in his club to make his fairies drool and behave, and introduced him to Kensington Kate and the finer points of classical music. Charlie was nineteen before he knew it, and had a good 'rep' for straight cards. He played a fair game of snooker and fought a few three-rounders at the Marshall Street Baths which boosted his image amongst the cobbles brawlers who loved nothing better than squaring up to bouncers in the Square Mile. Charlie preferred talk and ring-sense to skinning his knuckles on thick heads.

Then came the Kramer—Eyetie straightener and the start on the Ogle firm. *Good-bad old days,* thought Charlie. *But like Archie said: You can't go back . . . .*

'Charlie?'

The voice trembled and broke the muse. And Ingrid was in the doorway, standing on one foot.

'That's me,' said Charlie.

'I tried, I tried to go. But I couldn't . . . just like that.'

'You've lost a pom-pom.'

'I . . . fell up the stairs. The lift was too . . . small.'

'Hysterical claustrophobia.'

'Oh . . . .'

Ingrid's eyes seemed to leap across the room, as dark as old crystal and as liquid as quicksilver.

'Charlie . . . please?'

'That gets it said.'

Ingrid was in Charlie's arms, her mouth on his face and in his hair. The small of her back was cold when he found it under her coat. He applied pressure and she was in against him, closer than he'd allowed her before. His surprise evaporated as shared tenderness overtook them.

CHAPTER EIGHT

SAD SIDNEY SALT parked outside the City Hospital and chewed antacid tablets. His thin face mourned whatever his mood, and whatever he wore looked crumpled. For three years he was the scruffiest sapper in the British army, and only his genius with explosives saved him from the usual bull. He could blow an egg from its cup without breaking the shell and flicked beads of gelignite from sweating dynamite to hear them crack against the floor.

Sidney's only phobias were hospitals and being buried alive, and he waited until the last five minutes of visiting-time before he went up to the third-floor ward to find Limehouse Lou, and avoided eye-contact in case a casual glance transmitted terminal disease. He breathed in shallow sips, convinced the air was alive with killer germs. By the time he had climbed the three flights he was dizzy from self-induced oxygen starvation, and he leaned on the stairhead to blink the length of the ward.

Lou had a girl at his bedside and they rubbed noses like puppies in a basket, a marvellous excuse for Sidney to retreat. He left a scribbled note with the matron and went out to sit in his nondescript Ford to crunch BisoDols and sulk. Sidney didn't hold with mothers, wives or girlfriends. Villains just naturally got greedy when they were around.

Or, worse, boastful. Talking Jack the Lad nineteen to the dozen to impress some bit of fluff with all her brains under her girdle. The sort of tarts who wanted gold danglers and anything shiny they could plug into a kitchen socket.

Legions of bent faces had been greased up by disgruntled

birds. Like Pimlico Johnny when his Miriam threw a leg around Tommy Troy for the old afternoon rumpo and gave Tommy the idea that Pimlico was for the chop with the CID in case he found out and got heavy on the cobbles. And there was Lou acting daft over a whiff of lace knickers just when Sidney needed him as a second torch on the fires Connie Harold needed set.

Sidney gulped milk from a carton to settle his acid stomach and realised where he had seen Lou's girl before. His duodenal ulcer flared alight as he saw Tommy Troy reach for the pliers after finding out his wife was playing an away game with one of his ex-faces.

Sidney was about to drive away when Lou sat in the passenger seat, his face so pale his freckles were livid paint spots.

'Let's have it away, then, Sid.'

Sidney let the motor idle.

'You ain't even in street clobber. Ain't I gonna look tasty driving you about in pyjamas and a flash dressing-gown?'

'I discharged myself. And there's clobber at my drum, ain't there?'

'Sure you don't want me to drop you off at your tart's place? In Vallance Road? Help her pick her trousseau and your funeral director?'

'You seen Helen, that it?'

'With half the world. If your brains was dynamite, you wouldn't have enough to blow your hat off.'

'It ain't how you think,' said Lou.

Sidney belched long and loudly.

'What I think don't rate a carrot up a wild hare's arse. It's what Tommy Troy thinks that matters, Baby Brains. Sell your bollocks and buy some brains. Playing balcony scenes with Tommy's missus has you out of the car and me gone missing.'

'Coming from a berk who thinks playing with himself is a music lesson, that's bloody rich.'

'Maybe, but Tommy ain't climbing over my broken legs to get to you, right?'

Lou's hand dug into Sidney's upper thigh.

'Drive, Mister.'

'I'm driving, I'm driving.'

Sidney thought his femur was crushed. He followed City Road to Tower Bridge.

'All heart, ain't you, Sidney?'

'Only for me.'

'Then, we'll both mind our own business.'

'Don't everybody?'

Sidney took a backstreet and wished he could blow all overcoats to Kingdom Come, and Lou released his grip because his chest ached with exertion. He was weaker than he'd thought.

'This is a good earner, Lou. But no more pull-and-push, eh?'

'The monkey you're paying me'll get me where I'm going. You won't see me again.'

'Just don't tell me where, all right?'

Sidney took his Ford across the bridge. The Thames was a dull silver ribbon broken by lazy tidal action. Folds of muddy cloud blundered east on quartering winds, shredding to overcast over the Essex marshes.

Lou smelled Helen's fragrance on his fist. She'd promised to follow him when he got settled out of London. Her priest would accept letters at the church.

Sidney forgot his thigh to bring Lou up to date.

'Connie's brought the date forward. He's emptied the warehouses of all the long-firm bent gear, and the new insurance premium's due in three days' time. You up to this tickle, Lou? I can see your bones through your face.'

Lou's 'Yeah' didn't show his doubt.

'Wind on the shift is a sow. Does funny things to fires. Makes natural flues out of staircases and liftshafts. Pushes or draws flames through floor cavities and air-ducts. I've seen fires the brigade's put out with five appliances — not even a smoulder left — break out again half a street away. And no reason for it. Lint, wood-shavings, dust — even mouse-droppings can keep a fire smouldering. Everything burns, Lou. Soot in old chimneys, old birds' nests, gas in pipes people have capped and forgotten about. Even metal burns at the right temperature.'

'That right?' Lou was genuinely interested.

'Not many. Just look down-river to where the old spice warehouses were before they was bombed in 1940. They burned for days, and spice floats in the up-draughts like millions of match-heads. A pepper fire can blind you. Burning paint runs like lava and the fumes are poisonous. Empty propane-canisters explode like bombs, and if you rupture a gas-main say goodbye to half the street. Gas seeps up through earth, clay, building foundations — even water. Comes up where it can. And if that's near a naked flame or an electric motor — *whammo*, a bang that'll raise roofs and take out windows for six blocks. That's why yours truly, Sidney Salt, checks everything ten times over. Why I'm the best.'

'I thought you just set a match to rags and paraffin.'

'And leave a thousand clues for the firemen and insurance investigators? You leave them nothing suspicious. And you don't make bonfires of furniture, neither. That's a dead giveaway that somebody's been well at the naughties.'

'You could learn me a lot, Sid.'

'Not many I couldn't. There's another earner coming up right soon. For Bonar Tree and Ollie Oliphant. Some farmhouse out in the sticks. I could bring you in on that if you ain't sloped off by then.'

'I won't have.'

'And no more moody digs?'

Lou grinned and shook his head.

'Good boy. Have a barley-sugar. Good for the digestion.'

Sidney drove Limehouse to his mother's for clothes and then drove back to park outside a warehouse in Mitre Street.

'Beautiful in the City on a Sunday, ain't it? Nobody around until Monday morning. Yeah, this is my favourite time to work, Lou. No witnesses and hardly any busies.

Just us and the quiet and a lot of empty buildings. OK, open the bonnet and stick this note behind the wiper. Don't blank-look me, you daft halfpenny; it's so it looks like we've broken down if the law happens along, right? And where are we but phoning the AA?'

'Cunning stuff. And nobody sets fires in broad daylight, neither, that the size of it?'

'You're learning.'

Sidney gave Lou two sacks to carry.

The warehouse was five storeys of grey brick with an outside fire-escape. The brand-new illuminated sign had been Sidney's idea, and bolstered the illusion that Connie's long firm was expansionist in outlook.

Sidney strolled along the frontage and kicked the wired glass from a basement grating as casually as he'd crush a cigarette-butt. Nobody shouted and no alarms rang. Sidney toed stray glass shards through the hole and smeared the jagged edges of the broken window with grime from the pavement before letting Lou into the warehouse through a side-door.

For an hour they toured the building.

Sidney kicked holes in the hardboard over the fronts of the old fireplaces and had Lou disconnect the striplights to stop them coming on with the automatic timer. In the cellar, Sidney emptied the two sacks. He had baked transistors, radio parts, Sellotape, micromesh stockings and shreds of cardboard cartons together with old invoices in his oven at home to manufacture the detritus left by a fire. He sprayed petrol across the floor and over the walls, relying on natural evaporation to spread volatile fumes throughout the entire structure by nightfall.

Twenty minutes later, he and Lou were in the second Camberwell warehouse where they worked in much the same fashion. When Sidney was satisfied he took Lou to an illegal drinking club in Addison Road to kill time.

From the cover of the hospital portico, Gay Gordon watched Limehouse Lou and Sad Sidney argue together before they drove east. Then he waited for Helen to slip out through the casualty department and trailed her back to the Catholic church where Ida waited for her daughter-in-law to emerge from a very lengthy confessional. When Helen slipped into the church through a side-vestry, Gay Gordon went into the churchyard to urinate.

Careful not to splash his patent shoes, he desecrated the bones of a dyphtheria victim gone to her eternal rest in 1887, two days short of her eleventh birthday. A lick of steam rose from the marble as he zipped up, his face alive with ugly anticipation. He had confirmed Ida's suspicions and still had the pleasure of telling her to come.

Gordon had embraced the darker side of Calvinism in his native Glasgow, and equated kindness with weakness of the spirit. Plagued equally by his perverse sexuality and ungovernable jealousy, Gordon neither forgot nor forgave a slight. And since Jesse had met and fallen for the white-haired boy Gordon's emotional nose had been pushed firmly out of joint. And Helen's looks of quiet satisfaction had made his despair all the harder to take.

Gordon calculated he had lived 105 hours and 52 minutes of abject misery since Jesse Troy had shared his vodka and lime with Penny at Electric Raymond's party in Manor House. Turned into yesterday's man, Gordon had no way of hurting the boy or getting back at Jesse, but Helen was fair game now, and would serve his need to hurt somebody well.

Gordon hacked at the gravel with a heel. Scarred a virginal forehead in his imagination, blind to the stares of a winkle-man beyond the lych-gate. Gordon's tortured mind warped the congregation's hymn of devotion into a paean of praise for his crusade of vengeance against all womankind. Against Helen in particular. Limehouse Lou was a lesser daemon to be felled when the fountainhead of whoredom had been brought down.

Gordon would see Helen degraded as his stepmother should have been all those years before when he had been fifteen and his father had been dead for less than a day.

She had taken Gordon into his father's bed for comfort and introduced his penis into her cavernous vagina, trapping his rampant innocence for ever and for ever . . . .

Gordon had left home with all her housekeeping and funeral money and been picked up trying to sneak aboard a freighter bound for Buenos Aires and taken into care by the authorities, but the nightmares of the sobbing woman bearing down upon him never went away.

Gordon's malediction died away with the last chords of the hymn and left him detached and resolved. He smoothed his face and tie and went inside the church.

When he whispered into Ida's ear, light from the stained-glass window banded his face and flooded his colourless eyes with the glowing crimson of Christ's eternal wounds.

Absolving him of guilt.

Connie put the phone down after listening to Charlie Dance pass him a hot bubble from a contact in the Fraud Squad and rubbed goosebumps on his naked arms. Kelly turned away from him to feel for her slipper under the coffee cot before padding over to heat the percolator.

'We should get some carpet on this floor,' she said.

Connie admired her nakedness and wondered why Charlie Dance had marked his card about the Fraud Squad's big interest in finding Vic Dakin.

'That Charlie,' he said.

Kelly found cups and enjoyed Connie watching her.

'If the fraud busies make a dawn raid, ten to one they'll go to your house first. And won't that get up your Pauline's nose?'

'She'll shed ten stone and cry five gallons.'

'That's as maybe, and worth a grin or three, but you've got two fires and a lot of insurance money on the line. You can't let that quarter-million go walkies because you're knee-deep in busies hunting Vic Dakin, Con. And they'll do their damnedest to tie him into you, pet. You'd better have him do a runner abroad. Tonight.'

Light from the window bleached Kelly's frown.

'Yeah. Nice one, Kel.'

'Except he'd be back like a bad bun-penny. It's a permanent-losing job, Connie.'

Connie shook his head and his eyes marbled with laughter.

'And you're the girl who doesn't like me to starve the dogs once a week to keep them fierce. Shoot the bastard, Connie, and come back to bed, that the idea?'

'That's how it has to be, lover.'

Kelly's teeth were bone knives in her tight smile.

'That's where we think different. Boy and girl different. No company director's gonna blow himself up writing himself big fat cheques, now, is he?'

'Beautiful, Connie love . . . .'

'Get Mr Dakin for me, Miss Ketchum.'

'Certainly, Mr Harold.'

Kelly dialled Dakin's hotel and held the phone to Connie's ear, her rump hard in against his thighs.

'Victor, my son, something's come up . . . .'

'More than one thing,' Kelly hissed, reaching back.

Charlie finished talking to Connie Harold and would have gone back to his colour supplement if Ingrid hadn't slapped it towards the bedroom ceiling.

'What's your game?' he asked, looking simple.

'You did that for me. For my peace of mind.'

'Not me. I'm the bastard, remember?'

'Yes, you, you hard-nosed, soft-centred darling.' Ingrid bruised Charlie's nose with a plonking kiss. 'Connie has to let Vic go now, doesn't he?'

She threw her hair back and cuddled a pillow.

'If he doesn't want the law all over him before eight tomorrow morning, he will.'

'Special, that's you, Charlie.'

'Hungry more like. What's for tea, you idle wench?'

'Anything at all.' Ingrid's eyes shone.

'How about you on toast?'

'Coming right up.'

Ingrid pulled at the bows of her nightgown.

'Let them out one at a time, then. Don't want to be smothered . . . .'

The white-haired boy ate yoghurt in the lotus position as Jesse slept off Ida's Sunday roast.

Penny was jaded from an afternoon romp without penetration. He shifted slightly to favour his tender right buttock. Jesse bit when he was fellated and made love like he ate, butting around like a boar after truffles.

Penny licked the last of the curds from his spoon and wished he was still with Shane. Wished he hadn't met Jesse at Electric Raymond's party. Wished Charlie Dance had wanted him for himself.

Penny teased his inner thigh with a silver nail.

Instead he had ended up with a snoring animal no deodorant could sweeten in a houseful of Neanderthal shits.

He jabbed Jesse's foot with the spoon.

Jesse just snuffled and turned on his back.

Raised voices filtered up from the ground floor — a three-way squabble that had grown from the midday meal. Terrible Ida had fawned on Tommy, suffered Jesse, ignored Penny and snarled at Helen. Jesse hadn't even noticed the charged atmosphere, nor the looks of loathing and longing Gay Gordon had thrown in Penny's direction. When Jesse ate, he ate.

Furniture overturned with a thump, and Helen's scream choked off before becoming falsetto.

'Jesse, wake up.'

Jesse rolled and snorted.

'I paid for all night. Let me sleep, you slag.'

Penny was revolted.

'The charm of the man. You're not in the pit with some twopenny tom. You're at home with *me*. Or has that small fact galloped past you like a fiery fart on horseback?'

'I should kill you dead!'

Tommy's bellow pursued drumming high heels up

the stairwell.

'You whoring tart.'

Helen sobbed and lost a shoe, stumbled and screamed: 'Not me. You. It's you who tom-cats until the goldtops rattle on the doorstep, Tommy. You who gets his feet under other men's tables. I haven't forgotten you and Miriam Parsons. I just visited a nice boy you tossed aside and left to rot in hospital.'

Jesse scratched and belched drearily.

'Happens every Sunday there's nothing on the telly. At it like knives. Give us a back-rub, Pen.'

'You're the sick one, Tommy. You.'

'And getting sicker. Get back down here.'

Penny pointed his spoon at the door. 'That's normal? Give me an Earls Court brothel anytime. At least gay Aussies wait for the pubs to turn out before they use each other's heads as footballs.'

Jesse reached out an unwashed paw. 'C'mon, Pen.'

'You done my Tommy dirt, Helen girl. You and your quiet waters. It's the quiet ones that drops babies on your doorstep.'

A bedroom door slammed and a shoulder cannoned into it.

'Come out of there, Helen. You gypsy's melt.'

Tommy shouldered the door again.

'Keep it down out there,' Jesse bawled.

'Wind your own clock, Jesse.'

Jesse left the bed and broke wind at both ends.

'My house as much as yours, Bruv.'

On the landing he set his fists on his hips.

'She burn the custard again?'

'Jesse Troy,' Ida screamed through the banisters. 'Put some clothes on your body.'

'They're the exhibition, not bloody me.'

Jesse snatched a dressing-gown and got an arm into it. 'Custard nothing!'

Tommy punished the bedroom door with his fists.

'Her and that slag Limehouse been canoodling,' Ida called.

'Canoeing?'

Jesse fussed with a tangled sleeve.

Tommy put a fist through a door panel.

'Helen and fucking Limehouse have been well at it. Behind my sodding back.'

Penny glimpsed Gordon behind Ida on the half-landing and was repelled by his expression, was scalded by the cold saurian under the skin. Penny mewed into his fist and made himself small on Jesse's bed.

Tommy withdrew a bloody hand from the shattered panel.

'The whoring crab's cut me with my own whoring razor.'

Jesse's bulk tore the bedroom lock from its keeper.

'Cut my brother, would you?'

He hauled Helen into the passage and snatched the cut-throat away like an afterthought.

'Have her, Tom.'

The sound of Tommy's forehead slamming Helen's upturned face made Penny vomit. He fell into a whirlpool of nausea pursued by hard blows to ribcage and breast.

Hatred was a second presence in the hotel room.

Vic Dakin held the receiver long after Connie had stopped talking, and his healing scabs stung from quickening perspiration. He lit a cigar without tasting it, shaved without needing to, let ice melt in his drink and matched a tie to his shirt in an absent-minded stupor, mulling over Connie's strange change of heart.

Dakin could only believe that Kelly had addled Connie's brains with her demanding little body. They must have been on the nest all afternoon, rutting like badgers not six feet from where they had tortured and humiliated him.

Dakin mashed his cigar to brown flakes. Caught between fury and caution, he tried to work out why Connie wanted him to go to the Mitre Street warehouse immediately, and transfer all the funds from Common Market Traders through the Bank of Valletta to a company Connie had registered in Johannesburg.

Connie's voice came back, thickened by Kelly's clever little hands: 'Have the paperwork on my desk by Monday morning, Vic. You and temptation get along too well.'

Dakin tapped his teeth with a gold Parker. He already had facsimiles of the relevant directors' signatures, and he could easily forge them on a makeshift lightbox. And by pre-dating the irrevocable drafts he could present them for immediate encashment in Brussels the following morning. At the *precise* moment Connie expected him to walk into his office.

Dakin rubbed his thighs and giggled softly. By the time the drafts had been processed and presented to the defunct Maltese bank, Vic Dakin would have become M. Jacques Tournier and be sunning himself in Ceylon.

'My turn, *Mr* Connie-bastard-Harold.'

Dakin's muddy eyes still danced when he climbed the fire-escape in Mitre Street, too pleased with himself to notice the courting couple in the shadows or Sidney Salt's Ford coast to a halt on the far side of the street.

The beer in Sad Sidney's stomach turned acid when he spotted the couple in the warehouse doorway, and the pasties he'd eaten were as heavy as stones. Lou hissed through his teeth and suggested putting the frighteners on the lad and his girlfriend.

'Highly lovely, you twopenny twerp. Then you'd have two witnesses to pick you out in court. You been around them Troys too long. In this business you don't show yourself to nobody. Never.'

'We can't just sit here on our thumbs, Siddy.'

'We don't have to as it happens. We'll torch the Camberwell warehouse and come back later. By then love should have had its weary way.'

Three phone-booths later they found one the vandals had missed, and Lou dialled the Camberwell number whilst Sidney watched the southern rooftops.

Lou heard a click and the start of a warble before fat fried and the line went dead. He caught the flash of summer lightning from the corner of his eye, and low thunder rolled upwards. When he sat back in the Ford muted light played on the underside of the low cloud.

Sidney crunched a BisoDol.

'Easy, ain't it, Lou? One tiny spark of electricity, flash powder inside the bell of the phone, contact, and bingo.'

Lou's jaw had unhinged.

'Yeah,' he said. 'Yeah . . . .'

'If those kids have done eating each other, you can do it again.'

'Yeah . . . .'

Sidney fretted, knowing time was against him. But it was pleasant to see Lou so very impressed. The courting couple had left Mitre Street when they returned, but when they drove back to their working telephone the warehouse number was engaged.

Sidney began to fret seriously.

The gold Parker slipped from Dakin's fingers and rolled away.

His eyes smarted and would not behave.

He sat in scudding moonlight, head buoyant, limbs leaden. He thought somebody must have smashed a crate of industrial cleansing solvent. He had picked up the harsh odour when he reached the top-floor office, but now it was stronger, more pervasive. And his pen was at the bottom of a deep, dark, carpeted pool.

Dakin muzzily took stock.

He had emptied the safe of chequebooks and blank bank drafts, packed them in his briefcase and mentally calculated the amounts he would make their cashable values in the anonymous security of a hotel room. The Russell Hotel had a Turkish bath, so he would go there to steam some of his bruises away.

Dakin got up from the desk, but the floor smacked up into his knees and rolled him on to his side. His scrabbling fingers pulled the telephone to the floor and it burred impatiently.

'Answer yourself . . . bloody machine . . . .'

Dakin almost frowned. He had dragged his briefcase to the carpet for an important reason he no longer remembered. And there was a door he must find. He crawled on string and rubber limbs to a hard surface that would not yield. He took time to puzzle that out.

The vague image of a door and outside formed in his mind, but there were brilliant squirming things inside his eyelids.

A swollen heart hammered inside his constricting chest. His own blood was drowning him, and panic banged with his heart.

Dakin punched a cold metal horizontal bar. The emergency bar slammed up, and the door gaped.

Spilled out on to fretted cast iron, Dakin drank high-octane-flavoured air.

The fire-escape bit his back and rolling thighs as he flopped and floundered from landing to landing. Fell ever closer to the street. The night stank of petrol, and he thought Russian guards moved through winter trees to cut him off. His gasps of breath bayed like dogs.

Odessa was above him, and he wondered if the battered Ford in the street below was a mobile Russian patrol. A guard climbed from the car and lit a flare. Dakin let himself fall the last flight and clutched the briefcase to save it from Connie's electrodes.

'It's bloody engaged.'

Lou let Sidney jiggle the tines.

Sydney pushed Lou into the Ford and pulled away. They were over two hours behind schedule now, and the loss of telephonic contact meant they must go in on foot.

'And who was it left nothing to chance?' jeered Lou.

'Moonlight lovers and dodgy phones ain't down to me.'

Sidney swung into Mitre Street and rummaged in a bag on the back seat.

'Now you really earn your poppy, Limehouse son. Wind your window down, put on this glove and hold this rocket in line with that busted basement window.'

Lou stared.

'A kid's rocket? You plan to hit a window the size of a broken saucer twenty feet away with a kid's whoosher?'

'I ain't going no closer.'

Sidney lit the fuse.

A great golden shower filled the car. The firework rushed away in an eccentric curve, ricocheted off the warehouse and lost itself in the night.

'You bloody moved!' Sidney beat sparks from his lap.

Lou patted singed hair. 'Wouldn't you with half your head alight?'

'This next one'll get it done,' said Sidney.

'Only this bloody way.'

Lou slammed from the car and lit the rocket as he ran. A perfect underarm throw sent it through the broken pane. Lou peered inside to see where it had landed.

'Run!' Sidney bawled, trying for first gear. 'Run, you twopenny . . . .'

Expanding brilliance ate the night. A hammer of sound killed sight and hearing.

Sidney's head split the vinyl roofing, and the Ford stalled and lurched against a wall of hot air. He was rammed below the steering-column before being dumped bodily in the back seat. Hot embers set the fireworks alight, and Sidney was engulfed by showers of coloured light as the car lifted sideways and impacted against the railings of a dress manufactory. Every window in the street blew inwards.

Sidney slumped as all the breatheable air was consumed.

Bowled off his feet, Lou and the sky turned in slow circles. The stars and clouds were overlaid with colours he'd never seen before. His head filled with violent song without melody, and his jacket and a shoe sailed into the next street. Lou skinned his back when he bounced. Ground glass had formed an immediate glittering crust on the cobbles.

The warehouse came apart with monumental disregard

for time.

The turreted roof lifted on a raft of blast and slowly broke into tiles and beams and joists. A jet of flame blew the chimney-pots to dust, and columns of solid soot stabbed upwards as black exclamations. Expanding as it rose, a ball of incandescent vapour climbed the flue to dust bricks into powder and spread a dry red rain over the immediate neighbourhood.

A heating ventilator trailed yards of pipe across the street, ruptured a water-tank and buried itself in a stud-partitioned wall, starting an electrical fire.

Storey after storey, the warehouse floors heaved and collapsed, filling the gutted basement with blazing timber. Some of the super-heated baulks tumbled into the street to form eccentric bonfires. Smoke rolled in blinding banks, and invisible shrapnel hummed as it struck sparks from the cobbles. A gas-standard blown into the shape of a question-mark jetted flame into a fissure in the pavement. Concussed and dead pigeons made soft grey flops as they fell to earth.

Lou smelled coal-gas a bare moment before the underground main ignited and a massive secondary explosion tore a crater in the road.

Lou was snatched up again and blown through a wooden fence where stacked cardboard cartons broke his fall. He did not see a steel shutter slice through the Ford and neatly decapitate Sidney Salt. Sidney's head spun away through a marine broker's window and came to rest in a swivel chair where it smiled sadly at a portrait of Queen Elizabeth II.

Nor did Lou see Vic Dakin rolled to the corner of the street by the blast, gather up his briefcase and stagger off in search of a taxi to take him to Heathrow Airport.

In the scrapyard office across the river, Connie and Kelly heard the multiple explosion in their cot. Connie reared as the windows rattled and the Alsatians went wild with fear.

'A quarter-million earned. A bad penny lost. Not a

bad swap.'

Kelly responded by bucking faster with clenched teeth, her hair in wild disarray on the pillow.

Penny awoke in darkness and silence.

Ida played prize bingo every Sunday, the brothers would have gone drinking, and one of their overcoats would be guarding the house in front of the television. Penny found a lamp, and Jesse's bedroom leaped at him in shades of orange, wine and sepia. The shelves of pulp fiction and erotica. Nazi militaria and an original gouache male nude. The disordered wardrobes, ugly bed and matching side-tables. The tumble of discarded clothes over chairbacks.

The upper bedrooms were silent, and the television set chuckled from the ground floor.

Penny sluiced his face and combed his hair until it crackled. Then he scratched at the splintered door to Helen's bedroom. There was no response, and the door swung open at his touch. Nobody was in or near the bed, in either of the padded chairs or seated at the dressing-table in the spill of light from Casa Pupo lamps. Penny tried some of Helen's perfume and checked out her lipsticks, listening for movement in the *en suite* bathroom.

Water plopped, and a whisper of steam came under the door.

The thick carpet was wet under Penny's naked feet.

'The silly girl's left the tap running. Helen love?'

Penny pushed the door wide.

Helen lay in the bath with pretentious gold taps, and the water was pinker than the matching rose suite. The bruises over her closed eyes were a vague lilac and the broken skin was a dark strawberry. Her hair trailed in waterlogged bangs, the tips fanned out like submarine weed, moving slowly with the overflow. Her sleeping face was calm and pale, her bruised mouth a dreaming pucker that gave her a gently wanton look. Her outstretched arms floated palms down, and her ebony crucifix bobbed against a dark fistprint.

'Helen?'

Penny closed the hot tap and nudged Helen's shoulder.

The head lolled sideways. Trailed wet hair across the slowly opening mouth. The bruised torso rose and the small breasts came up with a thick red tidemark across the nipples. And very lazily the right shoulder dropped, rolling the left fist out over the edge of the bath still gripping the long-bladed knife Helen had plunged into her right armpit.

Penny kneeled on the spongy carpet. Read the words scrawled on the misted mirrors. Some were drawn in lip-gloss. Others were finger-painted in blood and had run with the condensation. He read Helen's last words aloud, his lips as bloodless as the limbs in the water.

Penny's mind and stomach were empty when he went slowly out and down the stairs, past Helen's lost shoe lying where Ida and Gordon had stood on the half-landing.

Gay Gordon sensed Penny in the doorway before he turned to see him. Bruce Forsyth bowed to live applause on the stage of the London Palladium as Penny offered his slender hand.

'Come with me. I've something to show you. Upstairs.'

Lou thought he was dead.

The crashing music inside his head could have been brazen trumpets from the walls of Paradise or a hellish choir calling him to Perdition. He was in limbo on a slab of refrigerated marble. If he was dead, there would be a tag on one of his toes to prove it. He lifted his head and a barrel of wet cement to look down the length of his body.

A sterile white room ebbed and flowed on incoming tumbles of pain as splintered bone grated in his shoulder. Agony made him Lou again, and he smelled his braised flesh under the gel and ice-packs. Saw again the fireball blow his senses into black tatters.

Voices muttered beyond a partition.

Lou lay very still to listen.

Doc Rudge said: 'A local finger-tame busy brought him here. I made the busy happy with fifty sovereigns and played the dumb old man. Seems it took twenty-seven fire-engines to put the fires out in Mitre Street, and almost as many for the Camberwell one. My question is: What's one of Tommy Troy's ex-overcoats doing outside a Connie Harold long firm when it blows?'

Charlie Dance yawned.

'Just another of the seven things in the world I don't know. You did right to call me, Doc.'

Lou heard notes crackle as they changed hands.

'There's a second face back in Mitre Street, but that one's a corpse without a head. The law's drawn a blank through CRO, so they're treating him as a motorist who ran out of luck. As a guessing man, I'd say different.'

'How different.'

'A torch who ran out of fuse?'

'Guess me a name.'

'Sad Sidney Salt.'

'That's quite a guess, Doc.'

'The busy gave me these antacid tablets. Salt chewed them all the time.'

'Then, I'm convinced.'

'Is this Tommy having a crack at Connie, Charlie?'

'Not with the strife he's got indoors. No, I'm betting it's a bent insurance tickle. Connie must be short of readies.'

'What strife, Charlie?'

'His old lady topped herself.'

'What? Terrible Ida?'

'No, Helen his missus. The Fortress is knee-deep in busies. Jesse even shipped his new fairy out the back door to keep himself smelling sweet.'

'How you get these hot bubbles baffles this old man.'

Doc Rudge clattered instruments in a steriliser.

'Carrier pigeons. But I'm no closer to who it was took a heavy dig at me and Archie. Can Lou talk?'

'See for yourself.'

Lou cracked a swimming eye and the two men hovered

in their own heat haze. His hand found Charlie's sleeve and words sighed close to Charlie's lowered face.

'Get to Pinky Bellaver . . . he promised Tommy your head for . . . Kosher's backing . . . mail train . . . and you got a grass in your firm . . . find him . . . you'll find who . . . .'

Lou fell in on himself. His strength gone.

Charlie and Rudge drifted through a white wall, and Lou heard Charlie say: 'That's decided me it's time for a seance at the seaside. A nice day out in Brighton making pies with Kosher Kramer's sand.'

'You'll get more than your name through a stick of rock if you go hunting Kosher on his own turf, Charlie. He's well forted up down there, take an old man's word.'

'When did a friendly chat come amiss? And Lou can't stay here. Your cheap busy will be back for more easy sovs. Drop Lou down to Stavros in Charing Cross. Lay on a nappy service with a mother's heart and a shut mouth.'

'Know the very nurse. But why d'you pick up all the shitty sticks, Charlie?'

Charlie's yawn was long and easy.

'So nobody picks up any of mine.'

The voices went away and a distant door slammed.

Lou resolved to live to see Tommy Troy in hell before he laid flowers where his heart had died.

CHAPTER NINE

VICTORIA STATION bustled with Monday-morning commuters arriving from the south. Charlie moved against the surge and lost Bulstrode and Quill to catch the Brighton Belle. He ate breakfast kippers with Nasty Nostrils and Sodbonce in the Pullman car before joining Johnny the Builder and Barry the Blag in their reserved first-class compartment.

Johnny dealt three hands and a dummy, liver spots on his quick fingers and his face thinner than his hair. Barry had a higher forehead, and there was grey in his ginger mop. He flicked a last card at Charlie and said: 'Give me the most northern training centre.'

Charlie fanned his hand.

'Dumbar. Length of Mildmay and jumps? I'll open for sixpence.'

'One mile two furlongs. Water jump, ditch and six sets of sticks. Your sixpence and sixpence and two cards,' Barry rapped back.

Johnny winked at nothing as usual.

Barry glanced at his cards.

'Is he bluffing, Chas? Johnny's always a millionaire on the first hand.'

'Is Charlie bluffing about Brighton? That's more to the point,' said Johnny. 'You need the runners and riders, right, Chas? That's why we're here, Barry. Ten to one Charlie don't come out to the course with us.'

'No bet,' said Barry. 'Your ante, Chas.'

'My shilling and up a monkey.'

Barry stacked. 'Let the millionaire take you.'

Johnny's eyes watered as if overwhelmed by sadness.

'Your bob and five hundred, and five hundred more. That's a grand to you, Charlie.'

'Turn you for the thousand.'

'Threes over bullets. A nice little house.'

Charlie threw in his two pairs.

'That's your outing paid for. Instant death, Barry? One hand face up. Just you and me.'

'And Johnny deals, right?' said Barry.

'Who else?'

'Two grand says I'm in.'

'Shuffle and deal, Johnny.' Charlie laid two blocks of Connie's money on the table.

Johnny snapped cards into neat rows, and Barry had a prial of sevens against Charlie's pair of jacks.

'You want to draw, Charlie?' Johnny asked.

'What for? You've got Barry's fourth seven three cards down, right?'

Johnny cut the seven without looking.

'You take all the fun out of skimming, Chas. And don't tell me an ordinary punter would have seen it.'

'You're still the smoothest, Johnny.'

Charlie pushed the money at Barry and took one of his Admirals.

'Except for you, Chas. You ever shuffle the pasteboards these days?'

'Only to make sure Ingrid's got enough for a new frock. She thinks she's won the dough and I ain't forever buying her presents, you know?'

'Nice kid.' Johnny lit himself an untipped Piccadilly. 'OK, Chas, business. You'll find Kosher stays mostly at the Pavilion Hotel. He almost owns it, and likes to sit around there with the local sweethearts. He's always mob-handed on the street, and has enough local filth in his pocket to whistle up blue serge if there's a naughty he don't want to handle. Kosher's got his back to the sea, so there's only three boundaries to his manor. With the coast road blocked and the railway station covered, there's only the one way back to the Smoke. Get my meaning?'

Charlie's nod was noncommittal, and Barry chipped in with: 'It's a tight little town. You can get your collar felt for parking your motor up wrong, for chatting up the wrong tom, or even for singing duff in a piano bar. Kosher likes a clean doorstep.'

'That takes heavy poppy.'

'You won't meet no hungry councillors, and the busies don't smoke cheap cigars.'

Johnny lit a fresh cigarette from his stub. 'And there's plenty of faces from the Smoke that use Brighton as a weekend watering-hole. You'll trip over faces from all the London manors. Kramer don't lord it, but he's got fingers in a lot of pies.'

Barry idly cut aces. 'He pulls strings like a puppeteer.'

'We're just telling you how it is, Charlie,' said Johnny. 'If Kosher looks at you sideways, have it away on your toes. Or you can bet your last groat you'll get leaned on while he's supping with straight citizens a good mile away.'

'Me and two overcoats ain't no invading army. Did either of you pass the word I was going down for a paddle?'

Johnny passed his hip-flask.

'Barry dropped the bubble last night when he booked us in at the Royal for dinner after the races. Said you was hot for a filly in the third and wanted to watch your money pass the tapes. Won't fool no one but won't harm, neither. Gives both sides an out from needing a face-off. You walk soft, Charlie, and you'll come back with a head to perch your hat on. What else can we tell you?'

Charlie wiped the flask off for Barry.

'Maybe I should wear a girl on each elbow. Give me a line-up on faces I might come chin to chin with.'

'On the earwig front there are the usual motley crew of grasses,' said Barry. 'Tommy Troy sends Silversleeves Sutton down there now and again for the odd squib he can glean. There's no heavy rabbit between Brighton and Bethnal Green, but they keep in touch. And Red and Pinky Bellaver come down from Catford every month or so. They could be a heavier link between the Troys and Kramer, but that's just guessing, right, Johnny?'

'Right. I've seen Red and Pinky at the races with Kramer, but that's nothing and everything. Nothing concrete. It'd help if we knew what you was angling for.'

Johnny nibbled the flask and wiped an amber pearl from his lip.

'Just general stuff, Johnny. How about the faces who tickle the trains?'

Barry fielded the question and the flask.

'Bonar Tree comes down for a good drink when him and Smiler and Alfie Horrabin have had a good blag off the rattlers. Alfie comes down with his wife for the sea air and a nice bit of Dover sole.'

Johnny wiped an eye and smiled sadly.

'If she ain't pulling the moodies on him. She's left him a couple of times. Never knew a wife like her. She's got enough hump to join the Camel Corps.'

'What about Ollie Oliphant? Eyetie Antoni?'

Barry choked on an intake of smoke.

'Ollie, yes. But Eyetie Antoni? Him and Kosher ain't met in nigh on twelve years. Their bad blood's so old it's as black as Newgate's knocker.'

Johnny rapped a fingernail on the table.

'Charlie's coming the old Chinese, Barry son. Pulling pudden to see who squeaks. Poker's the only game we play, Chas, so leave it out.'

Barry laughed, a shade pinker in the face.

'You ain't got much for your three and half grand, Chas. Ask us about ponies, punters or flat Welsh bitter beer, and we're your men. But not the SP on what the old firms are up to on the south coast. Archie gutted them years ago when they was full of piss and vinegar. Come and watch the ponies run. Leave old Kosher alone. Making waves at the seaside only gets you wet socks.'

Johnny looked sad and sour.

'King Canute in an overcoat. Stupid.'

'That a vote of confidence, Johnny?'

'I'll have confidence if you leave Kosher well alone. You wanna play some real cards or what?'

Charlie grinned at both men.

'No, nor two-up with my pennies. Go and see that Nasty and Soddy don't drink the Pullman dry. I need them halfway sensible.'

Johnny and Barry paused at the door. Two old uncles in a dark and strange new world. Johnny said: 'Don't do it, Chas. This is Crown and Anchor with Kramer's board and dice. His alley. His razors. And I thought you was old enough to shave yourself.'

'Get gone out of it, you old worrier.'

Charlie settled back to watch the suburbs peter out into rolling fields silvered by misty sunlight. Soothed by the rhythm of wheels and rails, he gathered his fragmented squibs into a loose whole and filled the gaps with questions.

Kramer linked through the Bellavers to Tommy Troy might bring Charlie back to Malcolm Sadler, or he might just find himself going through old washing Archie had left out in the weather to rot. The big question was whether Kosher had enough hate to come back at Archie after a long decade of seeming indifference.

Charlie picked up the cards, shuffled at speed and laid all four suits out in sequence with his eyes closed.

Then he dozed.

Vinnie Castle beat a pregnant woman to an empty phone-booth when he missed the Brighton train. He had only found out that Charlie was on the Brighton train that morning, and only because he'd phoned Doc Rudge to organise moving Lou to Charing Cross. He was dialling Queenie's number when Bulstrode crowded in behind him and cut him off.

'You got words, mouth? Tell them to me.'

Bulstrode strangled Vinnie with his own lapels, and Quill held the door closed from outside.

'One more porky and I'll knee your breakfast through your hat.'

'Don't get so aeriated, Buller.'

'Shut it. You've conned me with two duff bubbles. And that puts you at the top of my shit list, Castle. First there was no heroin at Windmill Street, and then — surprise, surprise — no Vic Dakin at Connie Harold's this morning. The Fraud Squad ain't pleased. Mr Lemmon ain't pleased. And me? I'm giving you the heavy finger.'

'It was a straight bubble. We must have both got turned over . . . .'

'Twice for me, you tosser. Now it's your turn.'

Bulstrode pulled Vinnie out on to the concourse and bundled him into a taxi as Quill told the cabbie to take them to Old Compton Street.

Vinnie blanched as he was sandwiched.

'What's your game, you two?'

Quill's small cigar reeked in the confined space.

'Think you're the only sod in shoes who can pull flankers? Here's us treating you to a nice sherbert ride when we should break your fingers for breaking our hearts. Time was, nasty felons like you was dragged to Tyburn tree on pallets with your arms and legs broke. They made certain-sure their villains hanged without fuss. It was more your slow strangulation then. Not a straight drop and a broken neck like today's enlightened times. The sports of them days made book on how long a felon would last on the rope before he choked his last. Made a day out for the whole family.'

'And you'd have them days back if you was in charge, which thank God you ain't,' Vinnie countered.

Quill's heel hacked his shins, and Bulstrode patted the back of Vinnie's head as he bowed over himself.

'Shut your clack.'

'You standing still for that, Buller?' Vinnie gasped.

Bulstrode shrugged.

'For what? Must have something in my eye. One of your porkies.'

The cab stopped in Old Compton Street, and Vinnie was hustled into a delicatessen hung with Italian sausage and ripe with strong cheese and ground coffee. Two old women haggled over the price of Parma ham as if the three men were invisible. A dark passage smelled of goat curds and furniture polish, and Vinnie fell into a back room with a small bar and sepia prints in black frames on brown walls.

A long and lean man with a lined face wore a trilby and braces over his pullover, sipped on stout without taking a dead butt from his mouth, and stroked the old cat on his lap.

Eyetie Antoni waved a long grey hand at the bar.

'You want drinks, have drinks, Mr Quill, Mr Bulstrode.'

A grey finger stabbed at Vinnie.

'You just talk.'

Vinnie said, 'About what?' and fed himself a Capstan.

'Is he kidding me?' Eyetie asked Bulstrode.

Quill snapped Vinnie's cigarette in two and tossed the pieces into a brass scuttle.

'Mouth up to the man. Coy earns you lumps,' he said.

'What d'you want? The price of coal or the shipping forecast?' Vinnie gave himself another cigarette. 'The frighteners don't make me a mind-reader.'

He thought Eyetie Antoni looked old and used up. He was as grey as a seal and his yellow eyes watered.

'Since when was you into friendly verbals with the straight law, Eyetie?'

'Since now, Smart Mouth. I had my crack at the top slot. Now it's comfort I'm after. War comes, we all lose. And Archie's Charlie making stupid in Brighton don't help. Why does he go down there when Archie ought to have the right faces up on meat-hooks, eh? Or maybe he's too old to keep the peace.'

'Archie's still the Man. And he ain't above marking your card permanent.' Vinnie blew smoke at Quill and Bulstrode. 'You and me verballing in front of these two makes no sense. Unless they've offered you some Donald Duck deal that puts our firm on a plate and you get left in peace.'

Eyetie's eyes dried and hardened, then softened and

saddened.

'I want it made clear there's no war in my corner. For thirty years I make favours and lend money to chaps who ate their porridge. I keep my word. That's honour and favours come back. I get my windows broke or my cat gets hurt, then you see how many friends Tony got. All the faces on all the firms owe Tony for something, eh? Even coppers have had a warm at my fire. Had a stout to keep out the cold when their helmets froze to their heads. They know my toms are clean and don't play the wardrobe mistress with the punters' wallets. And more than one copper has had a juicy freeman's in my cribs. I stop the fights, not start them, and my toms pay their fines good as gold. My spieler plays straight dice and the decks ain't shaved. My drinks ain't watered more than anyone else's. So why should Tony want wars?'

'Somebody does, Eyetie,' said Vinnie.

'Then, do good favours. Tell these straight busies who. Let them take the aggro off the streets. Leave us to get on with business.'

'Just like that.'

Eyetie shrugged and built a creamy head on his stout.

'I got the bad stomach. Three operations last year. Maybe they cut me again to get at the blockage. That's enough knives for Tony. Got a stomach so laced it's a regular roadmap. If Tony don't get the peace from Archie, I get my friends to make it bad for all the firms. My old man Alfredo went for the peace way back when I was too young to understand. Now I'm as old as he was when he died. I got the same crab in my belly, so I got the need for peace. Tony don't die from the wrong knife, eh?'

Vinnie snorted smoke.

'So you're a benign old pussycat, Eyetie. And maybe you can trust a handshake from Buller or Prophet here. Me, I'd want to deal with busies with more clout than these two before I coughed snide for empty promises. Get it said straight, Eyetie. You figure Kosher Kramer's on his way back into the Smoke with the Troys backing him. And

I'm supposed to swallow crow and cough snide on Archie to save your Italian arse. Buy yourself another parrot.'

'You'll cough,' said Quill.

'You've got more chance of growing a second navel,' Vinnie hissed.

'Mouth and trousers,' Quill said and made fists.

Vinnie shook his head at Bulstrode.

'Do us a favour, Buller. If I'm down for a good hiding, you do it. I ain't standing for Quill's paws on me.'

Eyetie uncapped another stout.

'Charlie sides with Kosher, eh? Tony don't like that.'

Vinnie forced a laugh.

'That kind of thinking earns you the paper hat, Eyetie. Charlie will laugh in your face when he gets back from his paddle.'

'If he gets back,' said Bulstrode.

Vinnie crossed fingers and spat three times.

'Give me my lumps or let me walk, Buller. A good whacking wipes out the two naughty bubbles, but it don't get me sniding on the firm, so what's it to be?'

'Good question,' said Quill.

Vinnie's stomach lurched as Quill fitted a brass duster over his knuckles.

'Good question . . . .'

Johnny the Builder bought five tickets as the racecourse bus left Brighton Station, and sat beside Charlie.

'We're spotted, Chas. A couple of faces at the barrier.'

'Three,' said Sodbonce.

Barry worried a nostril with a finger.

'Local faces and one from Catford.'

Nasty Nostrils studied form in a racing pink.

'I made a positive on Pinky Bellaver. And there's a law wagon up our exhaust. Three plain busies up.'

Charlie gave Nasty and Sodbonce a thousand each.

'I still fancy Sauceboat in the third. Get that on the nose for me. If I get lost in the crush, four o'clock in the music room at the Brighton Pavilion.'

'You ain't losing us,' said Sodbonce.

'And bring my winnings,' said Charlie. 'But if I'm not there by five take the train home. Right?'

The nods were slow in coming and the faces sulked.

The bus turned into a carpark where flags rapped in a stiff offshore wind and tipsters boasted at the tops of their voices. An escapologist rattled chains to gather a crowd and a Percy Dalton man bawled over his tray of peanuts. Hot dogs and onions cloyed the salt breeze rolling the white flanks of the marquees, and a photographer with monkeys and a macaw combed the crowd for children with indulgent parents.

The police car showed itself before parking behind a beer-tent, and Charlie sent Nasty and Sodbonce off with Johnny and Barry to check the first show of odds on the boards. Charlie climbed the stand to be alone with his race-card and a good view of the course. It wasn't long before three plain-clothes busies filtered up to flank him impassively. Time drifted with the listless punters and the busies edged closer. Charlie waved and Barry took pictures through a long lens.

'Now we're all on *Candid Camera,*' Charlie said to nobody in particular. 'Want to order your ten—eight glossy—unglazed now?'

A busy with flat features and a flatter voice said: 'Touting snaps without a licence? Prejudicial to the public order is that. And you've got nothing if the film goes missing.'

Charlie smiled to himself.

'There's more than one Brownie on you three. And you can't check the whole meet on your own.'

'Lovely speaking voice, ain't he?' said Flat Voice. 'A bit of a falsetto in there, would you say, chaps?'

The second busy said: 'If that's a heavy London face, I'll bob my hair and answer to Shirley. He looks like a big girl's blouse to me. Think he'd squeal if we squeezed his nuts?'

The third busy laughed because he liked the idea.

'A knee in the nuptials'll loosen his vocals.'

'Nothing like a knee in the nuptials,' agreed Flat Voice.

'It's got to be pink frillies and black bombazine under that cheap suit.'

'And lace around his Y-fronts.'

Charlie watched the runners and riders in the Silver Ring.

'You three are definitely bought and paid for. Leaves just the one question.'

A genteel group of flowered hats and civic chains had drifted into the reserved tier below. The champagne-and-mayoral-car set. They were ushered by a big man running to fat around the neck and waistcoat, his meaty shoulders squared by an angelically cut suit. A pork-pie hat sat on hair as black as dye could make it, and he lacked an earlobe on the right side of his face. Navy suede shoes did little to bring class to his money. He rolled a casual wrist and a dummy in camelhair danced off with the group's wagers.

'And what question would that be, sunshine?' asked Flat Voice.

Charlie pitched his voice to carry.

'Do we go all the way with the funny frighteners, or does somebody want to talk to somebody?'

The big man with scarred jowls and thoughtful eyes turned to look back and up. Recognition came with a slow nod and a slower smile. A masonic ring gleamed as a finger beckoned.

Flat Voice sniggered. 'Summoned to the presence. Well, well, scurry off to Mr Kramer, dearie.'

'See you three around.'

Charlie stayed where he was.

'Cautious, ain't he?' said the second busy.

The third toed a paper cup and laughed dryly.

'You'll see us, London. Bank on it.'

Flat Voice sauntered away, leaving the other two to throw meaningless backward glances. Charlie went down to shake hands with Kosher Kramer, who didn't bother with introductions.

'Travelling light, ain't you, young Charlie? Only two overcoats and two old tossers as company?'

'Saves train-fares and leaves more poppy for the

bookies, Kosh.'

'Champers, son?'

'I could murder a pint.'

'A cobbles thirst, eh? And why not?'

Kosher excused himself and walked Charlie down to the beer-tent for warm Bass in straight glasses.

'Am I pleased to see you, or what?'

'You got enough waves in the sea without my help.'

'I've got a good life, Charlie, and I wouldn't take kindly to that changing. Subbing out for council charities and paying off what passes for the law down here don't rub too raw.'

Kramer jerked his head at the reserved stand.

'Funny how the twinset-and-pearls mob love a reformed face with an open chequebook and a ready way in the kids' ward at Christmas. I hand out toys wholesale. All that old *bon noël*. The old Smoke don't sound the happy manor it once was, Charlie son.'

'Don't tell me you don't miss it.'

'Fog on Hackney marshes? Scratching about in slums for the half-crowns with a dozen baby-brained herberts looking to face me off just to say they squared up to Kosher Kramer before the cobbles came up a bit smartish? What's to miss?'

'Just that maybe.'

'You and Archie can have it. Look at my boat. A hundred and seventeen stitches went into this V-for-Victory I wear, and scars don't tan or grow hair. I shave round them and use tanning lotion in the summer. That's all the aggro I've got and all I need. I crept back to the Smoke once or twice and there's nothing left. Just dead streets full of brown faces rattling off at each other in language that sounds like they're picking cow turds out of their teeth. The smart yids have hopped off to Ilford, and the micks are cosied up in Kilburn or Camden Town. And have you seen Brixton? You need a bloody passport to buy a bag of greens off a stall. And who needs all them black looks?'

Kramer threw the last inch of his beer on to the yellow grass.

'Gnat's ullage. You and me'll have a wander, Charlie.'

'And your social commitments in the stand?'

'They're well sorted. Let's just leave your overcoats to outstare mine. We'll motor off for a decent gargle.'

'It's your manor, Kosher.'

'Can't say fairer. The Bentley's this way.'

The old Italian woman almost stopped Detective Inspector Lemmon reaching the brown back parlour, and shrill Neapolitan crowded in with him when he cracked the door. Vinnie stopped reaching for the poker, Quill's punch ducked into his pocket and Bulstrode pushed his drink away along the bar. Eyetie Antoni yelled, the woman closed herself out and Lemmon turned his hat one-handed.

'Run out of nice quiet police cells, have we? Or is this an economy drive against paperwork?'

Bulstrode and Quill decided silence was golden, Vinnie cuffed a damp forehead and Eyetie leered over his stout.

'Since you two are wondering how Uncle Theo found you, he'll tell you. A Black Rat clocked you ducking in here. A nasty, common traffic wally on a Noddy-bike thought I'd like to know two of his brave lads were supping ale with the Mussolini of Meard Street. And what do I find? You two about to duff our Vinnie for the pleasure it might afford a pimping, dicing mongrel with froth on his upper lip.'

Eyetie waved a grey hand.

'Nobody touch Vinnie. And you got no right to bust in my gaff righteous as a priest.'

'You want protection, Eyetie, buy yourself some bent law. God knows you're spoiled for choice there. Or have my lads given you to believe they're running in a selling-plate?'

Quill paled and Bulstrode came off the bar.

Eyetie wiped a damp eye. 'Who could afford such stallions?'

'Down to haggling over the price, were you?' said Lemmon.

'Leave it out, Guv.'

Bulstrode had flushed and perspired freely.

'And what's your price, Prophet? A warm tom and all the pasta you can eat?'

Quill swallowed, and Vinnie's sudden laugh made him flinch.

'Like Buller said, Mr Lemmon, leave it out. You're baying in the wrong forest. You lot have so little to go on you're at each other's throats looking for somebody to blame. I love seeing the law bite its own backside, but this is well out of order.'

'Who says your threepennorth's worth the waste of breath?'

'Nobody. But it ain't me who's desperate, is it? Eyetie would have to cheer up to be miserable, and you three are as popular as halitosis at a kissing contest.'

Lemmon tilted his chin and turned his hat.

'Then, you won't be swearing a complaint?'

'Straight-A right I won't. I don't want to be seen in private with you lot, let alone down the station in public. Let's just swallow and let me have it away on my toes.'

Vinnie found another Capstan to light.

'Stitching me up won't get you where you're going, Mr Lemmon. If you want a hot bubble, ask Eyetie about how he wants his New York cousins to come back into the London gambling scene fronted by an old-time movie star who can't get through a scene without flicking a coin? Give that to the heavy filth down at Special Branch and fatten your pension.'

Vinnie took pleasure from Eyetie's sullen anger.

Eyetie's expression was ugly and no longer looked old.

'Three nails and a hammer hangs you out to dry, Castle.'

'That'd sell tickets,' Vinnie said, his stomach cold.

Lemmon opened the parlour door.

'You two take Mr Castle out and buy him something expensively wet to make amends.'

'Another time,' said Vinnie, and bounced off Lemmon's forearm.

'Now. Eyetie and his Uncle Theo are going to have that little chat he's been longing for.'

Lemmon's sarcasm was as light as mother's pastry.

Over Burton's in a club bar, Kosher talked about his days in travelling boxing-booths and how his wife Rita still picked shrapnel out of his back from the flying bomb that knocked him down in Oxford Street and killed the two policemen chasing him.

In a club decorated with theatrical ephemera he reminded Charlie of the scalp that went wrong at Harringay greyhound arena. He laid the ball of a thumb close to a forefinger and said: 'You came close to getting lost permanent over that one, young Chas. Except that me and the Uncle from Peckham spoke up for you. Said you was a fast kid with a slow mouth who was clever beyond his tender years. They was heavy old lads in Hackney them days, and thought nothing of dumping a naughty face in the cockle-beds off Canvey. And being a kid wouldn't have saved you.'

'I wondered,' said Charlie. 'And I owe you one.'

Kosher cracked a depressed knuckle.

'That ain't why I told you. The point is that with different breaks things could have been well different. If you'd got lost permanent, and I'd had some patience, could have been me sitting alongside old Archie now. My old temper, you see? Rita said it was like having two people in the room when my rag went. It was well on the cards for me to have Cubby Colleano's spot when he died, but his manor and Toronto went to his nephews. Them Tonnas, Roger and Jesus. *Now* I can see why Archie wanted a family out there instead of me and my temper without a brother to watch my spine. *Now* I can. But not then.'

'Rankled, did it?'

'Not many. A good Yiddish boy, one of Archie's own, turned down for a couple of bloody Malts? I went bloody doolally-tap. Saw a hole in Soho and went for it. And there was plenty of hard young faces willing to back me against the old guard, and I got puffed up with myself. Happens, right? And I got well chastised for it, too. I was banged up in hospital and done my bird, and that tosser Eyetie got frostbite in Smithfield and learned how to grovel. Then I come down here, which ain't no bad thing.'

'If you say so, Kosh.'

'Bears repeating. It's you who's got the Troys and Harolds and the Gerrard Street Chinkies up your firm's jaxie — not mentioning the Eyeties. And them Brixton Zulus'll get organised once they run out of grannies' handbags. Your busted arm and rainbow eye don't shout peace in my ear. You hungry or what?'

Charlie said he could eat and they walked along the seafront to the Imperial where Kosher ordered oysters and stout to be followed by champagne and cold lobster in the shell.

'What else are you hungry for, Charlie?'

'Nothing.'

'Pleasure? Women?'

'A drink or three maybe.'

'Not something else?'

Charlie downed a last Portuguese oyster.

'Meaning what?'

Kosher's shrug was as elaborate as the violent tracery on his face. 'There's slow-mouthed and there's quick-eyed. You're fucking both, Mister.'

'You wouldn't want a dummy sitting in the chair you bad-tempered yourself out of, would you?'

'Truish not Jewish. And you ain't, are you, Charlie?'

'Don't kneel on a Muslim prayer-mat, neither. I'm just a fellow on a day out, eating lunch with a face who knows I owe him one.'

'You think I'm calling something in?'

'I think I don't know, that's what I think.'

'Question.'

Kramer raised a finger.

Charlie waited.

'If you ain't down here to wind me up or fumble my toms, what are you here for? Enemies or allies? What?'

'That about covers it.'

Kramer sucked fingers and remembered his napkin too late.

The V of scars stood out, white welting on old leather. 'You do get it said. What have you found?'

'Average oysters, great lobster.'

'And?'

'A face with a good life who's turned his back on the main event. Except he's got enough dough to buy me and Archie aggro. A face who's maybe financing a tickle big enough to lay a lot of heavy poppy on a lot of faces who ain't rightly fond of our firm. That's the definite maybe I've found. You have your big train tickle, Kosher, but keep the dough south of the Downs.'

'Wrong bait, wrong hook, wrong fish.' Kramer spoke a shade too easily. 'Didn't sound like calling in a favour, neither. More the heavy finger.'

'On my jack without a soldier in sight? In your manor with three finger-tame busies aching to turn my skull to eggshell? Pinky Bellaver haunting the station and trying to be invisible at the track? Him and Red are solid with the Troys, and you keep in touch with Tommy through them, right? They may call you a museum-piece out in the open, but behind the right door I ain't so sure. How different would that be, Kosh?'

'Well out of order. I get to ride the big dipper for free. I don't need your twists and turns. I ain't about to cross no deadline, but I won't help you, neither. Brighton ain't no closed manor and never can be. The Smoke faces swan down here for weekend naughties and a good drink. Some are proper oppos, others are just known faces. Don't read what ain't written, son. You figure you owe me, then pay it back by believing.'

'That ain't a lot for what my life's worth. But I'll shake on it and go home smiling.'

Kramer dug a toothpick into his smile and shook hands.
'You won't regret, Charlie son.'
'Time I was at the Pavilion to collect my faces and winnings.'
Kramer signed the bill and pushed his chair back.
'After you, Charlie.'

Bulstrode let Vinnie go to the gents' alone because there was no back way out of the club. Vinnie passed the toilet and went up two more floors. He pushed out through an emergency exit on to a flat roof, crossed a parapet with a sheer drop into D'Arblay Street, climbed an iron ladder and dropped through a fanlight into Armchair Doris's crib. Doris looked up from the film script she was typing with nothing but powder and rouge on her cheerful old face. She rattled a collection-tin at Vinnie and said: 'Don't forget the diver.'
'Use your phone, Doris?' Vinnie tucked a note into the slot.
'Business or pleasure?'
Like many ex-toms, Armchair Doris typed envelopes and manuscripts as a cover for her successful accommodation address.
'Pleasure's double,' she said and offered the tin.
'It's for Charlie.'
'Then, don't mention money.'
Doris tied on a plastic pixie hood and waddled towards the stairs.
'Slam the door on your way out. Charlie always comes free with old Armchair.'
Vinnie dialled, and Queenie's voice lashed at him.
'Where the sugar have you been? I thought you'd done a runner like the rest of the firm.'
'What?'
Vinnie's stomach rolled.
'Can't raise a single overcoat on our strength. Not even Foggy or Matt. I'm guarding Archie with my knitting-needles down here.'

'What about the freelancers?' Vinnie half-knew the answer.

'Nothing.'

'But Charlie's only got Soddy and Nasty. Where the hell is everybody?'

'Sold out. Gone on their holidays. Round somebody up, Vinnie, and get down here fast.'

'And Charlie?'

'He suckered himself in trouble, let him get out of it. I'd better see some muscle wearing our colours before the day's much older. You hear me?'

Vinnie came up with a lot of unanswered numbers before running into the street. He was flagging a cab when Quill grabbed him from behind.

'Going somewhere?'

'Archie's . . . . Christ, man, they're going to trigger Archie.'

Bulstrode flashed his warrant card at the cabbie and opened the door for Vinnie to stumble inside with his arm up his back.

'Battlebridge. *Fast!*'

'Over six miles is double the clock,' said the driver.

Quill gave Vinnie his arm back and stared the driver down.

'Just drive if you want to keep your licence.'

Quill settled back with the acceleration, hoping to witness the fall of an empire.

Kramer laughed when Sodbonce dismissed King George III's red and gold music room as 'a right royal load of brewer's posh gone Chinese', and was cordial at the station when he saw Charlie and his overcoats aboard the London train. He pinned carnations to their lapels, and his handshakes were firm and friendly.

'That was a fair old win at five to one in grands, Charlie. Shows Brighton's good for you.'

'Good reason for coming back.'

Laughter and scars creased Kramer's face.

'After you've got the Smoke sorted and calmed, eh?'

Charlie let Kramer favour him with a masonic handshake.

'Be lucky.'

Kramer waved and watched until a curve in the line took the train from sight.

'Sweaty old day. Now we can have a good drink.'

Sodbonce made himself comfortable on the first-class seats.

Nasty unbuttoned his waistcoat.

'Not many. Half of me's melted into my underwear. Never seen so many enemy overcoats. If looks was elbows, I'd have ten broken noses. But don't fret, Chas. We was nothing but mother's milk and seraphs' smiles.'

Sodbonce sniffed his carnation.

'Getting this far with just hard looks has done my brain in. We got Barry and Johnny away to Hove and a safe rattler home on the local line. Down the Pullman for a gargle, is it?'

Charlie shook his head, his slate eyes remote.

'No, and leave your coat on. Go get us a bottle from the buffet car and keep your minces peeled.'

He lit one of Soddy's Players from Nasty's stub and leaned back to wonder how long trouble would take coming. He showed no surprise when Nasty said: 'We're marked, ain't we, Chas?'

'What?'

'The carnations. Stands out a mile. Twice we've been clocked by faces in the corridor, so it's just a matter of waiting, right?'

'That's about the strength of it.'

Charlie stared out of the window. Grey fists of cloud punched south above fields of dull monochrome. Rooks rose from furrows like tatters of black rag, and the sun was a pale glare of white fire in the west. Charlie stared at his reflection in the window. It had the hollow gaze of a sick elder brother with no grapes and nothing to say on visiting day.

Sodbonce came back as the train plunged into a tunnel,

his face milky in the sudden tungsten light, and the whisky was a weapon he held by the neck.

'Indians,' he said. 'Custer's Last Stand with a cast of sodding thousands.'

'How many?' Charlie flowed to his feet like an edgy cat.

'I ran out of fucking fingers.'

'See any faces we know?'

'Masked with pick-handles? No chance.'

Nasty threw his carnation to the floor and rolled his overcoat around a forearm. A knife flicked open in his other hand.

'Run or stand, Chas? Pull the cord and have it away down the track?'

'In a tunnel? No chance.'

Charlie ripped the compartment door open and a length of ash skimmed his hair before jumping off the wall. Charlie flattened a nose under micromesh. A backside thudded to the floor and limbs flailed into the press of men behind.

'The guard's van. Move!'

There was a lot of hacking and weaving about as Charlie kicked kneecaps and Soddy and Nasty cleared the compartment. All three of them bored down the corridor, cannoning people aside.

Glass smashed and feet pounded behind them. Somebody took Nasty's whisky-bottle across the neck and fell down to vomit. A ticket inspector went a funny colour and locked himself in the toilet. A miniature poodle escaped a woman in furs and yapped at passing ankles. Charlie got his overcoats through a communicating door to earn precious seconds before the window was banged out by a stave. The communication cord was pulled, and brakes screamed and bound. Charlie bounced off a wall and sprawled headlong. Nasty rolled and landed on his feet with a lightness surprising in such a big man. Soddy had fallen into a carriage and wrestled with a couple of women who giggled and screamed and lost their 'Hello Sailor' hats.

Sodbonce swore and scrabbled away from a stabbing pick-handle. Nasty blocked a stave with the rolled overcoat, and Sodbonce reared up to bite into a thigh. Nasty's flick darted at a hard belly and his knee punished a crotch. The scream was like tearing silk.

Charlie drove a long right and felt the impact in his deltoid. Teeth cracked and a mouth made a wet O under a bloody stocking-mask. The opposition thrashed about and got in each other's way.

Charlie hauled Sodbonce to his feet and took a hard blow to the kidneys that stunned without pain. Nasty slashed to his rear as they ran the last yards to the guard's van.

The door ripped open and Charlie fell through with Sodbonce grunting in his ear. Hands pulled at them — passed them through a wall of men. Charlie glimpsed Pimlico's grin and Wally Harold's knuckles heavy with brass. Sharpened staves were passed to Nasty and Sodbonce, who grinned and blinked at Charlie.

'You cunning bastard, Charlie. You might have said we had some cavalry.'

'Could you have looked as bottle-tweaked as you do now?'

'Still well out of order.'

'You laced, Chas?' Pimlico asked.

'No, cut my fist on teeth.'

Charlie sank on a pile of newsprint and massaged the small of his back. Somebody put a cigarette in his mouth as Dublin Gerry led his team of relatives into the corridor. Nasty shouldered after them yelling for fair shares, and Charlie listened to thuds and wails as the opposition backed away down the train with nowhere to go.

He tied a handkerchief around his bloody knuckles and touched the carnation in his buttonhole. Kramer's big scarred smile was in the van with him, as genuine as a Kleenex banknote.

'Yeah, Kosher, I owe you one,' he said quietly. 'But for my todays or Archie's yesterdays?'

Stripes Flynn came into his mind to say, 'Show us some

hard,' and Fast Frankie breathed beer to say, 'I'm scared, but I ain't yellow. Take care of the little people, Chas, they're as much the firm as you are.' Limehouse Lou said, 'Give me Tommy and I'll give you the Troy firm,' his face as white as talcum and whiter than his pillow.

'And how hard is hard, Archie?'

Charlie dropped to the track and watched men being thrown from the train. A guard ran for the emergency telephone near the tunnel where a red light glared. Passengers peered from the carriages, pale faces in a row of dark aquariums. A horn blared from the road above the culvert and the roof of a pantechnicon showed above limes and birches.

Charlie walked past the sprawling men as Pimlico ripped their masks off. One of them was up on an elbow, red hair plastered around his mottled face. He spat blood and a tooth on to the rusty grass and watched Charlie with dreary anger.

'Hello, Pinky.'

Charlie flicked his cigarette-butt into a tangle of budding thorn.

'Looks like you came second. But your firm never was any good one-to-one, was it?'

Nasty Nostrils kicked a face to keep it quiet.

'Leave it out, Chas. You've won the straightener hands down. It's over, so let us walk,' said Pinky.

'When was twelve against three a straightener, Pinky?'

Pimlico stabbed his stave into Pinky's gut.

'Your walking days are over. Permanent.'

Pinky coughed bile on to the grass.

'No toppings, Chas. As Jesus lives, you can't.'

'Who ordered the muscle, Pinky?'

'Obvious, ain't it?'

Pimlico's stave dug into Pinky's throat.

'You want to gargle crooked?'

Pinky coughed and drooled.

'Everybody fancied it. Me, Red, Tommy. Even Kramer when it was put to him strong. Taking a crack at a wobbly firm on the skids is fair game, ain't it? We thought to have a final finisher. OK, so it works out you come up smelling of violets and we're out of order. That finishes it, right?'

'Look around, Bellaver. Do I look finished?'

'Fair dos, Chas. Let it sleep there, eh?'

'Not when you've earned a meat-hook up the khyber. Take him up the road, Pim. And make sure there's nothing left on that train that leads back to us.'

Wally Harold slammed carriage doors, and Dublin Gerry's team herded Pinky's men up the incline to the road.

Pinky squealed as Pimlico hauled him upright.

'Meat-hooks? *Christ*, Chas.'

Charlie's eyes were bleak.

'You was in on the Troubadour whacking, too. Hurt a lot of toms because they was easy. Oh yeah, you've earned a proper spanking.'

'No, Chas . . . .'

'Don't whine, Pinky. Whiners sicken me.'

Charlie climbed through trampled thorn and old grass to the road. When everybody was aboard the pantechnicon he locked the rear doors and climbed into the cab beside Froggy.

'Stripes's coldstore, Chas?'

'For starters.'

Charlie took a cigarette from the pack on the dash.

'Let's get home before some face sells London to the Yanks behind our backs.'

'We really showed 'em, Chas. Showed 'em good.'

'If you say so,' said Charlie. Far from satisfied.

Night winds brawled in from the North Sea and scattered raincloud over Essex.

When Lemmon arrived to take Quill and Bulstrode away from Archie's bedside, Archie sipped a medicinal gimlet as Vinnie dialled Charlie for him.

'Am I pleased with you, or what?'

Archie laughed when Charlie said he didn't know.

'You took our Vinnie right in. He didn't even have to act funny-worried to get the law scuttling over here on his coat-tail. They just naturally insisted. Nice one, that.'

Archie took a long bite from his drink.

'Lemmon was convinced your Brighton trip was down to you going off on your own bat and off your head. And I didn't let him think no different. How are them bastard freelancers of Troy's and Kramer's chilling down?'

Charlie heard Archie's voice harden.

'You could crack them into cocktails, Arch. I'll ship them over to the Fortress at first light. Troy ain't gonna do more than froth at the mouth with an unburied suicide in his front room. He'll swallow and bide his time. If anything, it's this train tickle he'll go after once he knows the strength of how much dough is involved.'

'Nobody knows that, Charlie.'

'Somebody always knows.'

'Are you giving me everything, young Charlie?'

There was a pause until Charlie said: 'Can't give you what I ain't got. G'night.'

Archie held the dead phone and his drink.

'A box of monkeys, that Charlie. A box of bloody monkeys . . . .'

'Yeah,' said Vinnie, wondering if there was a single straight line in Charlie's mind. Tomorrow sounded like a long hard day.

CHAPTER TEN

SODBONCE dropped Charlie in Weavers Field and parked in a side-street until he was needed. Muffled against persistent drizzle, Charlie walked his heavy fishing-bag past lock-ups without earning a glance from a coster setting his pony between the shafts of his cart. Somebody hammered a car panel and a goods train rolled wagons of aggregate towards Shadwell Basin as Charlie climbed an iron ladder to the top of the viaduct. The down-line signal swung to red as he crossed the track to look down into Vallance Road. The street was empty, and dim lights showed in the flats opposite the Fortress.

Charlie squatted behind a switching-box, pulled a high-velocity rifle from the fishing-bag and loaded it with soft-nosed ·30/30 shells designed to fragment on impact. He adjusted the scopesight and scanned the front of the Fortress with the stock hard in against his shoulder. Patterned curtains and dusty windows sprang at him, and he felt he could touch the mortar between the sooty bricks. He fed the first bullet into the breech and sat back to wait as the dawn quickened.

A whistling boy delivered newspapers, and a milk-float whined down Vallance Road to leave bottles on the doorsteps. Charlie wiped moisture from the rifle and practised patience. Minutes crawled and starlings came in a flock to settle in the Brady Street burial-ground. Charlie stopped himself from humming and smiled at the memory of Bulstrode's sleepy voice when he answered the anonymous call. Lemmon had come out of sleep faster but with no less puzzlement. Charlie was certain one of them would have called Quill. Not that it mattered. So long as there were witnesses to the shooting.

Charlie listened for engine noise and picked up the pantechnicon's comfortable diesel thump before it crossed beneath the viaduct and took its time parking outside the Fortress. There was a squeal of rubber, and Sodbonce reversed his saloon out of Weavers Field with the passenger door yawing. Froggy Farrell dropped from the cab of the pantechnicon and slammed himself into the saloon as Sodbonce roared off towards Roman Road.

Charlie picked up the police car as it slewed into Vallance Road from a side-street, coming fast. He waited until it had halted beyond the pantechnicon before opening fire. Aiming high, he lined up on the upper windows of the Troy house and systematically blew out the glass. His ears rang, and the slap and whack of the concussions drowned the sound of breaking glass. Charlie put two shots through the front-room windows and blew the milk-bottles from the doorstep.

Then he swung the rifle to cover the police car.

Bulstrode was at the wheel with Lemmon beside him. Quill, Dillman and Payne were crammed into the back seat and yelled silently.

Charlie set the crosshairs on Quill's forehead and squeezed off a last shot, hearing the soft click of an empty chamber.

Taking his time, Charlie zipped the rifle into the fishing-bag and collected all the used shell-cases. Then he went west along the viaduct in a ducking run. When he passed the rear of the Fortress he heard Jesse yelling and saw that one of his slugs had exited through a back window. A bright yellow curtain waved at him through a shattered pane.

Charlie jogged on.

The viaduct curved around to the rear of the burial-ground and overlooked stabling mews with the deep railway culverts of the Shoreditch spurline beyond.

Charlie swung over the parapet and dropped on to

overgrown rubble, staggered and kept his feet. He picked his way through discarded household rubbish at the edge of a carbreaker's yard, turned through an arch and made his way to a sliproad through parked coal-lorries. Sodbonce and Froggy picked him up on a humpbacked bridge, and they were well away before Lemmon's squad left the cover of their car.

Jesse Troy wished he could sleep. Wished it was time for breakfast. Wished there were more than two legs in his bed. He lit a small cigar and coughed himself upright to stub it out.

'Throat like sandpaper. Tongue like a tramdriver's glove.'

Jesse planned to make for Tommy's bathroom when he could breathe through congesting phlegm and reminded himself of the reason for his insomnia. Helen had marked the bathroom with her going, and even Ida wouldn't go in there. She'd rather use the downstairs sink to ablute herself than go into the room where Helen had bled herself to death.

Jesse laid a fresh match to the cigar but it was too mashed to draw. He shredded it and released a long satisfying stream of internal gas before lighting a fresh one.

Helen topping herself and Pinky's silence were driving Tommy mad.

Jesse figured the sooner she was planted the better he'd like it. Then maybe Tommy would really square things with the Harolds and that arrogant bastard Charlie Dance. And his spastic governor. Leaving the train straightener to Pinky might have been a real bloomer, and showed that Tommy wasn't thinking too straight. Tommy should have got his hooks into Brighton years before, and even if Kosher Kramer was a wanking geriatric dinosaur he was still laying out the heavy coin for the tasty rattler caper.

Jesse swung his legs to the floor and missed Penny.

He couldn't have the white-haired boy back until Tommy had dropped Helen's mortals, and Gay Gordon had promised Limehouse Lou's head on a platter, which wasn't sweetening Tommy's black mood none. Jesse thought Gordy was in line for a wreath of his own if he didn't get on the stick and come up with Lou's whereabouts smartish. Tommy was ready to blow, and Jesse wasn't about to let the blast come in his direction.

Jesse wreathed his bedside lamp with acrid smoke just as it exploded into fragments and his yellow curtains sucked themselves out through the window.

Jesse fell on his face and scrabbled for the door.

On the landing he yelled for Tommy. Called his mother.

Windows were caving in and holes were growing in the cavity walls.

Gordon swore from somewhere below, and Tommy was banging about in his bedroom. Jesse rolled down the stairs and burst into his mother's room. Ida snored peacefully, unaware of the glass and muck strewn over her counterpane or the ragged hole in the wall above her bed. Plaster dust writhed in a shaft of lateral light and settled on the polished surfaces.

Jesse barged out and collided with Gordon on the hall landing. The telephone was ringing, and a lake of dusty milk seeped under the front door.

'We haven't got a single shooter in the house because of the bloody dearly departed . . . .'

Gordon shut up as Tommy turned the corner above him.

'Shut that phone up, Gordy,' he snapped.

'It's right in front of the window.'

'Fucking well crawl!'

Tommy made fists.

'And get that milk mopped up, Jesse. I'm bringing *her* home from the undertaker's today. The bastarding bastards.'

Somebody hammered on the knocker.

'That ain't the fucking coalman, I know.'

Jesse threw tea-towels over the soggy doormat and stamped on them.

'And I ain't answering no door with just a thumb in my fist.'

Gordon crawled out of the front parlour and spread

himself against the passage wall.

'Now what is it?' Tommy snarled.

'An anonymous call, Tommy. Said have we made enough breakfast for a dozen extra bodies?'

'What the shit are you on about?'

'Not me, the anonymous. Have you seen the mess in there? They've shot the shit out of Ida's glass case of ornaments. Her shepherdess is nothing but the bottom of her frock and a bit of tree-stump. And her musical box with the dancing bear? That's—'

'Shut your weary Scotch cake.'

Tommy pushed Jesse and Gordon aside and banged the side of his fist against the front door.

'Who's out there?'

'Police.'

'Look out the window, Gordy.'

'Can't see nothing for this fucking great pantechnicon that's parked right across the window. And there's a lot of banging and commotion coming from inside that.'

'Use the spyhole, Tom,' suggested Jesse.

Tommy did so and said: 'It's that bloody DI Lemmon. Get the local filth down here in a hurry, I ain't having strange filth tracking up our carpets without no finger-tame cover. And tell them I want more than bloody uniformed wallies scratching themselves and looking dim. A shooter's been pushed through our letter-box, and that means Arthur-bloody-Ax down here in person.'

Lemmon punished the knocker some more.

'You letting them in, or what?' asked Jessie.

'Don't have to.' Bulstrode herded Gordon back into the hall. 'The window was more open than usual.'

Quill came out of the front room behind Bulstrode.

'Hope all that porcelain was insured.'

Bulstrode opened the front door, and Lemmon leaned against the railings as Dillman and Payne helped naked men from the back of the pantechnicon.

'Careful where they tread, lads. A lot of broken glass around the place.'

Tommy stared, his head pounding with disbelief. Pinky Bellaver hung between Dillman and Payne, his chapped hands and feet as red as his hair. Tommy's words were lost in cold, frustrated fury, and Lemmon tutted as if he understood.

'We'll have a chat while we wait for the ambulances,' Lemmon said as he followed the last naked man into the house.

'You can't build charges out of this,' Tommy snarled.

'Multiple indecent exposure?' Bulstrode suggested.

Tommy heard Ida on the stairs, her footfalls as violent as her language.

'All I need. Ma throwing a moody at a naked football team and the filth as linesmen.'

Then he was laughing as if something had broken inside.

Lemmon closed the front door with his back, stunned by the manic exhibition of unnatural glee.

Tommy's wildness left him when Ida screamed over the smashed chinaware as if the huddle of naked overcoats were just cardboard silhouettes. He took his dressing-gown cord in his fists and parted it like flimsy butchers' string.

'How can I bring my Helen home to *this*?'

Stavros leered at the two men in his office instead of the photogravure of a fifty-inch bosom spread across his desk. The Swedish traveller had promised Stavros 3-D nudes as an exclusive, and two faces he didn't know were of no interest to him. The slim one sported a suit, a mean pencil moustache and eyes like black seeds. The other man was comfortable roundels of hard fat, grizzled hair and a dimpled oriental smile that would not fade. Side by side they made a perfect figure 10.

'This is Stavros,' the fat one explained. 'The Turk.'

Stavros leaned on the inflated bosom and slid his foot close to the buzzer under his desk.

'And you want what?'

The slim one laid immaculate hands on the cheap desk.

'Tell Charlie we're here. Press the buzzer.'

'What buzzer?'

'And what Charlie, eh?'

The fat one's cheeks grew dimples.

Stavros sweated inside his stale shirt. The men could have been the Revenue or new faces on the Vice Squad.

'No Charlie,' Stavros agreed.

The fat one scratched a pectoral that did not move with his fingers.

'Tell Charlie that Pim sent us, Stavros.'

'Still no Charlie.'

The slim one scratched a nail along his moustache.

'Offer Stavros a gratuity, Ollie. Then he can buy shares in a soap factory.'

'How much of a gratuity?'

'Five tenners.'

The fat one fanned money.

'These whisper into your pocket, we whisper into Charlie's ear. Simple.'

Stavros licked his damp mouth and reached for the money. The slim man's hands darted to twist his nipples and pain paralysed his throat and scrotum. His foot danced on the buzzer in a riot of nerves and the office still revolved when he was dropped back into his chair. His thighs quivered and his calves jerked in spasm. Even Sergeant Mimi had not achieved such exquisite agony in the Istanbul prison.

The slim man leaned on the desk again.

'I can dislocate your kneecaps with my thumbs. Have your eyes out like shelling peas, only quicker. This Charlie you don't know taught me that trick. You want me to teach you, Turk?'

'Or how to kill your brain with a drinking-straw,' said the fat one. 'Why pretend to be deaf, dumb and blind when you can end up that way for real?'

Stavros shook his head and played for time.

'Both misters listen, eh? Dead for this Charlie I don't know, or dead for you, makes me dead, eh?'

'Loyal little bastard, ain't he?'

'And mortally afraid.'

Charlie aimed Connie's Beretta from the passage.

'Open the threads and let the loyal bastard pat you down.'

The slim one sneered when Stavros had patted him down.

'What now, Chas? Hands straight up, behind the head, or what when we go down into the cellar?'

'Just do it.'

In the bookstore Charlie pocketed the gun and shook hands with fat Ollie Oliphant and slim Bonar Tree.

'Quite an entrance. Thought you was gonna pull the Turk's chest out by the roots.'

'Couldn't look too friendly. And we'll leave the same way.'

Bonar Tree lit a cheroot, and Charlie took a Dunhill from Ollie.

When he had bloomed smoke over Ollie's lighter Charlie said: 'And who dreamed up the armpit straightener on the Brighton Belle?'

Bonar touched his moustache again.

'You've dry-cleaned Pinky Bellaver so you know the answer to that. Kosher's play, and nothing to do with me and Ollie, right? Think about it, Chas, when was we thud-and-blunder? You know our firm's MO.'

Charlie let Bonar watch him ponder the truth in what he had said.

Two years before, Bonar's firm had pulled a wages snatch at BOAC headquarters dressed as city gents. Rather than tamper with the padlock on the chained gate at the rear of the wages office, they had switched the chain itself with one fitted with a spring-loaded link, saving the need for duplicate keys. Sweet and simple except they hit too much security inside and ran rather than face odds of three to one.

When the law pulled them they earned Not Guiltys by coercing witnesses and bribing the evidence officer to switch a hat he held for one three sizes larger. Bonar had raised a laugh when he lost half his face trying it on for the prosecuting counsel. The chain itself had been produced in court and the 'expert' witness had missed the phoney link. On his way out as a free man, Bonar had sprung the link apart on the prosecution bench for the joy of seeing their faces fall.

Charlie nodded.

'No, I buy that as it happens. But it don't explain why you're showing your faces on my patch when I'm flavour of the month with the heavy filth.'

Bonar nodded back.

'The Smoke was never healthy for our firm. That's why we financed our next tickle in Brighton. And we don't plan to flush four months of hard graft down the lav because of flapping mouths.'

'Yeah, it rankles, but two firms on one train tickle, however big, is too many mouths. All right, so you need Alfie Horrabin's firm for the train itself, Ollie's transport, and you're the face with the inside info and the muscle, right, Bonar? Or am I guessing wrong?'

'That's some bloody guess,' Bonar snapped.

Charlie just looked at him.

'Maybe, but the tickle itself ain't the problem. It's what comes after you've tickled the train. Fact one: Kramer's already bubbled to the Troys. Fact two: once Tommy knows the strength of the dough involved, he'll be after your faces heavier than the filth. And fact three's obvious: Getting well away after the caper is where you'll come well unstuck.'

Charlie added a few more facts as Bonar and Ollie kept their hands and feet as still as their faces.

'Do we cancel, postpone, or what?' Ollie asked Bonar.

'Ask Chas.'

Charlie sat on a pile of old Hank Jansens.

'Depends when it's scheduled.'

'A week or three's time. Don't know for certain until our inside man tips us the nod. And, Charlie, I've never had better inside bubbles.'

Charlie turned the Dunhill in his mouth.

'Then, you go for it. But you allow for casualties. You

can't get all your faces and their dough abroad in one jump. Some won't even want to leave the country. And, sure as eggs, some of them have got to end up with the filth.'

'We can't draw straws for who gets his collar felt.'

Charlie smiled at Bonar's explosion of shock.

'You have already. Coming to me earns you a couple of long straws, right? I'll throw smokescreens so long as none of that heavy poppy earns me lumps in the Smoke.'

'That gets it said, Charlie,' Ollie said.

'So long as I get a nod.'

'So I'm nodding,' said Bonar.

'And me,' said Ollie.

'You still keen on having Pimlico as a second coachman?'

Bonar spat tobacco leaf out with his smoke.

'How many flies have you got on my wall, Charlie?'

'Not if you don't want Pim in,' said Ollie.

'Nothing like. Just let him think he's in on some country-house caper. That keeps him clean so far as grassing goes.'

'Nice one. You got it.'

'Now a bubble for you two. You've already had a casualty.'

Bonar and Ollie said 'Who?' together.

'Sad Sidney Salt's dead. Tag on his toe and everything. But I want that bubble to stay between us. Camberwell thinks there's another face on that slab, and I don't want that changed. You'll have to busk Sidney's part in the tickle right up to the last minute.'

Bonar snorted smoke.

'Some advice. Some favour. That's the smoothest part of our disappearing trick. Flash, bang, nothing left. We can't drop that for your amusement, Chas.'

Ollie lost a finger in a dimple.

'We'll figure a way, Bonar. It's one way of making sure who the casualties are. We cods it up for the few so the many get away clean.'

'Shitty but true,' Bonar admitted.

Ollie worried his dimple.

'We've got braggarts and dummies who'll crack, bubble to the law, piss their dough up against the first wall, or just plain fuck up. We got our losers, Bonar. Just let's make sure we don't lose alongside them. Right, Chas?'

'Not if you want to hire faces to have your hangovers for you when you're on the champagne-and-roses circuit.'

'That gets it said, Charlie.'

'I'll throw some curves for you if Sad Sidney "stays alive".'

'That's worth a handshake,' said Bonar.

'Glad we came.' Ollie offered his hand.

Charlie brought Connie's Beretta out of nowhere.

'Let's go fool the Turk again.'

They all went up the stairs looking sullen.

Tommy shaved with care, dressed in black and went below smoking a Havana he'd lifted from the office at the Philadelphia House.

Glaziers laid putty around new glass in the front room, and Ida was busy with the vacuum. Gordon talked to a local CID man in the hall, and Jessie played with a set of worry-beads outside the kitchen as he listened to the raised voices inside.

Tommy said: 'This whistle tasteful enough, you reckon?'

'Respectful, Bruv, that's the word. They've hauled the pantechnicon off to the police pound, and Pinky's mob have been ferried off to City Road Hospital.'

'Where's that flaming Lemmon?'

'Can't you hear? Getting a roasting from our local filth. He's well out of order and out of sorts.'

'Arthur Ax?'

'In full cry,' Jessie grinned.

Tommy cracked the kitchen door as Chief Inspector Ax said: '. . . You West End Central Cunts in Disguise are not the Flying Squad, the Vice Squad, or the Fraud Squad. They understood protocol. You understand nothing. You know nothing. You are . . . *nothing*. You have the gall to come swanning into my manor on the strength of an unlogged "anonymous" over the telephone—'

'Two actually,' Lemmon offered. 'My DC here—'

Arthur Ax bored on.

'. . . Just in time to witness an attack by rifle fire on one of my parishioners' houses. And what do you do, pray? You don't advertise your presence. You don't radio us through Central. You don't even pop your head round the door of the local nick. You do nothing about apprehending the shootist. No, you break into and enter a private dwelling without warrants. And with not so much as a "by your leave" you push innocent noses up against the wallpaper to ask a lot of irrelevant and impertinent questions of a family suffering a recent and harrowing bereavement. You assume also that an illegally parked vehicle outside the said dwelling is linked to the bereaved people inside that dwelling. How you plan to write this up for your superiors may be interesting, but it won't be half so telling as my own report on this sorry incident of blatant police harassment.'

'If I might—'

Ax's fist made cutlery jump in the table drawer.

'Don't interrupt a superior officer. You've already earned the whole ton of bricks. And even if there was something for you to investigate it was, and is, outside your very limited jurisdiction. An unlawful discharge of firearms in this manor is my responsibility and right, not yours. You could only assist me in any enquiries I may or may not make, *if* I so requested. I did not and do not make any such request. And even oddball morons like your squad couldn't in your wildest dreams make an indecent exposure charge stick against men, who, by their own admission, were stripped, robbed and held against their joint will in an enclosed vehicle by persons unknown. It was your squad who let the men out of the vehicle, so technically (and by heaven I'm tempted) you're open to the charge of exposing their nakedness to the public gaze. And the men themselves could bring a civil action against you. Do I make myself quite clear?'

Tommy closed the tirade away.

'Earns his dough, does Ax. Just see this circus is long gone by the time I come home from the undertaker's with . . . her. Right?'

'You got it, Tom.'

Tommy's sleepless eyes glittered.

'Then we start sorting.'

'About time,' said Jesse.

'More than about time.'

The drizzle died, and Soho glistened in late sunlight.

Vinnie Castle told Froggy to drive Fast Frankie Frewin home and went into Tatty Bogle's to wait for Wally Harold and Pimlico Johnny.

A weightlifter and some advertising men laughed over pints at the bar with some secretaries in mini-skirts. A pair of spades who pimped Ladbroke Grove teased Armchair Doris in their native Grenadan patois. Guitars and mumbled lyrics from the jukebox drove Vinnie and his Bacardi into a corner booth to worry over Charlie's sudden show of hard.

Froggy Farrell had crowed on *ad nauseum* about the shooting in Vallance Road after tickling Pinky Bellaver's gonads with a meat-hook in Stripes Flynn's Smithfield coldstore. If Froggy talked like that when he drove Fast Frankie home to Peckham, Vinnie knew of one ulcer that wouldn't sleep tonight, and he clicked his glass against his teeth. Archie had liked Charlie being hard. He'd laughed about it as he booked himself and Queenie on a flight to Malta and warned Vinnie not to say a dicky to Charlie until they were well gone.

'Can't have our Chas fretting his swede about me and the old woman when he's busy sorting. And I can still use the phone; it's me kneecaps that's broken, not me dialling finger.'

Vinnie's drink could have evaporated for all he tasted it.

Voices droned in the next booth as he flagged a refill.

Pimlico was frozen in the entrance with his eyes locked

on the booth next to Vinnie. He mouthed 'Filth' and went back outside.

Vinnie heard Bulstrode sort drinks for Quill, Dillman and Lemmon. That made it Payne's day off. Quill said: 'Here's the toast: Arthur Ax and his bent busies.'

Dillman sounded sick.

'Ain't there no straight law left?'

Quill gulped beer and broke wind.

'Only thee and me, lad.'

'And who's sure about thee?' Bulstrode asked.

Quill snorted froth. 'Ax will shuffle his police files and the Vallance Road Incident won't have happened. Save in our fevered imagination, that is.'

Bulstrode banged his glass down. 'All those wounds and abrasions have got to be on file at the City Road Hospital. And what's the betting they don't get themselves mysteriously burgled? Good mind to bloody lift them myself.'

'And because you're pure of heart the end would justify the means. That it, Buller?' Lemmon asked.

'Yeah, but I'm . . . .' Bulstrode's argument trailed away.

'As superior as your motivation?'

'What diff does it make, Guv? We're all back on Noddy bikes when Ax slams his report in.'

'What report? And who's got an untipped snout?'

'Ax's report,' Dillman said.

A lighter snapped, and Lemmon streamed words with smoke.

'There's more to coppering than paperwork and channels.'

'But you took twenty minutes of heavy finger right there in the bloody Fortress. Got right up my hopscotch.'

'Like I said, what report?'

Dillman didn't understand, and Lemmon watched Bulstrode shrug.

'Ax has earned us peace, you young berks. He'll have marked the Troys' cards as hard as he marked ours. Tommy can't even water an optic until Ax says he can. I'd say this was as good a time to book your annual holiday as any.'

'You're kidding,' said Bulstrode.
'I'm kidding.'
'Except you ain't.'
'Except just that. The bent law ain't stupid. Arthur Ax knows how vulnerable he is right now, and he doesn't plan to let Tommy crack heads or throw wobblies. Our Arthur's helping to bury a suicide on sacred turf, and Pinky's cuts and bruises won't be a cheap item on Tommy's shopping-list. The heavy finger'll be as far as it goes so long as we don't get caught playing Arthur's turf on the QT. All we've earned is breathing-space until after the Troy funeral. Let's not waste it, brave lads.'

Vinnie slipped from his booth and hurried towards Cambridge Circus through the last of the sunshine.

'You think the eyes and ears of the world heard enough?' Quill asked Lemmon.

'To quote his guvnor: "Oh blimey yeah." Your round, Prophet,' Lemmon said, reaching for another cigarette.

Ida Troy left beer and sandwiches in the living-room before turning in with a sleeping draught. Silversleeves Sutton sat facing Tommy, Jesse and Gordon, and tried not to stare at the coffin on trestles.

Tommy played with a black armband.

'I hope your ears have been working overtime, Sil.'

Silversleeves uncapped a light ale.

'Soho's a desert, Tom. You could run camels down Oxford Street without drawing a glance. Even the twopenny faces with nothing but bunny are nodding in their beer without a spare dicky. It's nervous. What can I tell you?'

'Who ain't on parade' Tommy's sleepless eyes rolled in dark sockets as if he tasted something inedible. 'Name names, Sil.'

'Connie Harold ain't about.'

'He's playing our turf in South Africa,' said Jesse.

'His brother Wally turns up now and again.'

Tommy shrugged. 'Who cares?'

Silversleeves sipped more ale.

'Eyetie Antoni looks like he's lost all his punters' money since Lemmon's squad have taken to being visible around his gaff.'

'Eyetie's nothing now. Not that you could lay a glove on him without half the ex-cons in the world queuing up to kick your legs away. Are the rattler firms showing their faces?'

Silversleeves nibbled his lip through a sandwich.

'They're more likely to show in Brighton, Tommy. But I did hear a casual bubble that Bonar Tree and Ollie Oliphant was seen ducking out of some porno shop off Charing Cross somewhere.'

Gordon leaned in over a crossed knee.

'With Pim in tow? Or Limehouse?'

Silversleeves tried a frown.

'I never heard that. Where'd you get it?'

'I didn't. I'm listening to you,' Gordon snapped.

'I said nothing like. All I heard about Pim was he had some country-house coaching to do. Ain't heard nothing about Limehouse.'

Jesse pointed a greasy finger round a sandwich.

'So tell us what you do know. Talk about trains. One special train.'

Silversleeves spread his hands in fright.

'What do I know from trains? Notch me up out of my league and I'll just get nosebleed. I can only give you street talk. If I'm drinking with Barry the Blag or Johnny the Builder, I'm invisible. I just listen and bring you what I get. If I noseprod too hard, they'll suss me as your snout and that's me finished. Look, Barry and Johnny are well in on all sides of the street, right? You want something special on trains, you pull them in personal and give them the sweat treatment, right? If there's anything going on a train, they'll know. I don't.'

Tommy stood to pace.

'That ain't a box of cornflakes on them trestles, Mister. I've got more than fresh putty in my windows to fret on, so how can I go boxing ears about the manors, eh? You and the likes of you got to earwig real handsome while I'm forted up in here, right?'

'But that'll take dough, Tommy.'

'So spend it, Silver. Recruit who you need. I want a grass at every important elbow night and day and dinner-times.'

Silversleeves's mind spun from the commission he'd earn.

'You got it, Tommy.'

'I'd better have.'

Gordon tapped Silversleeves's knee.

'He'd better have.'

'And here's some names for you. You listening?'

'Yeah, Tommy.'

'Bonar Tree and his soppy son . . . .'

'Smiler,' said Jesse.

'Smiler, yeah. Alfie Horrabin and that German Dennis geezer . . . .' Tommy clicked fingers at Jessie. 'And what's-his-face? That daft thick minder of German's . . . .'

'Popeye Greenland.'

'Him. Where German Dennis goes he won't be far behind. I want them all found and stuck to, right?'

'And keep your eyes peeled for Limehouse,' Jesse added.

'Specially him,' Gordon hissed.

Silversleeves sweated without control.

'I'll come up with . . . all them *and* your special rattler.'

Gordon pointed his finger at Silversleeves for all of them.

'See you do. We don't take kind to loud talk and nothing in the kitty. See you don't come up empty.'

Tommy dug fingers into Gordon's shoulder.

'No, we don't, Gordy. You came up empty on Limehouse when I wanted him planted before her lying back there in that coffin. So you ain't the one to shout the odds at our Sil, are you?'

'No, guess not, Tommy . . . .'

'Just give Silver some decent dough and see him out.'

'Yes, Tom.' Gordon bit the inside of his cheek and tasted blood.

Tommy gave him a dark and hollow look. ' "Yes,

Tom" is right.'

Silversleeves couldn't wait to be back in the street. He shuffled towards the door with: 'I'd like to pay me respects when you drop the coffin, Tommy. Three o'clock Friday, ain't it?'

'Appreciate that, Sil, but I want you earwigging the cobbles.'

'You got it, Tom.'

Silversleeves took his money into the warm night with fear and greed bubbling in his stomach. A train tickle with two firms up and the Troys wanting first blood was too rich for a small grass like Silversleeves, and he knew with dread certainty that he was as good as dead if he botched it. He could still feel Gay Gordon's dead eyes boring into his back long after he had turned the last corner in Vallance Road and trotted through gyppo barrows to the main road.

Back in the house, Gay Gordon watched Tommy pace as Jesse ate with his mouth open.

Tommy was on a talking jag.

'Kosher Kramer thought he was boxing clever with us when he let more than enough slip to nail Bonar and Alfie's firms to this train tickle. That kind of heavy dough'll take some heavy laundering abroad, right? And it's a duck's rear-end to a fried egg they ain't going through the Ogle firm for that, right? And if Connie Harold ain't in it's definitely down to German Dennis. And with two firms being shunted about that ties Oliphant and Pimlico Johnny into the tickle as first and second coachmen, right? Ties it all up in pink ribbon, does that.'

Gordon uncrossed a knee and said: 'Still means we can't hit the cobbles too soon.'

A nerve ticked in Tommy's jaw. 'Softly, softly advice from our Gordy?'

'Arthur Ax himself would stitch us if we hit the cobbles now.'

'Who's gonna tell him? You?'

'Nobody's telling nobody nothing.'

Tommy pointed both thumbs. 'Ain't they now? And I figured I was telling you.'

Jesse watched Tommy stroke the coffin. His brother had aged ten years in as many days.

'Let's sleep on it, Bruv.'

Tommy's hand lay on black polish.

'She's sleeping for all of us.'

'All the same, Bruv . . . .'

'No "all the same" about it. Them train bandits are all family men. Got wives and kids. Hard men fold if there's an accident in the school playground, if a kid gets splashed with acid in the home, or if a runaway motor goes up the pavement when somebody's missus is shoplifting a bit of supper. You see? We get the poppy or the train-ticklers start losing their dearly beloveds.'

'Don' mean we can't sleep on it, Bruv.'

Tommy's mouth writhed as he caressed the coffin.

'Ain't this the longest sleep there is? Why sleep on what we used to do without thinking about it? Or has your bottle gone, Jessie? Or is she dead on account your Scotch poof told naughty porkies about her? And how come Gordy couldn't find Limehouse? Afraid his story might be different, Gordy?'

Gordon swallowed air. 'No danger of that.'

'No danger of you burying that Lou before her like you swore you would,' said Tommy.

'Easy, Bruv. Gordy bubbled straight.'

'Fucking great. Fucking handsome. Fucking no danger there. A fucking relief all round. I'll scurf Ida out of kip and have her clap herself stupid.'

'Easy, Bruv,' Jesse soothed.

Tommy choked on anguish.

'How can this be good? Him sitting there and her lying here. Her gone and him breathing my air.'

Gordon's teeth met through his inner lip.

Tommy sagged across the coffin, and Jessie embraced him clumsily.

'Get it out, Tommy son.'

'You saw what she writ on the mirrors. All that fucking filth. All them lies I never knew she had in her. Must have had worms in her fucking head.'

'Yeah, Bruv . . . .'

'Worms. And he just sits there.'

Jesse sent Gordon away with a jerk of his head.

'Don't let me love nothing again.'

'No, Bruv . . . .'

'Fucking never.'

'No, Bruv.'

'Fucking promise.'

'Just you and me, Tom. You and me. Like always.'

Alone in the hallway, Gordon held himself and shook. Consumed by blind jealousy. Excluded from warped filial affection.

'You and me, right, Jesse?'

'You and me. Always.'

Vinnie Castle let DC Payne trail him to the Cambridge Club and left him standing in the dusk of Old Compton Street. Wally Harold was at the bar with a solitary pint.

'Pim ducked out of Tatty's when he clocked Lemmon's squad. Thought he'd come on here.'

Wally ordered Vinnie a white rum.

'He did. But only to say he was going out of town for a couple or three days with that Ollie Oliphant. Said you'd get the picture.'

'Framed and bloody varnished. That's bloody sudden.'

'Well, you know Pim. If he ain't wearing a wad on his hip he figures he's just another mumper on the skids. This country-house caper'll earn him enough beer vouchers until we get the one-arm bandit circuit sorted, so how bad?'

Vinnie lost the drink without tasting it. Knew he had to get to Charlie faster than fast. Somebody was about to nick a train, and the timing couldn't have been worse.

'Back later.'

Vinnie ran in search of a phone.

BOOK TWO

CHAPTER ELEVEN

THE CALL had come at three in the morning.

Lemmon made good time on the road to Aylesbury, and birdsong pecked the dawn as the eastern sky flamed and pearled. He parked on a verge beside a roadblock and nibbled at a yawn as a uniformed sergeant nodded over his warrant card.

'The Chief Constable of Buckinghamshire and Detective Chief Superintendent Cotton are up there under the bridge. They said for you to go straight on up, sir.'

'Thanks.'

Lemmon trudged through unseasonal chill and found the two men under Bridego railway viaduct. He peeled a glove and shook hands with CC Bunny Halliday and DCS Saul Cotton.

'Well met, Theo.'

Halliday could have been another sparrow greeting the day. He smiled across Lemmon at the head of the Flying Squad.

'DCS Cotton thinks you might be of some use to us. On the old QT, of course.'

Cotton nodded like a schoolmaster, his face puffed by a bad summer cold.

'It's just possible,' he admitted.

'In Buckinghamshire, sirs both?' Lemmon asked.

Halliday's laugh denied a sleepless night.

'I don't usually let you London wallahs grab off the plums in my manor, Theo. But this tickle is a trifle rich for our slender resources. These chummies planned too well *not* to have received excellent inside information.'

Lemmon looked out over hedgerows and rutted fields. 'About what? Sheep-stealing?'

Cotton pointed at the vaulted brickwork overhead.

'A mail train. They stopped it on a sixpence right where they wanted it. And no amateur separated the HVP coach and engine from the rest of the rolling stock.'

Cotton blew into a handkerchief.

'The last item we need is a noisy DI who ate a big breakfast. Join me on the track when you've briefed him, Halliday. *If* you still want him, that is.'

Cotton used the handkerchief again, studied it gloomily and went away up the incline.

'Glad you could join us, Theo.'

Lemmon grunted at empty fields.

'You've got the clout to order it, Bunny, even over Headmaster Cotton's pointed old head.'

'Suggested, Theo. World of difference.'

'You're a truly political animal. Even at grammar school you just had to take office. From milk monitor to head prefect, there you were, achieving away like mad. Squeaky-clean shoes and shiny, shiny badges. You haven't changed, Bunny.'

Bunny wagged a finger.

'The achiever's first law of survival. Surround yourself with the most able and add a whipping boy or two. But I never did oust you as captain of the first eleven, though.'

'In debate you had wings. On the rugby field, three left feet. You talked and I made the tries. It was a winning combination. What's an HVP coach?'

'High-Value Packages. Registered mail — that sort of thing.'

Bunny saw their past whip away with Lemmon's breath.

'But we're not talking about grannie's birthday pennies for Jack and Jill. The train was carrying 2.5 million of defaced currency south for incineration. That kind of money tends to weigh more heavily in the public consciousness than some small shopkeeper's cracked skull.'

Lemmon cracked his knuckles.

'So somebody did get hurt, but you only want to talk about the money.'

Bunny slapped his gloves together.

'Don't act the naïve cynic, Theo. Crimes against property always take precedence over crimes against the person. That's *the* fact of life. Screams of outrage from the establishment must always drown the crows of delight from the gutter press. We have to nail these bastards before Fleet Street turns them into latter-day Robin Hoods.'

'If this becomes a murder hunt, it'll temper the extreme views of both sides.'

'Take my word, Theo. The two and half mill will grab the headlines. Not the blood on the line.'

'Five bob says I hope you're wrong.'

'Can you work with Cotton?'

'Straight?'

'When was it ever otherwise between us?'

'Don't tempt me, Bunny. Nobody works *with* Cotton. You work under him or not at all. He takes scalps, not collars. All the limelight's his by divine right. He'll use me until I'm used up, then I'll be just another dogend on his office floor. This won't end with me smelling of violets.'

'You don't smell like that now, do you?' Halliday's question was silky. 'Otherwise you'd have made commander – not be some menial button-man with an inspector's pension. And you've no friends at court, have you?'

'Meaning I've no choice but to nod a lot.'

'That's the kind of thing, Theo. Walk the track with me.'

'Three bags full, sir.'

'If you say so.'

Halliday led off up the embankment where he scaled chippings down the incline.

'Where you've parked that scruffy motor of yours is where the chummies left their army vehicles whilst they stripped the HVP coach. A lorry and a couple of land-rovers we think. We're putting out television appeals for witnesses to army manoeuvres in the area. Not a bad cover the chummies chose, eh?'

'They'll have needed a lot of local garaging.'

'We thought of that.'

Cotton stood beneath a light gantry just south of Sears Crossing and pointed down the bank when Halliday and Lemmon joined him.

'That's where they waited for the train to stop at the signal they'd rigged to show red. They snatched the fireman when he came back to use the telephone. The local evidence officer found cigarette-butts in the grass. The chummies gave the fireman a smoke whilst they were bashing the driver's head in. Their own finger-tamed engine-driver couldn't make the engine run, so they got the regular driver awake and made him take them down the track. The poor basket flinched every time the interview-room door opened or closed. That's one man our chummies have broken.'

Again, Lemmon wondered why he was there.

'How many chummies were there?' he asked.

Cotton blasted air into his handkerchief.

'Fourteen, fifteen. It's either one big firm or a grab-bag of freelancers. And they're holed up not more than thirty minutes' drive from this spot.'

Halliday shivered inside his upturned collar.

'They hauled 180 High Value Package sacks down the embankment, and all we've got are eighty sorters who saw nothing, a bit of bloody cloth, a few scuffs in the turf, two cigarette-butts and tyre-tracks. Oh, and a mailsack they left by the pond.'

Cotton tapped a heel against a sleeper.

'According to the Post Office and British Railways, there could have been over five million aboard. Makes one think, eh?'

Lemmon stopped himself shrugging.

'A lot of heavy poppy.'

Bunny kept his smile despite the chill wind.

'The Treasury is terrified of copy-cat crimes once the amount of the haul gets out. They've passed their fears on to the Home Office, and I pass them on to you two. Slamming these chummies hard and fast is the only way of forestalling other similar attempts.'

Lemmon's grin was sour.

'Yeah, you're still talking about the money.'

'It's what makes the world go round, Theo. And that's why we want their noisome and troublesome arses in the dock at the Old Bailey fast. And it shouldn't matter to you *why* they draw massive sentences, just so long as they do. Property before people — despite the present faddish groundswell of silly socialism. Understand that and go far, Theo.'

'Bunny, Chief Constable, sir, you're a reactionary old fart.'

'Of course I am, dear old boy. And you'll be grateful for it when you see the enormous resources you'll have to nail these villains to the mast of the Ship of State. Wield the hammer and leave your idiotic views at home with your slippers. Don't cloud the issue with your painful honesty. You cannot afford it.'

Cotton's eyes reflected nothing but sky.

'My Flying Squad is manned by hardnoses and pirates. They know how to think like villains long enough to catch the bastards. But if a man walks through sewers for a living, then ordure is bound to rub off on even the whitest soul. Coppers buy villains, villains buy some of ours. Happens every day. Only thing left to squabble over is the price. Can you be bought, Inspector Lemmon?'

Lemmon chilled a back filling with a hard sip of air.

'Maybe nobody found my price.'

'Don't be flippant,' Bunny snapped.

'I wasn't. Corruption before breakfast is a bit hard to take, sirs both.'

Bunny lost patience.

'Hoity-toity. Just take your squad out of the usual channels. Information is leaking through too many holes in the system. We think we can trust you to get results without compromising the investigation proper. Is that oblique enough for your proper tight-buttocked mind?'

Lemmon scanned the Tring Canal and the road to Leighton Buzzard.

'A funny way for County and Met to carry on.'

'Unorthodox, but not without precedence, wouldn't you agree?' Bunny asked Cotton.

Cotton inspected his handkerchief for clues and lifted his blocked nostrils to a warm scurry of wind.

'Buy us some villains, Inspector Lemmon. Before the waters become as muddy as your name in certain quarters of the force. I can help you over one member who really has it in for you. No need for names, is there?'

Lemmon laughed into the wind.

'Arthur Ax isn't a name I mind spitting on.'

'But your spit hasn't the trajectory to hit the sole of his boot. Mine will drown him from a great height. You can consider Ax off your back before much longer. Not immediately, though; he has the Troys bottled up, and I like it that way. I make myself clear?'

'As crystal.'

Bunny looked at his half-hunter.

'Follow us along, Theo. Come and meet my local CID chaps and read over the relevant statements.'

Lemmon watched him link arms with Cotton to walk back to the black Rolls under Bridego Viaduct. A lark ascended from green corn to ride the first warm thermal of the day. Lemmon watched it climb in a spiral of song before he scanned the misty fields for something only he could see.

'Is this tickle down to you, Charlie? Did Archie teach you that well?'

The day died stillborn.

Cold inverted air had brought industrial pollution down from Luton and the Midlands beyond. Noon had been no brighter than the brief false dawn and the afternoon was a grey excuse of tainted fog.

Pimlico followed Ollie Oliphant's tail-lights down a

rutted lane under a stand of yew and willow, through a cattle-wallow and round a hard curve with a reverse camber. His bladder protested for the last mile of the cross-country route from Oxford where they had bought the two Aston Martins.

Pimlico grinned like a broken pot and knew he should have slept instead of playing the sandwich game on Dotty's water-bed; but to Pim's mind Dotty was worth more than some lost sleep, and her black pimp was coming home to a change of management. It made no difference to Pimlico that Dotty had sold her cherry for cash money; he could see nothing so awful when he'd sold his muscle to the highest bidder. And the ten grand he got for this tickle would set him up nicely in Charlie's slot-machine firm.

Pimlico followed Ollie up an incline where bald roots writhed from eroded soil. Both vehicles crested a razorback ridge, and Ollie's lights lost themselves in bracken and saplings. Pimlico took the drop as squarely as he could, pump-braking to stop side-slips on the boggy ground. Then the cars were through a copse of birch and into a lane bordered by baby oaks the dull copper of old pennies. Low branches slapped the cars and left smears of green mould on the paintwork. They chicaned down a muddy track and halted beside a wooden building where a khaki-drab lorry stood under a tarp nailed to poles.

Pimlico relieved himself against the offside wheel.

'Smells like a manure factory.'

Ollie's chubby smile drove crinkles into his sandy hair.

'It's what pigs make beside bacon.'

Pimlico stamped circulation back into his feet.

'What's that other pen-and-ink?'

Ollie's eyes made oriental curves.

'The chaps tried to burn some mail-sacks. Made too much black smoke, though.'

'Mail-bleeding-sacks? What's occurring?'

'Work it out. Come ahead.'

Pimlico barked a shin in a darkened passage.

'Pay the light bill, somebody.'

'Here.'

Ollie lifted a heavy blackout curtain, and Pimlico found himself in a long room crowded with men he knew by sight or reputation. A generator thumped and a rabbit bubbled in a pot. A retired engine-driver dealt himself a hand of patience, and Bonar Tree's four-man firm played Monopoly with real money, their gloves making them clumsy with cards and dice.

Pimlico shook hands around the table in a daze.

Bonar laughed at his surprise, and Alfie Horrabin gave Pimlico a beer and a sandwich, his brown berry of a face creased in smiles.

'Old home week, eh, young Pim? Look at the face on him, Ollie; you done well keeping him in the dark. Pimlico, if you hadn't been doing bird when this first come up, you'd have been in for a full-whack of 150,000 oncers. That's villas, class crumpet and a Ferrari. Still, ten grand ain't too shabby, right?'

Pimlico sank into a chair and let them all laugh at his lop-sided expression. Brixton Billy burned Paratroop Regiment uniforms in the fireplace, and Popeye Greenland lit a Woodbine with a blackened ten-shilling note. German Dennis counted notes on a trestle table, and Buster Brown packed them into suitcases and kitbags. Scottish, Irish and English currency was heaped on every available surface, and the too-badly soiled ones were scattered carelessly on the floor.

'Who brung the firms together, Ollie?' asked Pim as Alfie did a jig amongst tattered notes.

'Came natural, Pim. Bonar's firm got the inside tip, and Alfie had the expertise to work the rattler. German Dennis can launder the dough through his German-Swiss contacts, and he wanted Buster and Popeye in for crowd control. With us on the wheels it worked out neat.'

German Dennis looked up from his calculations.

'Over two mill so far.'

German Dennis was a South Londoner who earned his nickname from regular dipping trips to Oktoberfests where he did well until armed police caught him on a tram with several dozen wallets and banged him up in a Bavarian prison. Four years in a cell with an Austrian forger had perfected his French and German. He skimmed Pimlico a wad of notes.

'Only half what we expected. Should have been nearly six million. Still, buy yourself an aeroplane.'

Ollie snatched the money out of the air and weighed it.

'Maybe a plane ain't such a bad notion with the Old Bill on to our army vehicles dodge. We can't use the lorry or the land-rovers.'

Buster Brown punched a meaty thigh.

'I spent three days putting a false floor in that lorry.'

'Wasted your time, then, didn't you?'

'Shit and derision,' Buster explained.

Bonar Tree stopped haggling over Bond Street.

'You didn't get that out of a Christmas cracker, Ollie.'

'Monitored the police bands. They had an appeal for witnesses on the midday news. And that means there's no point in staying on at the farm over the weekend.'

Bonar agreed and offered another grand for Bond Street.

Brixton Billy traded glances with Alfie. A nerveless and natural actor, he had once faked a diabetic fit to distract the railway police from Alfie's activities in the guard's van of the Brighton Belle. Only when he was about to be pumped full of insulin did he jump from the moving ambulance. He winked solemnly at Pimlico and said: 'They'll have a helicopter up by then. Time we was all well gone.'

Buster got angry when faced with the need to think rapidly.

'You wanna tell us how?'

'Yeah.'

Popeye stood alongside Buster to flex his arms, reminding Pimlico of a pair of ugly bookends.

'There's the horsebox Pim drove up from the Smoke,' Bonar suggested.

Brixton snorted at that.

'Be serious, you clown. Fifteen grown faces in a horsebox with all that poppy? I can just see the law turning a blind eye to us lot coasting down Clapham High Street.'

Ollie cut the air with the edge of his hand.

'Academic. I had Pim dump it in Aylesbury on the way here.'

Popeye thought that was fine with him.

'Bang goes his ten-grand drink, then. No box, no poppy.'

'Yeah,' Buster agreed.

Unperturbed, Ollie winked at Pimlico.

'He'll be on a full earner before we're through. There are two Aston Martins outside. Me and Pim can buy another cash car tomorrow. We'll ferry you, or you can drive yourselves. Either way, we draw straws for who goes when and how. Fair?'

Bonar nodded for his whole firm.

'Fair. But don't buy another Aston Martin or we'll look like a bloody rally.'

Brixton thought that was fair comment.

'Get a saloon that'll take four faces and all their dough.'

Bonar threw white cards on to the Monopoly board.

'My Utilities and three grand for Bond Street, Smiler.'

Popeye crashed a fist on to the board.

'Sod sodding Bond Street. Let's get some deciding done.'

Smiler grinned at Popeye's stupidity.

'That's my top hat on the floor.'

'And my boot,' said Bonar. 'Whatever happened to sportsmanship?'

'Gone walkies with Popeye's brain,' said Smiler.

Popeye loomed over Smiler.

'And which cream puff's hiding behind his daddy, then?'

Bonar became quiet and dangerous, and Pimlico moved to cover his blind side.

'You're all meat and no gravy, Popeye. Go away and sit on your brains. Like now.'

Popeye resorted to bluster.

'Who's whack does the jam-jar come out of, then? I ain't whacking out for some snob-job of a Jag. Let that poxy solicitor who bought this place bring us some wheels. He's in for a full whack, so he can afford some wheels, right?'

Alfie played with his cap.

'I'm cycling out. You'll see my whack down to Bournemouth for me, won't you, Ollie?'

'Everybody should take care of his own whack,' said Popeye.

'Yeah,' Buster agreed. 'Definitely.'

German Dennis rubbed tired eyes.

'You two may be handy with a stave, but you've got fly-turds for intelligence. You want to get yourselves out with your dough without help, do it. You wouldn't get to the first main road. So don't tell your elders and betters how to get business done. Ollie's right; we'll need Pimlico, and that means a full whack. Right, Bonar?'

'I'll talk about it,' Bonar shrugged.

'Ten grand ain't a small drink,' Popeye insisted.

'Definitely.'

Buster blinked to keep up with the arguments.

'Will you take my dough for me?' Alfie asked Ollie.

'Sure. You lot get your deciding done. Me and Pim'll wait in the kitchen.'

Ollie ushered Pimlico out and they leaned either side of the cluttered sink.

'When thieves fall out, eh?' said Pimlico.

'When they've argued the toss they'll see you all right.'

Pimlico raked hair from his face.

'Only two million and it should have been six? Every grass in London and the Home Counties will be out for a slice of the action, if not the reward money. And the big firms'll want their cut. They won't have a friend they can trust, not even each other.'

Ollie looked and sounded comfortable.

'Ain't that always the way? All we have to do is box clever and don't run daft with fistfuls of money. Whatever you earn out of this, Pim, lose it. Forget it for a good long spell and go back to whatever you was doing before. You stay with Charlie's slot-machine tickle and look like butter wouldn't melt.'

'But there's a problem. Charlie. He'll have guessed what this was all about before I did.'

'So flaming what?'

'Charlie ain't no charitable organisation.'

Ollie rolled hands on his belly before pointing a steady finger close to Pimlico's nose.

'Listen up good. Apart from me, Charlie's the only face I know who ain't done time. That makes him a bit special in my book. Makes us closer than most brothers. If Charlie had wanted this caper, he'd have taken it. He didn't. He don't. He just don't want to see all kinds of funny money buying trouble in his manors, right? So keep that right up front of your suspicious bit of a brain. I ain't going down for this tickle, so don't make me regret I brought you in on it. I like to think I talk and trust where I know it ain't wasted.'

Pimlico washed beer over his tongue.

'I'm on your team, Ollie. We're thinking in the same street.'

Ollie nodded and toyed with a miniature cigar.

'See I don't regret, Pim. I want you thinking like our bike wheels are caught in the same tramlines. Come on, we've got some heavy coaching to do before we play millionaires.'

Sergeant Quill hanged Charlie Dance from a crude gallows with strokes of a ballpoint, Bulstrode tapped out a docket, Payne goosed a camera and Dillman blew moody rings at the silent telephones. The squad had little to do but contemplate their failures.

Quill added a vulture to his gallows.

Archie Ogle convalesced in Malta, and Connie Harold had disappeared to South Africa. The Troys kept a low profile, and Charlie Dance cruised Soho in Archie's white Rolls as if he owned the place.

Quill gave the vulture glasses and a trilby and thought about tomorrow's funeral. Half the villains in Christendom would be in black armbands when Tommy dropped Helen's coffin, and they'd have emptied Covent Garden of hothouse daisies to show respect for a girl they took no notice of when she'd been alive. All that floral cynicism, and an honest copper hardly rated a wilted tulip if he died during the course of duty. Quill drew a coffin under the gallows and an internal blinked silently.

'Your turn, Dillman.' Quill honoured the hangman with his own features. 'Probably a lost dog.'

'Or some moggie up a tree,' said Dillman.

Bulstrode used Tippex on a mistake.

'Or the Queen Mum inviting Buller to a dainty tea up the Palace.'

Payne focused a long lens through the window.

Quill put the phone to his face. 'Lost Property. Umbrellas speaking.'

'Repeat that if you want to get rained on.'

Quill paled. 'Yessir. Humorous quip. Sorry, Sir.'

Payne framed a shot of his desk calendar. 'Three redtops and a yoghurt, Milkman.'

'Since when did you have a sense of humour?' Lemmon asked from Aylesbury.

'How can I help you, Sir?'

'Are they all there?'

'Yessir.'

'Have yourselves and overnight bags at the Victoria helipad in one hour.'

'May I ask . . .?'

'You may not.'

'Thank you, Sir.'

'Haven't you seen the Stop Press?' Lemmon cleared down.

Payne looked up from his Pentax. 'Mothering Sunday. It wasn't . . . .'

'Wasn't it just,' said Quill. 'Christ, I get airsick.'

Bulstrode spilled correction fluid. 'You ain't flying off somewhere?'

Quill swept things into a drawer. 'We all are.'

'Not an out-of-towner when I've talked a certain little

darling into pulling my train to Paradise and back?'

'Different train. You can't cold-tap this one.'

Dillman's jaw dropped. 'That train?'

Quill dated an armaments docket above Lemmon's signature.

'Get that rubber-stamped downstairs. Move.'

Bulstrode exchanged casual sex for thoughts of promotion.

'Last one there patrols a duck reserve in the Orkneys.'

Pimlico hummed to keep himself awake.

German Dennis and Bonar Tree had slept all the way to Newhaven, no more company than their cases of money. They boarded a sleek sixty-footer without a backward glance, and Pimlico watched it cut out to sea in a chevron of white wake, making sixteen knots towards the Brittany coast, before he drove back to Buckinghamshire by a different route.

The coast road to Brighton had been a refrigerator, the fog closed in at Watford and was a blinding blanket when he reached Aylesbury.

Pimlico parked on a transport café forecourt and waited.

The café windows were yellow flags, and the tarps of the parked artics had the damp sheen of elephant hide in the tainted smog. The smell of fried food and overboiled tea churned Pimlico's stomach, and he rolled a cigarette to keep his hands busy.

A red Hillman stopped alongside his Aston Martin, and Ollie rolled down his window to say: 'Did they get away with their holiday money?'

'Clockwork. This smog's a bit tasty, though.'

'Same for the law. They can't use helicopters in this.' Ollie watched his rearview mirrors and stroked his wheel. 'Brixton Billy and Smiler took the other Aston, so they're well away. Alfie cycled to Oxford, so there's only Popeye and Buster at the farm. The rest of the daft tossers have gone to the solicitor's house in a van one of the wives drove up.'

Pimlico drummed on the dash. 'Too many people. What

about the army vehicles and the farm itself?'

Ollie lied as comfortably as an armchair storyteller: 'That's all down to Sidney Salt. All you have to do is get Popeye and Buster back to the Smoke. I've got the local traffic wallies up my exhaust, so it's time I showed them what a coachman with a set of tuned wheels can do. Draw them off your tail-lights.'

Pimlico felt breathless. 'Sidney Salt ain't coming, Ollie. Vinnie tipped me the nod the old tosser topped himself on a warehouse job three weeks back. I thought Vinnie would have told you.'

'How? I ain't been about, have I?'

Pimlico watched Ollie pretend to think, and his empty stomach snarled at him. The spectre of prison made him want to eat, to urinate, break wind or run into the anonymous night. He chewed a nail and did nothing.

Ollie stopped thinking to smile.

'Changes nothing, right? Get yourself a cup of tea and a seat by the café window. When I've drawn Tall John away, you get back to the farm and get them two clowns back to London.'

'I can't just leave you . . . .'

'Just do it,' Ollie snapped.

Pimlico locked his car and walked into steam and noise. The Beatles banged out from a jukebox and a pinball machine pinged up millions. Pimlico stirred his urn tea with a spoon chained to the counter, and a plump Kim Novak sandwiched burned bacon into sliced bread. In a window-seat he wiped a hole in condensation to watch Ollie create a speed-wobble as he drove away.

'Bloody cowboy,' said a lorry-driver. 'Screwing up a new car before it gets to the showroom. I hope the law turns him over.'

Pimlico refused a Woodbine and crossed his fingers.

'Me, too, brother.'

Ollie overtook two lorries on a blind curve and cut ahead of them on the straight. Air-brakes hissed as the leading lorry avoided jack-knifing and collision. Ollie ran up through the gears and closed on the next artic. Buffeted by backwash, he matched speed, his nose in against its tailgate. Ollie flicked out and braked hard before building speed. The police car on his tail seemed to reverse away as he accelerated into thick smog.

On a straight stretch Ollie killed his lights, swung into the hard shoulder and mounted a grass bank beside an elevated pedestrian walkway, reversing his direction with a hard swing of the wheel. Clods of grass screwed out from his rear wheels. He ground in a half-circle and turned his nose up the bank.

The police car belled past at seventy and lost itself in the murk.

Ollie snicked into first gear, hacked through a wooden fence and rolled to a halt on a feeder down-ramp, his VHF radio tuned to the police frequency.

A mobile gave the code for hot pursuit and Control acknowledged in a spray of static.

A second mobile gave co-ordinates for interception as it approached from the south-east. A third and fourth closed in from the west.

Ollie waited and hummed around an unlit Gold Flake.

Four minutes later a panda passed him, braking hard as it overshot. Ollie barrelled out and past with a coat of paint to spare. The panda stalled as the driver hovered between forward and reverse gears. Ollie leaned on his horn and swept out on to a dual carriageway.

He shaved the nose of a creeping family saloon and slewed into the fast lane ahead of another articulated lorry.

Horns blared and red lights bled into the overcast.

Ollie took the Hillman towards Oxford at 120 miles per hour. The second mobile was closing fast, and the third and fourth mobiles would intercept him at the next major intersection. He pumped his brakes to confuse the following police car, spun himself on to the central reservation and roared back the way he had come. The panda went past and speed-wobbled to a screaming halt with an artic trying not to climb over its boot. Ollie skipped through the oncoming traffic and made a hard, short turn. A Spitfire left tyrestripes as it swerved around him, and a coach threw up stones and weed as it carved furrows in the verge.

Ollie swept past the artic and panda as the police walked back to shout up into the artic's cab. Ahead were the revolving lights of a crash-tender and the milky swathe of panda headlights. Motorcycle outriders were flagging the traffic to a halt.

Ollie jumped the Hillman forward and arrowed into a concealed sliproad, the exit ramp of a service station closed for repairs. He rolled drums filled with concrete aside and put them back in a neat line when he had parked the Hillman on bare concrete beside rusted pumps.

A dog barked from an unseen kennel and the police bells gradually faded into traffic brawl as he stripped the car of his commercial delivery-plates.

Ollie locked the keys inside the Hillman and lit his Gold Flake.

'Pick the bones out of that,' he said.

The farmhouse reeked of bodies and oil-lamps.

Pimlico pushed Popeye Greenland in the chest and poked a finger at Buster Brown.

'You're both as pissed as puddens. If Bonar or German was here, you'd earn more than a paper hat, the pair of you.'

'So's he.'

Popeye slopped beer at Buster Brown, who fell into a chair laughing.

'So'm I.'

Popeye glared at Pimlico as if it was his fault that the room revolved.

'High and mighty Bonar-sodding-Tree and German-bleeding-Dennis are on their way to Portu-sodding-gal, ain't they? Gone off, the pair of them, and left me 'n' Buster here like a couple of lemons, jumping at every noise and with nothing else to do but gargle the bloody ullage. Who says the country's quiet, eh? Nothing but moos, pig-farts and miles of bloody trees swishing and banging about. 'S terrible.'

Pimlico tried to remember what he had touched.

'You should have cleaned this place up to stop the law from finding anything. You ain't even wearing your gloves.'

Popeye staggered in a half-circle.

' 'S all going whoosh in the morning. Bonar said. Your oh-so-clever-bloody-Bonar.'

Pimlico wiped off the chair he'd sat in.

'Bonar's wrong this time.'

'He's never wrong. Told me so. Sure as God's a bloody woman. Ain't that right, Popeye son?' said Buster.

'Never bloody wrong, Bonar.'

'Thassa truth.'

'What's the use?' Pimlico went into the kitchen where paper plates and congealed food was a foul clutter. He pocketed the Bass bottle he'd drunk from and decided he could afford to risk a bonfire. He smashed all the cups and glasses he could find and loaded the debris into orange-boxes heaped with bread-wrappers and egg-cartons. Stuffed a sleeping-bag with anything that would readily burn, hauled it all into the yard, doused it in cooking oil and set it alight. In the fitful glow he saw the yellow paint Buster had daubed on the lorry in an attempt to disguise it as a brick company vehicle, the raw scar where Brixton had buried the mail-sacks and frightened the engine-driver who thought it was his grave because he'd failed to move the train on to the viaduct.

Pimlico remembered Bonar Tree laughing at the driver's fear, but he'd take this madhouse a lot more seriously. Popeye and Buster giggling and knocking heads as if the whole caper was nothing more than a Crown and Anchor con in Crisp Street Market. Pimlico killed the idea of laying tyre-irons against their skulls and went back inside.

'Move it, you two.'

Popeye dragged his suitcase clumsily.

'Where's Ollie?'

'Saving our backsides with some fancy coachwork. Keep your voices down. Sound does funny things in the fog.' Pimlico knew dawn was a bare hour away.

'Pardon us for breathing.'

Buster sprawled against the car, tangled up with his kitbag.

Popeye giggled and his pink eyes rolled.

Pimlico got them into the car and slammed the boot on their money. The bonfire was well alight and black motes whirled in the tongues of flame. Once Pimlico was east of Luton he could run through Hatfield into Essex and clear the freakish local conditions. Then on into East London and relative safety.

He hoped.

CHAPTER TWELVE

HUMIDITY rose with the sun.

Vinnie nibbled Ingrid's toast as Doc Rudge cut the plaster from Charlie's arm.

'Swallow and talk to me, Vin.'

Charlie flexed fingers as his arm was turned between Doc Rudge's hands.

'Worked like a charm. Mrs Armitage identified Sad Sidney as her husband Alfred who went missing from home last April. Threw a lovely wobbly for the coroner and cremated the body yesterday afternoon. Tucked her five hundred up her knicker-leg and disappeared back to Romford right as ninepence.'

'One bent busy off your back, Doc.'

Charlie shrugged into a white shirt and tied a black tie.

Rudge's smile was a rictus of parchment and bone.

'So I kiss your feet, metaphorically speaking. You're going to the funeral in Bethnal Green?'

'I don't go to funerals. I promised Limehouse I'd look over the railings, check out the floral tributes to the late lamented Mrs Troy. Archie would have gone and looked solemn if he was here. Vinnie and Ingrid can do the honours instead.'

Vinnie fired a Player with a Swan Vesta.

'I don't trust Tommy. Even if funerals are neutral turf.'

'Tommy's more interested in the train money than starting naughties with us. He's got snouts all over the manors,' Charlie said as Ingrid left the bedroom to answer the phone in the living-room.

Vinnie grinned and said: 'All they'll end up with is string that's lost its balloon. More tall tales floating around

Soho than at a fishermen's outing. What with the Flying Squad and all them snouts eager to buy the drinks, you can get legless without the change of a tanner. The only missing faces are Lemmon's squad. Must have gone on their holidays or something.'

Charlie horned himself into black shoes.

'Work on that "or something", Vinnie. If Lemmon and Quill don't have Payne taking pictures all over the Troy funeral, you can bet your pension they're coming at us from an angle we haven't sussed.'

Ingrid came into the bedroom to ask Charlie for a private word. He followed her into the kitchen and her face was drawn when she closed the door with her back.

'Dotty's on the phone. Looking for Pim.'

'So?'

'She called me Gladys – Pim's sister's name. She's scared, Charlie, but she's thinking straight.'

Charlie chafed a wrist.

'Like somebody's listening over her shoulder?'

'Just . . . like that. I said to hold on . . . I'd find him.'

'You have, right?'

Charlie went into the living-room and held the phone to his face. He listened to Dotty breathe and thought he picked up a masculine whisper.

'Dotty love?'

'Pim? Is that you, Pim?'

'That's my name.'

'Can you come home . . . I mean to my place?'

'Why?'

'Please, Pim. I'll explain when you . . . get here.'

'Calm down. I've got some ducking and diving to do. And there's the funeral this afternoon.'

'You've . . . *got* to come, Pim.'

'Now, hold up them horses.'

'How soon can you . . . get here?'

Dotty's intakes of breath were louder and more distinct than her actual words.

'Hour maybe.'

'Christ, Pim . . . .'

Charlie put heat into his voice.

'I've got a business to run, you know. And if this is your daft goldfish drowning again I ain't gonna be pleased.'

'Please, please, Pim . . . .'

'Do my best, right?'

Charlie broke the connection with a slam and knuckled his upper lip. Deaf to Ingrid's pleas for information, he stared at her as if she were a trick of the light. Looked at his forearm as if he had never seen it before.

'Feel naked,' he said.

'Charlie?'

Ingrid skipped aside as Charlie walked through her. He hauled Vinnie off the bed and told him to whistle up Nasty and Sodbonce.

'You're taking Ingrid to the funeral with them in tow. And make double sure you're all seen, right?'

'Anything else while you're throwing a wobbly?'

'Will Bulstrode take a hot bubble from you after we conned him over that meet with Connie?'

'If it's hot enough.'

'You'll find him at Aylesbury nick. Give him Ollie Oliphant.'

'What?'

Charlie patted Vinnie's cheek.

'There's a good reason, son.'

'I don't like it, Chas.'

'Then, don't — just do it. And give me your throwing-shiv.'

'Since when did you go tooled up?'

Charlie ignored the question.

'Doc, my arm hurts. I want the plaster back on.'

He slapped Vinnie's knife into Rudge's palm.

'With this inside.'

'For why, Charlie?'

'There's this sick goldfish . . . .'

Sergeant Quill focused binoculars on Leatherslade Farm.

Cows lay in the lee of the hedge behind him and the farthest outbuildings were softened by morning haze. Dust had formed a skin over a puddle in the drive and browned the hedgerows. Rooks circled a stand of trees and wagtails hunted the furrows of a ploughed field.

Couch grass crackled under Quill's flak-jacket as he turned to watch a Post Office van bump towards the farm without hurry. Dillman climbed out with a registered parcel and whistled as he hammered on the front door. Quill checked the marksmen beside him. One covered Dillman with a scoped rifle and a second made controlled sweeps across the shuttered windows. Local CID men and more marksmen approached the rear of the building from the far trees.

Dillman knocked again, his whistle impatient.

They all waited, and nothing happened.

Come on, thought Quill, wishing he could smoke.

Dillman pulled a pencil from behind his ear and searched his pockets for a notification-of-delivery card. Listened for Payne's boot against the kitchen door.

Quill's elbow skidded in cowcake and he swore into his cuff.

The rooks were settling when a tearing lock sent them into the air like clamouring black rags.

Dillman threw himself aside. Drew a Smith & Wesson from his phoney package. Bulstrode dropped from the back of the Post Office van and levelled his revolver.

The farmhouse door shuddered on its hinges. Opened inwards.

Quill rolled upright and zig-zagged down the hill. Angled away from the marksmen's line of sight. Listened for gunfire that did not come.

He vaulted a fence and tore his trousers on a run of barbed wire. His boot plunged into a slick of deep mud. Held him immobile for a decade of seconds.

Swearing and panting, he heaved his foot from the gumboot, the boot from the mud, and arrived at the farmhouse panting with frustration. Bulstrode blocked his entry with a rigid forearm. His grin was boyish.

'Take off your other boot, Prophet. Can't have you trucking up the evidence for the forensic boys. It's the bloody motherload.'

Payne came to the door in his socks.

'Money everywhere. The place is a boar's nest. A million dabs and a sandwich with a bite out of it we can match a set of dentures to.'

Quill hauled off his second boot. The yard swarmed with Buckinghamshire police, and radio cars came down the track behind the Post Office van.

'Get one of them to swing in close. I want to tell our venereal leader personally. And he'll get the satisfaction of passing it on to Detective Chief Superintendent God Almighty Saul Cotton.'

'Uncle Theo's got that much coming to him. There'll be precious little else coming our way.'

Quill padded inside to sniff the stale litter.

Cotton and the local CID would take all the credit for finding the farm and putting names to all the faces Lemmon's squad had passed their way. And here all around Quill was the evidence to put all the chummies in the world behind bars. He drew on gloves and stirred paper bands on the soiled linoleum with a cautious finger. They were stamped with clearing-bank colophons and had banded the used notes to identify their points of origin. Quill straightened with a handful of them, his face thoughtful.

'What's a souvenir or three?' he asked softly.

When Bulstrode returned the bands were in Quill's wallet.

Safe against the day they might prove useful.

Charlie walked into Lowndes Square past the skeleton of a circular luxury hotel, a prime example of ugly commercial modernity that would soon dominate the surrounding elegant Georgian façades.

Idly wondering if the Archibald Ogle Complex would have any architectural merit once it had been thrown up,

Charlie crossed into Bolobec Street and entered a cobbled mews that had housed the gentry's horses before the Sloane Rangers moved in with their chintz curtains and geraniums.

Charlie gave Pim's name into a doorphone and was let into a cramped stairwell. He went up with his hands deep inside his pockets. Uncertain of the layout, he called: 'For someone who wanted me here sooner than yesterday, you ain't putting out the flags of welcome, Dotty Machin.'

'In here.'

Dotty's voice broke beyond a half-glazed door.

Charlie toed it open.

Dotty sat in a kitchen chair with dishevelled hair and mascara trailing her cheeks. The Negro pinning her arms had a shaved scalp and eyes without whites. He held an Italian flick-knife against Dotty's neck.

Charlie nodded to himself.

'Jonas the pimp, right?'

The knife flashed light.

'And you be the Peemleeco Johneee so big in Durham Gaol. From here you ain't nothing but sheet, man.'

'You planning to cut the merchandise you broke out for?'

'Me break out for this piece of white trash? I break out for *you*, man.'

'Why? I don't know you from a bar of coal-tar soap.'

Jonas looked sly.

'I know you bleed if I cut her.'

Charlie said nothing as the knife described a bright circle. Spittle formed a sticky web on Jonas's prominent lower lip.

'You the one thinks this whoring trash worth more than a few quids for the night, Mr Peem-lee-co. You the one who figure this nigger just roll over. Let you have her free, gratis, for nothing. Right, blood?'

'You cheap ginger biscuit. . . .' Charlie watched the blade dart across the white throat. 'OK. What d'you want?'

Jonas's smile was a slash in black vinyl.

'You ain't so brave with her face under my blade, huh? How much you worth to this whitey, Dotty sweetheart?

Hundreds? T'ousands and t'ousands?' A snicker of laughter stirred Dotty's hair. 'He can afford plenteee. Him earning bundles from that train. I know that. And me good friends spring me to get at all that dough.'

'What friends would they—?'

Charlie ducked into a crouch as a bludgeon swung where his head had been. He buried a heel in a groin and fell on his side. The bore of a gun screwed into his sideburn, gouging an earlobe. Charlie froze with halitosis gusting in his nostrils.

The sneer of a voice was pure cockney.

'Make me do it, Mister. Make me.'

'Not me, pal.'

'I'll spread your brains over her lap we don't get that money, Mister.'

'Get up, blood.' Jonas forearmed scum from his mouth.

Charlie staggered to get a look at the second man.

He had the golden eyes and dead yellow hair of an albino. His face was pocked with old acne, and teeth rotted in his smile.

'That Brock. And Brock don't like whitey,' Jonas said.

Brock told Charlie to strip.

Charlie dropped his hat, overcoat, jacket and trousers. Kicked off his black casuals. Pulled off his shirt and tie and stepped out of his jockey shorts.

'He dressed for his own funeral.' Brock searched the clothes for weapons and found nothing.

'Not now he naked. All Dotty see is all Dotty get, eh, blood? And you with a busted arm and all. You less than shit with nothing on your body.'

'Don't . . . *hurt* him,' Dotty wailed. 'He's not . . . .'

'Shut it!' Charlie ordered.

'He ain't what?' asked Jonas.

'Ain't scared of you.' Charlie watched the knife. 'You pair of tossing amateurs. If you broke out of Durham, I'm the Emperor of China. Jonas, you was released from open prison last week. Is that where you picked up this flyblown bag of offal?'

Jonas sniggered.

'Listen to whitey call the man with the blade names. You been keeping tabs on me, blood? Don't that just make me righter than right about you and this one here?'

Brock's Webley raked Charlie's spine.

'Maybe I break your other arm.'

'Then you'd have to do the digging.'

Jonas laid a hand on Dotty's blonde head.

'Now we getting to it. Where this money at?'

'A field in Essex. Leave her here and I'll take you right to it.'

Jonas wagged a finger and the knife.

'Cosier all together. You drive Dotty's Mini with Brock in front with you, Mr Peem-lee-co. Me and Dotty cuddle up in the back. It a long time since Jonas had hisself some white meat for his pleasure.' Jonas fondled a breast, his eyes on Charlie. 'Any objections, Peem-lee-co?'

'Oh blimey no,' Charlie said calmly.

'We wait for dark, then. Maybe I think of a way to 'muse meself. What you think, Peem-lee-co?'

'Probably.'

Charlie caught Dotty's eye and winked solemnly. Willing her to keep control.

Oldfield Sanatorium for Gentlefolk of the Masonic Order glowed in the Mini's heads before Charlie cut the engine and coasted under the elders.

'You can't do shit in the back of these baby cars,' Jonas grumbled. 'What's this shit, blood? A hospital?'

Charlie moved out from behind the wheel.

'They're all asleep. All we have to do is wade out to the island and get digging.'

'Stay put, blood. Brock, look around.'

Brock jerked his Webley at Dotty.

'What about her?'

'She comes, too.'

The men stripped to their shorts, and Dotty threw her dress into the back of the car.

Jonas tied his boots around his neck by the laces.

'Go ahead, blood. Slowly.'

Charlie crossed the sloping lawn and the gravel border. The water struck cold as he stepped down into mud and rotted leaves. Brock followed, outlined by lit hospital windows. The water deepened and Charlie lay forward into an easy swimming motion, careful not to outdistance the others. When he hauled himself out to shake himself, Brock's gun stayed locked on his heart.

'Which way, blood?'

Jonas pushed Dotty on to the island, and duckweed clung to his muscular torso like theatrical spangles.

A swan hissed from cover and a moorhen called plaintively.

Charlie pointed out a door in the Georgian folly.

'You'll have to pick the lock if you want tools.'

Brock cursed, and goosebumps stood out on his gun arm.

Jonas did something with the latch and tossed a pick and shovel at Charlie.

'Keep it simple, blood.'

Charlie went through Virginia creeper and paced random steps into a small clearing. He hacked the pick into the turf, lined it up with a chimney across the lake. Muttering calculations, he made a triangle of twigs. Crouched to squint this way and that. Then he straightened with the shovel gripped close to the blade.

'I dunno. It looks different at night.'

'Don't shit us,' Brock said.

'Then, you do it.'

'Do what?'

'Make a hypotenuse with three equal sides. The fourth being equal to the sum of both angles of the lateral measure. You want to dig in the wrong place?'

Jonas spat on the grass.

'I'll cut her, man.'

'Just see if Brock can align these markers with the pitch of the roof.'

'Lose the shovel, blood.'

Charlie tossed the shovel aside and scratched his plastered forearm. Damned Rudge for doing too good a job. His nails skidded on hard plaster as he pointed along the twigs for the albino.

Brock bent to look, thought better of it and straightened with a jerk, stabbing the Webley at Charlie.

Charlie drove a shoulder into Brock's stomach and mashed the albino's nose with a down-swinging arm.

Plaster cracked and made shrapnel.

Vinnie's knife spun off somewhere. Blood from Brock's burst forehead made a black fan in the moonlight, spattered the gun as it hit the turf.

Charlie heaved Brock aside, fell into a forward roll, gathered the Webley and swung it across to bear on Jonas.

Dotty had tried to run, Jonas gathered her by the waist and swung her around as a shield. Her teeth sank into his hand and his head jerked clear of her tousled hair.

Charlie expelled breath and fired.

The bullet tore into the pimp's left eye-socket and exited behind his ear as an explosion of hair, bone and streamers of grey tissue. Hurled on to tiptoe, Jonas threw his arms wide. Charlie drove two more bullets into his left pectoral.

Jonas bowled over and slammed the turf with his shoulders. Skidded to the water's edge with his boots bumping alongside his slack face. His head flopped into the water and sent rings out across the lake.

Brock was drooling mucus. Trying to rise.

Dotty's mouth was a widening black hole swallowing air to scream. Charlie took two steps through glue and clipped her on the point of her jaw. Watched her fall as his shots echoed back across the lake and chased off into the flatlands beyond the River Crouch.

Charlie watched Brock's face come up off his forearms with dreary eyes.

'Who pointed you at me? The name?'

Charlie barely recognised his own voice.

'Mmmmmmm.' Brock dribbled thick paste.

Charlie heeled him in the cheekbone.
'The name.'
'Mmmmmansssah Fedeee . . . .'
'Manchester Freddy?'
'Essssss . . . .'
Charlie felt Brock's collarbone snap when he swung the gun.
'He's only a pimp. A bloody Maltese pimp. He's only on the firm because he's married into the Tonna family . . . .'
'Immm nnnn Maweees Mawissss . . .,' Brock slobbered.
'Maltese Maurice?'
'Essss . . . .'
Charlie shook his streaming head. Squatted on the grass with his spiralling thoughts.
Maltese Maurice was a cousin of the Tonnas and was related to Manchester Freddy by marriage. He pimped out of King's Cross with a dozen toms, and Dotty Machin had got her start with him. Even Popeye Greenland's sister had walked the pavements for Maurice. And so had Armchair Doris in the old pre-war days before she got too old. Maltese Maurice and Manchester Freddy. Close friends of Kosher Kramer before Archie banished him to Brighton and the Tonnas used their influence with Archie to let Maurice and Freddy keep their London patches . . . .
Charlie's sweat dripped on the grass as everything made a kind of sense to him.
'All pimps together,' he said softly.
Brock was just a sprawl of moonlit nothing on the dewed turf.
Charlie turned the upturned face to pulp with two shots.
The body shuddered and lay still. The fingers and toes twitched once as the double echo raced east. There was a sighing silence until an ornamental fowl cried in distress.
Charlie threw the gun out into the dark lake, and the plop was a gentle full stop to the sudden violence. He cradled Dotty's head in his lap and picked duckweed out of her hair.
'Picked the wrong friends, didn't they, love?' he asked

as he lifted her.

When Dotty came round Charlie had left Battlebridge far behind and the two bodies floated on the lake with the rest of the flotsam.

'Climb into your dress, love. Don't want to give some traffic wally a reason to leave his wife.'

Dotty shuddered and wondered how she could live with what Charlie had done for her.

The lower walls of the interview room were painted hooker's green and were separated from the cream upper walls by a thick black line. The ceiling light was protected by iron mesh, and the tall single window had bars and reinforced glass.

Ollie Oliphant sat on a stained oak bench that matched the chairs Lemmon and Quill used. The table was tubular steel with a plastic top, and at its centre was an aluminium ashtray advertising a defunct brand of cigarettes. The uniformed constable at the door closed his eyes against the sunlight pouring through the window. Ollie's raised hands threw a shadow, and he worked his fingers into a rabbit with articulating ears. He had been at Aylesbury Police Station all morning, and was bored with the repetitive rhetoric.

Sergeant Quill said: 'Stands to reason they'd use the top coachman in the Smoke. Got to be you. Nobody else rates. You're it.'

Ollie said nothing. His knuckles made the rabbit's nose twitch.

'We can place faces from two firms at the farm. Lovely dabs. Fibres from their clothes. Even a pair of shoes with yellow paint on them. All you have to do is fill in a few details for us.'

Ollie gave the rabbit a tongue to waggle.

'That your answer, Oliphant?' Lemmon asked.

The rabbit nodded and licked its fur.

'There's no denying you gave those traffic wallies a run for their money. Nice coachwork. But we found the tyremarks *and* the Hillman you used. Matched the grass and mud from the skids to the car itself. Lovely forensic. Nothing to confuse a jury.'

The rabbit shook its head.

'Give us the other coachman and we'll see what we can do for you. Not in your class, is he? Heavy on the wheel.'

Ollie's rabbit became a hard V sign before he scratched his crotch, staring directly at Lemmon.

'Lose the playmates, or you get to talk to the whole bloody menagerie.'

'Outside.'

Lemmon offered Oliphant a Senior Service and they lit up as the door closed on Quill and the constable.

'You know you've got nothing, Mr Lemmon.'

'Enough to feel collars. But you'd know the names better than me.'

'I know a lot of people. Law of averages says some of them got to be naughty boys.'

'When did you last seen Bonar Tree?'

'Who?'

'Popeye Greenland? Brixton Billy?'

'Leave it out, Guv.'

'They're all for the jump.'

'Why tell me?'

'Better me than Cotton's pirates, Ollie. He won't make deals and stick to them like you know I will.'

Ollie picked tobacco from his lip. 'Just don't give me names I don't want to hear. I've gotta live out there. You don't. And don't give me all that police protection routine. That don't work.'

'We can place you at the farm with a hand tied. But if you get the word round . . . let the right faces know I'm ready to talk softly . . . they come in voluntarily . . . .'

'So that's how it is.'

'They come in voluntarily I'll see they get fair shakes. And the money has to come back. That's what'll nail them if they don't put up their hands. The money.'

'And you want me to put the word round, that it?'

'If I let you go.'

Ollie blew smoke where his rabbit had lived.

'A good thieftaker you may be. But if you've tied me to that Hillman you haven't done your homework. That car was nicked before I got to Oxford to pick it up. From outside a transport café. I phoned it in stolen to this very station. Check with the local traffic wallies.'

'If you're pulling my official pudden . . . .'

'My feet won't touch. I've never drawn bird in my life. But there's a few faces who'd just love to see me stitched up for a good stretch. You look where you got my name. You didn't pull it out of a hat. Look there, and you'll find a face with something to hide.'

'You give me the name.'

'And turn grass? Check your traffic records and let me get back to grafting for a living.'

'Charlie Dance is a name.'

'So is Charlie Peace and Jack the Ripper.'

'They're closed files. Charlie Dance is wide open. I don't think he likes you, Ollie.'

Ollie shrugged around an oriental smile.

'If you say so, Mister.'

Lemmon scraped his chair back.

'Just sit there and think of names.'

He went out, and the constable came back to squint in the sunlight. Ollie was showing him an ostrich when Quill put his head round the door.

'Hop it. You're free to go.'

'You should check out your snouts, Prophet,' Ollie said as they waited in the yard for a police car to take him to the railway station.

Quill watched the Humber pull away, certain Bulstrode had dropped another peg in Lemmon's estimation. As he went back inside he was called into Lemmon's office.

'Pity Oliphant wouldn't cough, Guv.'

Lemmon smiled over laced fingers.

'He's back on the streets where he belongs. With a few

names planted in his brainbox. By nightfall they'll be burning holes in his head. By tomorrow he'll be talking into the right ears. Just flushing the game from cover, Prophet. You can't shoot a sitting bird . . . .'

With sick certainty, Quill knew Bulstrode still smelled of violets. It was a struggle to keep his face pleasant.

Bulstrode had been parked in Middlesex Street for an hour when Vinnie Castle sat in beside him. The East End was icy after the sunshine in Aylesbury. 'About time you showed.' Bulstrode coughed into a Kleenex.

'The Met should spring for heaters in their Q-cars. No wonder you CID faces are always stuffed up with colds. A bit different from a postcard I got from Portugal this morning. This mate's sitting in the high eighties nuzzling señoritas.'

'This mate have a name?'

'Sarcasm, Buller?' Vinnie wiped the windscreen to check the street. 'This is like sitting inside an ice-lolly.'

'Tell me what you've got and let me get home to bed.'

'I gave you Ollie, so lay off the moodies.'

Bulstrode reached for another tissue.

'Much good it did me. He's already back on the street.'

'You losing him ain't down to me, Buller. You want this bubble or don't you?'

'I know the moon's green cheese, so don't let it be that.'

'It's an address in Islington. But you've got to be fast.'

Bulstrode sneezed violently.

'Will you pay attention?' Vinnie complained.

'Cotton gave me his cold. About all I will get from that face. Who's at this address in Islington?'

'Popeye Greenland.'

'And how much is that squib of not-a-lot gonna cost the taxpayers?'

'Nothing as it happens. I don't need your dough. Not now me and the ex-brother-in-law are on a nice little earner.'

'You and Pimlico? After your tart of a sister left him for a greasy bubble? And where's he got the capital for that?'

'Charlie and Wally Harold. And there's no collars there, Buller. It's a proper limited company and J. C. Hatton does the books. You want Popeye or don't you?'

Bulstrode nodded with watering eyes.

'He's at his sister's in Crowndale Road. In the attic behind a wardrobe in the upstairs bedroom. And get there soonest or he'll be well gone. Silversleeves earwigs for the Troys, right? He got Popeye's nephew pissed up in the Nell Gwynne. Had him boasting about his magic uncle and all the dough he's earned from this big tickle. Silversleeves phoned in to the Troys, Barry the Blag overheard and phoned me. Now I'm telling you. Move fast or Popeye's had it.'

'When were you the charity ward?'

Vinnie let himself out on to the cobbles.

'The Troys won't kiss Popeye to death, Buller. See if you can handle this without falling over your own size fourteens. And don't forget you've got bent law on all sides of you. There's more than one blue-serge face who'd blow the whistle on Popeye for a handful of sovs. And don't tell me I'm wrong, neither.'

He gave Bulstrode a look of disgust and walked away.

Bulstrode did not patch himself through to Scotland Yard. He went in search of a public telephone, suddenly trusting no one.

Vinnie watched him make his call and used the same box to contact Charlie and Ollie when he had driven away. The phone was still warm from Bulstrode's ear.

Popeye tossed and turned in the attic.

The gantry stoplight was a red eye as big as the moon.

He saw himself follow Brixton Billy down the halted train as one of Bonar's firm collared the fireman on the track and pitched him down the bank. Promised him a good drink if he behaved himself and kept his clack shut.

Popeye swarmed up into the engine as the driver kicked out at Brixton Billy. Almost dropped him on to the track with a heel to the kidneys. Popeye heaved Brixton back into the cab and whacked the driver's cap from his head with his stave, so he went down moaning and looking old in the hard moonlight.

And Bonar there saying, 'Don't hit him again. Get our driver up here and help with the uncoupling.' And the firms' driver fussing with levers and dials and gabbing on about building this vacuum. And this layout was more complicated than he was used to. And being told to get on with it without all the chat.

Then Popeye heaved and shoved at hooks and hoses where Alfie Horrabin told him to push and shove down between the mail-coach and the rest of the train. In the dark with the smell of diesel and his own sweat. All the time worrying if there was enough time, and whether another train would light them all up.

Then Brixton Billy said, 'Bring up the guns,' pretending to be tooled up to frighten the sorters inside the mail-coach. The doors opening and Popeye inside throwing sorters down on their faces and kicking the soles of their feet to keep them finger-tame.

And Alfie Horrabin saying, 'This is the HVP cage,' and Buster using the bolt-cutters where Alfie told him. Smiler rough-counting the sacks and Bonar wanting the real driver back at the controls because of the bloody vacuum. A long sweaty wait, and the carriages jerking hard as the train was finally separated and the engine and mail-coach rolled away down the line to the viaduct.

Making a line of men down the embankment to the lorry.

Popeye heaving sacks for two because Alfie looked like death and had no strength because his missus had gone off with some straight face she'd taken a shine to. Making Popeye heave for both of them he was so used up and trembling and sorry for himself. Scowling when Brixton wanted more speed with Bonar siding with him. Ticking off seconds on their stopwatches.

And the sacks getting heavier and heavier until Popeye's gloves shrank from the sweat that gummed his eyes almost shut. Still waiting for whistles to blow and boots to pound as the railway police and the proper busies got in amongst the firms to sort them out.

Popeye wishing he had a shooter. Knowing he would have used it on the driver and maybe the sorters. And knowing Bonar was right to put the block on using guns.

And Bonar saying, 'Time's up, chaps,' in a three-guinea voice with six sacks still on the coach. And the blessed relief of tumbling down the embankment into the lorry and bowling away down country lanes with Bonar dressed as a major in the leading land-rover. Standing up with a map and a torch as if he was really doing what real soldiers do.

Lovely. Sweet as you please.

Without the smell of another car or anything coming over the police band on the radios.

Popeye woke when a door closed below.

Sister Elsie's husband starting the day.

Soon Elsie would have bacon and tomatoes spitting on the stove as she yelled for the kids to get something hot inside them before they went off to the recreation centre. Getting them out from under her feet during the school holidays.

Popeye rolled a smoke and wound his clock. Waited for Elsie to bang on the ceiling with a broom when the house was empty and he could creep down for his breakfast.

Rain spotted the fanlight, and Popeye's belly rumbled.

There was nothing but silence below now that George and the kids had gone. And still no knocking broom.

Popeye got into his boots and donkey-jacket, wishing he had a shooter instead of his sap. There were footfalls on the stairs, and Elsie called through the bedroom wall: 'Breakfast, Popeye.'

Oh yes. And walk slap-bang into the filth.

Popeye eased the fanlight open and gripped the sill.

'Popeye, you sleeping?'

No, Popeye ain't.

Tommy Troy said, 'The kettle's boiled. Come on out before Elsie gets it over her head.'

Sorry, Elsie love . . . .

Popeye lay out along the wet roof and let himself slide down to the guttering. A tile dislodged and grated until he eased it back into place.

At least they can't touch the kids.

Popeye found the soil-pipe and swung down over the eaves. A lateral pipe took his weight and he got a hand to the ridge of the kitchen extension. Popeye straddled the pitch and walked crabwise to the garden eave, dropping on to the lawn without a sound.

Elsie made a sound like a fingernail on glass.

Bastard cowsons.

Popeye skirted cold-frames and went over the back wall.

He dropped into a cobbled alley and heard Jesse call his name from an upper window. Gay Gordon and two other faces were banging out of the scullery.

Talk about team-handed.

Popeye made a ducking run for the canal.

He found the missing rail in the iron fence and squeezed through. Flattened bushes where his Jack Russell usually rolled and scratched and watered the grass. Slid down a steep turfed bank. Something tore inside his sock as his ankle twisted under him. He hit the towpath and his world blackened with sudden pain.

He hobbled round a bench and blundered into a fisherman casting line over the brown water. A lead sinker hummed near Popeye's face as the fisherman sprawled across his canvas chair. Keep-net, bait-box and rod plopped into the canal.

Popeye hobbled towards the roadbridge and the shopping-precinct beyond. Looking for crowds of witnesses.

He was thumped in the back and a rock scaled into the water.

Jesse wished his aim had been better as he jumped the fisherman.

Popeye glanced over his shoulder and pounded on into a small boy on a wobbling bicycle. He threw the boy up the bank and the bicycle flipped into the canal.

An old woman shook her umbrella, and the pigeons

she fed took off with a clatter.

Popeye favoured his wrenched ankle as best he could. He went under a roadbridge and found the stepped path on the far side. A man came down the stairs to throw a fist at Popeye's head.

'Lay hands on my kid . . . .'

Popeye roundhoused the man in the face. Mashed nose cartilage.

'Have some of *that*.'

The man was rigid with shock when Popeye lifted him by the lapels and threw him over his shoulder. The man flopped into Jesse and Gordon. Jesse ducked against the wall, and Gordon's feet went out from under him as he lost a casual shoe. He hit the water trying to keep his watch dry.

Popeye went under Jesse's swing and sapped him across a kneecap. Jesse went down bawling, and Popeye hauled himself up the stepped path to run south along the main road. Two of Tommy's overcoats were sprinting from the municipal gardens to cut him off.

Popeye quickened his pace, agonised when his left foot touched the ground. He went east at the intersection and passed a run of small shops. A publican hosed his forecourt, and a chair propped the saloon bar open. Popeye ducked inside, kicked the chair away and threw the bolts as Jesse slammed the door with his shoulder.

Popeye leered at a thin girl cutting sandwiches behind the bar.

'Don't touch me.'

The girl brandished a ham knife.

Popeye ignored her.

He limped into a lounge overlooking the southern canal bank. A narrowboat chugged past with a mongrel in the stern and a man in a mackinaw at the tiller. Popeye went out on to a covered veranda.

On the far bank Gordon looked for his shoe and the man with a mashed nose calmed his crying son. The thin girl opened the cellar door and a large Dobermann romped into the lounge bar. Popeye slid the glazed door closed and the dog scrabbled at the glass, baying at him.

The thin girl opened the saloon-bar door, and Jesse and the publican came in shoulder to shoulder. Yelling.

Popeye swung from the veranda and let himself drop to the towpath.

The Dobermann howled as it was hit with a chair. Matched the sound Popeye made when his ankle fractured. There was no strength in his legs and his scrotum was on fire. With a huge effort of will he pulled himself towards the pub wall. Fought a dreary mist. Just resting for a bit. Just resting . . . .

Gay Gordon was swimming towards him.

Popeye thought he could sap him when he reached the bank.

But feet dropped beside him and he took a hard kick to the ribs.

Popeye's brain stopped caring as his eyes rolled to white.

'A nice dance you've led us.'

Jesse stamped on Popeye's ankle and set himself for a second kick.

A stained-glass galleon sailed over the hole Jesse had punched in the glass sea to reach the inside latch.

Lemmon crunched on green shards in a narrow passage where op-art wallpaper screamed at a cheerful yellow carpet. Quill took the stairs to the upper floors, and Lemmon followed low whimpers into a kitchen where an overripe woman with bleached hair lay beside a lit gas-stove. Bubble-and-squeak had burned itself black in the pan, and the linoleum was slick with oil spilled from a chip-fryer.

'Hello, Elsie.'

Lemmon told Bulstrode to bring a WPC inside and sent a mobile for Elsie's husband.

Elsie mewed deep in her throat, and her shapeless bosom strained against her threadbare dressing-gown. The candlewick had faded to the dead pink of an unwashed neck.

Hot fat had coagulated in her hair and formed grey scales on her round face. Her hands and feet were red and raw, and scald blisters had begun to form between her toes. The dimples in her lumpy knees squinted like malformed Chinamen as Lemmon crouched beside her.

'Elsie?' Lemmon touched her shoulder.

Elsie shrugged away and her eyes snapped with pain.

'Bloody Sergeant Lemmon. Toss off, bluebottle.'

'Same old Elsie. You used to be something to look at when you solicited commuters in Argyle Square for Maltese Maurice. Fifteen years ago you pulled more passengers than British Railways. Look at the state of you now.'

'You ain't improved with age, neither. I'm respectable married, so watch your clack.'

Elsie was between perms. She shook a tangle of frizz, grey and natural mouse from her bloated face.

'Who did this, Elsie?'

'Had an accident, didn't I? And how's it gonna look if you don't get me to hospital right fast?'

'Tell me who, Elsie.'

'Nobody done nothing.'

'And nobody touched your kids. This time.'

'Leave the kids out of it.'

'Sure, if the Troys will.'

'Go scratch, Sarge.'

'Detective Inspector now.'

'Then, I'm the Pope of Rome.'

Elsie swore without repetition.

'Where's Popeye?' asked Lemmon.

'Courting Olive Oil.'

'Don't you want him back? Alive?'

'Fish another pool, Lemmon.'

'Highly hilarious.'

Lemmon and the WPC helped Elsie into the tiny living-room and laid her on an uncut moquette couch. Elsie spat near the WPC's foot.

'And you can keep your hands off me, ducky. All you

uniformed tarts are lesbians. I don't turn tricks for your sort no more.'

The WPC flushed scarlet.

'Bullseye,' said Elsie.

Quill called from the top floor, and Lemmon went up to meet him. Payne shone his torch into a cavity beyond a wardrobe they had pulled away from the wall. Rain spat through a skylight, damping a mattress on the bare boards. The smell of confined masculinity lingered on the down-draught.

Payne flashed off exposures as Quill searched the bedroom.

Lemmon returned to the living-room with an old pigskin case stuffed with fat bundles of used notes.

'Holiday money, Elsie? You could buy the Kursaal with this lot.'

'Never seen it before.'

'But you'll want a receipt for it all the same?'

'I'm saying nothing.'

'Popeye's funeral. You want that on your conscience?'

'Go scratch.'

'You're nicked. Read her the necessary, Buller.'

Elsie's foul tirade coloured the WPC's cheeks again.

Bulstrode puffed air. 'That's saying nothing?'

'That's our Elsie,' said Lemmon. 'Popeye in a frock.'

Pimlico's nerves were shredded when Archie's Rolls picked him up in Brewer Street. Charlie nosed into traffic, and Vinnie said: 'How's Dotty?'

'Pulling moodies. What's it to you?' Pimlico hunched in the back to chew a nail.

'Nothing. Just asking.'

Charlie swung into Charing Cross Road and nothing more was said until he had parked illegally in John Adam Street. The old Armenian washed dishes in the same steam and Stavros sat at his desk in the same shirt. Customs had seized his last consignment of pornography and were not open to bribery.

'I told you, Stavvie.'

Charlie took one of Stavros's Pall Malls into the bookstore and lit it looking between Vinnie and Pimlico.

'Let's have it,' he said.

Vinnie sighed and said: 'Lemmon's squad missed Popeye, so he's on the missing-list. Elsie needs skin grafts, and Ollie's been hauled in by Cotton's pirates twice. The whole Met's offering deals. Like being offered green stamps in a bent supermarket. They picked Alfie Horrabin up in Brighton with his dough, and they collared Bonar's boy Smiler in his caravan with all *his* dough. There's talk that a couple of other faces want to deal with the Flying Squad – give back the dough for smaller sentences – but nothing definite.'

'They never think of afterwards,' said Charlie.

Pimlico snorted and looked at nothing.

'Spit it out, Pim.'

'Three mouths in this room. Mine stays closed.'

'You ain't the first face with woman trouble. Or maybe your nose is out of whack because Wally's flown out to South Africa?' said Vinnie. 'You and me can cope while he's sunning himself.'

'I want out,' said Pimlico. 'Just out.'

'Not without a proper "why" you don't.' Charlie's eyes could have been holes in the darkness.

'It ain't just Wally going off when my back was turned. Kelly had him back on the firm the minute I was gone. Had him on some scrap contract at an aircraft factory. Wally took the needle to a welder and tossed him thirty feet on to the concrete apron. His headaches and temper ain't improved since he earned that whacking in Camden Town. Maybe some sun will bake his brains better.'

Charlie breathed smoke. 'If that ain't it, what is?'

Pimlico said nothing.

'This ain't friendly, Pim,' said Vinnie.

'Let Pim get it said, Vin.'

Charlie eased ash from the Pall Mall and spread it to nothing with his shoe.

'Well, Pim?' he said.

'All *right*. Ollie's sweating for the filth. Popeye's under the hammer. Alfie and Smiler are well nicked. When's it my turn? I bubbled that tickle up to you, Charlie. Now you know.'

Vinnie's breath whistled. 'You're labelling Charlie *grass*?'

'If the cap fits.'

Vinnie's fists beat the air. 'Who d'you think kept the home fires burning when you was coaching villains about the Home Counties? Ask your Dotty about two black faces in Essex. Get her to give you the lie on that score.'

'Enough,' Charlie said.

'But Chas . . . .'

Charlie dangled a key for Vinnie to snatch. 'Straighten him out with Exhibit A.'

'A fucking pleasure.'

Vinnie went away to clang doors.

Charlie leaked smoke into the bookracks and his face closed in on itself. Stavros muttered into a telephone and the Gaggia hissed. Heels rapped in the corridor and Brixton Billy came in to stare at Pimlico, a tissue held to a fresh razor-nick. He leaned a hip near Charlie.

'Well, well,' he said. 'The boy wonder. All the piss and none of the vinegar. I told Ollie you wasn't ready to play with the big kids, but he would have you. And here's you bleating grass when Ollie's out there saving your collar.'

'Ollie was grassed to the law,' said Pimlico.

'To order. Somebody had to find out just how far the heavy filth would bend to make deals. Ollie does that every time he's pulled in by Scotland Yard. You think I'd have got into this caper without I had Charlie watching my back? I'd be losing fingernails to Troy's tarts if Charlie hadn't pulled me out of my drum. And wouldn't it be lovely if the law had copped Tommy's firm leaning on Popeye for his whack? Scratch them *and* Popeye. Job done, right? Except Lemmon's mob's too slow to catch a cold.'

'That don't mean Popeye wasn't grassed up.'

'By his *own*, you infant. His own family couldn't keep their clack shut. There's always cannon fodder on something this big, and Popeye volunteered himself because he's thicker than the head on a glass of Dublin Guinness. And ain't you the lucky one not to be playing Mutt and Jeff at Aylesbury nick? Or face down in Essex with a shiv in your liver?'

Pimlico could not take it all in.

Brixton Billy fingered his razor-nick.

'And they'll get Buster the same way. Him and money could never sit quiet. This tickle was grassed up long before you came in on it. In Brighton where the finance came from. It just so happens that some of us with a bit of nous under our haircuts pulled our own flanker. If you had half a brain, you'd get yourself lost abroad like I plan to. That's *after* you've done a handsome kneesbend to Charlie here.'

Stavros drew Charlie into the passage to talk fast with wild arm motions.

Vinnie shook his head at Pimlico.

'How're you gonna square this with Charlie?'

'Or any of us,' said Brixton.

'Take an ad in the *Police Gazette*?'

Pimlico wondered what Dotty was keeping from him. She was sleeping badly, and her sex drive had sunk to zero.

Charlie came back and said: 'Stavvie's about to entertain the Vice Squad. Time we was all somewhere else. Vinnie, you get Brixton away to Dover. I'll get the Rolls out of the way.'

'Shake, Chas?' said Pimlico.

Brixton Billy slapped Pimlico's hand aside.

'Get some growing-up done first. Only the big kids get to shake with the Man. Come on, Vin.'

Left alone, Pimlico bruised knuckles against a steel cabinet.

Popeye came back to pain.

Gay Gordon sneezed and wrung water from his jacket.

'How were we to know Popeye had his whack in the house with him?'

Jesse found no takers for his small cigars.

'Worry whether Elsie bubbles up to the heavy filth.'

'Not her. She was close-mouthed when she tommed for Maltese Maurice in King's Cross. She may be off the game, but she hates the law like poison.'

Tommy drummed the steering-wheel.

'We still come up empty.'

Gordon listened to his drowned watch.

'Not so empty. Popeye must know where the others are forted up.'

'Nice one, Gordy.'

Popeye smelled his own vomit as he was dragged from the black Bedford into blacker night. The flooded quarry shone like oiled silk, and ebony pyramids of shale hid it from the road. The sky above Ottershaw was starlit velvet, and Staines was a glare of sodium to the west. He glimpsed the contrail of a BEA jet before he was hooded and dragged through hills and valleys of hard aggregate towards a mutter that became a chuckle and grew into the downward bellow of a weir.

'This is where it ends, Popeye.'

The sluice vibrated under his one good foot and the hood sucked into his mouth when he sobbed for breath, tasting of dust and cheap dye. Lint clogged his blooded nose.

'Talk and save yourself. Brixton Billy wasn't home. You ain't dealing with little boys. Talk.'

Popeye was held out over an abyss of tumbling water as if he weighed less than his clothes. Icy spray clamped his swollen ankle, and he made a noise like Elsie when her hands were plunged into her chip-fryer.

Tommy had liked her for not talking. 'More balls than a pinball machine,' he had said as he worked on Popeye's broken ankle bones.

'Drop the bastard and let's get a drink,' said Jesse.

Tommy patted the hooded head.

'Five locks between you and Tower Bridge, Popeye.

You'll float through every one. When you surface in Rotherhithe you'll have bloated to five times your proper size. Be as grey as a cod's belly. All that gas in you'll turn your balls to balloons. You've seen a floater, Popeye. You told us over a drink once. A good big drink, you was so rattled over it. Dreamed about it, didn't you? Couldn't keep your breakfast down for days. You remember that.'

Popeye tried not to see himself fill with gas. His face turn to mush as his belly and limbs swelled and swelled . . . .

'I'll give you my whack. Take me home . . . .'

'The law got your whack. Remember, Floater?'

Popeye was lowered on one arm. The water creamed around his thighs and midriff. The sodden donkey-jacket dragged him lower and lower. The torrent turned him this way and that and he could no longer breath.

'Buster. I'll give you Buster.'

'Where is he?'

'Home first. Then you can have him.'

Don't let me tell them about the half of my whack I buried. Just Buster.

Popeye was landed, and his bloated ankle smacked hard timber. He was drowning in sputum, lint and brackish bile. He would die without sight, without air.

Home, home . . . .

Tommy told him things, and Popeye made promises they knew he would keep. The hood was torn away, and the Bedford bumped on to the Chertsey Road to follow its heads towards Staines. Popeye smelled Jesse light a small cigar and coughed himself senseless.

Then he was flipped into the road and skated to a halt under the lights of Islington Green. He crawled until he was found by a Special Constable, who phoned him in as a hit-and-run drunk with multiple injuries.

Quill, Dillman and Payne had caught last orders at the Cottage Club in Tottenham Court Road and supped moody pints as Maxie Hoffa cleared the bar of noisy medical students.

Maxie was closing the door when Lemmon eased him back inside and Bulstrode threw the bolts for him.

'You'll be with them,' said Maxie.

'No, they're with me.'

Lemmon leaned on the mahogany as if he had been there all night and was in no mood to change venues. He took one of Dillman's Gold Flakes and slid the pack to Bulstrode, who just stared at it, still seeing the Dover Road unfold and Detective Chief Superintendent Saul Cotton taking their prisoner like a confiscated bag of sweets.

'We was just drinking up, Guv,' said Quill.

'Why?'

'Thought we'd do a bit of overtime on the paperwork.'

Payne earned a withering look from Quill.

Lemmon looked at the malt optics.

'Paperwork? Know anything about any paperwork, Buller?'

'Nossir. Nothing.' Bulstrode's laugh had a lost sound.

'Quite a selection, Maxie. Better than that old tonk you punted out in your old Covent Garden spieler.'

Maxie closed the bar-flap.

'Then, we've both come up in the world, Mr.Lemmon. You don't even look like you any more.'

'I'm in disguise.' Lemmon's smile had no substance.

'Join us in a last one, Guv?' asked Quill.

Lemmon laid money on the bar.

'No. You'll join me in a first one. Mine's a Glenlivet. A very large Glenlivet. In a clean glass with a finger of fresh water. Not that rusty stuff you flavour the bitter with, Maxie.'

'Nice talk.'

Relieved to see Lemmon's tenner, Maxie was generous with the measure and slid Malvern water along the bar.

'Anything else?'

Lemmon sniffed, tasted and downed his drink.

'Do that again. Then give my brave lads whatever they want. Starting with young, sadder and wiser Bulstrode here.'

Maxie took whisky and uncapped soda down the bar.

Quill saw the dull red of Lemmon's neck. The nerve fluttering under his set jaw. The tightness around his eyes. White knuckles around his glass.

Bulstrode looked as if he'd won the ultimate paper hat.

Quill sipped air and whisky.

'What happened, Guv?' he asked.

'What didn't happen?'

Bulstrode ate whisky and plumed smoke.

'Another here in bigger glasses.' Lemmon knuckled the bar. 'A toast.'

He lit a second cigarette and let it burn beside the first.

'To the unsung and unwashed heroes who never make the headlines. Create them most certainly, but never make them. To us, brave lads.'

'What's he talking about?' Dillman asked Payne.

'Pissed, do you suppose?'

'In a sow's ear,' said Quill. 'He's pissed off. Not pissed.'

'Correct, Prophet.'

Lemmon drank and told Maxie to leave the bottle.

'A lovely anonymous call had me and Buller racing south. We collared Brixton Billy, and Cotton's pirates collared us. Very polite and very firm is Detective Chief Superintendent Cotton. "My prisoner, I think," he said. And left us with our own digits up our own situpons.'

Bulstrode's eyes were as dark as bitter aloes.

'We should have called him *after* the collar. He flew down and was a jump and skip behind us on the gang-plank. Had *us* escorted off like *we* was prisoners and escort. Hu-bloody-miliating.'

'So here we are, lads.' Lemmon had a third cigarette between his long brown fingers. 'Baby shadows under the machinery of justice, small enough to be swept under the carpet; too straight to earn the plaudits of recognition.'

Quill nodded over another drink.

'Tell me the old, old story.'

They all drank in a long silence.

Lemmon banged for a second bottle and found more money.

'I made formal protest of course. Even phoned a certain high-flyer in Buckinghamshire. One short, sweet telephone call. We are off the case. Off assignment. Our faces no longer fit, lads. The Home Office like their heroes to have easily spelled names like *Cotton.* My surname is the citrus you slice into ladies' drinks. Poor old Quill is a Victorian writing instrument. And Bulstrode here? "A Buller in a China Shop" makes a poor headline.'

Dillman sniggered and hiccuped.

'Then, I'm a flaming dildo. And our intrepid cameraman is a Payne in the proverbial.'

'I resemble that remark,' said Payne.

'So do you,' Dillman told him.

'Surplus to requirements. Again,' said Quill.

'Why, fuck it? Why?' Bulstrode bit his tongue.

Lemmon lit a fourth cigarette and laid it with the others.

'Rank wins out every time. The great thumb of power only presses downwards. Right on to our curly little heads. Even Brixton Billy laughed when he was bundled away by the Flying Squad.'

Lemmon puffed at his cigarettes in turn.

Bulstrode ordered a pint to chase the whiskies.

'Well, we must have made the fastest run to Dover and back since records began.'

Lemmon patted Bulstrode's shoulder and drank deeply.

'That's the way, son. Find a laugh where you can.'

'Maybe there's one in the bottom of this bottle.'

Bulstrode splashed the last of the whisky into glasses.

'That's a dead soldier,' Lemmon said. 'Time for me to wend my weary way to home and hearth. Sleep on my back to keep my everloving awake with my glottal yodels. Enjoy a hangover, and arrive back in the office on Monday morning as if this conversation never happened. Which it didn't.'

'Let me drive you, sir?' said Bulstrode.

'Fatal. Then we'd get into my cooking brandy. You'd tell me your life-story. I'd blab the secrets of the universe.'

Lemmon reset his hat and plodded to the door.

'Good night, guttersnipes of the lost legion.'

And he was gone into the night.

'He's human after all,' said Payne.

Dillman pushed his drink away.

'And hard as a pterodactyl's toenail. Had enough for one night.'

Bulstrode sank his beer chaser.

'Cotton's used us and blown us out as bubbles. He's done a deal with Bucks CID and rowed us out. We opened the doors and they've slammed them in our faces. They can have the kudos for this train job, but that's where it ends for this kiddy.'

Quill's laugh was cynical.

'Listen to the Masked Avenger. What'll you do? Write a letter to *The Times*? Complain to the Police Commissioner? The Met's big fleas and little fleas, not a bloody democracy. And you're infinitesimal in that order of lice.'

'And you'll take it lying down, will you?'

Quill patted the wallet under his coat and smiled like a corpse.

'There's more than one way of skinning a dead goat.'

'What a load of old taxidermy,' said Bulstrode.

'You're only a victim if you think like one, Buller.'

Pimlico bought cod and chips from the Chinaman at Fatface Carroli's and drove with the window down to keep the smell out of the upholstery. Ollie Oliphant was on the midnight flight to Buenos Aires, and Brixton Billy had been arrested on his way to the Continent. Another question-mark gnawed at Pimlico as he parked and let himself into the mews flat. Something closer to home.

Dotty fed a fresh millet spray into her canary's cage. She wore a housecoat and pyjamas and had not bothered with make-up. She brought plates to the table and pecked Pimlico's nose as he unwrapped the food.

'Very passionate, I don't think,' he said.

Dotty sat listlessly.

'This summer never got started. Joey would sing if there was some sunshine.'

'Wouldn't everybody?'

Pimlico stopped scrunching the newspaper into a ball when a Stop Press item caught his eye. He leaned near the waste-disposal to read it, scratched the back of his neck as the words drove nails into his head.

'You men and your papers. The times my ma found Dad reading one she'd lined a drawer with. He always said an old one was more interesting than today's.'

'Happen he's right.'

Pimlico broke batter with his knife and watched the fish steam.

'When did you say you went to Durham last?'

'Six, seven weeks ago.'

Dotty held the sauce-bottle over her plate with lowered eyes.

'And you told Jonas about us, right?'

'Sort of.'

'How sort of?'

'He was so full of going to an open prison.'

'But you told him.'

'I suppose . . . .'

'You talk in your sleep. Didn't make sense. And Vinnie said something about Charlie and two black faces.'

'What?'

Dotty speared a chip and forgot to eat it.

'Two black faces. Dead in Essex. Here in the paper.'

Dotty said nothing.

'Mean anything to you, girl?' Pimlico stabbed a finger at the greasy newsprint.

'You're shouting.'

'Look at the paper.'

'Why're you shouting at me?' Dotty's eyes brimmed and tears hung on her lashes.

Pimlico massaged a temple. 'Vinnie told me. And I gave Charlie the heavy finger.'

'Don't look ugly at me, Pim. Hit me, but don't push

your face at me like that.'

'Talk to me, girl.'

'Let's go away, Pim. To the sun. You got all that dough from your whack of the—'

Dotty froze. Knew she had given herself away. Tried to unbutton Pimlico's shirt.

'You know,' Pimlico said. No doubt left.

'I know I haven't been right for you. But in the sun I'll sleep. Do all the things you like best—'

'Stop it.'

'Don't you want me, Pim? I'll do anything you want. But don't make me say about Charlie. Please, Pim? Not about . . . Charlie . . .?'

Pimlico wrapped powerful arms around the thin shoulders, stroked the matted hair and found images in the curtains like pictures in a coal fire.

'Promise, Pim? Promise . . . .'

'I promise.'

Seeds cracked in the canary's beak and the food grew cold on the plates.

The night seemed very long for both of them.

CHAPTER THIRTEEN

WALLY HAROLD used the shower as a bludgeon to bring him awake.

The embassy party came back with the streaming water as the woman on the bed ordered breakfast in Afrikaans and asked 'Walter' how he liked his eggs. Wally knew he had boxed her compass handsomely on the spinning bed, but her nameless face was lost in the mad kaleidoscope of the last month. He towelled feeling into his legs and brought focus to the whirl of ministers and dignitaries Connie and Jorgesson had rubbed shoulders with the previous evening. The Prime Minister of South Africa had been there, and champagne had flowed like cheap pop for the two thousand guests.

Wally ignored the woman's sleepy 'Good morning, Walter' and padded out on to the hotel balcony.

The sun was already hot, and white puffballs of cloud beat gentle fists against the blue vastness above Johannesburg. The air was dry and clear, and traffic purled in orderly rows fourteen floors below.

Wally forced himself through fifty press-ups.

The sun beat on his freckled back as he pumped blood to his muscles and sense into his head. Then he showered again and lit a first cigarette. Connie may be right about the climate, but these plonk-swilling Dutchmen were definitely costing the Harold firm a financial arm and leg. Even Kelly had cabled her concern in snappy language, and Wally had to admit that even though she wasn't his favourite face of all time she was in Connie's corner when it mattered. Definitely.

Kelly was not only keeping the scrap, demolition and long firms afloat without any help at all from Connie, Harry or Sailor, she was also mothering Connie's kids in Denmark Hill, and doing a better job of it than daft Pauline ever had.

Not that Connie could see that; he was too blinded by the high life and the trips up-country where he'd picked diamonds up off the ground. Connie was all big talk about this company and that company, talking internationally as if he was straight and had a million in readies tucked down each sock.

Wally blew moody streams of smoke.

Connie had also gone soft in the head over Jorgesson's wife. He'd bought the happy couple a house and loaded it up with antiques as if pound notes were peanuts. Alicia Jorgesson just fluttered her lashes and Connie reached for money he didn't have to see her smile. Kelly would take one look and know what was occurring.

Wally flicked his cigarette-butt from the balcony and watched it sail into invisibility.

Knew he was doing no good being in South Africa.

He could see there was no way of controlling the faces they were dealing with. Ministers, justices . . . . They owned the police, and Wally knew the South African coppers used nutcrackers on the old family jewels when they went for a confession. Just for openers.

Wally lay on the hot terrazzo and bucked through fifty slow sit-ups.

Everything was too big. Too foreign.

Jorgesson had talked Connie into flying an English geologist out to assess the Mkuse site, and now there was serious talk of bridging a river and building a bloody airfield. And there was Harry and Sailor, dripping shooters and bandoliers like regular Buffalo Bills, rounding up kaffirs to dig exploratory trenches for perlite and clear the bush to start the airfield. And the only laugh for Wally had been how they had taught the Zulu workers to sing 'All Coppers Are Bastards' as they flogged about the place.

Wally refused to grunt as he strove towards fifty.
Fighting the hangover.
Driving himself.
And of all the companies in the world only one could make a machine to expand this perlite stuff into usable commercial form. Just one company, and it just happened to be Hungarian. A communist company the South Africans wouldn't touch with a dozen ten-foot poles. Wally knew Charlie Dance had acted smart when he'd handed Jorgesson over without a murmur.
The woman watched Wally exercise.
Her hair was long and sun-bleached, and her body was lush and toned by swimming. The crests of her full breasts were untanned, and the appendix scar on her taut belly lost itself in the fine down of her pubis. Only the slight gauntness of her neck showed she was close to forty. Cleansed of make-up, her eyes were light amber with understated white lashes.
'You keep yourself in good shape, Walter. I admire that. Too many men grow fat with their wealth.'
Still wondering what her name was, Wally flopped into a lounger, lit a second Stuyvesant and figured something had happened inside Connie's head when the old mother had died. Connie had soldiered on when brother Danny drowned in the Thames. Hadn't even broken stride when the old man popped off. But he'd sat with the old mother all through the night until she'd gone, and hadn't let the priest anywhere near her until it was all over. He'd laid her out alone, and gave Wally a right royal whacking when he'd caught his big brother weeping.
The woman put on a towelling robe to let the breakfast-trolley into the suite, and wheeled it across nibbling toast.
'Have you been with a Kaffir woman, Walter?'
'Have I bloody what?'
'Had a Black—'
'No! Nor Hindus nor Eskimos, neither. Two of your embassy faces pumped me about that last night. Wouldn't believe we wasn't throwing Black tarts to the pavement

every five minutes because it ain't against the law back home. I'm sure there's some who like making coffee-coloured kids, lady. But not this kiddy, and nobody who's true-blue white.'

Wally shook his head. What was he doing around these people? People who Connie thought enough of not to drop his aitches like a Christian any more? The woman said something in a half-amused way but she wasn't really smiling about it.

'What?'

'Naomi. My name is Naomi. I thought you'd forgotten. You really are rather a brute, aren't you?'

'Naomi. Right.'

'And you're a complete rotter.'

'Well, that's as may be, and you wouldn't be here if you wasn't partial to a bit of rough, would you? Or are you minding me for the syndicate? Seeing I don't nick the silver or goose your Kaffirs?'

'Rather than goose me? A gentleman wouldn't even think that.'

'You see any gentlemen, Naomi?'

'Only a boy in a man's body. You'll burn if you stay there. So many muscles and such tender skin. Have you forgotten you're to take me to a luncheon party?'

'Get one of your *svelte* gents to take you and come back after dark.'

Wally went inside to burn his mouth on freshly brewed coffee.

Naomi sat on the bed to decapitate a boiled egg.

'Conrad flew to Durban this morning and left you as my escort. Being boorish with me won't bring your memory back. Or cure your hangover.' Naomi tongued yolk from her upper lip. 'I'm no cheap pick-up. And I'm not trying to trap you into anything.'

'Who said you was?'

'You. Last night. All night. And again just now. Are you usually so paranoiac? Or is that a goody you save just for me?'

Wally grinned at the composed woman.
'Drink and the devil, Lady.'
'Naomi.'
'Naomi. Keep me off the sauce and I'm a darling.'
'You'll need to be. We're going to the De Wits' with Clive Spring and the Jorgessons.'
'Dirk? I can't stand that face. Nor his bit of a wife.'
'Nor can I much. She's my daughter. He's my son-in-law.' Naomi wagged her spoon. 'And no remarks. Alicia was seventeen when she married.'
'No cracks. But she could have done better.'
'She likes money as much as I do. But I was less blind. I was spring married to winter. Now I'm widowed and pleased with my lot. I can afford to be diverted by young men like yourself, and I have no thoughts of remarrying. Honest lust with partners of my choice will do until I feel the need for a companion to accompany me into extreme old age. Until then . . . .' Naomi tossed her head.
Wally scratched a pectoral.
'I've never had a bird come straight out with it before. Maybe you're all right after all. Yeah, could be.'
'I'll take that as a compliment. Money breeds directness in certain circles. You have much to learn about society, Walter.'
'And you'll learn me, right?'
'The word is "teach". And "possibly" is the answer to that question. If you're sweet to me in or out of company.' Naomi lay back showing a lot of tanned thigh. 'And you could start now.'
Wally lay on the bed and leaned on an elbow.
'Lesson for lesson, Lady.'
'I'm bargaining with a shopkeeper,' Naomi sighed.
'What's this De Wit face all about?'
'Colonel De Wit? He's a sort of policeman. Just accept that you and your brother need him if you want to keep your mineral rights.'
'There's a bent rozzer around every corner. Even here in sunny South Africa.'

'If you mean he's dishonest, you are very wrong. That notion is meaningless here. Just take my word for it. Take care you never ever say anything of the kind to his face.'

Wally scratched his cleft chin.

'You looked . . . scared, really scared, when you said that.'

Naomi rolled Wally on to his back and straddled him. Her face hovered above his, and her breasts were as warm as muffins against his chest.

'And rightly so. Keep your right-white mores to the fore in that man's company if you wish to prosper on your brother's behalf. He can destroy you both with a single call. Now, ask me nothing more. Please?'

'Yes, Ma'am.'

Wally thought Naomi shivered with more than rising need. She buried her face in the pillow and covered her fear with a show of levity.

'Shut up and consume me with fire.'

'Don't take the piss, love. I'm only one man. And I ain't got my Boy Scout kindling-sticks with me.'

'Second best again, eh?'

'Maybe *you* should try a Kaffir.'

Naomi's back ridged under the towelling.

'Don't talk like that.'

'We're all the same in the dark, right?'

Naomi's nails bit into Wally's shoulders.

'Some more than others, brute.'

'Easy with the spurs, lady. Soft skin, remember?'

'Only in parts, Walter. Only in parts . . . .'

The house was white stucco with a portico of slender wooden columns, a roof of red Spanish tile and tall shuttered windows. The manicured lawn sloped to embrace a pool of jade water scintillant with dancing stars of light. Jacaranda, yucca and palm bowered between ancient quiver-trees, casting shade over the marbled terrace where the luncheon party gathered amongst loungers and sunshades. The blooms of the flowering shrubs were raw flames of pigment, too harsh for eyes accustomed to the mellow autumnal shades of London parks and the dismal prospects south of the Thames.

Wally sat on a recumbent concrete lion with a beer he didn't want, seeing why Jorgesson's commissions and expenses grew higher with every demand as he strove to keep up with Johannesburg society. The guests smelled of money, and their self-confessed God-given right to minority rule made them walk high, wide and handsome without the natural grace of the real nobility back home.

To Wally they all seemed to wear uniforms under their clothes.

Their arrogance isolated him, caused him to miss British beer and drizzle, red buses with steamy windows; saveloys and pies at a coffee-stall, and the grind of barrows on cobbles.

'You aren't swimming.'

Naomi dripped over Wally's shoes.

'With scratches up my back and a lovebite the size of a hubcap on my shoulder?'

Wally poured beer into the flowerbed to see it darken the red earth.

'But you've spoken to De Wit?'

'I've listened to De Wit. More like "twenty questions" down the copshop than talking.'

Wally watched De Wit, a man with a farmer's face and a soldier's bearing, order drinks from a Black houseboy.

'He quite likes you, I think.'

Naomi dried herself with a fluffy towel. Made Wally want her again as her breasts moved with her arms, heavy inside the scrap of a bikini, the fine grain of her skin the gold of sandstone.

'He called you a rough diamond.'

'I'll bet he did.'

De Wit handed Malcolm Sadler a tall Pimms. The Englishman was heavier than Jorgesson and shorter than his host. His Mayfair accent and sober suit set him apart from the Afrikaaners as surely as Wally's dark mood excluded him.

Wally figured Sadler for a smiler you could strike matches on for a century without getting a spark. He was all the things Vic Dakin had pretended to be. But Vic was well dead and Malcolm Sadler was very much alive, and was no friend of Connie's or Wally's. Wally could see that plainer than Naomi's big breasts, but Connie was blind to it, like so many other great truths.

'What? Sorry?' Wally had missed Naomi's last remark.

'He's my daughter Alicia's godparent. He thinks the world of her.'

'Who, Sadler?'

'Colonel De Wit.'

'That's why he puts up with Dirk, eh?'

Jorgesson showed off on a low diving-platform. His small and dark elfin of a wife ignored his clowning with her hand over De Wit's. Their heads together like conspirators.

'He likes her all right.'

Wally took a passing Manhattan for something to hold. He was the only smoker there and was shy of lighting up.

'Winter and spring again, Naomi?'

Naomi's face was sun-dried bone.

'If you swallowed your spit, you'd poison yourself.'

'Would I? What about Alicia and your precious Colonel? Cuckolding Dirk without undoing a single bloody button. Doing it with their eyes.'

The light seemed to burn the flesh from Naomi's skull. She turned away with an abrupt strangled noise.

'I only guessed, Lady. You've made it obvious. And don't let the servants see you cry. I hear they love to gossip.'

'You foul-minded, unprincipled . . . .'

'Maybe. But that don't change what's happening.'

Wally swallowed, and the alcohol hit hard. His constitution no longer bounced.

'You just had to use my own words against me, didn't you?'

'I didn't give your daughter appetites like her mother's. Like De Wit and Sadler have different appetites. You all like to play the ends against the middle and want the biggest slice of what's going for yourself. And, apart from all of you screwing each other for sex or money, the biggest prize here and now is my brother's tail, right?'

'If you think that, why are you here?'

'Ain't that a question and a half? What am I doing here apart from not a lot? You wanna leave with me?'

'I've had more than enough of your diseased mind for company.'

'Your choice.'

Wally watered the flowers with the Manhattan and set the glass between the lion's stone paws.

'You can tell Connie – sorry, Con*rad* – I said my goodbyes like a proper chap.'

'Tell him yourself.'

Jorgesson had flopped into the pool and was a silver ghost in the glittering water. Clive Spring had joined Alicia and De Wit, and they quoted poetry at each other with practised ease. Spring's Welsh accent reminded Wally of Dylan Thomas's radio voice. Too well oiled to be authentic. Sadler said something clever enough to make the company laugh and Jorgesson spurted water into the air, his hair wet straw against the jade tiles. Their laughter wound down when Wally's shadow cut between them.

'Gotta go. Something came up. Business.'

Wally and De Wit cracked knuckles in a hard handshake.

'You'll come to dinner when your brother returns from Cape Town?'

'Nice one. But Con's in Durban.'

'And it's business before pleasure. He's very single-minded.'

Sadler waved a long drink in a plump hand.

'I can vouch for that. A lurcher after hares.'

Spring thought that was funny until Wally looked at him. Then he found the foliage in his drink fascinating.

Wally was close to dropping Spring into the pool a limb at a time. There was a slyness about the man that angered Wally. And the camera he always carried and used when his subjects didn't know.

'We both like rabbits. Thanks again, Mr De Wit.'

'My pleasure.'

De Wit didn't react to Wally ignoring his military title. His was just another face in the sunlight and could have been seeing far vistas or dark cells. There was nobody home behind the hooded eyes. Alicia had the same look when she watched her mother come up to take Wally's arm.

'Actually it's me, darlings. I have this frightful head, and Walter has offered to drive me home. I'll call you later, Alicia. Tomorrow.'

There were the usual goodbyes, and Naomi threw her car keys at Wally in the carport, slapped the roof of her white gullwing Mercedes and snapped: 'I suppose you can drive one of these?'

'If the rubber bands ain't perished.'

'I thought for a moment you were going to hit . . . .'

'So did Spring.'

Wally drove between confident estates and small exclusive houses in the weatherless weather. Found his way out on to a highway where knots of black children offered fruit and small birds for sale. He turned off into scrubland and let the motor idle above a deep kloof tangled by nondescript thorn. The air-conditioner hummed and the car ticked in the blanket of heat.

Wally lit a cigarette.

'What's De Wit's angle with Connie?'

'What could it be?'

'I'm asking you, Lady.'

'Nothing other than the desire to see your mining venture succeed. This is still a pioneering country. We all admire self-made men.'

'That's as phoney as your headache, Naomi.'

'And as phoney as you threatening Spring. And as silly as your not calling De Wit "Colonel".'

'With a nice little salute and a couple of "yessirs" thrown in, I suppose?'

'If you won't learn, you won't.'

'There's more going down here than I can see on the

surface, that I do know. What the hell do they think Connie is? A bloody Rotarian?'

'Is there any reason why they shouldn't? Sadler talks very highly of your brother. Almost too effusively sometimes. You're seeing shadows where there aren't any.'

'And you weren't shaking my bed apart this morning for fear of De Wit, eh?'

'Take me home.'

'And what about this Spring geezer? This rabbit who spouts poetry and reckons he can sneer at the likes of me?'

'Then will you take me home?'

'I'm listening, Lady.'

'Clive Spring is in public relations, and something of a features writer. He can get Conrad a lot of good column-inches here. We like to see a new millionaire flaunt the fact. Otherwise, how is society to know he is one? Clive can build Conrad into a public figure in a matter of months. Weeks.'

'And what have they got on you, girl?'

'What *could* they "have" on me?' Naomi almost met Wally's eyes.

'Maybe phoney headaches are a capital offence.'

'Take me home.'

'You ain't bedding me for fun and profit. Even if you do like it.'

'Take me home, you bastard.'

'Yeah. End of a perfect day.'

Wally turned the car in a veil of dust and sideslipped on to the highway. Pushed the pedal to the floor and hit 120 miles per hour until Naomi killed the ignition and the Mercedes coasted to a halt on the hard shoulder.

'You were the one in a hurry.'

'And get myself a traffic violation with you in my car? I'll drive.'

Wally still puzzled over that remark when Naomi stopped to drop him outside the Langham Hotel.

'I won't embarrass you by asking you in in daylight.'

Naomi stared over the wheel.

'And I shan't embarrass *you* by refusing.'

Wally got out and held the door.

'Why do I get the feeling I'll see you again? And not just because we both want it?'

'Wouldn't you love to be right about that?'

'Better than being wrong. And better than getting tight knickers because your Alicia's followed your road too close. Live honest with yourself and stop pretending. Christ, you'd think she'd taken De Wit away from *you*.'

Naomi's sudden look at Wally was white bone.

'Christ,' said Wally. 'She did.'

'Goodbye, my brutish friend.'

Naomi left tyrestripes and a curl of vapour behind. Her brakelights flared and she was gone in traffic.

Wally went into the Langham gnawing his lip.

The telephone in his room rang with the weary insistence of a machine that had been repeating itself for far too long.

'Hello.'

Wally jerked his ear away from static and bad temper.

'Calm down, Con. All I'm getting is snap, crackle and fucking pop.'

He realised that apart from the odd 'bloody' he hadn't sworn in Naomi's company.

Connie said 'Vic Dakin' as the sirens of all the fleets of the world whooped in the background.

'What about him?'

There was something about bank drafts. Post-dated cheques. Bad wallpaper hung from Florence to Brussels. All signed by Vic Dakin on irrevocable transfers. Connie's wallet had been sliced thin by a dead man.

'How thin, Connie?'

'. . . seen thinner Red Rizlas . . . .'

'What does Kelly say?'

'—cking unprintable . . . next flight home . . . . *You* sort it . . . . *You* . . . .'

The line degenerated into electronic birdsong and the turkey-gobble of interference. Died completely and left Wally with Vic Dakin somehow being alive.

Wally jiggled the tines. Asked for flight details at the desk.

Knew he'd be home for Christmas and didn't know Naomi's last name.

Shame, he thought. Distracted.

Charlie hit the water clean.

The bottom came up as a surge of dappled concrete. He touched and stayed under. Dribbled air as he swam under the Chinese bridge Queenie had commissioned and made for the shallows where Ingrid turned brown in the shade of banana trees. Queenie knitted something Archie would never wear, a bright turban over her white hair, glasses on the end of her nose.

Charlie floated on his back.

Geckos sunned themselves on the hot castellations of the boundary wall and early finches arrowed into the big palms to spend the night, safe from Maltese hunters who blew them apart with grapeshot.

Queenie's needles clacked as she purled and plained.

'You'll go all pruny if you stay in much longer.'

'Yes, Queenie.'

Charlie basked where he was.

Archie sat in a wheelchair at the far end of the pool. He wore sunhat and shorts, and his big belly was as brown as a Mexican pot. He leaned on a walking-cane and stared at the pool as if daring the waters to lap his feet.

An embolism had formed below his right knee ten days before, and he had known nothing for over a week. A naval surgeon saved him before the clots reached his heart; and now, speechless and forbidden to walk, he mended slowly, his brain alive behind silent lips.

Charlie watched the shadows move with the sun, listened to a celluloid ball chase its own echoes around the high boundary walls. Archie's Maltese minders played table-tennis in the sunroom, cutting shots like fencers. Charlie had checked them out with the Tonna brothers in Toronto and received a telexed testimonial.

'Time you girls changed for dinner.'

'Don't tire him, Charlie.'

Queenie's needles went quiet.

'I won't.'

The orange-trees released their bouquet with the setting sun as Queenie and Ingrid went into the villa. Charlie swam through pink light and leaned below the wheelchair to look up into faded green eyes.

'You scared me, old man.'

Eyes the colour of money said they knew.

'The trial's over, Arch. Brixton, Alfie and the lads drew thirty years apiece. They're all willing to pay the price to be sprung. Except Popeye. He's played the amnesiac over Ollie and Pim, but the sorry bastard's sent word his memory'll come back if he don't get sprung as a freemans. But, knowing Popeye, he'd hold a press conference the minute he hit Rio, bubble everybody down the drain. Don't see that leaves us much choice.'

The green eyes agreed.

'Bonar votes for hitting him inside. It's that or spring him.'

Archie's cane rapped twice.

'Then, he goes.'

Charlie wished Ingrid had left her cigarettes behind.

'A body that could have been Buster's turned up headless in Rotherhithe. There'll be plenty of takers to snuff Popeye once the bubble gets around he grassed Buster to the Troys.'

The eyes blinked and narrowed.

'The Harolds are in Jo'burg with this Sadler face. Vic Dakin must have got away with bundles of dough for Connie to send Wally back to sort it. Pim got that bubble to me. He's still hot as a pistol over Wally staying away so long, so that should be a reunion with a difference, eh?' Charlie grinned and sobered.

'Connie can't clear all that nicked earth-moving equipment through South African Customs for lack of poppy and proper documentation. He can't bribe the bribable without the readies in his hot little hand, right? And with Connie needing heavy funds fast he might just get Wally to start the cowboy action to get it for him. Question is which way will he jump? East or west?'

The faded eyes became distant.

The sky had darkened to royal purple, and a rare owl hooted from the bowers above the north tower.

Archie's cane pointed south.

'Brighton? He'll have his work cut out there, Arch. That's where you let the dregs of the old firms melt away. And like you said: "Always leave a man somewhere to run, or he'll have no choice but to come back at you." '

I did, said the eyes.

'There's still bundles of train-tickle money lying about, waiting to come on to the streets where we don't want it. How about we get it pointed towards Connie? Let him earn some early remissions for a few fellows who've had enough of Her Majesty's Pleasure? Better it ends up in South Africa than burning holes in our cobbles.'

Work on it, said the eyes.

'I'll have to delay Wally somehow. Give me time to get things rolling. Jesse's taken our fairy back into the Fortress, so the bubbles are coming out of there all right. And Limehouse Lou is a loaded gun ready to be pointed, but I'll keep him in trap three for a bit. You agree?'

Archie's cane rapped yes.

'I've done nothing about Kosher Kramer. Nor Manchester Freddy and Maltese Maurice. Do I take the gloves off or not?'

Not yet, said the eyes.

'I don't like leaving it lie, Arch.'

The eyes knew. Said: Patience, Charlie. Hold water.

'I'm gonna be busy enough when I fly back, eh?'

You are.

'Shall we join the ladies?'

Why not?

Charlie wheeled Archie through the fragrant garden as the rising moon took on brilliance. The board meeting was over.

Ingrid wondered how she could feel sick and ravenous at

the same time. Nausea bumped the back of her throat when she found Queenie admiring the dress she had laid out on the bed in her room.

'You were sick, sweetheart?'

'Too much sun.'

'The water's different here, too.'

'Yes.'

'And you should wash the fruit before you eat it.'

Sequins gleamed on black taffeta when Queenie turned the dress on its hanger.

'May I have that?' Ingrid smoothed her slip.

'I'll button you.' Queenie hooked hooks. 'A bit snug around your sit-upon.'

Ingrid twirled to check her stocking seams.

'Too much of your good cooking.'

'And it's too early to show.'

'What?'

Queenie's hand rose and fell in dismissal.

'I'm an old woman who's seen the elephant too many times. Charlie hasn't noticed, but what man does?'

Ingrid flushed and frowned.

'Queenie Ogle, if you say one single word—'

'You haven't told him. I thought not.'

'This may be a permissive society, but not in my heart of hearts. No, I haven't told him.'

'Maybe you should before he sees for himself.'

'And lose him? Have him get that cold look in his oh-so-cold grey eyes and say, "Wham-bam-thank-you-ma'am, there's the door"?'

'How d'you know he'll take it like that?'

'How? Would he be who he is, do what he does for Archie, if he wasn't *just* like that?'

'But how d'you know?'

'You're a stuck gramophone-needle. Would you have told Archie if it had been you?'

'With brass bands and flying flags I would, you silly bitch. A kid's what we both wanted and never had. The closest we've got to a son is Charlie. Your Charlie. If a baby don't bring you together, nothing will. And if it pushes you apart? It was happening anyway. You can't hold on to what you haven't got, sweetheart. But you have to know either way, right?'

'I suppose . . . .'

'Will you tell him, then?'

'I'd have to be good and tiddly.'

'Whatever. But remember the baby eats and drinks what you eat and drink.' Queenie's look was bitter-sweet. 'I'm an expert on other people's babies.'

'You could be any kind of mother to this one. If you want . . . .'

Ingrid kissed Queenie's seamed cheek.

'You'll keep it?' said Queenie.

'Yes.'

'Whatever he says?'

'Whatever he says. Of course.'

'No "of course" about it. And now we're both crying. Wash your face and we'll find a bottle to celebrate. What, I don't know.'

'Life?'

'That's corny. Even for a mother-to-be. But we'll drink to it.' Queenie opened the door for Ingrid, and neither of them saw Charlie flattened against the wall as they headed for the stairs.

Charlie found himself looking at a man in swimming-shorts with a comical look on his face. It was a reverse image of himself in the mirrored niche across the landing.

Charlie stared at Charlie, and the reflected one seemed to have all the answers.

Wally cleared Customs with a sick migraine a week later than he had planned. In Pimlico's Jaguar he said: 'Straight to Camberwell, son. No messing.'

Pimlico turned through Longford, away from the M4.

'Connie swanned back a couple of days ago. Me? I got to twiddle my thumbs for six days and nights because I was flown out on a dodgy excess-baggage ticket from

Dakin's old travel agency. And bloody why? Because Interpol and the Fraud Squad are investigating thousands of snide tickets. Picked me out at random.'

Wally blew smoke. Blind to Pimlico's silent disapproval.

'And now I've got to listen to bloody Kelly carp about all the earth-moving equipment she's shipped to Durban and can't pay the duty on because tricky Vicky cleaned out the piggy bank. *And* all the plant she's had nicked from motorway construction sites she *can't* ship because South African Customs want documents of origination and ownership she plain can't supply. It's just as bloody well the insurance money from the long-firm fires went into a different account, or Connie'd be right up the Mississippi without a banjo.'

There was more of the same before Pimlico pulled off on to the common land beyond Poyle.

'Couldn't you take a leak in the terminal, Pim?'

Wally followed Pimlico out on to grass stiff with frost.

Distant cows huffed white breath and a colt skipped about a mare.

'This is igloo-land after the jungle I've—'

Wally sat down hard and skidded on his buttocks. Pimlico's fist had taken him in the mouth. He stared at the green trail he had blazed, and cold struck up through his rimed trousers.

'What's your game? I ought to—'

Pimlico kicked the wind from Wally's lungs. Crouched on a ham to watch Wally sit up to hold himself.

'You want some more? Or you want to listen?'

Wally touched a swelling lip.

'I'll listen. One-sided chat anyhow.'

'OK. So don't thank me for climbing out of bed at five this morning. Or for driving all the way up from Brighton. Don't once ask how business has been since you been playing Tarzan in wogland. And don't just *don't* expect me to drop my marbles in the playground for your bloody brother. We got our own tickles to fret on.'

'Who said . . .?'

Pimlico ripped a frozen stalk of cow parsley from the turf and slashed the air with it.

'I'll take you to Camberwell to see Connie's crumpet. I'll even hold your coat when you pat her head and say, "Shame, darling". But I've made a meet with Charlie. And you're going to that. Any arguments and we're history, right?'

'But there's millions at stake . . . .'

'Ain't my millions. Nor yours.'

'But, Pim . . . .'

'And if this mining lark is so lucrative how is it the South Africans are handing it over on a plate? To a foreigner?'

'Connie knows.'

'Connie knows nothing.'

Wally pointed a heavy finger.

'He's my brother, Pim. Like you and me are brothers. The only difference is we chose each other, you and me. I got born alongside him. You've got a punch, you know that?'

'So long as you do.'

'You're taking a lot for granted I won't belt you back.'

'You can try.'

Wally offered his hand for a lift.

'Hell, no. But I'd like to sell tickets if you and Charlie ever squared off. Can I get up, or are you planning to kick my legs away?'

Pimlico stepped off a few paces.

'You can make it. And I saw that move in ten old John Wayne movies.'

Wally slapped his soaked backside.

'I can sort this Vic Dakin business *and* take care of us.'

'Not if Brighton goes sour. Kosher's crowd don't want our machines. And Charlie wants it sorted. Yesterday.'

Wally retucked his scarf and found his hat.

'Hitting me won't sort it.'

'Had to make you listen.'

'To what? Charlie comes first?'

'And because the Troys have laid a carpet of poppy in Brighton to keep us out. And sent a message it's their turf now. They're right cosied up with Kosher's firm.'

'You could have said that without the oliver in the mince.'

Wally stared into the neutral haze.

'So that's how they figure to make happy with Sadler. Play Jack the Lad out of the Smoke. Connie said they'd try something flash without dropping another bollock.'

'What are you wittering on about?'

Wally saw bands of colour as migraine clamped his head.

'Tommy reckons to get at Connie through us, that's all. And your precious Charlie. They've chosen the turf. All we gotta do is pile in with our soldiers and take a licking. Unless we box more than clever.'

'That's why Chas wants to see us. He's too smart to get caught that way. He knows it's no walk-over.'

'Is there anything else in your tiny mind, O Master of the Magic-flaming-Ring?'

'Yeah, don't smoke in my car.'

'Nice one. Welcome home, Wally,' Wally sneered.

'Welcome home, you fart. I've missed your ugly boat.'

'Stands out a sea-mile, does that.'

'And congratulate me. I got married.'

'Now, that' – Wally sat in the car – 'is real aggro.'

The stage at Mother's Club had new curtains.

The flats and backdrop of Highgate Hill where Dick Whittington turned again for fame and fortune in the City of London needed six feet of sky, a door for the medieval pub and numerals for the milestone. Electric Raymond sewed a tail on to a cat costume, and Kensington Kate sat in muted light from a niggered-pup with the white-haired boy. The same nude reclined on his painted pillows, and the same incense tickled Charlie's nose as he helped himself to coffee from the Cona.

Penny opened his silk blouse to show weals and scratches, the big blue pigeon's egg under his long white fringe.

Kate's nostrils pinched.

'Sorry in triplicate won't make this right, Charles.'

Charlie blew on his scalding drink.

'You're always formal when you chide me. Jesse's work?'

'His brother Tommy's. It was just after Helen's memorial service. I was upstairs. Changing for Jesse. He likes me in lingerie. They were things Helen gave me before she —'

'Slowly, son,' Charlie soothed.

'— killed herself. Tommy came into the bedroom. Just came in and went berserk. Screamed her name over and over again with spit jumping out of his mouth. Tore everything away. Looking . . . for her. And when he saw there was only me he started punching and punching. Ripping at me with his nails . . . .'

Penny gagged. Clicked his teeth.

'. . . Then Jesse came in at a run. Jumped at his brother. Trampled all over me like madmen. With Jesse holding Tommy around the chest. And Tommy hitting down anywhere he could. Head. Face. Shoulders. Kicking, too. The mirrors smashed. They fell over the bed, and the pillows burst. Feathers went everywhere. All over them. In their eyes. In their hair. Then Jesse hit Tommy with something hard. Tommy went down and went to pieces. Just sobbed and punched the bed. And Jesse held him like a little boy. Ida screamed for the others to do something. But nobody would come in. Not even Gordon. Then it got quiet. Like they were asleep. But they weren't. They were whispering as if they'd hidden something. Something special. Something only they knew about. Not Ida. Not me. Not anybody . . . .'

Penny sipped Charlie's coffee.

'Take your time, son.'

'And . . . when I looked they were holding something. A cigar-box, with rings and pieces of gold. Shiny things like that in it. Turning them. And touching them. Nodding and smiling. They were in another world. Like bad children . . . .'

Kate glanced at Charlie. Rubbed his neck as if bristle grew back into his skull.

Charlie drank coffee, but his mouth would not moisten.

'And then . . . slowly, and then all at once, they grew

up. Were men again. But private. Touching the things in the box as if they were . . . magic. It was . . . . I don't know. Just nasty.'

Charlie's 'uhuh' was taut.

'And they stayed on the bed with their foreheads touching. With white down drifting down all around them. And they made plans. Sometimes there were words. Mostly they sort of knew what the other brother was thinking. They mentioned Brighton and how many overcoats they could call on for a straightener. And talked about Sadler in mumbly voices. Too mumbly for me to hear. And Archie Ogle was finished. There was a contract on him. Who's Sadler and Archie Ogle, Charlie?'

'Nobody. What else?'

'And when they said your name, Charlie, they made a circle with their hands and . . . spat through it. Three times.'

'Romany rubbish,' said Kate. 'You'll have them burning feathers next.'

'They did.'

Kate rubbed his neck some more.

'And lit candles. And let the wax drip on something I couldn't see. And said he was dead. And said other names and said they were dead.'

Penny drank coffee and shuddered.

'What names?'

'Yours. And an Irish name. Who missed an old lady and shot . . . a horse . . . .' Penny touched his bruised forehead. 'Does that make . . . sense?'

'Dublin Gerry? Was that the name?'

'But he's—' Kate started.

'Shut it, Kate. Was that the name?'

'I . . . think so.'

Charlie's smile was a fleeting thing.

'Pull the trigger without triggering the target. Makes sense. If you're Irish.' He nudged Kate. 'And talking of Irish.'

'I've gone.'

Electric dropped his sewing and poured Jamieson's

over ice in a tall glass.

'I'm not going back. Money or no money.'

Penny shook like paper in the wind.

'No, son. You and Shane are going on holiday.'

Penny's smile was beatific.

'They said something about Manchester, too.'

'Manchester?' said Kate. 'They're bringing provincial overcoats in?'

Charlie shook his head.

'Not a town, Kate. A man. Wheel Penny away, old son. Pim and Wally are due here for a meet.'

Kate stood.

'Good. They can make their machine pay out better. My fairies aren't made of money.' The snap in his voice almost masked his pleasure. He rounded on Electric Raymond with: 'And if that cat's tail is on straight I'm Rita Hayworth.'

'And we loved you in *Pal Joey*.'

Electric handed Charlie his long Irish as Kate took Penny away up the stairs.

'You've pleased the old dear.'

'Fair exchange.'

Charlie toasted Dublin Gerry on a job badly done.

Connie glared at Wally, nodded at Pimlico, stuffed geological surveys into his briefcase and gave Kelly something to file. Harry the Crack and Sailor Mailer loaded purlite samples into a van in the yard.

'You've missed all the fatted calves, prodigal.'

'And who left me at Jan Smuts Airport without a dildo to dangle?'

Wally's head was a ballroom of angry echoes.

'You had Naomi Leathers to ease the wait.'

So that's her surname. 'And you weren't batting your eyes at her daughter Alicia?'

Kelly spiked a docket.

'Sounds fun. Do tell.'

Connie's eyes marbled.

'He's throwing dust to cover his own ricket. Alicia's only a kid.'

'Nineteen going on a thousand. You'd clean her clock. *If* Uncle De Wit don't clean yours first.'

'Well, tick-tock.'

Kelly answered the phone with a stiff back, and Connie stabbed his blotter with a stiffer finger.

'I wasn't back in this chair five minutes before West End Central was on my neck for a sweetener. You forgotten drinks for the boys in blue's first order of business?'

'We don't backhand the filth,' said Pimlico.

'Everybody needs sweetening. First law of villainy: buy the right copper.'

'Wasn't me got turned over by Vicky Dakin. And buying coppers ain't where it stops for you, is it? You want to buy whole governments. Let me off this carousel. I'm riding the dead horse.'

Wally's neck and earlobes flushed.

Connie pointed over both fists.

'And Charlie Dance ain't deader? Why don't you make one with the Troys and really cut my throat?'

'You don't need my help. You was the one who thought he had Dakin cut and dried, not this kiddy. Get your feet back on the cobbles where they belong. *We've* got the Troys on *our* doorstep because they won't come straight for you. Leave me and Pim to our straightener and get back to your big-deal scheming.'

'No straighteners. No Mickey Mouse. After Christmas maybe.' Connie sounded strangled.

'Easter? Whitsuntide? All Hallows?' asked Wally, and Pimlico snorted softly. 'So long as it ain't now. It's never *now* with you.'

'Straighteners ain't earners. I need dough, not aggro.'

'Then, earn it how we do. On the cobbles.'

'You'd choke if I didn't swallow for you,' Connie said.

'Don't big-brother me, Mister.'

Pimlico got his back against the wall as Harry and Sailor came in to block the door. Connie looked wild enough to try something hard and permanent.

'And don't Jack the Lad me,' said Connie. 'You two take on the Troys? You haven't the spit to lick a Penny Black. And Charlie's got you well finger-tamed. He's started you out of trap three and no back-up. Go away and be unlucky.'

'That's what Charlie said you'd say,' said Pimlico.

'Said what?'

'Said you'd be in the mood for an earner. You want one? You got one. He said.'

'Is that a message to me from him?' Connie asked.

'If you want it.'

'Like what? As if I'm interested.'

'Some boarders wanna go on their holidays. Without a striped suntan. It's an earner you could handle.'

Connie just stared, thinking hard.

Pimlico shrugged and rolled his shoulders.

'They want a foreign holiday. You want dough in wogland. One gets you the other.'

' "Charlie said," ' Connie sneered. 'All this "Charlie said" is giving me the heaves.'

Pimlico barely smiled.

'And I had you pegged higher than the Troys. But you and them are the same stamp. There ain't enough money in the whole world to make you or them happy. No highs. No lows. Just take it all because you want it. Unhappy on top. Unhappy anywhere. No, you ain't no better nor no worse than them. You're just the same. You through here, Wal?'

'Except I ain't walking around them two,' said Wally.

Kelly glared at Wally over Connie's shoulder.

'You could ask them to curtsy and stand aside.'

Mad lights stung Wally's eyes.

'She talks; you wear the frock. That it, Bruv?'

Connie's fists shook on his blotter.

'Easy, Greasy. You got a long way to slide.'

Wally stared at the men in the doorway.

'Anybody else got anything to say?'

Harry the Crack showed his palms and edged aside.

He wanted Wally off the firm without trouble. Wanted the top slot in South Africa keeping Dirk Jorgesson finger-tamed for Connie. Seeing that Alicia didn't play footsie under another table unless it was that phoney colonel's. Harry liked the life out there. Liked teaching the Kaffirs to play darts with six-inch nails and how to bawl ribald cockney songs as they sank their frothy Kaffir beer.

Sailor stayed mute. Eyes mean in his tanned face. He wanted to mix with Pimlico and Wally to show Connie what he could do. To show Connie that Sailor was better than both of them any day of the week and twice on Sundays.

Connie may have given a sign. Kelly hissed as Sailor became casual and made a show of looking at nothing through the grimed windows. Harry opened the door, and the tension guttered and died like a used candle.

Wally followed Pimlico into the yard.

'You'll be back. You'll come crawling,' Connie yelled.

Pimlico bundled Wally into the car and drove away fast. They were fifteen minutes behind schedule when he parked in Soho Square in plain view of Quill's vantage-point above the massage parlour south of the Fox building.

Quill lowered his binoculars.

'They're going to Mother's, Buller.'

'Five minutes behind the Troys. Do we steam in or sweat it?'

Quill's eyes shone like wet tarmac.

'If there's an affray, we won't need a warrant. Have the squad on stand-by.'

Electric Raymond flipped coasters on to the bar and wiped the mahogany with a bar-towel as Jesse came through the tables with Tommy, Gordon and three overcoats.

Kensington Kate ran scalding water into a pitcher and held it below the counter.

Jesse's smile was the yellow of old ivory in a face that

would not form a single expression. He seemed to be shaking apart from inside.

'A pound's worth of mixed drinks here, Electric.'

'Haven't seen you since my party three months back, Jesse dear. How's our Penny?'

The barb went deep, and Electric didn't seem to notice the harm he had caused. Kate worried a lip. Charlie Dance sat in a spotlight and was making no move to leave.

Tommy tapped the bar with a manicured nail.

'And you tarts wouldn't know about Penny, eh? You're still a comedian, Kate.'

'Only in the right company, Mr Troy dear. Five small iced pigeon's milks, is it? Or manly pints of cooking-bitter in grubby glasses with lipstick smears around the rims?'

'It'll be large vodkas,' said Electric. 'Don't mind her, boys.'

'Large *free* vodkas,' said Tommy.

'And you can get Penny out here as quick as you like.'

Jesse's face wouldn't compose itself. He sneer-smile-frowned with damp lips. His heavy eyebrows jumped like caterpillars with a multiple hotfoot.

Kate sighed and let more water into the pitcher.

'They say a refusal often offends. We haven't seen the little darling since — when was it, Electric?'

'My party in Manor House.'

'Her party in Manor House.'

'That right?'

Tommy emptied his glass and turned it in his hand.

'That's right,' Kate affirmed.

'Not since Jesse abducted the little darling and left us without a raffle prize.'

Tommy's smile had malice.

'I drink vodka in the Russian style. Means you don't get to use the same glass twice. Frederick March done it in a Garbo movie. All the officers had one swallow and whacked their glasses into the fireplace.'

Jesse swilled his drink.

'Penny was clocked coming in here.'

Kate's sarcasm deepened his baritone.

'Leading a slightly pink elephant by the trunk? On points in a tutu and prancing on moonbeams, I suppose.'

'You've been listening to the halt and blind, Jesse,' said Electric. 'We should chide you for that.'

An overcoat said, 'Anywhere on the top shelf, Tommy? Knock 'em down and win a packet of fags?'

Gordon liked that remark.

'If we play Russians, we'll not finish a bottle before your backbar was a disaster, Kate. All those wee glass animals and ballerinas. Your Guinness toucans. Your Johnny Walkers. All gone with the wind. Like Ida's did.'

'A smashing time was had by all,' said another overcoat.

'Last chance, Kate,' said Tommy.

Kate held the pitcher of scalding water at his side. Looked Tommy straight in the eye and said: 'We both know it won't make an infinitesimal jot of difference what I say or do, don't we? You'd still have to make your mark. I'm too old and too fey to spit into the wind or fart in the face of the inevitable. You just smash away, dear heart. My glass-salesman's sitting right behind you, and he gives me lovely rates for breakages. Don't you, Charles?'

'Oh blimey yeah.'

Charlie was a severed head in the spotlight.

Tommy turned easily, and short staves slid from overcoat sleeves into ready palms. Kate showed Jesse the pitcher of scalding water when he started across the bar, and Electric Raymond's kitchen knife was as long as a moonlit road.

Tommy wished he could see more than shadows around Charlie's smile.

'That can't be you, Charlie?'

'Run out of gaffs to smash in your manor, Tom?'

'Somebody upset the brother.'

'Not difficult as I hear it.'

'That's as maybe. But how is it that Archie's top monkey happens to be cosied up in this poofs' parlour at the very moment Jesse's special fairy goes walkies? I mean, a very nasty thought occurs, right? Like, could it be the special fairy we're looking for has been bubbling our secrets into your shell-like?'

'That's a lively imagination you've got there, Tommy. You should write gags for Kate's panto.'

Tommy looked at a fist. Opened it and put it into a pocket.

'Flying glass gets everywhere, Charlie. And Kate won't earn damages from the Arts Council. Just the paper hat from us.'

'Like that punter of yours who obliged you by throwing himself through his own plate-glass window to save you the bother? Twice? I heard they had to number the parts to put him back together again. Just like poor old Popeye Greenland.'

Tommy edged towards Charlie's table.

'What about Popeye?'

'On his way to the sluice when it happened. Pot-carrying for Her Majesty. Earned a sharpened spoon in the kidneys for threatening to bubble if he wasn't sprung for free. Touch and go in surgery, I heard. He got word out through his sister Elsie. You know her, Tommy. She's the one who's susceptible to burns in the kitchen.'

'And what if I do?'

'Elsie reckons Popeye wants to keep his clack shut and do the rest of his bird in solitary.'

Tommy rubbed his jaw with his free hand.

'You tell the bloke with the spoon I'll buy him a good drink if he does better next time.'

'Happens you couldn't buy him a drink. But you have one with me, that's if Electric will save that pig-sticker for cutting sandwiches.'

Jesse found his voice from somewhere.

'Let him hold his shiv until I shove it up sodomite valley for him. I want my Penny. Now.'

Tommy wore conceit like a cheap overcoat.

'You see, Charlie? He's well upset. So forget the silly sociables. You and the Dolly Sisters here are well overdue for a good hiding.'

Charlie said nothing and his face remained pleasant.

A silence gathered all by itself and the Cona bubbled like an upset stomach. The ceiling stayed where it was and the floor didn't quake.

Tommy's contracted pupils were as hard as the ends of freshly snapped pencils.

'The old bottle tweaking, Dance?'

Charlie's head shrugged against an unlit shoulder.

'For why? A nice fellow's never without friends. Penny ain't here and that shouldn't bother anyone but Jesse.'

'I'll show you bother.'

Jesse's face shook with emotional ague. His pink eyes snapped at nothing and his hands washed themselves sweaty. He looked ready to fall a long way into somewhere dark and unpleasant.

Charlie wondered how he could nudge him there.

'Love never runs smooth,' he said.

Tommy pointed a finger.

'It's you who's sweating.'

'You haven't looked in the doorway.'

'At what? I've got the front well covered.'

'You ain't looking.'

Wally stepped from the stairwell.

'He never did.'

'You never said truer, Wal.'

Pimlico nodded at Charlie and inspected Tommy as if he posed in a tailor's window.

'Does that coat come in bigger colours? Them padded shoulders an optional extra, or what? And, hello, here's some faces we usually only see the back of. Where'd you get this lot, Tommy? A job-lot from Mothercare?'

Tommy's fury paled his face.

'You owe me and Jesse for putting rent money on your Miriam's table, Pim. Don't prod your old friends.'

'Wasn't you prodding Miriam, Tommy? Didn't she welcome you with opened legs? So who owes who?'

Tommy bit into his half-smile. Stared at Pimlico with

raw hatred.

Jesse said 'Penny' and sighed.

'Get your mind out of your back pocket, Bruv. This face owes us.'

Pimlico leaned against the bar.

'So you reckon it's the husband who should pay for hot knickers and cosy cuddles? Like by not paddling at Brighton and not putting our machines in down there?'

'That and standing aside now,' said Tommy.

Pimlico let a stave out of his sleeve. Rolled it along the bar towards Jesse and tutted.

'Bit late for that. Your face on the door handed me this when I hooked him gentle. How'd you want to play this, Chas?'

Charlie remained still. 'A good host lets his guests choose the party games. It's up to Tommy. What's it to be? Musical headaches. Pin the tail on the tosser?'

Tommy's sneer almost came off.

'Comedian.'

Jesse knocked his stool over and grey tears trailed his face.

'You've got my Penny, you bastards . . . .'

His face caved in on itself and he sobbed as though he were alone.

'What have you girls said?' Pimlico asked Kate.

'That makes it a stand-off, Tommy. Pick up your marbles and go home,' said Charlie.

Kate stabbed the Pernod optic, and his hand shook as he added ice and water.

'Nine straights and not a fairy in sight? What kind of a name will Mother's get now?'

'Thirteen,' said Electric. 'The law's in.'

Quill's squad milled about on the stairs, and Bulstrode was saved from falling by Wally's stiff forearm.

'Nobody move,' Quill bawled. 'I have reason to believe —'

'Are you gentlemen members?' asked Kate.

'— there has been an affray in contravention and in breach of—'

Bulstrode straightened his tie.

'Hold it, Prophet.'

Kate insisted he see the gentlemen's cards.

'Not warrant cards,' Electric told Payne as he flashed his wallet.

Kate sighed at the ceiling.

'Fourteen straights and nobody drinking.'

'You!' Quill poked a hole in the air near Charlie's nose. 'Stand up. You're carrying a concealed weapon.'

Payne seared the bar with his flashgun, and light slicked the staves in the overcoats' hands.

'What are they?' asked Charlie. 'Lollipops?'

'Stand up.'

Charlie's head went into shadow, and Quill's hand was spotlit as he took Charlie's wallet.

Payne asked Tommy his name.

'Joe Loss. This is me orchestra.'

'You what?'

'It's an audition, you soppy copper,' said Electric.

Tommy found Pimlico over Payne's head.

'I want a straightener. You and me. No lawyers.'

Pimlico bared teeth.

'Pick your turf.'

Wally wandered to the bar and asked for a vodka to wash down a soluble aspirin.

'Get names and addresses,' Quill told Dillman.

Wally gargled vodka.

'Duke Ellington, Hollywood. Never black up for rehearsals.'

'Barbara Stanwyck,' said Electric. 'And she's Rita Hayworth this week, aren't you, petal?'

'Autograph, handsome?' Kate offered.

Jesse buried his nose in a handkerchief and snorted long and loud.

'Stagefright,' said Electric.

'You know who I am,' said Pimlico.

Paper bands fluttered to the carpet when Quill fumbled with notes and credit cards.

'What would you say they were, Buller?'

Bulstrode knelt beside the paper bands. Recognised the

colophon of a Scottish bank.

'Like Mr Dance has some explaining to do.'

'Now, ain't that a turn-up?' Quill crowed.

Bulstrode could not look at Quill. He blinked up at Charlie.

'He'd starve as a cardsharp,' Charlie said softly.

'We'll have to take you in, Charlie.'

'Suits me, as it happens,' said Charlie.

Bulstrode used tweezers to put the bands into an envelope.

'It don't sit right with me, Charlie,' he said.

Quill found his handcuffs and a printed caution.

'Turn around, Dance. Hands behind your back.'

'Out of order, Prophet,' said Bulstrode.

Quill just read from his card with his face lit from within.

Dillman fumbled with notebook and pencil.

'What do I write as the accused's reply?'

'Write nothing,' said Bulstrode as Quill's handcuffs snarled around Charlie's wrists.

'Write the Lord's Prayer for all I care,' said Quill. 'He's well nicked.'

'What are all these wooden clubs for?' asked Payne.

Kate swept from behind the bar to tweak Payne's cheek.

'Props, you sweet thing. Hand them in, boys. You know I don't like you playing with them. We're closing for rehearsals, but you can stay. That camera looks so professional.'

Payne coloured and went behind Bulstrode.

'You're swallowing this, Chas?' Pimlico asked.

'Why not?'

'Don't talk to the prisoner,' said Quill.

In the street Charlie sniffed the early-evening air. Smelled frost in the lowering scud of mist and chimney smoke.

'Breathe deep, Dance. That's the last free air you'll know for a couple or three decades.'

Charlie was ducked into a police car and sandwiched between Bulstrode and Dillman. He played a mental game of poker to pass the time and smooth his face, and didn't react to Quill's taunts.

BOOK THREE

CHAPTER FOURTEEN

THE CELL was just oblong of square and the light stayed on all night. It had a grey steel door with rounded bolts and a fisheye lens set in a concave oval viewing-port. The floor was brown composition with faint red figuring, and rolled up to make a hard sanitary skirting to the base of the tiled walls. The wooden bunk was three inches too short for Charlie and was deadbolted to the left-hand wall.

A fumigated mattress the thickness of an arrowroot biscuit and the brown of old faeces was tightly rolled beside a small rubberoid pillow with an off-white slip that also smelled of treated sewage.

The corner sink was stainless steel, and button taps dribbled lukewarm chlorinated water when leaned against. There was no mirror, no razor, and the soap was a hard slab of yellow sawdust that gave grudging lather and a swale that refused to wash away.

The toilet bowl was cantilevered white ceramic crazed by age and use. There had once been a window, but now there was raw brick beyond the thick steel bars.

The towel Charlie had been issued was the size of a large facecloth and its nap was as abrasive as a Brillo pad. He had shaved watched by a warder who took the razor away when he was finished. They had also taken his tie and belt and shoelaces.

Breakfast had been a compound of eggs, a sliver of fatty bacon, a cob of bread and a mug of dark tea sweetened with evaporated milk.

Somebody had cried during the night. The sobs had become long withdrawal moans. Then screams. Doors had clanged, a doctor called, and the weeping addict sedated enough not to dream vampires ate through his ribcage.

All Charlie needed was a Negro singing the blues and he could have believed Burt Lancaster reared canaries in an adjoining cell.

Charlie no longer cared what day it was.

He lay on the bunk and calculated complicated bets to keep his mind sharp.

A uniformed policeman slammed the door open and poked his head inside. It was a hard, shaven head and the eyes were tougher than nailheads. The jaw said: Don't look sideways at me. Don't even look at your own shoes. Look nowhere. Look smart. And jump when I say jump. I'm the man, and you're nothing but grist to my mill. Move when I say and not before. Wait for the command.

'Out,' he said, crashing a heel against the door.

Charlie was walked along a corridor of the same white tile and the same flooring. The stairs were spiralled and rang under his feet as he climbed two storeys to another door.

'Stand *still*!'

The screw opened the door with the right key on his jangling ring and hustled Charlie through, locking it with a deft twist.

This corridor was green and dull cream, and there was glass in some of the doors. Charlie glimpsed a pigeon on a sill beyond bars before he was sent into a room with two chairs and a wooden table. The tall window looked out on to a tiled light-well through more bars.

'Wait,' said the screw and went away.

Charlie waited.

High heels walked across the ceiling on linoleum and a filing-cabinet drawer slid on steel runners. Two fingers stabbed at a typewriter, and keys jangled as policemen in shirtsleeves strolled down the passage. A late bluebottle blundered against the window and flew away up the light-well. A light-switch clicked inside the cavity wall and a floor-joist creaked. Then nothing happened for a long time, and there was no clock to record the wasted minutes.

Then two men came in.

The tall one with a long face and grey receding hair took the chair in front of the window and the stout younger one stood at his side with a buff file and a large notebook. The tall one scraped his chair. Scratched an eyebrow and the bridge of his bony nose. Looked at the file the stout one placed on the table in front of him. He did not look at Charlie when he said: 'Sit down, Mr Dance. You may smoke.'

The stout one watched Charlie stay where he was through large tinted glasses with lenses the size of apples. His chubby leer let Charlie know they meant business — knew his hat size and his laundry number, how many fish there were in his aquarium and the titles of the books on his library shelf. He said: 'You heard the Detective Chief Superintendent, Dance. Sit.'

'Please,' said the long-faced DCS.

'Please?' said the stout one.

Charlie sat in a hard chair and watched for more bluebottles.

He was asked his full name, address, height, age, date of birth, even though it was typed on the form in front of them. He was told he was a remand prisoner, could wear his own clothes, order meals from outside, and had visiting rights.

'Can you account for your movements between 5 August and 9 August?'

'This year?'

'This year.'

'If I thought about it.'

'Do so.'

'OK.'

'Well?'

'Well, what?'

'The dates, Dance.'

'I'm thinking about it.'

'Slow, aren't we?' said the stout one.

'Slow enough to stand the three-card trick. Slow enough

to know you've got my passport and would oppose bail if I asked for it. Slow enough to know you two would like to play "nice" and "nasty" with me. The old Mutt and Jeff. Chubby there gets to be nasty. You get to be the placatory, avuncular one. Chubby yells and goes red in the face. You offer me a cigarette and fatherly advice. And tell me how hard you'll fight to get me a fair shake. I play the dumb yo-yo and end up wearing the paper hat. That act should have gone out with high-button boots and "Vote for Disraeli" posters, *Mr* Cotton.'

'You're not so slow you don't know who I am.'

The one with the long face found crumpled Gauloises and a box of matches.

'There's the snout. D'you want the avuncular advice?'

'Neither, thanks.'

'Independent, isn't he?' said the stout one.

Charlie folded his arms.

'Hasn't even yelled for a brief. Don't you know a bent solicitor?'

'Is there a straight one?'

'You sound like a couple of coppers I know.'

Cotton straightened a Gauloise and rolled it into his mouth without lighting it.

'Straight, are they?' said Charlie.

The stout one frowned and said nothing.

Cotton just looked at the file and said: 'Suppose I tell you you've been named as the laundry for the train tickle? All signed, sealed and delivered. You'll want to make a statement now. Get yourself a silk with a long line of objections.'

'No.'

'No?'

Charlie watched moisture darken the cigarette in Cotton's mouth.

'No. I like the quiet life. You have to prove I've done what you allege. Establish guilt without a shadow of doubt. Not just to your satisfaction. To the court's. I don't have to prove anything. Now or ever. And I don't need legal advice. Only the guilty or the innocent need all that nonsense. Remand away. Postpone. Adjourn. Do it up brown. Pleas of mitigation and cross-petitions are a pain. Me, I'll sit here with a paperback, three meals a day, lots of uniformed protection, solitude. And, more important, peace of mind.'

'Confident as well,' said the stout one. He leered and jabbed thick thumbs into his waistcoat pockets. 'You want the country drive, do you?'

Charlie shrugged at him.

'Sounds different.'

'You'll change your tune after a week in Brixton. Another in Maidstone. A third in Durham or Swansea. We can yo-yo you up and down the country from nick to nick until you think your head's twisting off at the shoulders.'

Charlie did not respond.

The stout one leaned forward from the waist.

'And on the way you can't help but meet up with faces who owe you more than a moody dig. Plenty of cons with sharpened spoons. A razor blade in a potato. They'll carve on you for the crack of saying they carved Charlie Dance. And if you live to go to trial you won't draw Number One Court at the Old Bailey, Mister. You'll shuffle into the dock of the crown court at Aylesbury. A nowhere place for a nowhere face. You could be on remand for a full calendar year. And there's no remission for that.'

'Want to reconsider, Dance?' Cotton asked.

Charlie uncoiled from his chair. Stared through the barred window. Watery light formed silent patterns on the white tiles. The bluebottle made a final circuit and went away in an upward spiral.

'Well, Dance?'

Cotton was ready to call a constable with shorthand.

'Who do I see about buying some decent Christmas cards?' Charlie said.

The stout one showed disappointment.

Cotton closed his files and shook his head.

'Hard-nosed and very, very stupid,' he said.
'With robins on logs,' Charlie smiled.

Silversleeves Sutton bought plaice and chips in Catford High Street. The headline on the newspaper wrapping was five days old and read: KENNEDY SHOT IN DALLAS.

Silversleeves wished the fish was as fresh.

He wove through the market in a bitter wind. Soho had been alive with advertising agencies starting their Christmas jollies early. Silversleeves had been punched by a model who shot arrows between cider-bottles in television commercials. How he had earned a split lip was lost in alcoholic haze, but Silversleeves knew the archer's muscles weren't painted on by Special Effects.

He pushed into the snug of the Minstrel Boy and got himself a pint of Younger's. Nobody bought him a gargle any more, and getting decent warehouse oddments to suitcase out in Oxford Street was almost impossible now he'd been marked as a Troy snout. When he'd been laying out the cash for information on the mail-train tickle he'd had friends coming out of his ears, but after the dough dried up and after Popeye got himself shivved doing porridge Silversleeves's face no longer fitted.

'Silver,' he told himself, 'you need another drink and a fat tickle.'

Tommy and Jesse Troy had changed over the recent months. Time was, when they talked of a straight straightener they'd meant it. Like talking hard at Pimlico for a neutral hand-to-hand on neutral turf. But that wasn't their style any more. Now they came out of the dark team-handed when they knew the face they'd challenged had his back well turned. And now they were slagged down by everybody what chance did Silversleeves have of changing firms? None. Even Johnny the Builder and Barry the Blag turned their backs. No, Silversleeves was stuck with the Troys, and the only way to get on an earner with them was to turn up Limehouse Lou or point out one of Pim's firm when he was on his own . . . .

Silversleeves leaned on the counter and craned to flag the barman in the saloon bar where the darts-players drank more doubles than they hit. Then he checked the public bar where a barmaid with a rear like a full moon watched two men check the coin-drop on a one-armed bandit.

Silversleeves knew his luck had changed.

Wally Harold lifted the machine back into place, and Vinnie Castle gave the barmaid some free discs.

'Have some free pulls, Maisie. Nothing's too good for our punters, and you could win.'

Maisie laughed like a throttled goat.

'And porkers might levitate, Vinnie Castle. I knew you when you had nothing in your pockets but mischief to get girls like me into trouble. And time was, I might have let you.'

'Time was, you should have.'

Maisie said something lost in racket from the saloon bar, and Silversleeves dialled the Vallance Street number. Ida passed him to Gordon, who finally handed him to Tommy.

'See they stay there,' Tommy ordered, and the phone went dead.

Sweating on the much-needed earner, Silversleeves broke the back of his last pound to send drinks across for Wally and Vinnie. Then he ducked outside before they spotted where the free round came from. It was much colder, and a parked Bedford with *Imperial Machines* lettered on the side ticked as it lost engine heat. Silversleeves sheltered in the doorway of a furniture store to watch all three entrances of the Minstrel Boy. Vinnie and Wally were misty patches beyond acid-etched glass.

Christmas lights flicked on and off in the store window, and a plastic Santa smiled beside cheap chairs that might hold together if they were sat in by a dwarf with no small change in his pocket.

Silversleeves sneered at the furniture.

And waited.

J. C. Hatton got Charlie's signature on the last document

and closed his briefcase with a loud double snap.

'You look — and I don't wish to strike a dismal note — distinctly jaded.'

'Then, don't.'

Charlie dredged up a wink for Ingrid, who suppressed tears.

'They only moved me from Maidstone last knockings yesterday. How did you find me so fast?'

'We're not entirely without influence, Charles. A chum of mine flew us down from London. Swansea has quite a decent airfield.'

'No problems on the firm?'

'The casinos take care of themselves as ever. The betting shops are marginally more profitable than the summer quarter. We've added yet another branch to our meat distributors. Nothing else bothers us overmuch.'

'Nothing from Toronto?'

'Golden silence, which is as it should be.'

'Keep tabs, J.C. Don't want no surprises.'

Hatton's wink barely fluttered his lashes. He patted Ingrid's hand and went into the passage.

'Hello, Funny Face.'

Charlie's hair was badly cropped, and his face was chapped from cold-shaving with a dull razor. His eyes were as vague as scraps of fog.

'Why wouldn't you let me come before?'

Ingrid's eyes brimmed without overflowing.

'You would have cried. Like now.'

'That's just me. Means nothing.'

'That kind of nothing sticks. After I've counted all the tiles in the cell, the lights are out, and I can't even read the graffiti on the ceiling. I still can't figure out how fellows get up there. Must be ten or twelve feet or—'

'In heaven's name, Charlie. Can't you—?'

'No, I can't. And nor can you. You've got two to look after, and I can't be there to see things are as they should be.'

Ingrid blinked.

'Yes, love. I know about the bundle of fun. I listen at

doors. My old mother never could break me of the habit.'

Ingrid turned shy and rewrapped her duster coat.

'It's beginning to show. I'm not holding you to anything. I wouldn't even—'

'Even if you could?'

'I suppose.'

'You're on the next flight to Malta. J.C. will fix it. There you'll be safe. And old Queenie'll have a fit if you don't pull a cracker with her. There's no choice, right?'

'That's what you want?'

'That's what I want.'

'But you here for Christmas. Charlie, I feel so inadequate.'

'Don't. Going without an apple, orange, a new penny and a piece of coal in my stocking won't hurt me. I'm in the best place, believe me.'

'Dotty says she'll swear on a stack of bibles you were—'

'Never heard of her. Go away now, Ing.'

'Mr Self-contained.'

Ingrid showed bitter need.

'Go away. Go away now.'

'Yes, Mein Führer. I always follow orders. Anything else I have to do?'

'Take care.'

'Anything else?'

'Yeah.'

Charlie stood and rapped on the door to the cells.

'I love you, you silly cow.'

'You . . . what?'

But Charlie had gone.

The screw watched Ingrid get hysterical with a blank face as he carefully closed and locked the door.

Cars and vans passed and kept going.

A mongrel with a bad hind leg damped a lamp-post, sniffed at the meagre mist he had raised and trotted off as if he knew where he was going.

Silversleeves leered at the dog.

A dark saloon coasted past, slowed almost to a standstill, gathered speed and lost itself down the street.

Silversleeves kept his brain warm with thoughts of money. Of the drinks money would buy. Rows and rows of bottles with the right labels. The best bonding. All his alone. In a darkened room where there were women who poured for him without drinking themselves. Who patted his hand and left fragrance close to his face without speaking or wanting him to talk. The dream had recurred all his life since puberty. When pathological shyness clamped him in a sure grip. Made him inarticulate and impotent around *them*.

Women.

In the street it was different.

There he was in charge.

He could silver-tongue them into passing the half-crowns at will, whatever he sold: stockings with crooked seams or legs of different length, blades that fitted no known razor, aftershave that smelled of goat curds — anything at all.

Silver-tongued Silversleeves, who could sell sand to Arabs and junk to women with locked purses.

The alcohol died, and Silversleeves knew he had caught cold. He shivered violently when Vinnie and Wally came out to laugh in the glow of the mongrel's lamp-post. Wally dropped a toolbox into the Bedford, making it bounce on its springs. They laughed at that and did not look up when the dark saloon reversed to a halt beside them, white smoke popping from the exhaust.

Something dark and metallic slid through the open rear window and all the flashguns in the world went off in a searing clap of white light. The concussion flattened Silversleeves's clothes against his chest, flexed the plate-glass window and rang in his ears like a million untuned bells.

Vinnie was lifted, hurled against the pub door. Small coins chimed on the pavement as the skirts of his topcoat blew into tatters along with gobbets of flesh from his thighs. The whole of his left leg showed through ruined trousers before he flopped. On to his haunches with his hands above his head.

Then he said 'Oh' as if somebody had stolen his last sweet and became a bundle of torn clothing on a discarded dummy.

Wally had not moved.

There were blood spots all over him. He swung a fist at the car roof. Dented the metal skin. But the saloon was already gathering speed. Slid away leaving a last coil of exhaust in the cold air. Then that was blown to nothing and the normal sounds of the night came back. Creeping like thieves.

Silversleeves found himself moving away.

Going anywhere.

Telling himself he was nothing to do with what happened.

They was just gonna rough him, wasn't they? Cut him a bit. Razor him. Break his head or his legs like usual. Not put a shooter to him. Not a shooter . . . .

He ran blindly. Did not see Wally trying to staunch the wound in Vinnie's groin with a red rag of shirt-tail. Or Maudie holding the head in her ample lap. Crying for the boy she had known all her life.

Pimlico just held the wheel.

The telephone was still a presence against his face.

Dotty's Mini found the green lights and the fast lanes without him. He could still see Dotty with street cold coming off her coat as the telephone told him about Vinnie in Wally's broken voice.

His belly just spilled out over his belt buckle, Pim. His legs was just meat open to the bone . . . .

Pimlico blinked to change the pictures in his head.

Blink. Vinnie aged eleven outside Southend Kursaal with a parakeet on each shoulder and a sock down. Another Vinnie nine years on, grinning in RAF blue. Both Vinnies framed in silver on his mother's mantelshelf.

Blink. Vinnie with last month's receipts from Imperial Machines. All ice-cream smiles because they were in profit.

Wally groaned. *His kneebone was on the pavement by*

his foot . . . like a bloody piece of cuttlefish . . . .

Blink. Vinnie kissing the bride outside Caxton Hall for the photographer. Dotty kissing him back with her skirt hiked to show her lucky blue garter.

'Who? Who did it?' Pimlico asked again in the speeding Mini.

Wally had choked with frustration.

The Troys, who else? . . . Plain as day and nasty as ninepence . . . . I was too slow . . . .

'Against a sawn-off?' Pimlico asked the streaming sodium lights of the somnolent City. Racing into Aldgate's cheerless glare of whelk- and coffee-stalls, Jewish and Chinese restaurants, Seamen's Missions, churches darkened by television and apathy.

At the City Hospital he abandoned the Mini in a surgeon's reserved space with the indicators blinking life from the battery. Ran up stone steps into the wet blanket smell of steam central heating. The hushed sounds of a hospital putting itself to sleep for the night.

A black student nurse pointed him towards the casualty ward, and he tried to slow to a walk. To show nothing in his face or manner to anyone. To himself,

Vinnie's mother was dwarfed by a brace of doctors and a young beat constable.

Pimlico reached for the double doors, was pulled into an alcove by Wally.

'Too much law for us, son.'

'I'm going—'

'Nowhere but out of here.'

'Don't stick your oar—'

'Arthur Ax has charge of the case, you berk. He's Troys' bought and paid for. Come away.'

Wally drew Pimlico down a metal staircase into the basement. Laundry made soiled white mountains, and dim service lights formed dark grottoes in the vaulted ceilings. Pimlico dragged his feet. Took a meaty slap across the face when Wally wheeled him about in the freezing carpark.

White breath gusted as Wally said: 'You'll only get collared by the local CID. End up down Leman Street nick playing "Twenty Questions" with the Cunts In Disguise. Vinnie's close to had it. Sweating for Arthur Ax under his lights won't help him. Right?'

Blink. 'You've seen him?'

'Told a nurse I was reporting for the local rag. I've got a date for Thursday night if I want it.'

'You're talking crumpet at a time—'

'With them ankles and a bum as big as all outdoors? It earned me the inside dope, that's all. Vinnie won't never walk straight again. Even if they save the one leg and his heart gets him through surgery.'

Pimlico could not stop blinking. The lights were crazy smears in the night. Glaring softly.

'You want back at them? Pim, you listening?'

Blink.

'You want another whacking?'

Blink. 'No.'

'In the jam-jar.'

Pimlico shrank into the Mini, and Wally drove to a lock-up garage off Roman Road. He closed and locked the doors and sat back in the car with a heavy fishing-bag across his lap.

'You want back at them, Pim? Hard?'

Pimlico's face was all hard planes in the spill of dipped heads.

'I can taste it.'

'Then, we scrub hitting Brighton. Tonight in Catford.'

'Just the two of us? I'm livid, not potty.'

'I've been on the telephone a lot. Got us a team.'

'Who?'

'All we need. I got enough shooters to start a war.'

Wally unzipped the fishing-bag to show Pimlico a pair of sawn-off ·410s, restocked and shortened twelve-bores, a ·38 Smith & Wesson on a ·45 frame, ammunition as red as blood.

'Look at Wally when he's talking. You hear me?'

Pimlico nodded, worked the pump action of a Remington, filled his pockets with cartridges.

'There's this club crying out for our machines and some heavy crowd-control. A firm of Troy's freelancers have got their elbows in the till. Costing the management an arm and a leg. It's perfect, Pim. They won't expect us to come back at them so fast. And there's no point going to Vallance Road; Troys tarts'll be nowhere near the Fortress tonight.'

'But Arthur Ax and his boys in blue will, right?'

'That's my old Pim. Thinking straight.'

Wally plumped shells into a twelve-bore and snapped it closed.

'Give me the faces and the club?'

'Called Captain Jones and the Ju-Ju Men or something poncey. And you'll like the who.'

Blink. Vinnie in a wheelchair. On crutches. No more fast swerves in front of the goalmouth at Highbury Fields.

'Pinky and Red Bellaver. That's who.'

Pimlico stopped blinking, and his vision was very clear indeed.

'Let's go.'

The sign was as vulgar as the club.

White bulbs chased themselves around a red neon monkey in a green palm on the illuminated fascia. Discouraged brown rubber plants nodded sagely from brass-bound tubs either side of an entrance tricked out in painted concrete bamboo. Woven bamboo trellised the lobby carpet, and the reception desk was faced with dyed reed. A black girl in a glitter-dust sarong took entrance fees without losing the basket of fruit she wore as a hat. Split bamboo covered the walls except where inset squares of rattan cane framed enlarged jungle-movie stills.

Hope grinned at Crosby in Bali, Sabu waved his steel tooth at Sheer Khan, Fay Wray screamed from Kong's fist, Bogart hauled *African Queen* through Hollywood reeds and Johnny Weismuller called elephants from the

Universal City waterfall.

Pinhole lights were stars in a black ceiling above palm-leaves on wooden poles. A poster advertised 'Jungle Jim's Bingo' on Tuesdays and listed forthcoming attractions in dayglo.

Wally and Pimlico drank at a bar where vines twisted, grapes hung in plastic clusters, and the barmen wore boleros and bow-ties over bare chests, and waitresses in grass skirts flitted through the tables as a trio played sugary numbers for the couples eating each other's faces on the dance-floor. A planter's veranda overlooked the dance-floor and a jungle battered by mechanical storms every hour on the hour.

Red and Pinky Bellaver drank at a long table on the veranda with a crowd of noisy faces. Pimlico spotted Kosher Kramer and three Maltese pimps in the company. One of them was Manchester Freddy, and Pimlico wondered why he was cosied up with a rival firm.

Wally downed a third vodka.

'Freddy's a fader, Pim. He'll never trade knuckles chin to chin.'

Pimlico swallowed Scotch and water.

'That's as maybe, but he's married into the Tonna family. He got their sister Fat Maria well up the dove and married her before Jesus and Roger shortened him by a couple of feet. Then they had to take him serious — take him into the family and give him a living. Before that he was a small-time pimp who did the best part of a five stretch for torching his tom's flat. Scarred her for life. He's rubbish, Wally, and him in this company don't sit right.'

'Then, he takes his chances like the rest of them,' said Wally.

Pimlico worried a knuckle between his teeth and took comfort from the shotgun under his coat. Harry the Crack and Sailor Mailer drifted to a side-table and were joined by Froggy Farrell and Nasty Nostrils.

'There's a sight you never thought you'd clock,' said Wally. 'Them faces at the same table. Have you ever seen

Harry use six-inch nails at a dart match? He can take a fag out of your mouth at thirty feet with a nail.'

Pimlico rolled cartridges in his pocket.

'Is that right?' he said for something to say.

'And there he is sitting over a drink with Nasty and Froggy like they was all West Ham supporters. Harry's dead keen on South Africa. Hot for living out there. Figures a small favour here'll keep me off Connie's firm and help get his feet well under the table. Sailor, too. That's how to work the oracle, Pim. Dangle the right carrot.'

'And Nasty and Froggy?'

Wally looked amused.

'Maybe Charlie figures you ain't allowed out alone.'

'There's still a good eight faces up there.'

'You can't count *pimps*. Scrub Freddy, Maltese Maurice and Johnny Valletta. Three brass monkeys in need of a good polish. Malts melt in the crowd. Not in your fist.'

'You got a carrot for Kosher?'

'Yeah, double-barrelled.'

Wally smoothed a bulging lapel.

'Fit, are you?'

The restaurant was closed. The trio finished their last set and dancers drifted towards the exits. Wally sauntered across the sprung floor and stepped on to the veranda.

'Thought I'd buy you chaps a gargle.'

Pinky was owlish with drink. His pocked face was flushed and he grinned with grey teeth.

'On our own turf? This ain't no railway line, right, Red?'

Red nodded with narrowed eyes.

'Seems we owe you . . . something, Harold. Maybe it is a drink with lumps in it.'

Wally smiled at that.

'But me and Pim's in company. Couldn't take a solitary bevy without the mates got one, too.'

Red's narrowed eyes flicked towards Pimlico. Swivelled to rest on Harry the Crack's table. Hovered there and came back to Wally's face.

'A regular little firm you've got there. A drink for them

won't break us. It's all earners out of our special services.'

'How special would they be, Red?' Wally winked at Kosher, who held a goblet of champagne in a hand covered in rings. The scarred face stayed neutral and the eyes could have been lead slugs.

'Dunno,' said Red. 'Nobody's ever put us to the test.'

'Maybe they're all little boys around here,' said Kosher.

Manchester Freddy liked that enough to repeat it. The Maltese smiled in waxy silence.

'You think they're little boys?'

Wally stabbed a finger towards Harry's table.

Red Bellaver leaned back in his chair, and the butt of a gun showed against his shirt.

'If they are choirboys, they can give us a bit of a song.'

'You wouldn't like the tune,' said Wally.

'I thought we was drinking,' Freddy said, wiping his pencil moustache with a damp finger. He called for a tray of pint glasses, upended a bottle of Stolichnaya over a glass and slammed it down in front of Wally. 'Have some of that.'

'Don't leave me out.' Pimlico emptied most of a bottle of Scotch into a straight glass and filled one for Freddy. His hand had lost its shake. 'Nor yourself, Freddy. Get that down you.'

Freddy's bow-tie bobbed as he swallowed. His eyes turned sullen as his hand twitched beside the huge Scotch. Unwilling to pick it up.

Wally chuckled.

'You're the host, Red. How do we get a good drink for everybody without more than dead soldiers on the table? Or is this little boy's bluff?'

Kosher shifted in his seat.

'Call the drinks in, Red. No room for bluff here.'

'We know that,' Pinky snapped. 'You wanna play games, we'll play games. You want drink for drink, you got drink for fucking drink.'

'If you've got the bottle for the bottles.' Freddy sniggered at his own wit. Earned a hot look from Pinky, a cool one from Kosher.

Wally called Harry's table across and said: 'Harry's partial to mother's ruin. Right, Harry?'

'Very, very dry.'

Harry looked huge in a camelhair coat. Dwarfed everyone at the long table. He draped an arm around Sailor's shoulder and laid a hand on Nasty's elbow. Jerked his head at Froggy.

'Sailor and Nasty like black velvets without the black.'

Red Bellaver made his eyes open wide.

'Champagne, Harry? In poofy little glasses with the old Kensington finger out?'

Pinky leered at his brother.

'They are choirboys.'

Harry just smiled.

'They'll take their bottles by the neck. Froggy'll knock off a bottle of Canadian Club. Freddy and Pim are all topped up. They can get stuck in while we're waiting for reinforcements from the bar. A reconnaissance drink for the firms. Or is the pimp's mouth the biggest thing about him?'

'I'll show you mouth.' Freddy took a long draught of Johnny Walker. Choked and held the alcohol in his throat until he got it down. His eyes watered and he sat heavily with a gasp. 'How's . . . that?'

'Pitiful,' Wally said. 'Which of my little boys is gonna show London can beat a Manchester melt any day?'

'Try here.'

Pimlico's spine was ice, and great balls of sweat ran down his back. Vinnie haunted him as he emptied his lungs, opened his throat and drained off the pint of whisky without a blink. Set the glass down without a tremor.

'Fucking Ada,' said Morrie Torrance.

'And her sister in the WAAFS,' Kosher added.

Wally banged the table.

'A pint here for Pim. Must need a beer chaser for that.'

Pimlico stayed upright without weaving.

'But not without a toast,' he said.

A pale waitress brought a tray of bottles and a pint of

lager and lost herself in plastic greenery. The bar staff had melted away. Red leered at his brother.

'What's the toast? His grey-haired old mother?'

Wally rapped the table again, and Froggy stripped foil caps from bottles, popped champagne corks.

'No,' Wally said. 'Nor slow greyhounds nor the price of pease pudding. Let's have all of you with full glasses. Malt whisky here for the Malts, Frog.'

'Don't take the piss,' Freddy mumbled.

'So long as you can swallow yours, Manchester. Only right you should match drinks with us. You offered the gargle.'

Red filled glasses for himself and Pinky.

'That much is right. But it's my firm you're drinking with, Harold.'

'Nice point of clarification there, Red. Needed to know.'

Pimlico held his glass up to the light.

'To your firm, Red. And to a face you'd have been proud to drink with. If he wasn't in surgery losing a leg. To Vinnie Castle, who got done tonight. Done from a moving car by faces who should rot in hell. Vinnie Castle.'

Red spilled ash down himself.

'Red's firm and Vinnie Castle,' Wally said, drinking.

'Seconded.'

Red nuzzled his drink, seeing everybody did the same. Three gulps in he gaped and stopped swallowing. Pinky did much the same. Freddy and the Maltese took less than a solid mouthful. Morrie Torrance made frogmouths into his lap, and Sailor coughed champagne on the floor. Harry turned away with puffed cheeks, and Froggy sneezed Canadian Club down his waistcoat. Kosher kept drinking until Pimlico finished his lager, upended his glass and set it on the table, then he sat back in his chair with a long belch and a look of odd admiration for Pimlico's capacity.

'To Red, Vinnie, and a change of management,' Pimlico said.

There was a silence that Red broke with a fulsome belch and 'Is that your idea of ho-fucking-ho, Mister?'

'Ain't a laugh left in the world,' Harry the Crack said.

Wally held a bottle of Stolichnaya by the neck and slammed it down on the table in front of the Bellavers.

'That's it for you boys. Pick up your marbles and trot off home. This your last free gargle in Catford. You're barred.'

'We ain't mean,' Harry said. 'You can have the dead soldiers as souvenirs.'

'You ain't right in the head, neither.'

Pinky scraped his chair back a millimetre. Harry leaned on the chairback and ground him to a halt.

Freddy waved a sloppy hand.

'Mouth and trousers never got baby a new bonnet. I drink what I like, when I like, where I like. I ain't just some fucking face. I'm—'

'Nothing.'

Pimlico swept Freddy's drink into his lap and slapped his face with a return swing. The slap lost itself in the palms and bamboo before anybody reacted.

'Out of order.'

Pinky crouched and pushed himself upright into the bottle Wally swung at him. Hit across the throat, Pinky slammed an arm into his brother's face and made sounds in his chest like glass grating under a heel.

'My suit. Thirty guineas of threads,' Freddy wailed.

Wally threw Pinky from the veranda and hurled the chair after him. Pinky hit the polished floor and was still skidding when he fired his sawn-off ·410 without bothering to aim. The chair still bounced when pellets sprayed the table. Morrie Torrance clapped a hand to his torn neck and looked stupefied.

Harry the Crack's left drove Red Bellaver into Wally's arms and they fell together in a thrash of legs and tumbling bottles. Kosher came out of his chair heaving the table over. He was no longer a slow and heavy middle-aged man. He head-butted Sailor, and cut-throat razors came out from behind his lapels.

Sailor turned to vomit champagne over Morrie Torrance. Morrie reared away to save his suit, tripped over Wally and Red, crashed down beside them and kicked Sailor's feet from under him.

Pinky tore holes in the air where they had all been a moment before.

Pimlico mashed Maltese Maurice's nose with an up-swinging right. Maurice flailed away as Johnny Valletta slashed at the air with a switchblade, trying for Pimlico's jugular. Pimlico decked him with his shotgun-butt. Johnny flopped into a cascade of glassware and a sudden swill of spilled alcohol, squealed as he ground glass into his buttocks.

Freddy fell behind the overturned table where Froggy caught at his ankle. Hauled himself up Freddy's body. Biting where he could not punch. Freddy used his nails like a hysterical woman, gouged Froggy's wrists and face.

Pimlico pointed the shotgun at Kosher to keep him away. Watched Wally punish Red's head against the floor. Saw Morrie and Sailor fight in their own puke. Let Johnny Valletta crawl for the exit trailing blood from badly slashed buttocks.

Harry the Crack had vaulted the rail and made a running kick at Pinky's head. His leg was in mid-air when Pinky fired one-handed. Hit in the thigh, Harry spiralled to the floor and took a second charge in the lower back.

Distracted, Pimlico barely dodged the cut-throats darting in crisscross near his face. One slashed through his lapel. The second blade nicked his shoulder. Kosher's bulk took him back a step. The razors slashed again, parting his hair.

Pimlico stabbed the shotgun into the big belly. Brought it up in a savage arc under Kosher's nose. Spattered himself with blood and phlegm from Kosher's nostrils and one ear. Kosher still came on, the razors cut ahead of him. Pimlico felt the Remington buck. Pumped the action automatically and fired again. Kosher stood still and shook his head. The front of his suit was peppered and blackened, and spurts of carmine ruined what was left of his white dress shirt. His jowls shook and turned grey under the dark beard stubble and the dead white scar tissue.

'Now, ain't that a turn-up,' he said dreamily.

Pimlico racked a third cartridge into the chamber, and the sound brought Kosher's eyes up.

'You won't need that, son,' Kosher said. 'You've done me handsome. Can I go home now?'

Pimlico nodded. At a loss to know what else to do.

Kosher held his belly and turned away very slowly. He winked at Pimlico and followed Johnny Valletta's red trail through the kitchens to the emergency exit. A leg went rubbery, and he saved himself with a monumental effort of will. Leaned into a crouch and kept walking until he turned from sight behind the plastic jungle where lightning flashed and rain hammered rock and palm and a volcano smoked sullenly.

Pimlico swung the shotgun to cover Wally. Sailor and Morrie were tumbling chairs about at the far end of the veranda, and Froggy was getting the best of Freddy. Maltese Maurice had disappeared, and Harry still lay on the dance-floor, searching for something inside his coat as Pinky reloaded and grinned his grey grin, deciding where he would shoot Harry next.

Pimlico felt the Scotch and lager hit him harder than the cold fact that he had finished Kosher Kramer. He saw Pinky as a blur of menace. Brought up his gun and shouted Pinky's name. It came out as a muddy croak.

Pinky ignored the shout. Took a step closer to Harry and brought his shotgun up to his shoulder.

Harry found what he was looking for, and his right hand darted forward with a delicate flick of the wrist. There was a blur and a light tick, and Pinky looked surprised. An inch of polished metal grew out of his button-down collar. He tried to look at it. Was still trying to look at it when a second six-inch nail went into his cheek below his right eye. He took a step away from the pain, thought better of it and made for Harry, the ·410 out ahead of him.

Pimlico threw his shotgun up into his shoulder, blinked uncontrollably again, sweat in his sockets, stinging his eyes.

A third nail hit Pinky in the heart. He let go of a long

breath and pitched on to his face. The shotgun skittered away and came to rest against Harry's foot. Harry bowed over himself and muttered an obscene prayer.

Pimlico slumped, remembered Wally and turned to cover him again. Wally had lost the bottle he had been laying alongside Red's face, and both men had their hands around Red's sawn-off. Wally jerked it away from his face and Pimlico saw both bores flash in concert.

Then he was reeled away. Found himself bowed over the overturned table. Deafened by shock and concussion he took a long time to move. His teeth ached from grinding together, and whatever he looked at swam too close to his eyes. He levered himself upright with the shotgun, and the club came back on a dark wave of nausea as he tried to remember who Vinnie was.

The breast of his topcoat was black with powder burns, and his raked ribs stung and pounded. More than sweat ran down his chest as somebody used his voice to tell him to finish something.

He shook sweat from his face in a fine spray, and the shotgun was too long and too heavy to lift. He let it drop and felt better about something.

Pimlico sagged against an upright, and plastic vine-leaves caressed his face. He hadn't the breath to blow them away.

Sailor kicked Morrie Torrance in the ribs like a robot footballer.

Froggy and Manchester Freddy still made shrill noises as they fought like old women.

Wally bounced Red Bellaver's head off the floor and kneed him in the crotch at the same time, his face manic. A cold breeze came through the emergency doors, snapped paper napkins from their holders and drifted them about the club like ghostly moths.

Pimlico was colder than he had ever been in his life. His lower gut burned like dry ice. He wished Dotty was there to warm him with her body and hot drinking chocolate. He walked and walked and walked with small pecking steps, leaned against glass doors until they parted for him. The rubber plants nodded, and the neon monkey was monochrome on the unlit sign.

Something that could have been a man lay on the driveway, and the sideburns and scars could have been Kosher's. The low bubbling voice that could have been Kosher's talked in a soft monotone to an uncaring sky.

'. . . should've stayed in Brighton where it was . . . safe . . . . Not listened to all that Jack-the-Lad chat from Tommy and Pinky and Red . . . . All those Toytown heroes with yards of rabbit and no mileage . . . except miles and miles of not a lot . . . .'

Pimlico heard without listening as he walked and walked and walked.

In the main road a belisha beacon winked at him.

A car at the kerb called his name.

He dared not look for fear of being seen.

So he walked and walked and tried to walk until he was herded into a saloon by a redhead who said not to struggle or the hole in Pimlico would tear him apart. He fell into a leather seat, and the world rolled on without any help from him. The somebody driving talked about phonecalls to Dotty and being at Charlie's flat when the news about Vinnie copping both barrels came in. How Wally had told Dotty and Dotty had called Charlie back and . . . .

Pimlico saw the driver would have real red hair and freckles in proper light. Sodium wasn't real light at all.

'You're limehouse lou and they killed vinnie,' Pimlico mumbled.

'Chas said this would happen.'

Lou worried a lip with uneven teeth and tooled the saloon towards Spitalfields.

'Charliedunnoeverything.'

'Don't talk, Pim.'

The handbrake ripped on, and Pimlico found oblivion as he was lifted. Then floor jogged under his face and an old voice told Lou to lay someone on a table in a searing white room.

'How can I use anaesthetic with all that alcohol in him? He'd drown in his own vomit if his heart didn't explode. Maybe novocaine locally. That's all. I don't even know his blood type to make a cross-match. He needs a proper hospital.'

'Taking him to hospital would be giving him to the law, Doc.'

'He'd be alive.'

'And captured. That'd kill Pim.'

Breath smelling of old library books gusted as Pimlico's eyelid was peeled for a penlight. The sweet odour of final corruption.

'I can only try.'

A metal probe went into Pimlico's groin, and he followed Vinnie down a long arcade where parakeets the colour of agony beat their wings at his nerve-endings and cracked lead pellets in beaks like bullet probes. Then he flew with them into a night without end. Was an Icarus falling into a dark sun where all the hues were black.

Black nothing.

Blink.

Gone.

Connie Harold stood at the window in shock.

The tall American from Florida had sipped iced water at the head of a teak conference-table and said: 'Our offer is one million dead.'

Dirk Jorgesson had doodled on his pad, and Kelly sat in her white dress contemplating her own cleavage. The other executives of the mining company were just a row of men in leather chairs with well-groomed faces and lightweight suits.

One million.

Connie used two fingers to open the slats of a fabric blind. Bleached his face with hard sunlight bounced from cement paths between landscaped palms and bird-of-paradise plants. The tom-cat smell of ground ivy blended with the bitter tang of flaking gum-trees. Flags of all nations batted on the poles facing the white sand beach. Sprinklers chattered arcs of spray over a brown lawn. A girl in Bermuda shorts carried a toy dog the colour of ivory. Her cinnamon hair streamed in the salt breeze. Connie watched her cross the manicured courtyard, sit in a tiny red car and drive herself out of his life.

His mouth was as dry as a stale crust.

'Dollars or sterling?'

Connie wondered if the girl would have thrown him a brilliant smile if she knew he was a millionaire for the want of a simple 'Yes'.

There was only vague shadow and an oil-spot where her car had been.

'Your national currency, of course.'

The man from Florida drew smiles from his board.

Connie closed the light out with slow fingers.

Part of him wanted the soft option with six zeros. A certified cheque small enough to fold into his wallet and sit against his chest when he walked out into the Nassau sunlight. Tiny beads of sweat pricked his eye sockets, drying almost before they'd formed in the arid conditioned air. Air without taste or smell. Filtered for the corporate nostrils of men used to buying what they wanted with signatures on oblongs of engraved paper. Thinking no more of a million than a coin flipped at a newsvendor.

Connie had thought money had a smell. Like the London cobbles or Namaqualand when he first walked there, the smell of wealth locked in the ground since it had been closed to prospectors in 1928. And Connie had opened it up. The question was for whom? For himself? Or these smooth corporate men breathing their dead air in a deader building?

Six zeros backing a lonely number one.

Why shouldn't a three or a five front those six zeros?

Connie went back to his chair and ran a thumb over brass nails and leather. Decided white was not Kelly's colour. It was too bleached for her dull olive skin. And Jorgesson looked like a reformed drunk in a borrowed suit.

It was almost time for Connie to make the last few rungs to the top alone. To discard the passengers riding on his coat-tails. The cautious part of his mind winced when he said: 'Thank you, gentlemen. We'll consider your offer.'

Connie shook hands around the table, and the man from Florida looked impressed as he scribbled on a business card and tucked it into Connie's top pocket.

'A little reminder,' he drawled as he walked Connie's party through a marbled hall of sober greys and golden hardwoods, waved their taxi from the compound with a reflective smile.

'A million, Conrad. One thousand thousands,' Jorgesson said. 'That calls for a methuselah of champagne, by damn.'

'Don't spend what you ain't got.'

Connie watched a shopping-precinct glide past. The Christmas decorations tawdry in the tropical sunlight. As tawdry as Kelly was beside Alicia Jorgesson. Alicia belonged in boardrooms and on elevated terraces above the city skyline. She and Naomi Leathers had that elusive quality Connie needed to own for himself.

Kelly yelped and snatched her hand from Connie's fist.

'Down, Tiger. Enough time for rough stuff later.'

She blew on small knuckles and dug a finger into Dirk's midriff.

'And who didn't want to fly out here to listen to what the Americans had to say, eh? Wait until I tell Alicia what a *dassie* you are.'

'What my wife thinks is of little moment,' Jorgesson said.

Connie made fists in his lap.

Maybe Jorgesson didn't care what Alicia thought, but Connie did. He wanted to see her eyes shine when he doubled and trebled millions. Wanted her admiration in the boardroom and in bed. Dirk saw nothing when Connie looked at Alicia, but De Wit did. And so did Clive Spring. Wally may think that Spring's nothing but a no-good ponce of a reporter who takes funny photos when people aren't looking, but Spring had admitted to doing bird for a Mayfair jewel-heist back in the fifties. Had started over fresh in South Africa after a five stretch in Maidstone. And if De Wit trusted him Connie had no option but to go along . . . .

'You ain't listening, Con.'

'So what if the Yanks do double their offer, Kel?'

'Two million ain't a "so what", Connie Harold.'

Kelly fanned her cleavage for Jorgesson's benefit.

'I'm sweating hot, ain't you?'

Connie knew Alicia wouldn't have said that if her knickers were alight. She'd have borne it with a sweet smile.

'Ain't you, Con?'

'No. And stop showing Dirk next week's washing.'

Connie threw money at the black driver and made for the hotel lift. In their suite he made a Tom Collins the way Naomi had taught him and told Kelly to come out of the shower to answer the phone.

'It's London. For you.'

Kelly was a bedraggled urchin in a huge bathtowel, and her thin wrist shook as she offered the receiver.

Connie stared at her.

'Well?'

'Wally's been nicked. For murder.'

Connie took the phone and turned the card the man from Florida had given him. It read: *You'll never forget the day you turned down a million.*

That was for certain, thought Connie as he waited for the line to clear.

CHAPTER FIFTEEN

DETECTIVE INSPECTOR LEMMON winced when the grey steel door closed him inside the grey windowless room. Claustrophobia was a second overcoat for the long dreadful moment it took to shrug the fear of confinement away. The grey electric clock on the grey wall ticked off seconds. The grey heating vents hummed as far doors slid and clanged and screws walked with measured tread.

'One away to you, Mister,' somebody yelled.

'One away to me. Step it out there, Mister.'

Lemmon laid his trilby on the grey steel table and found himself rolling a Player between his fingers. He laid the cigarette on the crown of his hat. Pulled a grey metal chair out from the table and did not sit in it. Felt he would take root if he sat in the empty room alone. Trapped in the greyness for as long as his heart held out in the featureless monochrome.

Even the tin ashtray had been painted grey.

He laid his cigarettes and matches beside the ashtray. The sailor with his HMS *Hero* hat in the roundel on the Player's pack took on a prison pallor. His scrap of green sea was frozen, and the lighthouse in the background seemed to gather grey fog. His neat naval beard became unkempt, and the blue eyes lost their keenness. Lemmon lit the cigarette on his hat and watched the grey smoke lose itself in the greater greyness of the ceiling.

A prison officer opened the door, said, 'Remand prisoner Dance,' and made a meal of rattling the lock before going away like a toy soldier with a steel spine.

Charlie's slate eyes were holes in his face. The same

colourless nothing of the interview room. He sat opposite Lemmon and said: 'Welcome to Auschwitz on the Congo. Capital of the West Indies and the armpit of noplace. Brixton.'

'I'm glad you decided to see me.'

Charlie's almost-smile was as shallow as the chrome on a Ford hubcap.

'You didn't have to dress. We're very informal here.'

Lemmon touched his black tie and starched collar.

'Formal dinner tonight. Smoke?'

Charlie lit a Player with a Swan Vesta that refused to snarl. When he broke the match it sighed apart instead of snapping.

'Everything rots in here. Given time.'

'A smart brief could have bailed you.'

'Is that right?'

'You chose this road, Charlie. Why?'

Charlie leaked smoke with a shrug.

Lemmon leaned forward.

'Just the two of us here, so let's play the truth game.'

'It's your twopence.'

'Buller talked to me after he heard about Vinnie Castle. In confidence. He talked about Quill. At Mother's Club.'

'And?'

'Cotton's pirates and the Bucks CID presented seventeen hundred pieces of evidence at Aylesbury crown court when they prosecuted the train-ticklers and earned them thirty apiece. Including a couple of faces *in absentia*. Could be a certain bag labelled 1693 is surplus to requirements. Could be a certain somebody not an arm's length from me could be home and free in no time at all. For a certain consideration.'

'Mr Clean offers a deal?'

'Gloves off, Charlie. I want your collar. But I want it straight.'

'What difference would it make?'

'To me? All the difference in the world.'

Charlie sighed smoke.

'What *do* you want?'

'Apart from you in here for the right reasons?' Lemmon came close to a smile and rubbed it out with a brown hand.

'Apart from that.'

'Clever old Charlie Dance who knew the bloodbath was coming and took a rigged fall to keep his firm's nose clean. Eating his porridge whilst the rubbish leaves its own claret on the cobbles. Kills itself off. Leaving you to pick up the pieces when it's all over. It's as clear as your barber's rash.'

Charlie did not touch his face.

'That'll go with a change of diet.'

'Only if you deal.'

'With you.'

'With me.'

Charlie's eyes could have been shards of ice.

'You're a still small voice in the wilderness, Mr Lemmon. How d'you figure to climb the wall between us when your own patch is a mud wallow? You can't kick Quill out to pasture without a nasty internal song and dance. Or the Sunday tabloids printing corruption headlines. I've got more chance of spanking him soundly than you ever have.'

'You lay a glove there . . . .'

'Me? Lay a hand on my old mate Prophet? Why would I do that when he'll fall apart like the house-of-cards of a case you've got against me. Your forensic wizards can't place me at that farm; I was never there. Nor on that viaduct. And if I'm supposed to have laundered the dough how come Cotton's pirates scooped up so much of it? And you won't find my dabs on the stuff that "fell" out of my wallet, neither. Some deal you're offering. You're as much in prison as I am. Only diff is I'll get out. You're a lifer with no chance of remission.'

Lemmon's breath whistled in his nostrils. Spots of heat burned his cheeks. His brown fists came together at the knuckles and squeezed his Player flat as they softly pounded the grey table. His shoulders spread inside his coat and a flush stained his thick neck. His lips parted from his teeth with a tiny pop of air.

'Vinnie Castle's on the critical-list. And you let it happen. Pimlico Parsons is on the missing-list with some serious holes in him, his dabs and blood type all over a sawn-off he dropped. Harry the Crack and Froggy Farrell are on the trot for the same affray, except it isn't that any more. It's a capital charge. Pinky Bellaver's on a slab with some interesting holes in him, and Kosher Kramer's wearing a tag on his big toe. And all due to your cleverness, Charlie. With him gone Brighton's a walk-over, and now you'll see Bethnal Green and Camberwell at each other's throat. Just like you planned.'

'You're right. If my homing pigeons let me down, I write my instructions in blood on paper aeroplanes. Fly them out through the bars. And a zephyr of wind comes out of the west and blows them straight into the right letter-box. Simple.'

'Play the simpleton. But you'll dance to another tune before you're much older, Charlie.'

Charlie's eyes went behind his lids and came back flinty.

'So what if Bethnal Green and Wandsworth kill each other off? Let them top themselves. Save the taxpayers a lot of poppy and cost a few bent briefs some fat fees. Then you can sleep nights and go back to worrying about motorists who use Guinness labels for tax discs.'

'I'll still have your firm to break apart.'

'If you want that, you'd best keep me right here.'

Lemmon picked up his hat, turned it and laid it back where it had been before.

'Full circle. I'll have you straight. No other way.'

'And you're here to salve *your* conscience, not mine.'

'A psychoanalyst with wide lapels, well, well.'

Charlie plumed lazy smoke.

'Nobody's goading you, Mister. Except the little man in the back of your head who comes out in your dreams. Tells you all the rotten things you push aside in daylight. He's the one who's looking at me now. Not the career copper who goes by the book and doesn't dare see his face in his shiny toecaps when he laces his boots of a morning. And the funny-sad thing is, if you'd learned to bend the rules straight off, you'd have your commander's pips by now. And just maybe have the clout to make your patch of copperdom as squeaky-clean as you'd like it.'

Lemmon paled and lit a Player from his stub. Charlie took it without thanks and said: 'Don't lose some dodgy evidence on my account. It's your lily-white integrity that's in jeopardy whatever you do. And that's your dilemma, isn't it? Lose it or use it, that junk of Quill's compromises you where you live. In your honourable heart. You're in a no-win all-lose cleft stick, you poor bastard.'

Lemmon had hold of Charlie's shirt-front, and a ham of a fist hovered mid-punch.

Charlie blew smoke at it.

'Go ahead. Compromise yourself a little more. The screws will back your story. Prisoners fall and hurt themselves here all the time. It's just part of the system. Go ahead and hit me. Join them all the way.'

Lemmon opened his fist and buried fingers in his hair.

'You cynical bastard. I almost . . . .'

'But not quite, Theo. Not quite. Come on, son. Like it or not, we're of a kind, you and I. I've learned to live in my mud wallow, that's all. I police my animals as best I can, but I let the mad dogs go to the dog-pound for the big chop.'

Lemmon tidied his hair with a steel comb.

'And you'd have made a good-bad copper like Prophet Quill? If that's your contention, it stinks.'

Charlie killed a long stub and took three cigarettes from Lemmon's pack with one fluid movement. He uncoiled from his chair tucking them into his shirt pocket.

'For later,' he said. 'All democracy is a compromise, Theo. Live with it.'

'Not your sick view of it.'

'Nobody cried for Stephen Ward when he suicided over the Christine Keeler case, but they hated Jack Profumo.

Not because he compromised state security by sleeping with whores who also bedded a Russian, but because he got caught out in a lie. Didn't do the honourable thing like putting a revolver in his mouth and kissing his brain goodbye. Before Cromwell and the Long Parliament *all* the kings of England ran police states. Only *they* called it Grace and Favour when they bribed rich allies with earldoms and changed the rules to suit themselves. Now we have elected government and the Queen is titular head of state. But all that means is her up the palace heads the armed forces. Means *they* can't use the military to declare a republic or a dictatorship. It doesn't mean *they* can't grab off the gravy. It's still jobs for the boys and knighthoods for the self-servers. And you never hear of a politician or a judge dying in penury, right? You take a leaf out of your mate's book — Whats-his-face, Bunny Halliday. He used you, didn't he? Maybe he owes you one or several back.'

Lemmon could have been a stone man in the grey room.

'You're playing marked cards, Charlie.'

'They ain't coming off the bottom of the deck. I'm a villain. I can afford to be honest.'

'You've got a sick view of the world.'

'It's a sick old world. And like Archie says: "I didn't make the times, but I take my profits from them." '

Something glowed in the depths of Lemmon's eyes. Twilight lit by inner lightning.

'Thanks, that makes it easier. You think Toronto's far enough away from Malta, Charlie? You think that maybe, just maybe old man Ogle can cut the mustard without you? I mean, what's another dead Maltese pimp to a man like Charlie Dance? Nothing.'

'It's still your twopence.'

'Got your attention, have I?'

A line as fine as the print on an insurance waiver creased Charlie's forehead before he smoothed it away.

'For the moment.'

'Johnny Valletta's some sort of cousin to Roger and

Jesus Tonna, isn't he? Or was. I must get the tense right. *Was* a sort of cousin.'

Charlie reached a cigarette from his pocket and held it like a pencil.

'So he's past tense. So what?'

'He bled to death in the same affray as Kosher and Pinky. Manchester Freddy was well upset about it. Talked nineteen to the dozen when we brought him round at the station in Catford. He figured Pimlico and Froggy were on your firm. That you had him and his unlovely friends hit on account of Vinnie Castle. And our Freddy only an innocent pimp out for a drink, too? I'd describe his demeanour as outraged. And that outrage has got to get passed on to Toronto, wouldn't you say?'

'I wouldn't say anything.'

'And you so full of words a moment ago.'

'That was then.'

'And this is now. Freddy's a talker, Charlie. A loud-mouth. And who else would he talk to over the Christmas goose but his in-laws in Toronto? Tell how Charlie Dance came close to having him killed alongside his prince of a cousin Johnny? And for no good reason he can see.'

'Keep talking.'

'We let Freddy go on his own recognisance with a few oblique pointers to help him on his way. Give me the right verbals and a signed statement I can use, and I could have you on a plane to Malta by . . . when? Christmas Eve tomorrow? Let's say Boxing Day?'

Charlie mashed the unlit Player and wiped tobacco shreds from his palm.

'Ring off, Mr Lemmon. Wrong number.'

Lemmon's fist made the steel door boom.

'One away to you, Mister.'

An hour later he was parking in Esher, and Charlie had begun to break up his cell.

There was snow in the fog.

Lemmon stamped slush from his galoshes as the bell-pull

chimed the first coda of a carol. Wishing he was home.

Elizabeth had insisted: 'Of course we must go. If Bunny Halliday wants you in your penguin-suit and me in my best black, then so be it. There are worse things than dull company and indifferent sherries, you know. Like being married to an able and lovable inspector who ought to be something more. I'm tired of your being passed over for promotion.'

'Sucking up to the After Eight set won't change that.'

'Good. I'll write a bread-and-butter acceptance,' and Elizabeth had confined herself to bed with a viral temperature of 102°.

A *svelte* young man in maroon and black took Lemmon's coat, hat and scarf, and left him in a library of rosewood, brass, and leather bindings. Apple logs snapped in a mock-Tudor chimney and marble knights supported a huge overmantel of swashes and armorials. Low chairs with carved backs crouched in dim corners and good period furniture stood about on Chinese carpets that were young when Richard Cœur de Lion romanced Blondin to the sound of lutes.

Conversation drifted through the panelling like surf on a distant shore as Lemmon warmed his hands and found Charlie's face in the leaping flames. Quill's eyes were in the hot motes spiralling past the blackened fireback, and Bulstrode's voice whispered with the crackling wood. The wail of a dryad in a haunted tree.

'Glenlivet and Malvern water.'

Bunny held identical drinks, his silver hair platinum in the firelight.

'I thought a quiet word before you met your host and hostess.'

He sat and waved Lemmon into a facing chair.

'I can make amends without apologising, I think.'

'I'll take the drink. That's real.'

Lemmon eased his jacket open, and a braces button bit his lower back.

'Cheers, then.' Bunny sipped delicately and said, 'Yummy.'

Lemmon looked attentive and thought: *Here it comes.*

'Your help over that little affair was invaluable, Theo. No shadow of a doubt. DCS Saul Cotton's praise was fulsome. But naughty old political expedients do have a way of muddying the water. Whatever one's best intentions may be. Your reward will come. But not quite in the way you or I may have envisaged. I should have broken silence earlier, but . . . .'

Bunny fluttered pink fingers and looked solemn in the uncertain light.

'You do understand, I'm sure.'

Grace and Favour, Charlie said from the fire.

What's changed?

'You'll make it clear, Bunny.'

Bunny offered cigars with a neat skim of the wrist.

'No? Pity, they're rather fine. It will, of course, mean you'll have to tread a very familiar path just *once* more.'

'Lousy with primroses and mud.'

'Pardon, old man?'

'Just something a villain told me not ninety minutes ago. You reminded me, that's all.'

Lemmon watched Bunny trim and light his cigar with the care of a neurosurgeon snipping a frontal lobe. Found himself prowling the carpet trailing monstrous and shifting shadows across the shelves of old volumes.

'That's very distracting, old man.'

Lemmon sat with a 'Sorry' and: 'What *do* you want, Bunny?'

Christ, Dance again. But there's nothing grey about this rich room. Nothing at all.

'We have most of the train chummies banged up now. And Cotton's confident he'll collar the rest. But there are some rather shadowy loose ends. The money, Theo. Seems much of it has gone missing somewhere. And we — that is, our masters in Whitehall — have the quaint but implacable notion we should recover it. One way . . . or the other. That seems to require the collaring of some very heavy gentlemen indeed. And not just the heavy sort of gentlemen you are familiar with in your line of business.'

Lemmon's knees ached from his clamped hands. He stamped a foot and felt pins and needles.

'Quite another league entirely,' said Bunny.

Lemmon rolled malt on his tongue and looked awake.

'We have a clandestine task force in mind. All low-key. And answerable to the Home Office only. You will remain what you seem as far as the lower echelons of the Metropolitan Police Force are concerned. But through me you will report directly to one other in Whitehall. He will be a simple report-gatherer as far as you are concerned; anything more about him is of no interest to you. And the collars, should they come, will, in all probability, not be yours.'

Lemmon thought of acres of primroses and said nothing.

Bunny stood to spread his coat-tails before the fire.

'There is much at stake here, Theo. More than you can probably imagine. This has been a terrible year for the country. One administration has revamped itself because of the Profumo Affair. A third man has been named in the Burgess—Maclean ménage. We've lost a good friend in the White House and now have to come to terms with his predecessor. And to go into the New Year with a police corruption scandal would change the face of British politics too rapidly for both sides of the House. Changes will come, Theo. Radical changes. But they must come by evolution and not by revolution. Given time there will be an enormous shake-up. Stories of graft and corruption are leaking out to my peers in the county constabularies. Too many stories. But before we clean house we have to strike at the root cause of that corruption. Outside the police force. You must help us to present an untarnished image to the great unwashed, the man in the street, the voter.'

Lemmon rolled his eyes. Looked coy. Shuffled his feet and said: 'What, little old me? Shucks, Mizz Scarlett.'

'By God, I could strike you.'

Bunny was no longer a bland pink fat-cat. His decorations no longer baubles on a baby-pink sash. There was a patina of blood on their gleaming faceted surfaces. The flushed jowls could have been carved from hard redwood. The moist eyes were crumbs of raw gypsum.

Lemmon swallowed whisky and tried not to stare, smoking a Player he did not remember lighting.

'Easy, old friend.'

Bunny's face changed without altering expression.

'What is so bloody difficult about making common cause with our masters, Theo? They want what we want: the heavy villains off the street. Whatever it takes. Just so long as there is no chance of them using legal technicalities or tales of bent coppers to set themselves free. Is that so very hard for you to comprehend? Am I talking to an honest fool or, as I had hoped, a man who loves truth enough to lie, cheat and perjure himself to maintain the greater truths at the cost of a few of the lesser ones?'

A lie is a lie is a lie . . . .

Bulstrode whispered in the chimney, and Charlie laughed with the jumping flames.

Democracy is a compromise. The old Grace and Favour. Jobs for the boys. Say yes and be a commander, son . . . .

Bunny's smile grew dimples.

'No buts, or back into obscurity you go, Theo.'

Lemmon heard himself say, 'And you believe this, my achieving friend. I've taken a good long squint at myself tonight. Helped by you and another bastard very like you. And that wife of mine with her suddenly convenient headache and heavy sniffles. You did get her to throw a wobbly tonight, didn't you? So us lads could chat in private? Don't answer; it doesn't matter. What does matter is that I'll make common cause with you, Halliday. I'll earn my fatter pension through your gilded back door. But — and it's a big but — you drop me halfway, leave me out in the cold for your political expedience, and I'll make you eat my whistle, badge and truncheon before I pull your plug.'

Bunny dimpled again.

'Applause, applause. I'll remember that little speech.'

Lemmon was suddenly jaded.

'When do I start as the Masked Avenger?'

'Now. Tonight. That's why you're here in this house. Thought you'd like a close look at someone you could well be netting for us. Your host.'

'Why? Is he an independent voter? Or a card-carrying commie who walks backwards with a sword for the Queen?'

Bunny linked arms with Lemmon and opened the library door.

'His name is Malcolm Sadler and he's our host. And I rather suspect he's sailing close to the legal wind in several seas. And because of him you could well earn a flight to South Africa.'

They walked into soft gales of polite laughter and the softer glow of chandeliers.

Charlie threw the second screw into the wall of his cell. Faked a trip and turned his head away from a rabbit punch aimed at the base of his skull. It took him high on the shoulder, and he was woozier than he expected when he flopped across his ripped mattress. Knees dug into his back, and the third screw kicked a rib before helping the first screw to handcuff Charlie's arms behind his back. They dragged him down to the infirmary and were waiting for the prison doctor to sedate Charlie when two escort officers came in behind the screw in charge of reception.

'What happened to him?'

'Went doolally. Right after that CID bloke interviewed him.'

The third screw rubbed a raw shoulder.

'Threw me about like a packet of cornflakes.'

'Caught me close to the family jewels. Can't rub that in public.'

The reception screw shook his head at the escort officers.

'I'd leave him overnight if I was you, lads. Let the MO give him a bye-byes shot. Nobody wants a raver in the Maria, do they?'

'He don't look nothing special,' said the escort officer with acne. 'Any road, they want him down at Maidstone chop-chop.'

'Waffor?' said the first screw.

The second escort officer looked at his clipboard, chewed a match at it and said, 'He's down for the yo-yo treatment. If they want him, we take him. There's the bloody rota if you want to see it. I ain't the Home Secretary, am I?'

'Who is? But you ought to let the MO see him before you cart him off.'

'He won't give us no bother, will you, sunshine?'

The first escort officer ruffled Charlie's hair, and the head lolled under his calloused palm.

'They don't none of them give *us* bother.'

The reception screw sighed and scratched the bald spot under his cap.

'Sign for him downstairs and he's yours. And don't bring him back. We got enough nutters who break up cells this time of the year. Christmas is always a bastard.'

They talked about lunatics on three staircases, and when the paperwork was completed Charlie felt night air in his face. The rear doors of a Black Maria opened and he was pushed up the steps. The yard was dusted with snow, and more flurried in a cold wind. Then the Medical Officer was there wanting to check Charlie out before he went into transit, talking down to the reception screw with an Oxford accent.

'Up you go, Charlie. Move your sodding legs.'

Charlie's head snapped up and he saw sweat on the first escort officer's lip. The sheen of spirit gum under his stage moustache.

'Move. Or I'll shiv you here, you flaming whore's melt.'

The second escort officer kicked at Charlie's ankles.

Charlie let himself fall on to his back. Braced his shoulders and threw both feet into the first escort officer's face. His wrists screamed inside the handcuffs and a cap sailed into the darkness. Charlie enjoyed the shock of his heel snapping a chin back. Scrabbled away from the Black Maria on elbows and heels.

The Oxford accent had risen in pitch, and the reception

screw was following it out of the door.

Something long and sharp flashed between Charlie's side and his right arm. A blade nipped his bicep and skidded away across his ribs before losing itself under the vehicle.

Charlie used the pain to summon everything he had.

Hoped it was enough.

Arched his spine and came up on to the balls of his feet. Rolled into the first escort officer as he made for the cab of the Black Maria. Brought him down with a leg scissors and kicked him in the crotch twice. Dropped on to the gaping mouth with all his weight behind his bent knees. Jumped away to get his back slammed up against the side of the phoney police vehicle to dodge the reception screw's lunge.

'They ain't real rozzers, you berk. I'm shivved.'

'You're a flaming nutter.'

Charlie gave the reception screw a flying head-butt and then the MO with the Oxford accent had Charlie all to himself.

A hypodermic gleamed when he spread his palms in the air.

'You're disturbed, old chap.'

'I'm stabbed, you medical moron.'

The MO watched Charlie slide down the side of the Black Maria. Leaving a snail's trail of crimson on the paintwork.

'Is that claret, or is that claret?'

Charlie's grin was lopsided.

'I'd call help if I was you, my old quack . . . thass Red Bellaver lying . . . there . . . before him and his oppo . . . have it away on their . . . toes . . . I could make them talk for you . . . for me actually . . . but there just ain't . . . the time . . . .'

The MO yelled inside the prison. Rang an alarm bell.

'. . . merry Chrissmasssss . . . .'

Charlie passed out with snow falling on his face.

Valletta simmered.

A furnace of marzipan buildings under a hot and white

Sahara sky. Whiter than snow and hotter than sand. The noonday promenade in Kingsway had been a listless mill of bored soldiery and young Maltese, all too jaded to flirt or exchange the usual ribald banter.

Ingrid sat in Queen Victoria's shadow with iced coffee and gâteau, resting before the drive back to Tarxien. She had bought silly, frivolous presents to amuse rather than impress.

A pair of wind-up tin mobsters that fired bubbles from tin machine-guns for Archie. Candy jewellery and home-baked gingerbread men decorated with Edwardian lithographs for Queenie. Silly things to match her mood of gay optimism. She turned the gold band on the third finger of her left hand. Pretended she had not bought it herself. Polished it slowly on her rising belly, enjoying the hot metal against the silk of her dress. The fine material against her skin.

The roly-poly doctor from Bugibba had told her she would carry the child well so long as she gave up tennis for swimming.

'And not too much love-making.'

He had looked over his half-glasses and wagged a finger.

'And not too little. A father needs his love, too, eh?'

His chocolate eyes and Hitler moustache had glistened with moisture as he closed his black bag.

'And you a Catholic, Dr Micalef,' Ingrid had teased.

'But a man first. God would see it my way. We talk all the time. Mostly I talk. He listens. And not always in church, eh?'

Then he had patted her head and left through Archie's rose-bower.

Another month and the baby would stir.

Ingrid longed to snuggle against Charlie's back so that he could share the kicks he had helped to create. And make love without pressing on her swelling belly.

Gently, gently . . . .

Ingrid blushed crimson. Watched by two young sappers with their soldier's haircuts and boyish faces. She poked her tongue at them and took her packages to her car.

Ingrid drove carefully. Avoided the many potholes and the carefree Maltese drivers who obeyed no rules. As if their battered Fords and Mercedes had one fast forward speed and brakes were an optional extra.

She parked in the meagre shade of the dusty orange-trees and prickly pear below the old rampart wall and toiled up the steep stone steps to a walled garden with the arms of the last Grand Master of Malta carved over the gate.

A fallen banana-frond had drowned in the shallows. The rest of the pool was an angry glitter spiked by dancing light. The honey walls shed heat into the fruit-trees Queenie had hung with coloured lights, and the statues in their niches wore bright party hats and sprigs of mistletoe. The fairy at the top of the twenty-foot Canadian pine spread her wings against the brazen sky, and her chintz skirt stirred in the molten breeze.

Missing Charlie, Ingrid walked through the games room. Walked softly in case Archie enjoyed an afternoon siesta on his fourposter. His speech improved slowly, and he made himself understood when he spoke with care. Queenie avoided sharp and angry raps of his cane by curbing her inclination to finish sentences for him.

Ingrid laid her packages on the kitchen table, filled the kettle for a cup of tea and listened for the clack of Queenie's needles.

The bougainvillaea tapped the kitchen wall, and a car with a riddled silencer chugged along the lower road near the megalithic temple. The ceiling fan beat the air as though it stirred syrup, and a pair of finches chirped in the red bracts outside the window. Ingrid decided that Queenie dozed and made tea through the strainer, practising the austerity of her childhood. Waste was a crime no matter what could be afforded.

She sliced a lemon when a brown hand clamped her mouth and an arm circled her waist.

Without thinking, and as shock scalded her, Ingrid drove the paring-knife over her shoulder. Felt it strike muscle.

Garlic breath made a hot, moist explosion against her neck as it was twisted aside. Grated bones against her skull. Tears popped from her eyes. She bit her tongue and hacked back with her heels.

They drummed uselessly against a man's legs, and her flip-flops dropped to the floor as she was lifted and thrown. A stream of hot Maltese followed her sprawl, and her head hit the limewashed wall a moment before the rest of her limbs caught up with her.

Ingrid curled over herself, protected her belly, but her head was lifted by the hair and a horny palm beat her face from side to side.

Red centipedes wriggled behind her eyelids amid bursting grey balloons of nausea. She went limp and was lifted by elbow and throat and dragged along the cool marble passage to the drawing-room where she was dumped in a heap on a scatter rug. Again she wrapped herself in a foetal curl and sobbed for breath, her eyes squeezed closed against the woolly nap of locally woven thread. Breathed for the baby and thought of rape.

'Bitch cut me good.'

Ingrid edged away from the voice, and her hand found the edge of an overscuffed chair. A shoe and a heavy cane.

'A fleabite.'

The second voice was unruffled and cold, a scratch of a voice in a deformed throat. Dry leaves rattling in a tomb.

A fruit-bowl hit the carpet with a roll of apples as the antimacassar was pulled from the coffee-table.

'Use this.'

Archie's hand squeezed Ingrid's shoulder and she laid her face against his leg, looked into his strong and tanned face for comfort. His eyes were pools of angry russet. A nerve ticked in the flap of skin under his right eyebrow. He stroked Ingrid's hair, his entire attention on the men in the middle of the long vaulted room.

'Sit . . . tight . . .,' he said slowly and quietly.

'Sound advice,' the dead voice scratched.

Ingrid cuddled her legs under her chin and looked

without wanting to.

A young Maltese with hot black eyes stuffed the balled antimacassar inside a tanned jacket. Blood was a ragged bloom on his torn lapel. He bared overwhite teeth and purple gums in a thin smooth face. The long-barrelled Savage he held on Queenie seemed too heavy for his lean olive hand.

The second man was older and taller and more olive. His face was all seams. The hollow cheeks were lightly pocked and his throat was a livid turkey-wattle. His black hair had red tints and laid too close to his skull to be real hair. His sideburns were as grey as the salt-and-pepper bristle on his neck. He looked at Ingrid's legs. Smiled at them with pale brown lips. One eye blinked and the other stared as cold and as unmoving as glass. Frozen in a socket the same rough texture as his ugly throat. His teeth worried a brown lower lip.

'You're looking at my eye. They all look at my eye. You want to see it closer, girly?'

Ingrid gulped bile. Drew strength from Archie's hand.

'Maybe I save her for last, eh, Mario?'

'Yeah, she goes last. She cut me good.'

'You can have her. After me.'

Queenie laughed suddenly. Just short of hysteria.

'After nobody. Somebody crossed your wires, Ugly.'

Archie tapped his cane.

'Acid . . . burns . . . .'

The man with the frozen eye almost touched his neck. Brought a revolver from somewhere instead. It blurred into his hand like an angry hummingbird. A flick of blue steel and it was there.

'You don't speak. Until it's time. The old lady shut up good, too. Live happy until it's time, too. Nor Girly.'

'Time . . . for what?'

Archie's cane went quiet.

'Mmy mmalts didn't just take off . . . for no good *reason*.'

'Slowly, Arch,' Queenie warned.

'Old lady don't say nothing,' said Frozen Eye.

Archie breathed carefully, his hand a clamp on Ingrid's shoulder.

'I get it. . . . Toronto sent them . . . Queenie. . . . Crossed wires is right. . . . They're on contract for . . . Roger and Jesus. . . .'

Mario shrugged and made himself wince.

'You'll talk when they come.'

'How mmuch to do a deal . . .?'

'No more talk.'

'Money always talks, Ugly,' said Queenie. She reached for her knitting-bag. 'D'you mind, since I ain't allowed to bunny?'

'Old lady stay quiet and make things.'

Frozen Eye's gun swung at Archie, down at Ingrid and across to Queenie. The fast, practised move of a man who hated wasted motion. Making shots. His hand flexed and the revolver spun and was gone. The good eye fixed on Ingrid's legs.

To divert him Archie asked for water.

'No water.' The eye ran up Ingrid's body to her mouth.

'The pattern's here somewhere.' Queenie rummaged in her knitting-bag.

Archie licked a dry mouth. 'Don't ffind it too . . . quick. She might finish that thing and I'd . . . have to wear . . . it. . . .'

'That ain't your worry, dad,' said Mario.

'Cold in Toronto, is it?' Queenie asked.

'Not as cold as you're gonna be,' Mario drawled.

The frozen eye looked at nothing and the blinking one moistened as Ingrid was told to stand up.

'Cold must be . . . mmurder on an acid . . . burn. Must burn colder than . . . hell. . . .'

Archie's fingers dug into Ingrid's shoulder, and he pointed his cane at Frozen Eye.

'You're Pru Mmizzi. . . . Has Roger fforgotten how ssmall this island is? . . . Hey . . . Mario . . . you won't make it out of the airport with that ffrozen . . . ffizzog . . . in tow. . . .'

'Shut it, dad.'

Pru Mizzi's throat crackled with dry leaves of laughter.

'You want lumps, old man? First her lumps. Then yours.'

'You'll get my knee where it matters, you gargoyle,' Ingrid said, dizzy with fear.

'That cuts it.'

Mario showed teeth and gum. 'What now, Pru?'

'She comes here.'

Mizzi tore Archie's cane away and it bounced off to crack a pane of window glass. He grabbed Ingrid's hair and pulled her towards him.

Ingrid buried teeth into a wiry groin.

The gun made its blur and searched for the nape of Ingrid's neck.

Archie fell forward and butted Mizzi in the abdomen.

Mizzi staggered. Kicked Ingrid off his leg as he was dragged to the floor by Archie's dead weight.

Mario was in motion. The Savage snapped out to train on Archie's scalp.

Queenie raised her knitting-bag and flame cut a black hole through the embroidered side.

Mario stood very straight. Looked puzzled when his tie jumped away from a second red bloom on his shirt-front. His white teeth snarled and ground together. Then he just stood there looking weary. A bored young man with nothing on his mind.

Mizzi rolled on a curved spine. His leg came free with a wet bite-mark on the left thigh. A ribbon of spittle spun from Ingrid's mouth as she held her kicked stomach. Settled on the floor with rigid care, whitened by pain and shock.

Mizzi's fast revolver shot Admiral Byng from the wall, and the walnut frame came to pieces. Archie's hair ruffled as crimson striped his scalp. Spattered the chairback. His meaty fists beat Mizzi's face, and slow grunts came from deep within him.

Queenie got down from her chair without hurry and fired into the top of Mizzi's shoulder.

Twice. With her tongue out.

The small nickel Beretta snapped in her tiny hand. No louder than a thirsty lapdog.

Mizzi's glass eye popped from the socket in a spurt of rich blood and rolled away. His head strained on his ugly neck and the wattled Adam's apple jerked aimlessly.

Queenie's next shot took him in the ear, knocked him on his side. The fast gun trembled in the olive fingers, then lay on the carpet under a slowly stilling hand.

Mario was trying to work out why his Savage pointed at his own foot. He was smiling apologetically when Queenie pumped two small-calibre bullets into his perfect teeth.

Mario coughed red bubbles. Sighed a last deep sigh of regret and fell on his face. He did not feel Queenie hit him with her embroidered bag or see hundreds of tiny beads bounce to all four corners of the room until Ingrid dragged herself across to pull her away.

Archie picked up the two revolvers and dragged himself back into his chair. And waited for the Tonna brothers.

Margot Sadler's eyes were oval, sharp, and very blue.

She looked at Lemmon as if he could be valued in gossip-column inches and her handshake was manly. Her no-nonsense voice was languorous and her drop-earrings could have paid off the national debt of a banana republic. Her hair and dress were black and sewn with seed-pearls, her wayward nose was a marvel of unrelated curves, and she smiled with far too many teeth. She had the brittle glitter of a faded *ingénue* who had sailed across footlights into the arms of money before she and the bit parts dried up, and her laugh said she knew that all too well and didn't give a damn.

At first glance, her husband was just a sleek executive with tinted hair and a face as solemn as organ music. His light tan had not penetrated the crow's-feet round his eyes and gave him the look of a startled somnambulist. His comfortable stomach fronted a hollow back and probably reduced his tailor to bitter tears. His nose was a careless afterthought with nostrils, and his mouth was just something he ate with. His chins were chins and his cool eyes flicked from face to face like flags in a department-store till.

Margot laughed and said, 'So you're Bunny's favourite copper. He dines out on you all the time.'

Bunny laughed back.

'Perhaps I should eat at home more often. One should not turn one's friends into anecdotes.'

Margot stage-managed drinks.

'You'd starve or die of boredom. And our buffet-table groans under the weight of the goodies thereon. Malcolm has decided to outdo the Guildhall yet again. Haven't you, darling?'

Sadler's eyes flicked and flicked away.

'Entertaining is an art. Like all things theatrical. One must get the props right. Mustn't one, *darling*?'

'Meeeow,' said Margot, her own eyes nailing Lemmon. 'Are we to be riveted by tales of police deduction, Inspector dear?'

'I never tell tales out of school. *Sub judice*, you know.'

'Such discretion. And such a bore. Malcolm was so looking forward to tales of thud and blunder. He eats a constant diet of *True Crime* stories. His bedside table is simply littered with the most lurid magazines.'

'This whisky sour is excellent, Mrs Sadler.' Lemmon hid a yawn in his cheek.

'Which means you won't talk about such things. Such a real disappointment for all of us. Poor Malcolm,' Margot said with a wide and insincere smile.

'One has to do something before dropping off to sleep.'

Sadler's glance brushed Lemmon's face before settling on a tall blonde in a sheer backless gown the turquoise of tropical seawater. Her tan was as permanent as his was transitory.

'Doesn't one? Who is that attractive creature?' There was mischief in Bunny's voice. 'She has the look of a wanton mermaid in that most stunning of gowns.'

Sadler's mouth tasted itself and said, 'Naomi Leathers.

She and her daughter are here on a shopping trip. And for Christmas of course. From South Africa. Business acquaintances in the loosest sense of the word. More friends of friends.'

'Loose precisely,' Margot muttered.

'Did you say something, darling?' Sadler asked.

'I?' said Margot.

'You,' said Sadler.

'Only that you adore all things criminal, *darling*. And there is nothing drearier than corpses over the consommé; death by ligature, garotte and hempen rope through the entrée; and gore, graves and ghoulish practices for dessert. And it is as well English is already a bastard tongue. Some of the people Malcolm invites to the house are really beyond the pale. . . . .'

'Cats', said Sadler, 'should stay in their baskets with their claws sheathed. Cats should look regal and not scratch Papa's furniture or his good humour. Cats who wail on walls get snipped by vets with small sharp knives. Cats—'

'Malcolm has been drinking wine. Well if not wisely,' Margot said.

'Cats,' Sadler said dreamily. 'Cats can use up their nine lives so very quickly. Then it's a sack and the canal at midnight. If you gentlemen will excuse me?'

Sadler drifted away and lost himself in a knot of guests near the blonde in the seawater dress.

'You two do have the knives out tonight,' Bunny said.

Margot's smile was as bright as a musical overture.

'And puss should play the dutiful wife as usual? Most especially on the eve before the eve of immaculate birth? Marriage is an interminable roadshow with the dullest notices, a dull script and an even duller cast of two.'

She drained her glass and whisked another from a passing tray.

'God and fishes, but I'm tired of this role.'

Bunny laid a pink hand on her slender wrist.

'Now, Margot. Santa doesn't come down the chimney for naughty girls with carrying voices. And jealous green isn't your colour. Sexual window-shopping is the last privilege left to the married man. And looking at the goods is so much better than the concomitant sordid scenes of an actual affair. A cat may look at a queen without designs on her crown.'

'Witty and empty,' said Margot. 'Like your smug old face.'

'Now I'm wounded,' Bunny mocked.

'And I adore you, too,' said Margot. 'But not tonight. If I stay here a moment longer, I shall scream blue bloody murder.'

'Do you have a telephone I could use?' said Lemmon.

'What? I mean . . . pardon?' said Margot.

'A telephone. Dial-dial-ring-ring-talk? Telephone? I'd like to tell my wife she's wrong. Very, very wrong. And I should like to come home and prove it to her. That and other things. I have the right coins to leave in the silver tray.'

'Now, *there* speaks a truly married man.'

Margot found another drink and ordered whisky sours for Bunny and Lemmon.

'Oh dear,' Bunny said.

'Tush,' said Margot. 'What's your first, Christian or given name, Married Man?'

'Theo,' said Lemmon.

'Come with me, married Theo. Then both Malcolm and Bunny will be free to watch Madam's dumplings boil out of that dress. Bunny might even give Malcolm's nervous little eyes a rest by ogling for him.'

'And double meeow to you, Margot dear.'

Bunny held his fresh drink and watched Margot lead Lemmon through a door that could have graced a cathedral. Then he slipped away to wake his driver and had himself driven home.

Elizabeth was snuggled up with hot milk and a paperback romance. She said fond goodnights in a yawny voice, blew a kiss and rang off.

Lemmon redialled, and Bulstrode said: 'Bulstrode.'

'It's me.'

Lemmon watched Margot eavesdrop as she roamed the anteroom plumping cushions. Silver gleamed in glass cabinets and the oiled panelling shone like dark waters in the dimmed light.

'Brixton have had an attempted break. Red Bellaver and Morrie Torrance tried to pull Charlie out.'

Lemmon kneaded nails in his stomach.

'And?'

'Charlie worked them over and bent a couple of screws. Took a shivving, but he's gonna live to annoy us another day.'

Lemmon squeezed the phone in his big brown hand.

'He's all right, then?'

'Stitches and sedation. MO said he was lucky.'

'He always was. And getting luckier.'

'Guv?' Bulstrode was puzzled by Lemmon's tone.

'That package. From the train.'

'Yessir?'

'Mark it "Lost in the Post" and do just that.'

'If you say so, Guv.'

'I say so.'

'And Charlie?'

'Leave him to due process. Now lose yourself for the rest of the holiday. Merry Christmas, son.'

'And you, Guv. And . . . thanks.'

'For what?'

Lemmon found Margot in the doorway beside a tapestry of medieval horsemen chasing stags through a forest of stylised trees.

'Where do I leave the gratuity?'

'Have the calls with the compliments of the season. Are you unwell? You seem very pale.'

Lemmon squeezed sweating temples.

'Must be I climbed too high and too fast up the social ladder. If I have a nosebleed, I'll spill Olympian ichor, not real blood at all. And if I fall from these golden rungs I'll leave the perfect outline of a failed copper in the gutter on my long drop into Hades. And who will pay Charon to ferry me across the River Styx to join the dead? And what will it matter anyway? It can only be a mirror image of all this. Good liquor in bad company. The same old Grace and Favour rules. That is how it works, isn't it?'

'Great good heavens. A copper with a classical bent. Yes, Married Man, those are the ground rules for the initiate.'

Lemmon shook his overheated face, looked into his empty glass for clues.

'Air and a drink are what you need, my lad.'

Margot led him down a dark passage and through glass doors into the hot smell of sweet sap and moist earth. The old-maid odours of orchids and tropical fish. Fleshy leaves dripped with moisture and fish swam in stone pools between banks of mature rare plants. Fog curled against the conservatory roof like primordial mist above a rainforest.

Lemmon slumped on a slatted bench, and Margot fixed iced drinks at a bar behind a fall of purple pitcher-plants.

'Here.' She handed Lemmon a frosted glass.

He savoured the clean astringency of limes laced with gin and could have been alone when he said: 'And she refreshed him with drink and silent company. And they dallied by the streams of the forest until it was time to leave that enchanted place, for it is known that Man may not remain too long away from his own time, his own people, for too long.'

Margot fed a carp by hand.

'That should end "For there lies Madness and Death". I'll raise a bumper to that merry thought.'

'Maybe it does. I read it somewhere.'

'And now you're going to ask me about my errant husband.'

'Am I?'

'Bunny Halliday didn't bring you here for no good reason. There's a reason for everything Bunny does.'

'Maybe, maybe not. A million maybes and not a truth to hang your hat on. And what are you going to ask me for? To fix a parking fine or two? An invitation to the

Black Museum?'

'Direct, aren't you, Married Man?'

'Mr Oblique, at your service.'

'Tush. It isn't me who needs information. It's the madam with the boiling muffins. I said I'd see what I could do.'

Margot sent ripples across the pond with a flick of a silver nail.

'Shall I ask? Or pander to your morbid mood?'

'Is she playing four legs in a bed with your husband?'

'She isn't. He'd like to.'

'I see.'

'No, married Theo. You do not see.'

'All right. I don't.'

'It is not all right.'

Lemmon offered his glass.

'This whirligig needs refreshing. Is there more lubricant?'

'Oodles and oodles.'

Margot poured from a silver Thermos, compensated for Lemmon's shaking hand.

'Poor Naomi. She has the rottenest luck with her casual consorts. If her brains were in her bra, she'd be in the genius class.'

'You're not that flat-chested.'

Margot's sigh could have filled a spinnaker.

'Liar.'

'I'd better go back to misquoting things, look sorry for myself. Nothing else seems to please you.'

Margot took a long frond and trapped it between her nose and upper lip, gave herself a long green moustache.

'A bosom of gigantic proportions isn't everything. I have other attributes. Not that bastard Malcolm sees them any more. Perhaps he never did. He prefers to saddle me with low-lifers from the East End for interminable weekends, and gloats until I could shriek. Awful people with eyes like boiled sweets and clammy hands.'

'I thought we were talking about the Muffin Lady?'

Lemmon accepted a refill from the bottomless shaker.

'But we are, married Theo. I just don't like linear

dialogue. What woman does?'

'No comment.'

'He's the brother of this man Malcolm has been cultivating for his own curious and perverse reasons.'

'Who is?'

'Naomi's bit of East End rough, darling. I'm telling you, aren't I?'

Margot released the frond and it swayed off into the humid green canopy to rattle in the shadows.

'If you say so,' Lemmon said.

'The brother of the one Malcolm has so much time for. The one with a name like two surnames. Walter, that's it. Walter Harold. There, I remembered.'

'You certainly did.'

Lemmon winked both eyes, thoroughly bemused.

'She, Naomi, met him — them — in South Africa. And had this, you know, thing with the brother.'

'The Muffin Lady and Wally Harold had a romp in South Africa. And she wants to know what?'

'Why he's been arrested.'

Lemmon tried not to stumble over words.

'That's one of the seven things in the world I don't . . . can't talk to you about. Save he's on a murder charge.'

'But Malcolm said it was over breakfast.'

'Was what over breakfast?'

'Your case, darling. Or, more precisely, Bunny's chum's case is what he said. He said, "Bunny's chum's handling that". That's what Malcolm said.'

'Bunny has dozens of chums. Bunny has chums like other people have mice.'

Margot's smile-frown was slightly myopic.

'So you can't help our Muffin Lady?'

'Why do you want to help a woman your husband lusts after anyway? I thought wives were pretty territorial. I know mine is.'

'Territorial about bastard Malcolm? My dear married Theo, bastard Malcolm could have starred in *Lawrence of Arabia*. I'm just the dressing on the top of his perverted sexual sandwich.'

Lemmon watched the drink soften the cross-hatching palms above his head.

'Poor Muffin Lady, and poor you,' he said solemnly.

Margot topped both glasses.

'Damn other people's indiscreet affairs. They so impinge on one's own. Don't they, married Theo?'

'Are you having an affair, Mrs Sadler?'

'Only if you ask me.'

'Ah.'

'And it's Margot. Don't be so stuffy. I mean, you're one of us now by your own admission.'

'I've been seduced once this evening already. Twice would be too much, thank you kindly. I like you, Margot. You're indulging me *and* patronising me.'

'I patronise the arts, not people. I'm drinking far too quickly with a tarnished knight without an escutcheon and no real dragons to fight. Poor married knight, Theo. And a tipsy wife, however badly used she may consider herself, should not go public with her soiled linen. And bastard Malcolm is not to be betrayed to. . . . .'

Margot swallowed the rest with her drink.

'The likes of me? Who's asking you to? I'm drinking with Solomon's wife and a lot of fish. In a jungle. Can't get drunk, though. Heat drives off the alcohol. Thiss iss juss coloured water. Cannibalism. Lemmon drinking lime.'

'I believe you,' Margot lied.

'You're right. I'm by-God drunk and nobody's asking anybody anything. And I can't pretend to romance another man's wife for shiny pips and a bigger pension. Too stuffy and middle-class. Even if I was led to it by an old school-chum with a phoney conscience and a pink sash. Sorry and all that, old girl.'

Margot arched an eyebrow over a blue oval eye.

'Is that what you thought you were doing? Well, you're making a perfectly rotten job of it. *If* you don't mind my saying so.'

'I don't if you don't. Thass fair.'

Margot emptied the Thermos over their glasses.

'Fine logic, Sherlock. Have a topper. Cheers, Sleuth.'

'Chuzz.'

'And now, if you'll lever your nose out of that drink, I'd like to be kissed rather firmly.'

'You're . . . smart lady. You know it wouldn't mean anything.'

'I shan't know that until I try, damn it.'

'True.'

'Well?'

'I'm extremely married.'

'Try anyway.'

Lemmon leaned into Margot's mouth. Tasted limes and Cognac and gin on her firm mouth before she ran her warm tongue against his teeth and her hard hips ground against him. They clung together in a locked sway as the humidity plopped all around them. Each salving the ache of profound solitude. Then they parted shakily and became strangers again.

Margot leaned on a long forearm and used the pond as a mirror to repair her lipstick.

Lemmon twirled his glass.

'Time for weary coppers to wend homeward.'

'What? No third-degree? Kiss and run and no rubber hoses? And I was so looking forward to a ghastly experience.'

'All frogs don't turn into princes. But don't stop looking, Margot.'

Margot grinned at her distorted reflection.

'I just kissed a bluebottle. Are any of them princes?'

'Stony ground for nobility, the filth.'

'Stony ground everywhere, Inspector Lemmon.'

'And a formal goodnight to you, Mrs Sadler.'

'Goodbye, married Theo.'

Out in the fog, Lemmon could just pick out the yellow glow of the conservatory above a wall and a gap between bald elms.

He drove home with his wheels close to the kerb.

Asleep beside Elizabeth, he dreamed Margot Sadler hunted crowned frogs through a grey steel jungle with a golden butterfly-net. Dislodged leaves like banknotes, all of them bearing Bunny's head in the Queen's roundel, and bearing the legend: *Grace and Favour*. Apes with screws' voices swung through the grey steel canopy crying, 'One away to you, Mister,' making the steel tree-trunks boom with their fists. Charlie was there leaving a spoor of bright red blood, confusing poor Margot who hacked about and got crosser and crosser and lonelier and lonelier in her search for a loving royal frog. And somehow Charlie had all the frogs and crowns and made Margot run in smaller and smaller circles until her unravelled hair spun itself into the cocoon of a black butterfly that flew into Lemmon's face and woke him with a monumental hangover on a disordered bed.

CHAPTER SIXTEEN

JANUARY HAD COME IN hard and smelled of spent cartridges.

Brixton glittered with frost under a sky greyer than his cell when Charlie heard the prison door slam him out into the real world.

There was nobody to meet him.

He took a taxi to Pimlico through silent early-morning streets and took the lift up to his flat where he drove must and silence away by floating Vivaldi's baroque arabesques on hot conducted air.

He lit the wall-length aquarium, and his Discus sailed through slate gorges and submarine weed. Circular rainbows with sad golden eyes. He made coffee to spice the antiseptic air. Smashed ice-cubes, salted a tequila glass and built a shaker of margaritas.

He booked a call to Malta and could not settle.

He wandered from room to room. Turned on lights and wound his collection of antique clocks. Straightened perfectly hung pictures. Turned back his bed to air and laid out a new towelling robe. A stranger in his own home.

He took the coffee and cocktails into the bathroom. Ran the taps. Broke open fresh bars of soap. Sprinkled bath essence into the foam and warmed towels over the heated rail.

In the living-room he stripped naked.

Slashed the clothes he had been wearing to ribbons with pinking shears and stuffed the rags into a plastic refuse-sack. Padded to the refuse-chute and listened to the sack slither down the shaft to boom into the basement garbage-bin.

Vivaldi's Winter gave way to Shostakovich's Spring as he lowered himself into fragrant suds and methodically scrubbed five prisons away between swallows of coffee and margaritas.

He scrubbed for a very long time and through several changes of hot water. Hard-towelled off until his skin glowed crimson.

He was almost drunk enough to sleep when the telephone rang and Queenie told him Ingrid had lost the baby, crying for both of them.

Charlie just listened until she was finished.

Then looked at nothing as the day became night filled with soft flurries of snow.

And at dawn he went hunting.

BOOK FOUR

CHAPTER SEVENTEEN

MARIA'S FAT ARM was across Freddy's face.

Smothering him.

He vowed to buy single beds for the trillionth time and made to shrug her away. She wouldn't shrug a damn, and the backs of her hands were stiff with male hair. A pad clamped his nose and mouth. Watered his eyes. He choked on cloying sweetness as he started up from the pillow. Pressed back and down, a red pole of light grew from below his feet. Whirled him through the floor on the spokes of a nebulous ferris-wheel. Spun into drugged twilight, he sneezed against a ribbed metal floor and was jogged by a van's suspension.

Stars jiggled in a swatch of night sky.

The cold bite of wind on his face and a shoulder ground against his crotch as he was carried across rubble, down creaking stairs. Flopped into a chair in a spill of torchlight. He was grateful ropes stopped him sliding on to his face until they constricted his chest, snagged his ankles and brought his feet off the floor.

The pad left his face and he smelled dead air, dry rot and the bitterness of wet coal. Ammonia seared his nostrils. Startled him aware.

And fear came with the cold.

The torch showed him a cellar floor black with coaldust. Panes of grey glass lying against a bunker. A rusty gas-meter and scales of fallen plaster. Fungus on the rafters and walls of crusted brick. Dusty cobwebs bellying in a draught that turned his feet to stones.

He remembered his name. Knew this was a mistake.

Tried to talk. But his tongue was just a thing he swallowed around. The torch clicked off, and a voice in the darkness said: 'Time to own up, Freddy.'

There was no face he could match to the quiet monotone.

To what? 'Wrong face . . . Mister. . . .'

'Now or later. You'll own up.'

Freddy said the three foulest words he knew.

The darkness sighed.

'You hear me, Mister? You ain't dealing with little boys.'

Freddy heard cracks in his bluster. The cold had cracked his lips.

'You hear me?'

The darkness stayed silent.

Freddy listened until his ears popped.

Nothing.

Then the saccharine-citrus stench of chloroform slammed against his face, and Manchester Freddy fell into a darker darkness in a long chime of silence.

'You'll talk.'

Charlie climbed stairs into a fresh fall of snow.

The house in Esher crouched in snow with dripping eaves.

The green-tiled roof ran between dunce-cap turrets and jabbed ornate lightning-conductors into snowcloud. The central mansard was bordered by finely scrolled ironwork with gilded spearheads. A weather-vane pointed its flag to the east, and Father Time leaned over a scythe wearing a snow skullcap.

A dying run of red creeper shed ice-melt on to the pitched portico, and icicles dripped themselves to death over wide stone steps leading to the heavily carved front door. Swiss shutters grafted on to the Tudoresque façade were folded back from the ground-floor windows, and heraldic lozenges set in the leaded glass leaked vague patterns of colour on to the snowbound lawn.

A lean-to garage of ship's timbers and more green tile housed a Porsche and a new Mercedes, and a chauffeur steamed frost from a maroon Daimler with an air-hose on a flagged drive. All that could be seen of the kitchen gardens and the rear grounds was bald elms and a conservatory roof above an arched wall with rubble infills.

Mature monkey-puzzle trees bordered the front-garden wall and spread their spiked branches over the pavement, low enough to graze pedestrians' faces. It was a suburban street where only the postman walked.

A Post Office van nosed into the kerb, offloaded a candy-striped tent and red folding barriers and drove away. Two men got out of an official red van, set the tent over a manhole and disappeared inside to locate the right circuitry and cut the house off from outside contact. The one with freckles and unnaturally black hair wore earphones, and the one with slate eyes sent feedback down the wires.

Inside, Malcolm Sadler dialled 0 to clear the line, and electronic discords fought the Talking Clock for his attention. He swore, pinched his mouth bloodless and earned a brilliant blue glare from his wife.

'Profanity changes nothing, Malcolm darling.'

Margot blew on silver nails.

'Take care, Cat. This house lives by the telephone.'

Sadler's mouth flushed as blood returned.

'The world's stock-markets are closed on Sundays. So be grateful there's at least one day in the week when you can't sell yourself short in Tokyo or New York. What with tin on Wednesday, and magnesium on Thursday, I can hardly keep up with your countless market shortfalls. That *is* the right phrase, isn't it, darling?'

Margot pouted into her mirror with a sardonic purr. Settled a black slip over her narrow hips and recrossed her legs with a hiss of nylon.

'*Short* falls?' she repeated.

'A momentary setback. And a subject high above your avaricious whiskers, Cat.'

Sadler worried a perfect knot into his shirt collar. Grunted over his folded belly when he tied his shoes.

'You *could* blame the Labour opposition, darling. You've

been far too nice about them since Gaitskell died and small fat Harold became leader. And that screaming skull Lord Home makes chubby little Wilson seem quite attractive by comparison. Perhaps we shall have a socialist government after the next general election. Then you'll really be "one of the lads" when you entertain your East End roughnecks, won't you?'

Sadler tried the phone again.

'You'll find most of them are emotional socialists and have rapidly moved to a conservatism far to the right of Genghis Khan. In their world, it takes more than a cut-glass accent and a stream of friendly bank managers to prevail against the opposition. Take care you don't brush their fur the wrong way, Cat.'

Margot eased into a very frilly black blouse, zipped into a charcoal-grey skirt and added four inches to her height with French heels.

'Will your robber barons require cutlery? Or will they eat their rancid faggots and pease-pudding with their fingers as usual? I forget the protocol, bastard darling, Malcolm sweetie.'

Sadler reached Margot in two strides. Moved quickly for his sleek bulk. Thick fingers twined into the hair at the back of Margot's neck. Twisted with a vicious upturn. A thick thumb and forefinger closed around her neck. Squeezed slowly, lifting her inch by inch from the floor.

'You go too far, Cat. Far too far. . . .'

Margot smelled breakfast marmalade on his breath, the harsh tang of witch hazel on his shaved cheeks.

'Just wifely cat noises . . . Mal . . . colm. . . .'

Margot's pointed toes tried for the floor. She thought of driving silver nails into the whites of his eyes. But her sight was gone in mist and her heart was a slowing engine.

He swore he'd never play this foul game again. . . .

She was plunged back to Biarritz when Malcolm and her wedding band were equally strange. Clever *ingénue* Margot who had avoided bedroom scenes with shy Malcolm until after altar pledges were notarised and she had tossed orange-blossom to her maids of honour. The champagne whirl into the bridal suite where Malcolm had pressed her face into the pillows and used her as if she were the chorus boy who had introduced them. Angry she had not embraced sapphism as he had supposed. Angrier still when she would not complete the triangle when the young man flew in the following day. The humiliation of nights on the couch as they used her bridal bed.

'Too catty to be wifely, Cat.'

Margot spun on the edge of consciousness as the voice brushed her with the threat of sadism.

'The cat must lap the milk of penitence. Lap it and drink it down like a good and dutiful queen. But true queens can have kittens. Can't they, cat? And this queen is barren. Not a real queen at all. Just a cat who pretends she had eggs. Just to bring Malcolm into her bed for her own lascivious ends. No son for Malcolm. Just a cat. . . . .'

'No . . . Malcolm . . . you swore. . . .'

'But it's yes, Malcolm. It's always to be yes for Malcolm.'

Agree before he peels your scalp like pith from an orange.

'Yesss . . . Malcolm. . . .'

'Again, Cat.'

'Yesss. . . .'

Sadler drove Margot to her knees. Made her crawl towards the bed.

'Nothing inside my cat but avarice. And the need for punishment. Now, what should that be, I wonder? Should Malcolm buy himself a new cat? Make the old eggless cat kiss the new cat's paws before the old cat laps milk from Malcolm's lap? H'm?'

The bed and Malcolm sighed as he lowered himself on to the counterpane, Margot's face trapped between his great thighs. He released the pressure on her throat and she drank in the smell of laundered sheets, Malcolm's oversweet male perfume.

Her face was slowly raised, and Sadler was a dark buddha against the hot orange of a stained-glass lozenge.

'Well, Cat?'

Feed his perverted fantasies . . . and live.

Say it and get it over with. . . .

'Yesss . . . Malcolm. . . .'

'Only yes, Margot cat? Barren cat?'

'Yesss, Malcolm. Please, please, Malcolm?'

'Margot cat wants to lap the milk of penitence?'

'Yes, please, Malcolm.'

Margot unbuttoned the pinstripe fly with dreary care.

Freed the half-risen member and took it into her quivering mouth very very slowly. Felt it become a hard pole against the roof of her mouth. And with her eyes locked on Sadler's shadowed face she lapped her milk like a good cat until he exploded against her tongue with a long guttural moan. Hammered his thighs against her face. Withdrew to glisten her cheeks with the last milky pulses from his flaccid erection. Turned Margot into a little girl being blooded by a foxtail on her first hunt in the long-gone mists of Surrey. She had cried for the red fox and a little for herself. Denied her father's need for a manly daughter.

The hands left her hair, and Margot was pushed on to her side with: 'Clean your whiskers, Puss.'

Margot crawled to the bathroom.

Wiped tears away with the semen and did not vomit until Sadler had gone below to swear at the dead telephone.

She repaired her make-up and changed into a pale oyster trouser-suit, and checked that the cold buffet had been properly laid out in the library where Bunny and Lemmon had had their private talk. Then she rebuilt her brittle shell with Cognac and fresh limes in the conservatory, and was halfway down a bottle when the telephone engineer with slate eyes scratched at the window.

Crystal Palace was Sunday-quiet under a fresh blanket of snow.

Bulstrode was kissing a plain-clothes WPC when Connie Harold parked his Vanden Plas beside the unmarked Q-car. The BBC transmitting mast cast blue shadows as Connie walked Pimlico across crackling snow and Bulstrode contacted Quill's mobile by radio. Dillman acknowledged as Connie climbed a bank to the footpath and said: 'If they gave the train robbers thirty apiece when there was only one driver with a cracked nut, what chance does Wally have? You only draw fifteen for murder, and you're out in eight. But they're after us in a big way. All the bloody way.'

Pimlico refused Connie's arm, favoured his right leg and held his tender groin on the bank, feeling the cold in his newly healed stomach. Doc Rudge had worked miracles and tutted sadly when Pimlico said he had to go out in the freezing weather.

Pimlico panted on the path, pulled his collar higher.

'That's why we're here, right?'

'Which way?' Connie's breath was tainted by Cuban tobacco.

'Around the tennis courts and the ornamental gardens.'

Pimlico kicked slush from his shoes.

The sky was a leaden sprawl of windless cloud, and the bald trees were black skeletons against the aching white of pristine snow.

Connie windmilled his arms.

'The law's as hard as the weather. Bubbles from my finger-tame busies are rarer than Russian Studebakers since Wally was collared. Thanks be to whatsit I squared that truce with Troy and his tarts; with Charlie-bloody-Dance banged up with a shiv in his derby, that's me home and free to take care of this bit of a farce before I gets back to my holdings in South Africa.'

Pimlico spat a hole in snow.

'Handshaking with the Troys? That buys you not a lot and less than nothing.'

'Buys me time. All you've bought me with your hard-nosing is Harry the Crack limping from buckshot wounds and crying for me to get him away to Jo'burg, you hiding out in Spitalfields, Sailor Mailer on the wanted list, and a brother banged up on a murder charge. What have you taught Wally except to elbow his own brother and never run from anything? That's got your little firm well up the pictures, and you out in the cold without a warmer.'

'Once Wally's back on the cobbles we'll get Imperial Machines sorted.'

'So long as Charlie Dance stays upright. And I don't give his chances more than a cold carrot. Come over to Uncle Con while he can still use you.'

'You'd use me all right. Forget it.'

'You're running out of shadows to hide in.'

Pimlico sniffed at the chill overcast.

'There's always more than smoke to your bonfires. You wouldn't be Connie Harold if there wasn't. You'd love me and Wally handling Kelly and the London end — you with clean hands when me and Wally really knock heads with the Troys. You out in wogland playing footsy with Jorgesson's wife, making her and making money.'

'That's nothing to you, Parsons.'

'You got that right. Save all your old tonk for the fish who swallow your old line.'

'All *right*.'

Connie skidded to a halt on the path beside the running-track. A man in orange strip padded round the invisible perimeter timing himself with a stopwatch.

'That's you and Wally both. Running going nowhere. I've given the Troys my share of Petticoat Lane. And I've given them a free road to Malcolm Sadler by elbowing him out of my mining deal. Two darling sweeteners they couldn't resist. But I need dough from somewhere else. And springing Bonar's boy Smiler would earn the right kind of poppy for starters. And Brixton Billy. And that ain't the half of it. There's a lovely earner out at National Car Parks Heathrow. The faces there have been fiddling the tills. Charge the motorists full whack and pay half into the firm. They're splitting two grand a week between six of them. I want half, and you can have a quarter of that for collecting once a week. How bad?'

'A half a monkey? Why so generous?'

Connie sneaked a sly glance at Pimlico.

'Because I know you'd collect, that's why. And if you

come in on springing Smiler and Brixton Billy—'

'You don't just hook them over the wall, you know. I've got the bottle but not the nous. You'd need someone like—'

Connie laughed smoke.

'Dublin Gerry? He's in.'

Pimlico stared and held his stomach.

'Gerry ain't fond of me, and if you're dealing with the Troys there's more to this than you're saying.'

'Ain't you the clever one?'

'Clever enough to know you've offered the Troys something more than a few stallholders' subs and Sadler, whoever he is.'

'So hurt your brain and tell me.'

'A share of South Africa. Got to be.'

'Right again.'

'They'll want more, whatever you offered.'

'But they'll take time wanting more.'

'No longer than the time it took to shake your paw, Con.'

Connie shook his head. Flipped his cigar-butt into a hedge laden with snow. Blue smoke curled from the crater.

Pimlico watched for shock in Connie's marbled eyes when he said: 'Gerry won't take shares as payment. He don't like me, and you say he's in, knowing you're hand-shaking the Troys. That it?'

'That's it.'

'And him knowing the Troys have got him marked for not triggering Charlie and Queenie Ogle?'

Connie's face almost stayed calm.

'You didn't know that, right?'

'It's a detail.'

'The main event more like.'

'Always the bloody Jeremiah. Gerry's a man who'll earn where there's a crust. Business is business.'

Connie looked out over the frozen ponds and the pre-historic lizards on their islands. Hoary with frost, the silent saurians raked the sky with fretted backs, ugly with menace under scales of peeling brown paint.

'Who put them things there?'

'They're Victorian. Something to do with the Great Exhibition of 1851.' Pimlico huffed breath over the crusted ice. 'I used to bring sandwiches and Tizer out here when I was a kid. Get in amongst them and pretend I was Stanley or Livingstone finding them for the first time.'

'Who'd *want* to find the buggers?'

'Weren't you *ever* a kid, Connie?'

'Too busy earning a crust for kids' stuff.' Connie clapped his gloves together. 'Where's this face anyway?'

'He'll be along. Walks his dog here every morning.'

Connie dribbled white breath.

'You want these earners?'

'Heathrow, yeah. But forget me ducking in and out of maximum-security prisons.'

'Mr Hard goes soft.' Connie cracked a puddle with his heel.

'Sensible ain't soft. You could find that out sudden.'

Connie almost grinned.

'Maybe, maybe not. Is this the face?'

Pimlico watched a man plod round the bend after a dog snapping at the snow. The bushes of rhododendron were fat white bouquets hung with icicles. The setter barked fearlessly at nothing and ignored the call to heel. The man snapped a leash at the setter and it bounded off a few steps, full of mischief.

'Nice dog.'

Connie blocked the path.

'A complete fool. But he makes me take my regular constitutional,' said the middle-aged man. Eyes friendly in a windburned face.

'Just a pup, eh?'

Connie saw Pimlico catch the setter's collar.

'My previous old friend died after thirteen years. I got this scamp to take his place.'

'Dogs do get to you, Mr Dalgliesh.'

The man looked puzzled.

'You know me?'

'A friend of mine does. You'll be looking at him from

the jury bench soon. And you could turn his misfortune to your advantage. A thousand favours. All with the Queen's head in the corner. All green. All cash. All my friend wants is a quick "Not Guilty" at Kingston crown court, have it away on his toes, and you could be back walking your dog with a nice little earner in your pocket.'

'I have been called for jury service. . . .'

Dalgliesh paled under his windburn and cast about for other people. There were only hedges and the giant concrete lizards.

'Let me pass.'

Connie put his face close to Dalgliesh, and his voice was low and confidential.

'I know of a dog. Got trapped under the ice. Couldn't get him out before he went down for the third time.'

'Happens to people just as easy,' said Pimlico.

'Hear your wife's a bit frail these days. Florence, ain't it? A fall at this time of the year, broken hip, nasty.'

'Fatal,' said Pimlico.

Dalgliesh looked jaundiced.

'We don't want to see Towser fall in, do we? Or your missus come a purler in the house while you're out trying to save your mutt? Course we don't,' said Connie.

'Looks thin here,' said Pimlico, stroking the puppy. 'Wouldn't hold his weight.'

Dalgliesh shrank inside his tweed coat as Connie's breath curled around his face.

'And you'd find yourself alone in the voting. If you was daft enough to go for a "Guilty". That's been well taken care of. One lady almost went under an Underground train before she got all wised up. Her nose was right on the rails. Electric sparks and goodbye just inches away. You don't go out with a bang, you know. You burn long and slow on electrified lines. A fact, that.'

Dalgliesh couldn't talk.

'You want us to give you chapter and verse on the rest of the jury?'

'I . . . no . . . I'm . . . convinced. . . .'

Connie tucked Dalgliesh inside his collar.

'Well, that's nice. Ain't that nice?'

'Nice,' said Pimlico, testing the ice with a toe.

'But, to make sure, there'll be somebody cruising about around your house every night. Number 41, right?'

'Oh . . . God. . . .'

'I think He's out to lunch. You take your dog straight home now. And walk careful. Treacherous, these paths.'

'Yes, yes, I'll. . . .'

'And keep an ear out for passing cars.'

'And hope they keep passing.' Pimlico dropped the setter, and it slid on the snow wagging a stump of a tail.

Dalgliesh leashed the dog and broke into a trot at the first bend. Left a coil of white breath in the grey air.

The park crackled and plopped in hard silence.

'Nice bloke.'

Connie's laugh found Dillman crouched beside a Sauropoda with young. Out of earshot of the preceding threats.

'Coming your way, Mobile 1,' he told Bulstrode.

'Snow's played havoc with the overhead wires.'

Charlie watched Margot Sadler take that in with slow blue myopic blinks. She wagged a finger beside her drink.

'Snow always brings this benighted country to a halt. And unions keep us stationary. Snow and unions. The British Diseases. Come in, come in.'

Charlie edged into the sub-tropical cloy of damp humus and orchids.

'Come along, Working Man.'

Margot wove through fleshy bowers and along a passage to the library. Waved her glass at a telephone on an escritoire.

'That's the one for His Master's Voice. There are six or seven others dotted around. And oodles of those jack-plug thingies. This house *lives* by the telephone.'

She crossed a languorous leg to watch Charlie unscrew the mouthpiece and thumb a bug into place. He added a miniature microphone to the skirting junction-box and asked where the other instruments were.

In the Chinese room she learned he was unmarried. In the master bedroom they were on Christian-name terms. In the panelled anteroom he admitted preferring whisky to gin, and back in the conservatory he accepted a small Irish to keep out the cold. Margot by that time held a longer drink and listened for sibilance in her speech with alcoholic care.

Charlie dialled a phoney service call to activate the bugs and Limehouse rang back to say a pink Cadillac had drawn up outside.

'Thanks, Exchange. Keep me posted.'

Charlie smiled at Margot Sadler.

'They're checking the circuits now. It could be an hour or so, so I'll get out from under your feet and wait in the van.'

'In this weather?'

A doorbell chimed, and Sadler let the Troys into the house. Their voices were dulled to baritone fuzz by the massed foliage and double glazing.

'You've got guests to look after.'

Charlie took a Perfectos Finos and held Margot's wrist to steady the lighter flame. Her cornflower eyes darkened as she blew smoke and the voices died behind the library door.

'I'd rather die of leprosy.' Margot shivered and held herself. 'Ignore them, they're an illusion.'

'I've got in-laws I can't stand myself.'

'Even yours can't be as Neanderthal as those people. I told you, they're but an illusion.'

Charlie pinged a nail against his glass.

'And this is reality?'

A carp cut a chevron as it arrowed between water-lilies, and Margot laughed without expression.

'There are two undeniable forces in my universe, Charlie. Age and gravity. They both pull you down in the end.'

'Black coffee won't change that, Lady. But it might give your liver—'

'A fallacious concept, Telephone Charlie. Watered drinks mean the alcohol assimilates in your bloodstream that much faster, that's all. Doesn't hit your liver in one great lump.'

Charlie heard the doorbell and transatlantic accents.

'No jollying you along, is there, Lady?'

He lifted the wallphone.

'Exchange?'

'Strangers to me, Chas. Came in a taxi and didn't get change of a fiver. Italians or Yanks maybe?'

'Out, exchange.'

'And don't call me "Lady". Makes me feel like a chipped remnant on a cheap market-stall.'

'All right.'

Margot spilled amber liquid near her glass and across an oyster thigh.

'Damn. I should rinse this at once.'

Charlie damped a bar towel and offered it. Margot grabbed Charlie's bicep, and her shakes jogged up into his shoulder. A nerve ticked near the bridge of her wayward nose, and her eyes swam with unshed tears.

Charlie heard forced laughter from the hall.

'Americans?'

'Canadians,' said Margot. 'Let it stain.'

Charlie got his hand back and dabbed the alcohol away.

'Nice things deserve nice treatment.'

'Frugal little soldier, aren't you?'

'Mother's little helper.'

'You're no telephone engineer,' Margot accused, her face chalky.

'No?' Charlie's neck bristled.

'No. You're one of Malcolm's legion of bleeding hearts who use their wiles to get him grounds for divorce.'

'Oh blimey yeah. It's the GPO's latest gimmick. Leave it out, Lady.'

Charlie watched the sorrowing face flit through half-formed expressions. None of them stable, none of them attractive.

'It's Margot. And when did you last help a woman sleep without the need of that last little drink to find oblivion?'

'Not this year, Lady.'

'Don't call me—'

'Then, act the lady you are. Then I'll maybe call you bloody Margot.'

Charlie held the moist blue eyes and plumed smoke from the side of his mouth.

'More than one of my mates has lost his job because some frustrated *hausfrau* asked for a bit of slap and tickle. And screamed rape when she didn't get it. Are you going to scream me out of a job?' Charlie was ready to choke Margot unconscious.

'Maybe I was thinking something like that. The reasons—'

'Are none of Charlie's business.'

Margot pinned a fleeting smile to her lips.

'And I thought one could be brutally frank with strangers.'

'Don't mean they won't lie to you.'

'Or I to them. So where's the harm?'

'In how many lies you don't admit to yourself.'

'Well, bravo with brass knobs.' Margot attempted a sneer when Charlie grinned. 'What's the Cheshire Cat for?'

'You. You'd run a mile if I laid a glove on you.'

'So that's what's at the back of your seedy little mind.'

'Nope. But it's at the front of yours.'

'Poo,' said Margot.

Charlie leaned a hip against the bar.

'Why is it rich women don't seem to have fun? You laugh, but it's just a sound. And your clothes are just clothes. You didn't have to save your pennies for them, so why take pride in what comes for free? The shops are full of nifty little numbers you can charge to the old man's account.'

Margot's eyes snapped. Roundels of anger burned the chalky cheeks.

'That's brutal, inaccurate and bloody smug. I've been down to my last pair of gloves and washed my dainties out in rooming-house sinks, you moron. Begged lifts in transport cafés when the entire cast has been abandoned without train fare home. Dirty theatres and dirtier digs. Leading men who wiped their personality off with their make-up. Managers with minds grubbier than their fingernails. You can't eat the tinsel dream when you're hungry, dirty and friendless. So stuff your inverted snobbery, Telephone Charlie.'

Charlie found another grin.

'There's always hope for somebody who can get that cross with herself. Means you still have some self-respect.'

'I'm cross with your impertinence. Not me.'

'No, you ain't. I'll soon be gone and forgotten. You'll still have to live with you.'

'A nice convolution, you viper.'

'Yes, Ma'am.'

Margot cocked an eyebrow.

'And now I'm supposed to kick you out. Let the silence come back and drown in this stuff. Pretend that rabble in the library isn't there. That my bastard husband didn't make me take his filthy. . . .'

Margot's shudder almost emptied her glass, and her high heels grated on the stone flags. Her sombre eyes darkened to match the witches'-butter algae on the side of the pool.

'None of your business, though, eh, Telephone Charlie?'

'No, Ma'am.'

Charlie held the wallphone to his ear. Heard Limehouse tell Sadler he'd be called when the circuits were restored. Added a 'sir' colder than the snow he crouched in.

'How's the front, Exchange?'

Lou described the overcoats outside as four broken circuits.

'Best stay inside, Service.'

'Stay inside, the man says.'

Charlie gnawed a thumb at the spot where Margot had sat. Her trousers were flung over the spikes of a yucca, and a damp ring marked the stone where her drink had rested. She waded across the central pool with a tray of drinks, four inches of white thigh showing above black stocking-tops.

'Paddling in high heels?'

Charlie shook his head. Reminded of another stretch of water. Black faces and the bore of a gun in moonlight.

Margot said 'Uhuh' and went through a thick fan of palm, green spears brushing the greener water.

'Mind the alligators, Charlie.'

Charlie took off his boots and socks, rolled up his trousers and followed her through the thick bower of fronds into a cocoon of eau-de-Nil light and cool russet shadows.

Margot was a little girl playing tea-parties.

Mixing drinks on a long tongue of rock carpeted with Korean moss. A dim yellow canebrake rustled in the windless air, and elephant-grey trunks with boles like ancient kneecaps twined and crooked into the dark canopy of varicoloured leaves. Irregular spills of water formed a small waterfall and drummed amongst glossy lily-pads, running off as fast marbles of mercury.

Charlie hauled himself on to springy moss, and his face brushed Margot's cleavage as she moved in against him, her voice muffled in his hair.

'Do I need this drink, Telephone Charlie?'

Margot cringed from her childish question. Feared scorn in her private everglade.

Instead, her hair was tumbled into soft falls around her face. A thumb ran down her nose to part her lips for a cool mouth tasting of peat fires. She leaned in to twine tongues as her back was bared and arched by a firm palm. Hard shoulder muscles bunched under her gently biting nails.

She rolled her head as the mouth enclosed an aching breast, once more panicked by the head prefect who suckled her budding mammaries after lights out, the Oxford graduate who knuckled her labia in the back seat of a rented tourer, the understudy who relieved her of innocence in the wings whilst the second lead was accused of murder most foul by a theatrical barrister, a last meaningless encounter before Malcolm turned her into a shrewish sophisticate who found oblivion and numbed peace with a cocktail-shaker.

Margot was lost in a thousand places and nowhere.

Her slip was a wisp of black silence beside her overturned drink, and sure stranger's hands kneaded the soft swells below her damp spine, brought her closer and closer to the erect man in a long upsurge of need, a need maddeningly tempered by the timeless dread of male invasion.

She drowned in her own hair and had visions of a rampant snake in a dark and liquid purse as she made a great salmon-leap across an infinite weir, fell ever upward to embrace a massive full stop to seven lean and celibate years.

Mounted on a great spur of rock she both rode and surrounded, she spiralled through the viridian canopy into the primordial boil of her own inner seas where a great rolling scald left her beached on the island moss. The incoming spasms died, and the locked loins pulsed to a halt as her fists opened like tired flowers and lay quietly beside her.

Then shyness came and she wanted to press her face into the ground, hidden in her tent of hair. But firm hands and slate eyes pinned her where she lay. Forced her to enjoy the last long quivers of a marvel forbidden her save in lonely orgasmic dreams.

Her need to say something tart emerged as a yawning sigh. As warm as her snuggle of contentment. As pneumatic as the opening conservatory door.

Sadler was a shadow through leaves. An indistinct reflection in the pool.

'Margot? Damn the woman, where are you?'

Margot laid a finger to Charlie's lips and deliberately slurred her words.

'Lying here with my lover, darling bastard, Malcolm sweetie.'

'The bitch is drunk,' Sadler said without surprise. 'Well, Cat, and where does your master find more ice? That moronic cook of yours has gone heaven knows where.'

'In the freezer, bastard love. Surely that fool of a chauffeur can put his hands on it. He finds the cooking-brandy readily enough.'

Margot belched lightly for effect. Flicked a nail against Charlie's pectoral and curled her stockinged heels against his buttocks. Enjoyed his flinch and the inadvertent buck between her thighs.

Sadler oiled his voice.

'Damn you, Puss. We have guests and my cat thinks herself safe.'

'Perfectly safe.'

Margot crossed her eyes, extended her tongue and grinned like a twelve-year-old.

'But guests go home, Puss. And then we shall see just how safe my cat is.'

The door hissed closed, and Sadler was gone.

Margot began to shake violently.

'Even the uninvited ones. Put me in your pocket, Telephone Charlie,' she whispered. 'Let me curl up like a dormouse in your teapot. I don't want to be a cat any more.'

Charlie held her until her face slept in the green twilight, shedding years as her eyes closed and her mouth slackened, seeing another more oval face, fuller breasts that had lactated in early pregnancy, longer legs with narrower feet without silver nail-gloss.

Until Mario and Pru Mizzi and the kick that miscarried his son. Turned him into just another crimson smear on that stone villa-floor.

The whirling tapes in Limehouse Lou's van recorded the Troys and the Tonnas in Sadler's library. Another nail in their collective coffin, courtesy of Charlie Dance.

But that cold comfort did not stop Charlie from feeling he had contracted a disease that made his neck permanently dirty.

Black ice was a hazard on the road to Stoke Mandeville.

Bulstrode walked the length of an airy ward of limbless ex-servicemen and found Vinnie Castle in an observation room overlooking a frozen valley six miles from Bridego Bridge.

A cold afternoon sun set fire to the sky behind purple hills. Gilded the naked elms and pastelled the snowscape with sage and violet.

Vinnie came out of a doze to thumb the magazines Bulstrode dropped into his lap. He had lost weight, but his smile was still brilliant.

'Nice of you to come in this humpty weather, Buller.'

'You're worth it, Ugly. When d'you get your tin leg?'

Vinnie's teeth were too white in his gaunt face.

'When the grafts take. The limbs are plastic nowadays. The doc figures he can fit a rubber lining so I can fill it with gin and be a walking distillery. And make me taller if I lose the other leg.'

Bulstrode shook his head.

'How d'you stay cheerful, son?'

A legless man with a mutilated face whined past in an electric wheelchair, working the controls with a three-fingered hand.

'That's how. Funny how it's the patients who cheer up the visitors.'

Vinnie peeled an orange, and Bulstrode refused a wedge.

'And I throw a wobbly when the gas bill's too high.'

'And how many more over how bad you and Lemmon are at banging up villains?'

Bulstrode touched his cigarettes and left them in his pocket.

'Charlie's out,' he said.

'That right?'

Vinnie dribbled juice through his smile. Wiped it off with a tissue.

'Am I sucking eggs, or what?' said Bulstrode.

'Yeah,' said Vinnie. 'I sort of heard he was back on the cobbles. Now you'll see some unhappy faces.'

'Tell him to hold off, Vin. We're getting there with the chapter and verse on Bethnal Green and Wandsworth. And you could drive a nail or three by fingering who triggered you. The Met won't stand still for another Mr Jones and the Ju-Ju Men.'

Vinnie snorted through orange-pith.

'Then I'd really be the one-legged man in that famous arse-kicking contest. The word of one man against half of bloody Bethnal Green? They'd have rigged the jury and be back on the cobbles before the judge disrobed and reached for the old Amontillado. Just like Connie's doing for brother Wally right now. And that's with your law firm right up their jaxies. Don't kid a kidder, Buller son.'

'Take the stand. We'll ring you with more blue serge than a Hendon review.'

'Even if I made the witness-box and bubbled honest, what then? I'd be just another grass waiting to be shivved rotten. And deserve it. We'll sort our own . . . unless you deal with the Man.'

'Archie?'

Vinnie wiped juice away with a pale hand.

'Charlie.'

Bulstrode stared. Washed his hands between his thighs and turned his signet ring.

'Since when did Charlie earn that specious accolade?'

'He's out earning it now, I shouldn't wonder.'

'I heard there was a hit in Malta.'

'Get away,' Vinnie said softly. 'That right?'

'Give me something, Vinnie. Something upright and still breathing. No more bodies with tagged toes. No more claret on the cobbles.'

'Talk to the Man.'

'About what? Exchanging Bethnal Green for one of ours? Quill's head on a silver salver like Salome had John the Baptist?'

'He might listen at that.'

'I'll bet.'

Bulstrode stood at the window where early stars faded into dull glittering strands in the upper darkness. His breath formed a patch of vapour on the glass and he drew a swastika in it without knowing why. Thought of minicabbing or pulling pints as an alternative lifestyle.

Vinnie said, 'You need a nice fresh corpse, a signed confession and the Troys with smoking shooters in their hands before you'll nail them. Unless. . . .'

Bulstrode bowed over Vinnie's wheelchair. His hands clamped the padded arms.

'I ought to drop you back in the sewer where I found you. A bad copper for two gobs of slime? Quill may be a lot of things, but up for grabs he ain't. And what would Charlie the Man want for the Harolds? The fucking Home Secretary up on pederasty charges citing all the kids in Dr Barnardo's? How do you sleep nights, Castle? How many of their pink pills does it take to turn your rotten brain off until breakfast?'

Vinnie's smile was just white teeth and hard eyes.

'I sleep just fine. Unless the pain has me ringing for the night-nurse. Or I get to thinking about the twenty more ops I've got coming. Or wondering if my heart'll stand up to it all. Or looking at my old mother going grey with worry over me. Missing the grandkids I'll never give her now I piss through a plastic pipe. Try living without an honest erection, Buller. Knowing you'll never make a woman, any woman go misty for your touch, you up inside her. Ask yourself how you'd see the world with your manhood blown away. All I've got is what you see. It's me who has to live with what I ain't got no more. One leg a memory, the other coming off below the knee in all probability. You man enough to swallow that? I am. But I'll never swallow shit again. How about you?'

Bulstrode's knuckles cracked when he let go of the chair. His heart filled his chest and there was the slightest flutter in his stimulated groin. The vague brush of unbidden sexual need. Made worse because Vinnie saw it in his flushed face. His breath whistled as he said: 'You bitter, bitter bastard.'

Vinnie's grin was as thin as bookbinders leather.

'Surprised, are we?'

'You think I like seeing you like this? Like the idea of the dozens of others chopped into raw liver like you? I'm a copper, son. A badge with a heart pinned to it. I want real justice, not the perverted crap you and yours go in for. You can't see how wrong you are. I pity you.'

'Pity I can do without. Or you bleeding reason all over me. I'm a face. Not a chunk of meat you can patronise with your Boy Scout cowcake. You wouldn't know street justice if it bit you in the back pocket. Deal or don't, it's down to you.'

Vinnie turned his wheelchair full circle before spinning himself back to his ward.

Bulstrode wiped the swastika out with his sleeve and watched the sun die with a crimson flourish.

Needing a woman very badly.

Jutting his plump lower lip, Malcolm Sadler drew the library curtains when the pink Cadillac followed the Tonnas' taxi out of the street. Toasted himself in five-star brandy. Celebrated the culmination of three long years of planning at the cost of several thousand grey cells and very little financial outlay.

For all their vicious armoury, his departed guests lacked protection from their one vulnerable spot. Their own monumental greed.

Once he had lured them out into the arid wasteland of international finance where the solid gold-blocked assets of bona-fide companies funded by their unlaundered money became ephemeral stock-quotations in shadowy paper companies, then he would have them. Then the stocks could convert to yen in Brazil. Become steel shares in Pensacola. Transform themselves to American dollars in Sydney, to Swiss francs in the Cayman Islands. Spinning from there into a flurry of numbered accounts spread between Cadiz and Rio de Janeiro. Lost to sight to all save the single responsible signatory. Himself.

Then, with split-second timing, he could pauper them – could control their various enterprises by using their own capital against them.

Sadler had the details down to the last decimal place committed to memory. Calculated it would take a single calendar year to bring his plans to fruition. Until then he would dangle golden carrots in front of the donkeys on his long, long line.

The Troys had wanted a club in the West End, so Sadler had given them the keys to Titania's Castle in Bond Street. The Tonnas had wanted the lion's share of Archie Ogle's casinos and the control of their new drugs network between the Philippines and Hong Kong. Sadler had agreed. Allowed them to front for him like so many dangerous puppets, grateful their massing assets were in his capable hands. Sadler let them paw over their paper profits and glory in their new-found respectability. Allowed them to strut and boast and think him the fool.

The brandy was golden fire on Sadler's tongue. Helped his heart to bump with controlled exitement.

Connie Harold's shambolic attempts to build an empire in South Africa would come to nothing without Sadler's expert hand on his shoulder, although Sadler knew he should have foreseen Conrad trying to go it alone — offering Sadler the Troys like bargain packets of soap powder. Connie had learned to handle Jorgesson very well, and turning down the American offer of a million said much for his doggedness. But his feelings for Alicia had caused some tension with De Wit.

Sadler's respect for De Wit was based on fear.

De Wit had a very long arm indeed. Not only in Africa but also throughout the South Americas where his Broederbond contacts were amongst the German expatriate élite of Paraguay and Brazil. Powerful men not to be dismissed lightly.

De Wit was Sadler's way of bringing Connie Harold to his knees when he had finally overextended himself. Then there would be all the time in the world to pick up the pieces of his embryonic but lucrative holdings.

Whistling tunelessly, Sadler went to bathe and change. The reckoning with Margot was still to come, and he wanted to be clean and rested for that pleasure.

The Barren Cat should have given Sadler grounds for a simple and inexpensive divorce and not wittered on about how devoted she was to Chartings Hall. It was just a house like any other. Sadler knew he could call upon the Troys to dispose of Margot for him, but he would rather find a way without being beholden to them.

Sadler frowned and scrubbed, and thought the problem through.

Then he went down into the hot odours of the conservatory to find the drunken bitch.

He laid his dressing-gown beside Margot's oyster trousers and took a long moment to enjoy his naked reflection before stepping into the warm water.

The stone floor was slick with silt, and he reminded himself to have the gardener syphon it out in the morning. Sadler would brook nothing less than perfection, and in that single regard Margot was an excellent housekeeper. It was such a pity she failed in so many other areas.

Sadler parted hanging fronds and skirted the rock where Margot lay curled up, breathing through her mouth, hair a black fan around her supine face.

Sadler breathed quietly, bit on pleased laughter as he moved silently through the water. The bruise on Margot's throat was just beginning to show, and he meant to kiss her there before strangling her awake.

Sadler sniffed the air. Caught the elusive musk of Margot and something other. A man-smell not his. He froze reaching for Margot's neck. Was thinking about telephone engineers when the back of his head exploded into a million disparate colours, each colour a different wavelength of pain.

His gasp did not reach the back of his teeth, was a hard bubble at the base of his tongue locked there by muscular spasm.

He tried to turn his head as chest hair brushed his shoulders and a great clamp at the base of his skull drove his face into the moss beside Margot's silver toes. A knee ground into the base of his spine and livid primaries burst around his fluttering eyeballs. Chopped behind both knees his legs turned to numbed flab.

He threw a wild backhand. Tried to gouge an eye or grasp hair. The arm was caught and turned against the joint. His elbow grated, stung his mind with the flare of pinched nerves and torn muscle, and hung in numbness.

Sadler's cry was as liquid as the slap of carp on still water.

His teeth scraped rock as his head was plunged into the pool. His ears sang with pressure and his world turned green. He saw his own toes flex in silt between another man's feet. A gout of air from his mouth boiled up around his face. Took sound to the surface and left him behind. His eyes bulged and tried to follow the bubbles, so Malcolm would drown in blindness. His nose smashed against the bottom, then he was back in tropical smells, breathing raggedly through his own blood. Angry enough to weep before he was plunged back into brackish water.

He lost all thoughts of living, part of the pool now, without substance. Survival meant nothing. Only wanting to float deeper and deeper in submarine greens where calm and sleep were down and down and down. . . .

Knuckles bruised his scalp. A hard palm slammed his face from side to side. Brought him back from his drowned paradise. Made him taste salty blood in his mouth, running warmth in his mashed nose. Made him fill his ironbound chest with precious oxygen and sob. Small tearing sounds smacking of humiliation profound enough to share with . . . Margot.

Sadler came out of mist to see his belly rise and fall with droplets running from it in thin streams. His useless legs hung from his hips as he lay arched over the edge of the pool.

The hand in his hair made him see his swollen genitals, puffing grotesquely from a hard downward pull that had driven him into limbo.

Then the hand released his hair. His head cracked against the hot flags and his useless hands were unable to cover his hurt. He could only breathe, see and hear.

Somebody said the bugs were cleared.

But that made no sense because they wriggled under Sadler's drooping lids.

'Can you hear me, animal?'

Sadler said he could hear perfectly well, being polite to avoid further pain.

'Don't make me come back,' said the quiet voice.

Sadler affirmed with nods. Was still nodding vigorously when the pneumatic door hissed closed on his uncontrolled weeping.

He called for a long time before he made Margot hear.

Lemmon sat Bulstrode beside his living-room fire with a stiff vodka and tonic whilst Elizabeth made coffee and Tony Bennett left his heart in San Francisco. When Elizabeth had brought them the Cona and cups on a tray, kissed Lemmon good night and gone to bed with a paperback romance, Bulstrode talked about Crystal Palace and Stoke Mandeville Hospital.

Lemmon smoked through it all in silence, nodded here and there, and said: 'We've got everything and nothing. We know a great deal and can prove nothing in a court of law. Doesn't mean we aren't winning, and we're not losing by a long chalk, either. Sooner or later, something will break our way. Then landslide.'

Bulstrode chewed a moody Player.

'When? The jury members Connie's nobbled won't even talk to us. Let alone bring charges of attempted bribery with threats of violence against the Harold firm. We're supposed to be the good guys in white hats. It's a bloody nightmare.'

'And it'll get worse before it gets better, Buller my son. Tall John Law's lost the respect of the man in the street. Even the law-abiding ones who work their eight-hour shifts, pay their taxes and hand lost property in at the local station. The tragedy is you aren't old enough to remember how it used to be. When the local beat copper knew everybody in the manor, and a clipped ear stopped more than one Jack the Lad from turning villain.

'When the villains themselves turned in the faces who used shooters in a robbery or turned one on a copper. When the toms told us about their dodgy tricks. Gave us the nod if there was a sexual pervert on their patch who might interfere with a decent girl. Or molest a child.

'You either get crazy-angry about it, or you become philosophical. Or do what Prophet did to Charlie Dance: plant evidence to nail him on a charge, any charge, rather than wait and get him straight. Or do what too many do: shrug and take all the bribes offered.'

'That's for the Arthur Axes of this world. Not us.'

'You say.'

Lemmon hid himself in a last gout of smoke and tossed the butt into the fire.

'You ain't helping me, Guv.'

'You want advice, you'll get it. Make out your report in triplicate about this jury-nobbling and hang fire. Let Wally Harold walk free.'

Bulstrode stared and lit another cigarette.

'I'll say this once, Buller. That's all. As soon as that jury comes in with a "Not Guilty" and Wally's back on the cobbles, then all those jurors will talk – not to us directly, but to friends and friends of friends. Shouldn't wonder if there wasn't a reporter or two in earshot, either. And the judiciary aren't stupid. Those judges talk to each other. Reach ears in rarefied places. We'd get slapped down if we made noises too soon. We just collate all the dribs and drabs and baby squibs and leave them in neatly labelled files. And once the faces on the Queen's Bench know there's monkey business going on they'll be ready for the next big case. They'll order us to protect the next jury. They'll order us to provide telephones in their homes, protect their children at school. And make damned certain their family doctors know the stress they're under. We'll lose this one, Buller. But not the next big one. Or the next or the next. You've got my word on that.'

'And Quill?'

'If Charlie wants Quill, he'll have him. He doesn't need our tacit consent. He's trying you out, that's all.'

'So I say what?'

Lemmon tapped a Player against a nail.

'You say "yes" without actually saying "yes".'

'A "yes" except it ain't?'

'That's the kind of thing.'

Bulstrode shrugged. 'I can try.'

'No, son. You can do it. Quill would make a pretty stringy Judas goat for Dance to chew on anyway. If Charlie means to give us the Troys on a plate, I won't say no. Anyway, I want to see how he plans to do it.'

'You must be more than just curious, Guv?'

'Why must I?'

'You must, that's all.'

Lemmon shook his head.

'Troy won't come down alone. I want to see some bent serge tumble out of Leman Street nick as well. I was ordered not to, but nobody ordered Charlie Dance to play the white man for them in Whitehall, did they?'

'That's a deep old game, Guv. Arthur Ax *and* the Troy firm? Wrapped up in the same pink ribbon? It's a neat trick, but it don't half make my bottle tweak.'

'Coffee?' Lemmon said comfortably.

The bitterly cold darkness had a sweet smell.

Children scuttled past his bed towards the suit draped over a chairback, and Freddy waited for the chink of pilfered small change.

I'll cure them where soft-headed Maria failed. Stealing from their father indeed. A few cracked bottoms would have them wailing Daddy had hard hands.

Maria would get that slow-eyed look and gather them to her big belly. All suffering and reproach.

Well, let her.

They were close enough now.

And Freddy swung . . . nothing.

His neck cracked with whiplash.

Rope sawed his throat and suspended his cold bare feet.

The darkness whirled black on black, and the puzzle he had to solve was lost in obsidian. Returning circulation reared him against a hard chairback, and the children scampered from his squall of terror with scratching nails and tiny squeaks.

If only he could touch the floor, he could grow back into a man. Stop being a helpless boy in a cat's-cradle of knotted hemp. The knots tightened when he struggled. Hurt his constricted bladder. Another humiliation.

Another childhood fear.

Freddy-wet-the-bed earning a whipping for nocturnal incontinence, peeling another layer of manhood away.

Poor Freddy wept for poor Freddy.

He caught the flick of a small yellow eye. Whiskers and a damp questing nose touched his foot. Distant artillery shook mortar from the unseen walls. The rats went away, and the cellar was lit by dim torchlight. Fragrant Virginia bloomed in his nose, and a series of clicks wound voices into the cellar. Sadler said something about drinks, and Tommy Troy said it was about bloody time he met Roger and Jesus Tonna.

Freddy heard Roger sit in a squeal of leather and click a lighter at a cigar.

'I'll shake hands when there's something to shake hands about. I've had the recent displeasure of having to shake Archie Ogle's hand. With two of my best torpedoes wasted right there on the rug. In the same goddamned room. Me and Jesus standing there with thumbs in our ears whilst that hoary old bastard held a goddamned Savage on us. Made us grovel and eat crow. And swear to Christ we had our wires crossed about Johnny Valletta. That we were just there to talk, not have him blown away. And Queenie knitting away and sneering at us the while. Sweating us like we were hustling toms in Charing Cross like the old days. Man, he *knew* about our drug contacts in the Philippines. The mother knew. So put your hand back on your pecker until me and Jesus hear some plain good news worth more than ten cents on the dollar.'

'Me and Roger ain't just birds-aturding, guys,' said Jesus. 'Just cut the smooth garbage and get to cases. All this goddamned "How's the family and the family cow" shoot. All we see is a gaggle of Limey nebishes ready to dip their beaks in our birdbath. And, guys, Archie Ogle ain't finished until he's *finished*. Like *finito*.'

Roger snapped fingers.

'Which of you guys has the brass balls to cut his legs out from under? And Dance. That guy has to go.'

Jesse Troy said something lost in babble, and Sadler emerged from hard asides with: 'Details later, gentlemen. You didn't fly three thousand miles with closed minds. Archie Ogle has bled you white for too many years. And quite rightly you resent the fact. Our terms would be infinitely more advantageous, and you both know it. The world has shrunk too far and too fast for any of you to sit in your own small —'

'Small?' Tommy snarled.

'— small territories, and think Jimmy-be-damned to my proposal of co-operating internationally. We can fly to New York more readily than drive to Aberdeen, Scotland. Gems stolen in Amsterdam can be fenced just as readily in Toronto or Karachi as they can in London. Bullion from Boston can reach here and be sold off in Pakistan before the American federal authorities have fed the details to Interpol. And hot money here is ice-cold in Johannesburg. We know that for a fact. We are negotiating such a transfer at present.'

'Train-robbery money, huh?' said Roger Tonna.

'The very same.'

'You think we didn't have the same deal with Ogle?'

Sadler cleared his throat.

'I note the use of past tense there, Mr Tonna.'

'That's still negotiable.'

'And didn't you pay upwards of seventy cents on the dollar?'

'Sure we did, smart-ass,' Jesus said. 'But once we tied in with you — *if* we tied in with you — the rate would climb right back up again. And we'd do the dead same thing to you guys. That's both of us between a rock and a hard place. Back to square-goddamned-one.'

'I have a solution. . . .'

The tape squabbled into high register as it was wound on to Roger saying: '. . . OK. But we get the whole skim from the London casinos. We know what they're grossing, pal. Freddy and Maurice have fed us the receipts for the last six months. You ain't the only one who don't leave diddly-squat to chance, big brain. But you guys get to handle Ogle's wooden overcoat. I'm sentimental about that hit. I've had my thumb up my arse once over that guy. Maybe if we'd come to you guys earlier. . . .'

Tommy's laugh was a hard bark.

'Maybe him and Charlie wouldn't have walked away from that café in Mafeking Street. You've listened to Manchester and that Maltese Maurice too long and too often, Tonna. You and Jesus both. Pimps are just pimps. And Freddy clawing up a face for you fifteen years ago don't cut the mustard this day and age. If his mouth was a shooter, Freddy could blow us all to shit and gone. But he ain't nothing but a tom-pedlar. You think we didn't figure it was him screwed up dropping bricks on the Ogle firm?'

Jesse butted in with: '*And* you fucked up letting Maurice send his baby coons after Pimlico Johnny Parsons. They met up with Charlie Dance instead. And *that* makes them history. One man ain't enough to drop that bastard. It's us who'll turn him into hung meat. Us. *After* we've turned Connie Harold into liver and lights.'

Roger spoke in a rush.

'You gotta clear the decks. Like now. That guy's begging for a concrete-kimono bye-bye. . . .'

'No deal otherwise,' Jesus added.

'Get Manchester Freddy, then,' Jesse hissed.

'We have to consolidate our South African dealings first. If we are to launder our money through Harold's mining cons. . . .'

Sadler's voice died in mid-sentence.

Freddy heard it keen into rewind. Winter wind in haunted eaves. A warm spurt of urine soaked his lap as he forced himself to look up into cold slate eyes.

'It wasn't that way at all, Charlie. . . .' The torch glared in Freddy's face. 'I had to do it for Maria . . . for the kids. . . . You don't know them, Charlie. . . . They'd have. . . .'

The stale air vibrated to the dull thump of a pile-driver, and the cellar shook with the rumble of earth-movers. Mortar dribbled in cavity walls and dust drifted from the rafters.

The damp patch between Freddy's thighs spread and chilled.

He knew with dread certainty where he was.

'You ain't brought me to Mafeking Street, Chas? You can't. Not leave poor old Freddy here to be . . . buried?'

Charlie let Freddy babble.

'Blame them, Charlie. Not little Freddy . . . not me . . . not meeeeeeeeeeeeeeeee. . . .'

A wall thundered apart, overhead timbers began to grind, and Freddy used all his breath in a long ululating scream.

When the torch clicked off, terror shattered his sanity like a dropped dish.

After a time the machines went quiet and the rats came back. By then Freddy was a catatonic with nothing behind his eyes but empty shadows, beyond recall when Charlie threw him into a black panel truck and drove east.

Feeling cheated.

CHAPTER EIGHTEEN

THREE MONTHS into his thirty-year sentence, Brixton Billy sewed ten stitches to the regulation inch in hemp and watched the fat screw the inmates called Kaiser Bill reach out his watch to tick off the final seconds of the work-period in the mailbag room.

Kaiser Bill counted silently as he habitually did, sitting in the oak chair on the dais like an overripe serge pear, walrus moustache moving with his lips. Kaiser Bill had greeted Brixton each afternoon for sixty-two days with: 'Try nicking these mailbags, son. See where it gets you,' adding a look of amused surprise as though taken unawares by his own ready wit.

Kaiser Bill ignored the accurate wall-clock above his head even though it kept scrupulous time. His father's watch was his pride and joy, and Brixton's offer of a full ounce of prison shag to the man who dipped it was unclaimed as yet. Another week and Brixton would double the prize. Anything to see the fat screw change his boring mannerisms.

Ninety days from thirty years left ten thousand and fifty days to serve. One thousand and forty-seven of those being Sundays. All those compulsory church services where news from the outside world was exchanged to the sound of hymns.

And 4 oz. of breakfast porridge a day meant Brixton would eat 115 lb. 4 oz. of oats a year, a staggering 3,457 lb. 8 oz. before he saw the outside world again. In excess of sixteen times his own body-weight.

Brixton amused himself with such numerical games to pass the time, despite warnings from older cons who knew such useless exercises led to mental disorder in a very short time.

Their sage advice was to do your bird one day at a time. Go in for running gags rather than dreams of release. Brixton ignored them. Thought of nothing else. Thought of exactly that as he watched Kaiser Bill mouth the last second and start to stand.

Brixton drove the big sewing-needle into his left palm with his leather pad. Spattered his work with sudden blood. Broke the Silence Rule with a yell of pain. Tucked the paper-twist of waterproofing grease into his cuff next to the twist of granulated sugar he had lifted from the canteen.

Twenty minutes later, his prizes tucked inside a fresh bandage, he was marched back to his high-security cell in C wing, Winsom Green Prison. Subjected to a complete body-search, stripped and sent into his cell wearing nothing but a vest, Brixton lay on his bunk and counted off the fifteen minutes to the next visual check on him. His eyes lidded, he saw the screw's eye in the observation port before it winked and went away. Brixton gave the screw enough time to get back to his chair at the end of the corridor, then blew the sugar under the cell door into the passage beyond. His early-warning system against surprise changes in schedule. He would hear the screws' boots crunch when they came to his door.

He spent the next several minutes smearing the ceiling light with the waterproofing grease. Dimming the light a little more with each application. The light stayed on twenty-four hours a day, and the cell had previously held Gordon Lonsdale, convicted of spying for the Russians.

A fervent patriot, Brixton was disgusted to be treated the same as a bloody traitor to his country, and saw no irony in his deep outrage. Nicking a few million banknotes destined for the official incinerator in no way compared with some sod jeopardising national security in Brixton's book, and made him sulky in rare depressed moments.

That and not seeing Smiler Tree, even though he was only four cells down on the opposite side of the corridor.

Smiler had had the horrors a couple of times during the early days, but there had been no sound out of him for weeks, and Brixton was not even certain he was still there. Though somebody was. He heard the cell open and close at regular times, and he was sure the screws would not go to such lengths just for his benefit.

Brixton logged the passing hours by the crunch of sugar every quarter-hour. Thought of escape to fill the time until nightfall. He had long ago realised that mid-week would be the best time. Security was almost doubled at weekends, and the screws were younger and tougher. And less friendly. Getting out of C wing itself was the biggest problem, and he had yet to solve it. Unless he had a shooter smuggled in. Shot his way out like Tom Mix. Something Brixton discounted out of hand.

He wanted *them* to find his locked cell empty and him long gone without a clue as to how he achieved the miracle. Until he wrote his memoirs from some distant sunny land where he could spend his whack in secure luxury. One of the reasons Connie Harold's straight firms in South Africa sounded so tempting. Put his whack into Connie's firms and skim profit without moving from his deckchair under some fig-tree. If that kind of a deal had come through Archie or Charlie, Brixton would have jumped at it. But it was Connie Harold, and Brixton knew as much about sunny South Africa as he did about the dark side of the moon. Maybe less.

Brixton dozed.

Going abroad had a temporary feel to it. He'd have to come home someday when the fuss had died down. There were always finger-tamed coppers in the Flying Squad willing to turn a blind eye for a big enough 'drink'. Just Brixton's luck to have his collar felt by bloody Theodore 'Mr Clean' Lemmon, and get handed straight over to DCS Cotton without the chance to offer a drink down the line to one of his more reasonable pirates.

Brixton sleepily broke the days down into minutes and seconds when a key grated in the lock.

Another bloody surprise search.

Except they ain't a bloody surprise to anyone.

Brixton rolled off his bunk and broke wind noisily — the only antisocial protest he could come up with on the spur of the moment — and stared into masked faces and a levelled gun.

'You're coming out.'

The strange voice was muffled by a woollen ski-mask.

Brixton's foul reply earned him a knee to the centre of equilibrium.

After that he had no breath to argue.

Wally saw Naomi Leathers walk in and forgot about drinking himself stupid.

The WELCOME HOME WALLY banner stretched the length of the prestige office suite overlooking Berkeley Square and billowed in hot convected air. Wally raised his glass to it and thought that the party was more of a puff for Connie's moving west into lahdie-land than a coming-out party for himself. Where, he wondered, were the reliable old faces from the old days? The Pims and Dottys? Wally didn't know half the faces surrounding him and didn't want to.

An alcoholic peer of the realm who 'guinea-pigged' for the new companies had his photograph taken with Connie and a cockney actress with a smile as wide as her famous bosom. Motor traders and long-firm smoothies mixed with local councillors angling for funds for the coming general election. Three CID faces from the City of London chatted with a supermarket magnate and a sprinkling of minor celebrities from the British film industry.

A Welsh actor in a beautifully engineered toupee who played screen heavies and revelled in rubbing shoulders with the real thing had already invited Connie and Wally on to a location shoot later in the year. The screenplay was about an air-crash survivor who becomes the leader of a pack of ferocious baboons, and sounded about as believable as a nun becoming mother of the year.

Wally had said it sounded 'ace', winked into Kelly's cleavage to cheer her up, and found himself in a corner with Harry the Crack, who was owlish with drink.

'Sorry you was the one to get your collar felt, Wal. Had our diffs, you and me, but 'sall inna past now, innit?'

Wally nodded, thought *Berk*, and watched Naomi. She and Margot Sadler stood apart with Dirk and Alicia Jorgesson. Hard put to understand much of the vulgar South London chirpiness surrounding them. Alicia was a fragile elfin beside Dirk's bulk, and Margot's slim severity enhanced Naomi's dress of white scalloped silk.

'Can't wait to get back to J'burg, Wal mate. Had this town up to my collar-stud. Get some sun on my poor old bod. Still got shotgun pellets coming out here and there. Bloody lucky dip some mornings.'

'That right?' Wally continued to watch Naomi. Saw her flush when she caught his eye. Grinned into his drink.

'Con squared the law so I could get here tonight. Says Tall John's well asleep now you've earned a "Not Guilty". I got well choked being cooped up in that safe gaff in Tooting. Not going out for a pint or a paper. Watching the wallpaper peel and all that kids' television. If I see another Andy-bloody-Pandy, I'll go doo-bloody-lally-tap.'

'My heart bleeds, Harry.'

'I know you had it worse, Wal. Don't think I don't. I just can't stand being banged up inside. That's why South Africa suits so well. All that bloody outside they got over there. Miles you can stretch your eyes on. Handsome.'

'When you going back out?' Wally asked, for something to say. Connie had edged close to Alicia. Had his arm round Dirk's shoulder.

Harry grabbed another pink champagne.

'Lahdie Tizer, this stuff. How'd they make it pink?'

'Fermented jelly beans, how do I know?'

'Yeah?' Harry got his drink and cigar tangled. His heavy eyebrows knitted in concentration. 'Going to get well pissed. You deserve that much, Wal. Not enough of the old mates here to lay on a good drunk for you. Here's to you, Mister. And to us getting our feet well under the table out there in wogland. Con says I can go flying off out there inna couple . . . days. Juss wish he dinn spenn s'much poppy on that Dirk an' his missus. Need every penny onna firm, y'know?'

'I reckon.'

Harry winked and breathed into Wally's face.

'That De Wit's the one to square. Heesa one with alla clout . . . see if I ain't right. Nuff said . . . word to the wise, eh, Mister?'

'Yeah.' Wally turned his face away from Harry's anti-social breath, saw Naomi's eyes dance when Connie said something that amused her.

'Ain't seena lass of that Sadler, neither. Not by . . . long old chalk. He was too well cosied to De Wit. Seef I ain't right, Mister. See if I ain't. . . .'

'You're right, Harry.'

Wally patted the owlish face and went over towards Naomi.

Harry sagged against a pillar and talked to his knuckles.

Margot swizzled her champagne with a pink stick and didn't nudge Naomi when she spotted Wally, and when Connie had said, 'My baby brother's my right hand,' Margot gave Naomi a drowsy look and said: 'I see the attraction, darling. We all congratulate you madly, Mr Harold. Your friend over there discussing philosophy with his hands is taking your return very seriously, is he not?'

'Traditional,' Wally said. 'Funny you being here now Con and your old man are divorced.'

'But that's only business, darling. And poor bastard Malcolm would have been here but for his recent accident. The poor old chap's been in bed for weeks with a nasty wrench of some sort. And I'm being comforted with a night out by my adorable friends here. Aren't I, darlings?'

Naomi moistened her mouth with champagne. Unable to meet Wally's direct gaze.

'Dirk insisted we come to be impressed with Conrad's new and glossy premises. Which we duly are. You look well, Walter.'

Wally felt himself warm and rise.

'You look as if you could go the distance yourself.'

Margot's laugh was a spray of tinkling barbs.

'You make Naomi sound like a bloodstock mare.'

'Happen she is,' said Wally. 'She could win my two thousand guineas any time.'

Margot arched an eyebrow.

'Such gallantry. And time to melt away. Come along, my dears. Time you introduced me to some of these theatricals. A little limelight and greasepaint might aid the digestion.'

She dragged Connie and the Jorgessons away to gossip with the Welsh toupee and the cockney bosom.

Wally watched Margot take control of the conversation. Saw Connie's arm circle Alicia's waist on Dirk's blind side.

'When did she last jump out of a cake? Mafeking Night, 1899?'

'Margot is highly intelligent. And, like most men, you fear a clever woman.'

'I ain't scared of you.'

'Means you think I'm stupid.'

'Means nothing of the sort. But if I was Connie I'd be running well away from that daughter of yours. He must be feeling a lot safer here than he does on your patch.'

'Much like yourself.'

Naomi's up-and-under look simmered.

Wally forced a smile, his eyebrows hard down.

'Could be you're right. Never said anything diff, did I? With Alicia in the middle, Kelly on one side and your Colonel on the other, poor old Con don't stand a chance. It'll burn itself out.'

Naomi chafed a wrist.

'They're still using me as fuel for their tacky emotional bonfire. And I was stupid enough to look forward to seeing you. I must be insane.'

'And here's me thinking the same thing. Funny that.'

'Singularly unfunny.'

Wally's frown darkened and deepened.

'I've just had ninety days of briefs, cells, screws, heavy law and heavier Latin. I could lose myself in a lot of friendly bottles like daft Harry over there, or phone a couple or three dozen tarts who'd come running to keep me company. One thing I won't do, and that's top the evening out with a woman with a serious case of the snits who can't keep her nose out of her daughter's laundry, right?'

'Are you telling me off, Walter?'

Wally pointed at a blank wall.

'No. Her over there with a banjo riding that camel in a bowl of custard. Of course I'm telling you off.'

'At which point I melt or stalk away.'

'I guess so. I know what I bloody want.'

'You'll have to say it, Walter.'

Wally lit a cigarette and held it away from Naomi's face.

'Wally,' he said. 'It's Wally who wants you to stay with him. Not this sodding Walter.'

'Very well. Wally it is. But don't dare shorten my name. One of those actresses actually called me "Gnomey".'

Wally grinned.

'Yeah, they would.'

'Your Harry just slid down the wall.'

'Ain't no law against it.'

'Shouldn't somebody prop him somewhere before he swallows his tongue or something?'

'Nope. Harry's dim. If he was a lightbulb, we'd all live in the dark. But he'll kip for an hour. Wake up as right as ninepence. Don't fret your head about Harry the Crack, or Connie, or Dirk, or Alicia, or. . . .'

'Point taken. And Naomi for Wally. Shake?'

'Little fingers,' said Wally.

'Now you can buy me a drink, sneak me away and be very, very animal with me.'

'I can only try, love.'

'But very, very hard.'

'They won't shoot this horse for not trying, love.'

They hooked pinkies and went looking for the right bottle.

Brixton's wrists and bandaged hand throbbed from the handcuffs. Smiler went past the opened cell door, his face as white and tight as his naked buttocks. The screw at the end of the passage was all the way down in his chair with a dark sapmark on his jaw.

Brixton stumbled at the stairhead. The tape over his mouth made breathing a positive act of will, thinking impossible.

The stairs went down for ever, and Brixton's snorting breath was the only sound in the silent cellblock. All the security doors were unmanned and hard open. The surveillance cameras slept with unlit 'ON' lights.

Then Brixton was outside. Chilled by night breeze and padding across tarmac.

A fat moon rode through mackerel cloud and etched the central prison yard with hard shadow. Brixton and Smiler were herded into the dark lee of high walls, ready to flee from sirens and the heavy tread of the regular patrol. The sudden sear of arcs turning night into day. Harsh commands to halt and lie spreadeagled on the floor.

Nothing happened, and they were safely inside A wing.

No torchlight. No shouts. Nothing.

The soft fall of a rope ladder came next, and Brixton swarmed up it with a hard hand pushing his buttocks. Another in the small of his back. Then the hard heave to flip him over the pitched capping stones. The cold slap of Edwardian slate against the inside of his thigh, shrinking his manhood like the unwanted sexual advances of a stone woman.

Brixton went down the other side of the high wall. Dropped into shadowed clutter. Sweated and shivered and skirted stands of old timber in a builder's yard. Frightened he might step in broken glass. Feeling vulnerable and foolish in his vest.

Was reminded of childhood dreams of flying where the

exhilaration of the high swoops across dark skies was spoiled by his partial nakedness and the rudely staring people below who ran to tell his mother about the third member he had grown in flight. And waking in his safe and overheated bed, face and penis blushing beneath the bedclothes. Exploring the mad stiffness of his tiny precocious member. The great fear of angry grownups censuring his fledgling sexual fantasies of soft roundnesses hiding warm and wet caves he could enter if he had the courage. Guilt and awe snuggling him in a foetal curl around the hard little monster between his thighs. Paring away another layer of precious childhood each time it happened.

There was a winding alley of smooth cobbles and then the grass and gravel of a canal towpath. The masked men hurried Brixton and Smiler past narrowboats into trees where two cars were parked without lights.

Smiler was bundled into the back of a Cortina, and Brixton was shoved aside when he tried to climb in beside him. The one with a gun ducked Brixton into a Jaguar and ground the bore into his ribs when he craned to see Smiler's look of mute fear before the Cortina swept him away. A second man took the Jaguar's wheel to drive with fast skill down too many back turnings without his heads on.

'Dress.'

Brixton jammed his feet into shoes and struggled into slacks. He was still buttoning himself into a shirt when the car stopped in a darkened road and he was bundled up a side-path into a terraced house. Guided into a curtained room he was sat in an armchair. He felt the thick pattern of moquette under his fingers and took comfort from stroking it.

A telephone was used for several short calls with long codes before it was put down with a light ping.

Then three men came into the room and switched the light on. The one with the gun tore the tape from Brixton's mouth and unlocked the cuffs. Dropped them in Brixton's lap.

'Souvenir,' he said. 'Cigarette?'

Brixton threw the cuffs from him. Touched his raw mouth.

'Depends who's asking.'

'You wanted out. You're out.'

'There's out and bloody out, ain't there? Could be I was better off where I was. Nobody was digging a shooter at me in C wing.'

'There's gratitude.' The voice was softly Irish.

The mask was peeled off and Dublin Gerry mocked Brixton with shamrock eyes. Tossed the revolver to the man behind Brixton's chair.

'You'd try the patience of all the saints, Billy boy.'

Froggy Farrell ruffled Brixton's hair.

'Out's out, Brix.'

Brixton jerked a thumb over his shoulder.

'Cocker there still has a shooter up my jaxie.'

Pimlico came around the armchair to plump the revolver in Brixton's lap, grinning at his jump of surprise.

'There's cockers and little boys, according to you. I hope this makes up for a couple of things.'

Brixton rubbed his sagging jaw.

'Could be, but why'd you bastards split me and Smiler up?'

Dublin Gerry played with a pack of Gallagher's Blue.

'Bonar's made special arrangements for Smiler. But you're a fish of a different colour. The way we figure it, Tommy lets you launder your whack through South Africa before you get lost in the shuffle.'

'That shuffle has a wet sound to it. Like I get to give the fish dancing lessons in concrete boots. Once I give up my whack, that's me down the Thomas Crapper with a long flush, right?'

Pimlico lit one of Gerry's cigarettes for Brixton with a Swan Vesta.

'That's why we pulled you out our way. You get to go missing, Brix, but not like Tommy Troy planned. Once we get you away from here, only I'll know where you are, apart from Charlie.'

Brixton looked at Gerry, Froggy and Pimlico in turn.

'I don't get it. Charlie, Tommy and Connie are all in on this? Since when was they handshaking?'

'They ain't,' Pimlico said. 'Tommy and Connie are playing at truces, but Charlie won't give them the time of day. And he ain't about to let you get lost permanent, neither. If he sees your whack safe to South Africa along with Bonar's contribution, Connie won't grumble, and Tommy can't. We just keep you on ice until the dough's delivered and we see how long it takes for Camberwell and Bethnal Green to start knocking heads again. You think I'd be here if I didn't figure I owed a favour to a face who opened my eyes to a couple of things?'

'And your whack, Pim?'

'Goes with yours when Charlie says, not before.'

Brixton nodded wearily.

'Let's just hope we're all trusting the right face.'

He was suddenly weary as the adrenalin drained away. The seedy room was just another cell, and the three men were just gaolers without uniforms. He saw a progression of such rooms, strobing past like windows in the longest train in the world. Rolling into a bleak future with him as the only passenger. And the past was another train on a parallel track. A weary shuffle of pasteboard dreams, all glitter and no substance. Yesterday's fragments that had tasted of success until reality left ashes on his imprisoned tongue. And now nobody would steal Kaiser Bill's watch.

Brixton opened his eyes and said: 'Which of you brave soldiers gets to tell Tommy Troy that Brixton Billy ain't for drowning?'

Dublin Gerry bowed from the waist.

'My pleasure.'

'Better make it a phone call. Or face him and his tarts on neutral turf. You head his shit-list, Gerry. Don't cut off your legs to spite that face.'

'Don't worry your head, Brix. Sure and wouldn't Bonar and Charlie make him eat coals in Hades if any of us earned a hard glance from the man?'

Brixton was too weary to argue. He shoved his hand out at Pimlico.

'Any chance of a cup o' tea? It's worth a handshake.'

'Thanks, Brix.'

Pimlico and Brixton cracked knuckles as Froggy put the kettle on.

The telephone said, 'They're out,' and went dead.

Killed a heartbeat.

Connie closed his eyes and spread his hands on the teak reception-desk. The party lost colour and sound and his limbs turned watery.

They're out thudded in his chest.

Brixton Billy had £200,000 salted, and even with a swingeing whack of ten per cent for the break itself the balance gave him the capital to bring the Nikex plant from Hungary to the Mkusi site.

They're out pearled his nose with moisture.

And Bonar Tree's escudos would grease the way to owning the Ghost Mountain site he and Dirk had been negotiating with a prospector from Pretoria.

They're out meant Pimlico's £100,000 would sweeten South African Customs and the Minister of Mines, consolidate his holdings here in London, cover Vic Dakin's thievery.

Connie's hands left perfect misty handprints on the gleaming teak, and he had the crazy notion he should preserve them in some fashion. Wanted to mark that single moment in time indelibly. Wanted to celebrate in a darkened room with Alicia and could not. Should tell Kelly and did not want to.

Everything is safe again. Nothing can stop me now.

All the same. . . .

Connie crossed his fingers when he gave Wally the news.

They're out.

Ingrid craned to see herself in the mirror above the big golden bed. A stranger with silver hair in a flame kimono.

Dotty played with the strobelights, and the Tonna brothers lounged in the lounge ignoring the women. Roger put down the telephone and chinked his glass against Jesus' with: 'They're out.'

Jesus pulled his grey moustache and watched the girl in the silver wig flicker in strobelights.

'So OK,' he said. 'Sadler figures this train-robbery scratch'll oil this South African mining deal before we walk in and take over. It's all too long-term for me, kiddo. I think we should grab and run. Get back on our own turf before all this local head-to-head bloodies up the cobbles.'

'Relax.' Roger rang down for more champagne.

'I've got that old feeling.'

'You feel shafted if your aftershave fails. We're sitting pretty. We've got chapter and verse on this guy Harold's operation, and the Troys are soldiering the sidewalks. We're in gravy, brother.'

'Not with Archie Ogle still upright we ain't. Our tails are still up for grabs. Don't ask me to swallow what smells bad, Roger. Hung meat ain't always venison.'

Roger was dismissive.

'Shadows at midnight. Only people playing grab-arse with us are those two broads Maurice sent over. The bugles would have blown long ago if Archie figured we weren't finger-tame. We're in his hotel and he's picking up the tab. The place is crawling with Troy's torpedoes. Even got his guys working the kitchens. Gold in Fort Knox, that's us.'

Jesus disagreed with a grunt.

'I don't take Sadler at face value, either. He's ducked us this trip and that "accident" of his vibes wrong. He gets hit once we've got solid control here. He was too clever by far, going after Archie's ankles through the betting shops.'

'That was when he knew no better. Hell, he's a corporation man. He'll learn street sense.'

Jesus rolled the empty Krug bottle in the ice-bucket.

'Like you've forgotten yours, Roger? You even look

like a goddamned banker nowadays. And this ain't the Savoy, right? First thing I do when we take over is get room service jumping.'

'You do that,' Roger laughed.

'And where the hell is Manchester Freddy? Troy was supposed to turn him up.'

'The hell with Freddy. He takes off when Maria's apron strings cut across his drinkbone. He's off on a drunk with a stray piece of tail. He'll turn up with the shakes and a cart-load of presents for his kids. You'll see.'

'You can't party with empty glasses, Mr Tonna.'

Dotty twirled an empty glass beside Roger's face.

Roger patted her cheek as somebody tapped on the door.

'No more you can, honey. Let the man with the bubbles in.'

He watched her sway across the carpet, her dress as yellow as her hair.

'Nice tush.'

'She's a bought-and-paid-for barracuda,' Jesus grunted.

Dotty wheeled a trolley across and handed Roger a chit.

'You have to sign this, Mr Tonna.'

'Christ, she can't even sign her own name,' Jesus sneered.

Roger scrawled his signature.

'You want a chess master from Mensa?'

Dotty dimpled. Eased the cork with a light pop and a wisp of mist.

'We don't have any of them on the books.'

'Other talents, huh?'

'Only the best for you gentlemen. Maurice's orders.'

Dotty poured wine and whispered an obscene promise in Roger's ear, flushing his lobes.

'The toast is pleasure.'

Roger and Jesus drank and their glasses were topped.

'You girls ain't taking the sauce,' Jesus said.

Ingrid drifted from the bedroom to tease his shaved neck. 'Your pleasure first. We'll have our bubbles . . . after.'

'After what?' Jesus leered, feeling the wine.

'Just . . . after.'

'You gents aren't talkers, are you?' asked Dotty.

Roger grinned and drained another glass of Krug.

'One demonstration coming up. For the honour of Toronto.'

He stood and weaved beside Dotty, more fuddled than he thought.

'Lean on me, baby,' Dotty cooed.

'Sure thing, sweet pea.'

Ingrid offered her hand to Jesus, and he blinked at the brilliant carmine nails. The couch was suddenly deeper and softer, and there was something he should worry about off in one of the shimmering corners of his mind.

Ingrid's oval face was a pretty blank and her bright red mouth was a jiggling red fish. Silver hair shone with alien brightness. All the pieces were there but somehow exploded into separate jewels of detail. Her dark eyes were twin moons hovering in the vibrant air and deep enough to drown in.

In the bedroom the eyes leaped with the crackling pulses of light, and he sprawled on to the golden lake of metallic comfort beside somebody who might have been Roger. A Roger who laughed when his robe was stripped away. Laughed at his own sleek limbs and grizzled chest.

Jesus saw his own body jump with electric blue light. Both motionless and in motion. His naked feet were as huge as picket fences and too high to see over. He washed clammy palms and the fingers entwined without his help. The wrongness of it all was hilarious and melancholy, and he wished Roger would stop laughing into his own navel.

Then the lights smoothed into long gentle strobes and dimmed to a cool dusk that no longer swooped him into a thousand dark corners. The circular bed was no longer a spinning carousel and the girls stood quietly, out of reach. Attractive flames of primary colour with all their softness gone, watching the man with slate eyes cross the lounge with silent grace.

Jesus screamed without sound and knew true fear for the first time in his adult life. Leaned on an elbow that slid away from him. Leaving him supine and helpless in a fogged drift of lysergic acid.

Jesus pawed his brother, and both men tried to swim away from the bed. Roger still laughed at things only he could see, but the weird chuckles were nothing at all to do with humour.

Charlie Dance drew up a golden chair and laid a long-barrelled Savage across his knees.

'Is this how it was when Archie waited for you bastards?'

Roger said something that never got started.

Jesus burned to tell his brother not to grovel. His head would not stop nodding over waterfalls of anxiety, and his tongue flapped behind clenched teeth. If he opened his mouth, it would scuttle off into a corner to hunt edible vowels. He fell against Roger and they held each other for comfort. Charlie's words glass-clothed their eardrums, and brain cells jumbled thought like balls in a bingo fountain.

'Archie couldn't talk, could he? Queenie had to find the words for him.'

Roger made sounds. The Savage had been used in Malta. Now it pointed its bore at him. A dark Cyclops staring into his very soul.

Ingrid ripped off the silver wig.

'Hurt them, Charlie. Hurt them the way they hurt me.'

'Your animals killed our child. Kicked it to death. They're long dead. But you're still alive. My lady don't like that.'

Jesus mewed into his naked lap. All the words he needed writhed like the hair on his thighs. He got a leg to the floor and cracked his nose against Roger's chin.

'Goodbye, Jesus.'

The room roared and flame came at him from a roll of smoke. He fell away as the gun jumped a second time. Felt nothing but nausea and mad dread.

'Goodbye, Roger.'

Roger saw the gun swing towards him. Tried to push himself away along the bed with legs of unco-ordinated string. Wanted to squeeze his eyes closed against the flash and whack of the concussion. Dared not miss the spit of fire and the hard double bark of powder stink. It was all he had. All there was left.

The Troys should come. Anybody. His mind embraced invented pain and he fell back into a last death throe that did not come. Charlie was still there and he saw himself in the mirrored ceiling. Naked and wretched.

And alive.

Charlie's voice boomed like the Wrath of God.

'She's seen you as you are. Stinking with fear. All your manhood gone. The memory of that will be enough to mend the hurt for her. But you'll never forget this moment, will you? You'll take it to the grave.'

Roger lay with Jesus, both of them leaking sweat and champagne and urine.

Dotty drew Ingrid away and they left the hotel suite without a backward glance.

Alive, thought Roger. *Alive with abiding humiliation.*

The same fearful thought glazed Jesus' eyes.

Why don't they come? Follow the shots and drag Charlie's carcass away?

Charlie seemed to read his mind.

'The hotel's closed for redecoration. You animals and one other are the only guests. I'll bring him. He'll be company for you.'

Who will, who will?

Roger and Jesus wanted a miracle when Charlie left them alone. Flailed on to the floor in a tangle of rubbery limbs. Roger butted the control panel, and lights revolved as he tried to crawl over Jesus and away from the bed.

Jesus sneezed into the carpet. Unable to scratch a nose wider than his face. There were vicious pins and needles in his fingers and toes, and every hair on his body was a barb in his flesh.

Forming consecutive thoughts was beyond both men. Their minds were blank scratch-pads that would only accept outside stimulus. And Charlie Dance was written large in indelible neon.

Moving further was beyond them.

And Charlie was back in the room, playing them the tape of their meeting with Sadler and the Troys. Damning them with their own words.

Jesus was flopped on to his back with his head propped against the bed. Roger was rolled in beside him, smelling of funk and defecation, and they found themselves staring at a slight figure in crumpled herring-bone. His thin face all hollows and his mouth a drooling pout. The eyes were just empty smudges of nothing.

They screamed silently as Charlie sat Manchester Freddy in the gold chair with his feet touching their naked soles.

'In a couple of hours you'll be able to walk. To start running. Don't be here when I come back. Nor anywhere I can find you.'

And for ninety-seven minutes Roger and Jesus watched Freddy sit very still and do nothing with an idiot's face.

Naomi came out of her white dress in a long tanned surge and moaned into Wally's neck on the reclining seats of Sadler's Daimler as they coupled with urgent need and little finesse, crashing to an abrupt orgasm.

'Too soon, too soon. . . .' Naomi beat a fist against Wally's chest.

'Can't argue with that, love.' Wally fought tender feeling. 'Short and very sweet.'

'Ninety days ends up as ninety seconds. Bloody pathetic.'

Naomi's bosom rolled in dim street-light, nipples still crested.

'And now you'll want to smoke and take me straight home.'

Wally tucked his cigarettes away.

'Stop telling me what I'll do next, woman.'

'Well, you will.'

'Maybe I've grown out of dirty dark doorways and rumpo in the backs of cars. Even with a class bird.'

'Am I a class bird?'

'There and back again.'

'That's nice,' Naomi purred, almost mollified.
'What are we arguing about, then?'
'Us? Nothing.'
'How come . . . ah, forget it.'
'You're smoking. Don't even know you're doing it.'
'It's me nerves.'
'You don't have any. Nerve, yes.'
'Thanks a bunch.'
'Was it awful? In prison?'
'Holiday camp with bars. Boredom and bars, 'sall.'
'Margot tried to find out where you were and what was happening to you. Through one of her police friends. You know, I don't even mind your cigarette smoke any more.'
Wally kept strain from his voice.
'What Tall John does she elbow with?'
'Tall what?'
'The law. Cop. Who does she know?'
'Everybody knows a policeman, my dear. God, your chest's gone as hard as a floor. Does it matter that I was curious to know how you were?'
'Does it matter?' Wally rolled his eyes in smoke. 'Who she rabbited to does. D'you know?'
'A chap named Lemmon. I only saw him the once at one of Margot's Christmas parties last year.'
'Never again?'
'Never.'
'Maybe it's all right. Maybe. . . .'
'When are you coming back to Jo'burg?'
'Putting on your little-girl voice don't rate eggs, Lady. Nor the fact I got a lot of business to catch up on. Three months off the cobbles is for ever in my game. I'll try, that's all I can say.'
'And they don't shoot horses for trying?'
'Yeah. You could stay on here. Get an apartment and keep a light burning for me. When I can get away.'
'Better be every night if I did.'
'Then, you will?'
'It would end in tears and you know it. Besides, I do

have commitments back home.'

'Bridge and bloody tennis parties? Leave it out.'

'I'm no social butterfly, you oaf. I have business interests I've too long neglected. Money needs to be tended like any crop. I am independent and wealthy, and this climate is absolutely filthy.'

Naomi shivered and snuggled closer.

Wally grinned and killed his cigarette-butt.

'There're ways of keeping a woman warm.'

'Not when it's over in a trice.'

'Over like what?'

'Like this.' Naomi's hand fell to find Wally erect. 'Where did that come from?'

'Probably a hitch-hiker. Shall I throw him out?'

'Throw yourself out. Leave him here.'

'And what do I do while you're busy with him?'

'You'll think of something.'

Wally reared as Naomi's mouth found him.

Closed his eyes and soared on surges from her clever tongue. Worried about Lemmon in Sadler's house and how much Sadler could have leaked to the filth about Connie's business. Knew he'd have to talk to Charlie if Connie wouldn't listen. Knowing Connie wouldn't listen. Knowing Kelly was unapproachable.

What a bloody tangle.

Wally raised Naomi's face and lifted her into his lap.

Why the hell don't I swan off and live off this amazing bird's dough in wogland? Forget all this pull-and-push. Fuck the fog and shooters and claret on the cobbles. . . .

Thought, *why not, why not, why not* as she came down on him with long and liquid thrusts of need.

Why sodding not?

Roger knew enough to pay off the cab three blocks from their destination. His eyes streamed as he rolled them at street-signs in darkest suburbia.

Jesus and Freddy had muddied themselves falling on a grass verge, and Jesus swore at invisible insects infesting his clothes. Freddy drooled and went where he was pushed, and Roger bit on the laughter that hurt his chest and mind. His mouth was bloody by the time he spotted the familiar monkey-puzzle trees and Father Time leaning on his scythe above Sadler's roof.

Jesus reached the gate first, stumbled up the flagged drive slapping his jacket, his brown scalp slick with sweat. Roger got Freddy round a gatepost and ducked him under a rake of sharp puzzle-leaves. Saw Jesus wore odd socks when he stretched for the bell-pull. Heard the dark across the street call his name.

Roger's mind screamed as he ducked and turned.

Saw a man in a navy topcoat point at him with slow deliberation. Saw slate eyes stare along a levelled revolver as light slicked the barrel and air whacked past his face. Saw Freddy jerk and weep at the crack of gunfire.

Roger heard Jesus grunt as he threw himself against the carved front door with half his skull gone and gobbets of flesh and grey ooze spattering the varnished wood. A second report pinned a red rosette between his shoulder-blades and arched his spine.

Freddy wept, hating the hard barks of sound.

Roger moved through glue. Started to pull Freddy down as he called to Charlie to stop and think. To talk. Heard his baritone squeal without authority. Saw the shine on Charlie's shoes as he shifted his stance. Saw a knuckle whiten as the bucking gun threw flame. A thermal fist set his chest alight and monumental pain threw him upright to embrace another bullet.

Roger folded over himself as a foggy cloak formed over his eyes. Jesus toppled from the steps and was a big loose doll with an unrecognisable face who dropped Roger on to cold flags beside a maroon car smelling of new rubber and bodywax.

Roger lay still. Too weary to feel anything but regret for all the fine things he would no longer enjoy.

He thought of breasts and flowers and fierce Tuscany wines. Of racing sulkies. Very long legs and lingerie. Of his grandson and saffron butterflies in a field of white daisies.

Charlie was gone in the darkness, and Freddy held the long-barrelled Savage, making Roger smile about cleverness.

Charlie *would* think of everything.

A family feud with two dead and no witnesses save an imbecile driven out of his mind by the man who actually pulled the trigger. With us gone, Toronto will revert to Archie. The drug circuit will fall into his lap, too.

Neat, Charlie. Very, very cleverrrrrrr. . . .

Roger died and his smile stayed behind.

Flecked by Jesus' blood.

Zipped back into her dress, Naomi repaired her make-up as Wally drove through the outskirts of Esher.

'I'll give you one small drink at Margot's whilst I call you a taxi.'

'Coo, thanks, Lady. Me inside that posh house without leg-irons and handcuffs. What a treat. Can I stand on the carpet and sit in a chair?'

'Why must our every meeting turn into a cockfight?'

'I thought class birds never talked shabby.'

'Depends on the company one keeps.' Naomi was still smiling when Wally coasted to a halt with deadened heads fifty yards from Sadler's house.

'Not a third time, you goat of a man?'

Wally peered through the windscreen.

'Shut it, love. Just a feeling. There's somebody out there. Ain't that Jesus and—?'

Rapid gunfire made Wally and Naomi flinch.

Wally held Naomi's head below the dash. Saw Jesus slam his face into the front door with his skull losing shape. Saw Roger snap upright and genuflect when two bullets smashed his chest. Skate on to his side as Jesus fell across him.

Then Manchester Freddy strolled aimlessly towards the car, his thin face mindless and a gun hanging from his hand. A navy coat showed in the shadows down the block and was gone into the greater darkness.

Wally swerved away from Freddy as he tried to lie along the bonnet. Left him collapsed in the kerb as he power-turned in tyre-scream, deaf to Naomi's questions. Cutting stoplights until he was deep into the friendly gloom of Wandsworth where he parked far away from his flat, wondering who the fourth man could have been.

Must have been.

Every national but the *Financial Times* made banner headlines of the double escape from Winsom Green Prison and carried bold-type theories about a shadowy mastermind beside old quarter-tones of Brixton and Smiler.

The death of two Canadian businessmen made the Stop Press of the London papers printed in Manchester, and missed the later editions because of a dispute between managements and the print unions.

The sanity hearing of Manchester Freddy Carpenter was reported a week later, almost as an oddity. Found unfit to plead, Freddy was installed at Broadmoor mental hospital with button-eaters, paper-tearers and silent starers as his unnoticed companions.

Their bodies claimed by shadowy 'relatives' in Malta, Roger and Jesus Tonna were interred in a plot overlooking the sewage outfalls above Marsa Creek. Their police files were officially stamped 'CLOSED' both sides of the Atlantic, and the vacuum their demise left was quickly filled by a subtle power-shift arranged by telex.

CHAPTER NINETEEN

BRIXTON BILLY'S BEARD was four days old when Pimlico drove him into the Knightsbridge mews outside Dotty's flat.

The run down from Birmingham had been brightened by radio reports of 150 armed police surrounding a country house in Stockbroker Surrey, and naval helicopters backing a similar operation at the Dorset estate of a foreign royal, which might well have created a minor international incident had he been in residence at the time.

As it was, there were red faces amongst police spokesmen, some prize dahlia corms were trampled, and an aged gardener was held at gunpoint until his identity could be established by the local vicar, who cycled over for that express purpose.

The evening television promised to be as entertaining.

Pimlico sounded a triple bleep on the horn and counted slowly to twenty. Dotty emerged with two large suitcases and a frivolous hat. When she had jammed the suitcases in the rear of her Mini she laid the hat on top of them and drove towards Cromwell Road and Heathrow Airport.

Pimlico told Brixton to say goodbye to his whack.

Brixton's imagination peopled the window boxes with angry law.

'Hope it's more a short *au revoir*. That Charlie moves double quick, don't he? I only told him where it was buried yesterday morning.'

'That's why Chas is Chas.'

Pimlico left the Jaguar in Dotty's parking-space and let Brixton into the flat. Fitful sunlight played on drawn curtains and flowered wallpaper. Roses twined on upholstery and forget-me-nots patterned the bathroom. The guest-room was a busy mixture of arum-lilies and scarlet pimpernels, and the pine bed was draped with a Union Jack bedspread. A blue sash proclaimed Queen Victoria Miss World, Disraeli held a pint of Watney's, and a sepia Buster Keaton ran from a phalanx of policemen. The wardrobe was full of clothes in Brixton's size.

Brixton bounced on the bed with a light ale.

'You and Dotty went to some trouble. But just her flying all that dough out solo don't sit right. Even if she is your missus.'

Pimlico popped a can of Long Life.

'She's got more escort than him up at Number Ten. Charlie's got all his overcoats riding shotgun. And a good few of Connie's lads. That dough's as safe as you are. And mine's gone, too. Ingrid's carrying it, and Wally's got some South African tart to include some in her luggage.'

'All in one jump?' Brixton shook his head. 'That Charlie.'

'It was that or take it out in penny packets. And the more time went by, the more chance there was of the Troys' tarts jumping it. And you.'

Brixton's gaze inverted.

'Wouldn't Tommy just love to dip his beak into all that hot poppy?' he said. 'I hope he's being kept well away.'

'He is, Brix.'

Pimlico thought of Dublin Gerry facing the Troys at the precise moment the SAA airliner left British airspace. Charlie had wanted Dublin to go in team-handed, but Gerry had insisted he got to gloat alone and turn the knife with Irish charm.

'Another beer, Brix?'

'Nope, too whacked out.'

Brixton lay back on the national flag and kicked off his shoes.

'Leave it to Charlie,' he said, and went to sleep.

Pimlico went out and closed the door. Rinsed the glasses and fed the canary. Glad of Brixton's faith in Charlie and disquieted by his own decision to launder his whack through Connie's mining enterprise. Musing over a second beer as Brixton snored.

At least Dotty and Ingrid were out of harm's way in South Africa. Now the cobbles could turn as red as they liked.

Dotty drove through Knightsbridge fighting panic.

The cases she had thought too heavy for her to carry had seemed to weigh nothing when she packed them in the Mini and laid her hat over them as Pimlico had told her to. She whirled through traffic trying not to think of the last time she and Pim had made love. How his stomach had knotted under pink scar tissue and ugly blue puckers. The grains of heavy buckshot that still worked their way to the surface to be picked out by tweezers. The way he muttered in his sleep afterwards, sweat shining on his face as he gripped the bedhead rails like cell bars. Perspiration running from his wide chest. Water on muscular stone.

The wrench of leaving her mews flat. Skipping down the stairs with Pimlico's assurances rolling through her mind.

How the flat was only wallpaper and four walls. And how a canary was only a canary. Replaceable, where she and Pimlico weren't. And the new life together in the sun had got to be better than whoring and pimping and big tickles that ended with the dawn frighteners and long cold train journeys for prison visits once a month. The future was making fat babies in the sun.

Wally's green and black Jaguar led Dotty to the start of the A4 where Archie's white Rolls swung in behind her Mini. Two motorcycles brought up the rear and there were other cars cruising the route to the airport. Dotty thought of flat tyres, fuel starvation and being a real mother as she passed some of the finest industrial architecture the thirties had produced, the rows of gabled houses built to overlook green fields that no longer existed.

Ingrid had said she wanted to try for another baby when the doctor said it would be safe. Dotty knew she was pretty and that Pim was strong, and they would make lovely babies together. Dotty was glad about Jonas and Brock and the Tonnas being dead. Glad that Manchester Freddy had gone potty and used a shooter on Jesus and Roger. That only left Maltese Maurice, and he should live just long enough to feel some of the misery he'd caused turning so many girls into toms for his beat.

There was sun in rusty fields of seeded cabbage. Fishermen on a canal bank. A whip of bare trees and slow Friesians grazing a paddock.

Dotty saw herself and Ingrid with prams in a playground.

Then overtook a lorry to follow Wally's Jaguar on to the perimeter road to the airport. The motorcyclists peeled off and went into the approach tunnel with a thunderous roar to alert the overcoats covering the rendezvous points ahead.

Dotty sensed there'd be no more adrenalin breakfasts waiting for the clock to tick past eight. No more carrying the strain through the rest of the day like an undigested meal. No more watching the rummage for evidence or the formal language of arrest before being taken into custody. Instead, Pim would mow a lawn and hang curtains with babies gurgling in a playpen.

The dream died as the plane crashed into a dark mountain in her mind and Dotty drove through a striped barrier to follow Wally's car up curving ramps to spaces reserved by an NCP man who had trolleys for the luggage. The multistorey carpark swarmed with hard, quiet men with busy eyes and nothing to say.

Ingrid got out of Archie's white Rolls to kiss Dotty, and Froggy, Sodbonce and Nasty Nostrils took the suitcases to the lift.

Dotty glimpsed Archie's white head before the car door closed and she asked where Charlie was.

Ingrid squeezed Dotty's arm.

'Around.'

Dotty said the tension was turning her milk to camel's water.

The NCP man stayed with the cars, eyes too big in his frightened olive face, as Ingrid and Dotty followed Wally and Naomi down cement stairs to the covered pedestrian ramp. When Wally had paid excess baggage on three of the suitcases at the SAA desk he made a face and a joke.

'Expensive playing it straight,' he said, suggesting a drink.

His humour escaped Naomi, who had already started to miss him.

Quill watched Wally introduce Naomi Leathers to Ingrid and Dotty and lead them away to find a bar. Without Payne there would be no photographs, without back-up there could be no arrests.

Quill angled closer as Wally led the women up to the horseshoe bar on the second level, unaware Charlie trailed him or that the anonymous call he'd received that morning had not come from Bulstrode talking through a handkerchief.

A late Lufthansa passenger was paged, Aussies from Kangaroo Valley drank from cans with brash flamboyance, and a party in African robes wheeled their duty-frees about in wire carts. Foreign students on 'stand by' slept on newspapers, stoic Germans ate overpriced gâteau in the cafeteria and Texans waiting for the Dallas flight looked jaded under their stetsons. An Afrikaans couple watched their baby scream from its folding chair whilst sullen Asiatics mopped between chairs and smoking-stands as though they had done nothing different for a thousand years.

Quill wondered what he was watching. Wished he could translate nods and handshakes into evidence. Have a pint himself or eat another breakfast. Since airport security was not controlled by the Metropolitan Police and the rest of Lemmon's squad was assigned elsewhere, Quill was just another private citizen on private property, and must conduct himself accordingly.

Quill watched a pair of Toytowns stroll past on the concourse below and sneered at them. They were just dropouts from the Met. Long on hair and short on brains. With the Toytown police bungling what passed for security at Heathrow, it was no wonder the wholesale thievery added up to millions each year. The Toytowns wouldn't go within fifty feet of a loading or unloading plane in case the unions accused them of 'harassment'. And meantime greedy fingers dipped into baggage to rip off the holiday-makers for untold millions, so it was no wonder to Quill that insurance claims and premiums had gone into orbit and nobody believed in copperdom any more.

Quill passed kiosks selling things only seen in airports, ducked through a news-stand and stared at an acre of camelhair. It was Sodbonce's chest, and Froggy and Nasty Nostrils stood at either side of him. Quill swallowed hard. They had all left their smiles at home.

'Hello, Prophet.'

'Going on your holidays?'

Nasty Nostrils played with a keyring on a carousel display.

'Keep it clean, lads.'

Quill dislodged a Travis McGee and a couple of Chandlers from a shelf. Sodbonce stood closer.

'Seeing somebody off, are we?'

'Could be.'

Quill swallowed tart bile.

Sodbonce put the paperbacks on a shelf.

'Happens we like you being here, Prophet. Right, Nasty?'

'Not many.'

'Lucky coincidence.'

'Except it ain't.'

Froggy jerked a thumb.

'There's a man wants to see you. Particular.'

'Very particular,' said Nasty.

'What man?' asked Quill. Knowing and unhappy.

'In the carpark. Man in a white Roller.'

'They're both white. Him and the Roller,' Sodbonce grinned.

Quill had backed as far as he could go. A counter cut at his buttocks and he jostled a Wrigley's display.

'Forget it,' he said.

'Call a Toytown, then.'

Sodbonce flicked Quill's tie out of his jacket.

'There's one. Shiny buttons, peaked hat and face to match.'

'Leave it out.'

'Call Toytown or walk.' Sodbonce laid a size-ten suede over Quill's size-seven Oxford. Draped a meaty arm around the slight shoulders as Froggy lifted Quill's warrant card and hid it in a pile of Monica Dickenses.

'Or limp.'

Sodbonce crushed Quill's foot.

'I'll . . . walk. . . .'

Quill soaked himself with popping sweat. His toes swelled and a fist of ice clenched his stomach. He was taken through automatic doors into dull sunlight where porters grinned over their trolleys as a Toytown told a motorist he couldn't park on yellow lines even if he was a close personal friend of BOAC's chairman.

Nasty's fingers met around Quill's bicep.

'Take a good long breath, Prophet. That is what you told our Chas? When you had him carted on your snide?'

Quill was crossed behind a black cab and walked into the shadows of the multistorey carpark. They clattered up cement stairs and between rows of cars. The NCP man was told to 'hop it', and Charlie came out of somewhere to lean against the white Rolls-Royce. An electric window whined open, and Quill saw Archie Ogle in the back seat. Frozen green eyes in a tanned face. Brandy and soda in a freckled fist.

Quill's mind tumbled over itself. Put himself back into bed with the telephone telling him he ought to go to Heathrow, that Bulstrode would meet him there to watch the SAA flight-desk. The puzzlement he had put aside because the whole squad was on surveillance in Bethnal Green with officers from Buckinghamshire. Quill spun back into the carpark to stare at Charlie Dance. Wanted to bluster and couldn't.

Charlie snapped fingers for a Gold Flake and blew out

a match in a hard puff of smoke.

'Mr Ogle's dead annoyed with you, Prophet. Won't even talk to you himself. Means I got to waste breath on you.'

Archie growled and sipped brandy.

'You and Maltese Maurice worked some naughties when you was a uniformed wally in King's Cross. Favours for favours, as Maurice so delicately puts it in his sworn affidavit. But, then, he's very delicate, is Maurice. Since his accident.'

Quill's small eyes widened.

Accident?

'All Maurice's toms declare you had some fine old Friday nights in their cribs. Dates, times, everything. You've been a very immoral lad.'

Quill blinked.

'Twenty-seven sworn statements before a Commissioner for Oaths and a couple of silks. They ought to keep you well busy with C12 or A10 or whatever Internal Affairs call themselves these days. And then there's your bank accounts.'

Quill blinked, wishing he could laugh. Scared to miss anything.

'Kept them a secret from yourself, did you?' said Charlie. 'Took us by surprise, too.'

'You've stitched me up?'

'Now, who'd believe that? A straight copper who's been salting dough away for two years and the bank statements lodged with a lawyer who don't know our firm from a bar of soap? That Mother Hubbard'll get lost in the rush when all that evidence gets slapped on the DPP's blotter. Your feet won't touch. Suspension on half-pay, and you calling Maurice and his toms liars won't be helped by bringing our firm into it, Prophet.'

Charlie leaked smoke through a tight smile.

Quill found the courage to snarl.

'I'll come after you, Charlie. However long it takes.'

'No, you won't.'

Quill sprang back when Charlie flicked ash. Took a short

hook to the stomach and fought to keep his breakfast. Suddenly on his knees he gaped at oily concrete.

'Suicides can't fight back.'

Quill's stomach was racked by long spurts of fire as he was lifted bodily. His ankles were roped together and his arms were pinioned behind his back. Held aloft, he was carried to the lifts and saw the OUT OF ORDER sign was a lie when Sodbonce opened the doors. A rope was tied off to a crossbar in the liftshaft and the dark hole came up at him in a surge of disbelief.

'Lose . . . him . . .,' Archie said with slow finality.

Quill tried to call Charlie. Or Archie. But nothing came as he was toppled into the void. Nothing but nausea and fury.

Falling, he embraced the coming end with anger. Found the breath to snarl at it.

Was jerked to halt. Blood rushed to his head and his neck whiplashed. He spun giddily with oily black cables smearing him. Fought blackout. Knew he must keep his nerve. Find the breath to call for help.

They were putting the frighteners on, that was all. They'd all be rolling about. Laughing up a storm. Thinking they'd drained old Prophet's bottle. Wrong, you bastards, thought Quill.

Wrong.

Then he heard the cage whine in the shaft above him and wondered what his last thought would be.

Naomi thought she quite liked Ingrid Dakin, but that Dotty Machin-Parsons was a petite blonde with a petit-pois mind.

Naomi hated all Dotty's fuss about crashing aircraft and not drinking the water abroad. As if she expected to squat at a waterhole and slake her thirst in the company of baboons and vervets. Naomi hated the thought of all those air-miles with that little goose for company instead of her loving clod Wally.

Naomi walked towards the whining aircraft. Wiped a

slick of moisture from her eye. Touched the bruise of Wally's farewell kiss. Blanked her face and rejected conversation. She stowed her coat and was grateful for the aisle separating her from Ingrid and Dotty. For the empty seat beside her. She refused a boiled sweet and buried her nose in an airline magazine. Daydreamed about honest sun on her face and servants who read her mind. Forced herself to forget about all that money in the rear baggage compartment. The shooting outside Margot's house. Wally driving her away without an explanation. Refusing to let her go back or even to telephone the Sadlers. And keeping Dirk and Alicia well away from reporters and the police.

All Naomi had for De Wit were some newspaper clippings and her own hazy recollection of gunfire. The small man called Freddy falling away from the car to roll in the gutter with empty eyes.

Naomi shuddered, knowing De Wit's debrief would be thorough and unpleasant. She kicked off her shoes and thought that at least playing house in Wally's tiny flat had been fun. Cooking basics on his funny little stove and going to bed in the long afternoons when the sun never showed at all. Even though it had been nothing more than a holiday romance, a shadow-dream that would fade like the last frame of an old movie, she had enjoyed every last moment of it.

'Have you fastened your seatbelt, Lady?'

Wally grinned down into Naomi's upturned face.

'What?'

The Super Constellation taxi'd towards the apron and the NO SMOKING signs were lit. There was no possible way Wally could leave the aircraft.

'You incredible twerp,' Naomi said, realising he was making the flight with her.

Lemmon climbed into the Post Office van and sat beside Dillman, who had earphones on as he fiddled with a directional receiver aimed at the Martyred Thomas. Payne's thousand-mill lens was trained on the saloon-bar entrance and his Pentax was loaded with 400 ASA film. In the lab it could be boosted to twice its speed with a slight loss of definition. The small mikes they had planted in the pub the previous night had picked up a whistling decorator who had left when the Troys went in and told him to 'sling his hook' just after noon.

'Anything new?'

Lemmon did not light a Player; they had all agreed not to smoke in the confined space. He had come from one of his 'meetings' at the Home Office where his files were accepted in silence by an anonymous official, and he had been given coffee in good china and solitude, before being let out into the street by the same silent man. Now and then Lemmon would get to talk to Bunny Halliday by phone, but he, too, said little that seemed relevant, apart from his usual 'Keep plugging away, Theo,' and the odd bouquet of flowers for Elizabeth when he was particularly pleased by the squad's progress. As usual, Bunny was only showing Lemmon a few of the cards he held against his chest.

'Nothing yet,' said Dillman. 'Just mutter and what sounded like a farting contest. And they're drinking in there.'

'Lucky old them. Can't even bust them for drinking on licensed premises out of hours.'

'It's a funny one, Guv. I get the feeling they're waiting for something to happen,' said Dillman.

'Ain't we all?' said Payne.

'Is Buller on station?'

'He's parked up east of us in an unmarked mobile, and he's tuned to our frequency. I've had an acknowledge.'

'And Quill?'

'No sign of him, Guv. Nothing on his answerphone, neither.'

Lemmon scrubbed his face with hot palms, and his jaw cracked when he yawned. He thought he would stroll off to Tubby Isaacs's stall for a bowl of eels and a smoke in the fresh air. A cup of lemon tea in one of the kosher cafés.

'I just hope Prophet—'

Lemmon broke off as Payne began shooting film. He craned to see through the two-way-mirrored window just as a tall stocky man pushed into the Martyred Thomas.

'I'd know the back of that head anywhere. Give us some sound, Dildo,' Lemmon breathed.

Dillman flipped on the speakers, and a needle danced on the volume dial as Jesse said, 'Hello, Mr Ax. Ain't this a s'prise, Tom?'

'Give the law a glass there, Gordy,' said Tommy.

'Not often we're graced, eh, lads?'

Arthur Ax cleared his throat. Scraped a chair aside and a length of timber skidded against plasterboard. Said: 'Nothing to drink on duty.'

Jesse laughed and snorted.

'Nicked, are we?'

'Not yet awhile. There *are* those who live in hopes. I could be one of them if my sweetener doesn't get to Jersey very, very soon.'

'You'll get your hotel in Guernsey. Matter of fact, we're hanging on here for some good news about that. Could even be a delivery. Poppy and that.'

'Don't let your bottle go, Arthur,' Jesse said.

'*Mr Ax* to you, Troy.'

'Yeah?' Tommy said lazily. '*Mister* gets earned around here. You'll earn a fucking *mister* so long as you keep the manor sweet when we're all moved up west. You're in as deep as us, Arthur mate. Don't crack on you ain't. You'll have to wait for your bootboys and chambermaids for fucking misters and tugged forelocks. Until then, Arthur mate, you're a bought-and-paid-for copper with forty grand coming his way as a kicker. How bad?'

'Finished?'

'Not by a long chalk, but, then, I ain't anxious to argue the toss with you. Stay by the phone. You could be a well-rich copper by sundown. Poppy straight from the sugar train.'

'And a drink wouldn't come amiss,' said Gordon.

'I'll call you,' Ax said. 'Get that clear. It's me who'll contact you. Not the other way around. I'm not jeopardising a thing at this stage.'

'Who'd want that? Nobody wants that, do they, lads?' asked Tommy.

'Tom's right there, Mister. Ain't you, Bruv?'

'Right as ninepence. Anything more, then, Arthur?'

'Nothing. . . .'

'All said, then.'

Lemmon had crushed his Player's pack, and his hand was mashing Dillman's shoulder.

'Get me some good snaps there, Payne.'

'Do we get Buller whistled up? Turn Ax over?'

'Not yet, my son. Not yet. This needs sleeping on.'

Lemmon watched Chief Inspector Ax hurry into the street turning up his collar. The Pentax took close-ups as Payne panned with the strolling policeman.

'Tell Buller to follow without making contact.'

'Acknowledged,' Bulstrode said over the radio patch.

'That's one copper too many in this world,' Jessie said with a long belch.

'But not for much longer, eh? Could give him to the Irishman,' said Tommy.

'Only if they took each other down.'

'Wouldn't that be a sweet old-fashioned thing?' Tommy said.

'And isn't science wonderful?' Lemmon listened to Bulstrode's engine over the patch.

Sweating and tense.

Wondering if he shouldn't swarm the area with uniforms.

Decided Yes.

The Martyred Thomas was forlorn in gathering dusk.

Decorators' dust-sheets flapped on the scaffolding and hardboard blinded the unglazed windows. The fascia boards had been removed, and blackened brick showed between the undercoated cornices.

Dublin Gerry stopped in shadow to admire his disappearing handiwork and gave Payne the chance to hack off some profiles before Gerry crossed the road.

'Anybody know him?' Lemmon asked.

Nobody did.

Tommy and Jesse sat in the dim light of the unfinished backbar to watch Gerry weave through ladders and scaffold boards and perch on a sawhorse in the heady reek of french polish and freshly planed mahogany.

Tommy tilted Scotch over shot-glasses.

'Welcome to the pub with no beer. You done good, Gerry son. The papers are still full of the break.'

Dublin Gerry took a glass and raised it.

'It'll die down when another nine-day wonder makes column-inches for John Q. Public to wrap his cod and chips in. Looks like the old insurance came across. Let's drink to the grand opening of the old Thomas.'

Jesse took whisky down.

'Be about a month. But some tosser's owed a permanent limp for it.'

'That right?' said Gerry.

'Yeah, yeah.' Tommy hated talking about the fire. 'What about Brixton's dough?'

'And Bonar's whack for Smiler,' asked Gordon.

Gerry began rolling an Old Holborn.

'There's good and bad news about that.'

Tommy rolled the gold band on his index finger.

'Without the Irish fife and drum, Dublin.'

Gerry teased tobacco flakes into shreds. Building tension with the cigarette.

'Straight you want it. Straight you'll get it. Bonar's escudos will get to Jo'burg in about a week. Not bad, seeing as how them Portuguese love the money rolling in and not out. Bonar's working the oracle though. There stands a clever man.'

Tommy stiffened in his chair.

'Since when was that poppy going direct to South Africa?' He hunched his shoulders at Jesse.

Gerry licked the gummed edge of a Job paper and rolled it into a neat tube. Pinched excess tobacco from the ends.

'Since Bonar figured you'd lean on Smiler to dip your snout into his whack. Smiler's the light of that man's life.'

'Fucking touching,' Jessie sneered.

'What am I smelling here?' said Tommy.

'A clever man being cautious. As cautious as Brixton Billy. And with reason.'

Gerry struck a Swan Vesta on his shoe and waited for the flame to burn evenly before touching it to his smoke.

The brothers exchanged looks with Gay Gordon, and Tommy cracked knuckles.

'How cautious is that, Dublin?'

'All the way.'

'All what fucking way?'

'Nobody believes your handshake, Tommy. Not Brixton, not Bonar Tree, not Connie Harold. And definitely not Charlie Dance.'

'Where's that face get into this?'

'By making sure you don't dip the whacks. Brixton Billy's out of Birmingham and safe. Smiler's well on his way to Portugal. And your cut of the whacks is where you can't touch it. Four miles up and flying towards Africa. Nobody's reneging; that's what was agreed. And you'll get yours when it's been laundered proper, not before.'

Jesse was pale, and his plump mouth was livid.

'Who brought Charlie Dance in?'

'Everybody.'

Tommy's face was bled meat.

'Name me names.'

'I have.'

'All of them?'

Tommy could not believe it.

'You ain't popular.'

Tommy pointed a thick finger.

'This is down to you, Dublin.'

'Why, because there's only me here? I was bought and

paid for and paid off. It's the big faces you have to make faces at. Not me. I've delivered the message and there's an end to it.'

'You figure you can waltz in here, tell *us* — tell *me* — we've been well and truly turned over, and figure you can just *walk*?'

Gerry let smoke through a lazy smile.

'Just an Irish herald, Tommy. Think about it. Charlie wanted the heavy poppy off the streets here, and he's done it. You and Connie want South Africa, he lets you have it. Right now, Charlie can buy you and sell you and give you back to yourselves. Here. He's got peace, and you faces are remittance men with your heavy poppy in a mine in wogland. Job done.'

'You still owe us one.'

'One what?'

'Who was it tried to pay us out in horsemeat for a hit on Dance and Ogle's old lady? You.'

'That debt's well overdue,' Jesse said.

'Well fucking overdue.'

Gerry lapped his drink and ate smoke.

'Over and done, Tommy. Unless you want to end up like the Tonna brothers.'

Jesse palmed a sweating face.

'Manchester Freddy went potty with a shooter. . . .'

'If you say so,' Gerry smiled.

'You ain't telling us. . . .'

'Toytown tales.' Tommy blanched all the same.

'Believe what you want. Roger and Jesus turn up dead on Sadler's doorstep. You've shook hands there, right? Shook hands everywhere and not meant it. Wanted to skim all the train whacks and own all the manors. Now your partners say you can't. So you roll your eyes and look for a scapegoat. Swallow it and count to a hundred. You'll see how it is and learn to live with it.'

'The bastard's enjoying himself, Tom.'

'I've got eyes.'

'So has he. Up to now.'

Gordon stroked the cut-throats behind his lapels.

Gerry tossed off his drink.

'And they're seeing straight. Anything happens to me, and you three'll go down faster than washing on a broken line.'

Tommy's hand shook as he drank. The whisky did nothing for him, but he could see the truth in what the Irishman was saying. The bigger *but* was that it was coming too hard and too fast for him. Everything was somehow slipping away. He had to crack skulls until it all fell back into place. He licked spilled whisky from his thumb and said: 'You set too much store in faces out of the country or well out of the running. There's just us and your tired old Irish charm here right now.'

Gerry sighed and stayed where he was.

Tommy poked another finger at him.

'Earn some remission on your debt. Give us Brixton and Smiler. That train poppy'd fly back here quick enough then.'

Jesse liked that.

'Nice one, Tom.'

Gerry shook his head.

'Take a good drink. Forget it.'

'More horsemeat earns you the paper hat,' said Tommy.

Gordon stroked his lapels.

Gerry shrugged and set his feet.

'I've wasted too much breath on you three-rounders. You're down and you don't know it. Every mother's son wants you finished and done with. And they don't care how you get taken off the streets. Their shooters or the law. One way or the other, you're history.'

Tommy's mouth worked into a bare smile.

'That gets it said, Gerry. And earns you a good last *drink*!'

The bottle swung and Gerry went under it in a hard crouch as Gordon's knee came up into his chest The razors came from behind the lapels in a double blur of borrowed fluorescence.

Gerry dropped a shoulder. Flicked his shot-glass into

Gordon's taut mouth. Heard it chink against tooth and gum. The knee skidded on a deltoid and Gerry stiff-fingered Gordon's crotch. A cut-throat flew off into pots of varnish and paint, and Gordon sat heavily, his torn mouth a hole in oatmeal.

Gerry banged the sawhorse into Tommy's next swing. The bottle shattered against steps where his head had been. Whisky stung the air, and Jesse's first punch missed. His second caved Gerry's front teeth in an implosion of shock.

Gerry kneedropped. Straight-armed Jesse to the heart through a swinging chairback. The chair disintegrated and a slat cut Gerry's eyebrow. A leg raked his cheek. Gerry rolled and toppled a scaffold board. Rolled again and kicked Tommy's legs out from under him. Pots scattered, and turpentine cartwheeled to make a stinking lake on the bare pine boards.

Gerry swallowed a bloody tooth and gagged as it stuck in his throat. Backed towards the saloon-bar door.

Tommy was coming to his feet and trod on Gay Gordon's hand. Jesse drew a long blade from a cardboard carton. Hurled the scabbard from an antique cavalry sword.

Gerry caught Tommy in the neck with a long kick. Jumped away and tangled an arm in a decorators' dust-sheet. Tore himself free as Tommy hunched his shoulders and windmilled punches. Slammed a foot into Tommy's armpit and backed clumsily as Gordon's long forward lunge glittered before contact.

The left hook cut instead of numbing.

A flap of meat hung over Gerry's collar and severed nerves screamed in lazy spits of blood. Gerry took another slash across the upper arm and followed through with combination punches that dropped Gordon in a flail of buckets and falling brooms.

Gerry feinted from the waist. Avoided Jesse's hooks and slashes with the sabre. The door was closer all the time and traffic brawled as the lights turned green. A bus changed gear and a horn bipped. Gerry shook blood from his eyes and skipped backwards. Kicked a bucket aside and felt for the brass handle. Skidded in turpentine and missed the swing of a baulk of sawn pine.

Tommy smashed the four-by-two across Gerry's right arm. Shattered bone. Drove him in a half-spin against the door in a daze that would not go away.

Something cleaved the air, and Gerry's face seemed to burst apart. His knees hit the floor and he fell on his side with his trapped right arm bent the wrong way. Bone splintered near his elbow. Ripped through tendon and knifed through his sleeve. Made him wail as he spattered himself with dark blood. Panted as he got his knees under him again. Only vaguely aware of the arcing knife that plunged into his face and pinned his head to the floor.

I should have listened, Charlie.

There were questions and breathing. No sensation save wood-shavings rustling under his trapped face. Keeping his eyes open was almost too much for his sapped mind to cope with. One was blinded anyway and wept around the blade through his cheek.

A longer blade hung in a shaft of light. Dust motes danced like liver spots. Jesse's hands were around the sharkskin haft. A gold tassle hung between the meaty knuckles.

Tommy bellowed madness.

The sabre hacked down through rib and lung and jammed in bone near Gerry's spine. The shock turned everything to silence. Gerry no longer owned a torso. No longer had legs. Just one good eye and his good left arm. It took Jesse by the throat and bulged the manic pink eyes. Locked off, the hand squeezed pith from a piece of rotten fruit.

The brothers leaned over Gerry in blessed silence. Turned the sabre. Sawed deeper. The point chunked into the floor and metal grated against bone. Splintered a floor board.

Spitted, Gerry watched his fingers open. His arm fell away. It was nothing to him any more. Spittle from Tommy's soundless shouts sprayed his upturned face. Pink froths of lung blood foamed in his open mouth.

Gerry fell away from it all. Did not hear a last clatter of air form a blood bubble over his lolling tongue.

The dark red ceiling came down to smother him and the body on the floor moved with the cut of the crimson blade long after Gerry had ceased to exist.

Dillman ripped the earphones off as Gerry's scream soared with the first downward plunge of the sabre. The sound went round the Post Office van as a whirlpool of terror. Payne took pictures of the closed door without knowing as Lemmon told all vehicles to converge. Now.

Bulstrode's Cortina mounted the pavement in a wide U-turn to make a bus-driver stamp on his brakes. Lemmon's hands slammed the rear doors open and turned his ankle on slick cobbles. Two pandas reached the intersection and began to bring order to the hooting traffic. A small man in a drab raincoat spun on his heels as Bulstrode bulled out of his vehicle. Threw his weight against the saloon-bar door and tumbled inside with Bulstrode three paces behind him. Payne got close-ups of Silversleeves Sutton before he fell inside the pub. The back of Bulstrode as he closed the gap, his tie streaming with his hair.

Lemmon hobbled through pedestrians, bringing up the rear.

Dillman sat and listened to the chop of metal against flesh with an ashen face, unable to react with anything but rapid blinks of his blue eyes.

Silversleeves had dressed over his pyjamas and hurried to the Martyred Thomas as soon as he had put the phone down from his cousin at Heathrow. A porter there, Silversleeves's cousin Willie, had seen Charlie's firm pick up Prophet Quill and Wally Harold catch the SAA flight.

'Has to be an earner of an earwig, right, Sil?' he had said. Silversleeves had said, 'Not many,' and kept repeating it as he hurried along Mile End Road.

Then Bulstrode had burned rubber in front of a bus, and pandas belling out of a side-street had panicked

Silversleeves into running into the pub instead of away from it.

He felt the door close on his back at the moment Jesse withdrew the sabre and severed Gerry's head with a savage downswing. Spattered Silversleeves with coagulating gore.

Silversleeves stared through blood measles. Said the road was thick with the filth as the head pinned to the floor stared one-eyed and grinned with broken red teeth. Kept him from seeing Gay Gordon crawl away behind the unfinished counter or minding the heavy thump between his shoulderblades as Bulstrode banged in behind him and allowed the small street trader to take comfort against his broad shirtfront.

Uniformed and plain-clothes police grappled Tommy to the floor and Jesse was backed against the bar, shedding sweat through freckles of blood as he made noises nobody wanted to hear. Cornered, he threw the sabre somewhere and tried to punch his way through a hardboarded window. Bowled uniforms aside like slack dummies. Ash cracked against his skull. Lignum vitae took the strength from his shoulders, and more heavy truncheon blows dropped him in a heap. His eyes rolled over Tommy and glared at Bulstrode and Lemmon. He hawked and spat with manic fury. Hit Lemmon's sleeve with a gobbet of phlegm before going limp, knees in his back and his arms handcuffed.

Unseen, Gay Gordon had crawled into the bar-well and dropped through the opened cellar-flap into the dark. With the sureness of practice he squeezed into the gap behind a large wine-rack and dropped into the vaulted cavity behind it. And waited.

Silversleeves smeared his face with a sleeve.

'Nothing to do with me, Guv,' he said hopefully.

'Cut yourself shaving, that it?'

Bulstrode wished he knew who the dead man was. Ambivalent about being too late to save him. Murder was a topping charge, and the Troys were caught dead to rights. A thousand Arthur Axes couldn't save them from the long drop and burial in lime.

Jesse wailed in mental twilight like an abandoned child.

Tommy just lay on the floor and ground his teeth.

Bulstrode got Payne taking pictures and said, 'What a frigging slaughterhouse.'

'Definitely nothing to do with me,' said Silversleeves.

Lemmon held the sabre by the tassle.

'This is one we won't lose in court,' he said, going over what he would say to Bunny and the silent man at the Home Office. Knowing he had most everything he needed to nail Arthur Ax. He bowed his head to let Dillman whisper something about Quill being rescued from a lift-shaft at Heathrow by firemen, and as he shook with nervous laughter one of the uniformed men was discreetly sick in a bucket of whitewash.

Gay Gordon did not move until three in the morning.

The CID had sealed the Martyred Thomas and left a constable and a sergeant to guard the building. The sergeant stood on the grating above the cellar and smoked where Gordon could not. Dropped his cigarette-butt into the shaft where they lay like fragrant rubies until they died. Cussed the cold when his constable patrolled past and hummed Max Bygraves medleys when he was alone.

Gordon crossed the cellar and quietly broke down a pile of wooden beer-crates he had used to block off the rear vaults. Eased himself over a dusty sill and closed the hole behind him with crates he had stacked on the opposite side.

No point in making them a present on my way out.

The golden rule in the Gorbals. When we was head to head with rival gangs in the derelict tenements. Always have a crafty way out if your mob got skinned. Ay.

Thick dust cushioned his footsteps as he wove through crusted arches scaled with mould. Feeling his way without showing a light. His outstretched hand touched the far wall and found the shutter of an old dumb waiter. It opened with a squeal and he froze for a millennia of seconds.

Listening.

The constable prowled the pavement overhead and the sergeant whistled to himself.

Gordon crawled into the dumb waiter and hunched small. Gingerly started himself upwards with the rope pulleys. Knew he should have oiled the tackle more often. Waxed the rope.

His tender groin pounded as hard as his heart, and fear of enclosed darkness sweated his scalp.

Just to be clean again. To languish in a bath and come out smelling of magnolias. Find somebody like that Penny waiting for me. Don't think about it. Or how bad things are with Tommy and Jesse banged up. They'll never get out. Don't think about it.

The ropes snagged and squealed when he was forced to haul on them with all his strength. Got them running free with a scream he thought could be heard in Brighton.

Don't think about it.

Pray if you must. Hail Mary, full of grace. . . .

No, cunt. You're parroting bitch Helen. Dead Helen. Helen in her RC pew and that face in the pink bathwater.

Don't think about it.

Just pull the ropes easy. Pull and ease off. Past the gym and up the shaft. Past this dead air. On and on and up and up to the top-floor offices.

All this bad air. Got to breathe.

Don't think about it.

The dumb waiter bumped to a halt.

Dead air smelled of old newspapers.

Gordon opened the hatch and sliced through wallpaper. Cutting carefully, keeping a straight edge. The square fell away and slithered against a skirting. Fresh air smelled sweet and made his own stink all the more improbable.

To be clean. . . .

Gordon climbed out on to a landing, and borrowed street-lights showed him the ladder to the fanlight. The CID seals on the outer office door.

Gordon gnawed his inner lip.

Cunting coppers. Hadn't banked on Tall John sealing the offices. There's hot water and clean clothes inside. Money and a shooter in the wall-safe.

Think, you dumb, muggled Jock.

Think.

The filth will be all over Ida like a blanket. You can't go near the Fortress. Or call cunting Arthur Ax. They'll not handle anything down at Leman Street for me now.

Think.

Nothing but bawbies and groats in your pockets and no face in Bethnal Green you can trust. No shooter nor lacer. Nothing but bare knucks and your muggled Jock brain.

Think, cunt, think.

You've got enough for cabfare to King's Cross. Hop a train back to Scotland. Wait. King's Cross. Argyle Square. Maltese Maurice. The only face who owes you one for past favours.

Maurice. Ay.

Gordon climbed to the fanlight and worked the rusty bolts.

Maltese Maurice.

CHAPTER TWENTY

THE GIRL with the pocked face chewed gum and said: 'It's twenty sovs or piss off, sunshine.'

Gordon's breath exploded in the early-morning darkness of Argyle Street as he snorted, 'I'm no kiltie just off the rattler from Aberdeen, henny lass. That's hard poppy you're talking.'

The girl slow-eyed Gordon.

'You say. It'd cost you a fiver for bed and breakfast around here without clean sheets. I'm worth fifteen more than that.'

'To who? Not to me. You'd only stick to five and hand the rest to Maurice.'

'Who's bleeding Maurice when he's home?'

'Your pimp. My mucker.'

'You and him mates? Never.'

'I told you.'

'I'd have seen you and him. Like together.'

'You would not.' Gordon's groin ached in the cold. 'Twenty sovs? Jesus.'

'It's the best room in the square, sunshine.'

'That makes it the first-floor front in Maurice's own drum, henny. The one with the musical bed and rampant stag wallpaper.'

The girl stopped chewing, and her big eyes hardened in a thick ring of mascara.

'Maybe you do know him?'

'Know who?'

'Him. Maurice.'

'Maybe you should give him a bell. He'd mark your

stupid face.'

'Wouldn't he, though.'

The girl looked thoughtful. Bit a nail and wet her lipstick.

'OK, sunshine. Ten it is. But nothing hard. Nothing violent.'

Gordon crackled a last pound note in his pocket.

'Wouldn't draw the wings from a fly. A straight up-and-downer, that's me. Come out of the road before it's time for breakfast.'

'Romantic little sod, ain't you?'

'Rudolph Valentino never paid for it in his life.'

'Another friend of Maurice's, I s'pose.'

'Ay, a West End face like me.'

The girl stuck her gum behind her ear.

'Come on, Big Dick. Let's get you out of the draught before a good sneeze knocks you over.'

Gordon made fists in his pockets.

'And you'd be the one to mother me, eh?'

'Not for no ten quid. Me name's Carlotta. Nice, ain't it?'

'And last week you was Charmian or Greta.'

Carlotta jangled keys.

'You want it or not?'

Gordon took her bony elbow.

'More than a free pint.'

Carlotta opened a peeling door on to boiling greens and tomcats. 'After you, Kiltie. You wouldn't be bad-looking if you wasn't so skinny like.'

'And Carlotta suits you, too. Exotic.'

'Yeah?'

'Ay.'

At the top of a flight of stairs Carlotta fumbled with a light and unlocked her room. Turned to bow Gordon inside and saw the dried blood and filth on his face. The brown stains on his collar and cuffs.

'Now, listen, sunshine—'

Gordon hit her in the throat. Chopped her hard behind the ear. Caught her and dragged her into the stale room. Dropped her on to the sagging bed, glad to let her go. The smell of her made him swallow hard. There were fresh track-marks on her wrists, and her nostrils were red from snorting coke.

That's how you keep them tame, eh, Maurice. Give them a habit they can't break. Ay, that was Tommy's idea, too. But he's gone and. . . .

Don't think about it.

Gordon tied Carlotta to the bedhead with her own tights. Gagged her with an unwashed pair of panties.

'Choke, you whore,' he said aloud, locking her in.

A Geordie voice complained in whispers as bedsprings protested. A cockney girl whined back as a strap slapped flesh. Gordon climbed stairs past snoring and the hoarse grunts of copulation. Two flights up he came to Maurice's flat. Used one of Carlotta's hair-grips to pick the lock. Took exactly eleven seconds to spring the door, slow by his standards.

Tired, he told himself in justification. Eased the door closed against the jamb and accustomed his eyes to the gloom. A wedge of light showed under a bedroom door, and the air was heavy with lavender polish.

Gordon risked the overhead light and showed himself the small neat sitting-room with its easy chairs and a sideboard of framed photographs. Maurice smiled beside the Tonnas at a sulky-race in Marsa, walked a horse with a winner's rosette on his lapel, leaned in bars in Canada, Malta and Soho, popped champagne with Gordon at a party in Manor House, wore funny hats with Manchester Freddy at a Greek restaurant in Peckham. Stood in a tuxedo surrounded by a flock of girls in spangles and feathers, and rode a fairground horse with a girl who might have been Carlotta before horse and smack took her looks and self-respect.

Gordon's stomach growled and he found the kitchen to rifle the fridge. Ate salami and drank milk to wash down stale cream crackers. Maurice hadn't shopped recently.

The old tosser was letting things slide. Must be snorting himself to go to sleep with the light on. Heroin's supposed to be a good sex aid for the over-forties.

Gordon grinned and helped himself to a sharp kitchen knife. Tucked it into his waistband where it was handy and cracked the bedroom door. Maurice lay on the bed in a dressing-gown, and his naked legs ended in white plaster bootees leaving his toes free to wriggle if they wanted to. His round face was rounder and one ear was the glossy purple of ripe aubergine. Crumbs of eyeball peered through black prunes of discoloured flesh, and his mouth was swollen and negroid.

Gordon ran fingers through his hair and stared.

'Have you earned the paper hat, or have you earned the paper hat?'

There was something wrong with Maurice's voice.

'Get gone out of . . . it . . . Gordy. They done me over. . . .'

That's as maybe. But I need poppy to do a hotsman.

Gordon took a step on to carpet thinking of self-preservation. Of how to ask Maurice for money without knowing who had worked him over.

'. . . Said they knew about Brock and Jonas . . . the casino receipts. . . . Told 'em dinn know nothing . . . but that Lou kept at me and at me ann at meee. . . .'

Lou?

Gordon's skin crawled hearing that name.

Don't think about it. Get the dough and get gone. Ay.

'Where's your dough stashed, Mo? I need—'

Gordon felt movement behind him. The slap of bare feet on linoleum. Then somebody was on his back and thin legs were around his waist, heels hammering his painful crotch. Nails dug into his face, and Carlotta's stench was all over him as she tried to drive a pair of pinking shears into his chest.

Didn't hit her hard enough. Must have cut herself free.

Gordon tried to scrape her off against the bed. Got the hand away from his face and turned the wrist until it cracked. Heaved the girl on top of Maurice, who sat upright to bellow softly before subsiding in an unconscious sprawl. Found the rank hair and jerked the spitting girl's face close to drive a short hook to the jaw. Clicked her teeth together just as she drove the shears into his ribs.

The whore's melt has cut me. Deep.

Gordon hit the girl again. Drove her face away over her shoulder at an odd angle. Smelled Carlotta on his fist when he let the body fall across Maurice. Wiped his hand on the garish pink bedspread thinking of money and where it might be hidden.

All pimps salt their money away. Ay.

Gordon ripped drawers out of a dressing-table. Left the shears where they had lodged until later when he could stop the bleeding. Let clothes fall in heaps and emptied the wardrobe. Opened shirt-boxes and found a coin collection. Emptied the gold and silver ones into his pocket. Discovered a wad of Maltese sterling in a leather collar-press and stuffed it into his shirt. In a suitcase he found the good stuff. Used fivers in rolls held by elastic bands.

Bloody thousands.

Gordon took all he could carry and pushed Carlotta aside to sit on the bed to look at the shears in his side.

Not too much blood, but I'll be a stuck pig unless I staunch the flow. Use a bath towel and Elastoplast. Take one of Mo's clean shirts. Pull the cunting shears out in the bathroom. Wash off the blood and clean up. Then have it away. Ay.

'As God makes them, so he pairs them,' somebody said.

Gordon saw Charlie lean in the doorway. Made a helpless gesture and thought to keep the bastard talking until he was less tired.

'If you done that to Maurice, you ain't no better than none of us, Charlie. Charlie Dance, the man who dinna ken the cowboy action.'

'Limehouse lost his temper. I'd have just killed him.'

'You don't want me, Charlie. Not now with—'

'You were in on what happened to Dublin Gerry.'

'Business, Charlie. Nothing personal in that.'

Gordon had to get to the bathroom. His bladder was

full, and fireflies burned and danced in his side. He watched Charlie walk round the bed to feel Carlotta's pulse.

'Pity she didn't do such a good job on you, Gordy. She's dead.'

Gordon blinked drearily. *It couldn't be.*

'This ain't no fob watch I'm wearing here. You don't want me, Charlie. I'm fucked and gone. All you do is let me walk.'

I can make it through the door. Throw the lock. Get down the stairs and shiv him if he comes after. Gut him through the banisters.

Charlie scratched his chin at the dead whore.

'You know where the door is,' he said softly.

'You won't regret, Chas.'

'Goodbye, Gordon.' Charlie just looked at the girl.

Gordon got to the bedroom door and held the lintel where he swayed. Saw another man in the sitting-room. A man in black with red hair and freckles and nothing in his hands but a pack of Capstan and matches.

'A last smoke before you go, Gordy,' said Lou. He lit and threw a cigarette on to the floor at Gordon's feet. 'Have that on Helen.'

'You'll not see me beg.'

Gordon bowed slowly and picked the Capstan off the carpet. Waited for the pain to leave before he straightened. Flicked the cigarette into Lou's face and punched the kitchen knife at him as he bobbed aside. Felt the blade strike nothing but air as Lou's foot drove the shears deep into his side with a light thud. Gordon was full of air he could not breathe. Unable to lower his arm he watched Lou wait for him to die with sad eyes in deep sockets.

Gordon refused to fall. To give in. He pointed at Lou and made small steps towards the dark staircase. Heard himself grab a final victory as he said: 'You never had her, Cunty. I took that away from you. You never had anything. And I did it. . . .'

Gordon could see the landing, but it stayed where it was. He was sinking to the floor, and something feminine shimmered as distant laughter tinkled from a face with hair as golden as the agony in his chest. Then he pitched forward on to the linoleum into infinity and beyond.

Charlie stepped round the body and found the smouldering Capstan. Put it in his mouth and drew on it. He had finished Maurice with pressure on his carotid artery, and it wouldn't take the law long to work out how Gordon had murdered him and the girl during the course of a burglary. It was as neat as he could make it.

'Where shall I drop you, son?'

Lou almost smiled.

'West End Central. Time I gave Mr Lemmon his "chapter and verse" on Tommy's tarts. Tie up the loose ends for him.'

'You don't have to. They're well nicked.'

Charlie wiped off anything he and Lou might have touched and led Lou down and out into the start of a bright summer's day.

'He was right, Gordy was. I never did have her.'

'No.'

'Makes it all the purer, though, don't it?'

Charlie nodded at the starlings flocking around the turrets of St Pancras Station.

'Two away to you, Mister,' he told the quickening sky. Not adding the girl to his tally.

CHAPTER TWENTY-ONE

MARGOT walked the river bottom below Chartings Hall and surprised a heron as mist retreated from the rising sun.

Malcolm would be awake soon, and the Andalusian cook would be preparing breakfast for him. Margot cut at the tall reeds with a hazel switch, calming herself after a sleepless night.

She had spent the previous morning in the confines of Lincoln's Inn with her legal adviser, whose conversation had been most illuminating. A dusty thumbprint on his half-glasses had blurred his right eye as he talked in a monotone in his dark panelled chambers, a Cyclopean pedant with the face of an ancient Druid and a voice as dry as his phraseology.

But sweet, Margot decided.

And desperately honest. And as ugly, sober and dull as Oscar Wilde's view of Dodge City.

She climbed the steps of the sunken garden to her favourite vantage-point. The shrubbery was bright with new leaf, and the view over the vales of Sussex was achingly green as the season ripened into early summer. Chartings's Jacobean brickwork and mortar were earthenware lined with biscuit, and the leaded windows were bright lozenges of reflected sky.

Margot knew she would not miss the house in Esher, even the sanctuary of her conservatory. The double shooting outside had soured her associations with that part of her life, but the loss of Chartings would be a tragedy of monumental proportions, far outweighing even Malcolm's previous brutality.

Margot said 'Ouch' softly and unclenched her fists. Her nails had scored her palms with deep crescents.

The gardener's old spaniel stalked flies on the lawn and an early bee blundered into a flowerbed. Pigeons from a nearby copse beat overhead and linnets spiralled from the cottages near the main road. The air was as clear and as fresh as any skiing resort Margot had visited, and she vowed to better Bastard Malcolm at his own devious game to keep her home.

Just to breathe rainwashed air and watch clouds chase olive shadows over the vales. Watch an old dog snap at insects on a lawn ruined by mole runs. Be mistress of my own destiny. Dream of another Telephone Charlie who may one day enjoy me on that same lumpy old run of lawn. Or anywhere else he might fancy.

Calling herself 'Fool', Margot scratched her wayward nose and went into the house to collect Malcolm's breakfast-tray and the morning papers, and was sitting on his bed when he emerged from his bathroom smoothing freshly shaven chins and the front of his very purple dressing-gown.

'Good morning, Wife.'

Sadler no longer called Margot 'Cat'.

'You're walking better.'

Margot poured his coffee and stirred in cream and sugar.

'Am I? Yes, I suppose I am.'

Sadler drank and smacked his lips, a mannerism Margot hated.

'You'll be well enough to resume travelling, I shouldn't wonder. All those foreign parts. . . .'

'I?'

'You, Malcolm.'

'You surprise me.'

Margot ploughed on through his negative responses.

'You and another, Malcolm. To Buenos Aires perhaps?'

Sadler stopped reaching for the newspapers.

'Buenos Aires, Margot? Why do you mention Buenos Aires so particularly?'

'The airline tickets in your bureau. Tickets purchased

on the domestic account. Not the business. Tickets, Malcolm. Plural rather than singular. You won't be travelling alone.'

'Ah.'

'Ah, indeed.'

Margot held out the pewter pot.

'More caffeine?'

Sadler offered his cup with a lifted brow.

'Two to Buenos Aires? And what might the significance of that piece of information be, I wonder?'

'I imagine it's where you plan to run with some female A. N. Other now that it's all up with your yobby friends.'

Sadler drank his second coffee back as he habitually did.

'Which friends would they be?'

Another bloody mannerism.

Margot opened the *Daily Express* and laid the *Daily Mirror* alongside it.

'These friends.'

Sadler saw Tommy Troy glare from beneath a blanket as police escorted him to a Black Maria. Jesse's grainy portrait sullen beside block headlines, his hair drooping spikes as he was frogmarched through drizzle. Ida cried into a handkerchief on courtyard steps as a beefy WPC held photographers back, their faces bleached by the flash of Speed Graphics. Tommy and Jesse flanking the cockney bosom in their nightclub. Posing with a knight who shone in popular television programmes and wrote pompous articles for the Sundays, whatever their political persuasion.

Sadler was the grey of the newsprint.

Margot watched his mouth blush and his jowls shudder. Saw coffee slop from his porcelain demitasse. Saw a thousand truths she had blocked out with brandy and self-delusion.

'How many photographs are you in, Malcolm?'

'Be quiet. . . .'

'That man Lemmon didn't let you take him in when he asked you about those men, the Tonnas, did he? Your claim to be too ill to talk to him made not a scrap of difference, did it?'

'Enough, Margot.'

'He knew you were lying from moment one. Saw through my unconvinced tears, too, didn't he? And they say the wife is always the last to know. A cliché and truism both.'

'I said *enough*.'

'You and your friends in high places. No such animals exist now, do they? Bunny Halliday hasn't accepted a single invitation since he brought his favourite copper into our circle, has he? Or any of the others you so confidently called your friends?'

'Shut up.' Sadler scanned the scant details. 'I have to *think*.'

'Of Argentina? Of divorcing me for your new travelling companion?'

'You will kindly close your very foolish mouth.'

'Yes, Malcolm, three bags full, Malcolm. That's what the old Margot would do. But not this one. Not now she knows she's a serious candidate for divorce or sudden death.'

'What drivel.'

'Was it one of your headlines here who was to convert me into a plausible "accident"?'

'You don't know what you're talking about.'

'You didn't fall in the conservatory. Was that mauling you took a warning not to cross them further?'

Sadler stood and promptly sat.

'You were dead drunk when I . . . fell. Nobody hurt me.'

'Lies, you liar.'

Sadler mumbled. Pawed his hair.

'I must think.'

'And this sudden flight to Buenos Aires? To sell my darling Chartings Hall to that awful farmer from Cheddington?'

'You know about that?'

'And how I do is simple. You put all your UK property into my name last year. A small matter of bad investment, remember? And yesterday I learned that silly drunken old Margot's signature is necessary to release the deeds of ownership so that the sale can go through. I signed over the Esher house, but my Chartings?'

Margot tossed her head. Dislodged a fat black curl.

'Not Chartings, Malcolm.'

Sadler's lips curled and quivered.

'You have no choice, my dutiful wife.'

'Wife in name only. We're talking property settlements. Not marital bliss. No more threats or brutality, Malcolm. One single bruise and I walk away with everything bearing my name. You'll get your divorce then — after I've taken your last solitary sixpence.'

'Will you now?' Sadler's doubled fists trembled in his lap. 'You utterly silly and thorough cow. All the courage in the world now you think you have the upper hand. And a fool of a solicitor to make your money-grubbing legal.'

'For the first time since our parody of a marriage started I feel I'm a person in my own right.'

'You, you degenerate bitch?'

'Me.'

'You joke of a woman.'

Margot smoothed her skirt with a sigh.

'Thank you, Malcolm. That makes it easier to leave.'

'Fornicatress.'

'I accept the gender, but the charge itself you must prove.'

Margot forced herself to hold Sadler's crumbling stare.

He licked a moist upper lip.

'Prove it, my pet? Didn't I see you reflected in the water under those bloody palms? Yes, my dearest dear, I saw. I wasn't sure until afterwards. Long afterwards. And you are quite right; my accident was no accident. I was fucked by the same bastard who fucked you.'

Telephone Charlie? Margot thought, not realising she said it aloud.

Sadler grinned like Blake's Tyger.

'Your penchant for giving pet names damns you. I thought on my bed of pain for weeks and was never sure until now. God, if only I'd known at the time. I could have had these men. . . .'

Sadler stabbed the half-tone Troys with a forefinger.

Margot thumbed a ticking eyelid.

'Had them kill us?'

'Why not, you bitching bitch? Your Telephone Charlie wants me dead. And now you're killing me by inches with your puerile notions of independence. That man, that man, that fucking man. . . .'

Sadler paced. His face dark with fear and malice.

Margot perspired. Chill as the sun rose through the leaded windows. Malcolm's fear fouled the timbered room and his swearing was a frightening novelty.

'You think you can keep Chartings Hall? You think, you really think you can live if I die? No witnesses, you dunce of a bitch. You go with me. Christ and double Christ, we both have to run. That man, that fucking man. . . .'

'Run? Run where? Why?' Margot did not comprehend.

'From him, from him.'

He made love to me. True, true loving.

Sadler turned on Margot with some of his old spirit.

'But Dance won't have it all his own way. Not by a very long chalk. I still have a long arm, Wife-in-name-only. I can reach out and hurt him the way he has dared to hurt me. My friends in South Africa will see to that. Charlie Dance is about to hurt.'

Charlie Dance?

Margot spun herself back to Wally Harold's 'Welcome Home' party. A Charlie Dance had been mentioned as she beamed through alcoholic mist. Wally himself had annoyed Conrad by saying: 'Charlie Dance promises the Troys as headlines, Mister, you'll *see* headlines.'

Margot whirled herself back to an erotic explosion on Korean moss and being cradled in strong arms whilst she slept. Until Malcolm's torn voice called her back to wade across the pool to where his naked feet jumped on the stone parapet. His chubby torso jerked under his fatter testicles and his head cracked against the heated flags in agony.

The awful pleasure of that moment.

The pleasure in Malcolm's pain.

Sweat blistered Margot's forehead.

'I don't understand. How deeply are you involved with these criminals if you talk of *hurt* in this way?'

'In over my head, Wife. I'm dead, you're equally dead if you don't sign those property deeds and share-blocks over to my brokers immediately. Two tickets to Buenos Aires, Margot. For you and me. You can't be left behind. He'd find you. And through you . . . *me*.'

Margot just sat. Very still. Composing herself.

Sadler paced and muttered and dry-washed his hands.

'What a pair we make,' Margot said at last. 'The man who would steal the world and an effeminate brewery.'

'Your salvation lies in signing your name. Not in stolen curtain speeches.'

'I believe you, God help me,' Margot whispered.

'Then, telephone your lawyer. Now.'

Margot studied a silver nail in a sunbeam.

'There will be certain conditions.'

Sadler stared. Unbelieving.

'What?'

'Write it all down, Malcolm. A private confession for me. Then I'll do it.'

Sadler's fists drummed his belly.

Nodded.

'You agree, bastard darling?'

Sadler nodded dumbly.

'Make the call.'

Margot went into her room to call Mr Thrupp. When he came on the line she said: 'How long will it take to process those papers I signed yesterday? Yes, all of them, including Chartings Hall. . . .'

'Three days, not allowing for the coming weekend.'

'Make that twenty-eight days, will you? And do make something up my husband will believe, should he telephone.'

'As you wish, Mrs Sadler.'

'I do so wish.'

'My pleasure.'

'There is one other thing. . . .'

'Yes?'

'Do you have a discreet enquiry agent? One who could locate somebody without hanging about in a shabby raincoat?'

Thrupp hawed, and his 'Yes' was cautious. Made it quite clear such activities were more the domain of less prestigious and, ah, lesser men in the lower echelons of his profession.

'But you can offer me such a service?'

Thrupp could indeed, and wrote *Charles Dance* on his memoranda-pad before Mrs Sadler rang off. He pondered his name for a long moment before unlocking a desk drawer, looking up a number and dialling J. C. Hatton in Esher. They talked in low tones for several minutes and came to a ready agreement in less than three minutes.

Margot cleared Malcolm's tray and smiled sweetly.

'All fixed. Now explain, please – about hurting Mr Dance in South Africa?'

And she listened with a fixed smile as Malcolm explained. Playing with her silver brooch with silver nails.

Arthur Ax feigned a migraine behind *The Times* until his wife went off to a WVS bridge party before allowing despair to drain his face of colour. The men from Internal Affairs and the cheerful one called Halliday had been overly polite when they made him read the transcript of the tapes Lemmon's squad had supplied. They agreed they couldn't use the tapes in a court of law when Ax tried to brazen it out, and their polite scorn had told him there were many other ways they could make a case against him.

Suspension on half-pay, his assets frozen and a full enquiry. Resignation? Out of the question, Chief Inspector. So sorry.

Sorry, my arse.

Arthur Ax saw his new life in the Channel Islands slip away and knew the lady who had promised to meet him in St Peter Port would find solace elsewhere with indecent haste.

Too many glands working for that one to live in celibacy or wait for me to come out of prison without a bloody sou. I know what prisoners do to disgraced coppers in the nick. I'd spend all my time in solitary and come out old, broke and broken. If I lived through it. . . .

Ax went into his wife's muddled kitchen where cakes and sponges cooled on wire trays, and rummaged in the cabinets and drawers until he found the things he needed. Then he undressed in the bedroom and hung his clothes in his wardrobe in his usual neat fashion. He laid his wallet and keys on his bedside table and decided against a note. They would get no help from him, he vowed, and stripped the cord from two pairs of pyjama trousers before locking himself in the bathroom.

When he had cleaned his teeth and combed his hair he sat on the toilet and lashed his feet to the bowl with one of the pyjama cords. The second he used to tie his neck to the cistern pipe so that he would not fall when he became unconscious. That was important to his orderly mind. He must maintain some dignity.

He filled a pair of Marigold gloves with cooking oil and trapped them between his knees whilst he prepared the plastic bags that were to go over his head. Four bags together ought to be strong enough, he decided, rolling the edges and fitting them on his head like a skullcap, ready to be pulled down.

Time of death ought to be exact, he thought, and smashed his wristwatch against the wall. The hands stopped at one-fourteen and Ax pushed the minute-hand forward two minutes to be as precise as possible.

No hesitation, Arthur. Do it.

Now.

Ax pulled the bags down over his face and expelled all his breath. When he breathed in, the bags sucked in against his face and blood pounded in his temples. He drove his hands into the rubber gloves and oil spurted out on to his forearms. He rubbed his hands together so that they, too, were slick with oil. His heart was a drum in his chest and his lungs ached for air. The panic he knew would come brought his hands up to tear at the bags but there was no purchase. He bucked against the cords and they cut into his ankles, tightened around his straining neck. His knees parted and his member rose, a magnificent final erection that would point in accusation at whoever found him. Hoping it would be his bloody awful wife, Arthur Ax bit through his tongue and lost consciousness. His arms and torso went slack and one of the oily gloves slipped to the floor with a rubbery slap he didn't hear. His knees sagged together and he farted long and loudly as his sphincter went slack.

Arthur Ax was clinically dead forty-seven seconds later than he had calculated and was not found until his wife had a neighbour kick the door in just after seven that evening, and Mrs Ax was still laughing hysterically when the police arrived with an ambulance twenty-five minutes later.

'He always was a pompous prick,' she said before they sedated her.

Colonel De Wit thought about Naomi Leathers as she cooled her heels in his waiting-room. Her skimpy report lay under his hand, and his displeasure showed as clenched muscles in his long jaw.

Naomi had been a fine mistress when she had been married to Damien Leathers the financier. A tigress between the sheets and a willing fly on the wall during those business meetings De Wit had been interested in. And just as useful to De Wit in other ways as her daughter Alicia was at present. It was clear that Naomi's work had deteriorated since De Wit's interest in Alicia had become more intimate, and it was as well her fear of him had not lessened, or even the scraps of information she now brought him would be even more worthless. More footling.

De Wit went to the window to stare down into the police compound where black prisoners washed a fleet of official cars. The big ceiling fan moved the air around without cooling his office, and small roundels of sweat grew under his armpits.

Women's emotions were troublesome, and their motivations were so transparent, so damned dishonest. All delusions without a shred of honesty. No wonder men grew beyond them so quickly and so readily. Women didn't mature and grow as men did, they shrivelled and wilted like Namaqualand daisies when the dry seasons came. Pretty and vivacious for such a short time whereas men put down deeper roots and threw up stronger branches to shield themselves from the hot rays of the sun of reality.

De Wit wished he had a decent intelligence network in Great Britain, especially now the damned socialists were in power with their dangerous and misguided policies of equality. Anti-apartheid groups were springing up all over London with the blessing of the Wilson government. Not the wind of change Harold Macmillan had prophesied. This wind blew chill for the only white tribe in Africa.

De Wit went back to his desk and tapped the file with a pencil, sighed and pressed the bell, and did not stand when Naomi was shown in. He made no comment when she sat across from him without invitation to do so. She was pale from her extended stay in England and wore powder blue to accentuate her blondeness. Her generous mouth pouted under the merest slick of lip-gloss.

De Wit tapped her report and watched her nervousness grow.

'My men tell me you brought one of the Englishmen with you,' he said with suddenness.

'Yes. He wishes to see you.'

'Without going through channels? Are you impertinent enough to believe my door is ever open to you?'

'I merely said I would ask if you would see him. Nothing more, Hendrik.'

'Hendrik is it now? Such familiarity. Has his great

cockney heart melted enough for him to ask me to give you away in the kirk?'

Naomi's face became scraped bone.

'You can be damned cruel, Colonel. It isn't Wal . . . Walter. It's his brother Conrad. You had said you wished to see him at the earliest moment. His anxiety to talk privately with you simply matches your own. Shall I tell him to go away?'

'I have constables to do that for me. If necessary. Did he tell you, his so dear friend and confessor, what it is he wants with me?'

'Only the barest ideas. It would be better if he—'

'Perhaps he *should* explain himself to me. After you explain this piece of silliness you sent me. Three sentences and a few newspaper cuttings? Nothing I couldn't and didn't get right here. And many days before you delivered this nonsense. Ach, Mrs Leathers, do you take me and our republic for a fool in a nation of fools?'

'No, not at all,' Naomi quavered. Chill in the heat.

'This report suggests otherwise. I am not well pleased with your notable lack of zeal. Not only as a public servant, but also as a grass-roots patriot who has set aside personal honour to save your personal fortune from being seized by the appropriate government department. Those discrepancies could well be resurrected at any time as you are well aware. Don't ask me always to turn a blind eye without you give me constant loyalty, my wealthy widow. Your late husband's memory would soon tarnish if the truth about his business dealings ever became known. You would be impoverished and the scandal would bar you from what we so tritely call "polite society". And I don't see you surviving such an eventuality, but, then, perhaps you do?'

Naomi felt the familiar weariness of defeat. The fact that she had supplied De Wit with the intelligence of her husband's perfidy in the first place crushed her spirit all the more.

Poor dear Damien, I sold us both out, she thought.

'What do you want from me, Hendrik?' she said.

'A small thing. You will stay very close to Conrad Harold. Very close indeed. What Alicia cannot glean from him, you will. I hope that is clear.'

'Can this wait for a few days? I did promise to go up-country with Wal . . . Walter and his two—'

'It will not wait. You must make your excuses.'

'Very well. Is there anything in particular you wish to know?'

'Just everything. We are never dealing with absolutes, my wealthy widow. Just keep your wits and your pencils sharp at all times. And pack a bag; you could well be flying to London. Clear?'

'Oh yes. Very.'

'Then, you may go. And send Mr Harold in on your way out.'

Naomi stood and held a handbag of brilliant blue feathers.

'Am I never to be free of Damien's past, Hendrik?'

De Wit's smile was bleak and his nod curt.

'I doubt it, my dear. I very much doubt it. Run along now.'

'Goodbye, Hendrik.' *You bastard.*

But De Wit was already looking past her, waiting for the Englishman to come in. Had already dismissed her from his mind. Naomi heard his cheerful greeting before the door closed on Connie's back. The offer of coffee or perhaps a cool drink before the rickety lift took her down to the street and the chance for quiet tears in her Mercedes as she pummelled the steering-wheel, blind to the staring Blacks.

Connie Harold quelled panic as he and Dit Wit crushed knuckles, refused a drink to keep his mind clear and sat in the chair Naomi had warmed for him. De Wit accepted a good cigar and they exchanged opening gambits and smoke across the pristine desk.

'This is all a bit complicated, Colonel.'

'Isn't anything worthwhile?'

'It ain't a parking ticket.'

'I would have thought not.'

'I brought a lot of pop . . . money into the country the day before yesterday. A lot of money. To finance the next stage of my mining interests. And I've had this, well, difficulty with the blokes in badges and buttons who've got something to do with exchange control. They've chucked a million forms at me, talked a lot of double dutch — no offence, just an expression — and, well, it's giving me the permanent wobblies.'

De Wit's smile was sly when he said he thought he might have heard something about it.

'And I still can't get through the restrictions on this plant I need from Hungary. Even the forms need forms, and my lawyers are running up fat bills without doing a hand's turn to straighten things. I don't know what it takes, Colonel, but whatever it costs I want it straightened.'

'Are you attempting to bribe me?' De Wit asked.

'I would if I thought that'd be what it took.'

Connie stopped himself pacing or raising his voice.

'You don't strike me as a man who can be bought, Colonel. But you'll trade, I reckon.'

De Wit went to the window. Kept his back to Connie when he said: 'Let me remind myself about you, my cockney friend. You've got the best part of four million acres of Namaqualand staked, and you've swept aside all the opposition Dirk Jorgesson had allowed to hamstring him. He was fortunate in his choice of partners finally. Except it was not his choice, but yours, eh? The Ministry of Mines has confirmed your rights to prospect and develop the sites at Mkuse and Meir, Portland Cement is very interested in your perlite, and the estimated turnover of your companies during the coming fiscal year is a cool £2.5 million. Correct?'

'Close enough.'

'There are inaccuracies?'

The question was sharp with surprise.

'Not one,' said Connie. Thinking, *Let the man talk. He*

wants something. Wait for the catch. He's done too much homework not to have a hook he wants baited.

'I ain't no small boy nicking toffee apples,' he added.

De Wit nodded out at the crashing heat.

'You wish to bring not only plant from an Iron Curtain country, but also two Hungarian experts who are probably agents of the Kremlin. My government's policy on that is very clear: Total embargo. And these many thousands of pounds in sterling you had brought in cannot be above question, can they? Yes, my friend, you need my protection and a great deal of help.'

'That gets it said.'

De Wit turned slowly and stroked a long upper lip.

'It must be abundantly clear that your criminal record is no secret to me, either. . . .'

That bloody Clive Spring, Connie thought.

'. . . From your first appearance at Tower Bridge juvenile court to your recent coercion of an entire jury to secure the release of your brother. Those facts alone should have barred your entry into this country without chance of appeal. So does it not strike you as strange that you are allowed to come and go with seeming impunity?'

'You're gonna tell me, right?'

'Unruffle your feathers. Don't act the injured party with me.'

'I'm calm enough. You just put me in the same class as Clive Spring. I understand it, but I don't have to like it.'

'He has his own peculiar talents, as you have yours. He is an asset, has made himself invaluable to me, and enjoys the protection of Republican Intelligence. Isn't that what you're asking for?'

Connie thought he must have misheard. Must still be jet-lagged.

'Have I missed the tram or what? You're like our mob, MI5?'

'Much more than that, Conrad. My department is a weapon I've forged to ensure the survival of an entire nation. The only white tribe in Africa. The only true

Christians on this dark continent. Republican Intelligence upholds racial and moral purity, suppresses socialism, liberalism, Black incursion and intermarriage with lesser races. All the things you appear to believe in, must believe in if you and your embryonic empire are to flourish. Look at your own country, choking itself to death with its mad notions of brotherhood and equality, giving your Black and Coloured immigrants equal rights in law. England is a museum of yesterdays without a tomorrow in sight. They've given away the birthright of the future generations because no socialist has the sense to see the wider issues of a nation within a community of nations. They talk of hospitals, welfare and schools, but they forget to look beyond their borders and see their enemies for what they are. They are criminals, neh?'

'I ain't arguing, but that's flying flags. It don't tell me what you want.'

De Wit's eyes hooded and flared.

'Obedience. Total and unquestioning. Without it you are finished in South Africa.'

Connie felt the floor dip under his feet.

The bastard means it.

'Are we talking money or what?' he asked.

'There will be "donations" to clandestine funds, but they are small nothings for the future. And you almost achieved what I need from you without knowing it, my London sparrow. Those cleverly forged documents you presented to clear your heavy plant through Customs? Next time, you will use that method to bring in items of interest to us. Armaments we are unable to purchase for ourselves.'

Connie had chewed through his cigar and soured his palate.

'Just like that?' he said sarcastically.

'Exactly like that,' said De Wit.

'And for that I get my Hungarians and their plant?'

'Why not?'

'And my money?'

'I could have taken your train robbery money any time

I chose or choose. Never forget that.'

Connie's 'Thanks' was as faint as he felt.

'There is a man in London who deals with an armaments firm in Hamburg. You will enquire about the availability of Bloodhound missiles and spare parts for our Centurion tanks. Do you need to take notes?'

Connie wiped his bitter mouth.

'A man who keeps the prices of hundreds of metals in his head can remember that little shopping-list, Colonel mate.'

De Wit nodded.

'We should be friends, Conrad. Don't make me your enemy.'

'There's no cherry in that cake, Colonel.'

'Meaning?'

'You're pulling the strings.'

Christ, Connie thought, *it's like hoping Julius Caesar keeps his thumb up when you're down in the Colosseum with a trident up your jaxie.*

'Keep that firmly in mind at all times. There are several Black political activist groups enjoying the protection of the Wilson government in London. Here is a list.'

Connie stared at the neatly typed addresses and sucked his teeth.

'What's the strength of this, then?'

'I want these offices burgled and every scrap of paper in them shipped back to me through this agency. Memorise the list; you can have nothing written down.'

'That I can handle with a hand tied.'

'Personally. No third parties.'

Connie agreed with a nod, too tired to argue.

De Wit opened a cabinet and chinked bottles.

'Now I imagine you'll accept that drink you so badly need?'

'Not many,' Connie said with feeling.

'When can you leave for London?'

'Couple of days?'

'There's a flight at midnight. Be on it.'

Connie accepted a tall Tom Collins.

Yessir, yessir, three bags full, he thought. *Bastard.*

Vinnie Castle covered a book of Robert Graves's poems with *Popular Mechanics* when Bulstrode whistled and threw a shadow across his wheelchair, grinning at his taste in literature.

'You'll be on Shakespeare next.'

Bulstrode wadded his jacket and lay on the grass.

'I got browned off with *Tit-Bits* and *Reveille.* Charlie and one of the doctors bring me things to read.'

Bulstrode chewed on a length of couch-grass.

'Your Charlie hasn't got time to skim a headline. Busier than ten hives of honey bees. No time for reading.'

'Is that right?' said Vinnie.

'Yeah, and our Prophet jumping down the shaft without waiting for the lift was only for openers. And he swears he doesn't know how he got there. How did Charlie get him so finger-tamed?'

'Like all of us, he has his ways.'

'Like nobody else, Mister.'

'It's your twopence, Buller. Your Mother Hubbard.'

Bulstrode rolled up on to an elbow to squint through dappled light.

'He's resigned the force, you know.'

'Who has?'

'Prophet. Gone off to Dorset to manage some trout streams. Out in the open air away from enclosed spaces. He missed his retirement dinner, too. Couldn't face the ride up to the top floor of the Hilton. Broke down and blubbed all over Dillman.'

'Poor old Dildo. Bet that took the shine out of his trousers.'

'Laugh and I'll kick your one good leg. They managed to save it, then?'

'And some other bits and pieces. And I ain't laughing at your precious Quill, neither. This is a smirk, part of my medical condition. And kicking all that expensive surgery'd be against the Hippocratic Oath. I've got more platinum in me than your average jeweller's window.'

'Remind me to hold you for ransom sometime.'

'I heard Limehouse turned Queen's.'

'Hundred and twenty-eight official statement forms filled with small writing and all usable in court. But never a mention of Argyle Square.'

'King's Cross ain't Bethnal Green, so why mention?'

'There's a funny story about that. Gordy and Maurice was thick as thieves long before Gordy went on the Troys' strength. He used to half-mind Maurice when the Elephant mob tried to push in on that manor, and Maurice liked him around the toms. A safe bet with him being a raving iron. And the fact that Gordy was very tasty in a cobbles straightener. Maurice offered Gordy to Archie first, did you know that? Charlie and Archie wasn't having any, so Gordy became one of Tommy's tarts instead.'

'Ain't funny in my book, Buller. Just sensible.'

'What's funny, my unidextered friend, is Gordon topping a mate and a tom for a couple of grand Maurice would have more than likely bunged him anyway. And then letting that skinny tom top him with a pair of scissors? It doesn't ring true. Forensic reckoned she couldn't have had the strength to stick him that well. Not bang nine inches of steel through his ribs and both lungs. But, then, people find a lot of strength when they're fighting for their lives. A bit like you, my little bantam.'

'And I love your smiling ways, too.'

'Seems those shears was slammed home by a size-nine shoe. We lifted street-dust from them.'

'So she was a whore with big plates. So what?'

'She was bare-footed when we found her.'

'Now, ain't that shocking? The other toms in that crib must have had her shoes away. There's no morality amongst them sort. Dear oh dearie me. Tut.'

'Lay off, Vinnie. We ought to nail all three of them on Limehouse. Lean on him and get to Charlie.'

'Back to Charlie, eh?'

'Back to Charlie.'

Vinnie shook his head and accepted a lit Dunhill.

'It's a sunny day, Buller. Plenty of shadows to chase if that's your pleasure. Me, I'd rather fish and wear a flat hat. I'd have more chance of earning a bit than you have of getting your hook into Charlie's mouth. You're a rotten fisherman anyway.'

'There's no statute of limitations on murder, Vin. That particular file might just stay open a lot of years.'

'We won't hold our breath, then, eh?'

Bulstrode's sudden grin made him boyish in the sunlight.

'Maybe not. And there's other fish to fry. Like this face Sadler and the Harolds.'

'Who?' said Vinnie.

'Damn but you're getting predictable. I've been around you too long, I guess.'

'That mean you ain't staying for tea? Even if I can con you a rosie and wad from one of the nurses?'

Bulstrode put his cigarettes away and shook grass clippings from his coat. Stood and brushed off his trousers, and watched Vinnie flick his cigarette-butt at a nearby chestnut.

'Answer me something straight for once, Vin?'

'Maybe.'

Vinnie shaded his eyes against glare.

'How is it Charlie earns loyalty? You know and I know he's topped a good half-dozen the hard way. Yet he holds Archie up as if he was still worth something, and I'll bet he never forgets flowers on Queenie's birthday. He's harder than the Harolds and rottener than the Troys, and yet you all look up to him. An immoral bastard like him. Why, for Christ's sake?'

Vinnie watched his cigarette-butt smoulder on a root.

'Who else is there?' he said quietly.

Dotty and Ingrid chattered as Wally drove Naomi's Mercedes west towards Zeerust, his face set in a rare sulk.

Bloody women. Say one thing. Do another.

Heat melted the straight brown road into upfalls of dun, and liquid snakes of shimmer layered the lower sky with false horizons. The veld was a winter-yellow sprawl of biscuit and saffron, distant acacias danced in the soft and molten air, and Wally dozed at the wheel with nothing to look at but noonday glare.

'Must be love, the way he's not listening,' said Dotty.

'Why wouldn't Naomi come?' Ingrid asked a second time.

Wally caught her eye in the rearview mirror.

'She's a woman, ain't she?'

Ingrid played with her white picture-hat.

'Well, it isn't every day you get invited to watch a film being made, and I'm sure she wanted to meet all those stars.'

Wally checked the roadmap against the highway.

'Business, she said. All-fired keen last night. This bloody morning. . . .' He shrugged. 'Women.'

Dotty bit into a chicken sandwich.

'Haven't *you* got it bad? No, Wally love, it's me she doesn't like.'

'Nonsense,' said Ingrid.

'Daft.' Wally swigged chilled beer from a bottle.

Dotty's laugh was a fall of tinkling water.

'Come on, you two. I'm jam-jars and she's chandeliers. My old mother scrubbed out for the likes of her and was glad of it. Class is class is class, and I ain't got it. I got Pim instead.'

'No argument there. You'll have him going straight next.'

'And why not, I'd like to know? Pim could if he wanted. And, Wally, you're both most of the way there without knowing it. And your Charlie's halfway a gentleman except he don't know it, Ing. We could all live the good life over here. I may be a daft moo but I can see that plain. So long as I don't have to wear long frocks and talk lahdie at plonk parties all the time.'

'It was De Wit talked her out of coming,' Wally said suddenly.

'What?'

'De Wit. Naomi goes all stiff when he's around. I'd like to know what makes that face tick. He's got her and her daughter both jumping through hoops.'

'I like him. Even if he is a copper.'

'You like everybody, Dot.'

Dotty brushed crumbs from her mouth.

'Naomi, too, as it happens. I was born loving everyone. Maybe that's why I've been such a naughty girl all my natural.'

'Until Pim,' Ingrid smiled.

'Until Pim. Yeah.'

'How can anybody like bloody De Wit? Or that tosspot Spring?'

'It doesn't cost anything to be polite, Wally,' said Dotty.

'Only an arm and a leg.'

'Ignore him, Dotty. He's angry because Naomi couldn't come with us. Let him sulk; he's not spoiling our weekend.'

'You're right, Ing. You and me are lucky to have the fellas we do. I'm even learning to knit things. And Wally could do worse than get his feet under Naomi's table. You can frown, Wally Harold, but she thinks the sun shines out of your elbow.'

'You're right,' said Wally.

'I am?'

'Yeah, you are a silly moo.'

Then they were all laughing with Wally trying not to let beer come back down his nose and to keep the car straight. There was an odd metallic clunk and the wheel went dead under his hands. The pedals were just pedals under his pumping feet as the car veered and slewed from side to side.

'Can't hold her.'

The Mercedes swung right to chop through scrub.

Carved a furrow through a bank of red earth.

Wally yelled, 'Hang on,' and hit his head on the dash.

The Mercedes crested a rise in free fall. Hung suspended, tipped left, skimmed an outcrop of rock and sailed on and down. A big grey baobab came up into the bonnet and crumpled it. The windscreen became flying crystal shards, and a gullwing door opened to throw Wally clear. He thought he saw Ingrid fall away on the other side before he was in red dust with flailing limbs.

Monkey-fruit rattled out of the baobab branches and bounced down the incline ahead of the falling car.

Wally heard metal and a woman scream. Stone teeth tore through his clothes and skinned his face. Thorn lashed up around him and he was caught up, head down over a long scar in the earth.

Winded and helpless, he heard the final grind of impact before a great brawl of high-octane hurled fragments of bodywork into the air. Flame came with a wave of heat, seared the scrub and rock, and the thorn-bush he was caught up in came alight like an untidy torch.

Wally threw himself outwards and watched himself fall a long way on to his face and continued to plunge into the dark of unconsciousness.

Wally came back to crawling in dusk and the smell of scorched earth. One arm was just hanging, and there was a lot of pain in his torn shoulder. He lay and thought about that for a long time before he got sensible enough to use what was left of his shirt to tie off his arm and pad out his broken collarbone. When he saw his blistered hands they began to hurt, too, and he stopped himself thinking about his face. There was a faint and persistent voice that called him back, and he began to crawl towards it.

The gully took a long time to scale, and when he did roll up over the edge he found the shell of the Mercedes in a blackened patch of burned scrub. He stumbled over a burst suitcase and saw what was left of Dotty lying in the back seat on naked springs with its hair and dress gone. The top of one shoe remained green. The rest was just bone and charcoal.

Wally took the time to be sick and listened for the voice again. Tried to call out and couldn't. Sucked on a stone to bring moisture into his mouth and called Ingrid, hoping the voice hadn't just been inside his head all the time.

There was darkness now and he had to listen hard.

The voice was low, conversational, and came from the

darkness of dark kloof. Stones rattled when Wally got too near the rim.

'Ing . . . rid?'

Was that me? Try again.

'Ingrid?'

Stronger. Better.

'Don't come any closer.'

'I'll climb down. . . .'

'No, Wally. I'm too far down and the sides keep falling in. I can see the stars and they're a comfort. Go for help.'

Help? Where?

'I can't just leave you.'

'Yes, you can. And you must. I'll wait here.'

'Do . . . are you hurt?'

'I can't feel anything, but I can move my head. Go along now, please. Go along. . . .'

'I'll hurry. . . . Swear. . . .'

'Take care, my dear.'

Wally could find no words. His eyes leaked and salt stung his burned cheeks. He shambled away and stumbled on to the empty highway to listen for traffic. He thought he had heard something in this distance, but which direction it may have come from defeated him. There were no lights. No houses. Just him and the brown road and the sky and the veld.

Wally began jogging towards the brightest sky in the heavens. Stumbled through the Lord's Prayer missing some of the lines. Trying to remember them was something to occupy his mind.

'Hallowed be . . . Thy Name . . .,' he chanted as he jogged on doggedly.

No accident, Wally son, he told himself when the words would no longer come. *That Merc didn't just go off the road by itself. But who'd come after us? Who'd want poor little Dotty dead? Somebody having a dig at Pim? Getting at Connie through me? Keep jogging. Keep jogging.*

Or Naomi. De Wit can't be that out of sorts with her. No, something else. Something other.

Keep jogging, son. Don't fall.

Ingrid? Ingrid to get at Charlie Dance?

Wally almost fell. Saved himself with his one good arm and kept going as all the stars in the universe wheeled overhead.

Who's got the arm to reach this far and have us over?

Who's got the nous to fix a jam-jar like that?

Wally saw Sadler and Spring with their heads together inside his head and couldn't lose them. Saw Charlie Dance in shadows with a levelled gun and no emotion on his face. Saw him pick up the phone and listen as he was told Ingrid was dead. Saw Charlie come after him without hurry. After all of them for the sake of the girl lying in a gully with a broken back and only poor old Wally to get her out.

Stay alive, girl. I'm running. See?

When Wally's footsteps died away Ingrid listened to the sides of the kloof crumble in slow drifts of dust and shale. Kept her eyes on the stars so far above her, wanting to touch them if only she could raise her hand. She could move nothing but her eyes, so she lay quietly with her panic whilst the small predators gathered and a hyena called his mate from a high kopje.

Come back for me, Wally.

Please?

Mercifully, nerve damage prevented her feeling the first rat begin to feed on her foot.

CHAPTER TWENTY-TWO

THE NIGHT SKY had pressed him down against the highway too many times, but he had to go with the blackened thing that had been Pim's wife padding alongside, haunting his conscience. Ingrid kept telling him to take care very quietly, and Wally wished her voice would go away. Begged her to as he reared towards the brightest star in a tangle of bedsheets.

A dark kloof split the brown road and became Naomi's cleavage in a dim bedroom as she laid a cold towel on his blazing forehead and hushed him with her soothing voice.

'You didn't come with us. You should have. . . .'

Wally shook sweat from his head and tousled hair.

'But then you'd be with them. The girls. The girls. Have they found the girls?'

'Long ago. Hush, it's only a bad dream.'

'How long ago? When?'

'A week ago. But you knew that, and you will again. Just a lapse of memory. You were in hospital then. It'll all come back to you.

Hospital?

'Gotta phone Pim, tell him. . . .'

'He knows, my dear.'

'And Charlie Dance. Explain to Charlie how it was. . . .'

'Conrad took care of that when we were in London. I told you about London. I came back yesterday, Conrad's coming today. Any moment now.'

'Connie told Charlie? Told Pim?'

'Yes, my dear.'

Wally's head slowly cleared and the burned thing no

longer lingered in the shadows.

'You shaved me this morning. Said my face was knitting nicely.'

'It is, my love.'

Charlie would not go away, and his shadows were darker over Naomi's shoulder. Wally pawed the air to bring him closer to explain something. But the shadows had not listened before. Would never listen.

'But they do know? They really know the girls are . . .?'

'They know.'

'And they are, right? They bloody are. . . .'

'Yes. The funeral's tomorrow in Kensal Green.'

A car door slammed, and steps hurried towards the house.

Wally shrank against the sopping pillows with haunted eyes.

'Charlie?' he wispered.

'No, my dear. Conrad.'

'Don't let Charlie in, love. Don't let him in.'

'Colonel De Wit's downstairs. You're quite safe.'

'Hold me, Naomi. For Chrissakes just hold me.'

And Naomi did as Connie and De Wit locked horns in her living-room.

Connie told Harry the Crack and Sailor Mailer to stay in the car, and he swallowed a benny to keep himself going as he went up the path to Naomi's house. The return flight had been savaged by storms, and bolt lightning had run the length of the aircraft. Sleep had been a stranger for four days now, and Connie wondered if he would ever close his eyes again.

Another day, another benny, he told himself wryly, wondering how long he could keep going like this. *Just to tuck up with Alicia and give her a proper seeing-to before sleeping the clock round. Some chance.*

The houseboy led Connie into a long cream and chocolate living-room where hunting trophies stared down with bright glass eyes. De Wit fixed Connie a long Tom Collins, his long face sombre.

'I hear you're fond of these.'
'You hear a lot of things.'
Connie rubbed gritty eyes, and his voice sharpened as the alcohol hit home with the benzadrine.
'First Wally, then London, right?'
'As you wish.'
De Wit jerked his glass at the ceiling.
'Your brother was extremely lucky; that's bad country up there. Just the other month the local Kaffirs burned a man and woman to death for practising witchcraft. Said the woman had made their children sick and the man had sent lightning to kill their cattle. They'll hang of course; we have to chastise them for the dangerous and savage *skepsels* they are. Your blacks don't do that in the Old Kent Road yet, eh?'
'Not without an argument, they don't.'
When did I ever see a cow trotting down the high street? Sides of beef hang on butchers' hooks and milk comes out of bottles where I come from, you Dutch berk.
'I had your brother brought back by helicopter and thought it best he recuperate here rather than in hospital. One of our medical staff comes in every day. He's strong, and he'll mend quickly. Naomi, broth and kindness should see to that.'
Connie ghosted a smile.
'He's too dumb to die.'
But something don't sit right here, Colonel my old cock. Like you're covering something up. Tucking our Wally up out of sight is only part of it. Got to be.
'Let me freshen your drink.'
'This one's melting nicely, thanks. I'll just look in on my baby bruv and have it away. Talk tomorrow.'
'Seeing him can wait until tomorrow; the talking can't. He's sedated, and better a woman's breast than yours, eh? Dirk's gone up to Meir for a few days, so you'll have your own breast waiting for you in Melrose.'
Connie said, 'Stop talking and say something.'
De Wit's harsh Afrikaans accent cut softly.

'Alicia can wait a little longer. She sits in her house surrounded by the English antiques you bought her. I approve of my god-daughter having the best that money can buy and, given time, I might approve of your liaison with her. I don't give up what is rightly mine readily, remember that.'

'Nor do I, Mister.'

'Clive Spring is very valuable to me.'

'What's that got to do with me and Alicia?'

'Nothing. Directly. But he has been overly zealous.'

'Like talking poetry and taking snaps with that bloody camera of his? The one that points one way and takes a picture somewhere else? All he's ever done around me is talk and drink too much, and boast about how he's a friend to the Blacks when it suits. It don't take a big brain to work out how he's suckering them daft bastards into bunnying up something you can use against them in court. All them house-arrests and detentions he reckons he's brought about don't rate beans to me, so why should I give a toss for what bloody Clive Spring gets up to?'

'To make that clear I have to go back in time. It was Spring who introduced Dirk to Malcolm Sadler, and had Sadler contact you and the Troys to finance his mining interests. And with my blessing. It was unfortunate for Dirk that he met that man of yours, Vic Dakin, and lost so heavily at the gaming-tables, because that brought a man called Charles Dance into the picture.'

Suspicion reddened Connie's earlobes. He crossed a leg and listened hard with breath whistling in his nostrils.

De Wit stood at the unlit fireplace between long elephant tusks and made the ice in his drink tinkle as he turned the glass with a casual wrist.

'Sadler has made several errors in judgement since then, only matched by your own stupidity in certain matters.'

Connie squeezed his empty glass and felt his heart trip in his chest. Wondered where all this was going.

'I blame myself,' De Wit said. 'I do not like to deal with Jews, and that clouded my own judgement. I dismissed the notion of dealing with the man Ogle for that reason but, then, I knew nothing of this man Dance. He has made it necessary for me to revise my plans quite drastically. Cut away a lot of dead wood.'

'That wouldn't include me, would it?' Connie asked.

'Not as yet, Conrad. But Sadler has become . . . an embarrassment?'

'I elbowed Sadler aside donkeys gone. If you know so much, you should know that.'

'You should have liquidated him.'

Connie shook his head and stared with nothing to say, and the start of a migraine coloured his peripheral vision. De Wit could have been lecturing boy soldiers in front of a blackboard.

'You're a criminal with delusions of grandeur, Conrad. You can only be of use to me if you have the will to keep all I have allowed you to accrue. Your mines and Alicia are at stake here, recognise that. And also recognise that you have no choice but to listen to what I have to tell you and do nothing whatsoever about it.'

Connie's teeth ground together. Nodded with marbled eyes.

'Your word, Conrad.'

'OK, for Chrissake.'

'Sadler was told not to make himself visible to Ogle or the man Dance, but he chose to ignore that advice, that directive. And the result was Dance bought and sold Jorgesson like a piece of prime meat. He became involved with the train robbery and was instrumental in getting your money here, something you could not have achieved yourself. And Sadler, in his infinite stupidity, thought to hit back at Dance and yourself for his own warped and selfish reasons. Ergo the car smash, which brings us back to Spring.'

'That Welsh offal?'

Connie was standing on shaking legs, his face suffused with rage and hypertension. The glass shattered in his hand, and blood ran down his cuff.

'Yes, Conrad. Spring thought to be of service to Sadler. It was he who effected your brother's accident.'

Effected? Connie thought. *What kind of language is that? Our Wally with a busted boat and second-degree burns, Dotty and Charlie's crumpet well dead. . . .*

'And you let it happen? You just stood there and let those two pissheads . . .?' he choked.

'I was not a party to it, Conrad. Nor did I condone it. You have to see the total picture. I needed a network of agents in London, and who better to choose than men like yourself who are already outside the law? Men who lie, cheat and kill for their own ends. Men who will do anything for profit. In one way you chose yourself, didn't you?'

The truth of that raced in Connie's head. To go after Spring would cost him everything he had so far achieved. And with the train robbery money gone there could be no going back to London. He would be a target for the rest of his life. There had to be a way of pulling his chestnuts out of the fire. But how? He looked at De Wit, hoping for answers.

De Wit handed Connie a bar towel to staunch the blood.

'You will work with Spring as I direct, and no harm must come to him, agreed?'

Connie wrapped his hand in the towel and flopped into a chair.

'Agreed.'

'You will burgle those offices in London.'

'I already turned one of them over. The stuff should arrive next week. And I've put feelers out on the armaments. Hamburg says "No problem".'

'Then, you have no problems yourself, do you? You can proceed with your mining operation as planned, and Clive Spring can continue to function without fear of reprisals from you.'

Connie thought of Charlie Dance. How he had looked when he heard about Ingrid's death. How he had looked from Harry to Sailor and back to himself, his eyes like wet slate as he asked oblique questions without emotion or inflection.

'I ain't the one you have to worry about, Colonel. Believe me.'

'A last drink before you go to Alicia?' said De Wit.

'Why not?'

If Charlie comes, and he will, he'll earn a six-foot hole in the bush. But how will take some thinking on, not that it ain't time that Harry and Sailor earned their poppy.

H'm.

But, first, a night with Alicia.

The drizzle drizzled and Kensal Green cemetery was a huddle of old memorials and headstones and dripping trees. The man by the railings wore a black armband and did not look at the woman who came along the pavement to share his umbrella. She listened to the reedy voice reading the burial service before saying: 'Rather rare, wouldn't you say?'

'It's just a funeral, Lady.'

'A double funeral I meant.'

'Two women. They were friends.'

'Close friends?'

'They would have thought so, but they're closer now. That's for ever out there, Lady.'

The woman's veil blew in against a wayward nose.

'Yes,' she said. 'I rather think it is.'

The man said nothing with a closed face.

'You knew them?'

'Yes.'

'Well?'

'One of them. But what man knows any woman well?'

'Some have . . . instincts.'

A man in black stepped from the distant umbrellas to sprinkle earth to the sound of the carrying pulpit voice.

'Does that man have . . . instincts?'

'Pim? Yeah, but his wife died instantly they say.'

'And your friend?'

'It was different for her. She was blown clear of the car

and went down into a deep gully. Her back was broken in the fall but she lingered for a couple of days. By then the rats and white ants had got to her. Both coffins came home marked "Unviewable". D'you carry cigarettes?'

'Sorry, I don't.'

' "Unviewable." That was hard to take. Until I learned to remember her the way she was . . . before.'

'A small comfort, but a comfort all the same.'

'Some. But not a lot.'

'You aren't going inside?'

'I don't go to funerals.'

'No other car was involved? In the accident, I mean?'

'No other car. Nobody for miles.'

'No, that fits. Loss of steering, no brakes. An impact explosion. The middle of uninhabited bush, survival prospects zero. Yes, that's how it must have been. Lonely and very, very terrible for her.'

'You ain't clairvoyant?'

The man's question was flat. Disinterested.

'Not I. And I'm a complete fool about machinery. I only know what my husband told me. And he only knows what Mr Spring told him over the telephone. That kind of accident is rare, Mr Spring said. Rare, but always . . . fatal.'

'Sounds like your Mr Spring was there.'

'My *husband's* Mr Spring.'

'Still sounds like he was there.'

'Doesn't it, though? He could have been following in another car. To make sure, you know?'

'He could have.'

'Was she very beautiful?'

'I . . . thought so.'

Drizzle followed a knot of mourners away to the chapel and the waiting limousines. Pimlico stayed where he was, his face wet from more than rain. His coat shone as the sun came from behind cloud to glisten in the droplets on the dark material.

'He'll need a friend,' said the woman.

'He's got one.'

The man held a railing with white knuckles.

'You?'

The man nodded. Unable to speak.

'I'm grateful you allowed a stranger to share this sad moment with you. Thank you.'

The man let his hand rise and fall, making a fist.

'Stopped raining.'

He folded his umbrella and shook droplets on to the sodden verge.

The woman almost touched his arm before stepping back.

'I have to go. I'm seeing my solicitor, Mr Thrupp of Lincoln's Inn, at four to finalise things. Leaving the country is such a wrench and, with the servants gone, packing is such a burden for a spoiled bitch like me. Just the two of us rattling around in that huge house for two whole weeks. You do understand?'

'Empty houses are all dark corners.'

'*Au revoir*, then.'

'Thanks . . . for dropping by.'

'If only things had been . . . different.'

'Carry cigarettes next time.'

'Next time, Charlie?'

'Goodbye, Margot.'

Vic Dakin sat on the veranda in a rattan peacock chair, his feet up on a cane stool, enjoying the cool morning air.

Rain had washed the foothills of haze, and the trees on the distant rim above the Yan Oya river were as clearly cut as Lotte Reininger stencils against an ocean of lapis lazuli sky. A single boa of cloud feathered out from the Buddhist temple on the high western tor, the thinning outer strands marzipanned by brazen sunlight. In the shadowed basin, still heavily dewed by a brisk downfall of seasonal rain, teapickers walked the long rows of *Thea sinensis*, bowing under their woven baskets, quick brown hands pecking out at the ripest plants.

The old woman who came with the rented bungalow brought tea and honey cakes on a tray and went away soundlessly, just another shadow in the heavily carved teak building. Stone elephants guarded the steps to the veranda and a tame mongoose hunted the crevices for snakes, one eye on Dakin's robe pocket where a fresh chicken's egg might be hidden. The mongoose showed his grey-white belly to the sun and washed his whiskers with hard swipes of his front paws, clucking and sneezing with pleasure.

Dakin sipped dark mashed tea and let honey cake melt on his tongue, cleansing his palate of last night's cigars.

The man on the bicycle would soon join him to drink endless glasses of tea and occasional Manhattans, and polish his rusty English whilst Dakin added to his Sinhalese vocabulary; each man only too anxious to fill his time with subjects other than crops, weather and local politics.

Dakin was lonely in exile, and Dr Ashram Jhanna was his only worthwhile companion.

True, Dakin enjoyed the nocturnal services of a young local girl, but she had no conversation in any language. Once she had bedded 'M. Tournier' she was off back to grandmother's house before the sun rose, her rupees tied in a red handkerchief, too wise to let the gossips see her leave the fat foreigner's house.

Even the rich silks Dakin had brought her from Colombo had been resold to put food on her grandmother's table for her hordes of brothers, sisters and cousins, and although she gymnastically strove to earn her money under the whirling bedroom fan she made no attempt to show Dakin any fondness. She wanted dowry enough to attract a certain estate-worker's younger son, not become permanent consort to an old foreigner who smelled like a wet elephant and tore holes in the night with his thudding snores.

Dakin mourned cynically.

After almost five months in Ceylon, I have a mongoose and Dr Ashram Jhanna (Retired).

Dakin no longer saw the *carte postale* view.

The heat jaded him, fear of reptiles kept him from walking the lush grounds, and sex without warm lies was as dull as combing dandruff from his thinning fringe.

Dakin whistled and held out the egg. Listened for Jhanna's squeaking bicycle.

The mongoose came in a short dash. Flowed to a halt with a bobbing head and erect whiskers. Nuzzled the egg and Dakin's plump knuckles, 'chitting' with mock anger at the oval 'enemy'.

'Chit yourself.'

Dakin watched the animal roll on to its back and lay the egg on the upturned belly. A natural juggler, the mongoose kicked the egg into the air and rolled to catch it between his shoulderblades. Caught it a moment before it hit the polished stone floor. Curled into a ball and bit a hole in the shell to lap the albumin, saving the yolk until last.

Dakin wagged a finger.

'Connie, you're a predator. Just like your namesake.'

A car exhaust exploded on the river road as it took a run at the steep gradient to the crest where Dakin sat. A familiar sound signature. The unmistakable sound of Probaka's pre-war bull-nosed Morris.

Probaka delivered mail and newspapers once a week, and shopped in the township when Dakin was too idle to make the tedious journey in the imported Renault he could not get serviced, even though the French attaché in Colombo had done his level best to be helpful. Bringing automobile parts that were not Empire- or British-made into the colony was frowned upon. The staff at the British High Commission had been quite snotty with the plump and balding 'Frenchman', as were the tea-company officials Dakin had tried to court socially. The memsahibs were the worst. They called him 'The Frog' behind his back and thought it to his face, alienating him further from the small and smaller-minded European community.

Even when Ceylon follows Mother India down the road to independence the tea companies' economic stranglehold will prevail. The British will still rule the island by pursestring. It might just as well be 1864 for the average native, instead of a full century later.

Is this me talking? Dakin wondered.

What the hell have I ever cared for the have-nots in this world? Ingrid and her dead mother wouldn't know me. I'm not sure I recognise myself any more.

The old Morris stalled outside the bungalow as it usually did, and Dakin heard Probaka kick the offside wing.

'As usual, eh, Connie?'

The mongoose listened with his head cocked.

Probaka loped down the path between the Butea trees. Called greetings and blessings to enlarge his gratuity. The mongoose took his egg off to a corner. Probaka did not only kick cars.

Dakin stood when he saw Europeans follow the Hindu deliveryman down the path just as the Tamil doctor wheeled his ancient Raleigh through the gate. Dakin cuffed the windchime for more tea.

Probaka slyly watched Dakin study the men behind him. Saw him pale under his deep tan and thought he might witness fine gossip in the making.

'I bring you more saabs, Saab. I bring them in my most wonderful very British motor-car.'

'For which I thank you,' Dakin said in dialect.

A languid blonde man in white strolled beside a short fussy man with large ears and a crumpled face, and a heavy brassbound briefcase cradled in his arms. Dakin knew the man in white was 'something' in the District Commissioner's office, and he had last seen J. C. Hatton when Quill's squad had raided the Windmill Street office and Connie had taken Dakin and Jorgesson back to South London where he fed voltage up into Dakin's. . . .

Dakin pinched a sweating brow. Paid Probaka for the newspapers, invited Jhanna to lean his bicycle in the usual place, and waved the two Englishmen into chairs.

Is my exile ended? he wondered.

Probaka took his money away to gossip over a glass of *char* with the old woman in the kitchen, and Jhanna took the mongoose on to his lap to play with his silver beard.

Holmes, the Englishman in white, said it was a sticky old day and one never really acclimatised, did one? He dabbed at a receding chin with a spotless handkerchief, and Hatton just looked desiccated.

Fine rain sped in with the tea, hammered the garden with brief energy and stopped, leaving the earth to steam as it dried.

Dakin crossed a hot thigh under his robe and sipped fresh mint tea.

'It's very good of you to come all this way to be sociable,' he said.

Holmes squirmed.

'Ah, not quite that, I'm afraid.'

'If the heat bothers you, perhaps you should have stayed in Surrey or wherever it was you were born.'

'Surrey?'

Jhanna adopted his music-hall English.

'Jolly fine cricket team, jolly very good. But I'm having to be warning you, this very moment and now, India has jolly splendid Test side this year.'

The mongoose nudged the cake on Jhanna's plate, smearing the willow pattern with yolk.

'These men will not talk cricket, my friend. Not with you, and most certainly *not* with a Frenchman,' Dakin said in rapid Tamil.

Jhanna wiped crumbs from a troubled mouth.

'They are bad tidings for you?' he said in the same tongue.

Dakin inclined his head.

'Damned if you don't speak the lingo,' said Holmes.

Jhanna ignored Holmes.

'Surrey is a rotten side this year anyway. Kent is the better team. If I may excuse myself, my friend, I will walk in your garden until they have gone.'

'It is they who should be excused, Ashram. We will talk just as soon as they have gone back to their safe unheathen compound where we cannot taint them with our un-Christian ways.'

Jhanna waved a long index finger.

'Take care, Victor, you are turning native.'

Holmes made a feeble effort at politeness.

'Don't let us drive you away, old chap. . . .'

Jhanna walked from the veranda with a stiff back.

'We will talk Pali, the sacred language of Buddha. To cleanse your house.'

He clucked, and the mongoose followed him into the trees.

Holmes shifted a buttock in a creak of rattan.

'Sorry to have offended the old fellow. They are damned touchy, though.'

Dakin shrugged and smiled to himself.

'His culture was old when your semi-illustrious forebears searched each other for lice and painted themselves woad blue. He also has a First from Edinburgh University and professed in Bombay for ten years. Not bad for a native, and a bloody sight better than your scraped Third from St Andrews, Holmes, *old* boy.'

Holmes coloured.

'But it is best he's gone. And do remember I could have had you brought down to the Hill Station under escort had I chosen. Made all this very official.'

'Decent that you didn't.'

'It is you who has the spot of bother, not I.'

'Ah,' Dakin mocked, swearing mentally.

Here it comes, my old Vic. The frighteners.

'Truth is, there's something anomalous about your papers, entry visa and so on. Even your nationality is in question. Truth is, you've caused a bit of a stir with the dear old bureaucrats down at the capital. And back in the old country. All beyond me of course, but they've sent a pretty stiff directive, and it's filtered down to me.' Holmes mopped the bridge of his nose.

'Ah,' Dakin teased again.

'They haven't quite declared you *persona non grata.*'

'Yet,' Dakin said, needing a drink very badly.

Holmes agreed with a nod.

'Not quite yet. It's the paperwork, you see. Takes time.'

'And I can always appeal.'

'Well, you *could*.'

'Or take refuge in the French embassy.'

'Ah, not that, you can't. Not actually an embassy, old man. And the French aren't that keen to take you in. Interpol and all that rot.'

Hatton ran a finger round his collar and pinched the knot of his tie. Cleared his throat and said: 'My legal advice to you is to co-operate. In the fullest sense of the word.'

Dakin chimed for drinks.

'Archie's parrot does talk. How've you worked this flanker of an oracle, J.C.? Fucking Inter-flaming-pol? You must have greased half the palms in the western hemisphere. You crafty old tosser.'

Straight back into the old cockney speech patterns as if I'd never been away. And Holmes looks like he's taken a wet kipper across the kisser. Sod his tight-knickered arse. Got a face like a boiled baby.

Holmes's hot and damp nose twitched.

'Interpol, quite. They seem to want you back in London rather badly. They had thought to send out some policemen, but Mr Hatton came instead. And the DC thought, well, you'd do the decent thing, seeing the way things are. . . .'

'The way things are? And would a toffee-nose like you ever know how things are the way they are? Speak English we can all understand. How exactly *are* things the way they are?'

Holmes slapped a leg.

'I rather think you have no choice in the matter. You go back to London at the first opportunity.'

Dakin slammed the windchime with a palm. The old woman came out of nowhere, and Dakin asked what everybody was having. Holmes wanted a whisky drowned in soda, and Hatton said he would suffer a small sherry. When they were served, the old woman went back to Probaka and their musical voices drifted on the warm morning air.

Dakin drank deeply to feel the fire of good brandy in his fluttering belly.

'Money buys choice, Holmes. How much do you earn a year? A thousand? Two? I'll treble it just to get that wizened old bastard out of my house. Forget the DC and the other form-fillers, take the money.'

'Ah, the bribe. The DC rather thought you'd try the old backhander. But even an *Oxford* Third has some backbone. No can do, Dakin or Tournier or whatever your real name is, and no apology.'

Dakin gulped his drink and padded across for a tall refill. Pleased he poured it without a tremor. Fear cut at the fatty tissue around his heart, biting like colic. The lush garden was a brilliant checkerboard of green through the teak lattices.

'What have they got in London?'

'Don't forget Milan, New York, Valletta and Rome,' Hatton said through slatted light.

'Rome?' Sweat prickled Dakin's spine.

'The piddling Old Masters fraud that ties you to the Troys.'

'And New York?'

'The airline-ticket frauds.'

'I don't go down alone, J.C.'

Hatton scratched his upper lip.

'Events have rather overtaken you there. Scotland Yard already have the Troys for murder; they need you to sew up the pieces relating to your involvement with Connie Harold.'

'Leaving Mr Chas Dance out of it, I suppose?'

'Do I know that gentleman?'

Hatton helped himself to another sherry, and Holmes denied himself a second Scotch.

'You have five days to put your affairs in order, Dakin. I shall have to leave a couple of my chaps with you, of course, for form's sake. They'll be discreet and a bit vague if asked why. Best for you, best for the colony.'

Dakin felt giddy. Blamed the brandy.

Holmes slapped his other leg.

'I'll just go and sweeten up old Jhanna. You and Mr Hatton will want a quiet word alone, I shouldn't wonder.'

'Don't bank on it,' Dakin snapped, watching him make his way through dappled shade.

Hatton polished his glasses and patted Dakin's hand. An uncharacteristic gesture.

'You've got five days to salt your poppy away, Vic. More than enough time if you haven't already. The filth will deal, you'll see. Turn Queen's Evidence and blame it all on Connie. You'll survive; you always have.'

'I wouldn't make it into court. Connie'd kill me dead.'

'I can gainsay that.'

'Backed by whose word?'

'Archie's, Charlie's. We've had tabs on you since you ducked out of Mitre Street and took a plane from Heathrow. You came here via Brussels and Karachi. Think straight; we could have given you to Connie any time we chose.'

'Why didn't you?' Dakin scrubbed sticky eyes.

'Because of Ingrid. More so now she's dead.'

Dakin didn't believe he heard aright until Hatton nodded solemnly, suddenly misted by tears Dakin never knew he had.

'Connie did it? Did he?'

'It amounts to the same thing, Vic.'

'She's worth five years with remission, right?'

'Charlie thinks so.'

Dakin made fists for the first time in his life and felt them pulse and swell with anger.

'We'll get 'em J.C., eh? Promise me that. We'll nail them to the cross?'

'Charlie's already working on it.'

'He should have dealt with me straight off.'

Hatton just smiled.

Dakin sighed.

'I guess not. And I can spend the five years totting the interest Connie's money's earning me. That should pass the time.'

When Probaka's Morris rattled back along the river road, Jhanna came back to find Dakin weeping with quiet desperation.

'They left policemen. That is bad.'

Dakin sobbed laughter.

'Not so bad with the Troys tucked up for murder.'

'Tucked up? In bed?'

Jhanna flinched when Dakin embraced him, completely bemused.

CHAPTER TWENTY-THREE

THE CHINAMAN in the shiny suit took himself down Old Compton Street past the phoney Post Office van, turned into Eyetie Antoni's delicatessen and waited for the two elderly women to terminate a squabble over the price of mozzarella. When they had wound down into sullen and breathless silence, he bowed, smiled with gold and porcelain teeth, and presented a card bearing his name under the red imprint of his family's *chop*.

'I, Fook', he said.

' 'S why they's so many of you buggers.' Eyetie's maternal aunt took the card through to the back parlour with a show of bad grace.

Fook's eyes glittered at the insult and decided her extreme age was reason enough not to kill her with the edge of his hand. Although a beating with bamboo wands, especially on the soles of her unbound feet, would sweeten her disposition. Masculine shouts brought the aunt scurrying, and she was servile when she ushered Fook down the dark passage. He liked that. It proved he was talking to the right people.

Eyetie set his Guinness aside to shake hands and bow and wave Aman Lee Fook to a seat opposite Archie Ogle. Archie snapped fingers at Fast Frankie Frewin to see him jump to serve Fook with a properly iced soda water. He had given Frankie 'the heavy finger' about his keeping 'face' with his old friend from Hong Kong with: 'Chinks is big on the old manners. The more "face" a face has in a Tong, the tattier he dresses, the quieter he is, and the more respect he expects and gets. Modesty goes with power, Frankie, so dress sober.'

Frankie found a corner to stand in, thinking: *And keep your mouth closed. Let them think you're stupid without opening your mouth to prove it, as the old mother used to say. Archie may be older and smarter than God's Uncle Jack, but he didn't ought to have kept this meet secret from our Chas. Charlie may be walking around with smoke in his eyes over his Ingrid's topping, but it don't mean he's gone daft or soft-centred. If anything, he's harder. You could cut diamonds on his minces. Just like this polite little Chink with eyes like bits of wet kerbstone.*

Frankie pretended to doze. Listened hard.

The opening pleasantries over, Archie talked opiates with Fook and Eyetie, described a courier network between New York, London and Amsterdam in such detail Frankie was more than ever convinced Archie had not been idle beside his swimming-pool all those months. And from what Fook said it was clear he and Arch had met in Valletta and Hong Kong and travelled to Pakistan more than once.

Horse from the Chinese mainland would come in shipments of edible seaweed, ginseng or frozen racehorse sperm. Eyetie's New York cousins had the East River ports squared through the dock unions, and one of Fook's factories was busily producing hollow madonnas for the first shipment to the New Jersey chapter. There was some problem supplying the West Coast through Baja California from bases further south in Lima and Buenos Aires, and Fook suspected the interference came from none of the usual government agencies. Archie agreed caution was necessary when they dug to discover who was blocking them, but his slow quiet voice was confident as he leaned on his heavy cane and held Fook's eyes with a smile.

Frankie was dizzy with all the geography, but he could not fail to see Archie was on top form and planned to present the whole deal as a *fait accompli* to Charlie when he was good and ready.

Like he's back and Charlie's just another overcoat on

the firm with a mouthful of 'yesses' when Archie snaps his pinkies. How long would Charlie swallow all that crow? Twenty minutes? Ten Christmases? And he never rated Eyetie as anything more than he looked, a second-stringer who dressed like a refugee from an Oxfam shop, so what happens if he's supposed to act as gopher between Antoni and this fucker Fook?

Frankie almost missed the profit projection Fook made for the first trading year in his quiet musical voice.

Eleven million plus? That's four train tickles in a row.

Nobody could elbow that. Not even Charlie. That kind of poppy turns any three-day sulk into a yahoo and a backflip. I'd even throw a leg over the old cow I'm married to for a slice of that kind of action. Moustache or no moustache. . . .

Frankie rubbed dry hands together as the meeting came to a close and remembered to let Fook refuse another drink of carbonated water. Caught a vague look of approval from Archie as he levered himself out of his seat and offered a big brown hand to the diminutive Chinese. They bowed with their heads almost touching, exchanging Cantonese as Eyetie toasted their success with a hand over their locked fists. Halfway through a second bow Archie's head snapped back as though he meant to bellow laughter at the ceiling. But his eyes had crossed and his jowls were the colour of old crusted port. His cane took Eyetie's stout from his hand and dashed it to the threadbare carpet, smashing the glass to smithereens against the brass scuttle. Fook hissed as his hand was crushed by Archie's grip and he staggered under Archie's falling bulk with the suffused head flopped over a thin shoulder. They hit the floor together and Archie made sounds like brakes binding on a steep hill before he went slack inside his clothes.

Frankie knew the heart had failed as he turned the body and felt for a pulse in the flaccid neck. He let Fook roll out from under the still body and get to his feet without help. Tried to force a pill through the locked teeth and knew it was too late when the mouth yawned and the swollen tongue poked out at him with a last sigh of dead breath.

Eyetie raked fingers through his hair.

'He ain't croaked? Say he ain't.'

Frankie sighed and laid a hand on the unmoving chest.

'Can't, can I?' he said.

'He can't die here. Not here.'

Fook said something that could have been a farewell.

Frankie's mind was in overdrive. This was one crisis he had to handle without running for help. There was no Vinnie to call on. No Charlie.

'Nor he won't, Eyetie. Get Froggy in here. We'll get him away in the Roller.'

'What about our deal? I can't tell New York "No". Not now I can't.'

You whingeing old tom. Got to get Doc Rudge.

Frankie reached the telephone off the bar and pointed a finger at Aman Lee Fook.

'The deal, Eyetie? He talks to Charlie, that's where your deal is, in Charlie's pocket.'

'How can that be?' Eyetie wailed.

'Because there ain't nobody else.'

Frankie dialled from memory.

'This is true?' Fook asked Eyetie.

'Not fucking many. Yes.'

'Then, you will get this Charlie. Now.'

Frankie told Doc to hold when he answered.

'He'll find you, Mister,' he said. 'Now get Froggy in here, Eyetie, you daft tart.'

Eyetie yelled for his aunt.

'I will not be hard to find,' said Fook.

'You can bank on that,' said Frankie. 'Hello, Doc. . . .'

'An unanswered phone is unlucky, Malcolm.'

'It's no longer our telephone, Margot. Let the incoming people answer the damned thing.'

Sadler forced a last suitcase into the maroon Daimler on the drive outside Chartings Hall.

Margot tried not to cry.

'Not until noon. Chartings is still mine until noon. And there are seventeen minutes to go.'

'My God, but you're a trial. Are we to have weeping fits all the way across the equator?'

'Shan't be a tick.'

Margot hurried through the empty hallway where Buhl cabinets and tapestries had flanked a grandmother clock with nursery rhyme characters on the face. The telephone rang from the centre of the withdrawing-room floor, lit by a dusty beam of sunlight. She lifted it as Malcolm slammed the boot closed, and the growl of a removal van became a persistent dull throb as it halted in the drive.

'You're blocking the drive.'

Sadler's challenge was answered by ripe and righteous cockney.

'Hello?'

Margot gave her number for the last time.

'If this is Chartings-bleeding-Hall we're in the right place, my old matey.'

'Mrs Sadler? Alfred Thrupp here.'

'But you're blocking my egress!'

'Your what, Squire?'

'My way out, you dunderhead.'

'Hello?'

'Sorry, Mr Thrupp, my husband is having a last fling in the drive.'

A removal man scratched his chin at his foreman.

'Is he talking English or what?'

'I was asked to call you at this precise moment by a Mr Dance, Mrs Sadler.'

'Who?'

Salt stung Margot's eyes, and she brushed a sleeve across her face and turned her back on the argument outside.

'Not so much of the name-calling, guvnor. We'll back her up.'

'Mr Charles Dance. He has instructed me to wish you *bon voyage* on his behalf. He did not wish to neglect your departure despite being out of the country himself.'

'How very like him,' said Margot, wondering if it was.

'A very personable gentleman, and I was paid very handsomely for such a pleasant task.'

'Did Mr Dance happen to say where he had gone?'

'South Africa, I think, if he said anything at all. . . .' Thrupp became as vague as J. C. Hatton had instructed him to be and Margot could almost see him frown behind misted bifocals. Heard him add his own best wishes and ring off a moment before the GPO severed the service with a loud click.

'Legally, you owe me fifteen minutes.'

Margot laid the dead instrument on the bare boards and listened as the house listened back. The fireplace sighed, a scale of soot fell on to the blackened hearth and a trapped bluebottle snarled in a pelmet. Margot brushed face-powder from her sleeve and went out into warm sunlight.

The removal van had backed into the trees, its long tailboard overhanging the ha-ha above the sunken tennis court where she had once worked on her backhand volleys. The foreman leaned against the unlettered side of his pantechnicon and blew on his knuckles as though he had just bruised them against a jaw.

Malcolm used the Daimler's horn to hurry Margot along.

'Really, Malcolm, you're the giddy limit. Three minutes is hardly a lifetime. . . .'

Margot slammed into the passenger seat and stared at the man beside her. Her heart bumped to a momentary halt and she froze with her hand on the door-handle.

'But you're not Malcolm. . . .'

Sodbonce patted his dark wig and the padding around his waist.

'Says so on my passport, Lady. Chas says I'll pass with my mouth shut closed, so you do the talking at the airport, right?'

Margot massaged her right breast.

'Where is . . . Malcolm?'

'Right here. Like I said.'

The foreman closed the big rear doors of the pantechnicon and banged on the side with: 'One away to you, Mister.'

Margot had seen him mourn alone at the cemetery in Kensal Green when she shared Charlie's umbrella outside the railings. Saw the dead face turn to her and nod at Sodbonce as he took the Daimler out of the gate with a cheery wave.

'Nice car. Handles lovely.'

'But this . . . isn't what I had in mind. . . .'

Margot's mind lurched as the car turned in a shower of gravel, leaning her outwards against the padded door.

'Shouldn't go to double funerals, then, should you?'

Sodbonce accelerated past hedgerows alive with finches, and the removal van trundled away towards the London Road in a spurt of blue diesel smoke. Turned a corner and was gone. Margot felt the shakes start in her knees and wrists as the enormity of what she had done bore down on her. She thought of asking Sodbonce to turn back, to stop the pantechnicon, to explain that it was all a mistake. Knowing she would only earn herself a short terminal ride beside her doomed husband. She looked ahead as the road unwound, thinking of life and the future and the infinite possibilities suddenly opened up to her. Listened to Sodbonce explain how things were to go in his cheerful and barbaric cockney.

'When we get to Buenos Aires I'll go missing. Bit of a swimming accident, I shouldn't wonder. Clothes on the beach and no body. You'll get the local coppers looking all over, post rewards and all that toffee, generally do it up brown, right? Hang about for a week or three before coming back. You can handle that. Charlie was well convinced you could. He ain't wrong is he?'

'I'm beginning to doubt if that's a possibility.'

Sodbonce sucked a tooth with a lopsided grin.

'There's millions who'd have to agree with you. Just you relax and leave everything to Uncle Soddy. I'm dead easy to get along with, and I've always fancied a bit of a conga in Rio. It is on the way, right?'

'It's on the way. What would have happened if I . . .?'

'Back there? If your bottle went? Two for the price of one. Would have been a shame 'cause Charlie must like you.'

'Does he . . . Malcolm?'

'That's me, ain't it? Yeah, as it happens. Rio for carnival. Nice one.'

Margot snuggled as the Daimler quietly ate the miles to Heathrow. Thoroughly content with her lot.

The solemn blue eyes of the Mares Serenitatis and Crisium regarded Connie from the August moon riding in the dark tidal swell of the Thames below Blackfriars Bridge. He had stared at the river for almost an hour, his elbows on the granite parapet, thinking things through.

Connie was exhausted physically and mentally, and too much benzedrine had strung his nerves to breaking-point. Fragments of recent events, snatches of wild conversation, of too many arguments and confrontations milled in a mad patchwork of meaningless complexity, and were further confused by his stubborn need to dip into them again and again; losing himself and the picture as a whole in small flashing jewels of irrelevant detail.

The long and wonderful last night of sexuality with his Alicia before they breakfasted with Wally and Naomi in her sunwashed yard. Wally being fed lightly coddled eggs, unable to use his heavily bandaged hands or do more than mumble through blistered lips as he stumbled through his night and day on the brown road under the bright star. Dribbling yolk as he said: '. . . and all the time there was this green car behind me. I could hear its tyres on the road before I heard the engine . . . always just out of sight . . . except for a couple of times when I hid in the bush to bring it closer . . . never really there when I tried to look at it. . . .'

And Naomi brushing hair from his blistered and skinned forehead. Dabbing his mouth with a napkin. Wally's despair and the bottomless look Connie could not match or hold as Alicia traded looks with her mother and stroked Connie's thigh under the sunsplashed tablecloth.

'. . . Good you wasn't there, Naomi. There was nothing left of that side of the car after it blew, and Dotty was just black, just burned to nothing. . . .'

The image swilled with the river, and Wally slept through the rest of the day without releasing Naomi's hand, unaware that Connie had to fly out that night for London on De Wit's orders. Stealing the afternoon in bed with Alicia, and Dirk suddenly in the doorway still dusty from the Meir site, the excitement of his discoveries there dying as he took in the last bumps and grinds before they noticed him. Dirk ignoring Connie. Rounding on Alicia with accusations about her affair with De Wit. Screaming: 'First the mother, then the daughter. Or did he have you both at the same time? Bloody lucky for me the man's not bisexual, or he'd climb my back like the bloody rock spider he is.'

Dirk spilling a sample of nitrate bentonite over the bed and his wife's damp body. Connie jumping to restrain him before Alicia's small fist bloodied Dirk's mouth. Her finger in Dirk's chest as she countered with: 'You *blaas japi*. You country boy. Rolling on the ground with Kaffirs instead of white women. You can't even have an affair with dignity yet you dare to blacken the name of a patriot? You're not fit to lick Uncle De Wit's boots.'

The thunder of Alicia's Afrikaans invective coming too fast for Connie to follow as dark wet cherries from Dirk's split lip dripped on to white carpet.

'And a cockney mongrel is better?'

Alicia with fists on her hips like a man.

'Any goatherd with an erection is better than you. I'd lift my skirts for Blacks rather than have you back in my bed. Go sleep in the garage like the *skepsel* you are. Or will you watch my "mongrel" take me here on the floor?'

Connie's laugh covering sudden Puritan shock. Pure little Alicia tumbled from her pedestal, replaced for ever by a woman of earth and passion. Words of his dead mother popping into his mind. Almost the last thing she said to him from her deathbed.

'A lady in the street, a mother in the house, and a whore in the bedroom. That's an ideal wife, lovely boy. . . .'

And Dirk running into the night pursued by Alicia's snarls.

The long flight home and Kelly producing the letter from a suit she was sending to the cleaner's. Alicia's frank sexual expressions in purple ink on lavender stationery. The blazing row that ended with Connie on the living-room couch until Kelly walked out in the morning. The crick in his neck that still bothered Connie eighteen hours later.

He flicked a tasteless cigar over the embankment as an empty train ground across the bridge to terminate at Holborn Viaduct.

Breaking into the ZAPU offices in King's Cross had been a doddle. But the offices of Christian Action in Amen Corner are in a different league. I just hope to Christ I can do better at Amnesty International for De Wit. Dirk's right, he is a bloody rock spider. I can feel him on my back now. . . . At least I've got duplicate keys to the office block backing on to Amnesty International's premises. . . .

His head pounding, Connie walked back to his Vanden Plas and did not see Nasty Nostrils's Minivan trail him to Fetter Lane and tuck itself behind a *People* delivery-truck.

Connie let himself into the deserted building and climbed to the top floor, reliving his final instructions to Harry the Crack and Sailor Mailer. Sure he had found the solution to his problems with both Charlie Dance and Dirk Jorgesson. When they were dead, Alicia would be his, and no more partners. . . ..

Connie went to the back of the building and opened a window high above the narrow courtyard separating the two buildings. No lights showed, and one of the windows across the way was open at the top.

Reach in with a coat-hanger and wallop. In.

Connie fetched the ladder he'd found in a caretaker's store and fed it out across the gap. Jammed it against the window-sill opposite and wiped off sweating hands that shook too much. He swallowed another benny and a downer to calm himself, washing them down with water from a tap in the cloakroom. Waited for the flare of light behind his eyes before ease came in a slow flood of well-being.

Takes longer every time, he thought, short of air.

He crawled out along the ladder four storeys above the ground and was across and inside the darkened offices before he knew it. Enjoyed a cigarette before going to work.

An hour later he dropped five plastic sacks of documents and photographs into the courtyard below and returned the way he had come. Tucked the ladder away and had a long swig of brandy from the hip-flask he had forgotten about. Hurried out of the building just as his euphoria warped to grinding fatigue. Locked up and buried the keys in a dustbin overflowing with old paper.

He was hauling the first two sacks out to his car when he walked into laughter. Late diners waiting for a taxi watched him throw what looked like rubbish into the back of his prestige car, and a woman in furs giggled.

Nasty Nostrils heard her say, 'The English eccentric isn't dead after all,' as he lay along his driving-seat with his mirror angled to see the street.

Connie slammed his boot and dropped behind the wheel, his judgement thrown by the woman and her hooray henrys, the constant jangle of Wally's hurt, Alicia's sleek body, De Wit's all-seeing eyes and his own exhaustion. Planned to rest up and come back for the rest later.

Sleep comes first, he told himself. *Tomorrow's soon enough to collect the rest.*

Nasty didn't give him the chance. He scooped up the sacks and drove them to Charlie at the Windmill Street office, correctly assuming Charlie would be more than interested in the contents, and when Connie went back to Fetter Lane after a sweating night of twists and turns he thought the sacks had been cleared by corporation dustmen.

Charlie leaned against a meat-locker in Smithfield and watched Sadler drowse at twenty thousand feet as he flew to the equator on an injection of scopolamine, still muttering after an hour of question and answer.

Charlie let him ramble as he had Fast Frankie and the Chinaman bring him up to date in Stripes Flynn's office over mugs of cocoa laced with rum.

Sadler dozed in a stream of consciousness he could not control.

The passenger with slate eyes made me talk and talk in gathering chill. Pressurised cabins are always cold at this altitude, but why sides of beef hung in the first-class aisles is as big a puzzle as the ancient steward checking my pulse and heartbeat with clouding breath that smelled of old books. He should have been retired from flying duties years before. This is an odd airline indeed, and Margot would have to complain since I'm too drifty to do it myself.

Drifty, drifty. . . .

Even odder how Chartings Hall exploded with Pimlico's left hook. Being thrown on sacking in a pantechnicon. Mewing behind a gag until the needle in the groin softened anxiety. Coming round strapped to a meat-trolley for take-off. Men packing a corpse in polythene and dry ice and laying it in a bronze coffin. The one with slate eyes who might be Margot's Telephone Charlie telling an oriental that Archie would die in Malta and be shipped back for burial when the time was ripe. All a matter of the right documentation and a phoney coffin being flown back from Hal Far.

Drifty and odd. . . .

But not quite as strange as slate eyes and the Chinese knowing how he had baulked Ogle's opening moves in South America using De Wit's expatriate Nazi contacts there. . . .

Sadler's eyes rolled with his mind.

He *had* talked to *someone*.

Realised he might *just* have mentioned *something* to Telephone Charlie. And it had been pleasant airing his knowledge about the Broederbond and Clive Spring's minor role in Republican Intelligence. Amusing to recount how Spring handled Conrad Harold. Had him praise a Black dissident when introduced to his wife after his trial. *The Kaffir mongrel had been guilty of course, and Conrad had lied like a Trojan. All part of RI recruitment techniques, and a pleasure to tell someone so anxious to learn. . . .*

Until I explained how I paid Spring handsomely to punish the man Dance in that clever and unusual way. . . .

'Shut the bastard the fuck up!'

Doc Rudge's hypodermic slammed Sadler into limbo just as Charlie stopped Pimlico burying a meat-hook into the drugged and garrulous face.

'Your way better be best, Chas.'

Pimlico's breath streamed in the frozen air, his face as dead as the face in the coffin. Knuckles whiter than his breath. Needing to fight Charlie to get to the man on the trolley who had his wife killed.

Fook watched Charlie's every move. How he was still and quiet and ready. Read every nuance of expression and body language like it was muscular prose. Assessed the cold control of the man beside Pimlico's hot madness and Doc Rudge's clinical detachment. How Charlie expected Pimlico to hand him the meat-hook without a word. The outstretched hand both gentle and demanding. Finally getting its own way.

Pimlico drooping at the shoulder.

Saying, 'Don't face me off like that again, Chas.'

'I won't.'

Fook grunted deep in his narrow chest at the calm lie. Smelled the raw carcasses on their hooks, the Buddhist in him offended by their bloody odour, the Tong in him excited by the prospect of working with the long-nosed and round-eyed Dance. The future could be pondered with serene optimism, he thought. Confident Dance would handle himself well in South Africa, even though the odds against him were enormous. It would be a great test for the man, and in prevailing he would be all the more useful to Aman Lee Fook and the Snake Tong. Eleven million was urine in the wind; his organisation made that amount in a single trading day from legitimate holdings. Fook was attracted by the need to expand into other areas for the exhilaration of the new and unknown, the vicarious excitement of seeing a man ready to take revenge without the usual assassin's paranoia.

It warmed his warrior's blood, and he was content to leave with the others to give Charlie a last few private moments with Archie's remains.

Night had come and gone, and Sadler was aware of what was happening to him. And could not scream or fight against what was inevitable.

Sandwiched between Charlie and Pimlico, the white Rolls-Royce had whirled him through the City to the Tower of London. Walked inside, Sadler had been sat on a bench by Bell Tower as Charlie and Pimlico puzzled over a crossword and the tourists thinned away. As the shadows lengthened they strolled him into the Chapel of St Peter ad Vincula and allowed themselves to be locked in by a whistling Beefeater to await the dark of the moon.

Stood in a corner without a sweet cigar to flavour the waiting, Sadler's drugged muscles were too relaxed to form words or cough to clear his gummy throat. Fitful moonglow splashed the painted altar with stained light and mocked his agnostic attempts to make amends, plead or call upon any deity to help him.

The Ceremony of the Keys passed with a brisk exchange of challenge and reply, the ravens slept on their perches below the White Tower, and the moon fell into the vague loom of the Thames beyond the curtain wall.

And Charlie Dance said: 'It's time.'

Sadler's masonic ring found its way on to Charlie's finger. He felt his clothes being stripped away, and the ancient floor flags struck cold beneath his naked feet. Pimlico opened the door with wire and an Allen key, and Sadler felt night air on his face in a great scald of fear. He was stumbled across cobbles and over metal hoops bordering a square of historic grass. He fell into a clumsy kneel on a square of stone flags, and his head was bowed over a brass plaque with a japanned inscription he knew without needing to read it. It marked the original site of the block where three of King Hal's wives had bared their necks for the Great Axe of State. Where his virginal daughter Elizabeth had finally rid herself of her tarnished favourite Essex after his monumental military blunders in Ireland.

Sadler's sobs emerged as silent trails of spittle.

Wind slapped them across his trembling chins as he tried to make sounds. Noises of any kind. His nose ran with mucus as Charlie Dance recited charges against him in a hating monotone of condemnation.

Sadler begged the voice and the trailing sputum to take themselves away. To give him back to himself. Allow him a last vestige of dignity before the end.

Pimlico's legs and an oak shaft formed a tripod of shadow in Sadler's peripheral vision. A dark axehead thumped against the grass, and the sharp leading edge shone. A last crescent of light before the total eclipse of Sadler's world, making him knowing and helpless and afraid.

He could not even flinch when Dance leaned down to speak close to his cheek, each word as sharply etched as the black and brass legend so near his face.

'You get to die twice, Sadler. And dead you're finally useful. . . .'

Useful? Useful dead?

The question screamed when Dance's breath retreated.

In God Almighty's Name? HOW?

A heel scraped on cobbles. Pimlico's smart black alligator shoes shifted. The axe rose and there was a grunt of hard exertion.

HOW?

The screaming question died in a fast whir of steel and the last shock of being nothing. Falling nowhere.

Sadler's head hit the brass plate with its right cheek and spun blind eyes upwards as dark arterial blood blackened the mossy lawn. His body toppled forward, and air bubbled in the neck-stump. Ordure soiled the flabby thighs as the arms spread themselves out across the York-stone flags with twitching fingers. The head stared and the body felt nothing as Pimlico severed the jerking hands with two quick strokes.

'It wasn't enough,' he said.

'What did you expect?'

Pimlico didn't know. He fed the axe into a sack with Sadler's clothes. Dropped the hands in and tied off the neck with stout twine.

'More. Something.'

'There isn't . . . anything.'

Charlie stripped off latex gloves when he had rolled the head into a heavy nylon container. Hefting it, he led off to the curtain wall near Traitor's Gate.

'Never, Chas?'

'No.'

Charlie sailed nylon cord into the dry moat and tested the grapnel's bite on the stone sill before sending Pimlico down into the darkness. Dropping after, he retrieved the grapnel and line and the container and paused to stare out over the cannon defending the reach above Tower Bridge.

'Just a feeling of loss. Hoping it's the last time.'

'But it ain't.'

'No. Maybe it never is.'

'I'm coming to South Africa, Chas. This won't stop me having that . . . last bastard.'

Charlie's grunt was almost a sigh. The night was heavy with things unsaid.

'I still miss her, Chas.'

'Maybe you won't . . . one day.'

'And nothing brings them back, right?'

'You got that right.'

They walked west along the embankment in silence and drove the Rolls across Chelsea Bridge to the coalyards of Battersea Power Station. Charlie flashed the heads when he parked and got out to strip naked alongside Pimlico, both of them dressing in new casual clothes. When they had bungled their soiled clothes into another sack a man in greasy coveralls took both sacks away to feed them into the incinerator, reducing them to anonymous white slag.

Pimlico took himself home and Charlie went to the Windmill Street office where Nasty Nostrils had crated up the Amnesty International documents ready to be delivered to Heathrow by special messenger, leaving a selection out for Charlie to pack into his attaché case.

There were four hours before his flight, and Charlie had a few things to tie up before he left. And coming back was something he didn't think about.

Eight straight hours had brightened Pimlico up.

He drove towards Heathrow, sorry he had not managed a brighter smile when Brixton Billy brought him tea in bed, his month-old beard shot through with grey and the bacon sandwiches cut as thick as doorsteps.

'You're a cross between Old Man Mose and the bloody Ancient Mariner, Brix.'

'And too old to be mothering you.'

Brixton poured strong tea into mugs and spooned sugar.

'You're looking at a retired schoolteacher off on his hiking holiday in France. I tried a monocle but it wouldn't stay in.'

Pimlico blew on his tea and automatically felt the cool side of the bed where Dotty usually lay. Felt the usual pang of loss and decided Brixton's tweed jacket with leather elbow-patches gave him a donnish air.

'So long as nobody asks you history or English questions, you'll make it. You're lost after twice two and "The cat sat on the mat".'

'Woodwork teachers don't know all that old toffee. A last shake and I'm off to Dover with me knapsack and roadmaps. Won't be no sweat once I get down the canals to Agde. I can get a job crewing on a yacht through the Med from there. Might even make it all the way to Cape Town by sea.'

Brixton shoved out his hand and spilled tea on the counterpane when he couldn't meet Pimlico's eye.

'Be lucky, you old tosser.'

'I'll light a candle for Dotty here and there, Pim. They go in for all that on the Continent, right?'

'Wouldn't hurt,' Pim had said.

'Yeah,' and Brixton had left abruptly, leaving his tea undrunk.

Pimlico parked in the multistorey carpark and took his bag across to the terminal. Spotted Charlie at the first-class desk as he passed, saw him keep the nylon container as hand-luggage when he went off through the departure gate with the check-in girl batting her eyelashes at him long after he had disappeared.

Pimlico grinned. It wouldn't take Charlie long to get squared away with something gorgeous when he felt able to put his mind to it. Still grinning, Pimlico slapped his ticket and passport on the tourist-class counter.

'Room for a little one?' he said.

The girl ignored Pimlico's wink and checked her passenger list.

Proves you gets what you pays for, Pimlico thought.

'Mr Parsons? John William Parsons?'

Now, where have I heard that tone of hobson's before?

'That's right.'

Pimlico turned to see an official with a hard salmon face and harder oyster eyes.

'Come with me, please, sir.'

'I ain't booked in proper yet.'

'All the same.'

The official pointed the way through a screened door, and Pimlico found himself in a hard white room with a lot of uniforms and Bulstrode.

'Now, what's your game, Buller?'

'Mine, or yours? You've been sussed, cocker.'

Bulstrode offered his cigarettes.

'Don't use 'em. And you better have more than Mickey Mouse in this rat trap for making me late for my flight.'

'To South Africa?'

'Correct.'

'You're not going.'

'Who says?'

Bulstrode tapped forms and a fat reference book.

'All this lot and me. We did get an anonymous on the old trombone, and how you hadn't declared your "previous" on your visa application. Then the South African embassy got on to us 'cause they'd had a call about this tasty villain trying to get into their country. But their call was from one of the tabloids, and the question was: Is South Africa a haven for Brit cons? Well, you can see, they'd be upset and want us to sort it all out this end.'

'And you're obliging, right?'

'Just part of my sunny disposition, Pim. And you didn't know you was travelling on a snide ticket, neither, eh?'

'That ticket come straight to me from—'

'Yes?'

Bulstrode looked interested.

Charlie got me the tickets, handled the visas. All that.

'Nothing,' Pimlico said.

'Funny thing, coincidence.'

'Is that what this is?'

'You turning up with the last of Vic Dakin's dodgy airline tickets on the very day we fly him home to face charges? I'd say so, wouldn't you?'

I wouldn't say nothing!

Pimlico turned one of Bulstrode's Dunhills between his knuckles whilst Bulstrode fumbled with Swan Vestas.

Charlie's stitched me up with all this tom-tit to keep me off that plane. Well out of the trouble he's flying into. I had the bottle for it, Chas. More than all the old toffee the law's about to put me through. They'll probably hammer me for parole violations, give me a compulsory medical so they can shine a torch up my jaxie to see if I'm smuggling illegal immigrants. Put me back in the slammer on technicalities. . . . Even baby bird'll give me grey hairs. Christ, Charlie, I ought to have this mob pull you off that plane. . . .

Pimlico drew flame from Bulstrode's match.

'Haven't had one of these in three years,' he said.

Bulstrode killed the match with a flourish.

'Myself, I never wanted white teeth enough to give up.'

Pimlico sighed in a gout of smoke.

'Bars and porridge attached to all this, is there?'

Bulstrode swivelled comfortably.

'Depends on you.'

'I don't trot hot bubbles.'

'Grassing ain't on my mind. Murder might be. Been a lot of heavy faces prancing back and fro to South Africa recently. Why was you hopping off out there?'

Pimlico shrugged to loosen tense shoulders. Glimpsed a forensic squad around a headless corpse at the Tower of London and thought Charlie must be stowing his nylon container under his seat. Figured Bulstrode couldn't know Charlie was aboard that plane, that he would have pulled him off double quick if he did.

'To see an elephant without looking through bars?'

'I believe *that* and you'll sell me a used car. I'm talking murder.'

'And these things are suicide.'

Pimlico stubbed the cigarette and didn't know what to do with his hands.

'Vic Dakin's talking straight murder.'

'That slag's a drunk driver when it comes to walking or talking straight. No chance. Dakin's got more curves than the Bluebell Girls.'

'Don't mean he ain't cut up rotten about his Ingrid. You and him ought to talk bereavement; you've got that in common.'

'He can scratch his own fur coat. They ain't my fleas.'

'You villains don't share your manly sobs, then?'

'You're well wrong there.'

'He wants it nailed to Connie's coat-tail, Pim.'

'With me as the hammer? No chance.'

'Better caution you, then. Before we both lose our sense of humour. Do I read from my card, or what?'

'Grass grows in parks, not in my north and south.'

'There's talking and talking. And – still off the record – all you have to do is convince our Vicky that Connie was in on her topping. Just quiet verbals, nothing written, right? He'll turn Queen's and you get to waltz out free than any pigeon strutting the cobbles. It's that or you fall for the eighteen months that's outstanding, pull another ninety days for a naughty passport and a probable year and a half for skipping during parole. And I haven't even started on your snide ticket. The airlines want to see some faces in the dock over that one. Don't let your face be one of them.'

I'm stitched up better than a hand-made suit, Pimlico thought bitterly, wanting more nails in more coffins. *Vic Dakin'll blame Connie Harold for everything anyway, so what difference would my threepennorth make? What should I do, Dotty? If you was here. . . . But you ain't, and Connie's got some blame due for that, right, love? Yeah.*

'OK, Buller. I'll talk to the slag. Alone. In private.'

'That's all it takes, Pim.'

All? Try standing where I am, Bulstrode.

A late call for the South African flight came over the Tannoy and sounded as distorted as Bulstrode's sense of justice to Pimlico's ear.

Be lucky for both of us, Charlie. You daft brave bastard.

CHAPTER TWENTY-FOUR

CHARLIE SHAVED and changed his shirt on the long descent to Jan Smuts Airport and was back in his seat for the bumpy landing. The Super Constellation taxi'd and the temperature aboard soared when the doors remained closed for fifteen interminable minutes. The first-class passengers milled about until they were asked to stand aside to allow a uniformed airline official aboard. He strode to where Charlie sat and frowned at him over a clipboard.

'Mr . . . King?' he asked officiously.

Charlie said he'd got that much right.

'Your passport please, Mr King?'

Charlie watched it being riffled through, was asked to 'Please follow me,' and went out and down steps into blazing noon shimmer. The concrete apron burned up through his shoes, and his scalp broke into sweat when security men with sidearms fell in on either side of him. They ushered Charlie through glazed doors into a shaded Customs hall, ignored the 'Whites Only' channel and lost the airline official when they turned Charlie up a flight of marble stairs. In a carpeted lobby they snapped salutes and sent Charlie into the shuttered light and expensive furniture of the VIP lounge, an overcool haven after the slamming heat of the airstrip.

'Welcome, Mr. King. I'm Lorenz Krepp. Treasury.'

The Afrikaaner wore an expensively cut suit of pale grey lightweight worsted, and the rose in his buttonhole was as waxy as a slick of butter on his narrow lapel. He waved Charlie into a pneumatic chair with a lethal Irish, sat opposite and made a tent of tanned fingers to beam over.

'This is Spring, my assistant,' he added.

Charlie nodded as if nothing mattered and made ice tinkle in his glass.

'Welcome to the Republic, Mr King.'

Spring did not offer to shake hands. He stood behind Krepp and toyed with a camera. A man who did not sweat, he licked a pale smile with a paler tongue, his skin untouched by the African sun. His bronze eyes flicked at Charlie as if he peered from under a rock.

Charlie ignored him and stared at Krepp.

'They kept my passport.'

'Naturally, Mr. King. Why should you be plagued by mundanities conjured by the bureaucratic mind? There are enough of *them* to take care of such trivia for you.'

Krepp oozed anxiety to please like sweat, and Charlie lashed at him with cold sarcasm.

'Aren't you one of *them* yourself?'

'Technically, my dear sir.'

'I made my own arrangements to be met. I hadn't banked on—'

'Our hospitality? Come now, Mr King, a leading financier like yourself cannot expect to come and go without some notice being taken. You must allow me the honour of oiling the way for you, eh? A small gesture of my humble regard for the great aid your people have afforded us in the arena of the . . . clandestine, shall we say?'

'I don't know what you're talking about.'

Krepp liked that.

'You see, Spring,' he said over a shoulder. 'Discretion, the hallmark of international banking. Hong Kong was most insistent that your privacy be considered sacrosanct. Most insistent, and quite rightly, may I say. True power does not need bread and circuses to amuse itself, neh, Mr King?'

Charlie savaged his drink and played along. It was clear that Fook had made himself useful by telex without being asked, and the nylon container by Charlie's foot began to burn a hole through his sock. It would have been pleasant to reach across and make Spring eat the camera he was so busy with.

'Hong Kong should not have bothered you,' he said.

'No trouble at all. They simply afforded me the pleasure of being useful in my own poor way.' Krepp skimmed his gold cigarette-case at Charlie. 'Turkish on the right, Virginia on the left.'

'Thanks.'

Charlie hoped his smile was enigmatic enough.

Krepp lit a Perfectos Finos for him with a gold Dunhill that tinkled a tune and returned Charlie's smile with interest.

'I should have offered you hospitality in my own home, but it was made clear to me that you would prefer the Langham Hotel. Also, that your social calendar has been firmly sketched in.'

'Wordy old Hong Kong,' said Charlie, his head buzzing. 'Shall we go?'

Krepp apologised for the short drive they must take to the bonded warehouse where Charlie's offloaded luggage was being processed through Customs. An air-conditioned limousine swept them across the airport to a long steel building where Customs men scurried with bills of lading and apologised for the several signatures needed to release the five crates and the long leatherette boxfile with ribbons and seals that contained Bonar Tree's escudos. Krepp countersigned with a gold pen and saw the crates loaded aboard a carrier vehicle to be delivered according to 'Mr King's' sealed instructions. Spring obligingly carried the boxfile of escudos on his lap when Charlie kept the container and his briefcase on his lap, and on the way to the hotel Krepp launched into his fondly held views on the current financial and political scene, summing up with:

'And is it not a tragedy that the international banking community is so hamstrung by the short-term placebos of the so-called Popular Left? Free trade was always the backbone of any successful regime, whatever its political hue, and no traditional statesman of the old school was ever so woefully ignorant of the need for a balanced foreign policy as these socialists we see in power in Britain these days. They see no further than the rickety fences surrounding their own national backyard, and ignore the needs and requirements of their international neighbours. They destroy honest argument with naïve hyperbole, bully when they should listen and discuss, and sulk when they do not understand. And does not their blanket offer of equality for all and sundry without the need to earn it kill off the individual's right to strive for excellence? To work for recognition in any field of endeavour like the arts, music or statesmanship? The trouble with the common man is that he is so very,. very common, and cannot perceive that only an informed and select élite can truly function for the common good. Am I to be considered no better than my clerks, my Kaffir gardener? Must we all sit in the dust with bowls of mealie-pap and deny our God-given talents by dropping standards to the lowest common denominator? Must excellence be swept away for the sake of the specious views of the mental pygmy? Should individual genius be lobotomised for the duration of this Golden Age of the Puerile? Shall we level all the mountains and live on the dull plain of mediocrity, subsisting on a diet of unrelieved boredom? Kill off all the eagles and allow the humble sparrow to prevail? Interbreed so that we leave the future to a mongrel race of small brown birds? Ach, the orchestra can only follow one baton, eh? And men such as you and I are born conductors, Mr King, and let them who can follow the score keep up as best they can on their chosen instruments, neh?'

'That gets it said.'

Charlie's bemused nod pleased Krepp.

'I knew you for a kindred spirit, Mr. King.'

'Almost a Broederbonder?' Charlie raised a hand in peace. 'The organisation that has no members and does not exist? But if it did exist you would be a senior member, I'm sure. Not that you can comment on that, eh?'

'Your own anonymity is precious, is it not, Mr King?'

'No more than yours.'

'A mere servant of the Treasury? Hardly.'

'A man can own more than one hat. But it's a hell of a trick to wear more than one at a time without looking like someone out of *Alice in Wonderland*.'

Charlie burned through another of Krepp's Perfectos Finos, allowed him to bully the hotel staff with teutonic efficiency, and Spring fixed them drinks as Black busboys filled the suite with fresh flowers. When the door closed on them Charlie laid a large manilla on the arm of Krepp's chair without comment.

'This is what?' he said warily.

'A sample of something that needs to find a home.'

Krepp weighed the big buff envelope on his palm.

'It bears no name or address.'

'Maybe because it's for eagles, not sparrows.'

Krepp's geniality thinned.

'You're teasing me with my own words, Mr King.'

'Not so as you'd notice. Just pick the right hat. One with colonel's stars on maybe.'

Charlie moved Spring away from the bar and stiffened his drink, watching Krepp's reflection rip the manila open in the mirror to leaf through papers and photographs before fanning them out on the floor at his feet.

'May I ask how you came by these?'

'Connie got careless. I got lucky.'

'You, too, wear more than one hat, Mr King.'

'Oh blimey yeah,' said Charlie, letting a silence gather as he met Krepp's eyes in the mirror. Krepp looked at the silent Spring and back at Charlie, put his drink aside and found a cigar to damp between pursed lips.

'Just what do you suppose these buy you?' he asked.

'Enough good will to get out of here in one piece.'

Spring started to say something and thought better of it. Charlie found complimentary cigarettes in a hardwood box and lit one. Shed his jacket and rolled his shirtsleeves. Turned on Krepp and grinned down at him.

'Customs men don't jump through hoops for bankers,

Mister. That makes you this toad's boss, right, Colonel De Wit?'

Krepp disappeared as De Wit shed the last vestiges of the assumed persona. He fingered the cigar, stroked a long upper lip and sat very straight in his chair.

'Quite an assumption, Mr Dance. Unfortunately for you, I have already taken custody of the five crates from the airport. That leaves you with very little to bargain with.'

'Waste paper. Check it out.'

De Wit snapped fingers, and Spring used the telephone to speak in clipped Afrikaans. Rang off and made a face at De Wit.

'Confirmed,' he sighed.

'Are we to know where the A1 documents are?' De Wit asked as he decided on another drink.

'Spread between here, Cape Town and Durban. I don't know how many law offices there are, but it should take you a couple or three months to ferret them out without my help. And even I don't know their exact location.'

De Wit nodded over the ice-bucket, was generous with soda and sliced limes and sat with a ramrod back.

'But your people in London do, eh? And they'll inform us when you're . . . safe? Very thorough, Mr Dance, but why did you consider that necessary?'

'What? With me as the young lady of Riga and you as the smile on the tiger? Leave it out, old son. You've finger-tamed Connie Harold into pulling naughty strokes all over London, and a lot of people have sunk money into his mine. I promised to watch their interests, and I couldn't do that under your hammer, could I?'

'Assuming that's true, I take it that your pretty box is the final payment?'

'Yeah, so let's hope Connie's hole in the ground ain't just a hole in the ground.'

De Wit allowed himself a short laugh.

'Come now, Dance. It would suit you very well to see this entire venture fail miserably. My sources are very definite about that. You wanted the money out of England, preferably lost for ever. If for no other reason than to teach your opposition a salutary lesson. You're a simple reactionary, aren't you? You want to avoid the revolution of change. Admit it.'

Charlie pointed a finger around his drink.

'Ain't that what you're doing right here? Keeping the *status quo* because your people can't handle change? Knowing that you wouldn't exist in ten years if you allowed a softening of attitudes to your policies? Don't kid a kidder, Colonel.'

'Do I sense disapproval?'

'No feelings either way. But you made waves in my town. Had berks like Sadler blundering about making trouble, cause a shooting war and me a lot of heavy aggro. Using amateurs like Sadler and Spring here, when you should have come to the pros. They're minnows in a river of pike.'

Spring muttered and fingered his camera. Spots of dull peach burned in his pale and sallow face when Charlie sneered smoke at him. De Wit leaned on an elbow, his farmer's face blank and brown, nothing in his narrow blue eyes.

'Are you planning to cause me some small . . . inconvenience?'

Charlie killed his stub in a ceramic tray.

'Where'd the profit be in that? You got it right the first time, Colonel. I want Connie's pack of cards to fall apart right enough, and I figure it will without any help from me. But I do have to look as if I'm keeping my part of the bargain, right? I have to walk around Mkuse and Ghost Mountain, inspect what there is to inspect and go back making happy noises. Let all this mining malarky grind to a halt in its own time and say "Shame" when all them long faces come looking for solace, hand out the fivers and put them all back to work for me. And in future, De Wit, you want something in my town, you come to the organ-grinder, not to his flaming monkey.'

De Wit showed mild surprise.

'You propose we should work together?'

'You think our worlds are so different? It's the winner who writes the histories, Colonel, not the loser. The Americans run around the globe pretending to be Coca-Cola salesmen, making noises like convenience food and fizzy drinks was the backbone of democracy when they subvert for their own ends. The Russians are close behind with their guns and butter and cynicism when they destabilise their poorer neighbours, again for their own ends; and us Brits have been well at the same game for three hundred years, so what's so different about what you're doing? You just joined the club a bit late, that's all. You want your patch, I want mine, how bad?'

'Well if crudely put, Mr Dance. Perhaps we ought to put that to the test, h'm?'

'So long as I can drink while you talk.'

Charlie mixed a gentle Irish and water.

'Do you know of a man named Dominic Keogh?'

'As it happens, why?'

Charlie wondered why De Wit was interested in Dublin Gerry's brother.

'A man capable of murder, would you say?'

'Well capable.'

'And competent?'

'He gets the job done.'

'That confirms my information. If I wanted him stopped from fulfilling a contract, could you handle that for me?'

'Money would have to change hands.'

De Wit shrugged that aside.

'I ask that because he and two other men have contracted to assassinate a political figure friendly to this regime. And since he is one of the few Black friends we have amongst our neighbours we cannot afford to lose him. I have warned his security personnel, but it would be simpler if the dogs were called off at source, wouldn't you say?'

Charlie thought better of lighting a fresh cigarette. He had checked back over the newspapers after Nasty brought him the sacks from the Amnesty International offices, and found that Connie could only have burgled one other building during his time in London.

'Them ZAPU papers came in handy, then?' he said.

De Wit put a lot of control into not reacting. Spring did it for him with burning cheeks and haunted eyes.

'Well?' said De Wit.

'I'll see what I can do. Is there a time limit on this?'

'Yesterday would be soon enough.'

'And I earn what out of it?'

'Freedom of movement, unless you wish me to lay on transport.'

'And have your tame constables breathing down my neck?'

De Wit had the grace to smile.

'Anonymity, Mr King?'

'A precious commodity, Mr Krepp.'

'You'll liaise with Spring here in the event you cannot reach me.'

'Fine,' Charlie said without shaking hands. And De Wit took Spring away, leaving Charlie with silence and the heady perfume of dozens of prime blooms.

De Wit watched Spring sag in the lift to the sound of Muzak violins.

'A knowing man, our Mr Dance,' he said.

Spring's mouth was dehydrated.

'He knows, Hendrik. That man *knows*.'

'Guesses perhaps. You got enough pictures?'

'What good are pictures if he . . .?'

'If he decides to ring your neck? Pray my people find those documents because he finds you, eh? Ach, Clive, the man is alone and friendless. What can he possibly do?'

Kill me, thought Spring. *Unless. . . .*

His brow was creased in thought as he followed De Wit to the black limousine.

Unless. . . .

Charlie had breakfasted and dressed when Harry the Crack

and Sailor Mailer came to collect the boxfile of escudos. They sat on the balcony under a striped awning with cold beers and their first cigarettes of the day, Sailor dark and withdrawn, Harry all smiles and suntan, Charlie quietly urbane.

'Playing Buffalo Bill up-country seems to agree with you both. How's Wally?' Charlie asked.

'Being nursed silly. Big girl that Naomi, eh?' said Harry.

He picked peeled skin from his nose, and Sailor gave him a silence to do it in. He pulled the ring from a second can and skyed it into space.

'Never met her,' said Charlie.

'So you ain't. He's missed something, eh, Sailor?'

'Just another lahdie scrubber after a bit of rough. That Wally's doing his brain in cosying up with her. He'd be better off back home like we all would.' Sailor wiped froth from his mouth with a calloused palm. 'And sitting here bunnying don't get that dough deposited at the bank like Connie wants. You forgotten who you work for, Harry?'

'Listen to face-ache? You wanna go running about in all this heat, have it away on your toes. It don't take two of us to make out a deposit slip. You got the car keys and the motor.'

Sailor stood and crushed his can. Pointed at Charlie.

'He's still the opposition, Aitch. This is just a truce till Con says otherwise. Right, Chas?'

'Maybe he'll let me know, too,' said Charlie.

'I don't doubt that.'

Sailor went away with a closed face and a stiff back, and Harry waited for the suite door to slam closed before he shook his head at Charlie.

'Missing his kids and missus. Ain't happy unless he's being nagged rotten and living off pie and chips, our Sailor. Gives him a fidgety mouth, so forget and forgive, eh, Chas?'

'Nothing. Ain't you missing the comforts of home?'

'Me and marriage never mixed. I tried it once, but it never took. Me on the couch and her upstairs in bed with six cats? Don't call that wedded bliss. No, this life suits and suits well, except for the potty way Connie's carrying on. Maybe I'm well out of order, but it could be I'm seeing the light for the first time.'

'That right?' Charlie sounded disinterested.

'I just don't want to be face down in pony knowing you'll end up smelling of violets. My gut's still only half-mended after that last crack at Mr Jones's club in Catford when I took a double dose of buckshot. And I could still get tucked up for that if I went back to the Smoke, right?'

'That's been well squared with Tall John.'

'Only if they don't change their minds. So, all right, I'm a tired overcoat looking for a way out. I'm coming up forty, Chas, long in the tooth for a cowboy hat and handing out big elbows to stroppy punters for baby earners. I want a bit of permanent.'

'Why tell me?'

'You're the man, that's why.'

'Tell that to Archie Ogle.'

'He ain't here; you are. Look, Chas, now Bonar's dough's in the bag, you could get to be yesterday's man right quick, you cotton? Connie's made noises about turning you over permanent. Here, before you get back home.'

'Sure of that, are you?'

'As sure as milk comes in pints.'

'OK, so I'm listening.'

'Yeah, with a shrug in your voice. We could handshake, Chas. Do each other some good. I get you off the hook out here, you keep a place warm for me on your firm if this mining toffee goes well wrong. I'll tell you what I told Wally, that De Wit and Jorgesson have got Connie well stitched up. Only Connie won't see it, and Wally's too humpty to take notice. They've both gone well soft over women and all them profits to see what's staring me in the face. I'll give you all of it if you handshake.'

'What does a handshake earn you?'

Harry reared back in surprise.

'Since when did you go back on a handshake? Your

rep's based on that. Firmer than concrete.'

Charlie listened to the rap of the striped awning. Sipped beer and lit one of Harry's Gold Flakes.

'Keep talking.'

'Get it said, right?' Harry scrubbed his head and opened another can.

'I'd say so.' Charlie flicked ash into the breeze.

'Connie don't like partners. Not in business. Not in bed. And that's Jorgesson on both counts, right?'

'So?'

'Connie had us put the frighteners on him. Break his windows in the middle of the night. Pump a few rounds into his house.'

Harry swallowed beer and belched softly.

'And?' Charlie prompted.

'Jorgesson shot back, and he's got this bloody great Alsatian. There was law all over the shop before we'd gone more than a hundred yards. But he's gotta go, Chas. And not just because of Connie having the big hots for Alicia, neither. With Dirk shoving up daisies I get the top spot out here, don't I? Get my feet well under the table. And that's me well set up for the rest of my natural.'

'So do it.'

Harry reddened and looked shifty.

'Ain't that easy, is it?'

'Not if your bottle's gone, no.'

'It ain't that so much as shoving the blame elsewhere. Where you'd maybe like it nailed. Get me?'

'Still your twopence, and you've got enough ale to lubricate your tonsils, Harry.'

'You ain't that slow, Charlie. You want who done your Ingrid, right? And I know who that was. So how would it be if I had a way of nailing him for topping Jorgesson?'

'You talk a good fight, Harry. That why your face is leaking?'

Charlie rapped Sadler's masonic ring against an eye-tooth. Stopped himself from kneeing Harry in half and throwing him bodily from the balcony.

'You'd make a pawnbroker sweat with them looks of yours.'
'Name me a name.'
'Won't do you any good. You can't lay a glove without my help, Chas.'
Charlie flowed upright, and his finger touched the tip of Harry's peeling nose. Harry crushed his can, and beer soaked his lightweight flannels.
'The name.'
'Spring. Connie let it slip after he saw how bad Wally was worked over. But you touch him straight and you'll have that De Wit well up your jaxie, and that's the final teddah, right? I can make it look like Spring triggered Jorgesson with his own shooter.'
'Give me a "how", Harry.'
'Spring loaned me a nice little Beretta when I lost my old Webley up at Mkuse. You see? We use it on Jorgesson and it turns up under Spring's pillow when we have Tall John Law waltz in on him. That way, you ain't laid a finger, De Wit can't save Spring from facing a topping charge, and we both get what we want. It's sweet as a nut.'
Charlie have Harry a long look and offered his hand.
'I'll buy it. But it's "we", Harry.'
'Wouldn't have it any other way. You won't regret.'
Harry pumped Charlie's arm up and down until Charlie looked at his wristwatch.
'When were you last at Jorgesson's?'
'In Melrose? Four, no, five nights back.'
'Have your car around front tonight around six. And bring Spring's shooter; we'll drive over for a recce.'
Harry drank up and brushed off his damp trousers.
'See you at six, then?'
'Oh, blimey yeah,' said Charlie. 'You can see yourself out?'
Harry took the lift to the ground floor and walked round to the hotel carpark where he leaned into a green Volvo. Spring sat at the wheel eating pistachios, his face stained green behind tinted glasses.

'We're under starter's orders, Clive my old Welsh harp.'
'He bought it?'
Spring's neck worked and his bony Adam's apple bobbed.
Harry had laughter locked in his chest. Already saw himself as Connie's partner with Jorgesson and Charlie out of the way.
'Bought it?' he said. 'Used all his pocket-money. But you better handle De Wit, son, or it's me and you for a serious up-and-downer.'
'No problem.'
Spring knew he would sleep well for the first time in days.

Charlie had binoculars trained on Jorgesson's house and he filled the car with dribbles of smoke. Melrose was a constellation of glow-worms in the warm and velvet night, and cicadas trilled and warbled in the brush beyond the verges. Harry took another nip from his hip-flask and shivered.
'You'd better lay off that stuff,' Charlie said, bobbing a Gold Flake stub on his lower lip.
'Settles my stomach, I told you.'
'You told me.'
Charlie lit a fresh cigarette and tossed the stub into the night.
'For someone who don't buy cigarettes, you get through the bastards at a rate of knots.'
'You told me. Where's the gun?'
Harry washed brandy into his mouth.
'Here where it always was. In my pocket. A shooter's only a shooter,' he mumbled. 'You've seen it. You've oiled it. You've bloody reloaded it. Even bloody polished the bullets. And it's still only a shooter.'
'It's a tool like any other tool, Harry. A dull chisel cuts the carpenter, not the wood. A lazy spring can jam a pistol. Dust can do the same. And forgetting to take the safety off can leave the face holding it with more than a daft look on his boat.'
'You told me that, too. And how you'd have preferred

a revolver on account of how they don't jam. Christ, Chas. . . .'

'Nerves, Harry. Just nerves.'

Harry wiped off the hip-flask and drained it.

'You? I've seen more nerves in a pulled tooth. Satisfied?' He shook the last drops of brandy on to the floor.

'They've just sat down to dinner. I say we go.'

'Yeah, then we can have a decent gargle at the hotel.'

'No, Aitch. Go in. Do it now.'

'But this was just a recce. I ain't—'

'Had enough to drink? Or d'you want to wait until the booze dies and you're all strung out wanting another soldier to kill?'

'I don't need a drink to—'

'Then, we make the hit. Let's go.'

'Don't push me, Dance.'

'Then, let me out. Forget it.'

'All-flaming-right, but it's—'

'I know. My responsibility.'

'Bear's-bloody-breath.'

Harry drove the car off the verge and coasted down into Melrose without lights. Hoped he sounded scared and drunk enough. A sideways glance at Dance reassured him: Charlie leaned back in his seat with half-closed eyes, humming something tuneless. He flicked his cigarette through the quarter-light, and sparks cascaded in the kerb.

Portrait of a man in control, Harry thought.

For maybe ten more minutes.

He halted the car on his handbrake and let the motor idle as Charlie had insisted. Opened the door and left it open when he stepped out, the Beretta a hard, cold friend in his hand as he waited for Charlie to round the bonnet and walk down the front path of Jorgesson's house ahead of him. He smelled roses and other fragrant blooms when he stepped into the bushes and let Charlie ring the door-bell.

The bastard's half in shadow.

'In the light, Chas. Where he can see you're friendly.'

Charlie centred himself under the porchlight when it

snapped on, and a dog bayed from the side of the house. Chains rattled and a lock was sprung, and the shadow of a man's head glanced off a lozenge of coloured glass set in the plain wooden door as it opened and swung inwards.

'Who's there?'

Recognising the voice, Charlie leaned further into the light.

'Hello, Dirk. Couldn't pass without stopping.'

Dirk flung the door wide and brought a heavy rifle up to waist height. Blinked and sneered at Charlie an instant before he found Harry off in the shadowed bushes.

'You?' he said to Charlie. And 'Harry? Christ, man. . . .'

Harry pointed the Beretta off into the flowerbed and suddenly sounded very amused and very sober.

'That's the bastard who shot up your house, Dirk. Now you can shoot him. Shoot the bastard, why don't you?'

Alicia called from somewhere inside, and the dog went crazy against the side-fence. Dirk pumped a ·30 30 round into the breech and cuddled the stock into his shoulder. Breathed out and hissed instead of shouting: 'You hairy-backed *rooinek* . . . *donner*. . . .'

His finger curled in against the trigger.

Charlie moved. Skimmed his hat back at Harry and ducked aside. Harry fended off the trilby and brought the Beretta around to bear. Swung a shade too wide and was correcting for a shot when Charlie went in low to mash Harry's larynx with stiffened fingers.

Harry tottered and took a knee up into the scrotum that raised him off the ground and turned his legs to rubbery tubes of hurting tissue that could not support him. He was puzzled when he tried to fall and couldn't. Wanted to grovel on the path and let it all happen to somebody else. But Charlie was in behind him and a shot squeezed itself off before Charlie took the Beretta away. Harry thought it lost itself in the hallway where Dirk was coming forward to shoot back.

Harry lost all interest when a steel arm locked across his impacted throat and he found himself sucking air through wells of salty warmth with Dirk planning to shoot Charlie despite Harry being between them.

Then the Beretta came up from somewhere below Harry's chin and put a spurt of flame into Dirk's waistline, jarring him back on his heels. A second shot blew a hole in flowered wallpaper as Dirk shook hair from his face and resighted. The bore of the rifle levelled with Harry's spangled eyes and stayed there until a third shot hit the big belly and drove a pearl button into Dirk's spleen. The rifle slid away down the path, and Harry slumped in Charlie's arms.

Dirk found himself looking at the ceiling, wondering why he had been allowed to be taken by surprise. Spring had promised something other.

Damn that rock spider of a Welshman, Dirk thought. *Didn't he promise Dance would come tomorrow . . . the next day? That he and Harry would swear he had needed to shoot in self-defence? Wasn't it a householder's right to shoot in defence of his property?*

Jorgesson did not see Charlie stamp Harry's feet into the soft flowerbed, leave perfect shoeprints in the soil and haul the big man away down the path.

Alicia's looking down at me . . . asking things I don't want to answer. . . . Of course I hurt . . . of course she should call the police . . . stupid woman . . . well rid of her. . . .

Jorgesson drifted towards death whilst Alicia became hysterical on the telephone and Harry gave hand-signals to Clive Spring's house, unable to talk.

Mrs Hannie De Wit left the telephone on the hall table and stalked back into the dining-room where her husband waited for her to serve dessert. She stood with hands on her ample hips and no longer cared that she sounded disagreeable.

'By the worm in God's apple, Hendrik,' she said, 'can we never have one hour of peace for dinner without some *dassie* of a government clerk calling to ruin our digestion?

I love my country enough to have you go out and die for it twice a week, but not during dinner, eh?'

De Wit looked over the half-glasses he used for reading.

'It's good of you to sacrifice me for the cause, Hannie. But who is calling?'

Mrs De Wit sat to dab her mouth with an orange napkin.

'When does one of your people give a name? I was schooled for too long to ask for names.'

De Wit pushed away from the table and wished his wife into a black Hades where nobody played bridge or spoke a word of Afrikaans. Somewhere like London where even the Kaffirs played card games like Christians. He listened to the voice from his office, grunted several times and massaged his long upper lip as it slicked with moisture. Said, 'Send my car and escort,' and went back through the dining-room.

'Important, I don't suppose, neh?'

Mrs De Wit expected the usual sour negative.

'Our god-daughter is widowed. I'd say that was important.'

'His heart?'

'Gunshot wounds. Don't wait up for me.'

De Wit went to change back into uniform and left his wife at the table where she smoothed her dress over her round belly and smiled at the candles.

The smile held a malicious and long-awaited delight.

'Well,' she said aloud. 'Two less legs in her bed for him to worry about.'

She reached for her husband's untouched dessert as his car raced down the drive without sirens, convinced the wrong person had died in the Jorgesson household. To compensate for that, she ate three more helpings of gâteau and clotted cream to ruin her heavy figure further.

It was a comforting revenge.

Spring's Dobermann went across the moonlit lawn in a silent run, guided by the man's scent. It located the dark figure against the storm fence under an old euphorbia-tree that bowered there and leaped for the throat. Something whipped in the darkness and tightened around the dog's neck, bringing it up short in mid-air. The wire tied off to the tree bit into the hard muscles and skidded the dog on its side just short of its target.

Charlie let it jump again and brained it with a rock. Struck again to make sure and left it where it fell, listening to the night. There was just the wind in the wild bamboo-hedges and the slower shush of the gums and acacias beyond the bungalow. The single-storey building was dark, and Charlie circled it twice before choosing a window with shutters and mosquito netting where the red steel alarm was located. The circuit was good by South African standards, and Charlie took fifteen minutes to bypass it before he slipped through into a modern kitchen that smelled of antiseptic chemicals instead of cooking. A bachelor smell no Black cook had been allowed to dispel with okra, yams or spiced meats, or brighten with singing.

Charlie hummed as he neutralised a separate alarm system outside a photographic darkroom, sprang the locked door and lit a viewing-plate to give him light to work by.

Strips of newly exposed 400 ASA film dried in a cabinet and Charlie found shots of himself at the airport with De Wit, the nylon container on the floor beside his foot. Charlie laid the film across his lighter-flame and watched it frizzle to black poodle hair.

Hundreds of negatives in a row of steel files were catalogued alphabetically. There were candid shots of Connie and his associates, hundreds of others of people Charlie neither knew nor cared about. Black faces talked earnestly with white, churchmen looked solemn over drinks, and exterior shots showed mixed ethnic groups entering or leaving buildings, all of them listed with care in a spiral-bound book in Spring's spidery script. The man was nothing if not thorough, but there was nothing under D for De Wit save for a small red star beside the initials

D.W. and a cross-reference to A. Charlie leafed back and found another red star beside A.J/D.W, which was meaningless until he found a thick album in a secret drawer of an escritoire in the living-room.

Bingo,' Charlie whispered to himself. 'Very gymnastic. Who'd think the old goat had it in him?'

The naked bodies were fuzzy on the beds in the three locations, but De Wit was clearly De Wit, and Alicia was very much Alicia, and Spring had tucked the negatives into the album's spine. Humming softly, Charlie took the album out to the car and brought Harry the Crack back into the house, sat him in a chair and went looking for the master bedroom.

Clive Spring came awake gaping for air with Charlie's fingers pinching his nostrils together. The Beretta slid into his suddenly opened mouth. His eyes opened slower but wider, and Spring tasted gun oil as he tried for night vision. Tasted the burned powder of spent cartridges. Smelled the peaty tang of good Irish. Knew the man drank and the gun had recently been fired.

'Get up, Mister.'

Spring nodded and cut his gum on the foresight. Gobbled when he tried to speak, muddled by the sleeping draught he had swallowed. The gun and a hand in his hair walked him into the living-room on tiptoe. The lamp on his escritoire was lit and showed up dust he had never noticed before. Made the nylon container into a belljar of luminescent light.

There were groans as hollow as promises, and Spring's brain was no longer dreary when he saw Harry flopped in a chair. Lying there as if his clothes were all that held him together. Hands on his lapels like broken crabs. Heels drumming on a nerve.

The gun sat Spring at his escritoire. Pressed against his balding temple and made him look at the container.

'Open it.'

The voice brooked no argument.

Spring's trembling hands released the astringent smell

of chemical. He peeled hard nylon edges apart and the pressure-seal hissed, stinging his nose and eyes with formaldehyde. Breathing was a grudging thing as he squinted down through tears at the bloated thing drowned in stinking liquid. A muddy dead eye stared back, and its twin made a lazy half-wink. There was congealed blood in the nose, and the mouth was parted in a humourless rictus that bared a long white molar and a chipped bicuspid. Face hair had grown after death, and Sadler's head needed a shave.

Spring fought vomit and lassitude as his mind formed mad arguments. An opening statement for the defence. All logical men were open to persuasion. He lifted his head to deliver it, but Charlie's fist drove him and his unspoken equivocation to the floor. Through the shock of pain the voice was as chill as a prefect in charge of a detention.

'Just say goodbye to your partner, Spring. Then it's all been said.'

Spring's mouth was too small for his tongue. He rolled his head against the floor, his need for answers to all these terrifying conundrums holding on to consciousness. He had to know where his dog was and why the alarms had failed. Why Dance was looking up numbers in a telephone directory, and why Harry pawed at his coat with sausage fingers. It all seemed so futile to Spring. His mind could not walk the tightrope of linear progressions, and the fault lay with everybody but himself. With Dance and De Wit and Sadler. With Harry who opened a small black wallet as if it was the answer to something important. What good was the sharpened silver nail he balanced in a shaky hand? No good at all.

Dance was dialling and listening and talking to a police station, reporting a prowler on the premises, giving Spring's own address and telephone number. And that was stupid with Spring's files open and his darkroom ready to be searched when they came. That must be stopped, but Spring's tongue scraped against coated teeth and would not articulate when Dance rang off and looked at him like some worthless thing.

Then there was a flick of silver light and Dance ducked with a dart buried in his upper arm. Harry was selecting another nail, and Dance was no longer where he had been. A long leg had struck out and Harry was smashing his chair to tinder as he took it back into the wall and drove the back of his head through a window-pane. Glass fell with him on to the polished boards, and his second nail had set the lightshade swinging above Dance's head. Dance turned Harry with his foot before hissing through clenched teeth at the nail buried in his deltoid. He mumbled something Spring did not catch and went away to root about in the darkroom. His shadow used pliers on the nail with a grunt of exertion, something metallic clattered in the sink, paper tissue was ripped from a roll and cold water ran as the shadow washed and packed the wound with a wad of mashed tissue.

Spring crawled for the door, unable to raise his head. He had reached the door-sill before he was chopped across the shoulders and hauled back inside. There was no feeling in his arms or torso as he was forced to watch Dance dab the Beretta with Harry's prints and drop it into the unconscious man's pocket with spare ammunition and negatives selected from the darkroom files.

'Get it now, Spring?'

Dance moved towards the paralysed man.

Spring did without wanting to. Jorgesson must be dead, and Harry was the prowler the police would find when they arrived. Forensic tests would tie him and Spring to the shooting in Melrose. Trace the Beretta back to himself, find Harry in possession of negs of Connie Harold in compromising situations, opening a barrel of worms that would involve them all. Unless he could think of a way out. Spring was still working on it when Dance took him out to a hired car he had parked down the block earlier in the day.

By the time the police had contacted De Wit, Spring and

Sadler's head were well on their way to Zeerust.

Wally's bright star was no longer a staring chip of ice in the black glacier of night. A bloated sun climbed out of a carmine haze, and wind stirred the veld like an old man breathing in shallow sleep. The eastern mountains had blued to ultramarine, and a red scar of light spread bloody fingers into low melancholy clouds, transforming them to bright banks of drifting peach.

The hired car threw a long shadow down the longer brown road, and a buzzard sailed in an early thermal like a ragged black pennant, too high to be disturbed by the sudden monumental grind of falling rock or the thick boil of dust throwing itself into the air. Thorn and brush ground into the deep kloof as a great wall of rock and shale scaled into the depths, and the rumbles were still dying away when the flutter of a distant helicopter grew out of the rising sun.

Charlie climbed back up to the road, rolled his shirt-sleeves down, retied his tie and brushed off his trousers. Lit Harry's last Gold Flake and held the hole in his shoulder as he leaned against the car.

The helicopter side-slipped to circle the kloof and landed on the road in a stew of brown dust. The rotors feathered, and men in olive fatigues dropped to the ground with levelled automatic weapons. The dust pall thinned, and Colonel De Wit came out of it stroking his long upper lip, a thumb hooked into a heavy black gunbelt.

'Mr King, I presume,' he said.

Charlie ignored him and the rising heat. Turned a masonic ring on his little finger.

The kloof gave off a last rumble and dust drifted over the blackened Mercedes below them. The scarred baobab it nuzzled shone like dirty milk, and De Wit sighed.

'Spring's down there,' he said. A statement.

Charlie said nothing. Savoured the smoke in his lungs.

'A gang of Blacks digging for a month might find him, I suppose. I think you'd better walk down there and join him, Mr Dance.'

Charlie looked at De Wit then. Streamed smoke and shook his head.

'No,' he said.

'But I insist.'

De Wit's nickel-plated army Colt came out of its holster, and Charlie's smile was a bare thing in his dust-streaked face.

'No, you don't. Your local coppers have got Harry Cracknell dead to rights on a murder charge, and he'll talk to save his scrag from the rope. You just get him talking right, and you could find yourself with a lot of new friends at Scotland Yard. Better friends than Spring or bloody Sadler were.'

'Past tense?' said De Wit.

'It was your house of cards, not mine. It's you who's not seeing the bigger picture, for all your clever talk. Harry used Spring's shooter on Jorgesson, and having that Welshman explaining that away in court wouldn't help you. Nor tying me into it. That'd bring us to why you, wearing your Mr Krepp hat, slid me into the country without formalities, right?'

'Not if you join Spring down there. You fall and die. Simple.'

'Simple-minded. Open the car boot. See what I liberated for you as a friendly gesture.'

De Wit turned the key and flipped open the album to see himself in grainy black and white.

'You and the widow Jorgesson well at it. How'd that have looked in the prosecution's hands, or on the wrong minister's desk?' Charlie did not mention the negatives he had posted to himself in London.

De Wit's eyes and mouth slitted. He had enemies within the Cabinet who would have used the material to catapult him into disgrace and obscurity. Spring's death in the kloof no longer required a reaction from him. He need only consider the best way of neutralising Dance.

Charlie slapped an envelope across a shot of Alicia's

rump raised in a motel room.

'And there's the first of the letters of introduction you'll need to collect your AI documents. You'll get the rest when I'm well out of South African airspace.'

De Wit looked out over the kloof at the distant mountains, and his Colt went back into its holster.

'You're on the next available flight. You were never in this country, *verstaan*?'

'Suits me, Colonel.'

'Congratulations, Mr Dance. You appear to have won.'

De Wit could have been admiring a carefully tended garden or a prettily engraved heirloom. He was taken unawares by Charlie's savagely controlled reaction.

'Won what? The right to stand side by side with you? Looking at a hole where what I ought to have cared for died? We're the losers, Colonel, you and me. We can only win by making the others lose. When did you last cry or laugh enough to crack a rib? Make love for the hell of it without awarding yourself points? Or just get drunk and not use the booze to turn off your brain? Don't talk to me about winning.'

De Wit made no sign he had heard. 'It's been a long twenty-four hours,' he said, lost in far blue escarpments.

Charlie took a last bite of fragrance and flicked his long cigarette-butt out and down at the baobab without seeing the view.

'I just hope she knows I did the best I could.'

'Who knows?' said De Wit. 'One of my men will take care of the hired car.' He led Charlie back to the helicopter with the album clamped under his arm, and they were whirled back the way they had come.

And below, strapped to the wheel of the burned-out Mercedes, Clive Spring gnawed at his gag and felt the first pangs of terminal thirst as the temperature climbed higher than the circling buzzard.

Knowing what must come with the darkness.

Charlie dumped his soiled clothes and padded into the

shower with a bottle of Irish to lay the dust, too tired to care that the scalding spray stung the wound in his arm.

Like iodine, he thought. *The more it stings, the more good it does you.*

He lathered the knife-scar Red Bellaver had given him in the yard of Brixton Prison and did not care that the whisky tasted of soap as he scrubbed himself pink again. He just wanted to be clean and drunk enough to sleep through the long flight home.

Two of De Wit's men had packed his case and waited outside the suite for him to dress and join them for the drive to the airport. It was refreshing to let someone else do the thinking for a change, and Charlie promised himself a long holiday after Archie's funeral. His limbs shook with exhaustion, and the bottle was heavy when he tilted it over the dark blue hole in his deltoid, cleansing it with alcohol, shuddering when it burned.

A ten-year old with a toffee-hammer could take me now.

Charlie shook spray from his hair and was liberal with shampoo. Fook and Eyetie Antoni's New York cousins could wait to finalise their plans for the drug deal. Charlie was only going along for Archie's sake, and planned to bow out as soon as he could without alienating the Chinese in Gerrard Street. There was enough money in the world without trading in opiates and the hallucinogens the trendies experimented with nowadays.

And what the hell's wrong with staying with booze, birds and baccy? It's a hard combination to beat, and where's the fun in giggling over the whorls in your thumb or finding patterns in a lightbulb more interesting than the girl you're turning on with? Dumb and antisocial. Kills brainbuds and conversation. And aren't people alone enough as it is without turning inside themselves with all that shit? Ingrid agrees; she. . . .

Charlie rinsed off and reached for a towel.

Don't think about it. About her.

He sensed the movement through the plastic curtain before something bellied the clinging folds towards him.

Slammed into his raised shoulder and ducking head. Snapped his face aside and numbed his whole right arm. Charlie fell with the curtain popping off its hooks all around him. Another blow took him in the lower back, and his legs skidded out from under him. Arms took his head in a lock and hauled him out on to slippery tiles where he was systematically kicked in the spine. Behind the knees. Draining him of strength.

Charlie still held the bottle and punched it back over his shoulder. Felt it impact against muscle and roll off somewhere. Heard breath expelled as the arms slackened around his neck. Turned a shoulder and popped a knuckle against a skull before the pressure came back and the knee in his back turned his legs to useless meat. Heard his own bawl of pain as he held on to the soil-pipe below the vanity suite with the last of his sapped strength until weakness and suds allowed him to be lifted bodily.

Charlie let his whole weight hang on the straining arms and saw Sailor Mailer's dark face beside his own in the mirror above the washbasin before he was turned and hurled out on to thick living-room carpet. Realised that Sailor had hidden himself somewhere in the suite whilst De Wit's men stripped the rooms of his personal effects. A kick rolled Charlie into a loose curl, and breeze from the balcony cooled his damp hair. The sliding windows had been closed, he was certain of that, and Sailor must have—

Charlie was kicked in the chest and heard himself try to draw breath into lungs turned solid by pain. Knew that Sailor meant to finish him with boot and sap before hurling him out and down on to the hot road surface fourteen floors below. Knew he was too used up to do much about it.

Charlie scrabbled away from the next kick and almost made it.

He upended a chair, and a cushion numbed the sap swung at his jaw, but not enough to stop him from being spreadeagled without the will to cover his exposed groin.

Sailor's boot rose in deliberate slow motion above Charlie's crotch, ready to stamp on his manhood. Charlie saw the back fillings in his opened mouth, the stiff hairs in his nostrils. Silly details that took his mind off the heavy boot. Then the contorted face jerked at the outer door as it splintered open and the door knob bounced across the floor. Sailor hacked down and his heel slammed into Charlie's upper thigh, missing his testicles by millimetres. Charlie jack-knifed over himself like a broken doll and fell away from another wild kick to the head, sensing the men falling into the suite behind him. Black shoes circled him and Sailor was backing away, thinking of survival instead of maiming Charlie. Sailor knocked against an ornamental table, and a crystal lamp shivered its drop-pendants. He launched himself forward, and his sap whirred as he swung it at the nearest head. It passed through thin air, and a solid fist mashed his mouth, spraying saliva from loose lips. The men were in close then, and all Charlie could see or hear was milling feet and the hard thud of fists on flesh. Then Sailor was down, and the men had his arms up his back as they dragged him towards the sliding windows. The curtains were drawn back and sunlight seared the room as Charlie tried to get a knee under him. He was still trying when Sailor sailed out over the balcony to make the traffic brake and horn from the street below.

'Another bloody suicide.'

The first man got Charlie upright and fed his useless legs into his underwear.

The second man laughed softly and got Charlie into his shirt.

'We put it down to the heat,' he said, buttoning carefully.

Charlie swayed between them as they zipped him into his trousers and tied his tie.

'Can you handle your socks yourself, *boet*?'

'Oh blimey yeah.'

Charlie passed out lacing his shoes and came to as the black limousine turned into the airport.

CHAPTER TWENTY-FIVE

CONNIE was pouring hot water over instant coffee when the front gate swung on its rusty hinge and post flopped through the letter-box on to the mat. He went down the passage licking marmalade from a thumb with Kelly's cat figure-of-eighting between his legs and mewing for his breakfast.

'Time Kel came and had you away, face-ache. With you still eating me out of house and home she must figure to get her feet back under my table. Some hopes, my old puss. You can tell her that from me. This time tomorrow I'll be landing in Jo'burg, and I ain't coming back for a good long stretch.'

Connie stooped to gather the usual bills and a large yellow envelope with a local postmark. He left the bills on the hall table and opened the yellow envelope with a kitchen knife. The cat pawed his trouser turn-up and wailed pathetically enough for Connie to discard the post and reach for a can of food from the fridge, spooning it out into a bowl.

'The hardest face in the Smoke hag-ridden by a moggy? Now who'd believe that?'

The cat went rigid when it was stroked, its nose deep in fish and meal. Connie straightened and rubbed his aching head.

'Typical woman. Get what you want from a man, and that's it. Nothing. Forget the bedroom, Mister, we're going to church. Well, at least you're company with my kids farmed out at my sister's and the bird I want in another country.'

Connie glanced at the clock as it ticked past eight.

'And it's too late for the dawn frighteners. Funny how the law loves to catch a villain in bed with last night's sand in his minces. Now, just listen to me, will you? Talking to a bleeding cat like it's sodding normal. Maybe they just ought to lock me up.'

He gulped coffee and remembered the envelope. Picked it up and slid photographs into his palm. For a moment they were just candid pornos of a couple on various beds. The man had the start of a belly and the woman was small and very agile. Then Alicia's face leaped at him as her nails dug into a muscular back and her legs clamped a thick waist. Her big eyes foggy with need and her teeth sunk into a grizzled neck. Biting as only she could bite. Straining under somebody who wasn't Connie Harold. Wasn't her husband. A man who looked like he wore a uniform under his clothes.

Connie spread the prints as if they burned him. Laid them out on to the work-surface and stared at them with ashes in his mouth and the beginning of a sick headache clouding his mind. He barely made it to the sink to vomit and kicked the cat's bowl apart without noticing. He was bowed there a long time. Until his stomach heaved with nothing left to void but strings of sour bile. He ran the tap over his head and took cold comfort from the icy water streaming down the sides of his face and swirling around the aluminium near his nose. The droplets ran in eccentric circles like wet lightning on the brushed metal, no two configurations the same, darting and dancing with liquid anarchy, much like his disordered thoughts.

Blame must go somewhere, Connie knew that much. He reared up and spattered the kitchen with water, made the cat run as water soaked its fur. He tore the envelope apart for a note, any clue as to who had sent the filthy evidence to him. There was nothing. Only the rows of grainy prints. Connie ripped them into smaller and smaller pieces. Ran to the lavatory and flushed them away. Pushed the bobbing pieces through the trap with a lavatory brush until there was nothing down there but innocent colourless water and featureless white porcelain.

Connie's head ballooned and split as his heart pumped blood too hard and too fast. He hypervented without knowing it, and his gorged face was bloated and feverish under his hands. He slumped on to the toilet seat with nerves tapping his feet on the cold linoleum. There was nothing to strangle but the cat. Nothing to hammer with his fists but tiled walls. Only yesterday he had received a long and fond letter from Alicia that mentioned Dirk's death almost in passing. Almost skimmed over Harry's arrest in favour of bald descriptions of her need to bed her beloved Conrad. Gave no reason for Sailor's silence.

Lies. And I swallowed them. Lies marching like soldiers. Rank after rank of them. Snapping salutes at me like they ended in two fingers. Up yours, Connie. Right up yours for believing Rudyard Kipling didn't have it right when he said: A woman's only a woman, but a good cigar's a smoke.

There was hammering that came from outside Connie's head. Hammering that had been going on for too long. He staggered to the front door, hoping it was some berk of a gasman wanting to read the meter. Somebody he could hand a tasty whack to. Anybody he could work over and leave crumpled in the gutter. He tore a nail on the latch getting the door open and blinked out at the tall man with the bland round face and the warrant he held like it was a blue riband for breeding a pedigree animal.

'Conrad William Harold,' he said. 'That is you?'

CID men were in the passage, and the cat streaked up the stairs ahead of them.

'Late for the dawn frighteners, Mr Lemmon,' Connie said, losing his fists behind his back.

'A lot of traffic coming in from the airport. Holiday season and all that.'

'The heavy Latin says you're coming in legal, that it?'

'I'd say so. After you.'

Lemmon followed Connie into his disordered lounge where chaos had gathered in the weeks since Kelly had left, and the remains of a forgotten meal congealed on top of the television set.

'Not much of a bachelor, are you, Connie?'

Lemmon perched on the arm of a fat flowered chair and lit a Player.

'If you've got something, spit it out.'

Connie stood beside his packed cases and watched Lemmon hand Dillman his passport and airline tickets.

'You won't be needing these where you're going.'

'Where's that, then?'

'West End Central first off. After you're charged we'll have to see where we tuck you up. Suffice it to say you'll be safe from harm. Like your ex-partners.'

Connie thumbed a pounding temple.

'I'm saying nothing to that. You'll get it said in your own good time anyway. Just let me get something for this blinding bonce-ache, will you.'

Lemmon sent Dillman out of the room.

'He'll do that. I want a quiet word before we go through the formal verbals.'

'Sounds like I ought to sit down for that.'

'Wouldn't hurt.' Lemmon's voice was as dry as the dust in a locked room. 'We've got you dead to rights on conspiracy charges allied to serious fraud, and your jury-rigging comes under the heading of conspiracy to pervert the course of justice. But what's so sweet for me, and so bitter for you, is that your ex-partners have got their stories straight, and it's all down to you on your lonesome ownsome.'

'That's twice you've said "ex-partners".'

'And now you've bitten. You had to know, didn't you? A Miss Kelly Ketchum ring a bell wtih you? She's been talking to us for— Well, how long is it since she waltzed out on you?'

'I don't believe that for—'

'Believe it, son, you're cooked in her slow oven. You know the saying about nothing like the wrath of a woman scorned? She was type-cast for the part.'

Connie slow-blinked at his fists. 'And?'

'Victor Gideon Dakin.'

'But he's—' Connie bit the inside of his lip. 'Nothing to do with me.'

'He says different, and at length. Chapter and verse. And, again, it's all down to you. You're a man without friends, Con.'

Connie just nodded at that. 'And?'

'There's over a hundred and seventeen charges right there. All provable. All substantiated by documentations and the oral and written statements of the aforementioned Ketchum and Dakin. But our star prize is Harry Cracknell. Your Harry the Crack. He talked up a storm when I saw him in Johannesburg. Yes, I've had a week out there, and he ties you to a murder he says he didn't do except you ordered it done. Our Harry wants to avoid the rope the South Africans are dangling for him, and they're willing to give him to us so long as we stop all this wild talk about there being some tie-up with Republican Intelligence, whatever that might be.'

Connie stood and trembled a finger close to Lemmon's face.

'There is, and you know it. If you've listened to Harry, you know there's a link to. . . .'

Lemmon watched Connie's mind catch up with his mouth. Saw him back into his chair with a solicitous smile.

'Just as I said, wild talk. And bringing all that up at the trial would do you no good at all. The twelve men and true in that jury are going to have a hard enough time following the straight evidence, without you confusing their honest little brains with talk of spies and gun-running. You'd best get that pill swallowed a bit quick.'

Connie wiped bitter scum from his mouth.

'You didn't happen to fall over a face called De Wit?'

'No, but he was mentioned. Harry talked long and loudly about him, but the coppers I liaised with said he was retired and lived on his farm as some kind of a recluse. I was even showed the records of serving policemen in the

South African force, and no De Wit was listed. Unless we counted a seventeen-year-old trainee constable in Pietermaritzburg. But, then, that's as wild as our Harry talking about Charlie Dance being a "Mr King" who was at the Jorgesson house when the shooting took place. I mean, I'd love to believe it, but wild talk isn't proof, is it? And I checked thoroughly; Charlie Dance was in Malta during that time. I've even seen the stamps in his passport.'

Dillman put his head round the door to hand in a glass of water and two Alka Seltzers, and Connie let them fizz as he ordered his thoughts.

'No De Wit and no Mr King, eh? Have you had the wool pulled, Mr Lemmon? I mean you *have*. You want me to swallow enough without I have to swallow that. I've got pictures of the bastard. In bed with. . . .' Connie blundered to a halt. He had no pictures.

'Yes?' asked Lemmon.

'Nothing.'

'Good. One odd thing I did turn up. There was a Mr King at the Langham Hotel, but he committed suicide the day after Jorgesson died. I saw the police blotter on that, and he did a flyer from the fourteenth floor. There were photographs, but not the sort you'd stick in the family album. Landing on your head from that height leaves little you'd want to remember.'

Connie drank the glass dry and knew who Mr King must be. Must have been. Sailor hadn't made it. And Harry was singing to save his neck. He felt everything he had been holding together with sheer willpower drain out from him like water through his fingers. Swirling away. The millions and Alicia were lost to him. All he had left was the street sense he had learned and the animal cunning he was born with. Potent weapons once he had rested up. They would see him through. Had to if he was to avoid a heavy sentence in maximum security.

'You're right, Mr Lemmon. Guns and spies would stick in the beak's craw. How much porridge am I looking at?'

'Your electric torture machine will make the headlines.

All them toenails you've used pliers on. But the heavy sentences come for the long-firm and airline-ticket frauds. Property before people, that's the law, Connie.'

'A couple of tens, then?'

'You won't get much change out of twenty-five long ones.'

'Then, I'll take a leaf out of Charlie Dance's book. Act the three brass monkeys and leave out hiring a brief. It worked for him, right?'

Lemmon almost nodded. Almost smiled.

'With a little help from his friends. And from a few who weren't. Yes, Charlie made it. That one time.'

'You're still after him, then?'

'More than ever.'

'That's a bit of a cheer-up, then. Charlie ain't all bloody violets. Handsome.'

'When we've tucked you up, there is only Charlie left.'

Connie's brittle laugh startled Lemmon into a frown.

'You get this Charlie, there's always another Charlie down the street. I ain't the last Connie Harold in the world, neither. The world's filled with Koshers, Tommys and Connies, old son. And you won't root them all out in a million years. There ain't enough straight coppers to do it, never will be. The corruption's gone too deep. I've bought MPs, mate, peers of the sodding realm; they've all got their price. And one day somebody'll meet your price, see if they don't. How does a hundred grand sound? Would that square you enough to drop this tonk long enough for me to get to the airport?'

Lemmon leaned in, and his frown deepened.

'You get to square the British public, chummy. You square them with heavy porridge because even you can't intimidate or bribe them all. No, it's tuck-up time for you.'

Connie shrugged.

'Funny how big things fall apart in a hurry.'

'Not funny, inevitable.'

'Could be. Read me the formals and let's get out of here. I hate this sodding house. Somebody else can pay the rates and do the washing-up. A guest of Her Majesty's got some sodding rights, right?'

'A few.'

Lemmon called Dillman in and read the formal caution, just as anxious to get out of the stale room as Connie.

Golder's Green crematorium lay in early-morning shadow, and a line of funeral limousines stretched back towards Finchley. Traffic was diverted for two miles in either direction, and security along the funeral route was tight enough for a royal progression or a visiting head of state. Uniformed police patrolled the perimeter and plain-clothes CID men mingled with the crowds of invited mourners. Press photographers were restricted to a roped podium, and keen strays looking for exclusive shots were escorted away by overcoats without a 'please' in them. Floral tributes covered a quarter of an acre inside the grounds and lined the white path winding up to the memorial chapel where DC Payne took candid shots of Queenie Ogle being escorted to her pew by Kensington Kate and Electric Raymond. The pallbearers were Nasty Nostrils and Sodbonce, Fast Frankie Frewin and Froggy Farrell, Pimlico Johnny Parsons and Aman Lee Fook, Eyetie Antoni and his American cousin Salvatore Castile. DC Brian Bulstrode wheeled Vinnie Castle, Johnny the Builder and Barry the Blag flanked a weeping Armchair Doris and Manchester Freddy's wife Maria, and they in turn were followed by Stripes Flynn's contingent from Smithfield, bookmakers, diamond merchants, club-owners and publicans, and those who could not be seated lined the walls or gathered outside, silent witnesses to the passing of an era.

J. C. Hatton gave a long and poignant eulogy, and a rabbi prayed for the departed soul as the bronze coffin slid away between slowly closing plush curtains. Queenie gave Electric her black-edged handkerchief to weep into and toured the mass of wreaths before being driven away to the funeral breakfast Charlie was to host in Park Lane.

Lemmon found Charlie back in the trees where he could see without being seen.

'You mind company?'

'Not if you're carrying cigarettes.'

'Used my last one.'

Lemmon crumpled his pack and put it back into his pocket.

'The king is dead, long live the king, Charlie?'

'Ends are only disguised beginnings, Theo. How did you enjoy South Africa?'

'It was enlightening. I suppose I'm getting better at the sensible compromise – that, or I'm learning Bunny Halliday's cold cynicism. Your prints were over everything I touched, Charlie. I just wish it was possible to nail you for it all, but you're protected by my masters' need for political expedience. You've heard that one before.'

'Somewhere, sometime. You wanted Connie stitched, he's well stitched; just don't be greedy, eh?'

'You can't hold the cobbles for ever, Charlie. One day we'll take them away from you.'

'When Queenie goes, maybe I'll let you. But change just makes change, nothing more, nothing less. The whole world hated the Union Jack when it flew over half the world, but the Pax Britannica lasted a hundred years. And when the last honest villain goes you'll have hard-nosed amateurs to deal with. A lot of nasty little nations who owe loyalty nowhere except to Number One. Then you'll have your work cut out, and you'll be thinking of today as the good-old-bad-old days. Better the devil you know, Mister.'

'You wouldn't want me to give up the fight, would you, Charlie? Let you have all your own way with your new friends from New York and Hong Kong? You've paraded them today to give me a good long squint at them, and that deserves a good straight fight surely?'

'It's your twopence, Mr Lemmon.'

'Whatever happened to Theo?'

'He talks off the record. You've just drawn the battle lines. We're squared off, and that suits me.'

'Me, too. Then, we're both happy. See you in court.'

'That's only a maybe, Mr Lemmon.'

'And time I wasn't here. Except for one last thing.'

'Oh?'

'Two, actually. I made Commander, and they've given me *carte blanche* to come after you any way I can.'

'Congrats, but I can't wish you luck, can I?'

'Not sincerely, no. And I've got a message for you, from a Mr Krepp. You remember him, don't you?'

Charlie's smile flitted, gone before it was formed.

'How could I? Never been in South Africa, have I?'

'That's true, but I'll tell you anyway. He said, and I quote: Tell him I found the loose spring in the Mercedes too late to mend it. You owe me a replacement part. Does that make sense?'

'Yeah.' Charlie's eyes hardened as briefly as he had smiled. 'It makes sense.'

'Keep your back to the wall, Charlie.'

'And you, Theo.'

Lemmon walked down the line of limousines and became just another bobbing head in the crowd. The last cars pulled away, and the stragglers followed in their own good time. Charlie listened to the pine-trees sigh in the breeze, crackling as they shed their needles around his feet. A cone thumped to the ground, and a grey squirrel flicked from sight.

Charlie took off the masonic ring and ground it into the needles, no longer needing trophies. He found a patch of sky through the nodding trees and smiled up into watery sunlight.

'One away to you, Mister,' he said softly. 'The best one,' making his final goodbye to Archie.

'I wasn't sure of the brand.'

A gloved hand offered Charlie a Player and he glimpsed a wayward nose through a black veil.

'You said to carry cigarettes next time.'

'Did I now?'

Charlie accepted a light from a gold Dunhill.

'Is this too soon?'

'For what?'
'Too soon for next time?'
'Only one way to find out.'
'How delicious. Do you plan to throw me to the ground here and now?'
'I think I'll contain myself until I've seen the floral tributes.'
'But there are thousands of them. Won't that take hours?'
'Half an hour maybe.'
'Then will you. . . .?'
'We'll see, won't we?'
'I'm trying not to pout.'
'There's a party after that in Park Lane.'
'Lovely. And after that, will you . . .?'
'After that? Yes.'
'D'you think I can contain myself until then?'
Charlie took Margot's arm and nodded.
'Oh blimey yeah,' he said.

THE END

THE SALAMANDRA GLASS

A.W. MYKEL

The heart-stopping novel of international suspense and intrigue by the author of *The Windchime Legacy*.

Michael Gladieux thought he'd finished with The Group, a highly specialised unit he'd served with in Vietnam . . . until his father is murdered, his body found with a note accusing him of Nazi collaboration during the war and a glass pendant anchored to his heart with a shiny steel spike.

Who was Michael's father? Why are Washington and The Group so interested? Michael's search for answers leads him on a terrifying quest – to find his father's killer. What he uncovers is far more deadly, as he becomes the one man capable of stopping the twisted legacy of THE SALAMANDRA GLASS

Rivals Ludlum at his best!

0 552 12417 6

£2.50

CORGI BOOKS

FREDERICK FORSYTH

THE MASTER STORYTELLER

The Day of the Jackal

One of the most celebrated thrillers ever written, THE DAY OF THE JACKAL is the electrifying story of an anonymous Englishman who, in the spring of 1963, was hired by Colonel Marc Rodin, Operations Chief of the O.A.S., to assassinate General de Gaulle.

'Mr. Forsyth is clever, very clever and immensely entertaining' *Daily Telegraph*

'In a class by itself. Unputdownable' *Sunday Times*

More than 7,500,000 copies of Frederick Forsyth's novels sold in Corgi

0 552 09121 9 £2.95

CORGI BOOKS

GIRI 義理

MARC OLDEN

"Ludlum, look out, Marc Olden is here"
Walter Wager, author of *Telefon*

GIRI
to the Japanese, a term meaning duty or loyalty, the most binding obligation of the samurai warriors. But to an American, it means something else – revenge!

Combining international intrigue, Oriental philosophy, deadly violence and burning passion, *Giri* is a gripping, fast-paced thriller in which East clashes with West, and the ageless code of the hunter versus the hunted is put to the ultimate test.

''Anybody who loved *Shibumi* and *The Ninja* shouldn't miss it''
James Patterson

0 552 12357 9 £2.95

CORGI BOOKS

EDWARD TOPOL &
FRIDRIKH NEZNANSKY

The ultimate Soviet thriller

'Fast moving and exciting . . . better than *Gorky Park*'
Good Book Guide

Much of this story is factually accurate – the names, the people and the places . . . the death of Brezhnev's brother-in-law was widely reported in the West. 'Death after long illness' said *Pravda* . . . although Andropov told Brezhnev it was suicide. Just *suppose* it was murder . . .

'Meaty entertainment'
Sunday Times

'Gripping and informative fiction that has an unexpected and chilling end'
Yorkshire Post

'Much more fun than *Gorky Park*'
The Spectator

0 552 12307 2 £2.50

CORGI BOOKS

A SELECTED LIST OF FINE TITLES AVAILABLE FROM CORGI BOOKS

THE PRICES SHOWN BELOW WERE CORRECT AT THE TIME OF GOING TO PRESS. HOWEVER TRANSWORLD PUBLISHERS RESERVE THE RIGHT TO SHOW NEW RETAIL PRICES ON COVERS WHICH MAY DIFFER FROM THOSE PREVIOUSLY ADVERTISED IN THE TEXT OR ELSEWHERE.

	Number	Title	Author	Price
☐	12639 X	**One Police Plaza**	*William J. Caunitz*	£2.50
☐	12550 4	**Lie Down With Lions**	*Ken Follett*	£2.95
☐	12610 1	**On Wings of Eagles**	*Ken Follett*	£2.95
☐	12180 0	**The Man from St. Petersburg**	*Ken Follett*	£2.95
☐	11810 9	**The Key to Rebecca**	*Ken Follett*	£2.95
☐	12569 5	**The Fourth Protocol**	*Frederick Forsyth*	£2.95
☐	12140 1	**No Comebacks**	*Frederick Forsyth*	£2.50
☐	11500 2	**The Devil's Alternative**	*Frederick Forsyth*	£2.95
☐	10244 X	**The Shepherd**	*Frederick Forsyth*	£1.95
☐	10050 1	**The Dogs of War**	*Frederick Forsyth*	£2.95
☐	09436 6	**The Odessa File**	*Frederick Forsyth*	£2.50
☐	09121 9	**The Day of the Jackal**	*Frederick Forsyth*	£2.95
☐	12417 6	**The Salamandra Glass**	*A. W. Mykel*	£2.50
☐	11850 8	**The Windchime Legacy**	*A. W. Mykel*	£1.75
☐	12541 5	**Dai-Sho**	*Marc Olden*	£2.50
☐	12357 9	**Giri**	*Marc Olden*	£2.95
☐	12662 4	**Gaijin**	*Marc Olden*	£2.95
☐	12584 9	**Deadly Games**	*Fridrikh Neznansky & Edward Topol*	£1.95
☐	12307 2	**Red Square**	*Fridrikh Neznansky & Edward Topol*	£2.50
☐	12583 0	**Submarine U-137**	*Edward Topol*	£2.50

All these books are available at your bookshop or newsagent, or can be ordered direct from the publisher. Just tick the titles you want and fill in the form below.

TRANSWORLD READER'S SERVICE, 61–63 Uxbridge Road, Ealing, London, W5 5SA

Please send a cheque or postal order, not cash. All cheques and postal orders must be in £ sterling and made payable to Transworld Publishers Ltd.
Please allow cost of book(s) plus the following for postage and packing:

U.K./Republic of Ireland Customers:
Orders in excess of £5; no charge
Orders under £5; add 50p

Overseas Customers:
All orders; add £1.50

NAME (Block Letters) ....

ADDRESS ....

....